Shadi Ahani

Borhgei.

Christmas

1896

CLAREMONT BOOKS

The Penguin Selected Works of Lewis Carroll

Lewis Carroll was the vigorously preserved pen-name of the Rev. Charles Lutwidge Dodgson. Born in 1832, he was educated at Rugby and Christ Church, Oxford, where he spent the rest of his life as lecturer in mathematics. In 1861 he took deacon's orders, but shyness and a constitutional stammer prevented him from seeking the priesthood. He never married but he was very fond of children and spent much of his time with them – the Alice books were originally written for the young daughters of Dr Liddell, the Dean of Christ Church. Besides his stories, Lewis Carroll also wrote nonsensical poems and parodies; in addition he published some learned mathematical treatises but these were of little significance beside his brilliantly absurd fiction. His prose and verse works include: *Phantasmagoria and Other Poems* (1869), *The Hunting of the Snark* (1876), and *Sylvie and Bruno* (1889). Charles Dodgson died in 1898.

THE PENGUIN SELECTED WORKS OF

Lewis Carroll

WITH AN INTRODUCTION BY

Alexander Woollcott

AND THE ILLUSTRATIONS BY

John Tenniel

CLAREMONT BOOKS

PENGUIN BOOKS

Published by the Penguin Group
Penguin Books Ltd, 27 Wrights Lane, London W8 5TZ, England
Penguin Books USA Inc., 375 Hudson Street, New York, New York 10014, USA
Penguin Books Australia Ltd, Ringwood, Victoria, Australia
Penguin Books Canada Ltd, 10 Alcorn Avenue, Toronto, Ontario, Canada M4V 3B2
Penguin Books (NZ) Ltd, 182-190 Wairau Road, Auckland 10, New Zealand

Penguin Books Ltd, Registered Offices: Harmondsworth, Middlesex, England

Published as *The Penguin Complete Lewis Carroll* in Penguin Books, 1982
Published under this title in Penguin Books, 1988

This edition published by Claremont Books,
an imprint of Godfrey Cave Associates Limited,
42 Bloomsbury Street, London WC1B 3QJ,
under licence from Penguin Books Ltd, 1995

ISBN 1 85471 476 7

CONTENTS

III. SYLVIE AND BRUNO

IV. SYLVIE AND BRUNO CONCLUDED

V. VERSE
THE HUNTING OF THE SNARK

THE PENGUIN SELECTED WORKS OF LEWIS CARROLL

INTRODUCTION

ON THE fourth of July, 1862, the Reverend Charles Lutwidge Dodgson, a young Oxford Don, who was then, and
for nearly half a century remained, Mathematical Lecturer of Christ Church, took the day off and went a-row-
ing with the small daughters of the Dean. That eventful
picnic was duly noted in his neat and interminable diary
that night. The entry runs thus:

"I made an expedition up the river to Godstow with the
three Liddells; we had tea on the bank there and did not
reach Christ Church until half-past eight."

But at that time he did not deem one subsequently en-
hanced detail of the day sufficiently important to be worth
chronicling. He said nothing of the fairy tale he began to
spin "all in the golden afternoon" there in the shadow of
the hayrick to which the four Argonauts retreated from
the heat of the sun. It was a tale about just such a little
girl as the gravely attentive Alice Liddell who used to
prod him when he ventured to let lapse for a time this
story of another Alice falling down a rabbit-hole into the
world of the unexpected. In response to such proddings,
he carried the story along on that and other afternoons
and finally committed it to manuscript as "Alice's Adventures Underground". Somewhat expanded this was published three years later under the *nom de guerre* of Lewis
Carroll and under the title of *Alice's Adventures in Wonderland*.

In the sixty years that have passed since then, this gay,
roving dream story and its sequel have seeped into the
folk-lore of the world. It has become as deeply rooted a
part of that folk lore as the legend of Cinderella or any
other tale first told back in the unfathomable past. Not

Tiny Tim, nor Falstaff, nor Rip Van Winkle, nor any other character wrought in the English tongue seems now a more permanent part of that tongue's heritage than do the high-handed Humpty Dumpty, the wistful Mad Hatter, the somewhat arbitrary Queen of Hearts, the evasive Cheshire Cat and the gently pathetic White Knight.

The tale has been read aloud in all the nurseries from Oxford town to the ends of the Empire. And there is no telling how many copies of it have been printed and sold. For when it was new, there was no binding law of international copyright and it was as much the prey of all the freebooters in America as was a somewhat kindred work of genius that came out of England a few years later—the nonsensical and lovely thing called *Pinafore*.

And the Alice books have known no frontier. If you poke about in the bookstalls on the Continent, you will stumble inevitably on *Alice's Abenteur im Wunderland*. Or *Le Aventure d'Alice nel Paese Meraviglie* (with illustrations, of course, by Giovanni Tenniel). You might even run into *La aventuroj de Alicio en Mirlando* which, if you must know, is life down a rabbit-hole as told in Esperanto. And you are certain to come upon *Les Aventures d'Alice au Pays de Merveilles* with one of the puns of the incorrigible Mock Turtle (Fausse-Tortue) rendered thus unrecognizable:

"La maitresse était une vieille tortue; nous l'appelions chélonée."

"Et pourquoi l'appeliez-vous chélonée, si ce n'était pas son nom?"

"Parcequ'on ne pouvait s'empêcher de s'écrier en la voyant: Quel long nez!" dit la Fausse-Tortue d'un ton fâché; "vous êtes vraiment bien bornée!"

Then the Alice books have been employed as scenarios for controversy. A long bibliography of such satires as *Alice in Kulturland* or *Malice in Blunderland* would indicate as much. The tale of Alice's adventure down the rabbit-hole and through the looking-glass is still a very source book for withering anecdotes in the House of

Commons or malignant cartoons in *Punch*; and even so sedate an orator as Woodrow Wilson, in speaking once of the ceaseless vigilance and aspiration required of a progressive, compared himself to the Red Queen, who, you will remember, had to run as fast as her legs would carry her if she wanted so much as to stay in the same place.

Plays have been wrought from the stuff of the Alice story. Some of these in London have been ambitious harlequinades. Irene Vanbrugh, for instance, could tell you how Lewis Carroll once watched her play the Knave of Hearts. More often, they have been sleazy, amateurish ventures, an outlet for the exhibitionism of grown-ups, who would then have the effrontery to say they were doing it to please the kiddies.

Even the symphony orchestras know Alice; for the chatter of the flowers in the looking-glass garden, the thunder of *Jabberwocky*, the hum of the looking-glass insects and the wistfulness of the White Knight have all been caught up in the lovely music of Deems Taylor. The artists have discovered it; and the book has even undergone the sometimes painful experience of being illustrated by Peter Newell.

Indeed, everything has befallen *Alice*, except the last thing—psychoanalysis. At least the new psychologists have not explored this dream book nor pawed over the gentle, shrinking celibate who wrote it. They have not subjected to their disconcerting scrutiny the extraordinary contrast between the cautious, prissy pace of the man and the mad, gay gait of the tale he told. They have not embarrassingly compared the Rev. Charles L. Dodgson with the immortal Lewis Carroll, two persons whom he himself never liked to see together.

One discrepancy between them has always been a subject of amused reflection—a discrepancy not unfamiliar to a generation which knows that one of its own most hilarious clowns is (in what is sometimes confusedly called real life) the professor of political economy at McGill

University. It was the dual nature which, when Lewis Carroll was asked to contribute to a philosophical symposium, compelled the Mathematical Lecturer of Christ Church to reply coldly:

> And what mean all these mysteries to me
> Whose life is full of indices and surds?
> $$x^2 + 7x + 53 = \tfrac{11}{3}$$

It was the discrepancy which once proved so embarrassing to him in his relations with his Queen. Victoria had been so good as to be delighted with Mr. Dodgson's photographs, for you may be sure that the then Prince of Wales, when he visited Oxford, did not get away without some samples of Mr. Dodgson's adroitness with a camera. Victoria even went so far as to say that Albert would have appreciated them highly. Then, when *Alice* was published and won her heart, she graciously suggested that Mr. Dodgson dedicate his next book to her. Unfortunately for Her Majesty, his next book was a mathematical opus entitled *An Elementary Treatise on Determinants*.

But the discrepancy which would more deeply interest those given to a new research into old lives lies in the fact that the man who wrote the most enchanting nonsense in the English language—a just description, surely, of the *Alice* books and *The Hunting of the Snark*—was a puttering, fussy, fastidious, didactic bachelor, who was almost painfully humourless in his relations with the grown-up world around him. You can see that much unconsciously revealed in the fatuous biography written a few months after Lewis Carroll's death in 1898 by his oblivious and too respectful nephew, who was awed by what he called the "purity and refinement" of his uncle's mind. That the shadow of a disappointment fell athwart the uncle's life, his nephew did detect; but he was the kind of biographer who would go on to say: "Those who loved him would not wish to lift the veil from these dead sanctities."

You must picture Lewis Carroll as living precisely in his quarters in the Tom Quad at Christ Church, all his life neatly pigeonholed, all the letters he wrote or received in thirty-seven years elaborately summarized and catalogued, so that by the time he died there were more than 98,000 cross references in the files of his correspondence. He was the kind of man who kept a diagram showing where you sat when you dined with him and what you ate, lest he serve you the same dish when you came again. He was the kind of man who, when an issue of *Jabberwocky*, the school paper of a Boston seminary, published a coarse anecdote from Washington's Diary, wrote to Boston a solemn rebuke of such indelicacy. He was the kind of man who gravely stipulated that no illustrations for a book of his be drawn on Sunday and who could indite the following reproach to a friend of his:

After changing my mind several times, I have at last decided to venture to ask a favour of you, and to trust that you will not misinterpret my motives in doing so.

The favour I would ask is, that you will not tell me any more stories, such as you did on Friday, of remarks which children are said to have made on very sacred subjects—remarks which most people would recognize as irreverent, if made by *grown-up* people, but which are assumed to be innocent when made by children who are unconscious of any irreverence, the strange conclusion being drawn that they are therefore innocent when *repeated* by a grown-up person.

The misinterpretation I would guard against is your supposing that I regard such repetition as always *wrong* in any grown-up person. Let me assure you that I do *not* so regard it. I am always willing to believe that those who repeat such stories differ wholly from myself in their views of what is, and what is not, fitting treatment of sacred things, and I fully recognize that what would certainly be wrong in *me*, is not necessarily so in *them*.

So I simply ask it as a personal favour to myself. The hearing of that anecdote gave me so much pain, and spoiled so much the pleasure of my tiny dinner-party, that I feel sure you will kindly spare me such in future.

Above all he was the kind of man who, in publishing his *Pillow Problems* (part of his series of *Curiosa Mathematica*) recommended these exercises in mental arithmetic not only as an agreeable diversion for a sleepless couch but, more especially, as a way of driving out the sceptical thoughts, the blasphemous thoughts, and "the unholy thoughts, which torture with their hateful presence the fancy that would fain be pure".

And yet in all the anthology of the gentlest art compiled by Mr. Lucas, there are no letters more charming or more frivolous than those which Lewis Carroll wrote to any one of the little girls in whose presence only he was a truly free spirit and at whose courts he was happy to play jester all his days in the land. Calverley, Ruskin, Millais, Tennyson, the Rossettis, Ellen Terry, these pass by in the long procession of his friends; but the greater part of his thought and his genius and his devotion was given to the children who one by one succeeded Alice Liddell in the garden of his friendship. He met them in railway carriages (for he always carried a few puzzles in his pocket against such chance encounters) and he scraped acquaintance with them on the beach, being well supplied always with safety pins in casè they wanted to go in wading. His letters to them would run like this:

November 30, 1879

I have been awfully busy, and I've had to write *heaps* of letters—wheelbarrows full, almost. And it tires me so that generally I go to bed again the next minute after I get up: and sometimes I go to bed again a minute *before* I get up! Did you ever hear of any one being so tired as *that?* . . .

Or like this:

December 26, 1886 ·

MY DEAR E——, —Though rushing, rapid rivers roar between us (if you refer to the map of England, I think you'll find that to be correct), we still remember each other, and feel a sort of shivery affection for each other. . . .

Or like this:

December 27, 1873

MY DEAR GAYNOR,—My name is spelt with a "G", that is to say "*Dodgson*". Any one who spells it the same as that wretch (I mean of course the Chairman of Committees in the House of Commons) offends me *deeply*, and *for ever!* It is a thing I *can* forget, but *never can forgive!* If you do it again, I shall call you "'aynor". Could you live happy with such a name?

As to dancing, my dear, I *never* dance, unless I am allowed to do it *in my own peculiar way*. There is no use trying to describe it: it has to be seen to be believed. The last house I tried it in, the floor broke through. But then it was a poor sort of floor—the beams were only six inches thick, hardly worth calling beams at all; stone arches are much more sensible, when any dancing, *of my peculiar kind*, is to be done. Did you ever see the Rhinoceros and the Hippopotamus, at the Zoological Gardens, trying to dance a minuet together? It is a touching sight.

Give any message from me to Amy that you think will be most likely to surprise her, and, believe me,

Your affectionate friend,

LEWIS CARROLL

Lewis Carroll's case was stated in his own words in one comment on *Alice*. He wrote:

"The why of this book cannot, and need not, be put into words. Those for whom a child's mind is a sealed book, and who see no divinity in a child's smile would read such words in vain; while for any one who has ever loved one true child, no words are needed. For he will have known the awe that falls on one in the presence of a spirit fresh from God's hands, on whom no shadow of sin, and but the outermost fringe of the shadow of sorrow, has yet fallen; he will have felt the bitter contrast between the selfishness that spoils his best deeds and the life that is but an overflowing love. For I think a child's first attitude to the world is a simple love for all living things. And he will have learned that the best work a man can do is when he works for love's sake only, with no thought of fame or gain or earthly reward. No deed of ours, I suppose, on this side of the grave, is really unselfish. Yet if one can put forth all one's powers in a task where nothing of reward is hoped for but a little child's whispered thanks and the airy touch of a little child's pure lips, one seems to come somewhere near to this."

The discrepancy between that solemn dedication and the irresponsible laughter of the book it referred to would, I fear, arouse the most animated curiosity in the clinic of a Dr. Edward Hiram Reede or the library of a Lytton Strachey. They can be pardoned an acute interest in the inner springs of any fellow man who has fallen into thinking of all life as a process of contamination and who, as Newman said of young Hurrell Froude at Oxford, has "a high, severe idea of the intrinsic excellence of virginity". But those of us whose own memories of childhood are inextricably interwoven with all the gay tapestry of *Alice in Wonderland* would rather leave unexplored the shy, retreating man who left so much bubbling laughter in his legacy to the world.

ALEXANDER WOOLLCOTT

I
Alice's Adventures
in
Wonderland

All in the golden afternoon
　　Full leisurely we glide;
For both our oars, with little skill,
　　By little arms are plied,
While little hands make vain pretence
　　Our wanderings to guide.

Ah, cruel Three! In such an hour,
　　Beneath such dreamy weather,
To beg a tale of breath too weak
　　To stir the tiniest feather!
Yet what can one poor voice avail
　　Against three tongues together?

Imperious Prima flashes forth
　　Her edict "to begin it":
In gentler tones Secunda hopes
　　"There will be nonsense in it!"
While Tertia interrupts the tale
　　Not *more* than once a minute.

Anon, to sudden silence won,
　　In fancy they pursue
The dream-child moving through a land
　　Of wonders wild and new,
In friendly chat with bird or beast—
　　And half believe it true.

And ever, as the story drained
　　The wells of fancy dry,
And faintly strove that weary one
　　To put the subject by,
"The rest next time—" "It *is* next time!"
　　The happy voices cry.

Thus grew the tale of Wonderland:
   Thus slowly, one by one,
Its quaint events were hammered out—
   And now the tale is done,
And home we steer, a merry crew,
   Beneath the setting sun.

Alice! A childish story take,
   And, with a gentle hand,
Lay it where Childhood's dreams are twined
   In Memory's mystic band.
Like pilgrim's wither'd wreath of flowers
   Pluck'd in a far-off land.

CHRISTMAS-GREETINGS

[FROM A FAIRY TO A CHILD]

LADY dear, if Fairies may
   For a moment lay aside
Cunning tricks and elfish play,
   'Tis at happy Christmas-tide.

We have heard the children say—
   Gentle children, whom we love—
Long ago, on Christmas-Day,
   Came a message from above.

Still, as Christmas-tide comes round,
   They remember it again—
Echo still the joyful sound
   "Peace on earth, good-will to men!"

Yet the hearts must child-like be
   Where such heavenly guests abide;
Unto children, in their glee,
   All the year is Christmas-tide.

Thus, forgetting tricks and play
   For a moment, Lady dear,
We would wish you, if we may,
   Merry Christmas, glad New Year!

Christmas, 1867.

CHAPTER I

Down the Rabbit-Hole

ALICE was beginning to get very tired of sitting by her sister on the bank and of having nothing to do: once or twice she had peeped into the book her sister was reading, but it had no pictures or conversations in it, "and what is the use of a book", thought Alice, "without pictures or conversations?"

So she was considering, in her own mind (as well as she could, for the hot day made her feel very sleepy and stupid), whether the pleasure of making a daisy-chain would be worth the trouble of getting up and picking the daisies, when suddenly a White Rabbit with pink eyes ran close by her.

There was nothing so *very* remarkable in that; nor did Alice think it so *very* much out of the way to hear the Rabbit say to itself "Oh dear! Oh dear! I shall be too late!" (when she thought it over afterwards it occurred to her that she ought to have wondered at this, but at the time it all seemed quite natural); but, when the Rabbit actually *took a watch out of its waistcoat-pocket*, and looked at it, and then hurried on, Alice started to her feet, for it flashed across her mind that she had never before seen a rabbit with either a waistcoat-pocket, or a watch to take out of it, and burning with curiosity, she ran across the field after it, and was just in time to see it pop down a large rabbit-hole under the hedge.

In another moment down went Alice after it, never once considering how in the world she was to get out again.

The rabbit-hole went straight on like a tunnel for some way, and then dipped suddenly down, so suddenly that Alice had not a moment to think about stopping herself before she found herself falling down what seemed to be a very deep well.

Either the well was very deep, or she fell very slowly, for she had plenty of time as she went down to look about her, and to wonder what was going to happen next. First, she tried to look down and make out what she was coming to, but it was too dark to see anything: then she looked at the sides of the well, and noticed that they were filled with cupboards and book-shelves: here and there she saw maps and pictures hung upon pegs. She took down a jar from one of the shelves as she passed: it was labelled "ORANGE MARMALADE" but to her great disappointment it was empty: she did not like to drop the jar, for fear of killing somebody underneath, so managed to put it into one of the cupboards as she fell past it.

"Well!" thought Alice to herself. "After such a fall as this, I shall think nothing of tumbling down-stairs! How brave they'll all think me at home! Why, I wouldn't say anything about it, even if I fell off the top of the house!" (Which was very likely true.)

Down, down, down. Would the fall *never* come to an end? "I wonder how many miles I've fallen by this time?" she said aloud. "I must be getting somewhere near the centre of the earth. Let me see: that would be four thousand miles down, I think—" (for, you see, Alice had learnt several things of this sort in her lessons in the school-room, and though this was not a *very* good opportunity for showing off her knowledge, as there was no one to listen to her, still it was good practice to say it over) "—yes, that's about the right distance—but then I wonder what Latitude or Longitude I've got to?" (Alice had not the slightest idea what Latitude was, or Longitude either, but she thought they were nice grand words to say.)

Presently she began again. "I wonder if I shall fall right *through* the earth! How funny it'll seem to come out among the people that walk with their heads downwards! The antipathies, I think—" (she was rather glad there *was* no one listening, this time, as it didn't sound at all the right word) "—but I shall have to ask them what the name of the country is, you know. Please, Ma'am, is this New Zealand? Or Australia?" (and she tried to curtsey as she spoke—fancy, *curtseying* as you're falling through the air! Do you think you could manage it?) "And what an ignorant little girl she'll think me for asking! No, it'll never do to ask: perhaps I shall see it written up somewhere."

Down, down, down. There was nothing else to do, so Alice soon began talking again. "Dinah'll miss me very much to-night, I should think!" (Dinah was the cat.) "I hope they'll remember her saucer of milk at tea-time. Dinah, my dear! I wish you were down here with me! There are no mice in the air, I'm afraid, but you might catch a bat, and that's very like a mouse, you know. But do cats eat bats, I wonder?" And here Alice began to get rather sleepy, and went on saying to herself, in a dreamy sort of way, "Do cats eat bats? Do cats eat bats?" and sometimes "Do bats eat cats?" for, you see, as she couldn't answer either question, it didn't much matter which way she put it. She felt that she was dozing off, and had just begun to dream that she was walking hand in hand with Dinah, and was saying to her, very earnestly, "Now, Dinah, tell me the truth: did you ever eat a bat?" when suddenly, thump! thump! down she came upon a heap of sticks and dry leaves, and the fall was over.

Alice was not a bit hurt, and she jumped up on to her feet in a moment: she looked up, but it was all dark over-head: before her was another long passage, and the White Rabbit was still in sight, hurrying down it. There was not a moment to be lost: away went Alice like the wind, and was just in time to hear it say, as it turned a corner, "Oh my ears and whiskers, how late it's getting!" She was close behind it when she turned the corner, but the Rabbit was no longer to be seen: she found herself in a long, low hall, which was lit up by a row of lamps hanging from the roof.

There were doors all round the hall, but they were all locked; and when Alice had been all the way down one side and up the other, trying every door, she walked sadly down the middle, wondering how she was ever to get out again.

Suddenly she came upon a little three-legged table, all made of solid glass: there was nothing on it but a tiny golden key, and Alice's first idea was that this might belong to one of the doors of the hall; but, alas! either the locks were too large, or the key was too small, but at any rate it would not open any of them. However, on the second time round, she came upon a low curtain she had not noticed before, and behind it was a little door about fifteen inches high: she tried the little golden key in the lock, and to her great delight it fitted!

Alice opened the door and found that it led into a small passage, not much larger than a rat-hole: she knelt down and looked along the passage into the loveliest garden you ever saw. How she longed to get out of that dark hall, and wander about among those beds of bright flowers and those cool fountains, but she could not even get her head through the doorway; "and even if my head *would* go through", thought poor Alice, "it would be of very little use without my shoulders. Oh, how I wish I could shut up like a telescope! I think I could, if I only knew how to begin." For, you see, so many out-of-the-way things had happened lately, that Alice had begun to think that very few things indeed were really impossible.

There seemed to be no use in waiting by the little door, so she went back to the table, half hoping she might find another key on it, or at any rate a book of rules for shutting people up like telescopes: this time she found a little bottle on it ("which certainly was not here before", said Alice), and tied around the neck of the bottle was a paper label, with the words "DRINK ME" beautifully printed on it in large letters.

It was all very well to say "Drink me", but the wise little Alice was not going to do *that* in a hurry. "No, I'll look first", she said, "and see whether it's marked '*poison*' or not"; for she had read several nice little stories about children who had got burnt, and eaten up by wild beasts, and other unpleasant things, all because they *would* not remember the simple rules their friends had taught them: such as, that a red-hot poker will burn you if you hold it too long; and that, if you cut your finger *very* deeply with a knife, it usually bleeds; and she had never forgotten

that, if you drink much from a bottle marked "poison", it is almost certain to disagree with you, sooner or later.

However, this bottle was *not* marked "poison", so Alice ventured to taste it, and, finding it very nice (it had, in fact, a sort of mixed flavour of cherry-tart, custard, pineapple, roast turkey, toffee, and hot buttered toast), she very soon finished it off.

*   *   *   *

    *   *   *

*   *   *   *

"What a curious feeling!" said Alice. "I must be shutting up like a telescope!"

And so it was indeed: she was now only ten inches high, and her face brightened up at the thought that she was now the right size for going through the little door into that lovely garden. First, however, she waited for a few minutes to see if she was going to shrink any further: she felt a little nervous about this; "for it might end, you know", said Alice to herself, "in my going out altogether, like a candle. I wonder what I should be like then?" And she tried to fancy what the flame of a candle looks like after the candle is blown out, for she could not remember ever having seen such a thing.

After a while, finding that nothing more happened, she decided on going into the garden at once; but, alas for poor Alice! when she got to the door, she found she had forgotten the little golden key, and when she went back to the table for it, she found she could not possibly reach it: she could see it quite plainly through the glass, and she tried her best to climb up one of the legs of the table, but it was too slippery; and when she had tired herself out with trying, the poor little thing sat down and cried.

"Come, there's no use in crying like that!" said Alice to herself rather sharply. "I advise you to leave off this minute!" She generally gave herself very good advice (though she very seldom followed it), and sometimes she scolded herself so severely as to bring tears into her eyes; and once she remembered trying to box her own ears for having cheated herself in a game of croquet she was playing against herself, for this curious child was very fond of pretending to be two people. "But it's no use now", thought poor Alice, "to pretend to be two people! Why, there's hardly enough of me left to make *one* respectable person!"

Soon her eye fell on a little glass box that was lying under the table: she opened it, and found in it a very small cake, on which the words "EAT ME" were beautifully marked in currants. "Well, I'll eat it," said Alice, "and if it makes me grow larger, I can reach the key; and if it makes me grow smaller, I can creep under the door: so either way I'll get into the garden, and I don't care which happens!"

She ate a little bit, and said anxiously to herself "Which way? Which way?", holding her hand on the top of her head to feel which way it was growing; and she was quite surprised to find that she remained the same size. To be sure, this is what generally happens when one eats cake; but Alice had got so much into the way of expecting nothing but out-of-the-way things to happen, that it seemed quite dull and stupid for life to go on in the common way.

So she set to work, and very soon finished off the cake.

       *   *   *   *
          *   *   *
       *   *   *   *

Chapter II

The Pool of Tears

"CURIOUSER and curiouser!" cried Alice (she was so much surprised, that for the moment she quite forgot how to speak good English). "Now, I'm opening out like the largest telescope that ever was! Good-bye, feet!" (for when she looked down at her feet, they seemed to be almost out of sight, they were getting so far off). "Oh, my poor little feet, I wonder who will put on your shoes and stockings for you now, dears? I'm sure *I* sha'n't be able! I shall be a great deal too far off to trouble myself about you: you must manage the best way you can—but I must be kind to them", thought Alice, "or perhaps they wo'n't walk the way I want to go! Let me see, I'll give them a new pair of boots every Christmas."

And she went on planning to herself how she would manage it. "They must go by the carrier," she thought; "and how funny it'll seem, sending presents to one's own feet! And how odd the directions will look!

Alice's Right Foot, Esq.
Hearthrug,
near the Fender,
(with Alice's love).

Oh dear, what nonsense I'm talking!"

23

Just at this moment her head struck against the roof of the hall: in fact she was now rather more than nine feet high, and she at once took up the little golden key and hurried off to the garden door.

Poor Alice! It was as much as she could do, lying down on one side, to look through into the garden with one eye; but to get through was more hopeless than ever: she sat down and began to cry again.

"You ought to be ashamed of yourself," said Alice, "a great girl like you", (she might well say this), "to go on crying in this way! Stop this moment, I tell you!" But she went on all the same, shedding gallons of tears, until there was a large pool around her, about four inches deep, and reaching half down the hall.

After a time she heard a little pattering of feet in the distance, and she hastily dried her eyes to see what was coming. It was the White Rabbit returning splendidly dressed, with a pair of white kid-gloves in one hand and a large fan in the other: he came trotting along in a great hurry, muttering to himself, as he came, "Oh! The Duchess, the Duchess! Oh! *Wo'n't* she be savage if I've kept her waiting!" Alice felt so desperate that she was ready to ask help of any one: so, when the Rabbit came near her, she began, in a low, timid voice, "If you please, Sir——" The Rabbit started violently, dropped the white kid-gloves and the fan, and scurried away into the darkness as hard as he could go.

Alice took up the fan and gloves and, as the hall was very hot, she kept fanning herself all the time she went on talking. "Dear, dear! How queer everything is to-day! And yesterday things went on just as usual, I wonder if I've changed in the night? Let me think: *was* I the same when I got up this morning? I almost think I can remember feeling a little different. But if I'm not the same, the next question is 'Who in the world am I?' Ah, *that's* the great puzzle!" And she began thinking over all the children she knew that were of the same age as herself, to see if she could have been changed for any of them.

"I'm sure I'm not Ada," she said, "for her hair goes in such long ringlets, and mine doesn't go in ringlets at all; and I'm sure I ca'n't be Mabel, for I know all sorts of things, and she, oh, she knows such a very little! Besides, *she's* she, and *I'm* I, and—oh dear, how puzzling it all is! I'll try if I know all the things I used to know. Let me see: four times five is twelve, and four times six is thirteen, and four times seven is—oh dear! I shall never get to twenty at that rate! However, the Multiplication-Table doesn't signify: let's try Geography. London is the capital of Paris, and Paris is the capital of Rome, and Rome—no, *that's* all wrong, I'm certain! I must have been changed for Mabel! I'll try and say '*How doth the little——*'," and she crossed her hands on her lap as if she were saying lessons, and began to repeat it, but her voice sounded hoarse and strange, and the words did not come the same as they used to do:

> "*How doth the little crocodile*
> *Improve his shining tail,*
> *And pour the waters of the Nile*
> *On every golden scale!*

> "*How cheerfully he seems to grin,*
> *How neatly spreads his claws,*
> *And welcomes little fishes in,*
> *With gently smiling jaws!*

"I'm sure those are not the right words," said poor Alice, and her eyes filled with tears again as she went on, "I must be Mabel after all, and I shall have to go and live in that poky little house, and have next to no toys to play with, and oh, ever so many lessons to learn! No, I've made up my mind about it: if I'm Mabel, I'll stay down here! It'll be no use their putting their heads down and saying 'Come up again, dear!' I shall only look up and say 'Who am I, then? Tell me that first, and then, if I like being that person, I'll come up: if not, I'll stay down here till I'm somebody else'—but, oh dear!" cried Alice, with a sudden burst of tears, "I do wish they *would* put their heads down! I am so *very* tired of being all alone here!"

As she said this she looked down at her hands, and was surprised to see that she had put on one of the Rabbit's little white kid-gloves while she was talking. "How *can* I have done that?" she thought. "I must be growing small again." She got up and went to the table to measure herself by it, and found that, as nearly as she could guess, she was now about two feet high, and was going on shrinking rapidly: she soon found out that the cause of this was the fan she was holding, and she dropped it hastily, just in time to save herself from shrinking away altogether.

"That *was* a narrow escape!" said Alice, a good deal frightened at the sudden change, but very glad to find herself still in existence. "And now for the garden!" And she ran with all speed back to the little door; but, alas! the little door was shut again, and the little golden key was lying on the glass table as before, "and things are

worse than ever," thought the poor child, "for I never was so small as this before, never! And I declare it's too bad, that it is!"

As she said these words her foot slipped, and in another moment, splash! she was up to her chin in salt-water. Her first idea was that she had somehow fallen into the sea, "and in that case I can go back by railway," she said to herself. (Alice had been to the seaside once in her life, and had come to the general conclusion that wherever you go to on the English coast, you find a number of bathing-machines in the sea, some children digging in the sand with wooden spades, then a row of lodging-houses, and behind them a railway station.) However, she soon made out that she was in the pool of tears which she had wept when she was nine feet high.

"I wish I hadn't cried so much!" said Alice, as she swam about, trying to find her way out. "I shall be punished for it now, I suppose, by being drowned in my own tears! That *will* be a queer thing, to be sure! However, everything is queer to-day."

Just then she heard something splashing about in the pool a little way off, and she swam nearer to make out what it was: at first she thought it must be a walrus or

hippopotamus, but then she remembered how small she was now, and she soon made out that it was only a mouse, that had slipped in like herself.

"Would it be of any use, now," thought Alice, "to speak to this mouse? Everything is so out-of-the-way down here, that I should think very likely it can talk: at any rate, there's no harm in trying." So she began: "O Mouse, do you know the way out of this pool? I am very tired of swimming about here, O Mouse!" (Alice thought this must be the right way of speaking to a mouse: she had never done such a thing before, but she remembered having seen, in her brother's Latin Grammar, "A mouse —of a mouse—to a mouse—a mouse—O mouse!") The mouse looked at her rather inquisitively, and seemed to her to wink with one of its little eyes, but it said nothing.

"Perhaps it doesn't understand English," thought Alice. "I daresay it's a French mouse, come over with William the Conqueror." (For, with all her knowledge of history, Alice had no very clear notion how long ago anything had happened.) So she began again: "Où est ma chatte?" which was the first sentence in her French lesson-book. The Mouse gave a sudden leap out of the water, and seemed to quiver all over with fright. "Oh, I beg your pardon!" cried Alice hastily, afraid that she had hurt the poor animal's feelings. "I quite forgot you didn't like cats."

"Not like cats!" cried the Mouse in a shrill passionate voice. "Would *you* like cats, if you were me?"

"Well, perhaps not," said Alice in a soothing tone: "don't be angry about it. And yet I wish I could show you our cat Dinah. I think you'd take a fancy to cats, if you could only see her. She is such a dear quiet thing", Alice went on, half to herself, as she swam lazily about in the pool, "and she sits purring so nicely by the fire, licking her paws and washing her face—and she is such a nice soft thing to nurse—and she's such a capital one for catching mice—oh, I beg your pardon!" cried Alice again, for this time the Mouse was bristling all over, and she felt certain it must be really offended. "We won't talk about her any more if you'd rather not."

"We, indeed!" cried the Mouse, who was trembling down to the end of its tail. "As if *I* would talk on such a subject! Our family always *hated* cats: nasty, low, vulgar things! Don't let me hear the name again!"

"I wo'n't indeed!" said Alice, in a great hurry to change the subject of conversation. "Are you—are you fond—of —of dogs?" The Mouse did not answer, so Alice went on eagerly: "There is such a nice little dog, near our house, I should like to show you! A little bright-eyed terrier, you know, with oh, such long curly brown hair! And it'll fetch things when you throw them, and it'll sit up and beg for its dinner, and all sorts of things—I ca'n't remember half of them—and it belongs to a farmer, you know, and he says it's so useful, it's worth a hundred pounds! He says it kills all the rats and—oh dear!" cried Alice in a sorrowful tone. "I'm afraid I've offended it again!" For the Mouse was swimming away from her as hard as it could go, and making quite a commotion in the pool as it went.

So she called softly after it, "Mouse dear! Do come back again, and we wo'n't talk about cats, or dogs either, if you don't like them!" When the Mouse heard this, it turned round and swam slowly back to her: its face was quite pale (with passion, Alice thought), and it said, in a low trembling voice, "Let us get to the shore, and then I'll tell you my history, and you'll understand why it is I hate cats and dogs."

It was high time to go, for the pool was getting quite crowded with the birds and animals that had fallen into it: there was a Duck and a Dodo, a Lory and an Eaglet, and several other curious creatures. Alice led the way, and the whole party swam to the shore.

Chapter III

A Caucus-Race and a Long Tale

THEY were indeed a queer-looking party that assembled on the bank—the birds with draggled feathers, the animals with their fur clinging close to them, and all dripping wet, cross, and uncomfortable.

The first question of course was, how to get dry again: they had a consultation about this, and after a few minutes it seemed quite natural to Alice to find herself talking familiarly with them, as if she had known them all her life. Indeed, she had quite a long argument with the Lory, who at last turned sulky, and would only say, "I'm older than you, and must know better." And this Alice would not allow, without knowing how old it was, and as the Lory positively refused to tell its age, there was no more to be said.

At last the Mouse, who seemed to be a person of some authority among them, called out "Sit down, all of you, and listen to me! *I'll* soon make you dry enough!" They all sat down at once, in a large ring, with the Mouse in the middle. Alice kept her eyes anxiously fixed on it, for she felt sure she would catch a bad cold if she did not get dry very soon.

"Ahem!" said the Mouse with an important air. "Are you all ready? This is the driest thing I know. Silence all round, if you please! 'William the Conqueror, whose cause was favoured by the pope, was soon submitted to by the English, who wanted leaders, and had been of late much accustomed to usurpation and conquest. Edwin and Morcar, the earls of Mercia and Northumbria——' "

"Ugh!" said the Lory, with a shiver.

"I beg your pardon!" said the Mouse, frowning, but very politely. "Did you speak?"

"Not I!" said the Lory, hastily.

"I thought you did," said the Mouse. "I proceed. 'Edwin and Morcar, the earls of Mercia and Northumbria, declared for him; and even Stigand, the patriotic archbishop of Canterbury, found it advisable——' "

"Found *what*?" said the Duck.

"Found *it*," the Mouse replied rather crossly: "of course you know what 'it' means."

"I know what 'it' means well enough, when *I* find a thing," said the Duck: "it's generally a frog, or a worm. The question is, what did the archbishop find?"

The Mouse did not notice this question, but hurriedly went on, " '—found it advisable to go with Edgar Atheling to meet William and offer him the crown. William's conduct at first was moderate. But the insolence of his Normans——' How are you getting on now, my dear?" it continued, turning to Alice as it spoke.

"As wet as ever," said Alice in a melancholy tone: "it doesn't seem to dry me at all."

"In that case," said the Dodo solemnly, rising to its

feet, "I move that the meeting adjourn, for the immediate adoption of more energetic remedies——"

"Speak English!" said the Eaglet. "I don't know the meaning of half those long words, and, what's more, I don't believe you do either!" And the Eaglet bent down its head to hide a smile: some of the other birds tittered audibly.

"What I was going to say", said the Dodo in an offended tone, "was, that the best thing to get us dry would be a Caucus-race."

"What *is* a Caucus-race?" said Alice; not that she much wanted to know, but the Dodo had paused as if it thought that *somebody* ought to speak, and no one else seemed inclined to say anything.

"Why," said the Dodo, "the best way to explain it is to do it." (And, as you might like to try the thing yourself some winter-day, I will tell you how the Dodo managed it.)

First it marked out a race-course, in a sort of circle, ("the exact shape doesn't matter," it said,) and then all the party were placed along the course, here and there. There was no "One, two, three, and away!" but they began running when they liked, and left off when they liked, so that it was not easy to know when the race was over. However, when they had been running half an hour or so, and were quite dry again, the Dodo suddenly called out "The race is over!" and they all crowded round it, panting, and asking "But who has won?"

This question the Dodo could not answer without a great deal of thought, and it stood for a long time with one finger pressed upon its forehead (the position in which you usually see Shakespeare, in the pictures of him), while the rest waited in silence. At last the Dodo said "*Everybody* has won, and *all* must have prizes."

"But who is to give the prizes?" quite a chorus of voices asked.

"Why, *she*, of course," said the Dodo, pointing to Alice

with one finger; and the whole party at once crowded round her, calling out, in a confused way, "Prizes! Prizes!"

Alice had no idea what to do, and in despair she put her hand in her pocket, and pulled out a box of comfits (luckily the salt-water had not got into it), and handed them round as prizes. There was exactly one a-piece, all round.

"But she must have a prize herself, you know," said the Mouse.

"Of course," the Dodo replied very gravely. "What else have you got in your pocket?" it went on, turning to Alice.

"Only a thimble," said Alice sadly.

"Hand it over here," said the Dodo.

Then they all crowded round her once more, while the Dodo solemnly presented the thimble, saying "We beg your acceptance of this elegant thimble"; and, when it had finished this short speech, they all cheered.

Alice thought the whole thing very absurd, but they all looked so grave that she did not dare to laugh; and, as she could not think of anything to say, she simply bowed, and took the thimble, looking as solemn as she could.

The next thing was to eat the comfits: this caused some noise and confusion, as the large birds complained that they could not taste theirs, and the small ones choked and had to be patted on the back. However, it was over at last, and they sat down again in a ring, and begged the Mouse to tell them something more.

"You promised to tell me your history, you know," said Alice, "and why it is you hate—C and D," she added in a whisper, half afraid that it would be offended again.

"Mine is a long and a sad tale!" said the Mouse, turning to Alice, and sighing.

"It *is* a long tail, certainly," said Alice, looking down with wonder at the Mouse's tail; "but why do you call it sad?" And she kept on puzzling about it while the Mouse was speaking, so that her idea of the tale was something like this:

"Fury said to
a mouse, That
he met in the
house, 'Let
us both go
to law: *I*
will prose-
cute *you*.
Come, I'll
take no de-
nial; We
must have
a trial:
For really
this morn-
ing I've
nothing
to do.'
Said the
mouse to
the cur,
'Such a
trial, dear
Sir, With
no jury
or judge,
would
be wast-
ing our
breath.'
'I'll be
judge,
I'll be
jury,'
Said
cun-
ning
old
Fury:
'I'll
try
the
whole
cause,
and
con-
demn
you to
death.' "

"You are not attending!" said the Mouse to Alice, severely. "What are you thinking of?"

"I beg your pardon," said Alice very humbly: "you had got to the fifth bend, I think?"

"I had *not*!" cried the Mouse, sharply and very angrily.

"A knot!" said Alice, always ready to make herself useful, and looking anxiously about her. "Oh, do let me help to undo it!"

"I shall do nothing of the sort," said the Mouse, getting up and walking away. "You insult me by talking such nonsense!"

"I didn't mean it!" pleaded poor Alice. "But you're so easily offended, you know!"

The Mouse only growled in reply.

"Please come back, and finish your story!" Alice called after it. And the others all joined in chorus "Yes, please do!" But the Mouse only shook its head impatiently, and walked a little quicker.

"What a pity it wouldn't stay!" sighed the Lory, as soon as it was quite out of sight. And an old Crab took the opportunity of saying to her daughter "Ah, my dear! Let this be a lesson to you never to lose *your* temper!" "Hold your tongue, Ma!" said the young Crab, a little snappishly. "You're enough to try the patience of an oyster!"

"I wish I had our Dinah here, I know I do!" said Alice aloud, addressing nobody in particular. "*She'd* soon fetch it back!"

"And who is Dinah, if I might venture to ask the question?" said the Lory.

Alice replied eagerly, for she was always ready to talk about her pet: "Dinah's our cat. And she's such a capital one for catching mice, you ca'n't think! And oh, I wish you could see her after the birds! Why, she'll eat a little bird as soon as look at it!"

This speech caused a remarkable sensation among the party. Some of the birds hurried off at once: one old Magpie began wrapping itself up very carefully, remarking "I really must be getting home: the night-air doesn't suit my throat!" And a Canary called out in a trembling voice, to its children, "Come away, my dears! It's high time you were all in bed!" On various pretexts they all moved off, and Alice was soon left alone.

"I wish I hadn't mentioned Dinah!" she said to herself in a melancholy tone. "Nobody seems to like her, down here, and I'm sure she's the best cat in the world! Oh, my dear Dinah! I wonder if I shall ever see you any more!" And here poor Alice began to cry again, for she felt very lonely and low-spirited. In a little while, however, she again heard a little pattering of footsteps in the distance, and she looked up eagerly, half hoping that the Mouse had changed his mind, and was coming back to finish his story.

CHAPTER IV

The Rabbit Sends in a Little Bill

IT was the White Rabbit, trotting slowly back again, and looking anxiously about as it went, as if it had lost something; and she heard it muttering to itself, "The Duchess! The Duchess! Oh my dear paws! Oh my fur and whiskers! She'll get me executed, as sure as ferrets are ferrets! Where *can* I have dropped them, I wonder?" Alice guessed in a moment that it was looking for the fan and the pair of white kid-gloves, and she very good-naturedly began hunting about for them, but they were nowhere to be seen—everything seemed to have changed since her swim in the pool; and the great hall, with the glass table and the little door, had vanished completely.

Very soon the Rabbit noticed Alice, as she went hunting about, and called out to her, in an angry tone, "Why, Mary Ann, what *are* you doing out here? Run home this moment, and fetch me a pair of gloves and a fan! Quick, now!" And Alice was so much frightened that she ran off at once in the direction it pointed to, without trying to explain the mistake that it had made.

"He took me for his housemaid," she said to herself as she ran. "How surprised he'll be when he finds out who I am! But I'd better take him his fan and gloves—that is, if I can find them." As she said this, she came upon a neat little house, on the door of which was a bright brass plate with the name "W. RABBIT" engraved upon it. She went in without knocking, and hurried upstairs, in great fear lest she should meet the real Mary Ann, and be turned out of the house before she had found the fan and gloves.

"How queer it seems", Alice said to herself, "to be going messages for a rabbit! I suppose Dinah'll be sending me on messages next!" and she began fancying the sort of thing that would happen: " 'Miss Alice! Come here directly, and get ready for your walk!' 'Coming in a minute, nurse! But I've got to watch this mouse-hole till Dinah comes back, and see that the mouse doesn't get out.' Only I don't think", Alice went on, "that they'd let Dinah stop in the house if it began ordering people about like that!"

By this time she had found her way into a tidy little room with a table in the window, and on it (as she had hoped) a fan and two or three pairs of tiny white kid-gloves: she took up the fan and a pair of the gloves, and was just going to leave the room, when her eye fell upon a little bottle that stood near the looking-glass, There was no label this time with the words "DRINK ME", but nevertheless she uncorked it and put it to her lips. "I know *something* interesting is sure to happen", she said to herself, "whenever I eat or drink anything: so I'll just see what this bottle does. I do hope it'll make me grow large again, for really I'm quite tired of being such a tiny little thing!"

It did so indeed, and much sooner than she had expected: before she had drunk half the bottle, she found her head pressing against the ceiling, and had to stoop to save her neck from being broken. She hastily put down the bottle, saying to herself "That's quite enough —I hope I sha'n't grow any more—As it is, I ca'n't get out at the door—I do wish I hadn't drunk quite so much!"

Alas! It was too late to wish that! She went on growing, and growing, and very soon had to kneel down on the floor: in another minute there was not even room for this, and she tried the effect of lying down with one elbow against the door, and the other arm curled round her head. Still she went on growing, and, as a last resource, she put one arm out of the window, and one foot up the chimney, and said to herself "Now I can do no more, whatever happens. What *will* become of me?"

Luckily for Alice, the little magic bottle had now had its full effect, and she grew no larger: still it was very uncomfortable, and, as there seemed to be no sort of chance of her ever getting out of the room again, no wonder she felt unhappy.

"It was much pleasanter at home", thought poor Alice, "when one wasn't always growing larger and smaller, and being ordered about by mice and rabbits. I almost wish I hadn't gone down that rabbit-hole—and yet—and yet— it's rather curious, you know, this sort of life! I do wonder

what *can* have happened to me! When I used to read fairy tales, I fancied that kind of thing never happened, and now here I am in the middle of one! There ought to be a book written about me, that there ought! And when I grow up, I'll write one—but I'm grown up now," she added in a sorrowful tone: "at least there's no room to grow up any more *here*."

"But then", thought Alice, "shall I *never* get any older than I am now? That'll be a comfort, one way—never to be an old woman—but then—always to have lessons to learn! Oh, I shouldn't like *that*!"

"Oh, you foolish Alice!" she answered herself. "How

can you learn lessons in here? Why, there's hardly room for *you*, and no room at all for any lesson-books!"

And so she went on, taking first one side and then the other, and making quite a conversation of it altogether;

but after a few minutes she heard a voice outside, and stopped to listen.

"Mary Ann! Mary Ann!" said the voice. "Fetch me my gloves this moment!" Then came a little pattering of feet on the stairs. Alice knew it was the Rabbit coming to look for her, and she trembled till she shook the house, quite forgetting that she was now about a thousand times as large as the Rabbit, and had no reason to be afraid of it.

Presently the Rabbit came up to the door, and tried to open it; but, as the door opened inwards, and Alice's elbow was pressed hard against it, that attempt proved a failure. Alice heard it say to itself "Then I'll go round and get in at the window."

"*That* you wo'n't!" thought Alice, and, after waiting till she fancied she heard the Rabbit just under the window, she suddenly spread out her hand, and made a snatch in the air. She did not get hold of anything, but she heard a little shriek and a fall, and a crash of broken glass, from which she concluded that it was just possible it had fallen into a cucumber-frame, or something of the sort.

Next came an angry voice—the Rabbit's—"Pat! Pat! Where are you?" And then a voice she had never heard before, "Sure then I'm here! Digging for apples, yer honour!"

"Digging for apples, indeed!" said the Rabbit angrily. "Here! Come help me out of *this*!" (Sounds of more broken glass.)

"Now tell me, Pat, what's that in the window?"

"Sure, it's an arm, yer honour!" (He pronounced it "arrum".)

"An arm, you goose! Who ever saw one that size? Why, it fills the whole window!"

"Sure, it does, yer honour: but it's an arm for all that."

"Well, it's got no business there, at any rate: go and take it away!"

There was a long silence after this, and Alice could only hear whispers now and then; such as "Sure, I don't like it, yer honour, at all, at all!" "Do as I tell you, you coward!" and at last she spread out her hand again, and made another snatch in the air. This time there were *two* little shrieks, and more sounds of broken glass. "What a number of cucumber-frames there must be!" thought Alice. "I wonder what they'll do next! As for pulling me out of the window, I only wish *they could*! I'm sure *I* don't want to stay in here any longer!"

She waited for some time without hearing anything more: at last came a rumbling of little cart-wheels, and the sound of a good many voices all talking together: she made out the words: "Where's the other ladder?—Why,

I hadn't to bring but one.
Bill's got the other—Bill! Fetch
it here, lad!—Here, put 'em up
at this corner—No, tie 'em together first—they don't reach
half high enough yet—Oh,
they'll do well enough. Don't
be particular—Here, Bill! Catch
hold of this rope—Will the roof
bear?—Mind that loose slate—
Oh, it's coming down! Heads
below!" (a loud crash)—
"Now, who did that?—It was
Bill, I fancy—Who's to go
down the chimney?—Nay, *I*
sha'n't! *You* do it!—*That* I
wo'n't, then!—Bill's got to go
down—Here, Bill! The master
says you've got to go down
the chimney!"

"Oh! So Bill's got to come
down the chimney, has he?"
said Alice to herself. "Why,
they seem to put everything
upon Bill! I wouldn't be in
Bill's place for a good deal; this
fireplace is narrow, to be sure;
but I *think* I can kick a little!"

She drew her foot as far down the chimney as she could,
and waited till she heard a little animal (she couldn't
guess of what sort it was) scratching and scrambling
about in the chimney close above her: then, saying to
herself "This is Bill," she gave one sharp kick, and waited
to see what would happen next.

The first thing she heard was a general chorus of
"There goes Bill!" then the Rabbit's voice alone—"Catch
him, you by the hedge!" then silence, and then another
confusion of voices—"Hold up his head—Brandy now—

Don't choke him—How was it, old fellow? What happened to you? Tell us all about it!"

Last came a little feeble, squeaking voice. ("That's Bill," thought Alice.) "Well, I hardly know—No more, thank ye; I'm better now—but I'm a deal too flustered to tell you—all I know is, something comes at me like a Jack-in-the-box, and up I goes like a sky-rocket!"

"So you did, old fellow!" said the others.

"We must burn the house down!" said the Rabbit's voice. And Alice called out, as loud as she could, "If you do, I'll set Dinah at you!"

There was a dead silence instantly, and Alice thought to herself "I wonder what they *will* do next! If they had any sense, they'd take the roof off." After a minute or two they began moving about again, and Alice heard the Rabbit say "A barrowful will do, to begin with."

"A barrowful of *what*?" thought Alice. But she had not long to doubt, for the next moment a shower of little pebbles came rattling in at the window, and some of them hit her in the face. "I'll put a stop to this," she said to herself, and shouted out "You'd better not do that again!" which produced another dead silence.

Alice noticed, with some surprise, that the pebbles were all turning into little cakes as they lay on the floor, and a bright idea came into her head. "If I eat one of these cakes", she thought, "it's sure to make *some* change in my size; and, as it ca'n't possibly make me larger, it must make me smaller, I suppose."

So she swallowed one of the cakes, and was delighted to find that she began shrinking directly. As soon as she was small enough to get through the door, she ran out of the house, and found quite a crowd of little animals and birds waiting outside. The poor little Lizard, Bill, was in the middle, being held up by two guinea-pigs, who were giving it something out of a bottle. They all made a rush at Alice the moment she appeared; but she ran off as hard as she could, and soon found herself safe in a thick wood.

"The first thing I've got to do", said Alice to herself, as

she wandered about in the wood, "is to grow to my right size again; and the second thing is to find my way into that lovely garden. I think that will be the best plan."

It sounded an excellent plan, no doubt, and very neatly and simply arranged: the only difficulty was, that she had not the smallest idea how to set about it; and, while she was peering about anxiously among the trees, a little sharp bark just over her head made her look up in a great hurry.

An enormous puppy was looking down at her with large round eyes, and feebly stretching out one paw, trying to touch her. "Poor little thing!" said Alice, in a coaxing tone, and she tried hard to whistle to it; but she was terribly frightened all the time at the thought that it might be hungry, in which case it would be very likely to eat her up in spite of all her coaxing.

Hardly knowing what she did, she picked up a little bit of stick, and held it out to the puppy: whereupon the puppy jumped into the air off all its feet at once, with a yelp of delight, and rushed at the stick, and made believe to worry it: then Alice dodged behind a great thistle, to keep herself from being run over; and, the moment she appeared on the other side, the puppy made another rush at the stick, and tumbled head over heels in its hurry to get hold of it: then Alice, thinking it was very like having a game of play with a cart-horse, and expecting every moment to be trampled under its feet, ran round the thistle again: then the puppy began a series of short charges at the stick, running a very little way forwards each time and a long way back, and barking hoarsely all the while, till at last it sat down a good way off, panting, with its tongue hanging out of its mouth, and its great eyes half shut.

This seemed to Alice a good opportunity for making her escape: so she set off at once, and ran till she was quite tired and out of breath, and till the puppy's bark sounded quite faint in the distance.

"And yet what a dear little puppy it was!" said Alice, as she leant against a buttercup to rest herself, and fanned herself with one of the leaves. "I should have liked teaching it tricks very much, if—if I'd only been the right size to do it! Oh dear! I'd nearly forgotten that I've got to grow up again! Let me see—how *is* it to be managed? I suppose I ought to eat or drink something or other; but the great question is 'What?'"

The great question certainly was "What?" Alice looked all round her at the flowers and the blades of grass, but she could not see anything that looked like the right thing to eat or drink under the circumstances. There was a large mushroom growing near her, about the same height as herself; and, when she had looked under it, and on both sides of it, and behind it, it occurred to her that she might as well look and see what was on top of it.

She stretched herself up on tiptoe, and peeped over the edge of the mushroom, and her eyes immediately met those of a large blue caterpillar, that was sitting on the top, with its arms folded, quietly smoking a long hookah, and taking not the smallest notice of her or of anything else.

CHAPTER V

Advice from a Caterpillar

THE Caterpillar and Alice looked at each other for some time in silence: at last the Caterpillar took the hookah out of its mouth, and addressed her in a languid, sleepy voice.

"Who are *you*?" said the Caterpillar.

This was not an encouraging opening for a conversation. Alice replied, rather shyly, "I—I hardly know, Sir, just at present—at least I know who I *was* when I got up this morning, but I think I must have been changed several times since then."

"What do you mean by that?" said the Caterpillar, sternly. "Explain yourself!"

"I ca'n't explain *myself*, I'm afraid, Sir," said Alice, "because I'm not myself, you see."

"I don't see," said the Caterpillar.

"I'm afraid I ca'n't put it more clearly," Alice replied, very politely, "for I ca'n't understand it myself, to begin with; and being so many different sizes in a day is very confusing."

"It isn't," said the Caterpillar.

"Well, perhaps you haven't found it so yet," said Alice; "but when you have to turn into a chrysalis—you will some day, you know—and then after that into a butterfly, I should think you'll feel it a little queer, wo'n't you?"

"Not a bit," said the Caterpillar.

"Well, perhaps *your* feelings may be different," said Alice: "all I know is, it would feel very queer to *me*."

"You!" said the Caterpillar contemptuously. "Who are *you*?"

Which brought them back again to the beginning of the conversation. Alice felt a little irritated at the Caterpillar's making such *very* short remarks, and she drew herself up and said, very gravely, "I think you ought to tell me who *you* are, first."

"Why?" said the Caterpillar.

Here was another puzzling question; and, as Alice could not think of any good reason, and the Caterpillar seemed to be in a *very* unpleasant state of mind, she turned away.

"Come back!" the Caterpillar called after her. "I've something important to say!"

This sounded promising, certainly. Alice turned and came back again.

"Keep your temper," said the Caterpillar.

"Is that all?" said Alice, swallowing down her anger as well as she could.

"No," said the Caterpillar.

Alice thought she might as well wait, as she had nothing else to do, and perhaps after all it might tell her something worth hearing. For some minutes it puffed away without speaking; but at last it unfolded its arms, took the hookah out of its mouth again, and said "So you think you're changed, do you?"

"I'm afraid I am, Sir," said Alice. "I ca'n't remember things as I used—and I don't keep the same size for ten minutes together!"

"Ca'n't remember *what* things?" said the Caterpillar.

"Well, I've tried to say '*How doth the little busy bee*', but it all came different!" Alice replied in a very melancholy voice.

"Repeat '*You are old, Father William*'," said the Caterpillar.

Alice folded her hands, and began:

"*You are old, Father William,*" *the young man said*
  "*And your hair has become very white;*
 And yet you incessantly stand on your head—
   Do you think, at your age, it is right?"

"In my youth", Father William replied to his son,
  "I feared it might injure the brain;
But, now that I'm perfectly sure I have none,
  Why, I do it again and again."

"You are old," said the youth, "as I mentioned before.
  And have grown most uncommonly fat;
Yet you turned a back-somersault in at the door—
  Pray, what is the reason of that?"

"In my youth", said the sage, as he shook his grey locks,
  "I kept all my limbs very supple
By the use of this ointment—one shilling the box—
  Allow me to sell you a couple?"

"You are old", said the youth, "and your jaws are too weak
  For anything tougher than suet;
Yet you finished the goose, with the bones and the beak—
  Pray, how did you manage to do it?"

"In my youth", said his father, "I took to the law,
  And argued each case with my wife;
And the muscular strength, which it gave to my jaw
  Has lasted the rest of my life."

"You are old," said the youth, "one would hardly suppose
  That your eye was as steady as ever;
Yet you balanced an eel on the end of your nose—
  What made you so awfully clever?"

"I have answered three questions, and that is enough,"
  Said his father, "Don't give yourself airs!
Do you think I can listen all day to such stuff?
  Be off, or I'll kick you down-stairs!"

"That is not said right," said the Caterpillar.

"Not *quite* right, I'm afraid," said Alice, timidly: "some of the words have got altered."

"It is wrong from beginning to end," said the Caterpillar, decidedly; and there was silence for some minutes.

The Caterpillar was the first to speak.

"What size do you want to be?" it asked.

"Oh, I'm not particular as to size," Alice hastily replied; "only one doesn't like changing so often, you know."

"I *don't* know," said the Caterpillar.

Alice said nothing: she had never been so much contradicted in all her life before, and she felt that she was losing her temper.

"Are you content now!" said the Caterpillar.

"Well, I should like to be a *little* larger, Sir, if you wouldn't mind," said Alice: "three inches is such a wretched height to be."

"It is a very good height indeed!" said the Caterpillar angrily, rearing itself upright as it spoke (it was exactly three inches high).

"But I'm not used to it!" pleaded poor Alice in a piteous tone. And she thought to herself "I wish the creatures wouldn't be so easily offended!"

"You'll get used to it in time," said the Caterpillar; and it put the hookah into its mouth, and began smoking again.

This time Alice waited patiently until it chose to speak again. In a minute or two the Caterpillar took the hookah out of its mouth, and yawned once or twice, and shook itself. Then it got down off the mushroom, and crawled away into the grass, merely remarking, as it went, "One side will make you grow taller, and the other side will make you grow shorter."

"One side of *what*? The other side of *what*?" thought Alice to herself.

"Of the mushroom," said the Caterpillar, just as if she had asked it aloud; and in another moment it was out of sight.

Alice remained looking thoughtfully at the mushroom for a minute, trying to make out which were the two sides of it; and, as it was perfectly round, she found this a very difficult question. However, at last she stretched her arms round it as far as they would go, and broke off a bit of the edge with each hand.

"And now which is which?" she said to herself, and nibbled a little of the right-hand bit to try the effect. The next moment she felt a violent blow underneath her chin: it had struck her foot!

She was a good deal frightened by this very sudden change, but she felt that there was no time to be lost, as she was shrinking rapidly: so she set to work at once to eat some of the other bit. Her chin was pressed so closely against her foot, that there was hardly room to open her mouth; but she did it at last, and managed to swallow a morsel of the left-hand bit.

*   *   *   *   *

*   *   *   *

*   *   *   *   *

"Come, my head's free at last!" said Alice in a tone of delight, which changed into alarm in another moment, when she found that her shoulders were nowhere to be found: all she could see, when she looked down, was an immense length of neck, which seemed to rise like a stalk out of a sea of green leaves that lay far below her.

"What *can* all that green stuff be?" said Alice. "And where *have* my shoulders got to? And oh, my poor hands, how is it I ca'n't see you?" She was moving them about, as she spoke, but no result seemed to follow, except a little shaking among the distant green leaves.

As there seemed to be no chance of getting her hands up to her head, she tried to get her head down to *them*, and was delighted to find that her neck would bend about easily in any direction, like a serpent. She had just succeeded in curving it down into a graceful zigzag, and was going to dive in among the leaves, which she found to be nothing but the tops of the trees under which she had been wandering, when a sharp hiss made her draw back in a hurry: a large pigeon had flown into her face, and was beating her violently with its wings.

"Serpent!" screamed the Pigeon.

"I'm *not* a serpent!" said Alice indignantly. "Let me alone!"

"Serpent, I say again!" repeated the Pigeon, but in a more subdued tone, and added, with a kind of sob, "I've tried every way, but nothing seems to suit them!"

"I haven't the least idea what you're talking about," said Alice.

"I've tried the roots of trees, and I've tried banks, and I've tried hedges," the Pigeon went on, without attending to her; "but those serpents! There's no pleasing them!"

Alice was more and more puzzled, but she thought there was no use in saying anything more till the Pigeon had finished.

"As if it wasn't trouble enough hatching the eggs," said the Pigeon; "but I must be on the look-out for serpents, night and day! Why, I haven't had a wink of sleep these three weeks!"

"I'm very sorry you've been annoyed," said Alice, who was beginning to see its meaning.

"And just as I'd taken the highest tree in the wood," continued the Pigeon, raising its voice to a shriek, "and just as I was thinking I should be free of them at last, they must needs come wriggling down from the sky! Ugh, Serpent!"

"But I'm *not* a serpent, I tell you!" said Alice. "I'm a—
I'm a——"

"Well! *What* are you?" said the Pigeon. "I can see
you're trying to invent something!"

"I—I'm a little girl," said Alice, rather doubtfully, as
she remembered the number of changes she had gone
through, that day.

"A likely story indeed!" said the Pigeon, in a tone of the
deepest contempt. "I've seen a good many little girls in
my time, but never *one* with such a neck as that! No, no!
You're a serpent; and there's no use denying it. I suppose
you'll be telling me next that you never tasted an egg!"

"I *have* tasted eggs, certainly," said Alice, who was a
very truthful child; "but little girls eat eggs quite as much
as serpents do, you know."

"I don't believe it," said the Pigeon; "but if they do,
then they're a kind of serpent: that's all I can say."

This was such a new idea to Alice, that she was quite
silent for a minute or two, which gave the Pigeon the opportunity of adding "You're looking for eggs, I know *that*
well enough; and what does it matter to me whether
you're a little girl or a serpent?"

"It matters a good deal to *me*," said Alice hastily; "but
I'm not looking for eggs, as it happens; and, if I was, I
shouldn't want *yours*: I don't like them raw."

"Well, be off, then!" said the Pigeon in a sulky tone, as
it settled down again into its nest. Alice crouched down
among the trees as well as she could, for her neck kept
getting entangled among the branches, and every now and
then she had to stop and untwist it. After a while she remembered that she still held the pieces of mushroom in
her hands, and she set to work very carefully, nibbling
first at one and then at the other, and growing sometimes
taller, and sometimes shorter, until she had succeeded in
bringing herself down to her usual height.

It was so long since she had been anything near the
right size, that it felt quite strange at first; but she got
used to it in a few minutes, and began talking to herself,

as usual, "Come, there's half my plan done now! How puzzling all these changes are! I'm never sure what I'm going to be, from one minute to another! However, I've got back to my right size: the next thing is, to get into that beautiful garden—how *is* that to be done, I wonder?" As she said this, she came suddenly upon an open place, with a little house in it about four feet high. "Whoever lives there," thought Alice, "it'll never do to come upon them *this* size: why, I should frighten them out of their wits!" So she began nibbling at the right-hand bit again, and did not venture to go near the house till she had brought herself down to nine inches high.

CHAPTER VI

Pig and Pepper

FOR a minute or two she stood looking at the house, and wondering what to do next, when suddenly a footman in livery came running out of the wood—(she considered him to be a footman because he was in livery: otherwise, judging by his face only, she would have called him a fish)—and rapped loudly at the door with his knuckles. It was opened by another footman in livery, with a round face, and large eyes like a frog; and both footmen, Alice noticed, had powdered hair that curled all over their heads. She felt very curious to know what it was all about, and crept a little way out of the wood to listen.

The Fish-Footman began by producing from under his arm a great letter, nearly as large as himself, and this he handed over to the other, saying, in a solemn tone, "For the Duchess. An invitation from the Queen to play croquet." The Frog-Footman repeated, in the same solemn tone, only changing the order of the words a little, "From the Queen. An invitation for the Duchess to play croquet."

Then they both bowed, and their curls got entangled together.

Alice laughed so much at this, that she had to run back into the wood for fear of their hearing her; and, when she next peeped out, the Fish-Footman was gone, and the other was sitting on the ground near the door, staring stupidly up into the sky.

Alice went timidly up to the door, and knocked.

"There's no sort of use in knocking," said the Footman, "and that for two reasons. First, because I'm on the same side of the door as you are: secondly, because they're making such a noise inside, no one could possibly hear you." And certainly there *was* a most extraordinary noise going on within—a constant howling and sneezing, and every now and then a great crash, as if a dish or kettle had been broken to pieces.

"Please, then," said Alice, "how am I to get in?"

"There might be some sense in your knocking", the Footman went on, without attending to her, "if we had the door between us. For instance, if you were *inside*, you might knock, and I could let you out, you know." He was looking up into the sky all the time he was speaking, and this Alice thought decidedly uncivil. "But perhaps he ca'n't help it," she said to herself; "his eyes are so *very* nearly at the top of his head. But at any rate he might answer questions.—How am I to get in?" she repeated, aloud.

"I shall sit here", the Footman remarked, "till to-morrow——"

At this moment the door of the house opened, and a large plate came skimming out, straight at the Footman's head: it just grazed his nose, and broke to pieces against one of the trees behind him.

"——or next day, maybe," the Footman continued in the same tone, exactly as if nothing had happened.

"How am I to get in?" asked Alice again, in a louder tone.

"*Are* you to get in at all?" said the Footman. "That's the first question, you know."

It was, no doubt: only Alice did not like to be told so. "It's really dreadful", she muttered to herself, "the way all the creatures argue. It's enough to drive one crazy!"

The Footman seemed to think this a good opportunity for repeating his remark, with variations. "I shall sit here," he said, "on and off, for days and days."

"But what am *I* to do?" said Alice.

"Anything you like," said the Footman, and began whistling.

"Oh, there's no use in talking to him," said Alice desperately: "he's perfectly idiotic!" And she opened the door and went in.

The door led right into a large kitchen, which was full

of smoke from one end to the other: the Duchess was sitting on a three-legged stool in the middle, nursing a baby: the cook was leaning over the fire, stirring a large cauldron which seemed to be full of soup.

"There's certainly too much pepper in that soup!" Alice said to herself, as well as she could for sneezing.

There was certainly too much of it in the *air*. Even the Duchess sneezed occasionally; and as for the baby, it was sneezing and howling alternately without a moment's pause. The only two creatures in the kitchen, that did *not* sneeze, were the cook, and a large cat, which was lying on the hearth and grinning from ear to ear.

"Please would you tell me", said Alice, a little timidly, for she was not quite sure whether it was good manners for her to speak first, "why your cat grins like that?"

"It's a Cheshire-Cat", said the Duchess, "and that's why. Pig!"

She said the last word with such sudden violence that Alice quite jumped; but she saw in another moment that it was addressed to the baby, and not to her, so she took courage, and went on again:

"I didn't know that Cheshire-Cats always grinned; in fact, I didn't know that cats *could* grin."

"They all can," said the Duchess; "and most of 'em do."

"I don't know of any that do," Alice said very politely, feeling quite pleased to have got into a conversation.

"You don't know much," said the Duchess; "and that's a fact."

Alice did not at all like the tone of this remark, and thought it would be as well to introduce some other subject of conversation. While she was trying to fix on one, the cook took the cauldron of soup off the fire, and at once set to work throwing everything within her reach at the Duchess and the baby—the fire-irons came first; then followed a shower of sauce-pans, plates, and dishes. The Duchess took no notice of them even when they hit her; and the baby was howling so much already, that it was quite impossible to say whether the blows hurt it or not.

"Oh, *please* mind what you're doing!" cried Alice, jumping up and down in an agony of terror. "Oh, there goes his *precious* nose!" as an unusually large saucepan flew close by it, and very nearly carried it off.

"If everybody minded their own business", the Duchess said, in a hoarse growl, "the world would go round a deal faster than it does."

"Which would *not* be an advantage," said Alice, who felt very glad to get an opportunity of showing off a little of her knowledge. "Just think what work it would make with the day and night! You see the earth takes twenty-four hours to turn round on its axis——"

"Talking of axes," said the Duchess, "chop off her head!"

Alice glanced rather anxiously at the cook, to see if she meant to take the hint; but the cook was busily stirring the soup, and seemed not to be listening, so she went on again: "Twenty-four hours, I *think*; or is it twelve? I——"

"Oh, don't bother *me!*" said the Duchess. "I never could abide figures!" And with that she began nursing her child again, singing a sort of lullaby to it as she did so, and giving it a violent shake at the end of every line:

> "*Speak roughly to your little boy,*
> *And beat him when he sneezes:*
> *He only does it to annoy,*
> *Because he knows it teases.*"

CHORUS

(in which the cook and the baby joined):
"*Wow! wow! wow!*"

While the Duchess sang the second verse of the song, she kept tossing the baby violently up and down, and the poor little thing howled so, that Alice could hardly hear the words:

> "*I speak severely to my boy,*
> *I beat him when he sneezes;*
> *For he can thoroughly enjoy*
> *The pepper when he pleases!*"

CHORUS

"*Wow! wow! wow!*"

"Here! You may nurse it a bit, if you like!" the Duchess said to Alice, flinging the baby at her as she spoke. "I must go and get ready to play croquet with the Queen," and she hurried out of the room. The cook threw a frying-pan after her as she went, but it just missed her.

Alice caught the baby with some difficulty, as it was a queer-shaped little creature, and held out its arms and legs in all directions, "just like a star-fish", thought Alice. The poor little thing was snorting like a steam-engine when she caught it, and kept doubling itself up and straightening itself out again, so that altogether, for the first minute or two, it was as much as she could do to hold it.

As soon as she had made out the proper way of nursing it (which was to twist it up into a sort of knot, and then keep tight hold of its right ear and left foot, so as to prevent its undoing itself), she carried it out into the open air. "If I don't take this child away with me," thought Alice, "they're sure to kill it in a day or two. Wouldn't

it be murder to leave it behind?" She said the last words out loud, and the little thing grunted in reply (it had left off sneezing by this time). "Don't grunt," said Alice; "that's not at all a proper way of expressing yourself."

The baby grunted again, and Alice looked very anxiously into its face to see what was the matter with it. There could be no doubt that it had a *very* turn-up nose, much more like a snout than a real nose: also its eyes were getting extremely small for a baby: altogether Alice did not like the look of the thing at all. "But perhaps it was only sobbing," she thought, and looked into its eyes again, to see if there were any tears.

No, there were no tears. "If you're going to turn into a pig, my dear," said Alice, seriously, "I'll have nothing more to do with you. Mind now!" The poor little thing sobbed again (or grunted, it was impossible to say which), and they went on for some while in silence.

Alice was just beginning to think to herself, "Now, what am I to do with this creature, when I get it home?" when it grunted again, so violently, that she looked down into its face in some alarm. This time there could be *no* mistake about it: it was neither more nor less than a pig, and she felt that it would be quite absurd for her to carry it any further.

So she set the little creature down, and felt quite relieved to see it trot away quietly into the wood. "If it had grown up", she said to herself, "it would have made a dreadfully ugly child: but it makes rather a handsome pig, I think." And she began thinking over other children she knew, who might do very well as pigs, and was just saying to herself "if one only knew the right way to change them——" when she was a little startled by seeing the Cheshire-Cat sitting on a bough of a tree a few yards off.

The Cat only grinned when it saw Alice. It looked good-natured, she thought: still it had *very* long claws and a great many teeth, so she felt that it ought to be treated with respect.

"Cheshire-Puss," she began, rather timidly, as she did not at all know whether it would like the name: however, it only grinned a little wider. "Come, it's pleased so far," thought Alice, and she went on. "Would you tell me, please, which way I ought to go from here?"

"That depends a good deal on where you want to get to," said the Cat.

"I don't much care where——" said Alice.

"Then it doesn't matter which way you go," said the Cat.

"——so long as I get *somewhere*," Alice added as an explanation.

"Oh, you're sure to do that", said the Cat, "if you only walk long enough."

Alice felt that this could not be denied, so she tried another question. "What sort of people live about here?"

"In *that* direction", the Cat said, waving its right paw round, "lives a Hatter: and in *that* direction", waving the other paw, "lives a March Hare. Visit either you like: they're both mad."

"But I don't want to go among mad people," Alice remarked.

"Oh, you ca'n't help that," said the Cat: "we're all mad here. I'm mad. You're mad."

"How do you know I'm mad?" said Alice.

"You must be", said the Cat, "or you wouldn't have come here."

Alice didn't think that proved it at all: however, she went on: "And how do you know that you're mad?"

"To begin with," said the Cat, "a dog's not mad. You grant that?"

"I suppose so," said Alice.

"Well, then," the Cat went on, "you see a dog growls when it's angry, and wags its tail when it's pleased. Now *I* growl when I'm pleased, and wag my tail when I'm angry. Therefore I'm mad."

"*I* call it purring, not growling," said Alice.

"Call it what you like," said the Cat. "Do you play croquet with the Queen to-day?"

"I should like it very much," said Alice, "but I haven't been invited yet."

"You'll see me there," said the Cat, and vanished.

Alice was not much surprised at this, she was getting so well used to queer things happening. While she was still looking at the place where it had been, it suddenly appeared again.

"By-the-bye, what became of the baby?" said the Cat. "I'd nearly forgotten to ask."

"It turned into a pig," Alice answered very quietly, just as if the Cat had come back in a natural way.

"I thought it would," said the Cat, and vanished again.

Alice waited a little, half expecting to see it again, but it did not appear, and after a minute or two she walked on in the direction in which the March Hare was said to live. "I've seen hatters before," she said to herself: "the March Hare will be much the most interesting, and perhaps, as this is May, it wo'n't be raving mad—at least not so mad as it was in March." As she said this, she looked up, and there was the Cat again, sitting on a branch of a tree.

"Did you say 'pig', or 'fig'?" said the Cat.

"I said 'pig'," replied Alice; "and I wish you wouldn't keep appearing and vanishing so suddenly: you make one quite giddy!"

"All right," said the Cat; and this time it vanished quite slowly, beginning with the end of the tail, and ending with the grin, which remained some time after the rest of it had gone.

"Well! I've often seen a cat without a grin," thought Alice; "but a grin without a cat! It's the most curious thing I ever saw in all my life!"

She had not gone much farther before she came in sight of the house of the March Hare: she thought it must be the right house, because the chimneys were shaped like ears and the roof was thatched with fur. It was so large a house, that she did not like to go nearer till she had nibbled some more of the left-hand bit of mushroom, and raised herself to about two feet high: even then she walked up towards it rather timidly, saying to herself "Suppose it should be raving mad after all! I almost wish I'd gone to see the Hatter instead!"

CHAPTER VII

A Mad Tea-Party

THERE was a table set out under a tree in front of the house, and the March Hare and the Hatter were having tea at it: a Dormouse was sitting between them, fast asleep, and the other two were using it as a cushion, resting their elbows on it, and talking over its head. "Very uncomfortable for the Dormouse," thought Alice; "only as it's asleep, I suppose it doesn't mind."

The table was a large one, but the three were all crowded together at one corner of it. "No room! No room!" they cried out when they saw Alice coming. "There's *plenty* of room!" said Alice indignantly, and she sat down in a large arm-chair at one end of the table.

"Have some wine," the March Hare said in an encouraging tone.

Alice looked all round the table, but there was nothing on it but tea. "I don't see any wine," she remarked.

"There isn't any," said the March Hare.

"Then it wasn't very civil of you to offer it," said Alice angrily.

"It wasn't very civil of you to sit down without being invited," said the March Hare.

"I didn't know it was *your* table," said Alice: "it's laid for a great many more than three."

"Your hair wants cutting," said the Hatter. He had been looking at Alice for some time with great curiosity, and this was his first speech.

"You should learn not to make personal remarks," Alice said with some severity: "It's very rude."

The Hatter opened his eyes very wide on hearing this; but all he *said* was "Why is a raven like a writing-desk?"

"Come, we shall have some fun now!" thought Alice.

"I'm glad they've begun asking riddles—I believe I can guess that," she added aloud.

"Do you mean that you think you can find out the answer to it?" said the March Hare.

"Exactly so," said Alice.

"Then you should say what you mean," the March Hare went on.

"I do," Alice hastily replied; "at least—at least I mean what I say—that's the same thing, you know."

"Not the same thing a bit!" said the Hatter. "Why, you might just as well say that 'I see what I eat' is the same thing as 'I eat what I see'!"

"You might just as well say", added the March Hare, "that 'I like what I get' is the same thing as 'I get what I like'!"

"You might just as well say", added the Dormouse, which seemed to be talking in its sleep, "that 'I breathe when I sleep' is the same thing as 'I sleep when I breathe'!"

"It *is* the same thing with you," said the Hatter, and

here the conversation dropped, and the party sat silent for a minute, while Alice thought over all she could remember about ravens and writing-desks, which wasn't much.

The Hatter was the first to break the silence. "What day of the month is it?" he said, turning to Alice: he had taken his watch out of his pocket, and was looking at it uneasily, shaking it every now and then, and holding it to his ear.

Alice considered a little, and then said "The fourth".

"Two days wrong!" sighed the Hatter. "I told you butter wouldn't suit the works!" he added, looking angrily at the March Hare.

"It was the *best* butter," the March Hare meekly replied.

"Yes, but some crumbs must have got in as well," the Hatter grumbled: "you shouldn't have put it in with the bread-knife."

The March Hare took the watch and looked at it gloomily: then he dipped it into his cup of tea, and looked at it again: but he could think of nothing better to say than his first remark, "It was the *best* butter, you know."

Alice had been looking over his shoulder with some curiosity. "What a funny watch!" she remarked. "It tells the day of the month, and doesn't tell what o'clock it is!"

"Why should it?" muttered the Hatter. "Does *your* watch tell you what year it is?"

"Of course not," Alice replied very readily: "but that's because it stays the same year for such a long time together."

"Which is just the case with *mine*," said the Hatter.

Alice felt dreadfully puzzled. The Hatter's remark seemed to her to have no sort of meaning in it, and yet it was certainly English. "I don't quite understand you," she said, as politely as she could.

"The Dormouse is asleep again," said the Hatter, and he poured a little hot tea upon its nose.

The Dormouse shook its head impatiently, and said,

without opening its eyes. "Of course, of course: just what I was going to remark myself."

"Have you guessed the riddle yet?" the Hatter said, turning to Alice again.

"No, I give it up," Alice replied. "What's the answer?"

"I haven't the slightest idea," said the Hatter.

"Nor I," said the March Hare.

Alice sighed wearily. "I think you might do something better with the time", she said, "than wasting it in asking riddles that have no answers."

"If you knew Time as well as I do," said the Hatter, "you wouldn't talk about wasting *it*. It's *him*."

"I don't know what you mean," said Alice.

"Of course you don't!" the Hatter said, tossing his head contemptuously. "I dare say you never even spoke to Time!"

"Perhaps not," Alice cautiously replied; "but I know I have to beat time when I learn music."

"Ah! That accounts for it," said the Hatter. "He wo'n't stand beating. Now, if you only kept on good terms with him, he'd do almost anything you liked with the clock. For instance, suppose it were nine o'clock in the morning, just time to begin lessons: you'd only have to whisper a hint to Time, and round goes the clock in a twinkling! Half-past one, time for dinner!"

("I only wish it was," the March Hare said to itself in a whisper.)

"That would be grand, certainly," said Alice thoughtfully; "but then—I shouldn't be hungry for it, you know."

"Not at first, perhaps," said the Hatter: "but you could keep it to half-past one as long as you liked."

"Is that the way *you* manage?" Alice asked.

The Hatter shook his head mournfully. "Not I!" he replied. "We quarreled last March——just before *he* went mad, you know——" (pointing with his teaspoon at the March Hare,) "——it was at the great concert given by the Queen of Hearts, and I had to sing

> '*Twinkle, twinkle, little bat!*
> *How I wonder what you're at!*'

You know the song, perhaps?"

"I've heard something like it," said Alice.

"It goes on, you know," the Hatter continued, "in this way:

> '*Up above the world you fly.*
> *Like a tea-tray in the sky.*
> *Twinkle, twinkle—*' "

Here the Dormouse shook itself, and began singing in its sleep "*Twinkle, twinkle, twinkle, twinkle——*" and went on so long that they had to pinch it to make it stop.

"Well, I'd hardly finished the first verse", said the Hatter, "when the Queen bawled out 'He's murdering the time! Off with his head!' "

"How dreadfully savage!" exclaimed Alice.

"And ever since that", the Hatter went on in a mournful tone, "he wo'n't do a thing I ask! It's always six o'clock now."

A bright idea came into Alice's head. "Is that the reason so many tea-things are put out here?" she asked.

"Yes, that's it," said the Hatter with a sigh: "it's always tea-time, and we've no time to wash the things between whiles."

"Then you keep moving round, I suppose?" said Alice.

"Exactly so," said the Hatter: "as the things get used up."

"But what happens when you come to the beginning again?" Alice ventured to ask.

"Suppose we change the subject," the March Hare interrupted, yawning. "I'm getting tired of this. I vote the young lady tells us a story."

"I'm afraid I don't know one," said Alice, rather alarmed at the proposal.

"Then the Dormouse shall!" they both cried. "Wake up, Dormouse!" And they pinched it on both sides at once.

The Dormouse slowly opened its eyes. "I wasn't asleep," it said in a hoarse, feeble voice, "I heard every word you fellows were saying."

"Tell us a story!" said the March Hare.

"Yes, please do!" pleaded Alice.

"And be quick about it", added the Hatter, "or you'll be asleep again before it's done."

"Once upon a time there were three little sisters," the Dormouse began in a great hurry; "and their names were Elsie, Lacie, and Tillie; and they lived at the bottom of a well——"

"What did they live on?" said Alice, who always took a great interest in questions of eating and drinking.

"They lived on treacle," said the Dormouse, after thinking a minute or two.

"They couldn't have done that, you know," Alice gently remarked. "They'd have been ill."

"So they were," said the Dormouse; "*very* ill."

Alice tried a little to fancy to herself what such an extraordinary way of living would be like, but it puzzled her too much: so she went on: "But why did they live at the bottom of a well?"

"Take some more tea," the March Hare said to Alice, very earnestly.

"I've had nothing yet," Alice replied in an offended tone: "so I ca'n't take more."

"You mean you ca'n't take *less*," said the Hatter: "it's very easy to take *more* than nothing."

"Nobody asked *your* opinion," said Alice.

"Who's making personal remarks now?" the Hatter asked triumphantly.

Alice did not quite know what to say to this: so she helped herself to some tea and bread-and-butter, and then turned to the Dormouse, and repeated her question. "Why did they live at the bottom of a well?"

The Dormouse again took a minute or two to think about it, and then said "It was a treacle-well."

"There's no such thing!" Alice was beginning very angrily, but the Hatter and the March Hare went "Sh! Sh!" and the Dormouse sulkily remarked "If you ca'n't be civil, you'd better finish the story for yourself."

"No, please go on!" Alice said very humbly. "I wo'n't interrupt you again. I dare say there may be *one*."

"One, indeed!" said the Dormouse indignantly. However, he consented to go on. "And so these three little sisters—they were learning to draw, you know——"

"What did they draw?" said Alice, quite forgetting her promise.

"Treacle," said the Dormouse, without considering at all, this time.

"I want a clean cup," interrupted the Hatter: "let's all move one place on."

He moved on as he spoke, and the Dormouse followed him: the March Hare moved into the Dormouse's place, and Alice rather unwillingly took the place of the March Hare. The Hatter was the only one who got any advantage from the change; and Alice was a good deal worse off than before, as the March Hare had just upset the milk-jug into his plate.

Alice did not wish to offend the Dormouse again, so she

began very cautiously: "But I don't understand. Where did they draw the treacle from?"

"You can draw water out of a water-well," said the Hatter; "so I should think you could draw treacle out of a treacle-well—eh, stupid?"

"But they were *in* the well," Alice said to the Dormouse, not choosing to notice this last remark.

"Of course they were," said the Dormouse: "well in."

This answer so confused poor Alice, that she let the Dormouse go on for some time without interrupting it.

"They were learning to draw," the Dormouse went on, yawning and rubbing its eyes, for it was getting very sleepy; "and they drew all manner of things—everything that begins with an M——"

"Why with an M?" said Alice.

"Why not?" said the March Hare.

Alice was silent.

The Dormouse had closed its eyes by this time, and was going off into a doze; but, on being pinched by the Hatter, it woke up again with a little shriek, and went on: "——that begins with an M, such as mouse-traps, and the moon, and memory, and muchness—you know you say things are 'much of a muchness'—did you ever see such a thing as a drawing of a muchness!"

"Really, now you ask me," said Alice, very much confused, "I don't think——"

"Then you shouldn't talk," said the Hatter.

This piece of rudeness was more than Alice could bear: she got up in great disgust, and walked off: the Dormouse fell asleep instantly, and neither of the others took the least notice of her going, though she looked back once or twice, half hoping that they would call after her: the last time she saw them, they were trying to put the Dormouse into the teapot.

"At any rate I'll never go *there* again!" said Alice, as she picked her way through the wood. "It's the stupidest tea-party I ever was at in all my life!"

Just as she said this, she noticed that one of the trees had a door leading right into it. "That's very curious!" she thought. "But everything's curious to-day. I think I may as well go in at once." And in she went.

Once more she found herself in the long hall, and close to the little glass table. "Now, I'll manage better this time," she said to herself, and began by taking the little golden key, and unlocking the door that led into the garden. Then she set to work nibbling at the mushroom (she had kept a piece of it in her pocket) till she was about a foot high: then she walked down the little passage; and *then*—she found herself at last in the beautiful garden, among the bright flower-beds and the cool fountains.

CHAPTER VIII

The Queen's Croquet Ground

A LARGE rose-tree stood near the entrace of the garden: the roses growing on it were white, but there were three gardeners at it, busily painting them red. Alice thought this a very curious thing, and she went nearer to watch them, and, just as she came up to them, she heard one of them say "Look out now, Five! Don't go splashing paint over me like that!"

"I couldn't help it," said Five, in a sulky tone. "Seven jogged my elbow."

On which Seven looked up and said "That's right, Five! Always lay the blame on others!"

"*You'd* better not talk!" said Five. "I heard the Queen say only yesterday you deserved to be beheaded."

"What for?" said the one who had spoken first.

"That's none of *your* business, Two!" said Seven.

"Yes, it *is* his business!" said Five. "And I'll tell him— it was for bringing the cook tulip-roots instead of onions."

Seven flung down his brush, and had just begun "Well,

of all the unjust things——" when his eye chanced to fall upon Alice, as she stood watching them, and he checked himself suddenly: the others looked round also, and all of them bowed low.

"Would you tell me, please," said Alice, a little timidly, "why you are painting those roses?"

Five and Seven said nothing, but looked at Two. Two began, in a low voice, "Why, the fact is, you see, Miss, this here ought to have been a *red* rose-tree, and we put a white one in by mistake; and, if the Queen was to find it out, we should all have our heads cut off, you know. So you see, Miss, we're doing our best, afore she comes, to——" At this moment, Five, who had been anxiously looking across the garden, called out "The Queen! The Queen!" and the three gardeners instantly threw themselves flat upon their faces. There was a sound of many footsteps, and Alice looked round, eager to see the Queen.

First came ten soldiers carrying clubs: these were all shaped like the three gardeners, oblong and flat, with their hands and feet at the corners: next the ten courtiers: these were ornamented all over with diamonds, and walked two and two, as the soldiers did. After these came the royal children: there were ten of them, and the little dears came jumping merrily along, hand in hand, in couples: they were all ornamented with hearts. Next came the guests, mostly Kings and Queens, and among them Alice recognized the White Rabbit: it was talking in a hurried nervous manner, smiling at everything that was said, and went by without noticing her. Then followed the Knave of Hearts, carrying the King's crown on a crimson velvet cushion; and, last of all this grand procession, came THE KING AND THE QUEEN OF HEARTS.

Alice was rather doubtful whether she ought not to lie down on her face like the three gardeners, but she could not remember ever having heard of such a rule at processions; "and besides, what would be the use of a procession", thought she, "if people had all to lie down on their faces, so that they couldn't see it?" So she stood where she was, and waited.

When the procession came opposite to Alice, they all stopped and looked at her, and the Queen said, severely, "Who is this?" She said it to the Knave of Hearts, who only bowed and smiled in reply.

"Idiot!" said the Queen, tossing her head impatiently; and, turning to Alice, she went on: "What's your name, child?"

"My name is Alice, so please your Majesty," said Alice very politely; but she added, to herself, "Why, they're only a pack of cards, after all. I needn't be afraid of them!"

"And who are *these*?" said the Queen, pointing to the three gardeners who were lying round the rose-tree; for, you see, as they were lying on their faces, and the pattern on their backs was the same as the rest of the pack, she could not tell whether they were gardeners, or soldiers, or courtiers, or three of her own children.

"How should *I* know?" said Alice, suprised at her own courage. "It's no business of *mine*."

The Queen turned crimson with fury, and, after glaring at her for a moment like a wild beast, began screaming "Off with her head! Off with——"

"Nonsense!" said Alice, very loudly and decidedly, and the Queen was silent.

The King laid his hand upon her arm, and timidly said "Consider, my dear: she is only a child!"

The Queen turned angrily away from him, and said to the Knave "Turn them over!"

The Knave did so, very carefully, with one foot.

"Get up!" said the Queen in a shrill, loud voice, and the three gardeners instantly jumped up, and began bowing to the King, the Queen, the royal children, and everybody else.

"Leave off that!" screamed the Queen. "You make me giddy." And then, turning to the rose-tree, she went on "What *have* you been doing here?"

"May it please your Majesty," said Two, in a very humble tone, going down on one knee as he spoke, "we were trying——"

"*I* see!" said the Queen, who had meanwhile been examining the roses. "Off with their heads!" and the procession moved on, three of the soldiers remaining behind to execute the unfortunate gardeners, who ran to Alice for protection.

"You sha'n't be beheaded!" said Alice, and she put them into a large flower-pot that stood near. The three soldiers wandered about for a minute or two, looking for them, and then quietly marched off after the others.

"Are their heads off?" shouted the Queen.

"Their heads are gone, if it please your Majesty!" the soldiers shouted in reply.

"That's right!" shouted the Queen. "Can you play croquet?"

The soldiers were silent, and looked at Alice, as the question was evidently meant for her.

"Yes!" shouted Alice.

"Come on, then!" roared the Queen, and Alice joined the procession, wondering very much what would happen next.

"It's—it's a very fine day!" said a timid voice at her side. She was walking by the White Rabbit, who was peeping anxiously into her face.

"Very," said Alice. "Where's the Duchess?"

"Hush! Hush!" said the Rabbit in a low hurried tone. He looked anxiously over his shoulder as he spoke, and then raised himself upon tiptoe, put his mouth close to her ear, and whispered "She's under sentence of execution."

"What for?" said Alice.

"Did you say 'What a pity!'?" the Rabbit asked.

"No, I didn't," said Alice. "I don't think it's at all a pity. I said 'What for?'"

"She boxed the Queen's ears——" the Rabbit began. Alice gave a little scream of laughter. "Oh, hush!" the Rabbit whispered in a frightened tone. "The Queen will hear you! You see she came rather late, and the Queen said——"

"Get to your places!" shouted the Queen in a voice of thunder, and people began running about in all directions, tumbling up against each other: however, they got settled down in a minute or two, and the game began.

Alice thought she had never seen such a curious croquet ground in her life: it was all ridges and furrows: the croquet balls were live hedgehogs, and the mallets live flamingoes, and the soldiers had to double themselves up and stand on their hands and feet, to make the arches.

The chief difficulty Alice found at first was in managing her flamingo: she succeeded in getting its body tucked away, comfortably enough, under her arm, with its legs hanging down, but generally, just as she had got its neck

nicely straightened out, and was going to give the hedgehog a blow with its head, it *would* twist itself round and look up in her face, with such a puzzled expression that she could not help bursting out laughing; and, when she had got its head down, and was going to begin again, it was very provoking to find that the hedgehog had unrolled itself, and was in the act of crawling away: besides all this, there was generally a ridge or a furrow in the way wherever she wanted to send the hedgehog to, and, as the doubled-up soldiers were always getting up and walking off to other parts of the ground, Alice soon came to the conclusion that it was a very difficult game indeed.

The players all played at once, without waiting for

turns, quarreling all the while, and fighting for the hedge-hogs; and in a very short time the Queen was in a furious passion, and went stamping about, and shouting "Off with his head!" or "Off with her head!" about once in a minute.

Alice began to feel very uneasy: to be sure, she had not as yet had any dispute with the Queen, but she knew that it might happen any minute, "and then", thought she, "what would become of me? They're dreadfully fond of beheading people here: the great wonder is, that there's any one left alive!"

She was looking about for some way of escape, and wondering whether she could get away without being seen, when she noticed a curious appearance in the air: it puzzled her very much at first, but after watching it a minute or two she made it out to be a grin, and she said to herself "It's the Cheshire-Cat: now I shall have some-body to talk to."

"How are you getting on?" said the Cat, as soon as there was mouth enough for it to speak with.

Alice waited till the eyes appeared, and then nodded. "It's no use speaking to it", she thought, "till its ears have come, or at least one of them." In another minute the whole head appeared, and then Alice put down her flam-ingo, and began an account of the game, feeling very glad she had some one to listen to her. The Cat seemed to think that there was enough of it now in sight, and no more of it appeared.

"I don't think they play at all fairly," Alice began, in rather a complaining tone, "and they all quarrel so dread-fully one ca'n't hear oneself speak—and they don't seem to have any rules in particular: at least, if there are, no-body attends to them—and you've no idea how confusing it is all the things being alive: for instance, there's the arch I've got to go through next walking about at the other end of the ground—and I should have croqueted the Queen's hedgehog just now, only it ran away when it saw mine coming!"

"How do you like the Queen?" said the Cat in a low voice.

"Not at all," said Alice: "she's so extremely——" Just then she noticed that the Queen was close behind her, listening: so she went on "——likely to win, that it's hardly worth while finishing the game."

The Queen smiled and passed on.

"Who *are* you talking to?" said the King, coming up to Alice, and looking at the Cat's head with great curiosity.

"It's a friend of mine—a Cheshire-Cat," said Alice: "allow me to introduce it."

"I don't like the look of it at all," said the King: "however, it may kiss my hand, if it likes."

"I'd rather not," the Cat remarked.

"Don't be impertinent," said the King, "and don't look at me like that!" He got behind Alice as he spoke.

"A cat may look at a king," said Alice. "I've read that in some book, but I don't remember where."

"Well, it must be removed," said the King very decidedly: and he called to the Queen, who was passing at the moment, "My dear! I wish you would have this cat removed!"

The Queen had only one way of settling all difficulties, great or small. "Off with his head!" she said without even looking around.

"I'll fetch the executioner myself," said the King eagerly, and he hurried off.

Alice thought she might as well go back and see how the game was going on, as she heard the Queen's voice in the distance, screaming with passion. She had already heard her sentence three of the players to be executed for having missed their turns, and she did not like the look of things at all, as the game was in such confusion that she never knew whether it was her turn or not. So she went off in search of her hedgehog.

The hedgehog was engaged in a fight with another hedgehog, which seemed to Alice an excellent opportunity for croqueting one of them with the other: the only difficulty was, that her flamingo was gone across the other side of the garden, where Alice could see it trying in a helpless sort of way to fly up into a tree.

By the time she had caught the flamingo and brought it back, the fight was over, and both the hedgehogs were out of sight: "but it doesn't matter much", thought Alice, "as all the arches are gone from this side of the ground." So she tucked it away under her arm, that it might not escape again, and went back to have a little more conversation with her friend.

When she got back to the Cheshire-Cat, she was surprised to find quite a large crowd collected round it: there was a dispute going on between the executioner, the

King, and the Queen, who were all talking at once, while all the rest were quite silent, and looked very uncomfortable.

The moment Alice appeared, she was appealed to by all three to settle the question, and they repeated their arguments to her, though, as they all spoke at once, she found it very hard to make out exactly what they said.

The executioner's argument was, that you couldn't cut off a head unless there was a body to cut it off from: that he had never had to do such a thing before, and he wasn't going to begin at *his* time of life.

The King's argument was that anything that had a head could be beheaded, and that you weren't to talk nonsense.

The Queen's argument was that, if something wasn't done about it in less than no time, she'd have everybody executed, all round. (It was this last remark that had made the whole party look so grave and anxious.)

Alice could think of nothing else to say but "It belongs to the Duchess: you'd better ask *her* about it."

"She's in prison," the Queen said to the executioner: "fetch her here." And the executioner went off like an arrow.

The Cat's head began fading away the moment he was gone, and, by the time he had come back with the Duchess, it had entirely disappeared: so the King and the executioner ran wildly up and down, looking for it, while the rest of the party went back to the game.

CHAPTER IX

The Mock Turtle's Story

"You ca'n't think how glad I am to see you again, you dear old thing!" said the Duchess, as she tucked her arm affectionately into Alice's, and they walked off together.

Alice was very glad to find her in such a pleasant temper, and thought to herself that perhaps it was only the pepper that had made her so savage when they met in the kitchen.

"When *I'm* a Duchess", she said to herself (not in a very hopeful tone, though), "I won't have any pepper in

my kitchen *at all*. Soup does very well without—Maybe it's always pepper that makes people hot-tempered," she went on, very much pleased at having found out a new kind of rule, "and vinegar that makes them sour—and camomile that makes them bitter—and—and barley-sugar and such things that make children sweet-tempered. I only wish people knew *that*: then they wouldn't be so stingy about it, you know——"

She had quite forgotten the Duchess by this time, and was a little startled when she heard her voice close to her ear. "You're thinking about something, my dear, and that makes you forget to talk. I ca'n't tell you just now what the moral of that is, but I shall remember it in a bit."

"Perhaps it hasn't one," Alice ventured to remark.

"Tut, tut, child!" said the Duchess. "Everything's got a moral, if only you can find it." And she squeezed herself up closer to Alice's side as she spoke.

Alice did not much like her keeping so close to her: first because the Duchess was *very* ugly; and secondly, because she was exactly the right height to rest her chin on Alice's shoulder, and it was an uncomfortably sharp chin. However, she did not like to be rude: so she bore it as well as she could.

"The game's going on rather better now," she said, by way of keeping up the conversation a little.

"'Tis so," said the Duchess: "and the moral of that is —'Oh, 'tis love, 'tis love, that makes the world go round!'"

"Somebody said", Alice whispered, "that it's done by everybody minding their own business!"

"Ah well! It means much the same thing," said the Duchess, digging her sharp little chin into Alice's shoulder as she added "and the moral of *that* is—'Take care of the sense and the sounds will take care of themselves.'"

"How fond she is of finding morals in things!" Alice thought to herself.

"I dare say you're wondering why I don't put my arm round your waist," the Duchess said, after a pause: "the reason is, that I'm doubtful about the temper of your flamingo. Shall I try the experiment?"

"He might bite," Alice cautiously replied, not feeling at all anxious to have the experiment tried.

"Very true," said the Duchess: "flamingoes and mustard both bite. And the moral of that is—'Birds of a feather flock together.'"

"Only mustard isn't a bird," Alice remarked.

"Right, as usual," said the Duchess: "what a clear way you have of putting things!"

"It's a mineral, I *think*," said Alice.

"Of course it is," said the Duchess, who seemed ready to agree to everything that Alice said: "there's a large mustard-machine near here. And the moral of that is— 'The more there is of mine, the less there is of yours.' "

"Oh, I know!" exclaimed Alice, who had not attended to this last remark. "It's a vegetable. It doesn't look like one, but it is."

"I quite agree with you," said the Duchess; "and the moral of that is—'Be what you would seem to be'—or, if you'd like it put more simply—'Never imagine yourself not to be otherwise than what it might appear to others that what you were or might have been was not otherwise than what you had been would have appeared to them to be otherwise.' "

"I think I should understand that better", Alice said very politely, "if I had it written down: but I ca'n't quite follow it as you say it."

"That's nothing to what I could say if I chose," the Duchess replied, in a pleased tone.

"Pray don't trouble yourself to say it any longer than that," said Alice.

"Oh, don't talk about trouble!" said the Duchess. "I make you a present of everything I've said as yet."

"A cheap sort of present!" thought Alice. "I'm glad people don't give birthday-presents like that!" But she did not venture to say it out loud.

"Thinking again?" the Duchess asked, with another dig of her sharp little chin.

"I've a right to think," said Alice sharply, for she was beginning to feel a little worried.

"Just about as much right", said the Duchess, "as pigs have to fly; and the m——"

But here, to Alice's great surprise, the Duchess's voice died away, even in the middle of her favourite word "moral", and the arm that was linked into hers began to tremble. Alice looked up, and there stood the Queen in front of them, with her arms folded, frowning like a thunder-storm.

"A fine day, your Majesty!" the Duchess began in a low, weak voice.

"Now, I give you fair warning," shouted the Queen, stamping on the ground as she spoke; "either you or your head must be off, and that in about half no time! Take your choice!"

The Duchess took her choice, and was gone in a moment.

"Let's go on with the game," the Queen said to Alice; and Alice was too much frightened to say a word, but slowly followed her back to the croquet ground.

The other guests had taken advantage of the Queen's absence, and were resting in the shade: however, the moment they saw her, they hurried back to the game, the Queen merely remarking that a moment's delay would cost them their lives.

All the time they were playing the Queen never left off quarreling with the other players and shouting "Off with his head!" or "Off with her head!" Those whom she sentenced were taken into custody by the soldiers, who of course had to leave off being arches to do this, so that, by the end of half an hour or so, there were no arches left, and all the players, except the King, the Queen, and Alice, were in custody and under sentence of execution.

Then the Queen left off, quite out of breath, and said to Alice, "Have you seen the Mock Turtle yet?"

"No," said Alice. "I don't even know what a Mock Turtle is."

"It's the thing Mock Turtle Soup is made from," said the Queen.

"I never saw one, or heard of one," said Alice.

"Come on, then," said the Queen, "and he shall tell you his history."

As they walked off together, Alice heard the King say in a low voice, to the company, generally, "You are all pardoned." "Come, *that's* a good thing!" she said to herself, for she had felt quite unhappy at the number of executions the Queen had ordered.

They very soon came upon a Gryphon, lying fast asleep in the sun. (If you don't know what a Gryphon is, look at the picture.) "Up, lazy thing!" said the Queen, "and take this young lady to see the Mock Turtle, and to

hear his history. I must go back and see after some executions I have ordered"; and she walked off, leaving Alice alone with the Gryphon. Alice did not quite like the look of the creature, but on the whole she thought it would be quite as safe to stay with it as to go after that savage Queen: so she waited.

The Gryphon sat up and rubbed its eyes: then it watched the Queen till she was out of sight then it chuckled. "What fun!" said the Gryphon, half to itself, half to Alice.

"What *is* the fun?" said Alice.

"Why, *she*," said the Gryphon. "It's all her fancy that: they never executes nobody, you know. Come on!"

"Everybody says 'come on!' here," thought Alice, as she went slowly after it: "I never was so ordered about before, in all my life, never!"

They had not gone far before they saw the Mock Turtle in the distance, sitting sad and lonely on a little ledge of rock, and, as they came nearer, Alice could hear him sighing as if his heart would break. She pitied him deeply. "What is his sorrow?" she asked the Gryphon. And the Gryphon answered, very nearly in the same words as before, "It's all his fancy, that: he hasn't got no sorrow, you know. Come on!"

So they went up to the Mock Turtle, who looked at them with large eyes full of tears, but said nothing.

"This here young lady," said the Gryphon, "she wants for to know your history, she do."

"I'll tell it her," said the Mock Turtle in a deep, hollow tone. "Sit down, both of you, and don't speak a word till I've finished."

So they sat down, and nobody spoke for some minutes. Alice thought to herself "I don't see how he can *ever* finish, if he doesn't begin." But she waited patiently.

"Once", said the Mock Turtle at last, with a deep sigh, "I was a real Turtle."

These words were followed by a very long silence, broken only by an occasional exclamation of "Hjckrrh!" from the Gryphon, and the constant heavy sobbing of the Mock Turtle. Alice was very nearly getting up and saying, "Thank you, Sir, for your interesting story," but she could not help thinking there *must* be more to come, so she sat still and said nothing.

"When we were little", the Mock Turtle went on at last, more calmly, though still sobbing a little now and then, "we went to school in the sea. The master was an old Turtle—we used to call him Tortoise——"

"Why did you call him Tortoise, if he wasn't one?" Alice asked.

"We called him Tortoise because he taught us," said the Mock Turtle angrily. "Really you are very dull!"

"You ought to be ashamed of yourself for asking such a simple question," added the Gryphon; and then they both sat silent and looked at poor Alice, who felt ready to sink into the earth. At last the Gryphon said to the Mock Turtle "Drive on, old fellow! Don't be all day about it!" and he went on in these words:

"Yes, we went to school in the sea, though you mayn't believe it——"

"I never said I didn't!" interrupted Alice.

"You did," said the Mock Turtle.

"Hold your tongue!" added the Gryphon, before Alice

could speak again. The Mock Turtle went on.

"We had the best of educations—in fact, we went to school every day——"

"*I've* been to a day-school, too," said Alice. "You needn't be so proud as all that."

"With extras?" asked the Mock Turtle, a little anxiously.

"Yes," said Alice: "we learned French and music."

"And washing?" said the Mock Turtle.

"Certainly not!" said Alice, indignantly.

"Ah! Then yours wasn't a really good school," said the Mock Turtle in a tone of great relief. "Now, at *ours*, they had, at the end of the bill, 'French, music *and* washing—extra'."

"You couldn't have wanted it much," said Alice; "living at the bottom of the sea."

"I couldn't afford to learn it," said the Mock Turtle with a sigh. "I only took the regular course."

"What was that?" inquired Alice.

"Reeling and Writhing, of course, to begin with," the Mock Turtle replied; "and then the different branches of Arithmetic—Ambition, Distraction, Uglification, and Derision."

"I never heard of 'Uglification'," Alice ventured to say. "What is it?"

The Gryphon lifted up both its paws in surprise. "Never heard of uglifying!" it exclaimed. "You know what to beautify is, I suppose?"

"Yes," said Alice doubtfully: "it means—to—make—anything—prettier."

"Well, then," the Gryphon went on, "if you don't know what to uglify is, you *are* a simpleton."

Alice did not feel encouraged to ask any more questions about it: so she turned to the Mock Turtle, and said "What else had you to learn?"

"Well, there was Mystery," the Mock Turtle replied, counting off the subjects on his flappers—"Mystery, ancient and modern, with Seaography: then Drawling—

the Drawling-master was an old conger-eel, that used to come once a week: *he* taught us Drawling, Stretching, and Fainting in Coils."

"What was *that* like?" said Alice.

"Well, I ca'n't show it you, myself," the Mock Turtle said "I'm too stiff. And the Gryphon never learnt it."

"Hadn't time," said the Gryphon: "I went to the Classical master, though. He was an old crab, *he* was."

"I never went to him," the Mock Turtle said with a sigh. "He taught Laughing and Grief, they used to say."

"So he did, so he did," said the Gryphon, sighing in his turn; and both creatures hid their faces in their paws.

"And how many hours a day did you do lessons?" said Alice, in a hurry to change the subject.

"Ten hours the first day," said the Mock Turtle: "nine the next, and so on."

"What a curious plan!" exclaimed Alice.

"That's the reason they're called lessons," the Gryphon remarked: "because they lessen from day to day."

This was quite a new idea to Alice, and she thought it over a little before she made her next remark. "Then the eleventh day must have been a holiday?"

"Of course it was," said the Mock Turtle.

"And how did you manage on the twelfth?" Alice went on eagerly.

"That's enough about lessons," the Gryphon interrupted in a very decided tone. "Tell her something about the games now."

CHAPTER X

The Lobster-Quadrille

THE Mock Turtle sighed deeply, and drew the back of one flapper across his eyes. He looked at Alice and tried to speak, but, for a minute or two, sobs choked his voice.

"Same as if he had a bone in his throat," said the Gryphon; and it set to work shaking him and punching him in the back. At last the Mock Turtle recovered his voice, and, with tears running down his cheeks, he went on again:

"You may not have lived much under the sea—" ("I haven't," said Alice)—"and perhaps you were never even introduced to a lobster—" (Alice began to say "I once tasted——" but checked herself hastily and said "No never") "—so you can have no idea what a delightful thing a Lobster-Quadrille is!"

"No, indeed," said Alice. "What sort of a dance is it?"

"Why," said the Gryphon, "you first form into a line along the sea-shore——"

"Two lines!" cried the Mock Turtle. "Seals, turtles, salmon, and so on: then, when you've cleared all the jelly-fish out of the way——"

"*That* generally takes some time," interrupted the Gryphon.

"—you advance twice——".

"Each with a lobster as a partner!" cried the Gryphon.

"Of course," the Mock Turtle said: "advance twice, set to partners——"

"—change lobsters, and retire in same order," continued the Gryphon.

"Then, you know," the Mock Turtle went on, "you throw the——"

"The lobsters!" shouted the Gryphon with a bound into the air.

"—as far out to sea as you can——"

"Swim after them!" screamed the Gryphon.

"Turn a somersault in the sea!" cried the Mock Turtle, capering wildly about.

"Change lobsters again!" yelled the Gryphon at the top of its voice.

"Back to land again, and—that's all the first figure," said the Mock Turtle, suddenly dropping his voice; and the two creatures, who had been jumping about like mad things all this time, sat down again very sadly and quietly and looked at Alice.

"It must be a very pretty dance," said Alice timidly.

"Would you like to see a little of it?" said the Mock Turtle.

"Very much indeed," said Alice.

"Come, let's try the first figure!" said the Mock Turtle to the Gryphon. "We can do it without lobsters, you know. Which shall sing?"

"Oh, *you* sing," said the Gryphon. "I've forgotten the words."

So they began solemnly dancing round and round Alice, every now and then treading on her toes when they passed too close, and waving their fore-paws to mark the

time, when the Mock Turtle sang this, very slowly and
sadly:

"Will you walk a little faster?" said a whiting to a snail,
"There's a porpoise close behind us, and he's treading on my
    tail.
See how eagerly the lobsters and the turtles all advance!
They are waiting on the shingle—will you come and join the
    dance?
    Will you, wo'n't you, will you, wo'n't you, will you join the
        dance?
    Will you, wo'n't you, will you, wo'n't you, wo'n't you join
        the dance?

"You can really have no notion how delightful it will be
"When they take us up and throw us, with the lobsters, out to
    sea!"
But the snail replied "Too far, too far!" and gave a look
    askance—
Said he thanked the whiting kindly, but he would not join the
    dance.
    Would not, could not, would not, could not, would not join
        the dance.
    Would not, could not, would not, could not, could not join
        the dance.

"What matters it how far we go?" his scaly friend replied.
"There is another shore, you know, upon the other side.
The further off from England the nearer is to France—
Then turn not pale, beloved snail, but come and join the dance.
    Will you, wo'n't you, will you, wo'n't you, will you join the
        dance?
    Will you, wo'n't you, will you, wo'n't you, wo'n't you join
        the dance?"

"Thank you, it's a very interesting dance to watch,"
said Alice, feeling very glad that it was over at last: "and
I do so like that curious song about the whiting!"

"Oh, as to the whiting," said the Mock Turtle, "they—
you've seen them, of course?"

"Yes," said Alice, "I've often seen them at dinn——"
she checked herself hastily.

"I don't know where Dinn may be," said the Mock Turtle; "but, if you've seen them so often, of course you know what they're like?"

"I believe so," Alice replied thoughtfully. "They have their tails in their mouths—and they re all over crumbs."

"You're wrong about the crumbs," said the Mock Turtle: "crumbs would all wash off in the sea. But they *have* their tails in their mouths; and the reason is——" here the Mock Turtle yawned and shut his eyes. "Tell her about the reason and all that," he said to the Gryphon.

"The reason is", said the Gryphon, "that they *would* go with the lobsters to the dance. So they got thrown out to sea. So they had to fall a long way. So they got their tails fast in their mouths. So they couldn't get them out again. That's all."

"Thank you," said Alice, "it's very interesting. I never knew so much about a whiting before."

"I can tell you more than that, if you like," said the Gryphon. "Do you know why it's called a whiting?"

"I never thought about it," said Alice. "Why?"

"*It does the boots and shoes*," the Gryphon replied very solemnly.

Alice was thoroughly puzzled. "Does the boots and shoes!" she repeated in a wondering tone.

"Why, what are *your* shoes done with?" said the Gryphon. "I mean, what makes them so shiny?"

Alice looked down at them, and considered a little before she gave her answer. "They're done with blacking, I believe."

"Boots and shoes under the sea", the Gryphon went on in a deep voice, "are done with whiting. Now you know."

"And what are they made of?" Alice asked in a tone of great curiosity.

"Soles and eels, of course," the Gryphon replied, rather impatiently: "any shrimp could have told you that."

"If I'd been the whiting", said Alice, whose thoughts were still running on the song, "I'd have said to the porpoise 'Keep back, please! We don't want *you* with us!' "

"They were obliged to have him with them," the Mock Turtle said. "No wise fish would go anywhere without a porpoise."

"Wouldn't it, really?" said Alice, in a tone of great surprise.

"Of course not," said the Mock Turtle. "Why, if a fish came to *me*, and told me he was going a journey, I should say 'With what porpoise?'"

"Don't you mean 'purpose'?" said Alice.

"I mean what I say," the Mock Turtle replied, in an offended tone. And the Gryphon added "Come, let's hear some of *your* adventures."

"I could tell you my adventures—beginning from this morning," said Alice a little timidly; "but it's no use going back to yesterday, because I was a different person then."

"Explain all that," said the Mock Turtle.

"No, no! The adventures first," said the Gryphon in an impatient tone: "explanations take such a dreadful time."

So Alice began telling them her adventures from the time when she first saw the White Rabbit. She was a little nervous about it, just at first, the two creatures got so close to her, one on each side, and opened their eyes and mouths so *very* wide; but she gained courage as she went on. Her listeners were perfectly quiet till she got to the part about her repeating "*You are old, Father William,*" to the Caterpillar, and the words all coming different, and then the Mock Turtle drew a long breath, and said "That's very curious!"

"It's all about as curious as it can be," said the Gryphon.

"It all came different!" the Mock Turtle repeated thoughtfully. "I should like to hear her try and repeat something now. Tell her to begin." He looked at the Gryphon as if he thought it had some kind of authority over Alice.

"Stand up and repeat ' *'Tis the voice of the sluggard*'," said the Gryphon.

"How the creatures order one about, and make one repeat lessons!" thought Alice. "I might just as well be at
school at once." However, she got up, and began to repeat it, but her head was so full of the Lobster-Quadrille,
that she hardly knew what she was saying; and the words
came very queer indeed:

> "'Tis the voice of the Lobster: I heard him declare
> 'You have baked me too brown, I must sugar my hair.'
> As a duck with his eyelids, so he with his nose
> Trims his belt and his buttons, and turns out his toes.
> When the sands are all dry, he is gay as a lark,
> And will talk in contemptuous tones of the Shark:
> But, when the tide rises and sharks are around,
> His voice has a timid and tremulous sound."

"That's different from what *I* used to say when I was a child," said the Gryphon.

"Well, *I* never heard it before," said the Mock Turtle; "but it sounds uncommon nonsense."

Alice said nothing: she had sat down with her face in her hands, wondering if anything would *ever* happen in a natural way again.

"I should like to have it explained," said the Mock Turtle.

"She ca'n't explain it," said the Gryphon hastily. "Go on with the next verse."

"But about his toes?" the Mock Turtle persisted. "How *could* he turn them out with his nose, you know?"

"It's the first position in dancing," Alice said; but she was dreadfully puzzled by the whole thing, and longed to change the subject.

"Go on with the next verse," the Gryphon repeated: "it begins *'I passed by his garden'*."

Alice did not dare to disobey, though she felt sure it would all come wrong, and she went on in a trembling voice:

> *"I passed by his garden, and marked, with one eye,*
> *How the Owl and the Panther were sharing a pie:*
> *The Panther took pie-crust, and gravy, and meat,*
> *While the Owl had the dish as its share of the treat.*
> *When the pie was all finished, the Owl, as a boon,*
> *Was kindly permitted to pocket the spoon:*
> *While the Panther received knife and fork with a growl,*
> *And concluded the banquet by —— "*

"What *is* the use of repeating all that stuff?" the Mock Turtle interrupted, "if you don't explain it as you go on? It's by far the most confusing thing that *I* ever heard!"

"Yes, I think you'd better leave off," said the Gryphon, and Alice was only too glad to do so.

"Shall we try another figure of the Lobster-Quadrille?" the Gryphon went on. "Or would you like the Mock Turtle to sing you another song?"

"Oh, a song, please, if the Mock Turtle would be so kind," Alice replied, so eagerly that the Gryphon said, in a rather offended tone, "Hm! No accounting for tastes! Sing her '*Turtle Soup*', will you, old fellow?"

The Mock Turtle sighed deeply, and began in a voice choked with sobs, to sing this:

> "*Beautiful Soup, so rich and green,*
> *Waiting in a hot tureen!*
> *Who for such dainties would not stoop?*
> *Soup of the evening, beautiful Soup!*
> *Soup of the evening, beautiful Soup!*
> *Beau—ootiful Soo—oop!*
> *Beau—ootiful Soo—oop!*
> *Soo—oop of the e—e—evening,*
> *Beautiful, beautiful Soup!*

> "*Beautiful Soup! Who cares for fish,*
> *Game, or any other dish?*
> *Who would not give all else for two p*
> *ennyworth only of beautiful Soup?*
> *Pennyworth only of beautiful Soup?*
> *Beau—ootiful Soo—oop!*
> *Beau—ootiful Soo—oop!*
> *Soo—oop of the e—e—evening,*
> *Beautiful beauti—FUL SOUP!*"

"Chorus again!" cried the Gryphon, and the Mock Turtle had just begun to repeat it, when a cry of "The trial's beginning!" was heard in the distance.

"Come on!" cried the Gryphon, and, taking Alice by the hand, it hurried off, without waiting for the end of the song.

"What trial is it?" Alice panted as she ran: but the Gryphon only answered "Come on!" and ran the faster, while more and more faintly came, carried on the breeze that followed them, the melancholy words:

> "*Soo—oop of the e—e—evening,*
> *Beautiful, beautiful Soup!*"

CHAPTER XI

Who Stole the Tarts?

THE King and Queen of Hearts were seated on their throne when they arrived, with a great crowd assembled about them—all sorts of little birds and beasts, as well as the whole pack of cards: the Knave was standing before them, in chains, with a soldier on each side to guard him; and near the King was the White Rabbit, with a trumpet in one hand, and a scroll of parchment in the other. In the very middle of the court was a table, with a large dish of tarts upon it: they looked so good, that it made Alice quite hungry to look at them—"I wish they'd get the trial done," she thought, "and hand round the refreshments!" But there seemed to be no chance of this; so she began looking at everything about her to pass away the time.

Alice had never been in a court of justice before, but she had read about them in books, and she was quite pleased to find that she knew the name of nearly everything there. "That's the judge," she said to herself, "because of his great wig."

The judge, by the way, was the King; and, as he wore his crown over the wig (look at the frontispiece if you want to see how he did it), he did not look at all comfortable, and it was certainly not becoming.

"And that's the jury-box," thought Alice; "and those twelve creatures," (she was obliged to say "creatures," you see, because some of them were animals, and some were birds,) "I suppose they are the jurors." She said this last word two or three times over to herself, being rather proud of it: for she thought, and rightly too, that very few little girls of her age knew the meaning of it at all. However, "jurymen" would have done just as well.

The twelve jurors were all writing very busily on slates. "What are they doing?" Alice whispered to the Gryphon.

"They ca'n't have anything to put down yet, before the trial's begun."

"They're putting down their names", the Gryphon whispered in reply, "for fear they should forget them before the end of the trial."

"Stupid things!" Alice began in a loud indignant voice; but she stopped herself hastily, for the White Rabbit cried

out "Silence in the court!" and the King put on his spectacles and looked anxiously round, to make out who was talking.

Alice could see, as well as if she were looking over their shoulders, that all the jurors were writing down "Stupid things!" on their slates, and she could even make out that one of them didn't know how to spell "stupid", and that he had to ask his neighbour to tell him. "A nice muddle their slates'll be in, before the trial's over!" thought Alice.

One of the jurors had a pencil that squeaked. This, of

course, Alice could *not* stand, and she went round the court and got behind him, and very soon found an opportunity of taking it away. She did it so quickly that the poor little juror (it was Bill, the Lizard) could not make out at all what had become of it; so, after hunting all about for it, he was obliged to write with one finger for the rest of the day; and this was of very little use, as it left no mark on the slate.

"Herald, read the accusation!" said the King.

On this the White Rabbit blew three blasts on the trumpet, and then unrolled the parchment-scroll, and read as follows:

> *"The Queen of Hearts, she made some tarts,*
> *All on a summer day:*
> *The Knave of Hearts, he stole those tarts*
> *And took them quite away!"*

"Consider your verdict," the King said to the jury.

"Not yet, not yet!" the Rabbit hastily interrupted. "There's a great deal to come before that!"

"Call the first witness," said the King; and the White Rabbit blew three blasts on the trumpet, and called out "First witness!"

The first witness was the Hatter. He came in with a teacup in one hand and a piece of bread-and-butter in the other. "I beg pardon, your Majesty," he began, "for bringing these in; but I hadn't quite finished my tea when I was sent for."

"You ought to have finished," said the King. "When did you begin?"

The Hatter looked at the March Hare, who had followed him into the court, arm-in-arm with the Dormouse. "Fourteenth of March, I *think* it was," he said.

"Fifteenth," said the March Hare.

"Sixteenth," said the Dormouse.

"Write that down," the King said to the jury; and the jury eagerly wrote down all three dates on their slates, and then added them up, and reduced the answer to shillings and pence.

"Take off your hat," the King said to the Hatter.

"It isn't mine," said the Hatter.

"*Stolen!*" the King exclaimed, turning to the jury, who instantly made a memorandum of the fact.

"I keep them to sell," the Hatter added as an explanation. "I've none of my own. I'm a hatter."

Here the Queen put on her spectacles, and began staring hard at the Hatter, who turned pale and fidgeted.

"Give your evidence," said the King; "and don't be nervous, or I'll have you executed on the spot."

This did not seem to encourage the witness at all: he kept shifting from one foot to the other, looking uneasily at the Queen, and in his confusion he bit a large piece out of his teacup instead of the bread-and-butter.

Just at this moment Alice felt a very curious sensation, which puzzled her a great deal until she made out what it was: she was beginning to grow larger again, and she thought at first she would get up and leave the court; but on second thoughts she decided to remain where she was as long as there was room for her.

"I wish you wouldn't squeeze so," said the Dormouse, who was sitting next to her. "I can hardly breathe."

"I ca'n't help it," said Alice very meekly: "I'm growing."

"You've no right to grow *here*," said the Dormouse.

"Don't talk nonsense," said Alice more boldly: "you know you're growing too."

"Yes, but *I* grow at a reasonable pace," said the Dormouse: "not in that ridiculous fashion." And he got up very sulkily and crossed over to the other side of the court.

All this time the Queen had never left off staring at the Hatter, and, just as the Dormouse crossed the court, she said, to one of the officers of the court, "Bring me the list of the singers in the last concert!" on which the wretched Hatter trembled so, that he shook off both his shoes.

"Give your evidence", the King repeated angrily, "or I'll have you executed, whether you are nervous or not."

"I'm a poor man, your Majesty," the Hatter began, in a trembling voice, "and I hadn't begun my tea—not above a week or so—and what with the bread-and-butter getting so thin—and the twinkling of the tea——"

"The twinkling of *what*?" said the King.

"It *began* with the tea," the Hatter replied.

"Of course twinkling *begins* with a T!" said the King sharply. "Do you take me for a dunce? Go on!"

"I'm a poor man," the Hatter went on, "and most things twinkled after that—only the March Hare said——"

"I didn't!" the March Hare interrupted in a great hurry.

"You did!" said the Hatter.

"I deny it!" said the March Hare.

"He denies it," said the King: "leave out that part."

"Well, at any rate, the Dormouse said——" the Hatter went on, looking anxiously round to see if he would deny it too; but the Dormouse denied nothing, being fast asleep.

"After that", continued the Hatter, "I cut some more bread-and-butter——"

"But what did the Dormouse say?" one of the jury asked.

"That I ca'n't remember", said the Hatter.

"You *must* remember", remarked the King, "or I'll have you executed."

The miserable Hatter dropped his teacup and bread-and-butter, and went down on one knee. "I'm a poor man, your Majesty," he began.

"You're a *very* poor *speaker*," said the King.

Here one of the guinea-pigs cheered, and was immediately suppressed by the officers of the court. (As that is rather a hard word, I will just explain to you how it was done. They had a large canvas bag, which tied up at the mouth with strings: into this they slipped the guinea-pig, head first, and then sat upon it.)

"I'm glad I've seen that done," thought Alice. "I've so often read in the newspapers, at the end of trials, 'There was some attempt at applause, which was immediately suppressed by the officers of the court,' and I never understood what it meant till now."

"If that's all you know about it, you may stand down," continued the King.

"I ca'n't go no lower," said the Hatter: "I'm on the floor, as it is."

"Then you may *sit* down," the King replied.

Here the other guinea-pig cheered, and was suppressed.

"Come, that finishes the guinea-pigs!" thought Alice. "Now we shall get on better."

"I'd rather finish my tea," said the Hatter, with an anxious look at the Queen, who was reading the list of singers.

"You may go," said the King, and the Hatter hurriedly left the court, without even waiting to put his shoes on.

"——and just take his head off outside," the Queen added to one of the officers; but the Hatter was out of sight before the officer could get to the door.

"Call the next witness!" said the King.

The next witness was the Duchess's cook. She carried the pepper-box in her hand, and Alice guessed who it was, even before she got into the court, by the way the people near the door began sneezing all at once.

"Give your evidence," said the King.

"Sha'n't," said the cook.

The King looked anxiously at the White Rabbit, who said, in a low voice, "Your Majesty must cross-examine *this* witness."

"Well, if I must, I must," the King said with a melancholy air, and, after folding his arms and frowning at the cook till his eyes were nearly out of sight, he said, in a deep voice, "What are tarts made of?"

"Pepper, mostly," said the cook.

"Treacle," said a sleepy voice behind her.

"Collar that Dormouse!" the Queen shrieked out. "Behead that Dormouse! Turn that Dormouse out of court! Suppress him! Pinch him! Off with his whiskers!"

For some minutes the whole court was in confusion, getting the Dormouse turned out, and, by the time they had settled down again, the cook had disappeared.

"Never mind!" said the King, with an air of great re-lief. "Call the next witness." And he added, in an under-tone to the Queen, "Really, my dear, *you* must cross-examine the next witness. It quite makes my forehead ache!"

Alice watched the White Rabbit as he fumbled over the list, feeling very curious to see what the next witness would be like, "—for they haven't got much evidence *yet*," she said to herself. Imagine her surprise, when the White Rabbit read out, at the top of his shrill little voice, the name "Alice!"

Chapter XII

Alice's Evidence

"Here!" cried Alice, quite forgetting in the flurry of the moment how large she had grown in the last few minutes, and she jumped up in such a hurry that she tipped over the jury-box with the edge of her skirt, upsetting all the jurymen on to the heads of the crowd below and there they lay sprawling about, reminding her very much of a globe of gold-fish she had accidentally upset the week before.

"Oh, I *beg* your pardon!" she exclaimed in a tone of great dismay, and began picking them up again as quick-ly as she could, for the accident of the gold-fish kept run-ning in her head, and she had a vague sort of idea that they must be collected at once and put 'back into the jury-box, or they would die.

"The trial cannot proceed", said the King, in a very grave voice, "until all the jurymen are back in their pro-per places—*all*," he repeated with great emphasis, looking hard at Alice as he said so.

Alice looked at the jury-box, and saw that, in her haste, she had put the Lizard in head downwards, and the poor

little thing was waving its tail about in a melancholy
way, being quite unable to move. She soon got it out
again, and put it right; "not that it signifies much," she
said to herself; "I should think it would be *quite* as much
use in the trial one way up as the other."

As soon as the jury had a little recovered from the shock
of being upset, and their slates and pencils had been
found and handed back to them, they set to work very
diligently to write out a history of the accident, all except
the Lizard, who seemed too much overcome to do any-

thing but sit with its mouth open, gazing up into the roof of the court.

"What do you know about this business?" the King said to Alice.

"Nothing," said Alice.

"Nothing whatever?" persisted the King.

"Nothing whatever," said Alice.

"That's very important," the King said, turning to the jury. They were just beginning to write this down on their slates, when the White Rabbit interrupted: "*Un*important, your Majesty means, of course," he said, in a very respectful tone, but frowning and making faces at him as he spoke.

"*Un*important, of course, I meant," the King hastily said, and went on to himself in an undertone, "important—unimportant—unimportant—important——" as if he were trying which word sounded best.

Some of the jury wrote it down "important", and some "unimportant". Alice could see this, as she was near enough to look over their slates; "but it doesn't matter a bit," she thought to herself.

At this moment the King, who had been for some time busily writing in his note-book, called out "Silence!" and read out from his book "Rule Forty-two. *All persons more than a mile high to leave the court.*"

Everybody looked at Alice.

"*I'm* not a mile high," said Alice.

"You are," said the King.

"Nearly two miles high," added the Queen.

"Well, I sha'n't go, at any rate," said Alice; "besides, that's not a regular rule: you invented it just now."

"It's the oldest rule in the book," said the King.

"Then it ought to be Number One," said Alice.

The King turned pale, and shut his note-book hastily. "Consider your verdict," he said to the jury, in a low trembling voice.

"There's more evidence to come yet, please your Majesty," said the White Rabbit, jumping up in a great hurry: "this paper has just been picked up."

"What's in it?" said the Queen.

"I haven't opened it yet," said the White Rabbit; "but it seems to be a letter, written by the prisoner to—to somebody."

"It must have been that," said the King, "unless it was written to nobody, which isn't usual, you know."

"Who is it directed to?" said one of the jurymen.

"It isn't directed at all," said the White Rabbit: "in fact, there's nothing written on the *outside*." He unfolded the paper as he spoke, and added "It isn't a letter, after all: it's a set of verses."

"Are they in the prisoner's handwriting?" asked another of the jurymen.

"No, they're not," said the White Rabbit, "and that's the queerest thing about it." (The jury all looked puzzled.)

"He must have imitated somebody else's hand," said the King. (The jury all brightened up again.)

"Please, your Majesty," said the Knave, "I didn't write it, and they ca'n't prove that I did: there's no name signed at the end."

"If you didn't sign it", said the King, "that only makes the matter worse. You *must* have meant some mischief, or else you'd have signed your name like an honest man."

There was a general clapping of hands at this: it was the first really clever thing the King had said that day.

"That *proves* his guilt, of course," said the Queen: "so, off with——"

"It doesn't prove anything of the sort!" said Alice. "Why, you don't even know what they're about!"

"Read them," said the King.

The White Rabbit put on his spectacles. "Where shall I begin, please your Majesty?" he asked.

"Begin at the beginning", the King said, very gravely, "and go on till you come to the end: then stop."

There was dead silence in the court, whilst the White Rabbit read out these verses:

"They told me you had been to her,
And mentioned me to him:
She gave me a good character,
But said I could not swim.

He sent them word I had not gone
(We know it to be true):
If she should push the matter on,
What would become of you?

I gave her one, they gave him two,
You gave us three or more;
They all returned from him to you,
Though they were mine before.

If I or she should chance to be
Involved in this affair,
He trusts to you to set them free,
Exactly as we were.

My notion was that you had been
(Before she had this fit)
An obstacle that came between
Him, and ourselves, and it.

Don't let him know she liked them best,
For this must ever be
A secret, kept from all the rest,
Between yourself and me."

"That's the most important piece of evidence we've heard yet," said the King, rubbing his hands; "so now let the jury——"

"If any one of them can explain it", said Alice, (she had grown so large in the last few minutes that she wasn't a bit afraid of interrupting him), "I'll give him sixpence. *I* don't believe there's an atom of meaning in it."

The jury all wrote down, on their slates, "*She* doesn't believe there's an atom of meaning in it," but none of them attempted to explain the paper.

"If there's no meaning in it," said the King, "that saves a world of trouble, you know, as we needn't try to find any. And yet I don't know," he went on, spreading out the verses on his knee, and looking at them with one eye; "I seem to see some meaning in them, after all. '—*said I could not swim* —' you ca'n't swim, can you?" he added, turning to the Knave.

The Knave shook his head sadly. "Do I look like it?" he said. (Which he certainly did *not*, being made entirely of cardboard.)

"All right, so far," said the King; and he went on muttering over the verses to himself: " '*We know it to be true*'—that's the jury, of course—'*If she should push the matter on*' —that must be the Queen —'*What would become of you?*'—What, indeed!—'*I gave her one, they gave him two*'—why, that must be what he did with the tarts, you know——"

"But it goes on '*they all returned from him to you,*' " said Alice.

"Why, there they are!" said the King triumphantly, pointing to the tarts on the table. "Nothing can be clearer than *that*. Then again—*'before she had this fit'*—you never had *fits*, my dear, I think?" he said to the Queen.

"Never!" said the Queen, furiously, throwing an inkstand at the Lizard as she spoke. (The unfortunate little Bill had left off writing on his slate with one finger, as he found it made no mark; but he now hastily began again, using the ink, that was trickling down his face, as long as it lasted.)

"Then the words don't *fit* you," said the King looking round the court with a smile. There was a dead silence.

"It's a pun!" the King added in an angry tone, and everybody laughed. "Let the jury consider their verdict," the King said, for about the twentieth time that day.

"No, no!" said the Queen. "Sentence first—verdict afterwards."

"Stuff and nonsense!" said Alice loudly. "The idea of having the sentence first!"

"Hold your tongue!" said the Queen, turning purple.

"I wo'n't!" said Alice.

"Off with her head!" the Queen shouted at the top of her voice. Nobody moved.

"Who cares for *you*?" said Alice (she had grown to her full size by this time). "You're nothing but a pack of cards!"

At this the whole pack rose up into the air, and came flying down upon her; she gave a little scream, half of fright and half of anger, and tried to beat them off, and found herself lying on the bank, with her head in the lap of her sister, who was gently brushing away some dead leaves that had fluttered down from the trees upon her face.

"Wake up, Alice dear!" said her sister. "Why, what a long sleep you've had!"

"Oh, I've had such a curious dream!" said Alice. And she told her sister, as well as she could remember them, all these strange Adventures of hers that you have just been reading about; and, when she had finished, her sister kissed her, and said "It *was* a curious dream, dear, certainly; but now run in to your tea: it's getting late." So Alice got up and ran off, thinking while she ran, as well she might, what a wonderful dream it had been.

But her sister sat still just as she left her, leaning her head on her hand, watching the setting sun, and thinking of little Alice and all her wonderful Adventures, till she

too began dreaming after a fashion, and this was her
dream:—

First, she dreamed about little Alice herself: once again
the tiny hands were clasped upon her knee, and the bright
eager eyes were looking up into hers—she could hear the
very tones of her voice, and see that queer little toss of her
head to keep back the wandering hair that *would* always
get into her eyes—and still as she listened, or seemed to
listen, the whole place around her became alive with the
strange creatures of her little sister's dream.

The long grass rustled at her feet as the White Rabbit
hurried by—the frightened Mouse splashed his way
through the neighbouring pool—she could hear the rattle
of the teacups as the March Hare and his friends shared
their never-ending meal, and the shrill voice of the Queen
ordering off her unfortunate guests to execution—once
more the pig-baby was sneezing on the Duchess's knee,
while plates and dishes crashed around it—once more the
shriek of the Gryphon, the squeaking of the Lizard's
slate-pencil, and the choking of the suppressed guinea-
pigs, filled the air, mixed up with the distant sob of the
miserable Mock Turtle.

So she sat on, with closed eyes, and half believed herself in Wonderland, though she knew she had but to open
them again, and all would change to dull reality—the
grass would be only rustling in the wind, and the pool
rippling to the waving of the reeds—the rattling teacups
would change to tinkling sheep-bells, and the Queen's
shrill cries to the voice of the shepherd-boy—and the
sneeze of the baby, the shriek of the Gryphon, and all the
other queer noises, would change (she knew) to the confused clamour of the busy farm-yard—while the lowing
of the cattle in the distance would take the place of the
Mock Turtle's heavy sobs.

Lastly, she pictured to herself how this same little sister
of hers would, in the after-time, be herself a grown woman; and how she would keep, through all her riper years,
the simple and loving heart of her childhood; and how

she would gather about her other little children, and make *their* eyes bright and eager with many a strange tale, perhaps even with the dream of Wonderland of long ago; and how she would feel with all their simple sorrows, and find a pleasure in all their simple joys, remembering her own child-life, and the happy summer days.

II
Through the
Looking-Glass

and what Alice found there

Child of the pure unclouded brow
    And dreaming eyes of wonder!
Though time be fleet, and I and thou
    Are half a life asunder,
Thy loving smile will surely hail
The love-gift of a fairy-tale.

I have not seen thy sunny face,
    Nor heard thy silver laughter:
No thought of me shall find a place
    In thy young life's hereafter—
Enough that now thou wilt not fail
To listen to my fairy-tale.

A tale begun in other days,
    When summer suns were glowing—
A simple chime, that served to time
    The rhythm of our rowing—
Whose echoes live in memory yet,
Though envious years would say "forget".

Come, hearken then, ere voice of dread,
    With bitter tidings laden,
Shall summon to unwelcome bed
    A melancholy maiden!
We are but older children, dear,
Who fret to find our bedtime near.

Without, the frost, the blinding snow,
    The storm-wind's moody madness—
Within, the firelight's ruddy glow,
    And childhood's nest of gladness.
The magic words shall hold thee fast:
Thou shalt not heed the raving blast.

And, though the shadow of a sigh
　　May tremble through the story,
For "happy summer days" gone by,
　　And vanish'd summer glory—
It shall not touch with breath of bale,
The pleasance of our fairy-tale.

W H I T E.

White Pawn (Alice) to play, and win in eleven moves.

PREFACE TO 1896 EDITION

As the chess-problem, given on the previous page, has puzzled some of my readers, it may be well to explain that it is correctly worked out, so far as the *moves* are concerned. The *alternation* of Red and White is perhaps not so strictly observed as it might be, and the "castling" of the three Queens is merely a way of saying that they entered the palace; but the "check" of the White King at move 6, the capture of the Red Knight at move 7, and the final "checkmate" of the Red King, will be found, by any one who will take the trouble to set the pieces and play the moves as directed, to be strictly in accordance with the laws of the game.

The new words, in the poem "Jabberwocky" (see p. 140), have given rise to some differences of opinion as to their pronunciation: so it may be well to give instructions on *that* point also. Pronounce "slithy" as if it were the two words "sly, the": make the "g" *hard* in "gyre" and "gimble": and pronounce "rath" to rhyme with "bath".

For this sixty-first thousand, fresh electrotypes have been taken from the wood-blocks (which, never having been used for printing from, are in as good condition as when first cut in 1871), and the whole book has been set up afresh with new type. If the artistic qualities of this reissue fall short, in any particular, of those possessed by the original issue, it will not be for want of painstaking on the part of author, publisher, or printer.

I take this opportunity of announcing that the Nursery "Alice", hitherto priced at four shillings, net, is now to be had on the same terms as the ordinary shilling picture-books—although I feel sure that it is, in every quality (except the *text* itself, in which I am not qualified to pronounce), greatly superior to them. Four shillings was a perfectly reasonable price to charge, considering the very heavy initial outlay I had incurred: still, as the Public have practically said, "We will *not* give more than a shilling for a picture-book, however artistically got-up," I am content to reckon my outlay on the book as so much dead loss, and, rather than let the little ones, for whom it was written, go without it, I am selling it at a price which is, to me, much the same thing as *giving* it away.

Christmas, 1896

CHAPTER I

Looking-Glass House

ONE thing was certain, that the *white* kitten had had nothing to do with it—it was the black kitten's fault entirely. For the white kitten had been having its face washed by the old cat for the last quarter of an hour (and bearing it pretty well, considering): so you see that it *couldn't* have had any hand in the mischief.

The way Dinah washed her children's faces was this: first she held the poor thing down by its ear with one paw, and then with the other paw she rubbed its face all over, the wrong way, beginning at the nose: and just now, as I said, she was hard at work on the white kitten, which was lying quite still and trying to purr—no doubt feeling that it was all meant for its good.

But the black kitten had been finished with earlier in the afternoon, and so, while Alice was sitting curled up in a corner of the great armchair, half talking to herself and half asleep, the kitten had been having a grand game of romps with the ball of worsted Alice had been trying to wind up, and had been rolling it up and down till it had all come undone again; and there it was, spread over the hearth-rug, all knots and tangles, with the kitten running after its own tail in the middle.

"Oh, you wicked, wicked little thing!" cried Alice, catching up the kitten, and giving it a little kiss to make

it understand that it was in disgrace. "Really, Dinah ought to have taught you better manners! You *ought*, Dinah, you know you ought!" she added, looking reproachfully at the old cat, and speaking in as cross a voice as she could manage—and then she scrambled back into the arm-chair, taking the kitten and the worsted with

her, and began winding up the ball again. But she didn't
get on very fast, as she was talking all the time, sometimes to the kitten, and sometimes to herself. Kitty sat
very demurely on her knee, pretending to watch the
progress of the winding, and now and then putting out
one paw and gently touching the ball, as if it would be
glad to help if it might.

"Do you know what to-morrow is, Kitty?" Alice began.
"You'd have guessed if you'd been up in the window with
me—only Dinah was making you tidy, so you couldn't. I
was watching the boys getting in sticks for the bonfire—
and it wants plenty of sticks, Kitty! Only it got so cold,
and it snowed so, they had to leave off. Never mind, we'll
go and see the bonfire to-morrow." Here Alice wound
two or three turns of the worsted round the kitten's neck,
just to see how it would look: this led to a scramble, in
which the ball rolled down upon the floor, and yards and
yards of it got unwound again.

"Do you know, I was so angry, Kitty," Alice went on,
as soon as they were comfortably settled again, "when I
saw all the mischief you had been doing, I was very
nearly opening the window, and putting you out into the
snow! And you'd have deserved it, you little mischievous
darling! What have you got to say for yourself? Now
don't interrupt me!" she went on, holding up one finger.
"I'm going to tell you all your faults. Number one: you
squeaked twice while Dinah was washing your face this
morning. Now you ca'n't deny it, Kitty: I heard you!
What's that you say?" (pretending that the kitten was
speaking). "Her paw went into your eye? Well, that's
your fault, for keeping your eyes open—if you'd shut
them tight up, it wouldn't have happened. Now don't
make any more excuses, but listen! Number two: you
pulled Snowdrop away by the tail just as I had put down
the saucer of milk before her! What, you were thirsty,
were you? How do you know she wasn't thirsty too? Now
for number three: you unwound every bit of the worsted
while I wasn't looking!

"That's three faults, Kitty, and you've not been punished for any of them yet. You know I'm saving up all your punishments for Wednesday week—Suppose they had saved up all *my* punishments?" she went on, talking more to herself than the kitten. "What *would* they do at the end of a year? I should be sent to prison, I suppose, when the day came. Or—let me see—suppose each punishment was to be going without a dinner: then, when the miserable day came, I should have to go without fifty dinners at once! Well, I shouldn't mind *that* much! I'd far rather go without them than eat them!

"Do you hear the snow against the window-panes, Kitty? How nice and soft it sounds! Just as if some one was kissing the window all over outside. I wonder if the snow *loves* the trees and fields, that it kisses them so gently? And then it covers them up snug, you know, with a white quilt; and perhaps it says 'Go to sleep, darlings, till the summer comes again.' And when they wake up in the summer, Kitty, they dress themselves all in green, and dance about—whenever the wind blows—oh, that's very pretty!" cried Alice, dropping the ball of worsted to clap her hands. "And I do so *wish* it was true! I'm sure the woods look sleepy in the autumn, when the leaves are getting brown.

"Kitty, can you play chess? Now, don't smile, my dear, I'm asking it seriously. Because, when we were playing just now, you watched just as if you understood it: and when I said 'Check!' you purred! Well, it *was* a nice check, Kitty, and really I might have won, if it hadn't been for that nasty Knight, that came wriggling down among my pieces. Kitty, dear, let's pretend——" And here I wish I could tell you half the things Alice used to say, beginning with her favourite phrase "Let's pretend". She had had quite a long argument with her sister only the day before—all because Alice had begun with "Let's pretend we're kings and queens"; and her sister, who liked being very exact, had argued that they couldn't, because there were only two of them, and Alice had been reduced at last to say "Well, *you* can be one of them, then, and *I'll* be all the rest." And once she had really frightened her old nurse by shouting suddenly in her ear, "Nurse! Do let's pretend that I'm a hungry hyæna, and you're a bone!"

But this is taking us away from Alice's speech to the kitten. "Let's pretend that you're the Red Queen, Kitty! Do you know, I think if you sat up and folded your arms, you'd look exactly like her. Now do try, there's a dear!" And Alice got the Red Queen off the table, and set it up before the kitten as a model for it to imitate: however, the thing didn't succeed, principally, Alice said, because the kitten wouldn't fold its arms properly. So, to punish it, she held it up to the Looking-glass, that it might see how sulky it was, "—and if you're not good directly," she added, "I'll put you through into Looking-glass House. How would you like *that*?

"Now, if you'll only attend, Kitty, and not talk so much, I'll tell you all my ideas about Looking-glass House. First, there's the room you can see through the glass—that's just the same as our drawing-room, only the things go the other way. I can see all of it when I get upon a chair—all but the bit just behind the fireplace. Oh! I do so wish I could see *that* bit! I want so much to know whether they've a fire in the winter: you never *can* tell, you know, unless our fire smokes, and then smoke comes up in that room too—but that may be only pretence, just to make it look as if they had a fire. Well then, the books are something like our books, only the words go the wrong way: I know *that*, because I've held up one of our books to the glass, and then they hold up one in the other room.

"How would you like to live in Looking-glass House, Kitty? I wonder if they'd give you milk in there? Perhaps Looking-glass milk isn't good to drink—but oh, Kitty, now we come to the passage. You can just see a little *peep* of the passage in Looking-glass House, if you leave the door of our drawing-room wide open: and it's very like

our passage as far as you can see, only you know it may
be quite different on beyond. Oh, Kitty, how nice it
would be if we could only get through into Looking-glass
House! I'm sure it's got, oh! such beautiful things in it!
Let's pretend there's a way of getting through into it,
somehow, Kitty. Let's pretend the glass has got all soft
like gauze, so that we can get through. Why, it's turning
into a sort of mist now, I declare! It'll be easy enough to
get through——'' She was up on the chimney-piece while
she said this, though she hardly knew how she had got

there. And certainly the glass *was* beginning to melt away,
just like a bright silvery mist.

In another moment Alice was through the glass, and
had jumped lightly down into the Looking-glass room.
The very first thing she did was to look whether there was
a fire in the fireplace, and she was quite pleased to find
that there was a real one, blazing away as brightly as the
one she had left behind. "So I shall be as warm here as I
was in the old room," thought Alice: "warmer, in fact,
because there'll be no one here to scold me away from the

fire. Oh, what fun it'll be, when they see me through the glass in here, and ca'n't get at me!"

Then she began looking about, and noticed that what could be seen from the old room was quite common and uninteresting, but that all the rest was as different as possible. For instance, the pictures on the wall next the fire seemed to be all alive, and the very clock on the chimney-piece (you know you can only see the back of it in the Looking-glass) had got the face of a little old man, and grinned at her.

"They don't keep this room so tidy as the other," Alice thought to herself, as she noticed several of the chessmen down in the hearth among the cinders; but in another moment, with a little "Oh!" of surprise, she was down on her hands and knees watching them. The chessmen were walking about, two and two!

"Here are the Red King and the Red Queen," Alice said (in a whisper, for fear of frightening them), "and there are the White King and the White Queen sitting on the edge of the shovel—and here are two Castles walking arm in arm—I don't think they can hear me," she went on, as she put her head closer down, "and I'm nearly sure they ca'n't see me, I feel somehow as if I was getting invisible——"

Here something began squeaking on the table behind Alice, and made her turn her head just in time to see one of the White Pawns roll over and begin kicking: she watched it with great curiosity to see what would happen next.

"It is the voice of my child!" the White Queen cried out, as she rushed past the King, so violently that she knocked him over among the cinders. "My precious Lily! My imperial kitten!" and she began scrambling wildly up the side of the fender.

"Imperial fiddlestick!" said the King, rubbing his nose, which had been hurt by the fall. He had a right to be a *little* annoyed with the Queen, for he was covered with ashes from head to foot.

Alice was very anxious to be of use, and, as the poor

little Lily was nearly screaming herself into a fit, she
hastily picked up the Queen and set her on the table by
the side of her noisy little daughter.

The Queen gasped, and sat down: the rapid journey
through the air had quite taken away her breath, and for
a minute or two she could do nothing but hug the little
Lily in silence. As soon as she had recovered her breath

a little, she called out to the White King, who was sitting
sulkily among the ashes, "Mind the volcano!"

"What volcano?" said the King, looking up anxiously
into the fire, as if he thought that was the most likely
place to find one.

"Blew—me—up," panted the Queen, who was still a
little out of breath. "Mind you come up—the regular way
—don't get blown up!"

Alice watched the White King as he slowly struggled
up from bar to bar, till at last she said "Why, you'll be
hours and hours getting to the table, at that rate. I'd far
better help you, hadn't I?" But the King took no notice

of the question: it was quite clear that he could neither
hear her nor see her.

So Alice picked him up very gently, and lifted him
across more slowly than she had lifted the Queen, that
she mightn't take his breath away; but, before she put
him on the table, she thought she might as well dust him
a little, he was so covered with ashes.

She said afterwards that she had never seen in all her
life such a face as the King made, when he found himself
held in the air by an invisible hand, and being dusted: he
was far too much astonished to cry out, but his eyes and
his mouth went on getting larger and larger, and rounder
and rounder, till her hand shook so with laughing that
she nearly let him drop upon the floor.

"Oh! *please* don't make such faces, my dear!" she cried
out, quite forgetting that the King couldn't hear her.
"You make me laugh so that I can hardly hold you! And
don't keep your mouth so wide open! All the ashes will

get into it—there, now I think you're tidy enough!" she added, as she smoothed his hair, and set him upon the table near the Queen.

The King immediately fell flat on his back, and lay perfectly still; and Alice was a little alarmed at what she had done, and went round the room to see if she could

find any water to throw over him. However, she could find nothing but a bottle of ink, and when she got back with it she found he had recovered, and he and the Queen were talking together in a frightened whisper—so low, that Alice could hardly hear what they said.

The King was saying "I assure you, my dear, I turned cold to the very ends of my whiskers!"

To which the Queen replied "You haven't got any whiskers."

"The horror of that moment", the King went on, "I shall never, *never* forget!"

"You will, though," the Queen said, "if you don't make a memorandum of it."

Alice looked on with great interest as the King took an enormous memorandum book out of his pocket, and began writing. A sudden thought struck her, and she took hold of the end of the pencil, which came some way over his shoulder, and began writing for him.

The poor King looked puzzled and unhappy, and struggled with the pencil for some time without saying anything; but Alice was too strong for him, and at last he panted out "My dear! I really *must* get a thinner pencil. I ca'n't manage this one a bit: it writes all manner of things that I don't intend——"

"What manner of things?" said the Queen, looking over the book (in which Alice had put '*The White Knight is sliding down the poker. He balances very badly*'). "That's not a memorandum of *your* feelings!"

There was a book lying near Alice on the table, and while she sat watching the White King (for she was still a little anxious about him, and had the ink all ready to throw over him, in case he fainted again), she turned over the leaves, to find some part that she could read, "—for it's all in some language I don't know," she said to herself.

It was like this.

ʏʞɔoᗯяƎᗺᗺA႟

'Ɐuɐ bɹᴉllᴉƃ' ɐuq ʇɥǝ slᴉʇɥʎ ʇoʌǝs
ᗡᴉp ƃʎɹǝ ɐuq ƃᴉɯplǝ ᴉu ʇɥǝ ʍɐqǝ:
Ɐll ɯᴉɯsʎ ʍǝɹǝ ʇɥǝ qoɹoƃoʌǝs'
Ɐuq ʇɥǝ ɯoɯǝ ɹɐʇɥs oนʇƃɹɐqǝ˙

She puzzled over this for some time, but at last a bright thought struck her. "Why, it's a Looking-glass book, of course! And, if I hold it up to a glass, the words will all go the right way again."

This was the poem that Alice read

JABBERWOCKY

'Twas brillig, and the slithy toves
Did gyre and gimble in the wabe:
All mimsy were the borogoves,
And the mome raths outgrabe.

"Beware the Jabberwock, my son!
The jaws that bite, the claws that catch!
Beware the Jubjub bird, and shun
The frumious Bandersnatch!"

He took his vorpal sword in hand:
Long time the manxome foe he sought—
So rested he by the Tumtum tree,
And stood awhile in thought.

And, as in uffish thought he stood,
The Jabberwock, with eyes of flame,
Came whiffling through the tulgey wood,
And burbled as it came!

One, two! One, two! And through and through
The vorpal blade went snicker-snack!
He left it dead, and with its head
He went galumphing back.

"And hast thou slain the Jabberwock?
Come to my arms, my beamish boy!
O frabjous day! Callooh! Callay!"
He chortled in his joy.

'Twas brillig, and the slithy toves
Did gyre and gimble in the wabe:
All mimsy were the borogoves,
And the mome raths outgrabe.

"It seems very pretty," she said when she had finished it, "but it's *rather* hard to understand!" (You see she didn't like to confess, even to herself, that she couldn't make it out at all.) "Somehow it seems to fill my head with ideas—only I don't exactly know what they are! However, *somebody* killed *something*: that's clear, at any rate——"

"But oh!" thought Alice, suddenly jumping up, "if I don't make haste, I shall have to go back through the Looking-glass, before I've seen what the rest of the house is like! Let's have a look at the garden first!" She was out of the room in a moment, and ran down stairs—or, at least, it wasn't exactly running, but a new invention for getting down stairs quickly and easily, as Alice said to herself. She just kept the tips of her fingers on the hand-rail, and floated gently down without even touching the stairs with her feet: then she floated on through the hall, and would have gone straight out at the door in the same way, if she hadn't caught hold of the door-post. She was getting a little giddy with so much floating in the air, and was rather glad to find herself walking again in the natural way.

CHAPTER II

The Garden of Live Flowers

"I SHOULD see the garden far better", said Alice to herself, "if I could get to the top of that hill; and here's a path that leads straight to it—at least, no, it doesn't do *that*——" (after going a few yards along the path, and turning several sharp corners), "but I suppose it will at last. But how curiously it twists! It's more like a corkscrew than a path! Well *this* turn goes to the hill, I suppose—no, it doesn't! This goes straight back to the house! Well then, I'll try it the other way."

And so she did: wandering up and down, and trying turn after turn, but always coming back to the house, do what she would. Indeed, once, when she turned a corner rather more quickly than usual, she ran against it before she could stop herself.

"It's no use talking about it," Alice said, looking up at the house and pretending it was arguing with her. "I'm *not* going in again yet. I know I should have to get through the Looking-glass again—back into the old room—and there'd be an end of all my adventures!"

So, resolutely turning her back upon the house, she set out once more down the path, determined to keep straight on till she got to the hill. For a few minutes all went on well, and she was just saying "I really *shall* do it this time

——" when the path gave a sudden twist and shook itself (as she described it afterwards), and the next moment she found herself actually walking in at the door.

"Oh, it's too bad!" she cried. "I never saw such a house for getting in the way! Never!"

However, there was the hill full in sight, so there was nothing to be done but start again. This time she came upon a large flower-bed, with a border of daisies, and a willow-tree growing in the middle.

"O Tiger-lily!" said Alice, addressing herself to one that

was waving gracefully about in the wind, "I *wish* you could talk!"

"We *can* talk", said the Tiger-lily, "when there's anybody worth talking to."

Alice was so astonished that she couldn't speak for a minute: it quite seemed to take her breath away. At length, as the Tiger-lily only went on waving about, she spoke again, in a timid voice—almost in a whisper. "And can *all* the flowers talk?"

"As well as *you* can," said the Tiger-lily. "And a great deal louder."

"It isn't manners for us to begin, you know," said the Rose, "and I really was wondering when you'd speak! Said I to myself, 'Her face has got *some* sense in it, though it's not a clever one!' Still, you're the right colour, and that goes a long way."

"I don't care about the colour," the Tiger-lily remarked. "If only her petals curled up a little more, she'd be all right."

Alice didn't like being criticised, so she began asking questions. "Aren't you sometimes frightened at being planted out here, with nobody to take care of you?"

"There's the tree in the middle," said the Rose. "What else is it good for?"

"But what could it do, if any danger came?" Alice asked.

"It could bark," said the Rose.

"It says 'Boughwough!'" cried a Daisy. "That's why its branches are called boughs!"

"Didn't you know *that*?" cried another Daisy. And here they all began shouting together, till the air seemed quite full of little shrill voices. "Silence, every one of you!" cried the Tiger-lily, waving itself passionately from side to side, and trembling with excitement. "They know I ca'n't get at them!" it panted, bending its quivering head towards Alice, "or they wouldn't dare to do it!"

"Never mind!" Alice said in a soothing tone, and, stooping down to the daisies, who were just beginning again, she whispered "If you don't hold your tongues, I'll pick you!"

There was silence in a moment, and several of the pink daisies turned white.

"That's right!" said the Tiger-lily. "The daisies are worst of all. When one speaks, they all begin together, and it's enough to make one wither to hear the way they go on!"

"How is it you can all talk so nicely?" Alice said, hoping to get it into a better temper by a compliment. "I've been in many gardens before, but none of the flowers could talk."

"Put your hand down, and feel the ground," said the Tiger-lily. "Then you'll know why."

Alice did so. "It's very hard," she said; "but I don't see what that has to do with it."

"In most gardens", the Tiger-lily said, "they make the beds too soft—so that the flowers are always asleep."

This sounded a very good reason, and Alice was quite pleased to know it. "I never thought of that before!" she said.

"It's *my* opinion that you never think *at all*," the Rose said, in a rather severe tone.

"I never saw anybody that looked stupider," a Violet said, so suddenly, that Alice quite jumped; for it hadn't spoken before.

"Hold *your* tongue!" cried the Tiger-lily. "As if *you* ever saw anybody! You keep your head under the leaves, and snore away there, till you know no more what's going on in the world, than if you were a bud!"

"Are there any more people in the garden besides me?" Alice said, not choosing to notice the Rose's last remark.

"There's one other flower in the garden that can move about like you," said the Rose. "I wonder how you do it —" ("You're always wondering," said the Tiger-lily), "but she's more bushy than you are."

"Is she like me?" Alice asked eagerly, for the thought crossed her mind, "There's another little girl in the garden, somewhere!"

"Well, she has the same awkward shape as you," the Rose said; "but she's redder—and her petals are shorter, I think."

"They're done up close, like a dahlia," said the Tiger-lily: "not tumbled about, like yours."

"But that's not *your* fault," the Rose added kindly. "You're beginning to fade, you know—and then one ca'n't help one's petals getting a little untidy."

Alice didn't like this idea at all: so, to change the subject, she asked "Does she ever come out here?"

"I daresay you'll see her soon," said the Rose. "She's one of the kind that has nine spikes, you know."

"Where does she wear them?" Alice asked with some curiosity.

"Why, all round her head, of course," the Rose replied.
"I was wondering *you* hadn't got some too. I thought it
was the regular rule."

"She's coming!" cried the Larkspur. "I hear her footstep, thump, thump, along the gravel-walk!"

Alice looked round eagerly and found that it was the
Red Queen. "She's grown a good deal!" was her first
remark. She had indeed: when Alice first found her in the
ashes, she had been only three inches high—and here she
was, half a head taller than Alice herself!

"It's the fresh air that does it," said the Rose: "wonderfully fine air it is, out here."

"I think I'll go and meet her," said Alice, for, though
the flowers were interesting enough, she felt that it would
be far grander to have a talk with a real Queen.

"You ca'n't possibly do that," said the Rose: "*I* should
advise you to walk the other way."

This sounded nonsense to Alice, so she said nothing,
but set off at once towards the Red Queen. To her surprise she lost sight of her in a moment, and found herself
walking in at the front-door again.

A little provoked, she drew back, and, after looking
everywhere for the Queen (whom she spied out at last, a
long way off), she thought she would try the plan, this
time, of walking in the opposite direction.

It succeeded beautifully. She had not been walking a
minute before she found herself face to face with the Red
Queen, and full in sight of the hill she had been so long
aiming at.

"Where do you come from?" said the Red Queen.
"And where are you going? Look up, speak nicely, and
don't twiddle your fingers all the time."

Alice attended to all these directions, and explained, as
well as she could, that she had lost her way.

"I don't know what you mean by *your* way," said the
Queen: "all the ways about here belong to *me*—but why
did you come out here at all?" she added in a kinder tone.
"Curtsey while you're thinking what to say. It saves time."

Alice wondered a little at this, but she was too much in awe of the Queen to disbelieve it. "I'll try it when I go home," she thought to herself, "the next time I'm a little late for dinner."

"It's time for you to answer now," the Queen said looking at her watch: "open your mouth a *little* wider when you speak, and always say 'your Majesty'."

"I only wanted to see what the garden was like, your Majesty——"

"That's right," said the Queen, patting her on the head, which Alice didn't like at all: "though, when you say 'garden'—*I've* seen gardens, compared with which this would be a wilderness."

Alice didn't dare to argue the point, but went on: "—and I thought I'd try and find my way to the top of that hill——"

"When you say 'hill'," the Queen interrupted, "*I* could show you hills, in comparison with which you'd call that a valley."

"No, I shouldn't," said Alice, surprised into contradicting her at last: "a hill *ca'n't* be a valley, you know. That would be nonsense——"

The Red Queen shook her head. "You may call it 'nonsense' if you like," she said, "but *I've* heard nonsense, compared with which that would be as sensible as a dictionary!"

Alice curtseyed again, as she was afraid from the Queen's tone that she was a *little* offended: and they walked on in silence till they got to the top of the little hill.

For some minutes Alice stood without speaking, looking out in all directions over the country—and a most curious country it was. There were a number of tiny little brooks running straight across it from side to side, and the ground between was divided up into squares by a number of little green hedges, that reached from brook to brook.

"I declare it's marked out just like a large chess-board!" Alice said at last. "There ought to be some men moving about somewhere—and so there are!" she added in a tone of delight, and her heart began to beat quick with excitement as she went on. "It's a great huge game of chess that's being played—all over the world—if this *is* the world at all, you know. Oh, what fun it is! How I *wish* I was one of them! I wouldn't mind being a Pawn, if only I might join—though of course I should *like* to be a Queen, best."

She glanced rather shyly at the real Queen as she said this, but her companion only smiled pleasantly, and said "That's easily managed. You can be the White Queen's Pawn, if you like, as Lily's too young to play: and you're in the Second Square to begin with: when you get to the Eighth Square you'll be a Queen——" Just at this moment, somehow or other, they began to run.

Alice never could quite make out, in thinking it over afterwards, how it was that they began: all she remembers is, that they were running hand in hand, and the Queen went so fast that it was all she could do to keep up with her: and still the Queen kept crying "Faster! Faster!" but Alice felt she *could not* go faster, though she had no breath left to say so.

The most curious part of the thing was, that the trees and the other things round them never changed their places at all: however fast they went, they never seemed to pass anything. "I wonder if all the things move along with us?" thought poor puzzled Alice. And the Queen seemed to guess her thoughts, for she cried "Faster! Don't try to talk!"

Not that Alice had any idea of doing *that*. She felt as if she would never be able to talk again, she was getting so much out of breath: and still the Queen cried "Faster! Faster!" and dragged her along. "Are we nearly there?" Alice managed to pant out at last.

"Nearly there!" the Queen repeated. "Why, we passed it ten minutes ago! Faster!" And they ran on for a time in silence, with the wind whistling in Alice's ears, and almost blowing her hair off her head, she fancied.

"Now! Now!" cried the Queen. "Faster! Faster!" And they went so fast that at last they seemed to skim through the air, hardly touching the ground with their feet, till suddenly, just as Alice was getting quite exhausted, they stopped, and she found herself sitting on the ground, breathless and giddy.

The Queen propped her up against a tree, and said kindly, "You may rest a little, now."

Alice looked round her in great surprise. "Why, I do believe we've been under this tree the whole time! Everything's just as it was!"

"Of course it is," said the Queen. "What would you have it?"

"Well, in *our* country", said Alice, still panting a little, "you'd generally get to somewhere else—if you ran very fast for a long time as we've been doing."

"A slow sort of country!" said the Queen. "Now, *here*, you see, it takes all the running *you* can do, to keep in the same place. If you want to get somewhere else, you must run at least twice as fast as that!"

"I'd rather not try, please!" said Alice. "I'm quite content to stay here—only I *am* so hot and thirsty!"

"I know what *you'd* like!" the Queen said good-naturedly, taking a little box out of her pocket. "Have a biscuit?"

Alice thought it would not be civil to say "No", though it wasn't at all what she wanted. She took it, and ate it as well as she could: and it was *very* dry: and she thought she had never been so nearly choked in all her life.

"While you're refreshing yourself", said the Queen, "I'll just take the measurements." And she took a ribbon out of her pocket, marked in inches, and began measuring the ground, and sticking little pegs in here and there.

"At the end of two yards", she said, putting in a peg to mark the distance, "I shall give you your directions—have another biscuit?"

"No, thank you," said Alice: "one's *quite* enough!"

"Thirst quenched, I hope?" said the Queen.

Alice did not know what to say to this, but luckily the Queen did not wait for an answer, but went on. "At the end of *three* yards I shall repeat them—for fear of your forgetting them. At the end of *four*, I shall say good-bye. And at the end of *five*, I shall go!"

She had got all the pegs put in by this time, and Alice

looked on with great interest as she returned to the tree, and then began slowly walking down the row.

At the two-yard peg she faced round, and said "A pawn goes two squares in its first move, you know. So you'll go *very* quickly through the Third Square—by railway, I should think—and you'll find yourself in the Fourth Square in no time. Well, *that* square belongs to Tweedledum and Tweedledee—the Fifth is mostly water —the Sixth belongs to Humpty Dumpty—But you make no remark?"

"I—I didn't know I had to make one—just then," Alice faltered out.

"You *should* have said," the Queen went on in a tone of grave reproof, " 'It's extremely kind of you to tell me all this'—however, we'll suppose it said—the Seventh Square is all forest—however, one of the Knights will show you the way—and in the Eighth Square we shall be Queens together, and it's all feasting and fun!" Alice got up and curtseyed, and sat down again.

At the next peg the Queen turned again, and this time she said "Speak in French when you ca'n't think of the English for a thing—turn out your toes as you walk—and remember who you are!" She did not wait for Alice to curtsey, this time, but walked on quickly to the next peg, where she turned for a moment to say "Good-bye", and then hurried on to the last.

How it happened, Alice never knew, but exactly as she came to the last peg, she was gone. Whether she vanished into the air, or whether she ran quickly into the wood ("and she *can* run very fast!" thought Alice), there was no way of guessing, but she was gone, and Alice began to remember that she was a Pawn, and that it would soon be time for her to move.

CHAPTER III

Looking-Glass Insects

OF course the first thing to do was to make a grand survey of the country she was going to travel through. "It's something very like learning geography," thought Alice, as she stood on tiptoe in hopes of being able to see a little further. "Principal rivers—there *are* none. Principal mountains—I'm on the only one, but I don't think it's got any name. Principal towns—why, what *are* those creatures, making honey down there? They ca'n't be bees—nobody ever saw bees a mile off, you know——" and for some time she stood silent, watching one of them that was bustling about among the flowers, poking its proboscis into them, "just as if it was a regular bee," thought Alice.

However, this was anything but a regular bee: in fact, it was an elephant—as Alice soon found out, though the idea quite took her breath away at first. "And what enormous flowers they must be!" was her next idea. "Something like cottages with the roofs taken off, and stalks put to them—and what quantities of honey they must make! I think I'll go down and—no, I wo'n't go *just* yet," she went on, checking herself just as she was beginning to run down the hill, and trying to find some excuse for turning shy so suddenly. "It'll never do to go down among them without a good long branch to brush them away—and what fun it'll be when they ask me how I liked my walk. I shall say 'Oh, I liked it well enough——' (here came the favourite little toss of the head), 'only it *was* so dusty and hot, and the elephants *did* tease so!' "

"I think I'll go down the other way," she said after a pause, "and perhaps I may visit the elephants later on. Besides, I *do* so want to get into the Third Square!"

So, with this excuse, she ran down the hill, and jumped over the first of the six little brooks.

*   *   *   *   *

*   *   *   *

*   *   *   *   *

"Tickets, please!" said the Guard, putting his head in at the window. In a moment everybody was holding out a ticket: they were about the same size as the people, and quite seemed to fill the carriage.

"Now then! Show your ticket, child!" the Guard went on, looking angrily at Alice. And a great many voices all said together ("like the chorus of a song," thought Alice) "Don't keep him waiting, child! Why, his time is worth a thousand pounds a minute!"

"I'm afraid I haven't got one," Alice said in a frightened tone: "there wasn't a ticket-office where I came from." And again the chorus of voices went on. "There wasn't room for one where she came from. The land there is worth a thousand pounds an inch!"

"Don't make excuses," said the Guard: "you should have bought one from the engine-driver." And once more the chorus of voices went on with "The man that drives the engine. Why, the smoke alone is worth a thousand pounds a puff!"

Alice thought to herself "Then there's no use in speaking." The voices didn't join in, *this* time, as she hadn't spoken, but, to her great surprise, they all *thought* in chorus (I hope you understand what *thinking in chorus* means—for I must confess that *I* don't), "Better say nothing at all. Language is worth a thousand pounds a word!"

"I shall dream about a thousand pounds to-night, I know I shall!" thought Alice.

All this time the Guard was looking at her, first through a telescope, then through a microscope, and then through an opera-glass. At last he said "You're travelling the wrong way," and shut up the window, and went away.

"So young a child", said the gentleman sitting opposite to her, (he was dressed in white paper), "ought to know which way she's going, even if she doesn't know her own name!"

A Goat that was sitting next to the gentleman in white, shut his eyes and said in a loud voice, "She ought to know

her way to the ticket-office, even if she doesn't know her alphabet!"

There was a Beetle sitting next the Goat (it was a very queer carriage-full of passengers altogether), and, as the rule seemed to be that they should all speak in turn, *he* went on with "She'll have to go back from here as luggage!"

Alice couldn't see who was sitting beyond the Beetle, but a hoarse voice spoke next. "Change engines——" it said, and there it choked and was obliged to leave off.

"It sounds like a horse," Alice thought to herself. And

an extremely small voice, close to her ear, said "You might make a joke on that—something about 'horse' and 'hoarse', you know."

Then a very gentle voice in the distance said, "She must be labelled 'Lass, with care', you know——"

And after that other voices went on ("What a number of people there are in the carriage!" thought Alice), saying "She must go by post, as she's got a head on her——" "She must be sent as a message by the telegraph——" "She must draw the train herself the rest of the way——", and so on.

But the gentleman dressed in white paper leaned forwards and whispered in her ear, "Never mind what they all say, my dear, but take a return-ticket every time the train stops."

"Indeed I sha'n't!" Alice said rather impatiently. "I don't belong to this railway journey at all—I was in a wood just now—and I wish I could get back there!"

"You might make a joke on *that*," said the little voice close to her ear: "something about 'you *would* if you could', you know."

"Don't tease so," said Alice, looking about in vain to see where the voice came from. "If you're so anxious to have a joke made, why don't you make one yourself?"

The little voice sighed deeply. It was *very* unhappy, evidently, and Alice would have said something pitying to comfort it, "if it would only sigh like other people!" she thought. But this was such a wonderfully small sigh, that she wouldn't have heard it at all, if it hadn't come *quite* close to her ear. The consequence of this was that it tickled her ear very much, and quite took off her thoughts from the unhappiness of the poor little creature.

"I know you are a friend," the little voice went on: "a dear friend, and an old friend. And you wo'n't hurt me, though I *am* an insect."

"What kind of insect?" Alice inquired, a little anxiously. What she really wanted to know was, whether it could sting or not, but she thought this wouldn't be quite a civil question to ask.

"What, then you don't——" the little voice began, when it was drowned by a shrill scream from the engine, and every-body jumped up in alarm, Alice among the rest.

The Horse, who had put his head out of the window, quietly drew it in and said "It's only a brook we have to jump over." Everybody seemed satisfied with this, though Alice felt a little nervous at the idea of trains jumping at all. "However, it'll take us into the Fourth Square, that's some comfort!" she said to herself. In another moment she felt the carriage rise straight up into the air, and in her fright she caught at the thing nearest to her hand, which happened to be the Goat's beard.

*　　　*　　　*　　　*　　　*

*　　　*　　　*　　　*

*　　　*　　　*　　　*　　　*

But the beard seemed to melt away as she touched it, and she found herself sitting quietly under a tree—while the Gnat (for that was the insect she had been talking to) was balancing itself on a twig just over her head, and fanning her with its wings.

It certainly was a *very* large Gnat: "about the size of a chicken," Alice thought. Still, she couldn't feel nervous with it, after they had been talking together so long.

"—then you don't like *all* insects?" the Gnat went on, as quietly as if nothing had happened.

"I like them when they can talk," Alice said. "None of them ever talk, where *I* come from."

"What sort of insects do you rejoice in, where *you* come from?" the Gnat inquired.

"I don't *rejoice* in insects at all," Alice explained, "be-cause I'm rather afraid of them—at least the large kinds. But I can tell you the names of some of them."

"Of course they answer to their names?" the Gnat remarked carelessly.

"I never knew them do it."

"What's the use of their having names", the Gnat said, "if they wo'n't answer to them?"

"No use to *them*," said Alice; "but it's useful to the

people that name them, I suppose. If not, why do things have names at all?"

"I ca'n't say," the Gnat replied. "Further on, in the wood down there, they've got no names—however, go on with your list of insects: you're wasting time."

"Well, there's the Horse-fly," Alice began, counting off the names on her fingers.

"All right," said the Gnat. "Half way up that bush, you'll see a Rocking-horse-fly, if you look. It's made entirely of wood, and gets about by swinging itself from branch to branch."

"What does it live on?" Alice asked, with great curiosity.

"Sap and sawdust," said the Gnat. "Go on with the list."

Alice looked at the Rocking-horse-fly with great interest, and made up her mind that it must have been just repainted, it looked so bright and sticky; and then she went on.

"And there's the Dragon-fly."

"Look on the branch above your head", said the Gnat, "and there you'll find a Snap-dragon-fly. Its body is made of plum-pudding, its wings of holly-leaves, and its head is a raisin burning in brandy.''

''And what does it live on?'' Alice asked, as before.

''Frumenty and mince-pie,'' the Gnat replied; ''and it makes its nest in a Christmas-box.''

''And then there's the Butterfly,'' Alice went on, after she had taken a good look at the insect with its head on

fire, and had thought to herself, ''I wonder if that's the reason insects are so fond of flying into candles—because they want to turn into Snap-dragon-flies!''

''Crawling at your feet'', said the Gnat (Alice drew her feet back in some alarm), ''you may observe a Bread-and-butter-fly. Its wings are thin slices of bread-and-butter, its body is a crust, and its head is a lump of sugar.''

''And what does *it* live on?''

''Weak tea with cream in it.''

A new difficulty came into Alice's head. ''Supposing it couldn't find any?'' she suggested.

''Then it would die, of course.''

''But that must happen very often,'' Alice remarked thoughtfully.

"It always happens," said the Gnat.

After this, Alice was silent for a minute or two pondering. The Gnat amused itself meanwhile by humming round and round her head: at last it settled again and remarked "I suppose you don't want to lose your name?"

"No, indeed," Alice said, a little anxiously.

"And yet I don't know," the Gnat went on in a careless

tone: "only think how convenient it would be if you could manage to go home without it! For instance, if the governess wanted to call you to your lessons, she would call out 'Come here——', and there she would have to leave off, because there wouldn't be any name for her to call, and of course you wouldn't have to go, you know."

"That would never do, I'm sure," said Alice: "the governess would never think of excusing me lessons for that. If she couldn't remember my name, she'd call me 'Miss', as the servants do."

"Well, if she said 'Miss', and didn't say anything more," the Gnat remarked, "of course you'd miss your lessons. That's a joke. I wish *you* had made it."

"Why do you wish *I* had made it?" Alice asked. "It's a very bad one."

But the Gnat only sighed deeply while two large tears come rolling down its cheeks.

"You shouldn't make jokes", Alice said, "if it makes you so unhappy."

Then came another of those melancholy little sighs, and this time the poor Gnat really seemed to have sighed itself away, for, when Alice looked up, there was nothing whatever to be seen on the twig, and, as she was getting quite chilly with sitting still so long, she got up and walked on.

She very soon came to an open field, with a wood on the other side of it: it looked much darker than the last wood, and Alice felt a little timid about going into it. However, on second thoughts, she made up her mind to go on: "for I certainly won't go *back*," she thought to herself, and this was the only way to the Eighth Square.

"This must be the wood", she said thoughtfully to herself, "where things have no names. I wonder what'll become of *my* name when I go in? I shouldn't like to lose it at all—because they'd have to give me another, and it would be almost certain to be an ugly one. But then the fun would be, trying to find the creature that had got my old name! That's just like the advertisements, you know, when people lose dogs—'*answers to the name of "Dash"*: *had on a brass collar*'—just fancy calling everything you met 'Alice', till one of them answered! Only they wouldn't answer at all, if they were wise."

She was rambling on in this way when she reached the wood: it looked very cool and shady. "Well, at any rate it's a great comfort," she said as she stepped under the trees, "after being so hot, to get into the—into the—into *what*?" she went on, rather surprised at not being able to think of the word. "I mean to get under the—under the—under *this*, you know!" putting her hand on the trunk of the tree. "What *does* it call itself, I wonder? I do believe it's got no name—why, to be sure it hasn't!"

She stood silent for a minute, thinking: then she suddenly began again. "Then it really *has* happened, after

all! And now, who am I? I *will* remember, if I can! I'm
determined to do it!" But being determined didn't help
her much, and all she could say, after a great deal of
puzzling, was "L, I *know* it begins with L!"

Just then a Fawn came wandering by: it looked at
Alice with its large gentle eyes, but didn't seem at all
frightened. "Here then! Here then!" Alice said, as she

held out her hand and tried to stroke it; but it only
started back a little, and then stood looking at her again.

"What do you call yourself?" the Fawn said at last.
Such a soft sweet voice it had!

"I wish I knew!" thought poor Alice. She answered,
rather sadly, "Nothing just now."

"Think again," it said: "that wo'n't do."

Alice thought, but nothing came of it. "Please, would

you tell me what *you* call yourself?" she said timidly. "I think that might help a little."

"I'll tell you, if you'll come a little further on," the Fawn said. "I ca'n't remember *here*."

So they walked on together through the wood, Alice with her arms clasped lovingly round the soft neck of the Fawn, till they came out into another open field, and here the Fawn gave a sudden bound into the air, and shook itself free from Alice's arm. "I'm a Fawn!" it cried out in a voice of delight. "And, dear me! you're a human child!" A sudden look of alarm came into its beautiful brown eyes, and in another moment it had darted away at full speed.

Alice stood looking after it, almost ready to cry with vexation at having lost her dear little fellow-traveler so suddenly. "However, I know my name now," she said: "that's *some* comfort. Alice—Alice—I won't forget it again. And now which of these finger-posts ought I to follow, I wonder?"

It was not a very difficult question to answer, as there was only one road through the wood, and the two finger-posts both pointed along it. "I'll settle it", Alice said to herself, "when the road divides and they point different ways."

But this did not seem likely to happen. She went on and on, a long way, but wherever the road divided, there were sure to be two finger-posts pointing the same way, one marked "TO TWEEDLEDUM'S HOUSE", and the other "TO THE HOUSE OF TWEEDLEDEE".

"I do believe", said Alice at last, "that they live in the *same* house! I wonder I never thought of that before— But I ca'n't stay there long. I'll just call and say 'How d'ye do?' and ask them the way out of the wood. If I could only get to the Eighth Square before it gets dark!" So she wandered on, talking to herself as she went, till, on turning a sharp corner, she came upon two fat little men, so suddenly that she could not help starting back, but in another moment she recovered herself, feeling sure that they must be

CHAPTER IV

Tweedledum and Tweedledee

THEY were standing under a tree, each with an arm round the other's neck, and Alice knew which was which in a moment, because one of them had 'DUM' embroidered on his collar, and the other 'DEE'. "I suppose

they've each got 'TWEEDLE' round at the back of the collar," she said to herself.

They stood so still that she quite forgot they were alive, and she was just going round to see if the word 'TWEEDLE' was written at the back of each collar, when she was startled by a voice coming from the one marked 'DUM'.

"If you think we're wax-works," he said, "you ought to pay, you know. Wax-works weren't made to be looked at for nothing. Nohow!"

"Contrariwise," added the one marked 'DEE', "if you think we're alive, you ought to speak."

"I'm sure I'm very sorry," was all Alice could say; for the words of the old song kept ringing through her head like the ticking of a clock, and she could hardly help saying them out loud:

> *"Tweedledum and Tweedledee*
> *Agreed to have a battle;*
> *For Tweedledum said Tweedledee*
> *Had spoiled his nice new rattle.*
>
> *Just then flew down a monstrous crow,*
> *As black as a tar-barrel;*
> *Which frightened both the heroes so,*
> *They quite forgot their quarrel."*

"I know what you're thinking about," said Tweedledum; "but it isn't so, nohow."

"Contrariwise," continued Tweedledee, "if it was so, it might be; and if it were so, it would be; but as it isn't, it ain't. That's logic."

"I was thinking," Alice said politely, "which is the best way out of this wood: it's getting so dark. Would you tell me, please?"

But the fat little men only looked at each other and grinned.

They looked so exactly like a couple of great schoolboys, that Alice couldn't help pointing her finger at Tweedledum, and saying "First Boy!"

"Nohow!" Tweedledum cried out briskly, and shut his mouth up again with a snap.

"Next Boy!" said Alice, passing on to Tweedledee, though she felt quite certain he would only shout out "Contrariwise!" and so he did.

"You've begun wrong!" cried Tweedledum. "The first thing in a visit is to say 'How d'ye do?' and shake hands!" And here the two brothers gave each other a hug, and then they held out the two hands that were free, to shake hands with her.

Alice did not like shaking hands with either of them first, for fear of hurting the other one's feelings; so, as the best way out of the difficulty, she took hold of both hands at once: the next moment they were dancing round in a ring. This seemed quite natural (she remembered afterwards), and she was not even surprised to hear music playing: it seemed to come from the tree under which they were dancing, and it was done (as well as she could make it out) by the branches rubbing one across the other, like fiddles and fiddle-sticks.

"But it certainly *was* funny", (Alice said afterwards, when she was telling her sister the history of all this), "to find myself singing '*Here we go round the mulberry bush*'. I don't know when I began it, but somehow I felt as if I'd been singing it a long long time!"

The other two dancers were fat, and very soon out of breath. "Four times round is enough for one dance," Tweedledum panted out, and they left off dancing as suddenly as they had begun: the music stopped at the same moment.

Then they let go of Alice's hands, and stood looking at her for a minute: there was a rather awkward pause, as Alice didn't know how to begin a conversation with people she had just been dancing with. "It would never do to say 'How d'ye do?' *now*," she said to herself: "we seem to have got beyond that, somehow!"

"I hope you're not much tired?" she said at last.

"Nohow. And thank you *very* much for asking," said Tweedledum.

"So *much* obliged!" added Tweedledee. "You like poetry?"

"Ye-es, pretty well—*some* poetry," Alice said doubtfully. "Would you tell me which road leads out of the wood?"

"What shall I repeat to her?" said Tweedledee, looking round at Tweedledum with great solemn eyes, and not noticing Alice's question.

"'*The Walrus and the Carpenter*' is the longest,"

Tweedledum replied, giving his brother an affectionate hug.

Tweedledee began instantly:

> *"The sun was shining——"*

Here Alice ventured to interrupt him. "If it's *very* long," she said, as politely as she could, "would you please tell me first which road——"

Tweedledee smiled gently, and began again:

> *"The sun was shining on the sea,*
> *Shining with all his might:*
> *He did his very best to make*
> *The billows smooth and bright—*
> *And this was odd, because it was*
> *The middle of the night.*
>
> *The moon was shining sulkily,*
> *Because she thought the sun*
> *Had got no business to be there*
> *After the day was done—*
> *'It's very rude of him', she said,*
> *'To come and spoil the fun!'*
>
> *The sea was wet as wet could be,*
> *The sands were dry as dry.*
> *You could not see a cloud, because*
> *No cloud was in the sky:*
> *No birds were flying overhead—*
> *There were no birds to fly.*
>
> *The Walrus and the Carpenter*
> *Were walking close at hand:*
> *They wept like anything to see*
> *Such quantities of sand:*
> *'If this were only cleared away,'*
> *They said, 'it would be grand!'*
>
> *'If seven maids with seven mops*
> *Swept it for half a year,*

Do you suppose', the Walrus said,
  'That they could get it clear?'
'I doubt it,' said the Carpenter,
  And shed a bitter tear.

'O Oysters, come and walk with us!'
  The Walrus did beseech.
'A pleasant walk, a pleasant talk,
  Along the briny beach:
We cannot do with more than four,
  To give a hand to each.'

The eldest Oyster looked at him,
  But never a word he said:
The eldest Oyster winked his eye,
  And shook his heavy head—
Meaning to say he did not choose
  To leave the oyster-bed.

But four young Oysters hurried up,
  All eager for the treat:
Their coats were brushed, their faces washed,
  Their shoes were clean and neat—
And this was odd, because, you know,
  They hadn't any feet.

Four other Oysters followed them,
    And yet another four;
And thick and fast they came at last,
    And more, and more, and more—
All hopping through the frothy waves,
    And scrambling to the shore.

The Walrus and the Carpenter
    Walked on a mile or so,
And then they rested on a rock
    Conveniently low:
And all the little Oysters stood
    And waited in a row.

'The time has come', the Walrus said,
    'To talk of many things:
Of shoes—and ships—and sealing wax—
    Of cabbages—and kings—
And why the sea is boiling hot—
    And whether pigs have wings.'

'But wait a bit,' the Oysters cried,
    'Before we have our chat;

For some of us are out of breath,
 And all of us are fat!'
'*No hurry!' said the Carpenter.*
 They thanked him much for that.

'*A loaf of bread', the Walrus said,*
 '*Is what we chiefly need:*
Pepper and vinegar besides
 Are very good indeed—
Now, if you're ready, Oysters dear,
 We can begin to feed.'

'*But not on us!' the Oysters cried,*
 Turning a little blue.
'*After such kindness, that would be*
 A dismal thing to do!'
'*The night is fine,' the Walrus said.*
 '*Do you admire the view?*

'*It was so kind of you to come!*
 And you are very nice!'
The Carpenter said nothing but
 '*Cut us another slice.*

I wish you were not quite so deaf—
I've had to ask you twice!'

'It seems a shame', the Walrus said,
'To play them such a trick.
After we've brought them out so far,
And made them trot so quick!'
The Carpenter said nothing but
'The butter's spread too thick!'

'I weep for you,' the Walrus said:
'I deeply sympathize.'
With sobs and tears he sorted out
Those of the largest size,
Holding his pocket-handkerchief
Before his streaming eyes.

'O Oysters,' said the Carpenter,
'You've had a pleasant run!
Shall we be trotting home again?'
But answer came there none—
And this was scarcely odd, because
They'd eaten every one."

"I like the Walrus best," said Alice: "because he was a *little* sorry for the poor oysters."

"He ate more than the Carpenter, though," said Tweedledee. "You see he held his handkerchief in front, so that the Carpenter couldn't count how many he took: contrariwise."

"That was mean!" Alice said indignantly. "Then I like the Carpenter best—if he didn't eat so many as the Walrus."

"But he ate as many as he could get," said Tweedledum.

This was a puzzler. After a pause, Alice began, "Well! They were *both* very unpleasant characters——" Here she checked herself in some alarm, at hearing something that sounded to her like the puffing of a large steam-engine in the wood near them, though she feared it was more likely to be a wild beast. "Are there any lions or tigers about here?" she asked timidly.

"It's only the Red King snoring," said Tweedledee.

"Come and look at him!" the brothers cried, and they each took one of Alice's hands, and led her up to where the King was sleeping.

"Isn't he a *lovely* sight?" said Tweedledum.

Alice couldn't say honestly that he was. He had a tall red night-cap on, with a tassel, and he was lying crumpled up into a sort of untidy heap, and snoring loud——"fit to snore his head off!" as Tweedledum remarked.

"I'm afraid he'll catch cold with lying on the damp grass," said Alice, who was a very thoughtful little girl.

"He's dreaming now," said Tweedledee: "and what do you think he's dreaming about?"

Alice said "Nobody can guess that."

"Why, about *you*!" Tweedledee exclaimed, clapping his hands triumphantly. "And if he left off dreaming about you, where do you suppose you'd be?"

"Where I am now, of course," said Alice.

"Not you!" Tweedledee retorted contemptuously. "You'd be nowhere. Why, you're only a sort of thing in his dream!"

"If that there King was to wake", added Tweedledum, "you'd go out—bang!—just like a candle!"

"I shouldn't!" Alice exclaimed indignantly. "Besides, if *I'm* only a sort of thing in his dream, what are *you*, I should like to know?"

"Ditto," said Tweedledum.

"Ditto, ditto!" cried Tweedledee.

He shouted this so loud that Alice couldn't help saying "Hush! You'll be waking him, I'm afraid, if you make so much noise."

"Well, it's no use *your* talking about waking him," said Tweedledum, "when you're only one of the things in his dream. You know very well you're not real."

"I *am* real!" said Alice, and began to cry.

"You wo'n't make yourself a bit realler by crying," Tweedledee remarked: "there's nothing to cry about."

"If I wasn't real", Alice said—half laughing through her tears, it all seemed so ridiculous—"I shouldn't be able to cry."

"I hope you don't suppose those are *real* tears?" Tweedledum interrupted in a tone of great contempt.

"I know they're talking nonsense," Alice thought to herself: "and it's foolish to cry about it." So she brushed away her tears, and went on, as cheerfully as she could, "At any rate, I'd better be getting out of the wood, for really it's coming on very dark. Do you think it's going to rain?"

Tweedledum spread a large umbrella over himself and his brother, and looked up into it. "No, I don't think it is," he said: "at least—not under *here*. Nohow."

"But it may rain *outside*?"

"It may—if it chooses," said Tweedledee: "we've no objection. Contrariwise."

"Selfish things!" thought Alice, and she was just going to say "Good-night" and leave them, when Tweedledum sprang out from under the umbrella, and seized her by the wrist.

"Do you see *that*?" he said, in a voice choking with passion, and his eyes grew large and yellow all in a moment, as he pointed with a trembling finger at a small white thing lying under the tree.

"It's only a rattle," Alice said, after a careful examina-

tion of the little white thing. "Not a rattle-*snake*, you know," she added hastily, thinking that he was frightened: "only an old rattle—quite old and broken."

"I know it was!" cried Tweedledum, beginning to stamp about wildly and tear his hair. "It's spoilt, of course!" Here he looked at Tweedledee, who immediately sat down on the ground, and tried to hide himself under the umbrella.

Alice laid her hand upon his arm and said, in a soothing tone, "You needn't be so angry about an old rattle."

"But it *isn't* old!" Tweedledum cried, in a greater fury than ever. "It's *new*, I tell you—I bought it yesterday—

my nice NEW RATTLE!" and his voice rose to a perfect scream.

All this time Tweedledee was trying his best to fold up the umbrella, with himself in it: which was such an extraordinary thing to do, that it quite took off Alice's attention from the angry brother. But he couldn't quite succeed, and it ended in his rolling over, bundling up in the umbrella, with only his head out: and there he lay, opening and shutting his mouth and his large eyes ——"looking more like a fish than anything else," Alice thought.

"Of course you agree to have a battle?" Tweedledum said in a calmer tone.

"I suppose so," the other sulkily replied, as he crawled out of the umbrella: "only *she* must help us to dress up, you know."

So the two brothers went off hand-in-hand into the wood, and returned in a minute with their arms full of things—such as bolsters, blankets, hearth-rugs, table-cloths, dish-covers, and coal-scuttles. "I hope you're a good hand at pinning and tying strings?" Tweedledum remarked. "Every one of these things has got to go on, somehow or other."

Alice said afterwards she had never seen such a fuss made about anything in all her life—the way those two bustled about—and the quantity of things they put on— and the trouble they gave her in tying strings and fastening buttons—"Really they'll be more like bundles of old clothes than anything else, by the time they're ready!" she said to herself, as she arranged a bolster round the neck of Tweedledee, "to keep his head from being cut off," as he said.

"You know," he added very gravely, "it's one of the most serious things that can possibly happen to one in a battle—to get one's head cut off."

Alice laughed loud: but she managed to turn it into a cough, for fear of hurting his feelings.

"Do I look very pale?" said Tweedledum, coming up to

have his helmet tied on. (He *called* it a helmet, though it certainly looked much more like a saucepan.)

"Well—yes—a *little*," Alice replied gently.

"I'm very brave, generally," he went on in a low voice: "only to-day I happen to have a headache."

"And *I've* got a toothache!" said Tweedledee, who had overheard the remark. "I'm far worse than you!"

"Then you'd better not fight to-day," said Alice, thinking it a good opportunity to make peace.

"We *must* have a bit of a fight, but I don't care about going on long," said Tweedledum. "What's the time now?"

Tweedledee looked at his watch, and said "Half-past four."

"Let's fight till six, and then have dinner," said Tweedledum.

"Very well," the other said, rather sadly: "and *she* can watch us—only you'd better not come *very* close," he added: "I generally hit every thing I can see—when I get really excited."

"And *I* hit every thing within reach," cried Tweedledum, "whether I can see it or not!"

Alice laughed. "You must hit the *trees* pretty often, I should think," she said.

Tweedledum looked round him with a satisfied smile. "I don't suppose", he said, "there'll be a tree left standing, for ever so far round, by the time we've finished!"

"And all about a rattle!" said Alice, still hoping to make them a *little* ashamed of fighting for such a trifle.

"I shouldn't have minded it so much", said Tweedledum, "if it hadn't been a new one."

"I wish the monstrous crow would come!" thought Alice.

"There's only one sword, you know," Tweedledum said to his brother: "but *you* can have the umbrella—it's quite as sharp. Only we must begin quick. It's getting as dark as it can."

"And darker," said Tweedledee.

It was getting dark so suddenly that Alice thought there must be a thunderstorm coming on. "What a thick black cloud that is!" she said. "And how fast it comes! Why, I do believe it's got wings!"

"It's the crow!" Tweedledum cried out in a shrill voice of alarm; and the two brothers took to their heels and were out of sight in a moment.

Alice ran a little way into the wood, and stopped under a large tree. "It can never get at me *here*," she thought: "it's far too large to squeeze itself in among the trees. But I wish it wouldn't flap its wings so—it makes quite a hurricane in the wood—here's somebody's shawl being blown away!"

Chapter V

Wool and Water

She caught the shawl as she spoke, and looked about for the owner: in another moment the White Queen came running wildly through the wood, with both arms stretched out wide, as if she were flying, and Alice very civilly went to meet her with the shawl.

"I'm very glad I happened to be in the way," Alice said, as she helped her to put on her shawl again.

The White Queen only looked at her in a helpless frightened sort of way, and kept repeating something in a whisper to herself that sounded like "Bread-and-butter, bread-and-butter", and Alice felt that if there was to be any conversation at all, she must manage it herself. So she began rather timidly: "Am I addressing the White Queen?"

"Well, yes, if you call that a-dressing," the Queen said. "It isn't *my* notion of the thing, at all."

Alice thought it would never do to have an argument at the very beginning of their conversation, so she smiled and said "If your Majesty will only tell me the right way to begin, I'll do it as well as I can."

"But I don't want it done at all!" groaned the poor Queen. "I've been a-dressing myself for the last two hours."

It would have been all the better, as it seemed to Alice, if she had got some one else to dress her, she was so dreadfully untidy. "Every single thing's crooked," Alice thought to herself, "and she's all over pins!——May I put your shawl straight for you?" she added aloud.

"I don't know what's the matter with it!" the Queen said, in a melancholy voice. "It's out of temper, I think. I've pinned it here, and I've pinned it there, but there's no pleasing it!"

"It *ca'n't* go straight, you know, if you pin it all on one side," Alice said, as she gently put it right for her; "and dear me, what a state your hair is in!"

"The brush has got entangled in it!" the Queen said with a sigh. "And I lost the comb yesterday."

Alice carefully released the brush, and did her best to get the hair into order. "Come, you look rather better

now!" she said, after altering most of the pins. "But really you should have a lady's-maid!"

"I'm sure I'll take *you* with pleasure!" the Queen said. "Two pence a week and jam every other day."

Alice couldn't help laughing, as she said "I don't want you to hire *me*—and I don't care for jam."

"It's very good jam," said the Queen.

"Well, I don't want any *to-day*, at any rate."

"You couldn't have it if you *did* want it," the Queen said. "The rule is, jam to-morrow and jam yesterday—but never jam *to-day*."

"It *must* come sometimes to 'jam to-day'," Alice objected.

"No, it ca'n't," said the Queen. "It's jam every *other* day: to-day isn't any other day, you know."

"I don't understand you," said Alice. "It's dreadfully confusing!"

"That's the effect of living backwards," the Queen said kindly: "it always makes one a little giddy at first——"

"Living backwards!" Alice repeated in great astonishment. "I never heard of such a thing!"

"—but there's one great advantage in it, that one's memory works both ways."

"I'm sure *mine* only works one way," Alice remarked. "I ca'n't remember things before they happen."

"It's a poor sort of memory that only works backwards," the Queen remarked.

"What sort of things do *you* remember best?" Alice ventured to ask.

"Oh, things that happened the week after next," the Queen replied in a careless tone. "For instance, now," she went on, sticking a large piece of plaster on her finger as she spoke, "there's the King's Messenger. He's in prison now, being punished: and the trial doesn't even begin till next Wednesday: and of course the crime comes last of all."

"Suppose he never commits the crime?" said Alice.

"That would be all the better, wouldn't it?" the Queen said, as she bound the plaster round her finger with a bit of ribbon.

Alice felt there was no denying *that*. "Of course it would be all the better," she said: "but it wouldn't be all the better his being punished."

"You're wrong *there*, at any rate," said the Queen. "Were *you* ever punished?"

"Only for faults," said Alice.

"And you were all the better for it, I know!" the Queen said triumphantly.

"Yes, but then I *had* done the things I was punished for," said Alice: "that makes all the difference."

"But if you *hadn't* done them", the Queen said, "that would have been better still; better, and better, and bet-

ter!" Her voice went higher with each "better", till it got quite to a squeak at last.

Alice was just beginning to say "There's a mistake somewhere———," when the Queen began screaming, so loud that she had to leave the sentence unfinished. "Oh, oh, oh!" shouted the Queen, shaking her hand about as if she wanted to shake it off. "My finger's bleeding! Oh, oh, oh, oh!"

Her screams were so exactly like the whistle of a steam-engine, that Alice had to hold both her hands over her ears.

"What *is* the matter?" she said, as soon as there was a chance of making herself heard. "Have you pricked your finger?"

"I haven't pricked it *yet*," the Queen said, "but I soon shall—oh, oh, oh!"

"When do you expect to do it?" Alice said, feeling very much inclined to laugh.

"When I fasten my shawl again," the poor Queen groaned out: "the brooch will come undone directly. Oh, oh!" As she said the words the brooch flew open, and the Queen clutched wildly at it, and tried to clasp it again.

"Take care!" cried Alice. "You're holding it all crooked!" And she caught at the brooch; but it was too late: the pin had slipped, and the Queen had pricked her finger.

"That accounts for the bleeding, you see," she said to Alice with a smile. "Now you understand the way things happen here."

"But why don't you scream *now*?" Alice asked, holding her hands ready to put over her ears again.

"Why, I've done all the screaming already," said the Queen. "What would be the good of having it all over again?"

By this time it was getting light. "The crow must have flown away, I think," said Alice: "I'm so glad it's gone. I thought it was the night coming on."

"I wish *I* could manage to be glad!" the Queen said. "Only I never can remember the rule. You must be very happy, living in this wood, and being glad whenever you like!"

"Only it is so *very* lonely here!" Alice said in a melancholy voice; and, at the thought of her loneliness, two large tears came rolling down her cheeks.

"Oh, don't go on like that!" cried the poor Queen, wringing her hands in despair. "Consider what a great girl you are. Consider what a long way you've come to-day. Consider what o'clock it is. Consider anything, only don't cry!"

Alice could not help laughing at this, even in the midst of her tears. "Can *you* keep from crying by considering things?" she asked.

"That's the way it's done," the Queen said with great decision: "nobody can do two things at once, you know. Let's consider your age to begin with—how old are you?"

"I'm seven and a half, exactly."

"You needn't say 'exactly'," the Queen remarked. "I can believe it without that. Now I'll give *you* something to believe. I'm just one hundred and one, five months and a day."

"I ca'n't believe *that*!" said Alice.

"Ca'n't you?" the Queen said in a pitying tone. "Try again: draw a long breath, and shut your eyes."

Alice laughed. "There's no use trying," she said "one *ca'n't* believe impossible things."

"I daresay you haven't had much practice," said the Queen. "When I was your age, I always did it for half-an-hour a day. Why, sometimes I've believed as many as six impossible things before breakfast. There goes the shawl again!"

The brooch had come undone as she spoke, and a sudden gust of wind blew the Queen's shawl across a little brook. The Queen spread out her arms again and went flying after it, and this time she succeeded in catching it herself. "I've got it!" she cried in triumphant tone. "Now you shall see me pin it on again, all by myself!"

"Then I hope your finger is better now?" Alice said very politely, as she crossed the little brook after the Queen.

*   *   *   *   *

*   *   *   *

*   *   *   *   *

"Oh, much better!" cried the Queen, her voice rising into a squeak as she went on. "Much be-etter! Be-etter! Be-e-e-etter! Be-e-ehh!" The last word ended in a long bleat, so like a sheep that Alice quite started.

She looked at the Queen, who seemed to have suddenly wrapped herself up in wool. Alice rubbed her eyes, and looked again. She couldn't make out what had happened at all. Was she in a shop? And was that really—was it really a *sheep* that was sitting on the other side of the counter? Rub as she would, she could make nothing more of it: she was in a little dark shop, leaning with her elbows on the counter, and opposite to her was an old Sheep, sitting in an arm-chair, knitting, and every now and then leaving off to look at her through a great pair of spectacles.

"What is it you want to buy?" the Sheep said at last, looking up for a moment from her knitting.

"I don't *quite* know yet," Alice said very gently. "I should like to look all round me first, if I might."

"You may look in front of you, and on both sides, if you like," said the Sheep; "but you ca'n't look *all* round you—unless you've got eyes at the back of your head."

But these, as it happened, Alice had *not* got: so she contented herself with turning round, looking at the shelves as she came to them.

The shop seemed to be full of all manner of curious things—but the oddest part of it all was that, whenever she looked hard at any shelf, to make out exactly what it had on it, that particular shelf was always quite empty, though the others round it were crowded as full as they could hold.

"Things flow about so here!" she said at last in a plaintive tone, after she had spent a minute or so in vainly pursuing a large bright thing that looked sometimes like a doll and sometimes like a work-box, and was always in the shelf next above the one she was looking at. "And this one is the most provoking of all—but I'll tell you what——" she added, as a sudden thought struck her.

"I'll follow it up to the very top shelf of all. It'll puzzle it
to go through the ceiling, I expect!"

But even this plan failed: the "thing" went through the
ceiling as quietly as possible, as if it were quite used to it.

"Are you a child or a teetotum?" the Sheep said, as she
took up another pair of needles. "You'll make me giddy
soon, if you go on turning round like that." She was now
working with fourteen pairs at once, and Alice couldn't
help looking at her in great astonishment.

"How *can* she knit with so many?" the puzzled child
thought to herself. "She gets more and more like a porcupine every minute!"

"Can you row?" the Sheep asked, handing her a pair of
knitting-needles as she spoke.

"Yes, a little—but not on land—and not with needles
——" Alice was beginning to say, when suddenly the
needles turned into oars in her hands, and she found they
were in a little boat, gliding along between banks: so
there was nothing for it but to do her best.

"Feather!" cried the Sheep, as she took up another pair
of needles.

This didn't sound like a remark that needed any answer: so Alice said nothing, but pulled away. There was
something very queer about the water, she thought, as
every now and then the oars got fast in it, and would
hardly come out again.

"Feather! Feather!" the Sheep cried again, taking
more needles. "You'll be catching a crab directly."

"A dear little crab!" thought Alice. "I should like that."

"Didn't you hear me say 'Feather'?" the Sheep cried
angrily, taking up quite a bunch of needles.

"Indeed I did," said Alice: "you've said it very often—
and very loud. Please where *are* the crabs?"

"In the water, of course!" said the Sheep, sticking
some of the needles into her hair, as her hands were full.
"Feather, I say!"

"*Why* do you say 'Feather' so often?" Alice asked at
last, rather vexed. "I'm not a bird!"

"You are," said the Sheep: "you're a little goose."

This offended Alice a little, so there was no more conversation for a minute or two, while the boat glided gently on, sometimes among beds of weeds (which made the
oars stick fast in the water, worse than ever), and sometimes under trees, but always with the same tall river-
banks frowning over their heads.

"Oh, please! There are some scented rushes!" Alice
cried in a sudden transport of delight. "There really are—
and *such* beauties!"

"You needn't say 'please' to *me* about 'em," the Sheep
said, without looking up from her knitting: "I didn't put
'em there, and I'm not going to take 'em away."

"No, but I meant—please, may we wait and pick

some?" Alice pleaded. "If you don't mind stopping the boat for a minute."

"How am _I_ to stop it?" said the Sheep. "If you leave off rowing, it'll stop of itself."

So the boat was left to drift down the stream as it would, till it glided gently in among the waving rushes. And then the little sleeves were carefully rolled up, and the little arms were plunged in elbow-deep, to get hold of the rushes a good long way down before breaking them off—and for a while Alice forgot all about the Sheep and the knitting, as she bent over the side of the boat, with just the ends of her tangled hair dipping into the water— while with bright eager eyes she caught at one bunch after another of the darling scented rushes.

"I only hope the boat wo'n't tipple over!" she said to herself. "Oh, _what_ a lovely one! Only I couldn't quite reach it." And it certainly _did_ seem a little provoking ("almost as if it happened on purpose," she thought) that, though she managed to pick plenty of beautiful rushes as the boat glided by, there was always a more lovely one that she couldn't reach.

"The prettiest are always further!" she said at last with a sigh at the obstinacy of the rushes in growing so far off, as, with flushed cheeks and dripping hair and hands, she scrambled back into her place, and began to arrange her new-found treasures.

What mattered it to her just then that the rushes had begun to fade, and to lose all their scent and beauty, from the very moment that she picked them? Even real scented rushes, you know, last only a very little while—and these, being dream-rushes, melted away almost like snow, as they lay in heaps at her feet—but Alice hardly noticed this, there were so many other curious things to think about.

They hadn't gone much farther before the blade of one of the oars got fast in the water and _wouldn't_ come out again (so Alice explained it afterwards), and the conse-quence was that the handle of it caught her under the chin, and, in spite of a series of little shrieks of "Oh, oh, oh!'' from poor Alice, it swept her straight off the seat, and down among the heap of rushes.

However, she wasn't a bit hurt, and was soon up again: the Sheep went on with her knitting all the while, just as if nothing had happened. "That was a nice crab you caught!'' she remarked, as Alice got back into her place, very much relieved to find herself still in the boat.

"Was it! I didn't see it,'' said Alice, peeping cautiously over the side of the boat into the dark water. "I wish it hadn't let go—I should so like a little crab to take home with me!" But the Sheep only laughed scornfully, and went on with her knitting.

"Are there many crabs here?" said Alice.

"Crabs, and all sorts of things," said the Sheep: "plenty of choice, only make up your mind. Now, what *do* you want to buy?"

"To buy!" Alice echoed in a tone that was half astonished and half frightened—for the oars, and the boat, and the river, had vanished all in a moment, and she was back again in the little dark shop.

"I should like to buy an egg, please," she said timidly. "How do you sell them?"

"Fivepence farthing for one—twopence for two," the Sheep replied.

"Then two are cheaper than one?" Alice said in a surprised tone, taking out her purse.

"Only you *must* eat them both, if you buy two," said the Sheep.

"Then I'll have *one*, please," said Alice, as she put the money down on the counter. For she thought to herself, "They mightn't be at all nice, you know."

The Sheep took the money, and put it away in a box: then she said "I never put things into people's hands—that would never do—you must get it for yourself." And so saying, she went off to the other end of the shop, and set the egg upright on a shelf.

"I wonder *why* it wouldn't do?" thought Alice, as she groped her way among the tables and chairs, for the shop was very dark towards the end. "The egg seems to get further away the more I walk towards it. Let me see, is this a chair? Why, it's got branches, I declare! How very odd to find trees growing here! And actually here's a little brook! Well, this is the very queerest shop I ever saw!"

* * * * *

* * * *

* * * * *

So she went on, wondering more and more at every step, as everything turned into a tree the moment she came up to it, and she quite expected the egg to do the same.

Chapter VI

Humpty Dumpty

HOWEVER, the egg only got larger and larger, and more and more human: when she had come within a few yards of it, she saw that it had eyes and a nose and mouth; and, when she had come close to it, she saw clearly that it was HUMPTY DUMPTY himself. "It ca'n't be anybody else!" she said to herself. "I'm as certain of it, as if his name were written all over his face!"

It might have been written a hundred times, easily, on that enormous face. Humpty Dumpty was sitting, with his legs crossed like a Turk, on the top of a high wall—such a narrow one that Alice quite wondered how he could keep his balance—and, as his eyes were steadily fixed in the opposite direction, and he didn't take the least notice of her, she thought he must be a stuffed figure, after all.

"And how exactly like an egg he is!" she said aloud, standing with her hands ready to catch him, for she was every moment expecting him to fall.

"It's *very* provoking", Humpty Dumpty said after a long silence, looking away from Alice as he spoke, "to be called an egg—*very*!"

"I said you *looked* like an egg, Sir," Alice gently explained. "And some eggs are very pretty, you know," she added, hoping to turn her remark into a sort of compliment.

"Some people", said Humpty Dumpty, looking away from her as usual, "have no more sense than a baby!"

Alice didn't know what to say to this: it wasn't at all like conversation, she thought, as he never said anything to *her*; in fact, his last remark was evidently addressed to a tree—so she stood and softly repeated to herself:

> "*Humpty Dumpty sat on a wall:*
> *Humpty Dumpty had a great fall.*
> *All the King's horses and all the King's men*
> *Couldn't put Humpty Dumpty in his place again.*

"That last line is much too long for the poetry," she added, almost out loud, forgetting that Humpty Dumpty would hear her.

"Don't stand chattering to yourself like that," Humpty Dumpty said, looking at her for the first time, "but tell me your name and your business."

"My *name* is Alice, but——"

"It's a stupid name enough!" Humpty Dumpty interrupted impatiently. "What does it mean?"

"*Must* a name mean something?" Alice asked doubtfully.

"Of course it must," Humpty Dumpty said with a short laugh: "*my* name means the shape I am—and a good handsome shape it is, too. With a name like yours, you might be any shape, almost."

"Why do you sit out here all alone?" said Alice, not wishing to begin an argument.

"Why, because there's nobody with me!" cried Humpty Dumpty. "Did you think I didn't know the answer to *that*? Ask another."

"Don't you think you'd be safer down on the ground?" Alice went on, not with any idea of making another riddle, but simply in her good-natured anxiety for the queer creature. "That wall is so *very* narrow!"

"What tremendously easy riddles you ask!" Humpty Dumpty growled out. "Of course I don't think so! Why, if ever I *did* fall off—which there's no chance of—but *if* I did——" Here he pursed up his lips, and looked so solemn and grand that Alice could hardly help laughing.

"*If* I *did* fall," he went on, "*the King has promised me*—ah, you may turn pale, if you like! You didn't think I was going to say that, did you? *The King has promised me—with his very own mouth*—to—to——"

"To send all his horses and all his men," Alice interrupted, rather unwisely.

"Now I declare that's too bad!" Humpty Dumpty cried, breaking into a sudden passion. "You've been listening at doors—and behind trees—and down chimneys—or you couldn't have known it!"

"I haven't indeed!" Alice said very gently. "It's in a book."

"Ah, well! They may write such things in a *book*," Humpty Dumpty said in a calmer tone. "That's what you call a History of England, that is. Now, take a good look at me! I'm one that has spoken to a King, *I* am: mayhap you'll never see such another: and, to show you I'm not proud, you may shake hands with me!" And he grinned almost from ear to ear, as he leant forwards (and as nearly as possible fell off the wall in doing so) and offered Alice his hand. She watched him a little anxiously as she took it. "If he smiled much more the ends of his mouth might meet behind," she thought: "And then I don't know *what* would happen to his head! I'm afraid it would come off!"

"Yes, all his horses and all his men," Humpty Dumpty went on. "They'd pick me up again in a minute, *they* would! However, this conversation is going on a little too fast: let's go back to the last remark but one."

"I'm afraid I ca'n't quite remember it," Alice said, very politely.

"In that case we start afresh," said Humpty Dumpty, "and it's my turn to choose a subject——" ("He talks about it just as if it was a game!" thought Alice.) "So here's a question for you. How old did you say you were?"

Alice made a short calculation, and said "Seven years and six months."

"Wrong!" Humpty Dumpty exclaimed triumphantly. "You never said a word like it!"

"I thought you meant 'How old *are* you?'" Alice explained.

"If I'd meant that, I'd have said it," said Humpty Dumpty.

Alice didn't want to begin another argument, so she said nothing.

"Seven years and six months!" Humpty Dumpty repeated thoughtfully. "An uncomfortable sort of age. Now if you'd asked *my* advice, I'd have said 'Leave off at seven'——but it's too late now."

"I never ask advice about growing," Alice said indignantly.

"Too proud?" the other enquired.

Alice felt even more indignant at this suggestion. "I mean", she said, "that one ca'n't help growing older."

"*One* ca'n't, perhaps," said Humpty Dumpty; "but *two*

can. With proper assistance, you might have left off at seven."

"What a beautiful belt you've got on!" Alice suddenly remarked. (They had had quite enough of the subject of age, she thought: and, if they really were to take turns in choosing subjects, it was *her* turn now.) "At least," she corrected herself on second thoughts, "a beautiful cravat, I should have said—no, a belt, I mean—I beg your pardon!" she added in dismay, for Humpty Dumpty looked thoroughly offended, and she began to wish she hadn't chosen that subject. "If only I knew", she thought to herself, "which was neck and which was waist!"

Evidently Humpty Dumpty was very angry, though he said nothing for a minute or two. When he *did* speak again, it was in a deep growl.

"It is a—*most—provoking*—thing", he said at last, "when a person doesn't know a cravat from a belt!"

"I know it's very ignorant of me," Alice said, in so humble a tone that Humpty Dumpty relented.

"It's a cravat, child, and a beautiful one, as you say. It's a present from the White King and Queen. There now!"

"Is it really?" said Alice, quite pleased to find that she *had* chosen a good subject after all.

"They gave it me," Humpty Dumpty continued thoughtfully as he crossed one knee over the other and clasped his hands round it, "they gave it me—for an un-birthday present."

"I beg your pardon?" Alice said with a puzzled air.

"I'm not offended," said Humpty Dumpty.

"I mean, what *is* an un-birthday present?"

"A present given when it isn't your birthday, of course."

Alice considered a little. "I like birthday presents best," she said at last.

"You don't know what you're talking about!" cried Humpty Dumpty. "How many days are there in a year?"

"Three hundred and sixty-five," said Alice.

"And how many birthdays have you?"

"One."

"And if you take one from three hundred and sixty-five what remains?"

"Three hundred and sixty-four, of course."

Humpty Dumpty looked doubtful. "I'd rather see that done on paper," he said.

Alice couldn't help smiling as she took out her memorandum book, and worked the sum for him:

$$
\begin{array}{r}
365 \\
1 \\
\hline
364 \\
\hline
\end{array}
$$

Humpty Dumpty took the book and looked at it carefully. "That seems to be done right——" he began.

"You're holding it upside down!" Alice interrupted.

"To be sure I was!" Humpty Dumpty said gaily as she turned it round for him. "I thought it looked a little queer. As I was saying, that *seems* to be done right—though I haven't time to look it over thoroughly just now—and that shows that there are three hundred and sixty-four days when you might get un-birthday presents——"

"Certainly," said Alice.

"And only *one* for birthday presents, you know. There's glory for you!"

"I don't know what you mean by 'glory'," Alice said.

Humpty Dumpty smiled contemptuously. "Of course you don't—till I tell you. I meant 'there's a nice knock-down argument for you!'"

"But 'glory' doesn't mean 'a nice knock-down argument'," Alice objected.

"When *I* use a word", Humpty Dumpty said, in rather a scornful tone, "it means just what I choose it to mean—neither more nor less."

"The question is", said Alice, "whether you *can* make words mean so many different things."

"The question is", said Humpty Dumpty, "which is to be master——that's all."

Alice was too much puzzled to say anything; so after a minute Humpty Dumpty began again. "They've a temper, some of them—particularly verbs: they're the proudest—adjectives you can do anything with, but not verbs—however, *I* can manage the whole lot of them! Impenetrability! That's what *I* say!"

"Would you tell me please," said Alice, "what that means?"

"Now you talk like a reasonable child," said Humpty Dumpty, looking very much pleased. "I meant by 'impenetrability' that we've had enough of that subject, and it would be just as well if you'd mention what you mean to do next, as I suppose you don't mean to stop here all the rest of your life."

"That's a great deal to make one word mean," Alice said in a thoughtful tone.

"When I make a word do a lot of work like that," said Humpty Dumpty, "I always pay it extra."

"Oh!" said Alice. She was too much puzzled to make any other remark.

"Ah, you should see 'em come round me of a Saturday night", Humpty Dumpty went on, wagging his head gravely from side to side, "for to get their wages, you know."

(Alice didn't venture to ask what he paid them with; and so you see I ca'n't tell *you*.)

"You seem very clever at explaining words, Sir," said Alice. "Would you kindly tell me the meaning of the poem called 'Jabberwocky'?"

"Let's hear it," said Humpty Dumpty. "I can explain all the poems that ever were invented—and a good many that haven't been invented just yet."

This sounded very hopeful, so Alice repeated the first verse:

" *'Twas brillig, and the slithy toves*
Did gyre and gimble in the wabe:
All mimsy were the borogoves,
And the mome raths outgrabe."

"That's enough to begin with," Humpty Dumpty interrupted: "there are plenty of hard words there. '*Brillig*' means four o'clock in the afternoon—the time when you begin *broiling* things for dinner."

"That'll do very well," said Alice: "and '*slithy*'?"

"Well, '*slithy*' means 'lithe and slimy'. 'Lithe' is the same as 'active'. You see it's like a portmanteau—there are two meanings packed up into one word."

"I see it now," Alice remarked thoughtfully: "and what are '*toves*'?"

"Well, *'toves'* are something like badgers—they're something like lizards—and they're something like corkscrews."

"They must be very curious-looking creatures."

"They are that," said Humpty Dumpty; "also they make their nests under sun-dials—also they live on cheese."

"And what's to *'gyre'* and to *'gimble'*?"

"To *'gyre'* is to go round and round like a gyroscope. To *'gimble'* is to make holes like a gimlet."

"And *'the wabe'* is the grass-plot round a sun-dial, I suppose?" said Alice, surprised at her own ingenuity.

"Of course it is. It's called *'wabe'* you know, because it goes a long way before it, and a long way behind it——"

"And a long way beyond it on each side," Alice added.

"Exactly so. Well then, *'mimsy'* is 'flimsy and miserable' (there's another portmanteau for you). And a *'borogove'* is a thin shabby-looking bird with its feathers sticking out all round—something like a live mop."

"And then *'mome raths'*?" said Alice. "I'm afraid I'm giving you a great deal of trouble."

"Well, a *'rath'* is a sort of green pig: but *'mome'* I'm not certain about. I think it's short for 'from home'—meaning that they'd lost their way, you know."

"And what does *'outgrabe'* mean?"

"Well, *'outgribing'* is something between bellowing and whistling, with a kind of sneeze in the middle: however, you'll hear it done, maybe—down in the wood yonder—and, when you've once heard it, you'll be *quite* content. Who's been repeating all that hard stuff to you?"

"I read it in a book," said Alice. "But I *had* some poetry repeated to me much easier than that, by—Tweedledee, I think it was."

"As to poetry, you know," said Humpty Dumpty, stretching out one of his great hands, "*I* can repeat poetry as well as other folk, if it comes to that——"

"Oh, it needn't come to that!" Alice hastily said, hoping to keep him from beginning.

"The piece I'm going to repeat", he went on without noticing her remark, "was written entirely for your amusement."

Alice felt that in that case she really *ought* to listen to it; so she sat down, and said "Thank you" rather sadly,

> *"In winter, when the fields are white,*
> *I sing this song for your delight ——*

only I don't sing it," he added, as an explanation.

"I see you don't," said Alice.

"If you can *see* whether I'm singing or not, you've sharper eyes than most," Humpty Dumpty remarked severely. Alice was silent.

> *"In spring, when woods are getting green,*
> *I'll try and tell you what I mean:"*

"Thank you very much," said Alice.

> *"In summer, when the days are long,*
> *Perhaps you'll understand the song:*
>
> *In autumn, when the leaves are brown,*
> *Take pen and ink, and write it down."*

"I will, if I can remember it so long," said Alice.

"You needn't go on making remarks like that," Humpty Dumpty said: "they're not sensible, and they put me out."

> *"I sent a message to the fish:*
> *I told them 'This is what I wish.'*
>
> *The little fishes of the sea,*
> *They sent an answer back to me.*
>
> *The little fishes' answer was*
> *'We cannot do it, Sir, because ——' "*

"I'm afraid I don't quite understand," said Alice.

"It gets easier further on," Humpty Dumpty replied.

"*I sent to them again to say*
'It will be better to obey'.

The fishes answered, with a grin,
'Why, what a temper you are in!'

I told them once, I told them twice:
They would not listen to advice.

I took a kettle large and new,
Fit for the deed I had to do.

My heart went hop, my heart went thump:
I filled the kettle at the pump.

Then some one came to me and said
'The little fishes are in bed.'

I said to him, I said it plain,
'Then you must wake them up again.'

> *I said it very loud and clear:*
> *I went and shouted in his ear."*

Humpty Dumpty raised his voice almost to a scream as he repeated this verse, and Alice thought, with a shudder, "I wouldn't have been the messenger for *anything!*"

> *"But he was very stiff and proud:*
> *He said, 'You needn't shout so loud!'*
>
> *And he was very proud and stiff:*
> *He said 'I'd go and wake them, if ——'*
>
> *I took a corkscrew from the shelf:*
> *I went to wake them up myself.*
>
> *And when I found the door was locked,*
> *I pulled and pushed and kicked and knocked.*
>
> *And when I found the door was shut,*
> *I tried to turn the handle, but ——"*

There was a long pause.

"Is that all?" Alice timidly asked.

"That's all," said Humpty Dumpty. "Good-bye."

This was rather sudden, Alice thought: but, after such a *very* strong hint that she ought to be going, she felt that it would hardly be civil to stay. So she got up, and held out her hand. "Good-bye, till we meet again!" she said as cheerfully as she could.

"I shouldn't know you again if we *did* meet," Humpty Dumpty replied in a discontented tone, giving her one of his fingers to shake: "you're so exactly like other people."

"The face is what one goes by, generally," Alice remarked in a thoughtful tone.

"That's just what I complain of," said Humpty Dumpty. "Your face is the same as everybody has—the two eyes, so——" (marking their places in the air with his thumb) "nose in the middle, mouth under. It's always the same. Now if you had the two eyes on the same side of the nose, for instance—or the mouth at the top—that would be *some* help."

"It wouldn't look nice," Alice objected. But Humpty Dumpty only shut his eyes, and said "Wait till you've tried."

Alice waited a minute to see if he would speak again, but, as he never opened his eyes or took any further notice of her, she said "Good-bye!" once more, and, getting no answer to this, she quietly walked away: but she couldn't help saying to herself, as she went, "of all the unsatisfactory——" (she repeated this aloud, as it was a great comfort to have such a long word to say) "of all the unsatisfactory people I *ever* met——" She never finished the sentence, for at this moment a heavy crash shook the forest from end to end.

Chapter VII

The Lion and the Unicorn

THE next moment soldiers came running through the wood, at first in twos and threes, then ten or twenty together, and at last in such crowds that they seemed to fill the whole forest. Alice got behind a tree, for fear of being run over, and watched them go by.

She thought that in all her life she had never seen soldiers so uncertain on their feet: they were always tripping over something or other, and whenever one went down, several more always fell over him, so that the ground was soon covered with little heaps of men.

Then came the horses. Having four feet, these managed rather better than the foot-soldiers; but even *they* stumbled now and then; and it seemed to be a regular rule that, whenever a horse stumbled, the rider fell off instantly. The confusion got worse every moment, and Alice was very glad to get out of the wood into an open place, where she found the White King seated on the ground, busily writing in his memorandum-book.

"I've sent them all!" the King cried in a tone of delight, on seeing Alice. "Did you happen to meet any soldiers, my dear, as you came through the wood?"

"Yes, I did," said Alice: "several thousand, I should think."

"Four thousand two hundred and seven, that's the exact number," the King said, referring to his book. "I couldn't send all the horses, you know, because two of them are wanted in the game. And I haven't sent the two

Messengers, either. They're both gone to the town. Just look along the road, and tell me if you can see either of them."

"I see nobody on the road," said Alice.

"I only wish I had such eyes," the King remarked in a fretful tone. "To be able to see Nobody! And at that distance too! Why, it's as much as I can do to see real people, by this light!"

All this was lost on Alice, who was still looking intently along the road, shading her eyes with one hand. "I see somebody now!" she exclaimed at last. "But he's coming very slowly—and what curious attitudes he goes into!" (For the Messenger kept skipping up and down, and wriggling like an eel, as he came along, with his great hands spread out like fans on each side.)

"Not at all," said the King. "He's an Anglo-Saxon Messenger—and those are Anglo-Saxon attitudes. He only does them when he's happy. His name is Haigha." (He pronounced it so as to rhyme with 'mayor'.)

"I love my love with an H," Alice couldn't help beginning, "because he is Happy. I hate him with an H, because he is Hideous. I fed him with—with—with Ham-sandwiches and Hay. His name is Haigha, and he lives ——"

"He lives on the Hill," the King remarked simply, without the least idea that he was joining in the game, while Alice was still hesitating for the name of a town beginning with H. "The other Messenger's called Hatta. I must have *two*, you know—to come and go. One to come, and one to go."

"I beg your pardon?" said Alice.

"It isn't respectable to beg," said the King.

"I only meant that I didn't understand," said Alice. "Why one to come and one to go?"

"Don't I tell you?" the King repeated impatiently. "I must have *two*—to fetch and carry. One to fetch, and one to carry."

At this moment the Messenger arrived: he was far too

much out of breath to say a word, and could only wave his hands about, and make the most fearful faces at the poor King.

"This young lady loves you with an H," the King said, introducing Alice in the hope of turning off the Messenger's attention from himself—but it was of no use—the Anglo-Saxon attitudes only got more extraordinary every moment, while the great eyes rolled wildly from side to side.

"You alarm me!" said the King. "I feel faint—Give me a ham-sandwich!"

On which the Messenger, to Alice's great amusement, opened a bag that hung round his neck, and handed a sandwich to the King, who devoured it greedily.

"Another sandwich!" said the King.

"There's nothing but hay left now," the Messenger said, peeping into the bag.

"Hay, then," the King murmured in a faint whisper.

Alice was glad to see that it revived him a good deal. "There's nothing like eating hay when you're faint," he remarked to her, as he munched away.

"I should think throwing cold water over you would be better," Alice suggested: "—or some sal-volatile."

"I didn't say there was nothing *better*," the King replied. "I said there was nothing *like* it." Which Alice did not venture to deny.

"Who did you pass on the road?" the King went on, holding out his hand to the Messenger for some hay.

"Nobody," said the Messenger.

"Quite right," said the King: "this young lady saw him too. So of course Nobody walks slower than you."

"I do my best," the Messenger said in a sullen tone. "I'm sure nobody walks much faster than I do!"

"He ca'n't do that," said the King, "or else he'd have been here first. However, now you've got your breath, you may tell us what's happened in the town."

"I'll whisper it," said the Messenger, putting his hands to his mouth in the shape of a trumpet and stooping so as to get close to the King's ear. Alice was sorry for this, as she wanted to hear the news too. However, instead of whispering, he simply shouted, at the top of his voice, "They're at it again!"

"Do you call *that* a whisper?" cried the poor King, jumping up and shaking himself. "If you do such a thing again I'll have you buttered! It went through and through my head like an earthquake!"

"It would have to be a very tiny earthquake!" thought Alice. "Who are at it again?" she ventured to ask.

"Why the Lion and the Unicorn, of course," said the King.

"Fighting for the crown?"

"Yes, to be sure," said the King: "and the best of the joke is, that it's *my* crown all the while! Let's run and see them." And they trotted off, Alice repeating to herself, as she ran, the words of the old song:

"The Lion and the Unicorn were fighting for the crown:
The Lion beat the Unicorn all round the town.
Some gave them white bread, some gave them brown:
Some gave them plum-cake and drummed them out of town."

"Does——the one——that wins——get the crown?"
she asked, as well as she could, for the run was putting
her quite out of breath.

"Dear me, no!" said the King. "What an idea!"

"Would you——be good enough——" Alice panted
out, after running a little further, "to stop a minute—just
to get—one's breath again?"

"I'm *good* enough," the King said, "only I'm not *strong*
enough. You see, a minute goes by so fearfully quick.
You might as well try to stop a Bandersnatch!"

Alice had no more breath for talking; so they trotted on
in silence, till they came into sight of a great crowd, in the
middle of which the Lion and Unicorn were fighting.
They were in such a cloud of dust, that at first Alice could
not make out which was which; but she soon managed to
distinguish the Unicorn by his horn.

They placed themselves close to where Hatta, the other
Messenger, was standing watching the fight, with a cup
of tea in one hand and a piece of bread-and-butter in the
other.

"He's only just out of prison, and he hadn't finished his
tea when he was sent in," Haigha whispered to Alice:
"and they only give them oyster-shells in there—so you
see he's very hungry and thirsty. How are you, dear
child?" he went on, putting his arm affectionately round
Hatta's neck.

Hatta looked round and nodded, and went on with his
bread-and-butter.

"Were you happy in prison, dear child?" said Haigha.

Hatta looked round once more, and this time a tear or
two trickled down his cheek; but not a word would he say.

"Speak, ca'n't you!" Haigha cried impatiently. But
Hatta only munched away, and drank some more tea.

"Speak, wo'n't you!" cried the King. "How are they getting on with the fight?"

Hatta made a desperate effort, and swallowed a large piece of bread-and-butter. "They're getting on very well," he said in a choking voice: "each of them has been down about eighty-seven times."

"Then I suppose they'll soon bring the white bread and the brown?" Alice ventured to remark.

"It's waiting for 'em now," said Hatta; "this is a bit of it as I'm eating."

There was a pause in the fight just then, and the Lion and the Unicorn sat down, panting, while the King called out "Ten minutes allowed for refreshments!" Haigha and Hatta set to work at once, carrying round trays of white and brown bread. Alice took a piece to taste, but it was *very* dry.

"I don't think they'll fight any more to-day," the King said to Hatta: "go and order the drums to begin." And Hatta went bounding away like a grasshopper.

For a minute or two Alice stood silent, watching him. Suddenly she brightened up. "Look, look!" she cried, pointing eagerly. "There's the White Queen running across the country! She came flying out of the wood over yonder—— How fast those Queens *can* run!"

"There's some enemy after her, no doubt," the King said, without even looking round. "That wood's full of them."

"But aren't you going to run and help her?" Alice asked, very much surprised at his taking it so quietly.

"No use, no use!" said the King. "She runs so fearfully quick. You :night as well try to catch a Bandersnatch! But I'll make a memorandum about her, if you like—— She's a dear good creature," he repeated softly to himself, as he opened his memorandum-book. "Do you spell 'creature' with a double 'e'?"

At this moment the Unicorn sauntered by them, with his hands in his pockets. "I had the best of it this time?" he said to the King, just glancing at him as he passed.

"A little—a little," the King replied, rather nervously. "You shouldn't have run him through with your horn, you know."

"It didn't hurt him," the Unicorn said carelessly, and he was going on, when his eye happened to fall upon Alice: he turned round instantly, and stood for some time looking at her with an air of the deepest disgust.

"What—is—this?" he said at last.

"This is a child!" Haigha replied eagerly, coming in front of Alice to introduce her, and spreading out both his hands towards her in an Anglo-Saxon attitude. "We only found it to-day. It's as large as life, and twice as natural!"

"I always thought they were fabulous monsters!" said the Unicorn. "Is it alive?"

"It can talk," said Haigha solemnly.

The Unicorn looked dreamily at Alice, and said "Talk, child."

Alice could not help her lips curling up into a smile as

she began: "Do you know, I always thought Unicorns were fabulous monsters, too? I never saw one alive before!"

"Well, now that we *have* seen each other," said the Unicorn, "if you'll believe in me, I'll believe in you. Is that a bargain?"

"Yes, if you like," said Alice.

"Come, fetch out the plum-cake, old man!" the Unicorn went on, turning from her to the King. "None of your brown bread for me!"

"Certainly—certainly!" the King muttered, and beckoned to Haigha. "Open the bag!" he whispered. "Quick! Not that one—that's full of hay!"

Haigha took a large cake out of the bag, and gave it to Alice to hold, while he got out a dish and carving-knife. How they all came out of it Alice couldn't guess. It was just like a conjuring trick, she thought.

The Lion had joined them while this was going on: he looked very tired and sleepy, and his eyes were half shut.

"What's this!" he said, blinking lazily at Alice, and speaking in a deep hollow tone that sounded like the tolling of a great bell.

"Ah, what *is* it, now?" the Unicorn cried eagerly. "You'll never guess! *I* couldn't."

The Lion looked at Alice wearily. "Are you animal— or vegetable—or mineral?" he said, yawning at every other word.

"It's a fabulous monster!" the Unicorn cried out, before Alice could reply.

"Then hand round the plum-cake, Monster," the Lion said, lying down and putting his chin on his paws. "And sit down, both of you," (to the King and the Unicorn): "fair play with the cake, you know!"

The King was evidently very uncomfortable at having to sit down between the two great creatures; but there was no other place for him.

"What a fight we might have for the crown, *now*!" the Unicorn said, looking slyly up at the crown, which the poor King was nearly shaking off his head, he trembled so much.

"I should win easy," said the Lion.

"I'm not so sure of that," said the Unicorn.

"Why, I beat you all round the town, you chicken!" the Lion replied angrily, half getting up as he spoke.

Here the King interrupted, to prevent the quarrel going on: he was very nervous, and his voice quite quivered. "All round the town?" he said. "That's a good long way. Did you go by the old bridge, or the market-place? You get the best view by the old bridge."

"I'm sure I don't know," the Lion growled out as he lay down again. "There was too much dust to see anything. What a time the Monster is, cutting up that cake!"

Alice had seated herself on the bank of a little brook, with the great dish on her knees, and was sawing away diligently with the knife. "It's very provoking!" she said, in reply to the Lion (she was getting quite used to being called 'the Monster'). "I've cut several slices already, but they always join on again!"

"You don't know how to manage Looking-glass cakes," the Unicorn remarked. "Hand it round first, and cut it afterwards."

This sounded nonsense, but Alice very obediently got up, and carried the dish round, and the cake divided itself

into three pieces as she did so. "*Now* cut it up," said the Lion, as she returned to her place with the empty dish.

"I say, this isn't fair!" cried the Unicorn, as Alice sat with the knife in her hand, very much puzzled how to begin. "The Monster has given the Lion twice as much as me!"

"She's kept none for herself, anyhow," said the Lion. "Do you like plum-cake, Monster?"

But before Alice could answer him, the drums began.

Where the noise came from, she couldn't make out: the air seemed full of it, and it rang through and through her head till she felt quite deafened. She started to her feet and sprang across the little brook in her terror, and had just time to see the Lion and the Unicorn rise to their

*   *   *   *   *

   *   *   *   *

*   *   *   *   *

feet, with angry looks at being interrupted in their feast, before she dropped to her knees, and put her hands over her ears, vainly trying to shut out the dreadful uproar.

"If *that* doesn't 'drum them out of town'," she thought to herself, "nothing ever will!"

Chapter VIII

"It's My Own Invention"

AFTER a while the noise seemed gradually to die away, till all was dead silence, and Alice lifted up her head in some alarm. There was no one to be seen, and her first thought was that she must have been dreaming about the Lion and the Unicorn and those queer Anglo-Saxon Messengers. However, there was the great dish still lying at her feet, on which she had tried to cut the plum-cake, "So I wasn't dreaming, after all," she said to herself, "unless—unless we're all part of the same dream. Only I do hope it's *my* dream, and not the Red King's! I don't like belonging to another person's dream," she went on in a rather complaining tone: "I've a great mind to go and wake him, and see what happens!"

At this moment her thoughts were interrupted by a

loud shouting of "Ahoy! Ahoy! Check!" and a Knight, dressed in crimson armour, came galloping down upon her, brandishing a great club. Just as he reached her, the horse stopped suddenly: "You're my prisoner!" the Knight cried, as he tumbled off his horse.

Startled as she was, Alice was more frightened for him than for herself at the moment, and watched him with some anxiety as he mounted again. As soon as he was comfortably in the saddle, he began once more "You're my——" but here another voice broke in "Ahoy! Ahoy! Check!" and Alice looked round in some surprise for the new enemy.

This time it was a White Knight. He drew up at Alice's side, and tumbled off his horse just as the Red Knight had done: then he got on again, and the two Knights sat and looked at each other for some time without speaking. Alice looked from one to the other in some bewilderment.

"She's *my* prisoner, you know!" the Red Knight said at last.

"Yes, but then *I* came and rescued her!" the White Knight replied.

"Well, we must fight for her, then," said the Red Knight, as he took up his helmet (which hung from the saddle, and was something the shape of a horse's head) and put it on.

"You will observe the Rules of Battle, of course?" the White Knight remarked, putting on his helmet too.

"I always do," said the Red Knight, and they began banging away at each other with such fury that Alice got behind a tree to be out of the way of the blows.

"I wonder, now, what the Rules of Battle are," she said to herself, as she watched the fight, timidly peeping out from her hiding-place. "One Rule seems to be, that if one Knight hits the other, he knocks him off his horse; and, if he misses, he tumbles off himself—and another Rule seems to be that they hold their clubs with their arms, as if they were Punch and Judy—— What a noise they make when they tumble! Just like a whole set of fire-irons falling into the fender! And how quiet the horses are! They let them get on and off them just as if they were tables!"

Another Rule of Battle, that Alice had not noticed, seemed to be that they always fell on their heads; and the battle ended with their both falling off in this way, side by side. When they got up again, they shook hands, and then the Red Knight mounted and galloped off.

"It was a glorious victory, wasn't it?" said the White Knight, as he came up panting.

"I don't know," Alice said doubtfully. "I don't want to be anybody's prisoner. I want to be a Queen."

"So you will, when you've crossed the next brook," said the White Knight. "I'll see you safe to the end of the wood—and then I must go back, you know. That's the end of my move."

"Thank you very much," said Alice. "May I help you off with your helmet?" It was evidently more than he could manage by himself: however she managed to shake him out of it at last.

"Now one can breathe more easily," said the Knight, putting back his shaggy hair with both hands, and turning his gentle face and large mild eyes to Alice. She thought she had never seen such a strange-looking soldier in all her life.

He was dressed in tin armour, which seemed to fit him very badly, and he had a queer-shaped little deal box fastened across his shoulders, upside-down, and with the lid hanging open. Alice looked at it with great curiosity.

"I see you're admiring my little box," the Knight said in a friendly tone. "It's my own invention—to keep clothes and sandwiches in. You see I carry it upside-down, so that the rain ca'n't get in."

"But the things can get *out*," Alice gently remarked. "Do you know the lid's open?"

"I didn't know it," the Knight said, a shade of vexation passing over his face. "Then all the things must have fallen out! And the box is no use without them." He unfastened it as he spoke, and was just going to throw it into the bushes, when a sudden thought seemed to strike him, and he hung it carefully on a tree. "Can you guess why I did that?" he said to Alice.

Alice shook her head.

"In hopes some bees may make a nest in it—then I should get the honey."

"But you've got a bee-hive—or something like one—fastened to the saddle," said Alice.

"Yes, it's a very good bee-hive," the Knight said in a discontented tone, "one of the best kind. But not a single bee has come near it yet. And the other thing is a mousetrap. I suppose the mice keep the bees out—or the bees keep the mice out, I don't know which."

"I was wondering what the mouse-trap was for," said Alice. "It isn't very likely there would be any mice on the horse's back."

"Not very likely, perhaps," said the Knight; "but, if they *do* come, I don't choose to have them running all about."

"You see," he went on after a pause, "it's as well to be provided for *everything*. That's the reason the horse has all those anklets round his feet."

"But what are they for?" Alice asked in a tone of great curiosity.

"To guard against the bites of sharks," the Knight replied. "It's an invention of my own. And now help me on. I'll go with you to the end of the wood—What's that dish for?"

"It's meant for plum-cake," said Alice.

"We'd better take it with us," the Knight said. "It'll come in handy if we find any plum-cake. Help me to get it into this bag."

This took a long time to manage, though Alice held the bag open very carefully, because the knight was so *very* awkward in putting in the dish: the first two or three times that he tried he fell in himself instead. "It's rather a tight fit, you see," he said, as they got it in at last; "there are so many candlesticks in the bag." And he hung it to the saddle, which was already loaded with bunches of carrots, and fire-irons, and many other things.

"I hope you've got your hair well fastened on?" he continued, as they set off.

"Only in the usual way," Alice said, smiling.

"That's hardly enough," he said, anxiously. "You see the wind is so *very* strong here. It's as strong as soup."

"Have you invented a plan for keeping the hair from being blown off?" Alice enquired.

"Not yet," said the Knight. "But I've got a plan for keeping it from *falling* off."

"I should like to hear it, very much."

"First you take an upright stick," said the Knight.

"Then you make your hair creep up it, like a fruit-tree. Now the reason hair falls off is because it hangs *down*— things never fall *upwards*, you know. It's a plan of my own invention. You may try it if you like."

It didn't sound a comfortable plan, Alice thought, and for a few minutes she walked on in silence, puzzling over

the idea, and every now and then stopping to help the poor Knight, who certainly was *not* a good rider.

Whenever the horse stopped (which it did very often), he fell off in front; and, whenever it went on again (which it generally did rather suddenly), he fell off behind. Otherwise he kept on pretty well, except that he had a habit of now and then falling off sideways; and, as he generally did this on the side on which Alice was walking, she soon found that it was the best plan not to walk *quite* close to the horse.

"I'm afraid you've not had much practice in riding," she ventured to say, as she was helping him up from his fifth tumble.

The Knight looked very much surprised, and a little offended at the remark. "What makes you say that?" he asked, as he scrambled back into the saddle, keeping hold of Alice's hair with one hand, to save himself from falling over on the other side.

"Because people don't fall off quite so often, when they've had much practice."

"I've had plenty of practice," the Knight said very gravely: "plenty of practice!"

Alice could think of nothing better to say than "Indeed?" but she said it as heartily as she could. They went on a little way in silence after this, the Knight with his eyes shut, muttering to himself, and Alice watching anxiously for the next tumble.

"The great art of riding", the Knight suddenly began in a loud voice, waving his right arm as he spoke, "is to keep——" Here the sentence ended as suddenly as it had begun, as the Knight fell heavily on the top of his head exactly in the path where Alice was walking. She was quite frightened this time, and said in an anxious tone, as she picked him up, "I hope no bones are broken?"

"None to speak of," the Knight said, as if he didn't mind breaking two or three of them. "The great art of riding, as I was saying, is—to keep your balance properly. Like this, you know——"

He let go the bridle, and stretched out both his arms to show Alice what he meant, and this time he fell flat on his back, right under the horse's feet.

"Plenty of practice!" he went on repeating, all the time that Alice was getting him on his feet again. "Plenty of practice!"

"It's too ridiculous!" cried Alice, losing all her patience this time. "You ought to have a wooden horse on wheels, that you ought!"

"Does that kind go smoothly?" the Knight asked in a

tone of great interest, clasping his arms round the horse's neck as he spoke, just in time to save himself from tumbling off again.

"Much more smoothly than a live horse," Alice said, with a little scream of laughter, in spite of all she could do to prevent it.

"I'll get one," the Knight said thoughtfully to himself. "One or two—several."

There was a short silence after this, and then the Knight went on again. "I'm a great hand at inventing things. Now, I daresay you noticed, the last time you picked me up, that I was looking rather thoughtful?"

"You *were* a little grave," said Alice.

"Well, just then I was inventing a new way of getting over a gate—would you like to hear it?"

"Very much indeed," Alice said politely.

"I'll tell you how I came to think of it," said the Knight. "You see, I said to myself 'The only difficulty is with the feet: the *head* is high enough already.' Now, first I put my head on the top of the gate—then the head's high enough—then I stand on my head—then the feet are high enough, you see—then I'm over, you see."

"Yes, I suppose you'd be over when· that was done," Alice said thoughtfully: "but don't you think it would be rather hard?"

"I haven't tried it yet," the Knight said, gravely; "so I ca'n't tell for certain—but I'm afraid it *would* be a little hard."

He looked so vexed at the idea, that Alice changed the subject hastily. "What a curious helmet you've got!" she said cheerfully. "Is that your invention too?"

The Knight looked down proudly at his helmet, which hung from the saddle. "Yes," he said; "but I've invented a better one than that—like a sugar-loaf. When I used to wear it, if I fell off the horse, it always touched the ground directly. So I had a *very* little way to fall, you see —But there *was* the danger of falling *into* it, to be· sure. That happened to me once—and the worst of it was, be-

fore I could get out again, the other White Knight came
and put it on. He thought it was his own helmet.''

The Knight looked so solemn about it that Alice did
not dare to laugh. "I'm afraid you must have hurt him,"
she said in a trembling voice, "being on the top of his
head."

"I had to kick him, of course," the Knight said, very
seriously. "And then he took the helmet off again—but it
took hours and hours to get me out. I was as fast as—as
lightning, you know."

"But that's a different kind of fastness," Alice objected.

The Knight shook his head. "It was all kinds of fastness with me, I can assure you!" he said. He raised his
hands in some excitement as he said this, and instantly
rolled out of the saddle, and fell headlong into a deep
ditch.

Alice ran to the side of the ditch to look for him. She
was rather startled by the fall, as for some time he had
kept on very well, and she was afraid that he really *was*
hurt this time. However, though she could see nothing
but the soles of his feet, she was much relieved to hear
that he was talking on in his usual tone. "All kinds of

fastness," he repeated: "but it was careless of him to put another man's helmet on—with the man in it, too."

"How *can* you go on talking so quietly, head downwards?" Alice asked, as she dragged him out by the feet, and laid him in a heap on the bank.

The Knight looked surprised at the question. "What does it matter where my body happens to be?" he said. "My mind goes on working all the same. In fact, the more head-downwards I am, the more I keep inventing new things."

"Now the cleverest thing of the sort that I ever did," he went on after a pause, "was inventing a new pudding during the meat-course."

"In time to have it cooked for the next course?" said Alice. "Well, that *was* quick work, certainly!"

"Well, not the *next* course," the Knight said in a slow thoughtful tone: "no, certainly not the next *course*."

"Then it would have to be the next day. I suppose you wouldn't have two pudding-courses in one dinner?"

"Well, not the *next* day," the Knight repeated as before: "not the next *day*. In fact," he went on, holding his head down, and his voice getting lower and lower, "I don't believe that pudding ever *was* cooked! In fact, I don't believe that pudding ever *will* be cooked! And yet it was a very clever pudding to invent."

"What did you mean it to be made of?" Alice asked, hoping to cheer him up, for the poor Knight seemed quite low-spirited about it.

"It began with blotting-paper," the Knight answered with a groan.

"That wouldn't be very nice, I'm afraid——"

"Not very nice *alone*," he interrupted, quite eagerly: "but you've no idea what a difference it makes, mixing it with other things—such as gunpowder and sealing-wax. And here I must leave you." They had just come to the end of the wood.

Alice could only look puzzled: she was thinking of the pudding.

"You are sad," the Knight said in an anxious tone: "let me sing you a song to comfort you."

"Is it very long?" Alice asked, for she had heard a good deal of poetry that day.

"It's long," said the Knight, "but it's very, *very* beautiful. Everybody that hears me sing it—either it brings the *tears* into their eyes, or else——"

"Or else what?" said Alice, for the Knight had made a sudden pause.

"Or else it doesn't, you know. The name of the song is called '*Haddocks' Eyes*'."

"Oh, that's the name of the song, is it?" Alice said, trying to feel interested.

"No, you don't understand," the Knight said, looking a little vexed. "That's what the name is *called*. The name really *is* '*The Aged Aged Man*'."

"Then I ought to have said 'That's what the *song* is called'?" Alice corrected herself.

"No, you oughtn't: that's quite another thing! The *song* is called '*Ways and Means*': but that's only what it's *called*, you know!"

"Well, what *is* the song, then?" said Alice, who was by this time completely bewildered.

"I was coming to that," the Knight said. "The song really *is* '*A-sitting On A Gate*': and the tune's my own invention."

So saying, he stopped his horse and let the reins fall on its neck: then, slowly beating time with one hand, and with a faint smile lighting up his gentle foolish face, as if he enjoyed the music of his song, he began.

Of all the strange things that Alice saw in her journey Through The Looking-Glass, this was the one that she always remembered most clearly. Years afterwards she could bring the whole scene back again, as if it had been only yesterday—the mild blue eyes and kindly smile of the Knight—the setting sun gleaming through his hair, and shining on his armour in a blaze of light that quite dazzled her—the horse quietly moving about, with the reins hanging loose on his neck, cropping the grass at her feet—and the black shadows of the forest behind—all this she took in like a picture, as, with one hand shading her eyes, she leant against a tree, watching the strange pair, and listening, in a half-dream, to the melancholy music of the song.

"But the tune *isn't* his own invention," she said to herself: "it's '*I give thee all, I can no more*'." She stood and listened very attentively, but no tears came into her eyes.

> "*I'll tell thee everything I can:*
> *There's little to relate.*
> *I saw an aged aged man,*
> *A-sitting on a gate.*
> '*Who are you, aged man?*' *I said.*
> '*And how is it you live?*'
> *And his answer trickled through my head,*
> *Like water through a sieve.*
>
> *He said* '*I look for butterflies*
> *That sleep among the wheat:*
> *I make them into mutton-pies,*
> *And sell them in the street.*
> *I sell them unto men*', *he said,*
> '*Who sail on stormy seas;*
> *And that's the way I get my bread—*
> *A trifle, if you please.*'
>
> *But I was thinking of a plan*
> *To dye one's whiskers green,*
> *And always use so large a fan*
> *That they could not be seen.*
> *So, having no reply to give*
> *To what the old man said,*
> *I cried* '*Come, tell me how you live!*'
> *And thumped him on the head.*
>
> *His accents mild took up the tale:*
> *He said* '*I go my ways,*
> *And when I find a mountain-rill,*
> *I set it in a blaze;*

And thence they make a stuff they call
  Rowland's Macassar-Oil—
Yet twopence-halfpenny is all
  They give me for my toil.'

But I was thinking of a way
  To feed oneself on batter,
And so go on from day to day
  Getting a little fatter.
I shook him well from side to side,
  Until his face was blue:
'Come, tell me how you live,' I cried,
  'And what it is you do!'

He said 'I hunt for haddocks' eyes
  Among the heather bright,
And work them into waistcoat-buttons
  In the silent night.
And these I do not sell for gold
  Or coin of silvery shine,
But for a copper halfpenny,
  And that will purchase nine.

'I sometimes dig for buttered rolls,
   Or set limed twigs for crabs:
I sometimes search the grassy knolls
   For wheels of Hansom-cabs.
And that's the way' (he gave a wink)
   'By which I get my wealth—
And very gladly will I drink
   Your Honour's noble health.'

I heard him then, for I had just
   Completed my design
To keep the Menai bridge from rust
   By boiling it in wine.
I thanked him much for telling me
   The way he got his wealth,
But chiefly for his wish that he
   Might drink my noble health.

And now, if e'er by chance I put
   My fingers into glue,
Or madly squeeze a right-hand foot
   Into a left-hand shoe,
Or if I drop upon my toe
   A very heavy weight,
I weep, for it reminds me so
Of that old man I used to know——
Whose look was mild, whose speech was slow,
Whose hair was whiter than the snow,
Whose face was very like a crow,
With eyes, like cinders, all aglow,
Who seemed distracted with his woe,
Who rocked his body to and fro,
And muttered mumblingly and low,
As if his mouth were full of dough,
Who snorted like a buffalo——
That summer evening long ago,
   A-sitting on a gate.''

As the Knight sang the last words of the ballad, he gathered up the reins, and turned his horse's head along the road by which they had come. "You've only a few yards to go," he said, "down the hill and over that little brook, and then you'll be a Queen——But you'll stay and see me off first?" he added as Alice turned with an eager look in the direction to which he pointed. "I sha'n't be long. You'll wait and wave your handkerchief when I get to that turn in the road! I think it'll encourage me, you see."

"Of course I'll wait," said Alice: "and thank you very

much for coming so far—and for the song—I liked it very much."

"I hope so," the Knight said doubtfully: "but you didn't cry so much as I thought you would."

So they shook hands, and then the Knight rode slowly away into the forest. "It wo'n't take long to see him *off*, I expect," Alice said to herself, as she stood watching him. "There he goes! Right on his head as usual! However, he gets on again pretty easily—that comes of having so many things hung round the horse——" So she went on talking to herself, as she watched the horse walking leisurely along the road, and the Knight tumbling off, first on one side and then on the other. After the fourth or fifth tumble he reached the turn, and then she waved her handkerchief to him, and waited till he was out of sight.

"I hope it encouraged him," she said, as she turned to run down the hill: "and now for the last brook, and to be a Queen! How grand it sounds!" A very few steps brought her to the edge of the brook. "The Eighth Square at last!" she cried as she bounded across,

  *   *   *   *   *

   *   *   *   *

  *   *   *   *   *

and threw herself down to rest on a lawn as soft as moss, with little flowerbeds dotted about it here and there. "Oh, how glad I am to get here! And what *is* this on my head?" she exclaimed in a tone of dismay, as she put her hands up to something very heavy, that fitted tight all around her head.

"But how *can* it have got there without my knowing it?" she said to herself, as she lifted it off, and set it on her lap to make out what it could possibly be.

It was a golden crown.

Chapter IX

Queen Alice

"Well, this *is* grand!" said Alice. "I never expected I should be a Queen so soon—and I'll tell you what it is, your Majesty," she went on, in a severe tone (she was always rather fond of scolding herself), "It'll never do for you to be lolling about on the grass like that! Queens have to be dignified, you know!"

So she got up and walked about—rather stiffly just at first, as she was afraid that the crown might come off: but she comforted herself with the thought that there was nobody to see her, "and if I really am a Queen", she said as she sat down again, "I shall be able to manage it quite well in time."

Everything was happening so oddly that she didn't feel a bit surprised at finding the Red Queen and the White Queen sitting close to her, one on each side: she would have liked very much to ask them how they came there, but she feared it would not be quite civil. However, there would be no harm, she thought, in asking if the game was over. "Please, would you tell me——" she began, looking timidly at the Red Queen.

"Speak when you're spoken to!" the Queen sharply interrupted her.

"But if everybody obeyed that rule," said Alice, who was always ready for a little argument, "and if you only spoke when you were spoken to, and the other person always waited for *you* to begin, you see nobody would ever say anything, so that——"

"Ridiculous!" cried the Queen. "Why, don't you see, child——" here she broke off with a frown, and, after thinking for a minute, suddenly changed the subject of the conversation. "What do you mean by 'If you really are a Queen'? What right have you to call yourself so? You ca'n't be a Queen, you know, till you've passed the proper examination. And the sooner we begin it, the better."

"I only said 'if'!" poor Alice pleaded in a piteous tone.

The two Queens looked at each other, and the Red Queen remarked, with a little shudder, "She *says* she only said 'if'——"

"But she said a great deal more than that!" the White Queen moaned, wringing her hands. "Oh, ever so much more than that!"

"So you did, you know," the Red Queen said to Alice.

"Always speak the truth—think before you speak—and write it down afterwards."

"I'm sure I didn't mean——" Alice was beginning, but the Red Queen interrupted her impatiently.

"That's just what I complain of! You *should* have meant! What do you suppose is the use of a child without any meaning? Even a joke should have some meaning—

and a child's more important than a joke, I hope. You couldn't deny that, even if you tried with both hands."

"I don't deny things with my *hands*," Alice objected.

"Nobody said you did," said the Red Queen. "I said you couldn't if you tried."

"She's in that state of mind", said the White Queen, "that she wants to deny *something*—only she doesn't know what to deny!"

"A nasty, vicious temper," the Red Queen remarked; and then there was an uncomfortable silence for a minute or two.

The Red Queen broke the silence by saying, to the White Queen, "I invite you to Alice's dinner-party this afternoon."

The White Queen smiled feebly, and said "And I invite *you*."

"I didn't know I was to have a party at all," said Alice; "but, if there *is* to be one, I think *I* ought to invite the guests."

"We gave you the opportunity of doing it," the Red Queen remarked: "but I daresay you've not had many lessons in manners yet."

"Manners are not taught in lessons," said Alice. "Lessons teach you to do sums, and things of that sort."

"Can you do Addition?" the White Queen asked. "What's one and one and one and one and one and one and one and one and one and one?"

"I don't know," said Alice. "I lost count."

"She ca'n't do Addition," the Red Queen interrupted. "Can you do Subtraction? Take nine from eight."

"Nine from eight I ca'n't, you know," Alice replied very readily: "but——"

"She ca'n't do Subtraction," said the White Queen. "Can you do Division? Divide a loaf by a knife—what's the answer to *that*?"

"I suppose——" Alice was beginning, but the Red Queen answered for her. "Bread-and-butter, of course. Try another Subtraction sum. Take a bone from a dog: what remains?"

Alice considered. "The bone wouldn't remain, of course, if I took it—and the dog wouldn't remain: it would come to bite me—and I'm sure *I* shouldn't remain!"

"Then you think nothing would remain?" said the Red Queen.

"I think that's the answer."

"Wrong, as usual," said the Red Queen: "the dog's temper would remain."

"But I don't see how——"

"Why, look here!" the Red Queen cried. "The dog would lose its temper, wouldn't it?"

"Perhaps it would," Alice replied cautiously.

"Then if the dog went away, its temper would remain!" the Queen exclaimed triumphantly.

Alice said, as gravely as she could, "They might go different ways." But she couldn't help thinking to herself "What dreadful nonsense we *are* talking!"

"She ca'n't do sums a *bit*!" the Queens said together, with great emphasis.

"Can *you* do sums?" Alice said, turning suddenly on the White Queen, for she didn't like being found fault with so much.

The Queen gasped and shut her eyes. "I can do Addition", she said, "if you give me time—but I ca'n't do Subtraction under *any* circumstances!"

"Of course you know your ABC?" said the Red Queen.

"To be sure I do," said Alice.

"So do I," the White Queen whispered: "we'll often say it over together, dear. And I'll tell you a secret—I can read words of one letter! Isn't *that* grand? However, don't be discouraged. You'll come to it in time."

Here the Red Queen began again. "Can you answer useful questions?" she said. "How is bread made?"

"I know *that*!" Alice cried eagerly. "You take some flour——"

"Where do you pick the flower?" the White Queen asked: "In a garden or in the hedges?"

"Well, it isn't *picked* at all," Alice explained: "it's *ground*——"

"How many acres of ground?" said the White Queen. "You mustn't leave out so many things."

"Fan her head!" the Red Queen anxiously interrupted. "She'll be feverish after so much thinking." So they set to work and fanned her with bunches of leaves, till she had to beg them to leave off, it blew her hair about so.

"She's all right again now," said the Red Queen. "Do you know Languages? What's the French for fiddle-de-dee?"

"Fiddle-de-dee's not English," Alice replied gravely.

"Who ever said it was?" said the Red Queen.

Alice thought she saw a way out of the difficulty, this time. "If you'll tell me what language 'fiddle-de-dee' is, I'll tell you the French for it!" she exclaimed triumphantly.

But the Red Queen drew herself up rather stiffly, and said, "Queens never make bargains."

"I wish Queens never asked questions," Alice thought to herself.

"Don't let us quarrel," the White Queen said in an anxious tone. "What is the cause of lightning?"

"The cause of lightning", Alice said very decidedly, for she felt quite certain about this, "is the thunder—no, no!" she hastily corrected herself. "I meant the other way."

"It's too late to correct it," said the Red Queen: "when you've once said a thing, that fixes it, and you must take the consequences."

"Which reminds me——" the White Queen said, looking down and nervously clasping and unclasping her hands, "we had *such* a thunderstorm last Tuesday—I mean one of the last set of Tuesdays, you know."

Alice was puzzled. "In *our* country", she remarked, "there's only one day at a time."

The Red Queen said "That's a poor thin way of doing things. Now *here*, we mostly have days and nights two or three at a time, and sometimes in the winter we take as many as five nights together—for warmth, you know."

"Are five nights warmer than one night, then?" Alice ventured to ask.

"Five times as warm, of course."

"But they should be five times as *cold*. by the same rule——"

"Just so!" cried the Red Queen. "Five times as warm, *and* five times as cold—just as I'm five times as rich as you are, *and* five times as clever!"

Alice sighed and gave it up. "It's exactly like a riddle with no answer!" she thought.

"Humpty Dumpty saw it too," the White Queen went

on in a low voice, more as if she were talking to herself.
"He came to the door with a corkscrew in his hand——"

"What did he want?" said the Red Queen.

"He said he *would* come in," the White Queen went
on, "because he was looking for a hippopotamus. Now,
as it happened, there wasn't such a thing in the house,
that morning."

"Is there generally?" Alice asked in an astonished tone.

"Well, only on Thursdays," said the Queen.

"I know what he came for," said Alice: "he wanted to
punish the fish, because——"

Here the White Queen began again. "It was *such* a
thunderstorm, you ca'n't think!" ("She *never* could, you
know," said the Red Queen.) "And part of the roof came
off, and ever so much thunder got in—and it went rolling
round the room in great lumps—and knocking over the
tables and things—till I was so frightened, I couldn't remember my own name!"

Alice thought to herself "I never should *try* to remember my name in the middle of an accident! Where would
be the use of it?" but she did not say this aloud, for fear
of hurting the poor Queen's feelings.

"Your Majesty must excuse her," the Red Queen said
to Alice, taking one of the White Queen's hands in her
own, and gently stroking it: "she means well, but she
ca'n't help saying foolish things as a general rule."

The White Queen looked timidly at Alice, who felt she
ought to say something kind, but really couldn't think of
anything at the moment.

"She never was really well brought up," the Red Queen
went on: "but it's amazing how good-tempered she is!
Pat her on the head, and see how pleased she'll be!" But
this was more than Alice had courage to do.

"A little kindness—and putting her hair in papers—
would do wonders with her——"

The White Queen gave a deep sigh, and laid her head
on Alice's shoulder. "I *am* so sleepy!" she moaned.

"She's tired, poor thing!" said the Red Queen. "Smooth

her hair—lend her your nightcap—and sing her a soothing lullaby."

"I haven't got a nightcap with me," said Alice, as she tried to obey the first direction: "and I don't know any soothing lullabies."

"I must do it myself, then," said the Red Queen, and she began:

> *"Hush-a-by lady, in Alice's lap!*
> *Till the feast's ready, we've time for a nap.*
> *When the feast's over, we'll go to the ball—*
> *Red Queen, and White Queen, and Alice, and all!*

"And now you know the words," she added, as she put her head down on Alice's other shoulder, "just sing it through to *me*. I'm getting sleepy, too." In another moment both Queens were fast asleep, and snoring loud.

"What *am* I to do?" exclaimed Alice, looking about in great perplexity, as first one round head, and then the other, rolled down from her shoulder, and lay like a heavy lump in her lap. "I don't think it *ever* happened before, that any one had to take care of two Queens asleep at once! No, not in all the History of England—it couldn't,

you know, because there never was more than one Queen
at a time. Do wake up, you heavy things!" she went on in
an impatient tone; but there was no answer but a gentle
snoring.

The snoring got more distinct every minute, and sounded more like a tune: at last she could even make out

words, and she listened so eagerly that, when the two
great heads suddenly vanished from her lap, she hardly
missed them.

She was standing before an arched doorway, over which
were the words "QUEEN ALICE" in large letters, and
on each side of the arch there was a bell-handle; one was

marked "Visitors' Bell", and the other "Servants' Bell".

"I'll wait till the song's over," thought Alice, "and then I'll ring the—the—*which* bell must I ring?" she went on, very much puzzled by the names. "I'm not a visitor, and I'm not a servant. There *ought* to be one marked 'Queen', you know——"

Just then the door opened a little way, and a creature with a long beak put its head out for a moment and said "No admittance till the week after next!" and shut the door again with a bang.

Alice knocked and rang in vain for a long time; but at last a very old Frog, who was sitting under a tree, got up and hobbled slowly towards her: he was dressed in bright yellow, and had enormous boots on.

"What is it, now?" the Frog said in a deep hoarse whisper.

Alice turned round, ready to find fault with anybody. "Where's the servant whose business it is to answer the door?" she began angrily.

"Which door?" said the Frog.

Alice almost stamped with irritation at the slow drawl in which he spoke. "*This* door, of course!"

The Frog looked at the door with his large dull eyes for a minute: then he went nearer and rubbed it with his thumb, as if he were trying whether the paint would come off: then he looked at Alice.

"To answer the door?" he said. "What's it been asking of?" He was so hoarse that Alice could scarcely hear him.

"I don't know what you mean," she said.

"I speaks English, doesn't I?" the Frog went on. "Or are you deaf? What did it ask you?"

"Nothing!" Alice said impatiently. "I've been knocking at it!"

"Shouldn't do that—shouldn't do that——" the Frog muttered. "Wexes it, you know." Then he went up and gave the door a kick with one of his great feet. "You let *it* alone," he panted out, as he hobbled back to his tree, "and it'll let *you* alone, you know."

At this moment the door was flung open, and a shrill voice was heard singing:

"To the Looking-Glass world it was Alice that said
'I've a sceptre in hand, I've a crown on my head.
Let the Looking-Glass creatures, whatever they be
Come and dine with the Red Queen, the White Queen, and
*   me!'"*

And hundreds of voices joined in the chorus:

"Then fill up the glasses as quick as you can,
And sprinkle the table with buttons and bran:
Put cats in the coffee, and mice in the tea—
And welcome Queen Alice with thirty-times-three!"

Then followed a confused noise of cheering, and Alice thought to herself "Thirty times three makes ninety. I wonder if any one's counting?" In a minute there was silence again, and the same shrill voice sang another verse:

" 'O Looking-Glass creatures', quoth Alice, 'draw near!
'Tis an honour to see me, a favour to hear:
'Tis a privilege high to have dinner and tea
Along with the Red Queen, the White Queen, and me!'"

Then came the chorus again:

"Then fill up the glasses with treacle and ink,
Or anything else that is pleasant to drink:
Mix sand with the cider, and wool with the wine—
And welcome Queen Alice with ninety-times-nine!"

"Ninety times nine!" Alice repeated in despair. "Oh, that'll never be done! I'd better go in at once——" and in she went, and there was a dead silence the moment she appeared.

Alice glanced nervously along the table, as she walked up the large hall, and noticed that there were about fifty guests, of all kinds: some were animals, some birds, and there were even a few flowers among them. "I'm glad they've come without waiting to be asked," she thought:

"I should never have known who were the right people to invite!"

There were three chairs at the head of the table: the Red and White Queens had already taken two of them, but the middle one was empty. Alice sat down in it, rather uncomfortable at the silence, and longing for some one to speak.

At last the Red Queen began. "You've missed the soup and fish," she said. "Put on the joint!" And the waiters set a leg of mutton before Alice, who looked at it rather anxiously, as she had never had to carve a joint before.

"You look a little shy: let me introduce you to that leg of mutton," said the Red Queen. "Alice——Mutton: Mutton——Alice." The leg of mutton got up in the dish and made a little bow to Alice! and Alice returned the bow, not knowing whether to be frightened or amused.

"May I give you a slice?" she said, taking up the knife and fork, and looking from one Queen to the other.

"Certainly not," the Red Queen said very, decidedly: "it isn't etiquette to cut anyone you've been introduced to. Remove the joint!" And the waiters carried it off, and brought a large plum-pudding in its place.

"I won't be introduced to the pudding, please," Alice said rather hastily, "or we shall get no dinner at all. May I give you some?"

But the Red Queen looked sulky, and growled "Pudding——Alice: Alice——Pudding. Remove the pudding!" and the waiters took it away so quickly that Alice couldn't return its bow.

However, she didn't see why the Red Queen should be the only one to give orders; so, as an experiment, she called out "Waiter! Bring back the pudding!" and there it was again in a moment, like a conjuring trick. It was so large that she couldn't help feeling a *little* shy with it, as she had been with the mutton; however, she conquered her shyness by a great effort, and cut a slice and handed it to the Red Queen.

"What impertinence!" said the Pudding. "I wonder

how you'd like it, if I were.to cut a slice out of *you*, you creature!"

It spoke in a thick, suety sort of voice, and Alice hadn't a word to say in reply: she could only sit and look at it and gasp.

"Make a remark," said the Red Queen: "it's ridiculous to leave all the conversation to the pudding!"

"Do you know, I've had such a quantity of poetry repeated to me to-day," Alice began, a little frightened at finding that, the moment she opened her lips, there was dead silence, and all eyes were fixed upon her; "and it's a very curious thing, I think—every poem was about fishes in some way. Do you know why they're so fond of fishes, all about here?"

She spoke to the Red Queen, whose answer was a little wide of the mark. "As to fishes," she said, very slowly and solemnly, putting her mouth close to Alice's ear, "her

White Majesty knows a lovely riddle—all in poetry—all
about fishes. Shall she repeat it?"

"Her Red Majesty's very kind to mention it," the White
Queen murmured into Alice's other ear, in a voice like
the cooing of a pigeon. "It would be *such* a treat! May I?"

"Please do," Alice said very politely.

The White Queen laughed with delight, and stroked
Alice's cheek. Then she began:

> " *'First, the fish must be caught.'*
> *That is easy: a baby, I think, could have caught it.*
> *'Next, the fish must be bought.'*
> *That is easy: a penny, I think, would have bought it.*
>
> *'Now cook me the fish!'*
> *That is easy, and will not take more than a minute.*
> *'Let it lie in a dish!'*
> *That is easy, because it already is in it.*
>
> *'Bring it here! Let me sup!'*
> *It is easy to set such a dish on the table.*
> *'Take the dish-cover up!'*
> *Ah, that is so hard that I fear I'm unable!*
>
> *For it holds it like glue—*
> *Holds the lid to the dish, while it lies in the middle:*
> *Which is easiest to do,*
> *Un-dish-cover the fish, or dishcover the riddle?"*

"Take a minute to think about it, and then guess," said
the Red Queen. "Meanwhile, we'll drink your health—
Queen Alice's health!" she screamed at the top of her
voice, and all the guests began drinking it directly, and
very queerly they managed it: some of them put their
glasses upon their heads like extinguishers, and drank all
that trickled down their faces—others upset the de-
canters, and drank the wine as it ran off the edges of the
table—and three of them (who looked like kangaroos)
scrambled into the dish of roast mutton, and began
eagerly lapping up the gravy, "just like pigs in a trough!"
thought Alice.

"You ought to return thanks in a neat speech," the Red Queen said, frowning at Alice as she spoke.

"We must support you, you know," the White Queen whispered, as Alice got up to do it, very obediently, but a little frightened.

"Thank you very much," she whispered in

reply, "but I can do quite well without."

"That wouldn't be at all the thing," the Red Queen said very decidedly: so Alice tried to submit to it with a good grace.

("And they *did* push so!" she said afterwards, when she

was telling her sister the history of the feast. "You would have thought they wanted to squeeze me flat!")

In fact it was rather difficult for her to keep in her place while she made her speech: the two Queens pushed her so, one on each side, that they nearly lifted her up into the air. "I rise to return thanks——" Alice began: and she really *did* rise as she spoke, several inches; but she got hold of the edge of the table, and managed to pull herself down again.

"Take care of yourself!" screamed the White Queen, seizing Alice's hair with both her hands. "Something's going to happen!"

And then (as Alice afterwards described it) all sorts of things happened in a moment. The candles all grew up to the ceiling, looking something like a bed of rushes with fireworks at the top. As to the bottles, they each took a pair of plates, which they hastily fitted on as wings, and so, with forks for legs, went fluttering about in all directions: "and very like birds they look," Alice thought to herself, as well as she could in the dreadful confusion that was beginning.

At this moment she heard a hoarse laugh at her side, and turned to see what was the matter with the White Queen; but, instead of the Queen, there was the leg of mutton sitting in the chair. "Here I am!" cried a voice from the soup-tureen, and Alice turned again, just in time to see the Queen's broad good-natured face grinning at her for a moment over the edge of the tureen, before she disappeared into the soup.

There was not a moment to be lost. Already several of the guests were lying down in the dishes, and the soup-ladle was walking up the table towards Alice's chair, and beckoning to her impatiently to get out of its way.

"I ca'n't stand this any longer!" she cried, as she jumped up and seized the tablecloth with both hands: one good pull, and plates, dishes, guests, and candles came crashing down together in a heap on the floor.

"And as for *you*," she went on, turning fiercely upon

the Red Queen, whom she considered as the cause of all
the mischief—but the Queen was no longer at her side—
she had suddenly dwindled down to the size of a little
doll, and was now on the table, merrily running round
and round after her own shawl, which was trailing behind her.

At any other time, Alice would have felt surprised at
this, but she was far too much excited to be surprised at
anything *now*. "As for *you*," she repeated, catching hold
of the little creature in the very act of jumping over a
bottle which had just lighted upon the table, "I'll shake
you into a kitten, that I will!"

Chapter X

Shaking

SHE took her off the table as she spoke, and shook her backwards and forwards with all her might.

The Red Queen made no resistance whatever: only her face grew very small, and her eyes got large and green: and still, as Alice went on shaking her, she kept on growing shorter—and fatter—and softer—and rounder—and——

Chapter XI

Waking

——and it really *was* a kitten, after all.

Chapter XII

Which Dreamed It?

"Your Red Majesty shouldn't purr so loud," Alice said, rubbing her eyes, and addressing the kitten, respectfully, yet with some severity. "You woke me out of oh! such a nice dream! And you've been along with me, Kitty—all through the Looking-glass world. Did you know it, dear?"

It is a very inconvenient habit of kittens (Alice had once made the remark) that, whatever you say to them, they *always* purr. "If they would only purr for 'yes', and mew for 'no', or any rule of that sort," she had said, "so that one could keep up a conversation! But how *can* you talk with a person if they *always* say the same thing?"

On this occasion the kitten only purred: and it was impossible to guess whether it meant "yes" or "no".

So Alice hunted among the chessmen on the table till she had found the Red Queen: then she went down on her knees on the hearth-rug, and put the kitten and the Queen to look at each other. "Now, Kitty!" she cried, clapping her hands triumphantly. "Confess that was what you turned into!"

("But it wouldn't look at it," she said, when she was explaining the thing afterwards to her sister: "it turned away its head, and pretended not to see it: but it looked a *little* ashamed of itself, so I think it *must* have been the Red Queen.")

"Sit up a little more stiffly, dear!" Alice cried with a merry laugh. "And curtsey while you're thinking what to—what to purr. It saves time, remember!" And she caught it up and gave it one little kiss, "just in honour of its having been a Red Queen".

"Snowdrop, my pet!" she went on, looking over her shoulder at the White Kitten, which was still patiently undergoing its toilet, "when *will* Dinah have finished with your White Majesty, I wonder? That must be the reason you were so untidy in my dream.——Dinah! Do you know that you're scrubbing a White Queen? Really, it's most disrespectful of you!"

"And what did *Dinah* turn to, I wonder?" she prattled on, as she settled comfortably down, with one elbow on the rug, and her chin in her hand, to watch the kittens.

"Tell me, Dinah, did you turn to Humpty Dumpty? I *think* you did—however, you'd better not mention it to your friends just yet, for I'm not sure.

"By the way, Kitty, if only you'd been really with me in my dream, there was one thing you *would* have enjoyed ——I had such a quantity of poetry said to me, all about fishes! To-morrow morning you shall have a real treat. All the time you're eating your breakfast, I'll repeat 'The Walrus and the Carpenter' to you; and then you can make believe it's oysters, dear!

"Now, Kitty, let's consider who it was that dreamed it all. This is a serious question, my dear, and you should *not* go on licking your paw like that—as if Dinah hadn't washed you this morning! You see, Kitty, it *must* have been either me or the Red King. He was part of my dream, of course—but then I was part of his dream, too! *Was* it the Red King, Kitty? You were his wife, my dear, so you ought to know——Oh, Kitty, *do* help to settle it! I'm sure your paw can wait!" But the provoking kitten only began on the other paw, and pretended it hadn't heard the question.

Which do *you* think it was?

A BOAT, beneath a sunny sky
Lingering onward dreamily
In an evening of July—

Children three that nestle near,
Eager eye and willing ear,
Pleased a simple tale to hear—

Long has paled that sunny sky:
Echoes fade and memories die:
Autumn frosts have slain July.

Still she haunts me, phantomwise.
Alice moving under skies
Never seen by waking·eyes.

Children yet, the tale to hear,
Eager eye and willing ear,
Lovingly shall nestle near.

In a Wonderland they lie,
Dreaming as the days go by,
Dreaming as the summers die:

Ever drifting down the stream—
Lingering in the golden gleam—
Life, what is it but a dream?

Editor's note: The initial letters of this poem
when read downward give the full name of
the original Alice—Alice Pleasance Liddell.

III
Sylvie and Bruno

Is all our Life, then, but a dream
Seen faintly in the golden gleam
Athwart Time's dark resistless stream?

Bowed to the earth with bitter woe,
Or laughing at some raree-show,
We flutter idly to and fro.

Man's little Day in haste we spend,
And, from its merry noontide, send
No glance to meet the silent end.

PREFACE

THE descriptions, at pp. 452, 453, of Sunday as spent by children of the last generation, are quoted *verbatim* from a speech made to me by a child-friend and a letter written to me by a lady-friend.

The Chapters, headed "Fairy Sylvie" and "Bruno's Revenge", are a reprint, with a few alterations, of a little fairy-tale which I wrote in the year 1867, at the request of the late Mrs. Gatty, for "Aunt Judy's Magazine", which she was then editing.

It was in 1874, I believe, that the idea first occurred to me of making it the nucleus of a longer story. As the years went on, I jotted down, at odd moments, all sorts of odd ideas, and fragments of dialogue, that occurred to me—who knows how?—with a transitory suddenness that left me no choice but either to record them then and there, or to abandon them to oblivion. Sometimes one could trace to their source these random flashes of thought—as being suggested by the book one was reading, or struck out from the "flint" of one's own mind by the "steel" of a friend's chance remark—but they had also a way of their own, of occurring, *à propos* of nothing—specimens of that hopelessly illogical phenomenon, "an effect without a cause". Such, for example, was the last line of "The Hunting of the Snark", which came into my head (as I have already related in "The Theatre" for April, 1887) quite suddenly, during a solitary walk; and such, again, have been passages which occurred in *dreams*, and which I cannot trace to any antecedent cause whatever. There are at least *two* instances of such dream-suggestions in this book—one, my Lady's remark, "it often runs in families, just as a love for pastry does", at p. 306; the other, Eric Lindon's *badinage* about having been in domestic service, at p. 425.

And thus it came to pass that I found myself at last in possession of a huge unwieldy mass of litterature—if the reader will kindly excuse the spelling—which only needed stringing together, upon the thread of a consecutive story, to constitute the book I hoped to write. Only! The task, at first, seemed absolutely hopeless, and gave me a far clearer idea, than I ever had before, of the meaning of the word "chaos": and I think it must have been ten years, or more, before I had succeeded in classifying these odds-and-ends sufficiently to see what sort of a story they indicated: for the story had to grow out of the incidents, not the incidents out of the story.

I am telling all this, in no spirit of egoism, but because I really believe that some of my readers will be interested in these details of the "genesis" of a book, which looks so simple and straight-forward a matter, when completed, that they might suppose it to have been written straight off, page by page, as one would write a letter, beginning at the beginning and ending at the end.

It is, no doubt, *possible* to write a story in that way: and, if it be not vanity to say so, I believe that I could, myself,—if I were in the unfortunate position (for I do hold it to be a real misfortune) of being obliged to produce a given amount of fiction in a given time that I could "fulfil my task", and produce my "tale of bricks", as other slaves have done. One thing, at any rate I could guarantee as to the story so produced—that it should be utterly commonplace, should contain no new ideas whatever, and should be very very weary reading!

This species of literature has received the very appropriate name of "padding"—which might fitly be defined as "that which all can write and none can read". That the present volume contains *no* such writing I dare not avow: sometimes, in order to bring a picture into its proper place, it has been necessary to eke out a page with two or three extra lines: but I can honestly say I have put in no more than I was absolutely compelled to do.

My readers may perhaps like to amuse themselves by

trying to detect, in a given passage, the one piece of "padding" it contains. While arranging the "slips" into pages, I found that the passage, which now extends from the top of p. 280 to the middle of p. 282, was 3 lines too short. I supplied the deficiency, not by interpolating a word here and a word there, but by writing in 3 consecutive lines. Now can my readers guess *which* they are?

A harder puzzle—if a harder be desired—would be to determine, as to the Gardener's Song, in *which* cases (if any) the stanza was adapted to the surrounding text, and in *which* (if any) the text was adapted to the stanza.

Perhaps the hardest thing in all literature—at least *I* have found it so: by no voluntary effort can I accomplish it: I have to take it as it comes—is to write anything *original*. And perhaps the easiest is, when once an original line has been struck out, to follow it up, and to write any amount more to the same tune. I do not know if "Alice in Wonderland" was an *original* story—I was, at least, no *conscious* imitator in writing it—but I do know that, since it came out, something like a dozen story-books have appeared, on identically the same pattern. The path I timidly explored—believing myself to be "the first that ever burst into that silent sea"—is now a beaten high-road: all the way-side flowers have long ago been trampled into the dust: and it would be courting disaster for me to attempt that style again.

Hence it is that, in "Sylvie and Bruno", I have striven —with I know not what success—to strike out yet another new path: be it bad or good, it is the best I can do. It is written, not for money, and not for fame, but in the hope of supplying, for the children whom I love, some thoughts that may suit those hours of innocent merriment which are the very life of Childhood: and also, in the hope of suggesting, to them and to others, some thoughts that may prove, I would fain hope, not wholly out of harmony with the graver cadences of Life.

If I have not already exhausted the patience of my readers, I would like to seize this opportunity—perhaps the last I shall have of addressing so many friends at once —of putting on record some ideas that have occurred to me, as to books desirable to be written—which I should much like to *attempt*, but may not ever have the time or power to carry through—in the hope that, if *I* should fail (and the years are gliding away *very* fast) to finish the task I have set myself, other hands may take it up.

First, a Child's Bible. The only real *essentials* of this would be, carefully selected passages, suitable for a child's reading, and pictures. One principle of selection, which I would adopt, would be that Religion should be put before a child as a revelation of *love*—no need to pain and puzzle the young mind with the history of crime and punishment. (On such a principle I should, for example, omit the history of the Flood.) The supplying of the pictures would involve no great difficulty: no new ones would be needed: hundreds of excellent pictures already exist, the copyright of which has long ago expired, and which simply need photo-zincography, or some similar process, for their successful reproduction. The book should be handy in size—with a pretty attractive-looking cover—in a clear legible type—and, above all, with abundance of pictures, pictures, pictures!

Secondly, a book of pieces selected from the Bible—not single texts, but passages of from 10 to 20 verses each—to be committed to memory. Such passages would be found useful, to repeat to one's self and to ponder over, on many occasions when reading is difficult, if not impossible: for instance, when lying awake at night—on a railway-journey—when taking a solitary walk—in old age, when eye-sight is failing or wholly lost—and, best of all, when illness, while incapacitating us for reading or any other occupation, condemns us to lie awake through many weary silent hours: at such a time how keenly one may realize the truth of David's rapturous cry *"O how sweet are thy words unto my throat: yea, sweeter than honey unto my mouth!"*

I have said "passages", rather than single texts, because we have no means of *recalling* single texts: memory needs *links*, and here are none: one may have a hundred texts stored in the memory, and not be able to recall, at will, more than half-a-dozen—and those by mere chance: whereas, once get hold of any portion of a *chapter* that has been committed to memory, and the whole can be recovered: all hangs together.

Thirdly, a collection of passages, both prose and verse, from books other than the Bible. There is not perhaps much, in what is called "un-inspired" literature (a misnomer, I hold: if Shakespeare was not inspired, one may well doubt if any man ever was), that will bear the process of being pondered over, a hundred times: still there *are* such passages—enough, I think, to make a goodly store for the memory.

These two books—of sacred, and secular, passages for memory—will serve other good purposes besides merely occupying vacant hours: they will help to keep at bay many anxious thoughts, worrying thoughts, uncharitable thoughts, unholy thoughts. Let me say this, in better words than my own, by copying a passage from that most interesting book, Robertson's Lectures on the Epistles to the Corinthians, Lecture XLIX. "If a man finds himself haunted by evil desires and unholy images, which will generally be at periodical hours, let him commit to memory passages of Scripture, or passages from the best writers in verse or prose. Let him store his mind with these, as safeguards to repeat when he lies awake in some restless night, or when despairing imaginations, or gloomy, suicidal thoughts, beset him. Let these be to him the sword, turning everywhere to keep the way of the Garden of Life from the intrusion of profaner footsteps."

Fourthly, a "Shakespeare" for girls: that is, an edition in which everything, not suitable for the perusal of girls of (say) from 10 to 17, should be omitted. Few children under 10 would be likely to understand or enjoy the greatest of poets: and those, who have passed out of girlhood, may safely be left to read Shakespeare, in any edition, "expurgated" or not, that they may prefer; but it seems a pity that so many children, in the intermediate stage, should be debarred from a great pleasure for want of an edition suitable to them. Neither Bowdler's, Chambers's, Brandram's, nor Cundell's "Boudoir" Shakespeare, seems to me to meet the want: they are not sufficiently "expurgated". Bowdler's is the most extraordinary of all: looking through it, I am filled with a deep sense of wonder, considering what he has left in, that he should have cut *anything* out! Besides relentlessly erasing all that is unsuitable on the score of reverence or decency, I should be inclined to omit also all that seems too difficult, or not likely to interest young readers. The resulting book might be slightly fragmentary: but it would be a real treasure to all British maidens who have any taste for poetry.

If it be needful to apologize to any one for the new departure I have taken in this story—by introducing, along with what will, I hope, prove to be acceptable nonsense for children, some of the graver thoughts of human life—it must be to one who has learned the Art of keeping such thoughts wholly at a distance in hours of mirth and careless ease. To him such a mixture will seem, no doubt, illjudged and repulsive. And that such an Art *exists* I do not dispute: with youth, good health, and sufficient money, it seems quite possible to lead, for years together, a life of unmixed gaiety—with the exception of one solemn fact, with which we are liable to be confronted at *any* moment, even in the midst of the most brilliant company or the most sparkling entertainment. A man may fix his own times for admitting serious thought, for attending public worship, for prayer, for reading the Bible: all such matters he can defer to that "convenient season", which is so apt never to occur at all: but he cannot defer, for one single moment, the necessity of attending to a message,

which may come before he has finished reading this page,
"this night shall thy soul be required of thee."

The ever-present sense of this grim possibility has been,
in all ages,[1] an incubus that men have striven to shake off.
Few more interesting subjects of enquiry could be found,
by a student of history, than the various weapons that
have been used against this shadowy foe. Saddest of all
must have been the thoughts of those who saw indeed an
existence beyond the grave, but an existence far more
terrible than annihilation—an existence as filmy, im-
palpable, all but invisible spectres, drifting about, through
endless ages, in a world of shadows, with nothing to do,
nothing to hope for, nothing to love! In the midst of the
gay verses of that genial "bon vivant" Horace, there
stands one dreary word whose utter sadness goes to one's
heart. It is the word *"exilium"* in the well-known passage

> *Omnes eodem cogimur, omnium*
> *Versatur urnâ serius ocius*
> *Sors exitura et nos in æternum*
> *Exilium impositura cymbæ.*

Yes, to him this present life—spite of all its weariness
and all its sorrow—was the only life worth having: all else
was "exile"! Does it not seem almost incredible that one,
holding such a creed, should ever have smiled?

And many in this day, I fear, even though believing in
an existence beyond the grave far more real than Horace
ever dreamed of, yet regard it as a sort of "exile" from all
the joys of life, and so adopt Horace's theory, and say "let
us eat and drink, for to-morrow we die".

We go to entertainments, such as the theatre—I say
"we", for *I* also go to the play, whenever I get a chance of
seeing a really good one—and keep at arm's length, if
possible, the thought that we may not return alive. Yet
how do you know—dear friend, whose patience has

[1] At the moment, when I had written these words, there was a
knock at the door, and a telegram was brought me, announcing
the sudden death of a dear friend.

carried you through this garrulous preface—that it may not be *your* lot, when mirth is fastest and most furious, to feel the sharp pang, or the deadly faintness, which heralds the final crisis—to see, with vague wonder, anxious friends bending over you—to hear their troubled whispers —perhaps yourself to shape the question, with trembling lips, "Is it serious?" and to be told "Yes: the end is near" (and oh, how different all Life will look when those words are said!)—how do you know, I say, that all this may not happen to *you*, this night?

And *dare* you, knowing this, say to yourself "Well, perhaps it *is* an immoral play: perhaps the situations *are* a little too 'risky', the dialogue a little too strong, the 'business' a little too suggestive. I don't say that conscience is *quite* easy: but the piece is so clever, I must see it this once! I'll begin a stricter life to-morrow." *To-morrow, and to-morrow, and to-morrow!*

> "*Who sins in hope, who, sinning, says,*
> '*Sorrow for sin God's judgement stays!*'
> *Against God's Spirit he lies; quite stops*
> *Mercy with insult; dares, and drops,*
> *Like a scorch'd fly, that spins in vain*
> *Upon the axis of its pain,*
> *Then takes its doom, to limp and crawl,*
> *Blind and forgot, from fall to fall.*"

Let me pause for a moment to say that I believe this thought, of the possibility of death—if calmly realized, and steadily faced—would be one of the best possible tests as to our going to any scene of amusement being right or wrong. If the thought of sudden death acquires, for *you*, a special horror when imagined as happening in a *theatre*, then be very sure the theatre is harmful for *you*, however harmless it may be for others; and that *you* are incurring a deadly peril in going. Be sure the safest rule is that we should not dare to *live* in any scene in which we dare not *die*.

But, once realize what the true object *is* in life—that it

is *not* pleasure, *not* knowledge, *not* even fame itself, "that last infirmity of noble minds"—but that it *is* the development of *character*, the rising to a higher, nobler, purer standard, the building-up of the perfect *Man*—and then, so long as we feel that this is going on, and will (we trust) go on for evermore, death has for us no terror; it is not a shadow, but a light; not an end, but a beginning!

One other matter may perhaps seem to call for apology —that I should have treated with such entire want of sympathy the British passion for "Sport", which no doubt has been in by-gone days, and is still, in some forms of it, an excellent school for hardihood and for coolness in moments of danger. But I am not entirely without sympathy for *genuine* "Sport": I can heartily admire the courage of the man who, with severe bodily toil, and at the risk of his life, hunts down some "man-eating" tiger: and I can heartily sympathize with him when he exults in the glorious excitement of the chase and the hand-to-hand struggle with the monster brought to bay. But I can but look with deep wonder and sorrow on the hunter who, at his ease and in safety, can find pleasure in what involves, for some defenceless creature, wild terror and a death of agony: deeper, if the hunter be one who has pledged himself to preach to men the Religion of universal Love: deepest of all, if it be one of those *"tender and delicate"* beings, whose very name serves as a symbol of Love —*"thy love to me was wonderful, passing the love of women"* —whose mission here is surely to help and comfort all that are in pain or sorrow!

> *"Farewell, farewell! but this I tell*
> *To thee, thou Wedding-Guest!*
> *He prayeth well, who loveth well*
> *Both man and bird and beast.*
>
> *He prayeth best, who loveth best*
> *All things both great and small;*
> *For the dear God who loveth us,*
> *He made and loveth all."*

Chapter I

Less Bread! More Taxes!

—AND then all the people cheered again, and one man, who was more excited than the rest, flung his hat high into the air, and shouted (as well as I could make out) "Who roar for the Sub-Warden?" *Everybody* roared, but whether it was for the Sub-Warden, or not, did not clearly appear: some were shouting "Bread!" and some "Taxes!", but no one seemed to know what it was they really wanted.

All this I saw from the open window of the Warden's breakfast-saloon, looking across the shoulder of the Lord Chancellor, who had sprung to his feet the moment the shouting began, almost as if he had been expecting it, and had rushed to the window which commanded the best view of the market-place.

"What *can* it all mean?" he kept repeating to himself, as, with his hands clasped behind him, and his gown floating in the air, he paced rapidly up and down the room. "I never heard such shouting before—and at this time of the morning, too! And with such unanimity! Doesn't it strike *you* as very remarkable?"

I represented, modestly, that to *my* ears it appeared that they were shouting for different things, but the Chancellor would not listen to my suggestion for a moment. "They all shout the same words, I assure you!" he said: then, leaning well out of the window, he whispered to a man who was standing close underneath, "Keep 'em together, ca'n't you? The Warden will be here directly. Give 'em the signal for the march up!" All this was evidently not meant for *my* ears, but I could scarcely help hearing it, considering that my chin was almost on the Chancellor's shoulder.

The "march up" was a very curious sight: a straggling procession of men, marching two and two, began from the other side of the market-place, and advanced in an irregular zig-zag fashion towards the Palace, wildly tacking from side to side, like a sailing vessel making way against an unfavourable wind—so that the head of the procession was often further from us at the end of one tack than it had been at the end of the previous one.

Yet it was evident that all was being done under orders, for I noticed that all eyes were fixed on the man who stood just under the window, and to whom the Chancellor was continually whispering. This man held his hat in one hand and a little green flag in the other: whenever he waved the flag the procession advanced a little nearer, when he dipped it they sidled a little farther off, and whenever he waved his hat they all raised a hoarse cheer. "Hoo-roah!" they cried, carefully keeping time with the hat as it bobbed up and down. "Hoo-roah! Noo! Consti! Tooshun! Less! Bread! More! Taxes!"

"That'll do, that'll do!" the Chancellor whispered. "Let 'em rest a bit till I give you the word. He's not here yet!" But at this moment the great folding-doors of the saloon were flung open, and he turned with a guilty start to receive His High Excellency. However it was only Bruno, and the Chancellor gave a little gasp of relieved anxiety.

"Morning!" said the little fellow, addressing the remark, in a general sort of way, to the Chancellor and the waiters. "Doos oo know where Sylvie is? I's looking for Sylvie!"

"She's with the Warden, I believe, y'reince!" the Chancellor replied with a low bow. There was, no doubt, a certain amount of absurdity in applying this title (which, as of course you see without my telling you, was nothing but "your Royal Highness" condensed into one syllable) to a small creature whose father was merely the Warden of Outland: still, large excuse must be made for a man who had passed several years at the Court of Fairyland,

and had there acquired the almost impossible art of pronouncing five syllables as one.

But the bow was lost upon Bruno, who had run out of the room, even while the great feat of The Unpronounceable Monosyllable was being triumphantly performed.

Just then, a single voice in the distance was understood to shout 'A speech from the Chancellor!" "Certainly, my friends!" the Chancellor replied with extraordinary promptitude. "You shall have a speech!" Here one of the waiters, who had been for some minutes busy making a queer-looking mixture of egg and sherry, respectfully presented it on a large silver salver. The Chancellor took it haughtily, drank it off thoughtfully, smiled benevolently on the happy waiter as he set down the empty glass, and began. To the best of my recollection this is what he said.

"Ahem! Ahem! Ahem! Fellow-sufferers, or rather suffering fellows——" ("Don't call 'em names!" muttered the man under the window. "I didn't say *felons*!" the Chancellor explained.) "You may be sure that I always sympa——" (" 'Ear, 'ear!" shouted the crowd, so loudly as quite to drown the orator's thin squeaky voice) "—that I always sympa——" he repeated. ("Don't simper quite so much!" said the man under the window. "It makes yer look a hidiot!" And, all this time, " 'Ear, 'ear!" went rumbling round the market-place, like a peal of thunder.) "That I always *sympathize*!" yelled the Chancellor, the first moment there was silence. "But your *true* friend is the *Sub-Warden*! Day and night he is brooding on your wrongs—I should say your *rights*—that is to say your *wrongs*—no, I mean your *rights*——" ("Don't talk no more!" growled the man under the window. "You're making a mess of it!") At this moment the Sub-Warden entered the saloon. He was a thin man, with a mean and crafty face, and a greenish-yellow complexion; and he crossed the room very slowly, looking suspiciously about him as if he thought there might be a savage dog hidden somewhere. "Bravo!" he cried, patting the Chancellor on the back. "You did that speech very well indeed. Why, you're a born orator, man!"

"Oh, that's nothing!" the Chancellor replied, modestly, with downcast eyes. "Most orators are *born*, you know." The Sub-Warden thoughtfully rubbed his chin. "Why, so they are!" he admitted. "I never considered it in that light. Still, you did it very well. A word in your ear!"

The rest of their conversation was all in whispers: so, as I could hear no more, I thought I would go and find Bruno.

I found the little fellow standing in the passage, and being addressed by one of the men in livery, who stood before him, nearly bent double from extreme respectfulness, with his hands hanging in front of him like the fins of a fish. "His High Excellency", this respectful man was saying, "is in his Study, y'reince!" (He didn't pronounce this quite so well as the Chancellor.) Thither Bruno trotted, and I thought it well to follow him.

The Warden, a tall dignified man with a grave but very pleasant face, was seated before a writing-table, which was covered with papers, and holding on his knee one of the sweetest and loveliest little maidens it has ever been my lot to see. She looked four or five years older than Bruno, but she had the same rosy cheeks and sparkling eyes, and the same wealth of curly brown hair. Her eager smiling face was turned upwards towards her father's, and it was a pretty sight to see the mutual love with which the two faces—one in the Spring of Life, the other in its late Autumn—were gazing on each other.

"No, you've never seen him," the old man was saying: "you couldn't, you know, he's been away so long—traveling from land to land, and seeking for health, more years than you've been alive, little Sylvie!"

Here Bruno climbed upon his other knee, and a good deal of kissing, on a rather complicated system, was the result.

"He only came back last night," said the Warden, when the kissing was over: "he's been traveling post-haste, for the last thousand miles or so, in order to be here on Sylvie's birthday. But he's a very early riser, and I dare say he's in the Library already. Come with me and see him. He's always kind to children. You'll be sure to like him."

"Has the Other Professor come too?" Bruno asked in an awe-struck voice.

"Yes, they arrived together. The Other Professor is—well, you wo'n't like him quite so much, perhaps. He's a little more *dreamy*, you know."

"I wiss *Sylvie* was a little more dreamy," said Bruno.

"What *do* you mean, Bruno?" said Sylvie.

Bruno went on addressing his father. "She says she *ca'n't*, oo know. But I thinks it isn't *ca'n't*, it's *wo'n't*."

"Says she *ca'n't* dream!" the puzzled Warden repeated.

"She *do* say it," Bruno persisted. "When I says to her 'Let's stop lessons!', she says 'Oh, I ca'n't *dream* of letting oo stop yet!' "

"He always wants to stop lessons", Sylvie explained, "five minutes after we begin!"

"Five minutes' lessons a day!" said the Warden. "You wo'n't learn much at *that* rate, little man!"

"That's just what Sylvie says," Bruno rejoined. "She says I *wo'n't* learn my lessons. And I tells her, over and over, I *ca'n't* learn 'em. And what does oo think she says? She says 'It isn't *ca'n't*, it's *wo'n't*!' "

"Let's go and see the Professor," the Warden said, wisely avoiding further discussion. The children got down off his knees, each secured a hand, and the happy trio set off for the Library—followed by me. I had come to the conclusion by this time that none of the party (except, for a few moments, the Lord Chancellor) was in the least able to see me.

"What's the matter with him?" Sylvie asked, walking with a little extra sedateness, by way of example to Bruno at the other side, who never ceased jumping up and down.

"What *was* the matter—but I hope he's all right now—was lumbago, and rheumatism, and that kind of thing. He's been curing *himself*, you know: he's a very learned doctor. Why, he's actually *invented* three new diseases, besides a new way of breaking your collar-bone!"

"Is it a nice way?" said Bruno.

"Well, hum, not *very*," the Warden said, as we entered the Library. "And here *is* the Professor. Good morning, Professor! Hope you're quite rested after your journey!"

A jolly-looking, fat little man, in a flowery dressing-gown, with a large book under each arm, came trotting in at the other end of the room, and was going straight across without taking any notice of the children. "I'm looking for Vol. Three," he said. "Do you happen to have seen it?"

"You don't see my *children*, Professor!" the Warden exclaimed, taking him by the shoulders and turning him round to face them.

The Professor laughed violently: then he gazed at them through his great spectacles, for a minute or two, without speaking.

At last he addressed Bruno. "I hope you have had a good night, my child?"

Bruno looked puzzled. "I's had the same night *oo've* had," he replied. "There's only been *one* night since yesterday!"

It was the Professor's turn to look puzzled now. He took off his spectacles, and rubbed them with his handkerchief. Then he gazed at them again. Then he turned to the Warden. "Are they bound?" he enquired.

"No, we aren't," said Bruno, who thought himself quite able to answer *this* question.

The Professor shook his head sadly. "Not even half-bound?"

"Why *would* we be half-bound?" said Bruno. "We're not prisoners!"

But the Professor had forgotten all about them by this time, and was speaking to the Warden again. "You'll be glad to hear", he was saying, "that the Barometer's beginning to move——"

"Well, which way?" said the Warden—adding to the

children,"Not that *I* care, you know. Only *he* thinks it affects the weather. He's a wonderfully clever man, you know. Sometimes he says things that only the Other Professor can understand: Sometimes he says things that *nobody* can understand! Which way is it, Professor? Up or down?"

"Neither!" said the Professor, gently clapping his hands. "It's going sideways—if I may so express myself."

"And what kind of weather does *that* produce?" said the Warden. "Listen children! Now you'll hear something worth knowing!"

"Horizontal weather," said the Professor, and made straight for the door, very nearly trampling on Bruno, who had only just time to get out of his way.

"*Isn't* he learned?" the Warden said, looking after him with admiring eyes. "Positively he runs over with learning!"

"But he needn't run over *me!*" said Bruno.

The Professor was back in a moment: he had changed his dressing-gown for a frock-coat, and had put on a pair of very strange-looking boots, the tops of which were open umbrellas. "I thought you'd like to see them," he said. "*These* are the boots for horizontal weather!"

"But what's the use of wearing umbrellas round one's knees?"

"In *ordinary* rain," the Professor admitted, "they would *not* be of much use. But if ever it rained *horizontally*, you know, they would be invaluable—simply invaluable!"

"Take the Professor to the breakfast-saloon, children," said the Warden. "And tell them not to wait for me. I had breakfast early, as I've some business to attend to." The children seized the Professor's hands, as familiarly as if they had known him for years, and hurried him away. I followed respectfully behind.

CHAPTER II

L'Amie Inconnue

AS we entered the breakfast saloon, the Professor was saying "—and he had breakfast by himself, early: so he begged you wouldn't wait for him, my Lady. This way, my Lady," he added, "this way!" And then, with (as it seemed to me) most superfluous politeness, he flung open the door of my compartment, and ushered in "—a young and lovely lady!" I muttered to myself with some bitterness. "And this is, of course, the opening scene of Vol. I. *She* is the Heroine. And *I* am one of those subordinate characters that only turn up when needed for the development of her destiny, and whose final appearance is outside the church, waiting to greet the Happy Pair!"

"Yes, my lady, change at Fayfield," were the next words I heard (oh that too obsequious Guard!), "next station but one." And the door closed, and the lady settled down into her corner, and the monotonous throb of the engine (making one feel as if the train were some gigantic monster, whose very circulation we could feel) proclaimed that we were once more speeding on our way. "The lady had a perfectly formed nose," I caught myself saying to myself, "hazel eyes, and lips——" and here it occurred to me that to see, for myself, what "the lady" was really like, would be more satisfactory than much speculation.

I looked round cautiously, and—was entirely disappointed of my hope. The veil, which shrouded her whole face, was too thick for me to see more than the glitter of bright eyes and the hazy outline of what *might* be a lovely oval face, but might also, unfortunately, be an equally *un*lovely one. I closed my eyes again, saying to myself "—couldn't have a better chance for an experiment in Telepathy! I'll *think out* her face and afterwards test the portrait with the original."

At first, no result at all crowned my efforts, though I

"divided my swift mind", now hither, now thither, in a way that I felt sure would have made Æneas green with envy: but the dimly-seen oval remained as provokingly blank as ever—a mere Ellipse, as if in some mathematical diagram, without even the Foci that might be made to do duty as a nose and a mouth. Gradually, however, the conviction came upon me that I could, by a certain concentration of thought, *think the veil away*, and so get a glimpse of the mysterious face—as to which the two questions, "is she pretty?" and "is she plain?", still hung suspended, in my mind, in beautiful equipoise.

Success was partial—and fitful—still there *was* a result: ever and anon, the veil seemed to vanish, in a sudden flash of light: but, before I could fully realize the face, all was dark again. In each such glimpse, the face seemed to grow more childish and more innocent: and, when I had at last *thought* the veil entirely away, it was, unmistakeably, the sweet face of little Sylvie!

"So, either I've been dreaming about Sylvie," I said to myself, "and this is the reality. Or else I've really been with Sylvie, and this is a dream! Is Life itself a dream, I wonder?"

To occupy the time, I got out the letter which had caused me to take this sudden railway-journey from my London home down to a strange fishing-town on the North coast, and read it over again:

"DEAR OLD FRIEND,

"*I'm sure it will be as great a pleasure to me, as it can possibly be to you, to meet once more after so many years: and of course I shall be ready to give you all the benefit of such medical skill as I have: only, you know, one mustn't violate professional etiquette! And you are already in the hands of a first-rate London doctor, with whom it would be utter affectation for me to pretend to compete. (I make no doubt he is right in saying the heart is affected: all your symptoms point that way.) One thing, at any rate, I have already done in my doctorial capacity— secured you a bedroom on the ground-floor, so that you will not need to ascend the stairs at all.*

"*I shall expect you by last train on Friday, in accordance with your letter: and, till then, I shall say, in the words of the old song, 'Oh for Friday nicht! Friday's lang a-coming!'*

"*Yours always,*

"ARTHUR FORESTER

"*P.S. Do you believe in Fate?*"

This Postscript puzzled me sorely. "He is far too sensible a man", I thought, "to have become a Fatalist. And yet what else can he mean by it?" And, as I folded up the letter and put it away, I inadvertently repeated the words aloud. "Do you believe in Fate?"

The fair "Incognita" turned her head quickly at the sudden question. "No, I don't!" she said with a smile. "Do you?"

"I—I didn't mean to ask the question!" I stammered, a little taken aback at having begun a conversation in so unconventional a fashion.

The lady's smile became a laugh—not a mocking laugh, but the laugh of a happy child who is perfectly at her ease. "Didn't you?" she said. "Then it was a case of what you Doctors call 'unconscious cerebration'?"

"I am no Doctor," I replied. "Do I look so like one? Or what makes you think it?"

She pointed to the book I had been reading, which was so lying that its title, "Diseases of the Heart", was plainly visible.

"One needn't be a *Doctor*", I said, "to take an interest in medical books. There's another class of readers, who are yet more deeply interested——"

"You mean the *Patients*?" she interrupted, while a look of tender pity gave new sweetness to her face. "But", with an evident wish to avoid a possibly painful topic, "one needn't be *either*, to take an interest in books of *Science*. Which contain the greatest amount of Science, do you think, the books, or the minds?"

"Rather a profound question for a lady!" I said to my-

self, holding, with the conceit so natural to Man, that
Woman's intellect is essentially shallow. And I considered
a minute before replying. "If you mean *living* minds, I
don't think it's possible to decide. There is so much *written* Science that no living person has ever *read*: and there
is so much *thought-out* Science that hasn't yet been *written*. But, if you mean the whole human race, then I think
the *minds* have it: everything, recorded in *books*, must
have once been in some *mind*, you know."

"Isn't that rather like one of the Rules in Algebra?"
my Lady enquired. ("*Algebra* too!" I thought with increasing wonder.) "I mean, if we consider thoughts as
factors, may we not say that the Least Common Multiple
of all the *minds* contains that of all the books; but not the
other way?"

"Certainly we may!" I replied, delighted with the illus-
tration. "And what a grand thing it would be", I went on
dreamily, thinking aloud rather than talking, "if we could
only *apply* that Rule to books! You know, in finding the
Least Common Multiple, we strike out a quantity wherever it occurs, except in the term where it is raised to its
highest power. So we should have to erase every recorded
thought, except in the sentence where it is expressed with
the greatest intensity."

My Lady laughed merrily. "*Some* books would be
reduced to blank paper, I'm afraid!" she said.

"They would. Most libraries would be terribly diminished in *bulk*. But just think what they would gain in
quality!"

"When will it be done?" she eagerly asked. "If there's
any chance of it in *my* time, I think I'll leave off reading,
and wait for it!"

"Well, perhaps in another thousand years or so——"

"Then there's no use waiting!" said my Lady. "Let's
sit down. Uggug, my pet, come and sit by me!"

"Anywhere but by *me*!" growled the Sub-Warden.
"The little wretch always manages to upset his coffee!"

I guessed at once (as perhaps the reader will also have

guessed, if, like myself, he is *very* clever at drawing conclusions) that my Lady was the Sub-Warden's wife, and
that Uggug (a hideous fat boy, about the same age as
Sylvie, with the expression of a prize-pig) was their son.
Sylvie and Bruno, with the Lord Chancellor, made up a
party of seven.

"And you actually got a plunge-bath every morning?"
said the Sub-Warden, seemingly in continuation of a
conversation with the Professor. "Even at the little
roadside-inns?"

"Oh, certainly, certainly!" the Professor replied with a
smile on his jolly face. "Allow me to explain. It is, in fact,
a very simple problem in Hydrodynamics. (That means a
combination of Water and Strength.) If we take a plunge-
bath, and a man of great strength (such as myself) about
to plunge into it, we have a perfect example of this
science. I am bound to admit", the Professor continued,
in a lower tone and with downcast eyes, "that we need a
man of *remarkable* strength. He must be able to spring
from the floor to about twice his own height, gradually
turning over as he rises, so as to come down again head
first."

"Why, you need a *flea*, not a *man*!" exclaimed the Sub-
Warden.

"Pardon me," said the Professor. "This particular kind
of bath is *not* adapted for a flea. Let us suppose", he continued, folding his table-napkin into a graceful festoon,
"that this represents what is perhaps *the* necessity of this
Age—the Active Tourist's Portable Bath. You may describe it briefly, if you like," looking at the Chancellor,
"by the letters A. T. P. B."

The Chancellor, much disconcerted at finding everybody looking at him, could only murmur, in a shy
whisper, "Precisely so!"

"One great advantage of this plunge-bath", continued
the Professor, "is that it requires only half-a-gallon of
water——"

"I don't call it a *plunge*-bath", His Sub-Excellency

remarked, "unless your Active Tourist goes *right under!*"

"But he *does* go right under," the old man gently replied. "The A. T. hangs up the P. B. on a nail—*thus.* He then empties the water-jug into it—places the empty jug below the bag—leaps into the air—descends head-first into the bag—the water rises round him to the top of the bag—and there you are!" he triumphantly concluded. "The A. T. is as much under water as if he'd gone a mile or two down into the Atlantic!"

"And he's drowned, let us say, in about four minutes——"

"By no means!" the Professor answered with a proud smile. "After about a minute, he quietly turns a tap at the lower end of the P. B.—all the water runs back into the jug—and there you are again!"

"But how in the world is he to get *out* of the bag again?"

"*That,* I take it," said the Professor, "is the most beautiful part of the whole invention. All the way up the P. B. inside, are loops for the thumbs; so it's something like going up-stairs, only perhaps less comfortable; and, by the time the A. T. has risen out of the bag, all but his head, he's sure to topple over, one way or the other—the Law of Gravity secures *that.* And there he is on the floor again!"

"A little bruised, perhaps?"

"Well, yes, a little bruised; but *having had his plunge-bath:* that's the great thing."

"Wonderful! It's almost beyond belief!" murmured the Sub-Warden. The Professor took it as a compliment, and bowed with a gratified smile.

"*Quite* beyond belief!" my Lady added—meaning, no doubt, to be more complimentary still. The Professor bowed, but he didn't smile *this* time.

"I can assure you", he said earnestly, "that, *provided the bath was made,* I used it every morning. I certainly *ordered* it—*that* I am clear about—my only doubt is, whether the man ever finished making it. It's difficult to remember, after so many years——"

At this moment the door, very slowly and creakingly, began to open, and Sylvie and Bruno jumped up, and ran to meet the well-known footstep.

Chapter III

Birthday-Presents

"It's my brother!" the Sub-Warden exclaimed, in a warning whisper. "Speak out and be quick about it!"

The appeal was evidently addressed to the Lord Chancellor, who instantly replied, in a shrill monotone, like a little boy repeating the alphabet, "As I was remarking, your Sub-Excellency, this portentous movement——"

"You began too soon!" the other interrupted, scarcely able to restrain himself to a whisper, so great was his excitement. "He couldn't have heard you. Begin again!"

"As I was remarking," chanted the obedient Lord Chancellor, "this portentous movement has already assumed the dimensions of a Revolution!"

"And what *are* the dimensions of a Revolution?" The voice was genial and mellow, and the face of the tall dignified old man, who had just entered the room, leading Sylvie by the hand, and with Bruno riding triumphantly on his shoulder, was too noble and gentle to have scared a less guilty man: but the Lord Chancellor turned pale instantly, and could hardly articulate the words "The dimensions—your—your High Excellency? I—I—scarcely comprehend!"

"Well, the length, breadth, and thickness, if you like it better!" And the old man smiled, half-contemptuously.

The Lord Chancellor recovered himself with a great effort, and pointed to the open window. "If your High Excellency will listen for a moment to the shouts of the

exasperated populace—" ("of the exasperated populace!" the Sub-Warden repeated in a louder tone, as the
Lord Chancellor, being in a state of abject terror, had
dropped almost into a whisper) "—you will understand
what it is they want."

And at that moment there surged into the room a
hoarse confused cry, in which the only clearly audible
words were "Less—bread—More—taxes!" The old man
laughed heartily. "What in the world——" he was beginning: but the Chancellor heard him not. "Some mistake!"
he muttered, hurrying to the window, from which he
shortly returned with an air of relief. "*Now* listen!" he
exclaimed, holding up his hand impressively. And now
the words came quite distinctly, and with the regularity
of the ticking of a clock, "More—bread—Less—taxes!"

"More bread!" the Warden repeated in astonishment.
"Why, the new Government Bakery was opened only last
week, and I gave orders to sell the bread at cost-price
during the present scarcity! What *can* they expect more?"

"The Bakery's closed, y'reince!" the Chancellor said,
more loudly and clearly than he had spoken yet. He was
emboldened by the consciousness that *here*, at least, he
had evidence to produce: and he placed in the Warden's
hands a few printed notices, that were lying ready, with
some open ledgers, on a side-table.

"Yes, yes, *I* see!" the Warden muttered, glancing carelessly through them. "Order countermanded by my
brother, and supposed to be *my* doing! Rather sharp practice! It's all right!" he added in a louder tone. "My name
is signed to it: so I take it on myself. But what do you
mean by 'Less Taxes'? How *can* they be less? I abolished
the last of them a month ago!"

"It's been put on again, y'reince, and by y'reince's
own orders!" and other printed notices were submitted
for inspection.

The Warden, whilst looking them over, glanced once
or twice at the Sub-Warden, who had seated himself before one of the open ledgers, and was quite absorbed in

adding it up; but he merely repeated "It's all right. I accept it as my doing."

"And they do say", the Chancellor went on sheepishly —looking much more like a convicted thief than an Officer of State, "that a change of Government, by the abolition of the Sub-Warden—I mean," he hastily added, on seeing the Warden's look of astonishment, "the abolition of the *office* of Sub-Warden, and giving the present holder the right to act as *Vice*-Warden whenever the Warden is absent—would appease all this seedling discontent. I mean," he added, glancing at a paper he held in his hand, "all this *seething* discontent!"

"For fifteen years", put in a deep but very harsh voice, "my husband has been acting as Sub-Warden. It is too long! It is much too long!" My Lady was a vast creature at all times: but, when she frowned and folded her arms, as now, she looked more gigantic than ever, and made one try to fancy what a haystack would look like, if out of temper.

"He would distinguish himself as a Vice!" my Lady proceeded, being far too stupid to see the double meaning of her words. "There has been no such Vice in Outland for many a long year, as he would be!"

"What course would *you* suggest, Sister?" the Warden mildly enquired.

My Lady stamped, which was undignified: and snorted, which was ungraceful. "This is no *jesting* matter!" she bellowed.

"I will consult my brother," said the Warden. "Brother!"

"——and seven makes a hundred and ninety-four, which is sixteen and twopence," the Sub-Warden replied. "Put down two and carry sixteen."

The Chancellor raised his hands and eyebrows, lost in admiration. "*Such* a man of business!" he murmured.

"Brother, could I have a word with you in my Study?" the Warden said in a louder tone. The Sub-Warden rose with alacrity, and the two left the room together.

My Lady turned to the Professor, who had uncovered the urn, and was taking its temperature with his pocket-thermometer. "Professor!" she began, so loudly and suddenly that even Uggug, who had gone to sleep in his chair, left off snoring and opened one eye. The Professor pocketed his thermometer in a moment, clasped his hands, and put his head on one side with a meek smile.

"You were teaching my son before breakfast, I believe?" my Lady loftily remarked. "I hope he strikes you as having talent?"

"Oh, very much so indeed, my Lady!" the Professor hastily replied, unconsciously rubbing his ear, while some painful recollection seemed to cross his mind. "I was very forcibly struck by His Magnificence, I assure you!"

"He is a charming boy!" my Lady exclaimed. "Even his snores are more musical than those of other boys!"

If that *were* so, the Professor seemed to think, the snores of *other* boys must be something too awful to be endured: but he was a cautious man, and he said nothing.

"And he's so clever!" my Lady continued "No one will enjoy your Lecture more—by the way, have you fixed the time for it yet? You've never given one, you know: and it was promised years ago, before you——"

"Yes, yes, my Lady, *I* know! Perhaps next Tuesday—or Tuesday week——"

"That will do very well," said my Lady, graciously. "Of course you will let the Other Professor lecture as well?"

"I think *not*, my Lady," the Professor said with some hesitation. "You see, he always stands with his back to the audience. It does very well for *reciting;* but for *lecturing*——"

"You are quite right," said my Lady. "And, now I come to think of it, there would hardly be time for more than *one* Lecture. And it will go off all the better, if we begin with a Banquet, and a Fancy-dress Ball——"

"It will indeed!" the Professor cried, with enthusiasm.

"I shall come as a Grass-hopper," my Lady calmly proceeded. "What shall *you* come as, Professor?"

The Professor smiled feebly. "I shall come as—as early as I can, my Lady!"

"You mustn't come in before the doors are opened," said my Lady.

"I ca'n't," said the Professor. "Excuse me a moment. As this is Lady Sylvie's birthday, I would like to——" and he rushed away.

Bruno began feeling in his pockets, looking more and more melancholy as he did so: then he put his thumb in his mouth, and considered for a minute: then he quietly left the room.

He had hardly done so before the Professor was back again, quite out of breath. "Wishing you many happy returns of the day, my dear child!" he went on, addressing the smiling little girl, who had run to meet him. "Allow me to give you a birthday-present. It's a second-hand pin-cushion, my dear. And it only cost fourpence-halfpenny!"

"Thank you, it's *very* pretty!" And Sylvie rewarded the old man with a hearty kiss.

"And the *pins* they gave me for nothing!" the Professor added in high glee. "Fifteen of em, and only *one* bent!"

"I'll make the bent one into a *hook*!" said Sylvie. "To catch Bruno with, when he runs away from his lessons!"

"You ca'n't guess what *my* present is!" said Uggug, who had taken the butter-dish from the table, and was standing behind her, with a wicked leer on his face.

"No, I ca'n't guess," Sylvie said without looking up. She was still examining the Professor's pincushion.

"It's *this*!" cried the bad boy, exultingly, as he emptied the dish over her, and then, with a grin of delight at his own cleverness, looked round for applause.

Sylvie coloured crimson, as she shook off the butter from her frock: but she kept her lips tight shut, and walked away to the window, where she stood looking out and trying to recover her temper.

Uggug's triumph was a very short one: the Sub-Warden had returned, just in time to be a witness of his dear child's playfulness, and in another moment a skilfully applied box on the ear had changed his grin of delight into a howl of pain.

"My darling!" cried his mother, enfolding him in her fat arms. "Did they box his ears for nothing? A precious pet!"

"It's not for *nothing!*" growled the angry father. "Are you aware, Madam, that *I* pay the house-bills, out of a fixed annual sum? The loss of all that wasted butter falls on *me*! Do you hear, Madam!"

"Hold your tongue, Sir!" My Lady spoke very quietly —almost in a whisper. But there was something in her *look* which silenced him. "Don't you see it was only a *joke*? And a very clever one, too! He only meant that he loved nobody *but* her! And, instead of being pleased with the compliment, the spiteful little thing has gone away in a huff!"

The Sub-Warden was a very good hand at changing a subject. He walked across to the window. "My dear," he said, "is that a *pig* that I see down below, rooting about among your flower-beds?"

"A *pig*!" shrieked my Lady, rushing madly to the window, and almost pushing her husband out, in her anxiety to see for herself. "Whose pig is it? How did it get in? Where's that crazy Gardener gone?"

At this moment Bruno re-entered the room, and passing Uggug (who was blubbering his loudest, in the hope of attracting notice) as if he was quite used to that sort of thing, he ran up to Sylvie and threw his arms round her. "I went to my toy-cupboard", he said with a very sorrowful face, "to see if there were *somefin* fit for a present for oo! And there isn't *nuffin!* They's *all* broken, every one! And I haven't got *no* money left, to buy oo a birthday-present! And I ca'n't give oo nuffin but *this!*" ("*This*" was a very earnest hug and a kiss.)

"Oh, thank you, darling!" cried Sylvie. "I like *your* present best of all!" (But if so, why did she give it back so quickly?)

His Sub-Excellency turned and patted the two children on the head with his long lean hands. "Go away, dears!" he said. "There's business to talk over."

Sylvie and Bruno went away hand in hand: but, on reaching the door, Sylvie came back again and went up to Uggug timidly. "I don't mind about the butter," she said, "and I—I'm sorry he hurt you!" And she tried to shake hands with the little ruffian: but Uggug only blubbered louder, and wouldn't make friends. Sylvie left the room with a sigh.

The Sub-Warden glared angrily at his weeping son. "Leave the room, Sirrah!" he said, as loud as he dared. His wife was still leaning out of the window, and kept repeating "I *ca'n't* see that pig! Where *is* it?"

"It's moved to the right—now it's gone a little to the left," said the Sub-Warden: but he had his back to the window, and was making signals to the Lord Chancellor, pointing to Uggug and the door, with many a cunning nod and wink.

The Chancellor caught his meaning at last, and crossing the room, took that interesting child by the ear—the next moment he and Uggug were out of the room, and the door shut behind them: but not before one piercing yell had rung through the room, and reached the ears of the fond mother.

"What *is* that hideous noise?" she fiercely asked, turning upon her startled husband.

"It's some hyæna—or other," replied the Sub-Warden, looking vaguely up to the ceiling, as if that was where they usually were to be found. "Let us to business, my dear. Here comes the Warden." And he picked up from the floor a wandering scrap of manuscript, on which I just caught the words "after which Election duly holden the said Sibimet and Tabikat his wife may at their pleasure assume Imperial——" before, with a guilty look, he crumpled it up in his hand.

CHAPTER IV

A Cunning Conspiracy

THE Warden entered at this moment: and close behind him came the Lord Chancellor, a little flushed and out of breath, and adjusting his wig, which appeared to have been dragged partly off his head.

"But where is my precious child?" my Lady enquired, as the four took their seats at the small side-table devoted to ledgers and bundles and bills.

"He left the room a few minutes ago—with the Lord Chancellor," the Sub-Warden briefly explained.

"Ah!" said my Lady, graciously smiling on that high official. "Your Lordship has a very *taking* way with children! I doubt if any one could *gain the ear* of my darling Uggug so quickly as *you* can!" For an entirely stupid woman, my Lady's remarks were curiously full of meaning, of which she herself was wholly unconscious.

The Chancellor bowed, but with a very uneasy air. "I think the Warden was about to speak," he remarked, evidently anxious to change the subject.

But my Lady would not be checked. "He is a clever boy," she continued with enthusiasm, "but he needs a man like your Lordship to *draw him out!*"

The Chancellor bit his lip, and was silent. He evidently feared that, stupid as she looked, she understood what she said *this* time, and was having a joke at his expense. He might have spared himself all anxiety: whatever accidental meaning her *words* might have, she *herself* never meant anything at all.

"It is all settled!" the Warden announced, wasting no time over preliminaries. "The Sub-Wardenship is abolished, and my brother is appointed to act as Vice-Warden whenever I am absent. So, as I am going abroad for a while, he will enter on his new duties at once."

"And there will really be a Vice after all?" my Lady enquired.

"I hope so!" the Warden smilingly replied.

My Lady looked much pleased, and tried to clap her hands: but you might as well have knocked two feather-beds together, for any noise it made. "When my husband is Vice", she said, "it will be the same as if we had a *hundred* Vices!"

"Hear, hear!" cried the Sub-Warden.

"You seem to think it very remarkable", my Lady remarked with some severity, "that your wife should speak the truth!"

"No, not *remarkable* at all!" her husband anxiously explained. "*Nothing* is remarkable that *you* say, sweet one!"

My Lady smiled approval of the sentiment, and went on. "And am I Vice-Wardeness?"

"If you choose to use that title," said the Warden: "but 'Your Excellency' will be the proper style of address. And I trust that both '*His* Excellency' and '*Her* Excellency' will observe the Agreement I have drawn up. The provision I am *most* anxious about is this." He unrolled a large parchment scroll, and read aloud the words " '*item*, that we will be kind to the poor'. The Chancellor worded it for me," he added, glancing at that great Functionary. "I suppose, now, that word '*item*' has some deep legal meaning?"

"Undoubtedly!" replied the Chancellor, as articulately as he could with a pen between his lips. He was nervously rolling and unrolling several other scrolls, and making room among them for the one the Warden had just handed to him. "These are merely the rough copies," he explained: "and, as soon as I have put in the final corrections—" making a great commotion among the different parchments, "—a semi-colon or two that I have accidentally omitted—" here he darted about, pen in hand, from one part of the scroll to another, spreading sheets of blotting-paper over his corrections, "all will be ready for signing."

"Should it not be read out, first?" my Lady enquired.

"No need, no need!" the Sub-Warden and the Chancellor exclaimed at the same moment, with feverish eagerness.

"No need at all," the Warden gently assented. "Your husband and I have gone through it together. It provides that he shall exercise the full authority of Warden, and shall have the disposal of the annual revenue attached to the office, until my return, or, failing that, until Bruno comes of age: and that he shall then hand over, to myself or to Bruno as the case may be, the Wardenship, the unspent revenue, and the contents of the Treasury, which are to be preserved, intact, under his guardianship."

All this time the Sub-Warden was busy, with the Chancellor's help, shifting the papers from side to side, and pointing out to the Warden the place where he was to sign. He then signed it himself, and my Lady and the Chancellor added their names as witnesses.

"Short partings are best," said the Warden. "All is ready for my journey. My children are waiting below to see me off." He gravely kissed my Lady, shook hands with his brother and the Chancellor, and left the room.

The three waited in silence till the sound of wheels announced that the Warden was out of hearing: then, to my surprise, they broke into peals of uncontrollable laughter.

"What a game, oh, what a game!" cried the Chancellor. And he and the Vice Warden joined hands, and skipped wildly about the room. My Lady was too dignified to skip, but she laughed like the neighing of a horse, and waved her handkerchief above her head: it was clear to her very limited understanding that *something* very clever had been done, but what it *was* she had yet to learn.

"You said I should hear all about it when the Warden had gone," she remarked, as soon as she could make herself heard.

"And so you shall, Tabby!" her husband graciously replied, as he removed the blotting paper, and showed the two parchments lying side by side. "This is the one he read but didn't sign: and this is the one he signed but didn't read! You see it was all covered up, except the place for signing the names——"

"Yes, yes!" my Lady interrupted eagerly, and began comparing the two Agreements. " '*Item*, that he shall exercise the authority of Warden, in the Warden's absence.' Why, that's been changed into 'shall be absolute governor for life, with the title of Emperor, if elected to that office by the people.' What! Are you *Emperor*, darling?"

"Not yet, dear," the Vice-Warden replied. "It wo'n't do to let this paper be seen, just at present. All in good time."

My Lady nodded, and read on. " '*Item*, that we will be kind to the poor.' Why, that's omitted altogether!"

"Course it is!" said her husband. "*We're* not going to bother about the wretches!"

"*Good*," said my Lady, with emphasis, and read on again. " '*Item*, that the contents of the Treasury be preserved intact.' Why, that's altered into 'shall be at the absolute disposal of the Vice-Warden'! Well, Sibby, that *was* a clever trick! *All* the Jewels, only think! May I go and put them on directly?"

"Well, not *just* yet, Lovey," her husband uneasily replied "You see the public mind isn't quite ripe for it yet. We must feel our way. Of course we'll have the coach-and-four out, at once. And I'll take the title of Emperor, as soon as we can safely hold an Election. But they'll hardly stand our using the *Jewels*, as long as they know the Warden's alive. We must spread a report of his death. A little Conspiracy——"

"A Conspiracy!" cried the delighted lady, clapping her hands. "Of all things, I *do* like a Conspiracy! It's so interesting!"

The Vice-Warden and the Chancellor interchanged a wink or two. "Let her conspire to her heart's content!" the cunning Chancellor whispered. "It'll do no harm!"

"And when will the Conspiracy——"

"Hist!" her husband hastily interrupted her, as the door opened, and Sylvie and Bruno came in, with their arms twined lovingly round each other—Bruno sobbing convulsively, with his face hidden on his sister's shoulder, and Sylvie more grave and quiet, but with tears streaming down her cheeks.

"Mustn't cry like that!" the Vice-Warden said sharply, but without any effect on the weeping children. "Cheer 'em up a bit!" he hinted to my Lady.

"*Cake!*" my Lady muttered to herself with great decision, crossing the room and opening a cupboard, from which she presently returned with two slices of plum-cake. "Eat, and don't cry!" were her short and simple orders: and the poor children sat down side by side, but seemed in no mood for eating.

For the second time the door opened—or rather was *burst* open, this time, as Uggug rushed violently into the room, shouting "that old Beggar's come again!"

"He's not to have any food——" the Vice-Warden was beginning, but the Chancellor interrupted him. "It's all right," he said, in a low voice: "the servants have their orders."

"He's just under here," said Uggug, who had gone to the window, and was looking down into the court-yard.

"Where, my darling?" said his fond mother, flinging her arms round the neck of the little monster. All of us (except Sylvie and Bruno, who took no notice of what was going on) followed her to the window. The old Beggar looked up at us with hungry eyes. "Only a crust of bread, your Highness!" he pleaded. He was a fine old man, but looked sadly ill and worn. "A crust of bread is what I crave!" he repeated. "A single crust and a little water!"

"Here's some water, drink this!" Uggug bellowed, emptying a jug of water over his head.

"Well done, my boy!" cried the Vice-Warden. "That's the way to settle such folk!"

"Clever boy!" the Wardeness chimed in. "*Hasn't* he good spirits?"

"Take a stick to him!" shouted the Vice-Warden, as

the old Beggar shook the water from his ragged cloak, and again gazed meekly upwards.

"Take a red-hot poker to him!" my Lady again chimed in.

Possibly there was no red-hot poker handy: but some *sticks* were forthcoming in a moment, and threatening faces surrounded the poor old wanderer, who waved them back with quiet dignity. "No need to break my old bones," he said. "I am going. Not even a crust!"

"Poor, *poor* old man!" exclaimed a little voice at my side, half choked with sobs. Bruno was at the window, trying to throw out his slice of plum-cake, but Sylvie held him back.

"He *shall* have my cake!" Bruno cried, passionately struggling out of Sylvie's arms.

"Yes, yes, darling!" Sylvie gently pleaded. "But don't *throw* it out! He's gone away, don't you see? Let's go after him." And she led him out of the room, unnoticed by the rest of the party, who were wholly absorbed in watching the old Beggar.

The Conspirators returned to their seats, and continued their conversation in an undertone, so as not to be heard by Uggug, who was still standing at the window.

"By the way, there was something about Bruno succeeding to the Wardenship," said my Lady. "How does *that* stand in the new Agreement?"

The Chancellor chuckled. "Just the same, word for word," he said, "with *one* exception, my Lady. Instead of 'Bruno', I've taken the liberty to put in—" he dropped his voice to a whisper, "—to put in 'Uggug', you know!"

"Uggug, indeed!" I exclaimed, in a burst of indignation I could no longer control. To bring out even that one word seemed a gigantic effort: but, the cry once uttered, all effort ceased at once: a sudden gust swept away the whole scene, and I found myself sitting up, staring at the young lady in the opposite corner of the carriage, who had now thrown back her veil, and was looking at me with an expression of amused surprise.

CHAPTER V

A Beggar's Palace

THAT I had said *something*, in the act of waking, I felt sure: the hoarse stifled cry was still ringing in my ears, even if the startled look of my fellow-traveler had not been evidence enough: but what could I possibly say by way of apology?

"I hope I didn't frighten you?" I stammered out at last. "I have no idea what I said. I was dreaming."

"You said '*Uggug indeed!*'" the young lady replied, with quivering lips that *would* curve themselves into a smile, in spite of all her efforts to look grave. "At least— you didn't *say* it—you *shouted* it!"

"I'm very sorry," was all I could say, feeling very penitent and helpless. "She *has* Sylvie's eyes!" I thought to myself, half-doubting whether, even now, I were fairly awake. "And that sweet look of innocent wonder is all Sylvie's, too. But Sylvie *hasn't* got that calm resolute mouth—nor that far-away look of dreamy sadness, like one that has had some deep sorrow, very long ago——" And the thick-coming fancies almost prevented my hearing the lady's next words.

"If you had had a 'Shilling Dreadful' in your hand," she proceeded, "something about Ghosts—or Dynamite —or Midnight Murder—one could understand it: those things aren't worth the shilling, unless they give one a Nightmare. But really—with only a *medical treatise*, you know——" and she glanced, with a pretty shrug of contempt, at the book over which I had fallen asleep.

Her friendliness, and utter unreserve, took me aback for a moment; yet there was no touch of forwardness, or boldness, about the child—for child, almost, she seemed to be: I guessed her at scarcely over twenty—all was the innocent frankness of some angelic visitant, new to the ways of earth and the conventionalisms—or, if you will, the barbarisms—of Society. "Even so", I mused, "will *Sylvie* look and speak, in another ten years."

"You don't care for Ghosts, then," I ventured to suggest, "unless they are really terrifying?"

"Quite so," the lady assented. "The regular Railway-Ghosts—I mean the Ghosts of ordinary Railway-literature—are very poor affairs. I feel inclined to say, with Alexander Selkirk, 'Their tameness is shocking to me'! And they never do any Midnight Murders. They couldn't 'welter in gore', to save their lives!"

" 'Weltering in gore' is a very expressive phrase, certainly. Can it be done in *any* fluid, I wonder?"

"I think *not*," the lady readily replied—quite as if she had thought it out, long ago. "It has to be something *thick*. For instance, you might welter in bread-sauce. That, being *white*, would be more suitable for a Ghost, supposing it wished to welter!"

"You have a real good *terrifying* Ghost in that book?" I hinted.

"How *could* you guess?" she exclaimed with the most engaging frankness, and placed the volume in my hands. I opened it eagerly, with a not unpleasant thrill (like what a good ghost-story gives one) at the "uncanny" coincidence of my having so unexpectedly divined the subject of her studies.

It was a book of Domestic Cookery, open at the article "Bread Sauce".

I returned the book, looking, I suppose, a little blank, as the lady laughed merrily at my discomfiture. "It's far more exciting than some of the modern ghosts, I assure you! Now there was a Ghost last month—I don't mean a *real* Ghost in—in Supernature—but in a Magazine. It was a perfectly *flavourless* Ghost. It wouldn't have frightened a mouse! It wasn't a Ghost that one would even offer a chair to!"

"Three score years and ten, baldness, and spectacles, have their advantages after all!" I said to myself. "Instead of a bashful youth and maiden, gasping out mono-

syllables at awful intervals, here we have an old man and
a child, quite at their ease, talking as if they had known
each other for years! Then you think", I continued aloud,
"that we ought *sometimes* to ask a Ghost to sit down?
But have we any authority for it? In Shakespeare, for
instance—there are plenty of ghosts *there*—does Shakespeare ever give the stage-direction '*hands chair to
Ghost*'?"

The lady looked puzzled and thoughtful for a moment:
then she *almost* clapped her hands. "Yes, yes, he *does!*"
she cried. "He makes Hamlet say '*Rest, rest, perturbed
Spirit!*'"

"And that, I suppose, means an easy-chair?"

"An American rocking-chair, I *think*——"

"Fayfield Junction, my Lady, change for Elveston!"
the guard announced, flinging open the door of the carriage: and we soon found ourselves, with all our portable
property around us, on the platform.

The accommodation, provided for passengers waiting
at this Junction, was distinctly inadequate—a single
wooden bench, apparently intended for three sitters only:
and even this was already partially occupied by a very
old man, in a smock frock, who sat, with rounded shoulders and drooping head, and with hands clasped on the
top of his stick so as to make a sort of pillow for that
wrinkled face with its look of patient weariness.

"Come, you be off!" the Station-master roughly accosted the poor old man. "You be off, and make way for
your betters! This way, my Lady!" he added in a perfectly different tone. "If your Ladyship will take a seat,
the train will be up in a few minutes." The cringing
servility of his manner was due, no doubt, to the address
legible on the pile of luggage, which announced their
owner to be "Lady Muriel Orme, passenger to Elveston,
via Fayfield Junction".

As I watched the old man slowly rise to his feet, and
hobble a few paces down the platform, the lines came
to my lips:

"From sackcloth couch the Monk arose,
With toil his stiffen'd limbs he rear'd;
A hundred years had flung their snows
On his thin locks and floating beard."

But the lady scarcely noticed the little incident. After one glance at the "banished man" who stood tremulously leaning on his stick, she turned to me. "This is *not* an American rocking-chair, by any means! Yet may I say," slightly changing her place, so as to make room for me beside her, "may I say, in Hamlet's words, 'Rest, rest ——' " she broke off with a silvery laugh.

" '—perturbed Spirit!' " I finished the sentence for her. "Yes, that describes a railway-traveler *exactly*! And here is an instance of it," I added, as the tiny local train drew up alongside the platform, and the porters bustled about, opening carriage-doors—one of them helping the poor old man to hoist himself into a third-class carriage, while another of them obsequiously conducted the lady and myself into a first-class.

She paused, before following him, to watch the progress of the other passenger. "Poor old man!" she said. "How weak and ill he looks! It was a shame to let him be turned away like that. I'm very sorry——" At this moment it dawned on me that these words were not addressed to *me*, but that she was unconsciously thinking aloud. I moved away a few steps, and waited to follow her into the carriage, where I resumed the conversation.

"Shakespeare *must* have traveled by rail, if only in a dream: 'perturbed Spirit' is such a happy phrase."

" 'Perturbed' referring, no doubt," she rejoined, "to the sensational booklets, peculiar to the Rail. If Steam has done nothing else, it has at least added a whole new Species of English Literature!"

"No doubt of it," I echoed. "The true origin of all our medical books—and all our cookery-books——"

"No, no!" she broke in merrily. "I didn't mean *our* Literature! *We* are quite abnormal. But the booklets— the little thrilling romances, where the Murder comes at page fifteen, and the Wedding at page forty—surely *they* are due to Steam?"

"And when we travel by Electricity—if I may venture to develop your theory—we shall have leaflets instead of booklets, and the Murder and the Wedding will come on the same page."

"A development worthy of Darwin!" the lady exclaimed enthusiastically. "Only *you* reverse his theory. Instead of developing a mouse into an elephant, you would develop an elephant into a mouse!" But here we plunged into a tunnel, and I leaned back and closed my eyes for a moment, trying to recall a few of the incidents of my recent dream.

"I thought I saw——" I murmured sleepily: and then the phrase insisted on conjugating itself, and ran into "you thought you saw—he thought he saw——" and then it suddenly went off into a song:

> "*He thought he saw an Elephant,*
> *That practised on a fife:*
> *He looked again, and found it was*
> *A letter from his wife.*
> '*At length I realise*', *he said,*
> '*The bitterness of Life!*' "

And what a wild being it was who sang these wild words! A Gardener he seemed to be—yet surely a mad one, by the way he brandished his rake—madder, by the way he broke, ever and anon, into a frantic jig—maddest of all, by the shriek in which he brought out the last words of the stanza!

It was so far a description of himself that he had the *feet* of an Elephant: but the rest of him was skin and bone: and the wisps of loose straw, that bristled all about him, suggested that he had been originally stuffed with it, and that nearly all the stuffing had come out.

Sylvie and Bruno waited patiently till the end of the first verse. Then Sylvie advanced alone (Bruno having

suddenly turned shy) and timidly introduced herself
with the words "Please, I'm Sylvie!"

"And who's that other thing?" said the Gardener.

"What thing?" said Sylvie, looking round. "Oh, that's
Bruno. He's my brother."

"Was he your brother yesterday?" the Gardener
anxiously enquired.

"Course I were!" cried Bruno, who had gradually crept
nearer, and didn't at all like being talked about without
having his share in the conversation.

"Ah, well!" the Gardener said with a kind of groan.
"Things change so, here. Whenever I look again it's sure
to be something different! Yet I does my duty! I gets up
wriggle-early at five——"

"If I was *oo*," said Bruno, "I wouldn't wriggle so early.
It's as bad as being a worm!" he added, in an undertone
to Sylvie.

"But you shouldn't be lazy in the morning, Bruno,"
said Sylvie. "Remember, it's the *early* bird that picks up
the worm!"

"It may, if it likes!" Bruno said with a slight yawn.
"I don't like eating worms, one bit. I always stop in bed
till the early bird has picked them up!"

"I wonder you've the face to tell me such fibs!" cried
the Gardener.

To which Bruno wisely replied, "Oo don't want a *face*
to tell fibs wiz—only a *mouf*."

Sylvie discreetly changed the subject. "And did you
plant all these flowers?" she said. "What a lovely garden
you've made! Do you know, I'd like to live here *always*!"

"In the winter-nights——" the Gardener was beginning.

"But I'd nearly forgotten what we came about!" Sylvie
interrupted. "Would you please let us through into the
road? There's a poor old beggar just gone out—and he's
very hungry—and Bruno wants to give him his cake,
you know!"

"It's as much as my place is worth!" the Gardener

muttered, taking a key from his pocket, and beginning to unlock a door in the garden-wall.

"How much *are* it wurf?" Bruno innocently enquired.

But the Gardener only grinned. "That's a secret!" he said. "Mind you come back quick!" he called after the children, as they passed out into the road. I had just time to follow them, before he shut the door again.

We hurried down the road, and very soon caught sight of the old Beggar, about a quarter of a mile ahead of us, and the children at once set off running to overtake him. Lightly and swiftly they skimmed over the ground, and I could not in the least understand how it was I kept up with them so easily. But the unsolved problem did not worry me so much as at another time it might have done, there were so many other things to attend to.

The old Beggar must have been very deaf, as he paid no attention whatever to Bruno's eager shouting, but trudged wearily on, never pausing until the child got in front of him and held up the slice of cake. The poor little fellow was quite out of breath, and could only utter the one word "Cake!"—not with the gloomy decision with which Her Excellency had so lately pronounced it, but with a sweet childish timidity, looking up into the old man's face with eyes that loved "all things both great and small".

The old man snatched it from him, and devoured it greedily, as some hungry wild beast might have done, but never a word of thanks did he give his little bene-factor—only growled "More, more!" and glared at the half-frightened children.

"There *is* no more!" Sylvie said with tears in her eyes. "I'd eaten mine. It was a shame to let you be turned away like that. I'm very sorry——"

I lost the rest of the sentence, for my mind had re-curred, with a great shock of surprise, to Lady Muriel Orme, who had so lately uttered these very words of Sylvie's—yes, and in Sylvie's own voice, and with Sylvie's gentle pleading eyes!

"Follow me!" were the next words I heard, as the old man waved his hand, with a dignified grace that ill suited his ragged dress, over a bush, that stood by the road side, which began instantly to sink into the earth. At another time I might have doubted the evidence of my eyes, or at least have felt some astonishment: but, in *this* strange scene, my whole being seemed absorbed in strong curiosity as to what would happen next.

When the bush had sunk quite out of our sight, marble steps were seen, leading downwards into darkness. The old man led the way, and we eagerly followed.

The staircase was so dark, at first, that I could only just see the forms of the children as, hand-in-hand, they groped their way down after their guide: but it got lighter every moment, with a strange silvery brightness, that seemed to exist in the air, as there were no lamps visible; and, when at last we reached a level floor, the room, we found ourselves in, was almost as light as day.

It was eight-sided, having in each angle a slender pillar, round which silken draperies were twined. The wall between the pillars was entirely covered, to the height of six or seven feet, with creepers, from which hung quantities of ripe fruit and of brilliant flowers, that almost hid the leaves. In another place, perchance, I might have wondered to see fruit and flowers growing together: here, my chief wonder was that neither fruit nor flowers were such as I had ever seen before. Higher up, each wall contained a circular window of coloured glass; and over all was an arched roof, that seemed to be spangled all over with jewels.

With hardly less wonder, I turned this way and that, trying to make out how in the world we had come in: for there was no door: and all the walls were thickly covered with the lovely creepers.

"We are safe here, my darlings!" said the old man, laying a hand on Sylvie's shoulder, and bending down to kiss her. Sylvie drew back hastily, with an offended air:

but in another moment, with a glad cry of "Why, it's *Father*!", she had run into his arms.

"Father! Father!" Bruno repeated: and, while the happy children were being hugged and kissed, I could but rub my eyes and say "Where, then, are the rags gone to?"; for the old man was now dressed in royal robes that glittered with jewels and gold embroidery, and wore a circlet of gold around his head.

CHAPTER VI

The Magic Locket

"WHERE are we, father?" Sylvie whispered, with her arms twined closely around the old man's neck, and with her rosy cheek lovingly pressed to his.

"In Elfland, darling. It's one of the provinces of Fairyland."

"But I thought Elfland was *ever* so far from Outland: and we've come such a *tiny* little way!"

"You came by the Royal Road, sweet one. Only those of royal blood can travel along it: but *you've* been royal ever since I was made King of Elfland—that's nearly a month ago. They sent *two* ambassadors, to make sure that their invitation to me, to be their new King, should reach me. One was a Prince; so *he* was able to come by the Royal Road, and to come invisibly to all but me: the other was a Baron; so *he* had to come by the common road, and I dare say he hasn't even *arrived* yet."

"Then how far have we come?" Sylvie enquired.

"Just a thousand miles, sweet one, since the Gardener unlocked that door for you."

"A thousand miles!" Bruno repeated. "And may I eat one?"

"Eat a *mile*, little rogue?"

"No," said Bruno. "I mean may I eat one of that fruits?"

"Yes, child," said the father: "and then you'll find out what *Pleasure* is like—the Pleasure we all seek so madly, and enjoy so mournfully!"

Bruno ran eagerly to the wall, and picked a fruit that was *shaped* something like a banana, but had the *colour* of a strawberry.

He ate it with beaming looks, that became gradually more gloomy, and were very blank indeed by the time he had finished.

"It hasn't got no taste at all!" he complained. "I couldn't feel nuffin in my mouf! It's a—what's that hard word, Sylvie?"

"It was a *Phlizz*," Sylvie gravely replied. "Are they *all* like that, father?"

"They're all like that to *you*, darling, because you don't belong to Elfland—yet. But to *me* they are real."

Bruno looked puzzled. "I'll try anuvver kind of fruits!" he said, and jumped down off the King's knee. "There's some lovely striped ones, just like a rainbow!" And off he ran.

Meanwhile the Fairy-King and Sylvie were talking together, but in such low tones that I could not catch the words: so I followed Bruno, who was picking and eating other kinds of fruit, in the vain hope of finding *some* that had a taste. I tried to pick some myself—but it was like grasping air, and I soon gave up the attempt and returned to Sylvie.

"Look well at it, my darling," the old man was saying, "and tell me how you like it."

"It's just *lovely*," cried Sylvie delightedly. "Bruno, come and look!" And she held up, so that he might see the light through it, a heart-shaped Locket, apparently cut out of a single jewel, of a rich blue colour, with a slender gold chain attached to it.

"It are welly pretty," Bruno more soberly remarked: and he began spelling out some words inscribed on it.

"All—will—love—Sylvie," he made them out at last. "And so they doos!" he cried, clasping his arms round her neck. "*Everybody* loves Sylvie!"

"But *we* love her best, don't we, Bruno?" said the old King, as he took possession of the Locket. "Now, Sylvie, look at *this*." And he showed her, lying on the palm of his hand, a Locket of a deep crimson colour, the same shape as the blue one, and, like it, attached to a slender golden chain.

"Lovelier and lovelier!" exclaimed Sylvie, clasping her hands in ecstasy. "Look, Bruno!"

"And there's words on this one, too," said Bruno. "Sylvie—will—love—all."

"Now you see the difference," said the old man: "different colours and different words. Choose one of them, darling. I'll give you whichever you like best."

Sylvie whispered the words, several times over, with a thoughtful smile, and then made her decision. "It's *very* nice to be loved," she said: "but it's nicer to love other people! May I have the red one, Father?"

The old man said nothing: but I could see his eyes fill with tears, as he bent his head and pressed his lips to her forehead in a long loving kiss. Then he undid the chain, and showed her how to fasten it round her neck, and to hide it away under the edge of her frock. "It's for you to *keep*, you know," he said in a low voice, "not for other people to *see*. You'll remember how to use it?"

"Yes, I'll remember," said Sylvie.

"And now, darlings, it's time for you to go back, or they'll be missing you, and then that poor Gardener will get into trouble!"

Once more a feeling of wonder rose in my mind as to how in the world we were to *get* back again—since I took it for granted that wherever the children went, *I* was to go—but no shadow of doubt seemed to cross *their* minds, as they hugged and kissed him, murmuring, over and over again, "Good-bye, darling Father!" And then, suddenly and swiftly, the darkness of midnight seemed to close in upon us, and through the darkness harshly rang a strange wild song:

> *"He thought he saw a Buffalo*
> *Upon the chimney-piece:*
> *He looked again, and found it was*
> *His Sister's Husband's Niece.*
> *'Unless you leave this house', he said,*
> *'I'll send for the Police!'"*

"That was *me!*" he added, looking out at us, through the half-opened door, as we stood waiting in the road. "And that's what I'd have done—as sure as potatoes aren't radishes—if she hadn't have tooken herself off! But I always loves my *pay-rints* like anything."

"Who *are* oor *pay-rints?*" said Bruno.

"Them as pay *rint* for me, of course!" the Gardener replied. "You can come in now, if you like."

He flung the door open as he spoke, and we got out, a little dazzled and stupefied (at least *I* felt so) at the sudden transition from the half-darkness of the railway-carriage to the brilliantly-lighted platform of Elveston Station.

A footman, in a handsome livery, came forward and respectfully touched his hat. "The carriage is here, my Lady," he said, taking from her the wraps and small articles she was carrying: and Lady Muriel, after shaking hands and bidding me "Good-night!" with a pleasant smile, followed him.

It was with a somewhat blank and lonely feeling that I betook myself to the van from which the luggage was being taken out: and, after giving directions to have my boxes sent after me, I made my way on foot to Arthur's lodgings, and soon lost my lonely feeling in the hearty welcome my old friend gave me, and the cosy warmth and cheerful light of the little sitting-room into which he led me.

"Little, as you see, but quite enough for us two. Now, take the easy-chair, old fellow, and let's have another look at you! Well, you *do* look a bit pulled down!" and he put on a solemn professional air. "I prescribe Ozone, *quant. suff.* Social dissipation, *fiant pilulæ quam plurimæ:* to be taken, feasting, three times a day!"

"But, Doctor!" I remonstrated. "Society doesn't 'receive' three times a day!"

"That's all *you* know about it!" the young Doctor gaily replied. "At home, lawn-tennis, 3 P.M. At home, kettledrum, 5 P.M. At home, music (Elveston doesn't give dinners), 8 P.M. Carriages at 10. There you are!"

It sounded very pleasant, I was obliged to admit. "And I know some of the *lady*-society already," I added. "One of them came in the same carriage with me."

"What was she like? Then perhaps I can identify her."

"The *name* was Lady Muriel Orme. As to what she was *like*—well, *I* thought her very beautiful. Do you know her?"

"Yes—I do know her." And the grave Doctor coloured slightly as he added "Yes, I agree with you. She *is* beautiful."

"*I* quite lost my heart to her!" I went on mischievously. "We talked——"

"Have some supper!" Arthur interrupted with an air of relief, as the maid entered with the tray. And he steadily resisted all my attempts to return to the subject of Lady Muriel until the evening had almost worn itself away. Then, as we sat gazing into the fire, and conversation was lapsing into silence, he made a hurried confession.

"I hadn't meant to tell you anything about her", he said (naming no names, as if there were only one "she" in the world!) "till you had seen more of her, and formed your own judgment of her: but somehow you surprised it out of me. And I've not breathed a word of it to any one else. But I can trust *you* with a secret, old friend! Yes! It's true of *me*, what I suppose *you* said in jest."

"In the merest jest, believe me!" I said earnestly. "Why, man, I'm three times her age! But if she's

your choice, then I'm sure she's all that is good and—"
"—and sweet," Arthur went on, "and pure, and self-denying, and true-hearted, and——" he broke off hastily, as if he could not trust himself to say more on a subject so sacred and so precious. Silence followed: and I leaned back drowsily in my easy-chair, filled with bright and beautiful imaginings of Arthur and his lady-love, and of all the peace and happiness in store for them.

I pictured them to myself walking together, lingeringly and lovingly, under arching trees, in a sweet garden of their own, and welcomed back by their faithful gardener, on their return from some brief excursion.

It seemed natural enough that the gardener should be filled with exuberant delight at the return of so gracious a master and mistress—and how strangely childlike they looked! I could have taken them for Sylvie and Bruno —less natural that he should show it by such wild dances, such crazy songs!

> *"He thought he saw a Rattlesnake*
> *That questioned him in Greek:*
> *He looked again, and found it was*
> *The Middle of Next Week.*
> *'The one thing I regret', he said,*
> *'Is that it cannot speak!'"*

—least natural of all that the Vice-Warden and "my Lady" should be standing close beside me, discussing an open letter, which had just been handed to him by the Professor, who stood, meekly waiting, a few yards off.

"If it were not for those two brats", I heard him mutter, glancing savagely at Sylvie and Bruno, who were courteously listening to the Gardener's song, "there would be no difficulty whatever."

"Let's hear that bit of the letter again," said my Lady. And the Vice-Warden read aloud:

"—and we therefore entreat you graciously to accept the Kingship, to which you have been unanimously elected by the Council of Elfland: and that you will allow your son Bruno—of whose goodness, cleverness, and beauty, reports have reached us—to be regarded as Heir-Apparent."

"But what's the difficulty?" said my Lady.

"Why, don't you see? The Ambassador, that brought this, is waiting in the house: and he's sure to see Sylvie and Bruno: and then, when he sees Uggug, and remembers all that about 'goodness, cleverness, and beauty,' why, he's sure to——"

"And *where* will you find a better boy than *Uggug*?" my Lady indignantly interrupted. "Or a wittier, or a lovelier?"

To all of which the Vice-Warden simply replied "Don't you be a great blethering goose! Our only chance is to keep those two brats out of sight. If *you* can manage *that*, you may leave the rest to *me*. I'll make him believe Uggug to be a model of cleverness and all that."

"We must change his name to Bruno, of course?" said my Lady.

The Vice-Warden rubbed his chin. "Humph! No!" he said musingly. "Wouldn't do. The boy's such an utter idiot, he'd never learn to answer to it."

"*Idiot*, indeed!" cried my Lady. "He's no more an idiot than *I* am!"

"You're right, my dear," the Vice-Warden soothingly replied. "He isn't, indeed!"

My Lady was appeased. "Let's go in and receive the Ambassador," she said, and beckoned to the Professor. "Which room is he waiting in?" she inquired.

"In the Library, Madam."

"And *what* did you say his name was?" said the Vice-Warden.

The Professor referred to a card he held in his hand. "His Adiposity the Baron Doppelgeist."

"Why does he come with such a funny name?" said my Lady.

"He couldn't well change it on the journey," the Professor meekly replied, "because of the luggage."

"*You* go and receive him", my Lady said to the Vice-Warden, "and *I'll* attend to the children."

CHAPTER VII

The Baron's Embassy

I WAS following the Vice-Warden, but, on second thoughts, went after my Lady, being curious to see how she would manage to keep the children out of sight.

I found her holding Sylvie's hand, and with her other hand stroking Bruno's hair in a most tender and motherly fashion: both children were looking bewildered and half-frightened.

"My own darlings," she was saying, "I've been planning a little treat for you! The Professor shall take you a long walk into the woods this beautiful evening: and you shall take a basket of food with you, and have a little picnic down by the river!"

Bruno jumped, and clapped his hands. "That *are* nice!" he cried. "Aren't it, Sylvie?"

Sylvie, who hadn't quite lost her surprised look, put up her mouth for a kiss. "Thank you *very* much," she said earnestly.

My Lady turned her head away to conceal the broad grin of triumph that spread over her vast face, like a ripple on a lake. "Little simpletons!" she muttered to herself, as she marched up to the house. I followed her in.

"Quite so, your Excellency," the Baron was saying as we entered the Library. "All the infantry were under *my* command." He turned, and was duly presented to my Lady.

"A *military* hero?" said my Lady. The fat little man simpered. "Well, yes," he replied, modestly casting down his eyes. "My ancestors were all famous for military genius."

My Lady smiled graciously. "It often runs in families." she remarked: "just as a love for pastry does."

The Baron looked slightly offended, and the Vice-Warden discreetly changed the subject. "Dinner will soon be ready," he said. "May I have the honour of conducting your Adiposity to the guest-chamber?"

"Certainly, certainly!" the Baron eagerly assented. "It would never do to keep *dinner* waiting!" And he almost trotted out of the room after the Vice-Warden.

He was back again so speedily that the Vice-Warden had barely time to explain to my Lady that her remark about "a love for pastry" was "unfortunate. You might have seen, with half an eye," he added, "that that's *his* line. Military genius, indeed! Pooh!"

"Dinner ready yet?" the Baron enquired, as he hurried into the room.

"Will be in a few minutes," the Vice-Warden replied. "Meanwhile, let's take a turn in the garden. You were telling me," he continued, as the trio left the house, "something about a great battle in which you had the command of the infantry——"

"True," said the Baron. "The enemy, as I was saying, far outnumbered us: but I marched my men right into the middle of—what's that?" the Military Hero exclaimed in agitated tones, drawing back behind the Vice-Warden, as a strange creature rushed wildly upon them, brandishing a spade.

"It's only the Gardener!" the Vice-Warden replied in an encouraging tone. "Quite harmless, I assure you. Hark, he's singing! It's his favourite amusement."

And once more those shrill discordant tones rang out:

> *"He thought he saw a Banker's Clerk*
> *Descending from the bus:*
> *He looked again, and found it was*
> *A Hippopotamus:*
> *'If this should stay to dine', he said,*
> *'There wo'n't be much for us!'"*

Throwing away the spade, he broke into a frantic jig, snapping his fingers, and repeating, again and again

*"There wo'n't be much for us!
There wo'n't be much for us!"*

Once more the Baron looked slightly offended, but the Vice-Warden hastily explained that the song had no allusion to *him*, and in fact had no meaning at all. "You didn't mean anything by it, now *did* you?" He appealed to the Gardener, who had finished his song, and stood, balancing himself on one leg, and looking at them, with his mouth open.

"I never means nothing," said the Gardener: and Uggug luckily came up at the moment, and gave the conversation a new turn.

"Allow me to present my son," said the Vice-Warden; adding, in a whisper, "one of the best and cleverest boys that ever lived! I'll contrive for you to see some of his cleverness. He knows everything that other boys *don't* know; and in archery, in fishing, in painting, and in music, his skill is—but you shall judge for yourself. You see that target over there? He shall shoot an arrow at it. Dear boy," he went on aloud, "his Adiposity would like to see you shoot. Bring his Highness' bow and arrows!"

Uggug looked very sulky as he received the bow and arrow, and prepared to shoot. Just as the arrow left the bow, the Vice-Warden trod heavily on the toe of the Baron, who yelled with the pain.

"Ten thousand pardons!" he exclaimed. "I stepped back in my excitement. See! It is a bull's-eye!"

The Baron gazed in astonishment. "He held the bow so awkwardly, it seemed impossible!" he muttered. But there was no room for doubt: there was the arrow, right in the centre of the bull's-eye!

"The lake is close by," continued the Vice-Warden. "Bring his Highness' fishing-rod!" And Uggug most unwillingly held the rod, and dangled the fly over the water.

"A beetle on your arm!" cried my Lady, pinching the

door Baron's arm worse than if ten lobsters had seized it at once. "*That* kind is poisonous," she explained. "But *what* a pity! You missed seeing the fish pulled out!"

An enormous dead cod-fish was lying on the bank, with the hook in its mouth.

"I had always fancied", the Baron faltered, "that cod were *salt*-water fish?"

"Not in *this* country," said the Vice-Warden. "Shall we go in? Ask my son some question on the way—*any* subject you like!" And the sulky boy was violently shoved forwards to walk at the Baron's side.

"Could your Highness tell me", the Baron cautiously began, "how much seven times nine would come to?"

"Turn to the left!" cried the Vice-Warden, hastily stepping forwards to show the way—so hastily, that he ran against his unfortunate guest, who fell heavily on his face.

"*So* sorry!" my Lady exclaimed, as she and her husband helped him to his feet again. "My son was in the act of saying 'sixty-three' as you fell!"

The Baron said nothing: he was covered with dust, and seemed much hurt, both in body and mind. However, when they had got him into the house, and given him a good brushing, matters looked a little better.

Dinner was served in due course, and every fresh dish seemed to increase the good-humour of the Baron: but all efforts, to get him to express his opinion as to Uggug's cleverness, were in vain, until that interesting youth had left the room, and was seen from the open window, prowling about the lawn with a little basket, which he was filling with frogs.

"So fond of Natural History as he is, dear boy!" said the doting mother. "Now *do* tell us, Baron, what you think of him!"

"To be perfectly candid," said the cautious Baron, "I would like a *little* more evidence. I think you mentioned his skill in—"

"Music?" said the Vice-Warden. "Why, he's simply a prodigy! You shall hear him play the piano." And he walked to the window. "Ug—I mean my boy! Come in for a minute, *and bring the music-master with you*! To turn over the music for him," he added as an explanation.

Uggug, having filled his basket with frogs, had no objection to obey, and soon appeared in the room, followed by a fierce-looking little man, who asked the Vice-Warden "Vot music vill you haf?"

"The Sonata that His Highness plays so charmingly," said the Vice-Warden.

"His Highness haf not—" the music-master began, but was sharply stopped by the Vice-Warden.

"Silence, Sir! Go and turn over the music for His Highness. My dear," (to the Wardeness) "will you show him what to do? And meanwhile, Baron, I'll just show you a most interesting map we have—of Outland, and Fairyland, and that sort of thing."

By the time my Lady had returned from explaining things to the music-master, the map had been hung up, and the Baron was already much bewildered by the Vice-Warden's habit of pointing to one place while he shouted out the name of another.

My Lady joining in, pointing out other places, and shouting other names, only made matters worse; and at last the Baron, in despair, took to pointing out places for himself, and feebly asked "Is that great yellow splotch *Fairyland*?"

"Yes, that's Fairyland," said the Vice-Warden: "and you might as well give him a hint," he muttered to my Lady, "about going back to-morrow. He eats like a shark! It would hardly do for *me* to mention it."

His wife caught the idea, and at once began giving hints of the most subtle and delicate kind. "Just see what a short way it is back to Fairyland! Why, if you started to-morrow morning, you'd get there in very little more than a week!"

The Baron looked incredulous. "It took me a full month to *come*," he said.

"But it's ever so much shorter, going *back*, you know!"

The Baron looked appealingly to the Vice-Warden, who chimed in readily. "You can go back *five* times, in the time it took you to come here *once*—if you start to-morrow morning!"

All this time the Sonata was pealing through the room. The Baron could not help admitting to himself that it was being magnificently played: but he tried in vain to get a glimpse of the youthful performer. Every time he had nearly succeeded in catching sight of him, either the Vice-Warden or his wife was sure to get in the way, pointing out some new place on the map, and deafening him with some new name.

He gave in at last, wished a hasty good-night, and left the room, while his host and hostess interchanged looks of triumph.

"Deftly done!" cried the Vice-Warden. "Craftily con-trived! But what means all that tramping on the stairs?" He half-opened the door, looked out, and added in a tone of dismay, "The Baron's boxes are being carried down!"

"And what means all that rumbling of wheels?" cried my Lady. She peeped through the window curtains. "The Baron's carriage has come round!" she groaned.

At this moment the door opened: a fat, furious face looked in: a voice, hoarse with passion, thundered out the words "My room is full of frogs—I leave you!" and the door closed again.

And still the noble Sonata went pealing through the room: but it was *Arthur's* masterly touch that roused the echoes, and thrilled my very soul with the tender music of the immortal "Sonata Pathetique": and it was not till the last note had died away that the tired but happy traveler could bring himself to utter the words "good-night!" and to seek his much-needed pillow.

Chapter VIII

A Ride on a Lion

THE next day glided away, pleasantly enough, partly in settling myself in my new quarters, and partly in strolling round the neighbourhood, under Arthur's guidance, and trying to form a general idea of Elveston and its inhabitants. When five o'clock arrived, Arthur proposed—without any embarrassment this time—to take me with him up to "the Hall", in order that I might make acquaintance with the Earl of Ainslie, who had taken it for the season, and renew acquaintance with his daughter Lady Muriel.

My first impressions of the gentle, dignified, and yet genial old man were entirely favourable: and the *real* satisfaction that showed itself on his daughter's face, as she met me with the words "this is indeed an unlooked-for pleasure!", was very soothing for whatever remains of personal vanity the failures and disappointments of many long years, and much buffeting with a rough world, had left in me.

Yet I noted, and was glad to note, evidence of a far deeper feeling than mere friendly regard, in her meeting with Arthur—though this was, as I gathered, an almost daily occurrence—and the conversation between them, in which the Earl and I were only occasional sharers, had an ease and a spontaneity rarely met with except between *very* old friends: and, as I knew that they had not known each other for a longer period than the summer which was now rounding into autumn, I felt certain that "Love", and Love alone, could explain the phenomenon.

"How convenient it would be", Lady Muriel laughingly remarked, *à propos* of my having insisted on saving her the trouble of carrying a cup of tea across the room to the Earl, "if cups of tea had no weight at all! Then perhaps ladies would *sometimes* be permitted to carry them for short distances!"

"One can easily imagine a situation", said Arthur, "where things would *necessarily* have no weight, relatively to each other, though each would have its usual weight, looked at by itself."

"Some desperate paradox!" said the Earl. "Tell us how it could be. We shall never guess it."

"Well, suppose this house, just as it is, placed a few billion miles above a planet, and with nothing else near enough to disturb it: of course it falls *to* the planet?"

The Earl nodded. "Of course—though it might take some centuries to do it."

"And is five-o'clock-tea to be going on all the while?" said Lady Muriel.

"That, and other things," said Arthur. "The inhabitants would live their lives, grow up and die, and still the house would be falling, falling, falling! But now as to the relative weight of things. Nothing can be *heavy*, you know, except by *trying* to fall, and being prevented from doing so. You all grant that?"

We all granted that.

"Well, now, if I take this book, and hold it out at arm's length, of course I feel its *weight*. It is trying to fall, and I prevent it. And, if I let go, it falls to the floor. But, if we were all falling together, it couldn't be *trying* to fall any quicker, you know: for, if I let go, what more could it do than fall? And, as my hand would be falling too—at the same rate—it would never leave it, for that would be to get ahead of it in the race. And it could never overtake the falling floor!"

"I see it clearly," said Lady Muriel. "But it makes one dizzy to think of such things! How *can* you make us do it?"

"There is a more curious idea yet," I ventured to say. "Suppose a cord fastened to the house, from below, and pulled down by some one on the planet. Then of course the *house* goes faster than its natural rate of falling: but the furniture—with our noble selves—would go on falling at their old pace, and would therefore be left behind."

"Practically, we should rise to the ceiling," said the Earl. "The inevitable result of which would be concussion of brain."

"To avoid that," said Arthur, "let us have the furniture fixed to the floor, and ourselves tied down to the furniture. Then the five-o'clock-tea could go on in peace."

"With one little drawback!" Lady Muriel gaily interrupted. "We should take the *cups* down with us: but what about the *tea*?"

"I had forgotten the *tea*," Arthur confessed. "*That*, no doubt, would rise to the ceiling—unless you chose to drink it on the way!"

"Which, I think, is *quite* nonsense enough for one while!" said the Earl. "What news does this gentleman bring us from the great world of London?"

This drew *me* into the conversation, which now took a more conventional tone. After a while, Arthur gave the signal for our departure, and in the cool of the evening we strolled down to the beach, enjoying the silence, broken only by the murmur of the sea and the far-away music of some fishermen's song, almost as much as our late pleasant talk.

We sat down among the rocks, by a little pool, so rich in animal, vegetable, and zoöphytic—or whatever is the right word—life, that I became entranced in the study of it, and, when Arthur proposed returning to our lodgings, I begged to be left there for a while, to watch and muse alone.

The fishermen's song grew ever nearer and clearer, as their boat stood in for the beach; and I would have gone down to see them land their cargo of fish, had not the microcosm at my feet stirred my curiosity yet more keenly.

One ancient crab, that was for ever shuffling frantically from side to side of the pool, had particularly fascinated me: there was a vacancy in its stare, and an aimless violence in its behaviour, that irresistibly recalled the Gardener who had befriended Sylvie and Bruno: and, as I gazed, I caught the concluding notes of the tune of his crazy song.

The silence that followed was broken by the sweet voice of Sylvie. "Would you please let us out into the road?"

"What! After that old beggar again?" the Gardener yelled, and began singing:

> *"He thought he saw a Kangaroo*
> *That worked a coffee-mill:*
> *He looked again, and found it was*
> *A Vegetable-Pill.*
> *'Were I to swallow this', he said,*
> *'I should be very ill!'"*

"We don't want him to swallow *anything*," Sylvie explained. "He's not hungry. But we want to see him. So will you please——"

"Certainly!" the Gardener promptly replied. "I *always* please. Never displeases nobody. There you are!" And he flung the door open, and let us out upon the dusty high-road.

We soon found our way to the bush, which had so mysteriously sunk into the ground: and here Sylvie drew the Magic Locket from its hiding-place, turned it over with a thoughtful air, and at last appealed to Bruno in a rather helpless way. "What *was* it we had to do with it, Bruno? It's all gone out of my head!"

"Kiss it!" was Bruno's invariable recipe in cases of doubt and difficulty. Sylvie kissed it, but no result followed.

"Rub it the wrong way," was Bruno's next suggestion.

"Which *is* the wrong way?" Sylvie most reasonably enquired. The obvious plan was to try *both* ways.

Rubbing from left to right had no visible effect whatever.

From right to left—"Oh, stop, Sylvie!" Bruno cried in sudden alarm. "Whatever *is* going to happen?"

For a number of trees, on the neighbouring hillside, were moving slowly upwards, in solemn procession: while a mild little brook, that had been rippling at our feet a moment before, began to swell, and foam, and hiss, and bubble, in a truly alarming fashion.

"Rub it some other way!" cried Bruno. "Try up-and-down! Quick!"

It was a happy thought. Up-and-down did it: and the landscape, which had been showing signs of mental aberration in various directions, returned to its normal condition of sobriety—with the exception of a small yellowish-brown mouse, which continued to run wildly up and down the road, lashing its tail like a little lion.

"Let's follow it," said Sylvie: and this also turned out a happy thought. The mouse at once settled down into a business-like jog-trot, with which we could easily keep pace. The only phenomenon, that gave me any uneasiness, was the rapid increase in the *size* of the little creature we were following, which became every moment more and more like a real lion.

Soon the transformation was complete: and a noble lion stood patiently waiting for us to come up with it. No thought of fear seemed to occur to the children, who patted and stroked it as if it had been a Shetland-pony.

"Help me up!" cried Bruno. And in another moment Sylvie had lifted him upon the broad back of the gentle beast, and seated herself behind him, pillion-fashion. Bruno took a good handful of mane in each hand, and made believe to guide this new kind of steed. "Gee-up!" seemed quite sufficient by way of *verbal* direction: the lion at once broke into an easy canter, and we soon found ourselves in the depths of the forest. I say *"we"*, for I am certain that *I* accompanied them—though *how* I managed to keep up with a cantering lion I am wholly unable to explain. But I was certainly one of the party when we came upon an old beggar-man cutting sticks, at whose feet the lion made a profound obeisance, Sylvie and Bruno at the same moment dismounting, and leaping into the arms of their father.

"From bad to worse!" the old man said to himself,

dreamily, when the children had finished their rather confused account of the Ambassador's visit, gathered no doubt from general report, as they had not seen him themselves. "From bad to worse! That is their destiny. I see it, but I cannot alter it. The selfishness of a mean and crafty man—the selfishness of an ambitious and silly woman—the selfishness of a spiteful and loveless child— all tend one way, from bad to worse! And you, my darlings, must suffer it awhile, I fear. Yet, when things are at their worst, you can come to me. I can do but little as yet——"

Gathering up a handful of dust and scattering it in the air, he slowly and solemnly pronounced some words that sounded like a charm, the children looking on in awe-struck silence:

> "Let craft, ambition, spite,
> Be quenched in Reason's night,
> Till weakness turn to might,
> Till what is dark be light,
> Till what is wrong be right!"

The cloud of dust spread itself out through the air, as if it were alive, forming curious shapes that were for ever changing into others.

"It makes letters! It makes words!" Bruno whispered, as he clung, half-frightened, to Sylvie. "Only I ca'n't make them out! Read them, Sylvie!"

"I'll try," Sylvie gravely replied. "Wait a minute—if only I could see that word——"

"I should be very ill!" a discordant voice yelled in our ears.

> " 'Were I to swallow this', he said,
> 'I should be very ill!' "

CHAPTER IX

A Jester and a Bear

YES, we were in the garden once more: and, to escape that horrid discordant voice, we hurried indoors, and found ourselves in the library—Uggug blubbering, the Professor standing by with a bewildered air, and my Lady, with her arms clasped round her son's neck, repeating, over and over again, "and *did* they give him nasty lessons to learn? My own pretty pet!"

"What's all this noise about?" the Vice-Warden angrily enquired, as he strode into the room. "And who put the hat-stand here?" And he hung his hat up on Bruno, who was standing in the middle of the room, too much astonished by the sudden change of scene to make any attempt at removing it, though it came down to his shoulders, making him look something like a small candle with a large extinguisher over it.

The Professor mildly explained that His Highness had been graciously pleased to say he wouldn't do his lessons.

"Do your lessons this instant, you young cub!" thundered the Vice-Warden. "And take *this*!" and a resounding box on the ear made the unfortunate Professor reel across the room.

"Save me!" faltered the poor old man, as he sank, half-fainting, at my Lady's feet.

"Shave you? Of course I will!" my Lady replied, as she lifted him into a chair, and pinned an anti-macassar round his neck. "Where's the razor?"

The Vice-Warden meanwhile had got hold of Uggug, and was belabouring him with his umbrella. "Who left this loose nail in the floor?" he shouted. "Hammer it in, I say! Hammer it in!" Blow after blow fell on the writhing Uggug, till he dropped howling to the floor.

Then his father turned to the "shaving" scene which was being enacted, and roared with laughter. "Excuse

317

me, dear, I ca'n't help it!" he said as soon as he could speak. "You *are* such an utter donkey! Kiss me, Tabby!"

And he flung his arms round the neck of the terrified Professor, who raised a wild shriek, but whether he received the threatened kiss or not I was unable to see, as Bruno, who had by this time released himself from his extinguisher, rushed headlong out of the room, followed by Sylvie; and I was so fearful of being left alone among all these crazy creatures that I hurried after them.

"We must go to Father!" Sylvie panted, as they ran down the garden. "I'm *sure* things are at their worst! I'll ask the Gardener to let us out again."

"But we ca'n't *walk* all the way!" Bruno whimpered. "How I *wiss* we had a coach-and-four, like Uncle!"

And, shrill and wild, rang through the air the familiar voice:

> *"He thought he saw a Coach-and-Four*
> *That stood beside his bed:*
> *He looked again, and found it was*
> *A Bear without a Head.*
> *'Poor thing,' he said, 'poor silly thing!*
> *It's waiting to be fed!'"*

"No, I ca'n't let you out again!" he said, before the children could speak. "The Vice-Warden gave it me, he did, for letting you out last time! So be off with you!" And, turning away from them, he began digging frantically in the middle of a gravel-walk, singing, over and over again,

> *"'Poor thing,' he said, 'poor silly thing!*
> *It's waiting to be fed!'"*

but in a more musical tone than the shrill screech in which he had begun.

The music grew fuller and richer at every moment: other manly voices joined in the refrain: and soon I heard the heavy thud that told me the boat had touched the beach, and the harsh grating of the shingle as the men dragged it up. I roused myself, and, after lending them a hand in hauling up their boat, I lingered yet awhile to watch them disembark a goodly assortment of the hard-won "treasures of the deep".

When at last I reached our lodgings I was tired and sleepy, and glad enough to settle down again into the easy-chair, while Arthur hospitably went to his cupboard, to get me out some cake and wine, without which, he declared, he could not, as a doctor, permit my going to bed.

And how that cupboard-door *did* creak! It surely could not be *Arthur*, who was opening and shutting it so often, moving so restlessly about, and muttering like the soliloquy of a tragedy-queen!

No, it was a *female* voice. Also the figure—half-hidden by the cupboard-door—was a *female* figure, massive, and in flowing robes. Could it be the landlady? The door opened, and a strange man entered the room.

"What *is* that donkey doing?" he said to himself, pausing, aghast, on the threshold.

The lady, thus rudely referred to, was his wife. She had got one of the cupboards open, and stood with her back to him, smoothing down a sheet of brown paper on one of the shelves, and whispering to herself "So, so! Deftly done! Craftily contrived!"

Her loving husband stole behind her on tip-toe, and tapped her on the head. "Boh!" he playfully shouted at her ear. "Never tell me again I ca'n't say 'boh' to a goose!"

My Lady wrung her hands. "Discovered!" she groaned. "Yet no—he is one of us! Reveal it not, oh Man! Let it bide its time!"

"Reveal *what* not?" her husband testily replied, dragging out the sheet of brown paper. "What are you hiding here, my Lady? I insist upon knowing!"

My Lady cast down her eyes, and spoke in the littlest of little voices. "Don't make fun of it, Benjamin!" she pleaded. "It's—it's—don't you understand? It's a DAGGER!"

"And what's *that* for?" sneered His Excellency. "We've only got to make people *think* he's dead! We haven't got to *kill* him! And made of tin, too!" he snarled, contemptuously bending the blade round his thumb. Now, Madam, you'll be good enough to explain. First, what do you call me *Benjamin* for?"

"It's part of the Conspiracy, Love! One *must* have an alias, you know——"

"Oh, an *alias*, is it? Well! And next, what did you get this dagger for? Come, no evasions? You ca'n't deceive *me*!"

"I got it for—for—for——" the detected Conspirator stammered, trying her best to put on the assassin-expression that she had been practising at the looking-glass. "For——"

"For *what*, Madam!"

"Well, for eighteenpence, if you *must* know, dearest! That's what I got it for, on my——"

"Now *don't* say your Word and Honour!" groaned the other Conspirator. "Why, they aren't worth half the money, put together!"

"On my *birthday*," my Lady concluded in a meek whisper. "One *must* have a dagger, you know. It's part of the——"

"Oh, don't talk of Conspiracies!" her husband savagely interrupted, as he tossed the dagger into the cupboard. "You know about as much how to manage a Conspiracy as if you were a chicken. Why, the first thing is to get a disguise. Now, just look at this!"

And with pardonable pride he fitted on the cap and bells, and the rest of the Fool's dress, and winked at her, and put his tongue in his cheek. "Is *that* the sort of thing, now?" he demanded.

My Lady's eyes flashed with all a Conspirator's enthusiasm. "The very thing!" she exclaimed, clapping her hands. "You do look, oh, such a *perfect* Fool!"

The Fool smiled a doubtful smile. He was not quite clear whether it was a compliment or not, to express it

so plainly. "You mean a Jester? Yes, that's what I intended. And what do you think *your* disguise is to be?"
And he proceeded to unfold the parcel, the lady watching
him in rapture.

"Oh, how lovely!" she cried, when at last the dress was
unfolded. "What a *splendid* disguise! An Esquimaux
peasant-woman!"

"An Esquimaux peasant, indeed!" growled the other.
"Here, put it on, and look at yourself in the glass. Why,
it's a *Bear*, ca'n't you use your eyes?" He checked himself
suddenly, as a harsh voice yelled through the room

> "*He looked again, and found it was*
> *A Bear without a Head!*"

But it was only the Gardener, singing under the open
window. The Vice-Warden stole on tip-toe to the window.
and closed it noiselessly, before he ventured to go on!
"Yes, Lovey, a *Bear*: but not without a *head*, I hope,
You're the Bear, and me the Keeper. And if any one
knows us, they'll have sharp eyes, that's all!"

"I shall have to practise the steps a bit," my Lady said,
looking out through the Bear's mouth: "one ca'n't help
being rather human just at first, you know. And of course
you'll say, 'Come up, Bruin!', won't you?"

"Yes, of course," replied the Keeper, laying hold of the
chain, that hung from the Bear's collar, with one hand,
while with the other he cracked a little whip. "Now go
round the room in a sort of a dancing attitude. Very
good, my dear, very good. Come up, Bruin! Come up,
I say!"

He roared out the last words for the benefit of Uggug,
who had just come into the room, and was now standing,
with his hands spread out, and eyes and mouth wide
open, the very picture of stupid amazement. "Oh, my!"
was all he could gasp out.

The Keeper pretended to be adjusting the bear's collar,
which gave him an opportunity of whispering, unheard
by Uggug, "*my* fault, I'm afraid! Quite forgot to fasten

the door. Plot's ruined if *he* finds it out! Keep it up a minute or two longer. Be savage!" Then, while seeming to pull it back with all his strength, he let it advance upon the scared boy: my Lady, with admirable presence of mind, kept up what she no doubt intended for a savage growl, though it was more like the purring of a cat: and Uggug backed out of the room with such haste that he tripped over the mat, and was heard to fall heavily outside—an accident to which even his doting mother paid no heed, in the excitement of the moment.

The Vice-Warden shut and bolted the door. "Off with the disguises!" he panted. "There's not a moment to lose.. He's sure to fetch the Professor, and we couldn't take *him* in, you know!" And in another minute the disguises were stowed away in the cupboard, the door unbolted, and the two Conspirators seated lovingly side-by-side on the sofa, earnestly discussing a book the Vice-Warden had hastily snatched off the table, which proved to be the City-Directory of the capital of Outland.

The door opened, very slowly and cautiously, and the Professor peeped in, Uggug's stupid face being just visible behind him.

"It is a beautiful arrangement!" the Vice-Warden was saying with enthusiasm. "You see, my precious one, that there are fifteen houses in Green Street, *before* you turn into West Street."

"*Fifteen* houses! Is it *possible*?" my Lady replied. "I thought it was fourteen!" And, so intent were they on this interesting question, that neither of them even looked up till the Professor, leading Uggug by the hand, stood close before them.

My Lady was the first to notice their approach. "Why, here's the Professor!" she exclaimed in her blandest tones. "And my precious child too! Are lessons over?"

"A strange thing has happened!" the Professor began in a trembling tone. "His Exalted Fatness" (this was one of Uggug's many titles) "tells me he has just seen, in this very room, a Dancing-Bear and a Court-Jester!"

The Vice-Warden and his wife shook with well-acted merriment.

"Not in *this* room, darling!" said the fond mother. "We've been sitting here this hour or more, reading——," here she referred to the book lying on her lap, "——reading the—the City-Directory."

"Let me feel your pulse, my boy!" said the anxious father. "Now put out your tongue. Ah, I thought so! He's a little feverish, Professor, and has had a bad dream. Put him to bed at once, and give him a cooling draught."

"I ain't been dreaming!" his Exalted Fatness remonstrated, as the Professor led him away.

"Bad grammar, Sir!" his father remarked with some sternness. "Kindly attend to *that* little matter, Professor, as soon as you have corrected the feverishness. And, by the way, Professor!" (The Professor left his distinguished pupil standing at the door, and meekly returned.) "There is a rumour afloat, that the people wish to elect an—in point of fact, an—you understand that I mean an——"

"Not *another Professor!*" the poor old man exclaimed in horror.

"No! Certainly not!" the Vice-Warden eagerly explained. "Merely an *Emperor*, you understand."

"An *Emperor!*" cried the astonished Professor, holding his head between his hands, as if he expected it to come to pieces with the shock. "What will the Warden——"

"Why, the *Warden* will most likely *be* the new Emperor!" my Lady explained. "Where could we find a better? Unless, perhaps——" she glanced at her husband.

"Where, indeed!" the Professor fervently responded, quite failing to take the hint.

The Vice-Warden resumed the thread of his discourse. "The reason I mentioned it, Professor, was to ask *you* to be so kind as to preside at the Election. You see it would make the thing *respectable*—no suspicion of anything underhand——"

"I fear I ca'n't, your Excellency!" the old man faltered. "What will the Warden——"

"True, true!" the Vice-Warden interrupted. "Your position, as Court-Professor, makes it awkward, I admit. Well, well! Then the Election shall be held without you."

"Better so, than if it were held *within* me!" the Professor murmured with a bewildered air, as if he hardly knew what he was saying. "Bed, I think your Highness said, and a cooling-draught?" And he wandered dreamily back to where Uggug sulkily awaited him.

I followed them out of the room, and down the passage, the Professor murmuring to himself, all the time, as a kind of aid to his feeble memory, "C, C, C; Couch, Cooling-Draught, Correct-Grammar", till, in turning a corner, he met Sylvie and Bruno, so suddenly that the startled Professor let go of his fat pupil, who instantly took to his heels.

Chapter X

The Other Professor

"We were looking for you!" cried Sylvie, in a tone of great relief. "We *do* want you so much, you ca'n't think!"

"What is it, dear children?" the Professor asked, beaming on them with a very different look from what Uggug ever got from him.

"We want you to speak to the Gardener for us," Sylvie said, as she and Bruno took the old man's hands and led him into the hall.

"He's ever so unkind!" Bruno mournfully added. "They's *all* unkind to us, now that Father's gone. The Lion were *much* nicer!"

"But you must explain to me, please," the Professor said with an anxious look, "*which* is the Lion, and *which* is the Gardener. It's *most* important not to get two such animals confused together. And one's very liable to do it in their case—both having mouths, you know——"

"Doos oo *always* confuses two animals together?" Bruno asked.

"Pretty often, I'm afraid," the Professor candidly confessed. "Now, for instance, there's the rabbit-hutch and the hall-clock." The Professor pointed them out. "One gets a little confused with *them*—both having doors, you know. Now, only yesterday—would you believe it?—I put some lettuces into the clock, and tried to wind up the rabbit!"

"Did the rabbit *go*, after oo wounded it up?" said Bruno.

The Professor clasped his hands on the top of his head, and groaned. "Go? I should think it *did* go! Why, it's *gone*! And where ever it's gone to—that's what I ca'n't find out! I've done my best—I've read all the article 'Rabbit' in the great dictionary—Come in!"

"Only the tailor, Sir, with your little bill," said a meek voice outside the door.

"Ah, well, I can soon settle *his* business," the Professor said to the children, "if you'll just wait a minute. How much is it, this year, my man?" The tailor had come in while he was speaking.

"Well, it's been a doubling so many years, you see," the tailor replied, a little gruffly, "and I think I'd like the money now. It's two thousand pound, it is!"

"Oh, that's nothing!" the Professor carelessly remarked, feeling in his pocket, as if he always carried at least *that* amount about with him. "But wouldn't you like to wait just another year, and make it *four* thousand? Just think how rich you'd be! Why, you might be a *King*, if you liked!"

"I don't know as I'd care about being a *King*," the man said thoughtfully. "But it *dew* sound a powerful sight o' money! Well, I think I'll wait——"

"Of course you will!" said the Professor. "There's good sense in *you*, I see. Good-day to you, my man!"

"Will you ever have to pay him that four thousand pounds?" Sylvie asked as the door closed on the departing creditor.

"*Never*, my child!" the Professor replied emphatically. "He'll go on doubling it, till he dies. You see it's *always* worth while waiting another year, to get twice as much money! And now what would you like to do, my little friends? Shall I take you to see the Other Professor? This would be an excellent opportunity for a visit," he said to himself, glancing at his watch: "he generally takes a short rest—of fourteen minutes and a half—about this time."

Bruno hastily went round to Sylvie, who was standing at the other side of the Professor, and put his hand into hers. "I *thinks* we'd like to go," he said doubtfully: "only please let's go all together. It's best to be on the safe side, oo know!"

"Why, you talk as if you were *Sylvie*!" exclaimed the Professor.

"I know I did," Bruno replied very humbly. "I quite forgotted I wasn't Sylvie. Only I fought he might be rarver fierce!"

The Professor laughed a jolly laugh. "Oh, he's quite tame!" he said. "He never bites. He's only a little—a little *dreamy*, you know." He took hold of Bruno's other hand, and led the children down a long passage I had never noticed before—not that there was anything remarkable in *that*: I was constantly coming on new rooms and passages in that mysterious Palace, and very seldom succeeded in finding the old ones again.

Near the end of the passage the Professor stopped. "This is his room," he said, pointing to the solid wall.

"We ca'n't get in through *there*!" Bruno exclaimed.

Sylvie said nothing, till she had carefully examined whether the wall opened anywhere. Then she laughed merrily. "You're playing us a trick, you dear old thing!" she said. "There's no *door* here!"

"There isn't any door to the room," said the Professor. "We shall have to climb in at the window."

So we went into the garden, and soon found the window of the Other Professor's room. It was a ground-floor window, and stood invitingly open: the Professor first lifted the two children in, and then he and I climbed in after them.

The Other Professor was seated at a table, with a large book open before him, on which his forehead was resting: he had clasped his arms round the book, and was snoring heavily. "He usually reads like that", the Professor remarked, "when the book's very interesting: and then sometimes it's very difficult to get him to attend!"

This seemed to be one of the difficult times: the Professor lifted him up, once or twice, and shook him violently: but he always returned to his book the moment he was let go of, and showed by his heavy breathing that the book was as interesting as ever.

"How dreamy he is!" the Professor exclaimed. "He must have got to a *very* interesting part of the book!" And he rained quite a shower of thumps on the Other Professor's back, shouting "Hoy! Hoy!" all the time. "Isn't it *wonderful* that he should be so dreamy?" he said to Bruno.

"If he's always as *sleepy* as that," Bruno remarked, "a *course* he's dreamy!"

"But what are we to *do*?" said the Professor. "You see he's quite wrapped up in the book!"

"Suppose oo *shuts* the book?" Bruno suggested.

"That's it!" cried the delighted Professor. "Of course that'll do it!" And he shut up the book so quickly that he caught the Other Professor's nose between the leaves, and gave it a severe pinch.

The Other Professor instantly rose to his feet, and carried the book away to the end of the room, where he put it back in its place in the book-case. "I've been reading for eighteen hours and three-quarters," he said, "and now I shall rest for fourteen minutes and a half. Is the Lecture all ready?"

"Very nearly," the Professor humbly replied. "I shall

ask you to give me a hint or two—there will be a few little difficulties——"

"And a Banquet, I think you said?"

"Oh, yes! The Banquet comes *first*, of course. People never enjoy Abstract Science, you know, when they're ravenous with hunger. And then there's the Fancy-Dress-Ball. Oh, there'll be lots of entertainment!"

"Where will the Ball come in?" said the Other Professor.

"I *think* it had better come at the beginning of the Banquet—it brings people together so nicely, you know."

"Yes, that's the right order. First the Meeting: then the Eating: then the Treating—for I'm sure any Lecture *you* give us will be a treat!" said the Other Professor, who had been standing with his back to us all this time, occupying himself in taking the books out, one by one, and turning them upside-down. An easel, with a blackboard on it, stood near him: and, every time that he turned a book upside-down, he made a mark on the board with a piece of chalk.

"And as to the 'Pig-Tale'—which *you* have so kindly promised to give us——" the Professor went on, thoughtfully rubbing his chin. "I think that had better come at the *end* of the Banquet: then people can listen to it quietly."

"Shall I *sing* it?" the Other Professor asked, with a smile of delight.

"If you *can*," the Professor replied, cautiously.

"Let me try," said the Other Professor, seating himself at the pianoforte. "For the sake of argument, let us assume that it begins on A flat." And he struck the note in question. "La, la, la! I think that's within an octave of it." He struck the note again, and appealed to Bruno, who was standing at his side. "Did I sing it like *that*, my child?"

"No, oo didn't," Bruno replied with great decision. "It were more like a duck."

"Single notes are apt to have that effect," the Other Professor said with a sigh. "Let me try a whole verse.

> There was a Pig, that sat alone,
>   Beside a ruined Pump.
> By day and night he made his moan:
> It would have stirred a heart of stone
> To see him wring his hoofs and groan,
>   Because he could not jump.

Would you call that a tune, Professor?" he asked, when he had finished.

The Professor considered a little. "Well," he said at last, "some of the notes are the same as others—and some are different—but I should hardly call it a *tune*."

"Let me try it a bit by myself," said the Other Professor. And he began touching the notes here and there, and humming to himself like an angry bluebottle.

"How do you like his singing?" the Professor asked the children in a low voice.

"It isn't very *beautiful*," Sylvie said, hesitatingly.

"It's very extremely *ugly*!" Bruno said, without any hesitation at all.

"All extremes are bad," the Professor said, very gravely. "For instance, Sobriety is a very good thing, when practised *in moderation*: but even Sobriety, when carried to an *extreme*, has its disadvantages."

"What are its disadvantages?" was the question that rose in my mind—and, as usual, Bruno asked it for me. "What *are* its lizard bandages?"

"Well, this is *one* of them," said the Professor. "When a man's tipsy (that's one extreme, you know), he sees one thing as two. But, when he's *extremely* sober (that's the other extreme), he sees two things as one. It's equally inconvenient, whichever happens."

"What does 'illconvenient' mean?" Bruno whispered to Sylvie.

"The difference between 'convenient' and 'inconvenient' is best explained by an example," said the Other

Professor, who had overheard the question. "If you'll just think over any Poem that contains the two words—such as——"

The Professor put his hands over his ears, with a look of dismay. "If you once let him begin a *Poem*," he said to Sylvie, "he'll never leave off again! He never does!"

"Did he ever begin a Poem and not leave off again?" Sylvie enquired.

"Three times," said the Professor.

Bruno raised himself on tiptoe, till his lips were on a level with Sylvie's ear. "What became of them three Poems?" he whispered. "Is he saying them all now?"

"Hush!" said Sylvie. "The Other Professor is speaking!"

"I'll say it very quick," murmured the Other Professor, with downcast eyes, and melancholy voice, which contrasted oddly with his face, as he had forgotten to leave off smiling. ("At least it wasn't exactly a *smile*," as Sylvie said afterwards: "it looked as if his mouth was made that shape.")

"Go on then," said the Professor. "*What must be must be.*"

"Remember that!" Sylvie whispered to Bruno. "It's a very good rule for whenever you hurt yourself."

"And it's a very good rule for whenever I make a noise," said the saucy little fellow. "So *you* remember it too, Miss!"

"Whatever *do* you mean?" said Sylvie, trying to frown, a thing she never managed particularly well.

"Oftens and oftens," said Bruno, "haven't oo told me 'There mustn't be so much noise, Bruno!' when I've tolded oo 'There *must*!' Why, there isn't no rules at all about 'There mustn't'! But oo never believes *me*!"

"As if any one *could* believe *you*, you wicked wicked boy!" said Sylvie. The *words* were severe enough, but I am of opinion that, when you are really *anxious* to impress a criminal with a sense of his guilt, you ought not to pronounce the sentence with your lips *quite* close to his cheek—since a kiss at the end of it, however accidental, weakens the effect terribly.

Chapter XI

Peter and Paul

"As I was saying," the Other Professor resumed, "if you'll just think over any Poem, that contains the words —such as

> *'Peter is poor,' said noble Paul,*
> *'And I have always been his friend:*
> *And, though my means to give are small,*
> *At least I can afford to lend.*
> *How few, in this cold age of greed,*
> *Do good, except on selfish grounds!*
> *But I can feel for Peter's need,*
> *And I WILL LEND HIM FIFTY POUNDS!'*

> *How great was Peter's joy to find*
> *His friend in such a genial vein!*
> *How cheerfully the bond he signed,*
> *To pay the money back again!*
> *'We ca'n't', said Paul, 'be too precise:*
> *'Tis best to fix the very day:*
> *So, by a learned friend's advice,*
> *I've made it Noon, the Fourth of May.'*

> *'But this is April!' Peter said.*
> *'The First of April, as I think.*
> *Five little weeks will soon be fled:*
> *One scarcely will have time to wink!*
> *Give me a year to speculate—*
> *To buy and sell—to drive a trade—'*
> *Said Paul 'I cannot change the date.*
> *On May the Fourth it must be paid.'*

'*Well, well!*' *said Peter, with a sigh.*
  '*Hand me the cash, and I will go.*
I'll form a Joint-Stock Company,
  And turn an honest pound or so.'
'*I'm grieved*', *said Paul, '*to seem unkind:
  The money shall of course be lent:
But, for a week or two, I find
  It will not be convenient.'

So, week by week, poor Peter came
  And turned in heaviness away;
For still the answer was the same,
  '*I cannot manage it to-day.*'
And now the April showers were dry—
  The five short weeks were nearly spent—
Yet still he got the old reply,
  '*It is not quite convenient!*'

The Fourth arrived, and punctual Paul
  Came, with his legal friend, at noon.
'*I thought it best*', *said he, '*to call:
  One cannot settle things too soon.'
Poor Peter shuddered in despair:
  His flowing locks he wildly tore:
And very soon his yellow hair
  Was lying all about the floor.

The legal friend was standing by,
  With sudden pity half unmanned:
The tear-drop trembled in his eye,
  The signed agreement in his hand:
But when at length the legal soul
  Resumed its customary force,
'*The Law*', *he said, '*we can't control:
  Pay, or the Law must take its course!'

*Said Paul '*How bitterly I rue
  That fatal morning when I called!
Consider, Peter, what you do!
  You wo'n't be richer when you're bald!

Think you, by rending curls away,
  To make your difficulties less?
Forbear this violence, I pray:
  You do but add to my distress!'

'Not willingly would I inflict',
  Said Peter, 'on that noble heart
One needless pang. Yet why so strict?
  Is this *to act a friendly part?*
However legal it may be
  To pay what never has been lent,
This style of business seems to me
  Extremely inconvenient!

'No Nobleness of soul have I,
  Like some *that in this Age are found!'*
(Paul blushed in sheer humility,
  And cast his eyes upon the ground.)
'This debt will simply swallow all,
  And make my life a life of woe!'
'Nay, nay, my Peter!' answered Paul.
  'You must not rail on Fortune so!

'You have enough to eat and drink:
  You are respected in the world:
And at the barber's, as I think,
  You often get your whiskers curled.
Though Nobleness you ca'n't attain—
  To any very great extent—
The path of Honesty is plain,
  However inconvenient!'

' 'Tis true', said Peter, 'I'm alive:
  I keep my station in the world:
Once in the week I just contrive
  To get my whiskers oiled and curled.
But my assets are very low:
  My little income's overspent:
To trench on capital, you know,
  Is always inconvenient!'

'*But pay your debts!*' *cried honest Paul.*
    '*My gentle Peter, pay your debts!*
What matter if it swallows all
    That you describe as your "assets"?
Already you're an hour behind:
    Yet Generosity is best.
It pinches me—but never mind!
    I WILL NOT CHARGE YOU INTEREST!'

'*How good! How great!*' *poor Peter cried.*
    '*Yet I must sell my Sunday wig—*
The scarf-pin that has been my pride—
    My grand piano—and my pig!'
Full soon his property took wings:
    And daily, as each treasure went,
He sighed to find the state of things
    Grow less and less convenient.

Weeks grew to months, and months to years:
    Peter was worn to skin and bone:
And once he even said, with tears,
    '*Remember, Paul, that promised Loan!*'
Said Paul '*I'll lend you, when I can,*
    All the spare money I have got—
Ah, Peter, you're a happy man!
    Yours is an enviable lot!

'*I'm getting stout, as you may see:*
    It is but seldom I am well:
I cannot feel my ancient glee
    In listening to the dinner-bell:
But you, you gambol like a boy,
    Your figure is so spare and light:
The dinner-bell's a note of joy
    To such a healthy appetite!'

Said Peter '*I am well aware*
    Mine is a state of happiness:
And yet how gladly could I spare
    Some of the comforts I possess!

What you call healthy appetite
   I feel as Hunger's savage tooth:
And, when no dinner is in sight,
   The dinner-bell's a sound of ruth!

'*No scare-crow would accept this coat:*
   Such boots as these you seldom see,
Ah, Paul, a single five-pound note
   Would make another man of me!'
Said Paul '*It fills me with surprise*
   To hear you talk in such a tone:
I fear you scarcely realize
   The blessings that are all your own!

'*You're safe from being overfed:*
   You're sweetly picturesque in rags:
You never know the aching head
   That comes along with money-bags:
And you have time to cultivate
   That best of qualities, Content—
For which you'll find your present state
   Remarkably convenient!'

Said Peter '*Though I cannot sound*
   The depths of such a man as you,
Yet in your character I've found
   An inconsistency or two.
You seem to have long years to spare
   When there's a promise to fulfil:
And yet how punctual you were
   In calling with that little bill!'

'*One ca'n't be too deliberate*',
   Said Paul, 'in parting with one's pelf.
With bills, as you correctly state,
   I'm punctuality itself.
A man may surely claim his dues:
   But, when there's money to be lent,
A man must be allowed to choose
   Such times as are convenient!'

It chanced one day, as Peter sat
  Gnawing a crust—his usual meal—
Paul bustled in to have a chat,
  And grasped his hand with friendly zeal
'I knew', said he, 'your frugal ways:
  So, that I might not wound your pride
By bringing strangers in to gaze,
  I've left my legal friend outside!

'You well remember, I am sure,
  When first your wealth began to go,
And people sneered at one so poor,
  I never used my Peter so!
And when you'd lost your little all,
  And found yourself a thing despised,
I need not ask you to recall
  How tenderly I sympathized!

'Then the advice I've poured on you,
  So full of wisdom and of wit:
All given gratis, though 'tis true
  I might have fairly charged for it!
But I refrain from mentioning
  Full many a deed I might relate—
For boasting is a kind of thing
  That I particularly hate.

'How vast the total sum appears
  Of all the kindnesses I've done,
From Childhood's half-forgotten years
  Down to that Loan of April One!
That Fifty Pounds! You little guessed
  How deep it drained my slender store:
But there's a heart within this breast,
  And I WILL LEND YOU FIFTY MORE!'

'Not so,' was Peter's mild reply,
  His cheeks all wet with grateful tears:
'No man recalls, so well as I,
  Your services in bygone years:

And this new offer, I admit,
    Is very very kindly meant—
  Still, to avail myself of it
      Would not be quite convenient!'

"You'll see in a moment what the difference is between 'convenient' and 'inconvenient'. You quite understand it now, don't you?" he added, looking kindly at Bruno, who was sitting, at Sylvie's side, on the floor.

"Yes," said Bruno, very quietly. Such a short speech was very unusual, for him: but just then he seemed, I fancied, a little exhausted. In fact, he climbed up into Sylvie's lap as he spoke, and rested his head against her shoulder. "What a many verses it was!" he whispered.

CHAPTER XII

A Musical Gardener

THE Other Professor regarded him with some anxiety. "The smaller animal ought to go to bed *at once*," he said with an air of authority.

"Why *at once?*" said the Professor.

"Because he ca'n't go at twice," said the Other Professor.

The Professor gently clapped his hands. "Isn't he *wonderful!*" he said to Sylvie. "Nobody else could have thought of the reason, so quick. Why, *of course* he ca'n't go at twice! It would hurt him to be divided."

This remark woke up Bruno, suddenly and completely. "I don't want to be *divided*," he said decisively.

"It does very well on a *diagram*," said the Other Professor. "I could show it you in a minute, only the chalk's a little blunt."

"Take care!" Sylvie anxiously exclaimed, as he began, rather clumsily, to point it. "You'll cut your finger off, if you hold the knife so!"

"If oo cuts it off, will oo give it to *me*, please?" Bruno thoughtfully added.

"It's like this," said the Other Professor, hastily drawing a long line upon the black board, and marking the letters "*A*", "*B*", at the two ends, and "*C*" in the middle: "let me explain it to you. If *AB* were to be divided into two parts at *C*———"

"It would be drownded," Bruno pronounced confidently.

The Other Professor gasped. "*What* would be drownded?"

"Why the bumble-bee, of course!" said Bruno. "And the two bits would sink down in the sea!"

Here the Professor interfered, as the Other Professor was evidently too much puzzled to go on with his diagram.

"When I said it would *hurt* him, I was merely referring to the action of the nerves———"

The Other Professor brightened up in a moment. "The action of the nerves", he began eagerly, "is curiously slow in some people. I had a friend, once, that if you burnt him with a red-hot poker, it would take years and years before he felt it!"

"And if you only *pinched* him?" queried Sylvie.

"Then it would take ever so much longer, of course. In fact, I doubt if the man *himself* would ever feel it, at all. His grandchildren might."

"I wouldn't like to be the grandchild of a pinched grandfather, would *you*, Mister Sir?" Bruno whispered. "It might come just when you wanted to be happy!"

That would be awkward, I admitted, taking it quite as a matter of course that he had so suddenly caught sight of me. "But don't you *always* want to be happy, Bruno?"

"Not *always*," Bruno said thoughtfully. "Sometimes, when I's *too* happy, I wants to be a little miserable. Then I just tell Sylvie about it, oo know, and Sylvie sets me some lessons. Then it's all right."

"I'm sorry you don't like lessons," I said. "You should copy Sylvie. *She's* always as busy as the day is long!"

"Well, so am *I!*" said Bruno.

"No, no!" Sylvie corrected him. "*You're* as busy as the day is *short!*"

"Well, what's the difference?" Bruno asked. "Mister Sir, isn't the day as short as it's long? I mean, isn't it the *same* length?"

Never having considered the question in this light, I suggested that they had better ask the Professor; and they ran off in a moment to appeal to their old friend. The Professor left off polishing his spectacles to consider. "My dears," he said after a minute, "the day is the same length as anything that is the same length as *it*." And he resumed his never-ending task of polishing.

The children returned, slowly and thoughtfully, to report his answer. "*Isn't* he wise?" Sylvie asked in an awe-struck whisper. "If *I* was as wise as *that*, I should have a headache all day long, I *know* I should!"

"You appear to be talking to somebody—that isn't here," the Professor said, turning round to the children. "Who is it?"

Bruno looked puzzled. "I never talks to nobody when he isn't here!" he replied. "It isn't good manners. Oo should always wait till he comes, before oo talks to him!"

The Professor looked anxiously in my direction, and seemed to look through and through me without seeing me. "Then who are you talking to?" he said. "There isn't anybody here, you know, except the Other Professor— and *he* isn't here!" he added wildly, turning round and round like a teetotum. "Children! Help to look for him! Quick! He's got lost again!"

The children were on their feet in a moment.

"Where shall we look?" said Sylvie.

"Anywhere!" shouted the excited Professor. "Only be quick about it!" And he began trotting round and round the room, lifting up the chairs, and shaking them.

Bruno took a very small book out of the bookcase, opened it, and shook it in imitation of the Professor. "He isn't *here*," he said.

"He *ca'n't* be there, Bruno!" Sylvie said indignantly.

"Course he ca'n't!" said Bruno. "I should have shooked him out, if he'd been in there!"

"Has he ever been lost before?" Sylvie enquired, turning up a corner of the hearth-rug, and peeping under it.

"Once before," said the Professor: "he once lost himself in a wood——"

"And couldn't he find his-self again?" said Bruno. "Why didn't he shout? He'd be sure to hear his-self, 'cause he couldn't be far off, oo know."

"Let's try shouting," said the Professor.

"What shall we shout?" said Sylvie.

"On second thoughts, *don't* shout," the Professor replied. "The Vice-Warden might hear you. He's getting awfully strict!"

This reminded the poor children of all the troubles, about which they had come to their old friend. Bruno sat down on the floor and began crying. "He *is* so cruel!" he sobbed. "And he lets Uggug take away *all* my toys! And such horrid meals!"

"What did you have for dinner to-day?" said the Professor.

"A little piece of a dead crow," was Bruno's mournful reply.

"He means rook-pie," Sylvie explained.

"It *were* a dead crow," Bruno persisted. "And there were a apple-pudding—and Uggug ate it all—and I got nuffin but a crust! And I asked for a orange—and—didn't get it!" And the poor little fellow buried his face in Sylvie's lap, who kept gently stroking his hair, as she went on. "It's all true, Professor dear! They *do* treat my darling Bruno very badly! And they're not kind to *me* either," she added in a lower tone, as if *that* were a thing of much less importance.

The Professor got out a large red silk handkerchief, and

wiped his eyes. "I wish I could help you, dear children!" he said. "But what *can* I do?"

"We know the way to Fairyland—where Father's gone —quite well," said Sylvie: "if only the Gardener would let us out."

"Wo'n't he open the door for you?" said the Professor.

"Not for *us*," said Sylvie: "but I'm sure he would for *you*. Do come and ask him, Professor dear!"

"I'll come this minute!" said the Professor.

Bruno sat up and dried his eyes. "*Isn't* he kind, Mister Sir?"

"He is *indeed*," said I. But the Professor took no notice of my remark. He had put on a beautiful cap with a long tassel, and was selecting one of the Other Professor's walking sticks, from a stand in the corner of the room. "A thick stick in one's hand makes people respectful," he was saying to himself. "Come along, dear children!" And we all went out into the garden together.

"I shall address him, first of all," the Professor explained as we went along, "with a few playful remarks on the weather. I shall then question him about the Other Professor. This will have a double advantage. First, it will open the conversation (you ca'n't even drink a bottle of wine without opening it first): and secondly, if he's seen the Other Professor, we shall find him that way: and, if he hasn't, we sha'n't."

On our way, we passed the target, at which Uggug had been made to shoot during the Ambassador's visit.

"See!" said the Professor, pointing out a hole in the middle of the bull's-eye. "His Imperial Fatness had only *one* shot at it; and he went in just *here!*"

Bruno carefully examined the hole. "Couldn't go in *there*," he whispered to me. "He are too *fat!*"

We had no sort of difficulty in *finding* the Gardener. Though he was hidden from us by some trees, that harsh voice of his served to direct us; and, as we drew nearer, the words of his song became more and more plainly audible:

"He thought he saw an Albatross
That fluttered round the lamp:
He looked again, and found it was
A Penny-Postage-Stamp.
'You'd best be getting home,' he said:
'The nights are very damp!' "

"Would it be afraid of catching cold?" said Bruno.

"If it got *very* damp", Sylvie suggested, "it might stick to something, you know."

"And *that* somefin would have to go by the post, whatever it was!" Bruno eagerly exclaimed. "Suppose it was a cow! Wouldn't it be *dreadful* for the other things!"

"And all these things happened to *him*," said the Professor. "That's what makes the song so interesting."

"He must have had a very curious life," said Sylvie.

"You may say that!" the Professor heartily rejoined.

"Of course she may!" cried Bruno.

By this time we had come up to the Gardener, who was standing on one leg, as usual, and busily employed in watering a bed of flowers with an empty watering-can.

"It hasn't got no water in it!" Bruno explained to him, pulling his sleeve to attract his attention.

"It's lighter to hold," said the Gardener. "A lot of water in it makes one's arms ache." And he went on with his work, singing softly to himself

"The nights are very damp!"

"In digging things out of the ground—which you probably do now and then," the Professor began in a loud voice; "in making things into heaps—which no doubt you often do; and in kicking things about with one heel— which you seem never to leave off doing; have you ever happened to notice another Professor, something like me, but different?"

"Never!" shouted the Gardener, so loudly and violently that we all drew back in alarm. "There ain't such a thing!"

"We will try a less exciting topic," the Professor mildly remarked to the children. "You were asking——"

"We asked him to let us through the garden-door," said Sylvie: "but he wouldn't: but perhaps he would for *you!*"

The Professor put the request, very humbly and courteously.

"I wouldn't mind letting *you* out," said the Gardener. "But I mustn't open the door for *children*. D'you think I'd disobey the *Rules?* Not for one-and-sixpence!"

The Professor cautiously produced a couple of shillings.

"That'll do it!" the Gardener shouted, as he hurled the watering-can across the flower-bed, and produced a handful of keys—one large one, and a number of small ones.

"But look here, Professor dear!" whispered Sylvie. "He needn't open the door for *us*, at all. We can go out with *you*."

"True, dear child!" the Professor thankfully replied, as he replaced the coins in his pocket. "That saves two shillings!" And he took the children's hands, that they might all go out together when the door was opened. This, however, did not seem a very likely event, though the Gardener patiently tried all the small keys, over and over again.

At last the Professor ventured on a gentle suggestion. "Why not try the *large* one? I have often observed that a door unlocks *much* more nicely with its *own* key."

The very first trial of the large key proved a success: the Gardener opened the door, and held out his hand for the money.

The Professor shook his head. "You are acting by *Rule*", he explained, "in opening the door for *me*. And now it's open, we are going out by *Rule*—the Rule of *Three*."

The Gardener looked puzzled, and let us go out; but as he locked the door behind us, we heard him singing thoughtfully to himself:

"He thought he saw a Garden-Door
That opened with a key:
He looked again, and found it was
A Double Rule of Three:
'And all its mystery', he said,
'Is clear as day to me!' "

"I shall now return," said the Professor, when we had walked a few yards: "you see, it's impossible to read *here*, for all my books are in the house."

But the children still kept fast hold of his hands. *"Do* come with us!" Sylvie entreated with tears in her eyes.

"Well, well!" said the good-natured old man. "Perhaps I'll come after you, some day soon. But I *must* go back, *now*. You see I left off at a comma, and it's so awkward not knowing how the sentence finishes! Besides, you've got to go through Dogland first, and I'm always a little nervous about dogs. But it'll be quite easy to come, as soon as I've completed my new invention—for carrying one's-*self*, you know. It wants just a *little* more working out."

"Won't that be very tiring, to carry *yourself?*" Sylvie enquired.

"Well, no, my child. You see, whatever fatigue one incurs by *carrying*, one saves by *being carried!* Good-bye, dears! Good-bye, Sir!" he added to my intense surprise, giving my hand an affectionate squeeze.

"Good-bye, Professor!" I replied, but my voice sounded strange and far away, and the children took not the slightest notice of our farewell. Evidently they neither saw me nor heard me, as, with their arms lovingly twined round each other, they marched boldly on.

Chapter XIII

A Visit to Dogland

"THERE'S a house, away there to the left," said Sylvie after we had walked what seemed to me about fifty miles. "Let's go and ask for a night's lodging."

"It looks a very comfable house," Bruno said, as we turned into the road leading up to it. 'I doos hope the Dogs will be kind to us, I *is* so tired and hungry!"

A Mastiff, dressed in a scarlet collar, and carrying a musket, was pacing up and down, like a sentinel, in front of the entrance. He started, on catching sight of the children, and came forwards to meet them, keeping his musket pointed straight at Bruno, who stood quite still, though he turned pale and kept tight hold of Sylvie's hand, while the Sentinel walked solemnly round and round them, and looked at them from all points of view.

"Oobooh, hooh boohooyah!" he growled at last. "Woobah yahwah oobooh! Bow wahbah woobooyah? Bow wow?" he asked Bruno, severely.

Of course *Bruno* understood all this, easily enough. All Fairies understand Doggee—that is, Dog-language. But, as *you* may find it a little difficult, just at first, I had better put it into English for you. "Humans, I verily believe! A couple of stray Humans! What Dog do you belong to? What do you want?"

"We don't belong to a *Dog!*" Bruno began, in Doggee. ("Peoples *never* belongs to Dogs!" he whispered to Sylvie.)

But Sylvie hastily checked him, for fear of hurting the Mastiff's feelings. "Please, we want a little food, and a night's lodging—if there's room in the house," she added timidly. Sylvie spoke Doggee very prettily: but I think it's almost better, for *you*, to give the conversation in English.

"The *house*, indeed!" growled the Sentinel. "Have you never seen a *Palace* in your life? Come along with me! His Majesty must settle what's to be done with you."

345

They followed him through the entrance-hall, down a long passage, and into a magnificent Saloon, around which were grouped dogs of all sorts and sizes. Two splendid Blood-hounds were solemnly sitting up, one on each side of the crown-bearer. Two or three Bull-dogs— whom I guessed to be the Body-Guard of the King—were waiting in grim silence: in fact the only voices at all plainly audible were those of two little dogs, who had mounted a settee, and were holding a lively discussion that looked very like a quarrel.

"Lords and Ladies in Waiting, and various Court Officials," our guide gruffly remarked, as he led us in. Of *me* the Courtiers took no notice whatever: but Sylvie and Bruno were the subject of many inquisitive looks, and many whispered remarks, of which I only distinctly caught *one*—made by a sly-looking Dachshund to his friend—"Bah wooh wahyah hoobah Oobooh, *hah* bah?" ("She's not such a bad-looking Human, *is* she?")

Leaving the new arrivals in the centre of the Saloon, the Sentinel advanced to a door, at the further end of it, which bore an inscription, painted on it in Doggee, "Royal Kennel—Scratch and Yell."

Before doing this, the Sentinel turned to the children, and said "Give me your names."

"We'd rather not!" Bruno exclaimed, pulling Sylvie away from the door. "We want them ourselves. Come back, Sylvie! Come quick!"

"Nonsense!" said Sylvie very decidedly: and gave their names in Doggee.

Then the Sentinel scratched violently at the door, and gave a yell that made Bruno shiver from head to foot.

"Hooyah wah!" said a deep voice inside. (That's Doggee for "Come in!")

"It's the King himself!" the Mastiff whispered in an awestruck tone. "Take off your wigs, and lay them humbly at his paws." (What *we* should call "at his *feet*".)

Sylvie was just going to explain, very politely, that really they *couldn't* perform *that* ceremony, because their wigs wouldn't come off, when the door of the Royal Kennel opened, and an enormous Newfoundland Dog put his head out. "Bow wow?" was his first question.

"When His Majesty speaks to you", the Sentinel hastily whispered to Bruno, "you should prick up your ears!"

Bruno looked doubtfully at Sylvie. "I'd rather not, please," he said. "It would hurt."

"It doesn't hurt a bit!" the Sentinel said with some indignation. "Look! It's like this!" And he pricked up his ears like two railway signals.

Sylvie gently explained matters. "I'm afraid we ca'n't manage it," she said in a low voice. "I'm very sorry: but our ears haven't got the right——" she wanted to say "machinery" in Doggee: but she had forgotten the word, and could only think of "steam-engine".

The Sentinel repeated Sylvie's explanation to the King.

"Ca'n't prick up their ears without a steam-engine!" His Majesty exclaimed. "They *must* be curious creatures! I must have a look at them!" And he came out of his Kennel, and walked solemnly up to the children.

What was the amazement—not to say the horror—of the whole assembly, when Sylvie actually *patted His Majesty on the head*, while Bruno seized his long ears and pretended to tie them together under his chin!

The Sentinel groaned aloud: a beautiful Greyhound— who appeared to be one of the Ladies in Waiting—fainted away: and all the other Courtiers hastily drew back, and left plenty of room for the huge Newfoundland to spring upon the audacious strangers, and tear them limb from limb.

Only—he didn't. On the contrary His Majesty actually *smiled*—so far as a Dog *can* smile—and (the other Dogs couldn't believe their eyes, but it was true, all the same) His Majesty *wagged his tail!*

"Yah! Hooh hahwooh!" (that is "Well! I never!") was the universal cry.

His Majesty looked round him severely, and gave a slight growl, which produced instant silence. "Conduct *my friends* to the banqueting-hall!" he said, laying such an emphasis on *"my friends"* that several of the dogs rolled over helplessly on their backs and began to lick Bruno's feet.

A procession was formed, but I only ventured to follow as far as the *door* of the banqueting-hall, so furious was the uproar of barking dogs within. So I sat down by the King, who seemed to have gone to sleep, and waited till the children returned to say good-night, when His Majesty got up and shook himself.

"Time for bed!" he said with a sleepy yawn. "The attendants will show you your room," he added, aside, to Sylvie and Bruno. "Bring lights!" And, with a dignified air, he held out his paw for them to kiss.

But the children were evidently not well practised in Court-manners. Sylvie simply stroked the great paw: Bruno hugged it: the Master of Ceremonies looked shocked.

All this time Dog-waiters, in splendid livery, were running up with lighted candles: but, as fast as they put them upon the table, other waiters ran away with them, so that there never seemed to be one for *me*, though the Master kept nudging me with his elbow, and repeating "I ca'n't let you sleep *here!* You're not in *bed*, you know!"

I made a great effort, and just succeeded in getting out the words "I know I'm not. I'm in an arm-chair."

"Well, forty winks will do you no harm," the Master said, and left me. I could scarcely hear his words: and no wonder: he was leaning over the side of a ship, that was miles away from the pier on which I stood. The ship passed over the horizon, and I sank back into the arm-chair.

The next thing I remember is that it was morning: breakfast was just over: Sylvie was lifting Bruno down from a high chair, and saying to a Spaniel, who was regarding them with a most benevolent smile, "Yes, thank you, we've had a *very* nice breakfast. Haven't we, Bruno?"

"There was too many bones in the——" Bruno began, but Sylvie frowned at him, and laid her finger on her lips, for, at this moment, the travelers were waited on by a very dignified officer, the Head-Growler, whose duty it was, first to conduct them to the King to bid him farewell, and then to escort them to the boundary of Dogland. The great Newfoundland received them most affably, but, instead of saying "good-bye", he startled the Head-Growler into giving three savage growls, by announcing that he would escort them himself.

"It is a most unusual proceeding, your Majesty!" the Head-Growler exclaimed, almost choking with vexation at being set aside, for he had put on his best Court-suit, made entirely of cat-skins, for the occasion.

"I shall escort them myself," His Majesty repeated, gently but firmly, laying aside the Royal robes, and changing his crown for a small coronet, "and you may stay at home."

"I *are* glad!" Bruno whispered to Sylvie, when they had got well out of hearing. "He were so *welly* cross!" And he not only patted their Royal escort, but even hugged him round the neck in the exuberance of his delight.

His Majesty calmly wagged the Royal tail. "It's quite a relief", he said, "getting away from that Palace now and then! Royal Dogs have a dull life of it, I can tell you! Would you mind" (this to Sylvie, in a low voice, and looking a little shy and embarrassed) "would you mind the trouble of just throwing that stick for me to fetch?"

Sylvie was too much astonished to do anything for a moment: it sounded such a monstrous impossibility that a *King* should wish to run after a stick. But *Bruno* was equal to the occasion, and with a glad shout of "Hi then! Fetch it, good Doggie!" he hurled it over a clump of bushes. The next moment the Monarch of Dogland had bounded over the bushes, and picked up the stick, and came galloping back to the children with it in his mouth. Bruno took it from him with great decision. "Beg for it"!

he insisted; and His Majesty begged. "Paw!" commanded Sylvie; and His Majesty gave his paw. In short, the solemn ceremony of escorting the travelers to the boundaries of Dogland became one long uproarious game of play!

"But business is business!" the Dog-King said at last. "And I must go back to mine. I couldn't come any further," he added, consulting a dog-watch, which hung on a chain round his neck, "not even if there were a *Cat* in sight!"

They took an affectionate farewell of His Majesty, and trudged on.

"That *were* a dear dog!" Bruno exclaimed. "Has we to go far, Sylvie? I's tired!"

"Not much further, darling!" Sylvie gently replied. "Do you see that shining, just beyond those trees? I'm almost *sure* it's the gate of Fairyland! I know it's all golden—Father told me so—and so bright, so bright!" she went on dreamily.

"It dazzles!" said Bruno, shading his eyes with one little hand, while the other clung tightly to Sylvie's hand, as if he were half-alarmed at her strange manner.

For the child moved on as if walking in her sleep, her large eyes gazing into the far distance, and her breath coming and going in quick pantings of eager delight. I knew, by some mysterious mental light, that a great change was taking place in my sweet little friend (for such I loved to think her) and that she was passing from the condition of a mere Outland Sprite into the true Fairy-nature.

Upon Bruno the change came later: but it was completed in both before they reached the golden gate, through which I knew it would be impossible for *me* to follow. I could but stand outside, and take a last look at the two sweet children, ere they disappeared within, and the golden gate closed with a bang.

And with *such* a bang! "It never *will* shut like any other cupboard-door," Arthur explained. "There's something wrong with the hinge. However, here's the cake and wine. And you've had your forty winks. So you really *must* get off to bed, old man! You're fit for nothing else. Witness my hand, Arthur Forester, M.D."

By this time I was wide-awake again. "Not *quite* yet!" I pleaded. "Really I'm not sleepy now. And it isn't midnight yet."

"Well, I did want to say another word to you," Arthur replied in a relenting tone, as he supplied me with the supper he had prescribed. "Only I thought you were too sleepy for it to-night."

We took our midnight meal almost in silence; for an unusual nervousness seemed to have seized on my old friend.

"What kind of a night is it?" he asked, rising and undrawing the window-curtains, apparently to change the subject for a minute. I followed him to the window, and we stood together, looking out, in silence.

"When I first spoke to you about——" Arthur began, after a long and embarrassing silence, "that is, when we first talked about her—for I think it was *you* that introduced the subject—my own position in life forbade me to do more than worship her from a distance: and I was turning over plans for leaving this place finally, and settling somewhere out of all chance of meeting her again. That seemed to be my only chance of usefulness in life."

"Would that have been wise?" I said. "To leave yourself no hope at all?"

"There *was* no hope to leave," Arthur firmly replied, though his eyes glittered with tears as he gazed upwards into the midnight sky, from which one solitary star, the glorious "Vega", blazed out in fitful splendour through the driving clouds. "She was like that star to me—bright, beautiful, and pure, but out of reach, out of reach!"

He drew the curtains again, and we returned to our places by the fireside.

"What I wanted to tell you was this," he resumed. "I heard this evening from my solicitor. I can't go into the details of the business, but the upshot is that my worldly wealth is much more than I thought, and I am (or shall soon be) in a position to offer marriage, without imprudence, to any lady, even if she brought nothing, I doubt if there would be anything on *her* side: the Earl is poor, I believe. But I should have enough for both, even if health failed."

"I wish you all happiness in your married life!" I cried. "Shall you speak to the Earl to-morrow?"

"Not yet awhile," said Arthur. "He is very friendly, but I dare not think he means more than that, as yet. And as for—as for Lady Muriel, try as I may, I *cannot* read her feelings towards me. If there *is* love, she is hiding it! No, I must wait, I must wait!"

I did not like to press any further advice on my friend, whose judgment, I felt, was so much more sober and thoughtful than my own; and we parted without more words on the subject that had now absorbed his thoughts, nay, his very life.

The next morning a letter from *my* solicitor arrived, summoning me to town on important business.

Chapter XIV

Fairy-Sylvie

FOR a full month the business, for which I had returned to London, detained me there: and even then it was only the urgent advice of my physician that induced me to leave it unfinished and pay another visit to Elveston.

Arthur had written once or twice during the month; but in none of his letters was there any mention of Lady Muriel. Still, I did not augur ill from his silence: to me it looked like the natural action of a lover, who, even while his heart was singing "She is mine", would fear to paint his happiness in the cold phrases of a written letter, but would wait to tell it by word of mouth. "Yes," I thought, "I am to hear his song of triumph from his own lips!"

The night I arrived we had much to say on other matters: and, tired with the journey, I went to bed early, leaving the happy secret still untold. Next day, however, as we chatted on over the remains of luncheon, I ventured to put the momentous question. "Well, old friend, you have told me nothing of Lady Muriel—nor when the happy day is to be?"

"The happy day", Arthur said, looking unexpectedly grave, "is yet in the dim future. We need to know—or, rather, *she* needs to know *me* better. I know *her* sweet nature, thoroughly, by this time. But I dare not speak till I am sure that my love is returned."

"Don't wait too long!" I said gaily. "Faint heart never won fair lady!"

"It *is* 'faint heart' perhaps. But really I *dare* not speak just yet."

"But meanwhile", I pleaded, "you are running a risk that perhaps you have not thought of. Some other man——"

"No," said Arthur firmly. "She is heart-whole: I am sure of that. Yet, if she loves another better than me, so be it! I will not spoil her happiness. The secret shall die with me. But she is my first—and my *only* love!"

"That is all very beautiful *sentiment*," I said, "but it is not *practical*. It is not like *you*.

> *He either fears his fate too much*
> *Or his desert is small,*
> *Who dares not put it to the touch,*
> *To win or lose it all.*"

"I *dare* not ask the question whether there is another!" he said passionately. "It would break my heart to know it!"

"Yet is it wise to leave it unasked? You must not waste your life upon an 'if'!"

"I tell you I *dare* not!"

"May *I* find it out for you?" I asked, with the freedom of an old friend.

"No, no!" he replied with a pained look. "I entreat you to say nothing. Let it wait."

"As you please," I said: and judged it best to say no more just then. "But this evening", I thought, "I will call on the Earl. I may be able to *see* how the land lies, without so much as saying a word!"

It was a very hot afternoon—too hot to go for a walk or do anything—or else it wouldn't have happened, I believe.

In the first place, I want to know—dear Child who reads this!—why Fairies should always be teaching *us* to do our duty, and lecturing *us* when we go wrong, and we should never teach them anything? You can't mean to say that Fairies are never greedy, or selfish, or cross, or deceitful, because that would be nonsense, you know. Well then, don't you think they might be all the better for a little lecturing and punishing now and then?

I really don't see why it shouldn't be tried, and I'm almost sure that, if you could only catch a Fairy, and put it in the corner, and give it nothing but bread and water for a day or two, you'd find it quite an improved character —it would take down its conceit a little, at all events.

The next question is, what is the best time for seeing Fairies? I believe I can tell you all about that.

The first rule is, that it must be a *very* hot day—that we may consider as settled: and you must be just a *little* sleepy—but not too sleepy to keep your eyes open, mind. Well, and you ought to feel a little—what one may call "fairyish"—the Scotch call it "eerie", and perhaps that's a prettier word; if you don't know what it means, I'm afraid I can hardly explain it; you must wait till you meet a Fairy, and then you'll know.

And the last rule is, that the crickets should not be chirping. I can't stop to explain that: you must take it on trust for the present.

So, if all these things happen together, you have a good chance of seeing a Fairy—or at least a much better chance than if they didn't.

The first thing I noticed, as I went lazily along through an open place in the wood, was a large Beetle lying struggling on its back, and I went down upon one knee to help the poor thing to its feet again. In some things, you know, you ca'n't be quite sure what an insect would like: for instance, I never could quite settle, supposing I were a moth, whether I would rather be kept out of the candle, or be allowed to fly straight in and get burnt—or again, supposing I were a spider, I'm not sure if I should be *quite* pleased to have my web torn down, and the fly let loose— but I feel quite certain that, if I were a beetle and had rolled over on my back, I should always be glad to be helped up again.

So, as I was saying, I had gone down upon one knee and was just reaching out a little stick to turn the Beetle over, when I saw a sight that made me draw back hastily and hold my breath, for fear of making any noise and frightening the little creature away.

Not that she looked as if she would be easily frightened: she seemed so good and gentle that I'm sure she would never expect that any one could wish to hurt her. She was only a few inches high, and was dressed in green, so that you really would hardly have noticed her among the long grass; and she was so delicate and graceful that she quite seemed to belong to the place, almost as if she were one of the flowers. I may tell you, besides, that she had no wings (I don't believe in Fairies with wings), and that she had quantities of long brown hair and large earnest brown eyes, and then I shall have done all I can to give you an idea of her.

Sylvie (I found out her name afterwards) had knelt down, just as I was doing, to help the Beetle; but it needed more than a little stick for *her* to get it on its legs again; it was as much as she could do, with both arms, to roll the heavy thing over; and all the while she was talk-

ing to it, half scolding and half comforting, as a nurse
might do with a child that had fallen down.

"There, there! You needn't cry so much about it.
You're not killed yet—though if you were, you couldn't
cry, you know, and so it's a general rule against crying,
my dear! And how did you come to tumble over? But I
can see well enough how it was—I needn't ask you that—
walking over sand-pits with your chin in the air, as usual.
Of course if you go among sand-pits like that, you must
expect to tumble. You should look."

The Beetle murmured something that sounded like "I
did look," and Sylvie went on again.

"But I know you didn't! You never do! You always
walk with your chin up—you're so dreadfully conceited.
Well, let's see how many legs are broken this time. Why,
none of them, I declare! And what's the good of having
six legs, my dear, if you can only kick them all about in
the air when you tumble? Legs are meant to walk with,
you know. Now don't begin putting out your wings yet;
I've more to say. Go to the frog that lives behind that
buttercup—give him my compliments—Sylvie's compliments—can you say 'compliments'?"

The Beetle tried, and, I suppose, succeeded.

"Yes, that's right. And tell him he's to give you some of
that salve I left with him yesterday. And you'd better get
him to rub it in for you. He's got rather cold hands, but
you mustn't mind that."

I think the Beetle must have shuddered at this idea, for
Sylvie went on in a graver tone. "Now you needn't pretend to be so particular as all that, as if you were too
grand to be rubbed by a frog. The fact is, you ought to be
very much obliged to him. Suppose you could get nobody
but a toad to do it, how would you like *that?*"

There was a little pause, and then Sylvie added "Now
you may go. Be a good beetle, and don't keep your chin
in the air." And then began one of those performances of
humming, and whizzing, and restless banging about, such
as a beetle indulges in when it has decided to flying, bun

hasn't quite made up its mind which way to go. At last, in one of its awkward zig-zags, it managed to fly right into my face, and, by the time I had recovered from the shock, the little Fairy was gone.

I looked about in all directions for the little creature, but there was no trace of her—and my "eerie" feeling was quite gone off, and the crickets were chirping again merrily—so I knew she was really gone.

And now I've got time to tell you the rule about the crickets. They always leave off chirping when a Fairy goes by—because a Fairy's a kind of queen over them, I suppose—at all events it's a much grander thing than a cricket—so whenever you're walking out, and the crickets suddenly leave off chirping, you may be sure that they see a Fairy.

I walked on sadly enough, you may be sure. However, I comforted myself with thinking "It's been a very wonderful afternoon, so far. I'll just go quietly on and look about me, and I shouldn't wonder if I were to come across another Fairy somewhere."

Peering about in this way, I happened to notice a plant with rounded leaves, and with queer little holes cut in the middle of several of them. "Ah, the leafcutter bee! ' I carelessly remarked—you know I am very learned in Natural History (for instance, I can always tell kittens from chickens at one glance)—and I was passing on, when a sudden thought made me stoop down and examine the leaves.

Then a little thrill of delight ran through me—for I noticed that the holes were all arranged so as to form letters; there were three leaves side by side, with "B", "R", and "U" marked on them, and after some search I found two more, which contained an "N" and an "O".

And then, all in a moment, a flash of inner light seemed to illumine a part of my life that had all but faded into oblivion—the strange visions I had experienced during my journey to Elveston: and with a thrill of delight I thought "Those visions are destined to be linked with my waking life!"

By this time the "eerie" feeling had come back again, and I suddenly observed that no crickets were chirping, so I felt quite sure that "Bruno" was somewhere very near.

And so indeed he was—so near that I had very nearly walked over him without seeing him; which would have been dreadful, always supposing that Fairies *can* be walked over—my own belief is that they are something of the nature of Will-o'-the-Wisps: and there's no walking over *them.*

Think of any pretty little boy you know, with rosy cheeks, large dark eyes, and tangled brown hair, and then fancy him made small enough to go comfortably into a coffee-cup, and you'll have a very fair idea of him.

"What's you name, little one?" I began, in as soft a voice as I could manage. And, by the way, why is it we always begin by asking little children their names? Is it because we fancy a name will help to make them a little bigger? You never thought of asking a real large man his name, now, did you? But, however that may be, I felt it quite necessary to know *his* name; so, as he didn't answer my question, I asked it again a little louder. "What's your name, my little man?"

"What's oors?" he said, without looking up.

I told him my name quite gently, for he was much too small to be angry with.

"Duke of Anything?" he asked, just looking at me for a moment, and then going on with his work.

"Not Duke at all," I said, a little ashamed of having to confess it.

"Oo're big enough to be two Dukes," said the little creature. "I suppose oo're Sir Something, then?"

"No," I said, feeling more and more ashamed. "I haven't got any title."

The Fairy seemed to think that in that case I really wasn't worth the trouble of talking to, for he quietly went on digging, and tearing the flowers to pieces.

After a few minutes I tried again. "*Please* tell me what your name is."

"Bruno," the little fellow answered, very readily. "Why didn't oo say 'please' before?"

"That's something like what we used to be taught in the nursery," I thought to myself, looking back through the long years (about a hundred of them, since you ask the question), to the time when I was a little child. And here an idea came into my head, and I asked him "Aren't you one of the Fairies that teach children to be good?"

"Well, we have to do that sometimes," said Bruno, "and a dreadful bother it is." As he said this, he savagely tore a heartsease in two, and trampled on the pieces.

"What *are* you doing there, Bruno?" I said.

"Spoiling Sylvie's garden," was all the answer Bruno would give at first. But, as he went on tearing up the flowers, he muttered to himself "The nasty cross thing—wouldn't let me go and play this morning—said I must finish my lessons first—lessons, indeed! I'll vex her finely, though!"

"Oh, Bruno, you shouldn't do that!" I cried. "Don't you know that's revenge? And revenge is a wicked, cruel, dangerous thing!"

"River-edge?" said Bruno. "What a funny word! I suppose oo call it cruel and dangerous 'cause, if oo wented too far and tumbleded in, oo'd get drownded."

"No, not river-edge," I explained: "revenge" (saying the word very slowly). But I couldn't help thinking that Bruno's explanation did very well for either word.

"Oh!" said Bruno, opening his eyes very wide, but without trying to repeat the word.

"Come! Try to pronounce it, Bruno!" I said, cheerfully. "Re-venge, re-venge."

But Bruno only tossed his little head, and said he couldn't; that his mouth wasn't the right shape for words of that kind. And the more I laughed, the more sulky the little fellow got about it.

"Well, never mind, my little man!" I said. "Shall I help you with that job?"

"Yes, please," Bruno said, quite pacified. "Only I wiss I could think of somefin to vex her more than this. Oo don't know how hard it is to make her angry!"

"Now listen to me, Bruno, and I'll teach you quite a splendid kind of revenge!"

"Somefin that'll vex her finely?" he asked with gleaming eyes.

"Something that will vex her finely. First, we'll get up all the weeds in her garden. See, there are a good many at this end—quite hiding the flowers."

"But *that* won't vex her!" said Bruno.

"After that", I said, without noticing the remark, "we'll water this highest bed—up here. You see it's getting quite dry and dusty."

Bruno looked at me inquisitively, but he said nothing this time.

"Then after that," I went on, "the walks want sweeping a bit; and I think you might cut down that tall nettle —it's so close to the garden that it's quite in the way——"

"What *is* oo talking about?" Bruno impatiently interrupted me. "All that won't vex her a bit!"

"Won't it?" I said, innocently. "Then, after that, suppose we put in some of those coloured pebbles—just to mark the divisions between the different kinds of flowers, you know. That'll have a very pretty effect."

Bruno turned round and had another good stare at me. At last there came an odd little twinkle into his eyes, and he said, with quite a new meaning in his voice, "That'll do nicely. Let's put 'em in rows—all the red together, and all the blue together."

"That'll do capitally," I said; "and then—what kind of flowers does Sylvie like best?"

Bruno had to put his thumb in his mouth and consider a little before he could answer. "Violets," he said, at last.

"There's a beautiful bed of violets down by the brook——"

"Oh, let's fetch 'em!" cried Bruno, giving a little skip into the air. "Here! Catch hold of my hand, and I'll help oo along. The grass is rather thick down that way."

I couldn't help laughing at his having so entirely forgotten what a big creature he was talking to. "No, not yet, Bruno," I said: "we must consider what's the right thing to do first. You see we've got quite a business before us."

"Yes, let's consider," said Bruno, putting his thumb into his mouth again, and sitting down upon a dead mouse.

"What do you keep that mouse for?" I said. "You should either bury it, or else throw it into the brook."

"Why, it's to measure with!" cried Bruno. "How ever would oo do a garden without one? We make each bed three mouses and a half long, and two mouses wide."

I stopped him, as he was dragging it off by the tail to show me how it was used, for I was half afraid the "eerie" feeling might go off before we had finished the garden, and in that case I should see no more of him or Sylvie. "I think the best way will be for *you* to weed the beds, while *I* sort out these pebbles, ready to mark the walks with."

"That's it!" cried Bruno. "And I'll tell oo about the caterpillars while we work."

"Ah, let's hear about the caterpillars," I said as I drew the pebbles together into a heap and began dividing them into colours.

And Bruno went on in a low, rapid tone, more as if he were talking to himself. "Yesterday I saw two little caterpillars, when I was sitting by the brook, just where oo go into the wood. They were quite green, and they had yellow eyes, and they didn't see *me*. And one of them had got a moth's wing to carry—a great brown moth's wing, oo know, all dry, with feathers. So he couldn't want it to eat, I should think—perhaps he meant to make a cloak for the winter?"

"Perhaps," I said, for Bruno had twisted up the last word into a sort of question, and was looking at me for an answer.

One word was quite enough for the little fellow, and he went on merrily. "Well, and so he didn't want the other caterpillar to see the moth's wing, oo know—so what must he do but try to carry it with all his left legs, and he tried to walk on the other set. Of course he toppled over after that."

"After what?" I said, catching at the last word, for, to tell the truth, I hadn't been attending much.

"He toppled over," Bruno repeated, very gravely, "and if *oo* ever saw a caterpillar topple over, oo'd know it's a welly serious thing, and not sit grinning like that—and I sha'n't tell oo no more!"

"Indeed and indeed, Bruno, I didn't mean to grin. See, I'm quite grave again now."

But Bruno only folded his arms, and said "Don't tell *me*. I see a little twinkle in one of oor eyes—just like the moon."

"Why do you think I'm like the moon, Bruno?" I asked.

"Oor face is large and round like the moon," Bruno answered, looking at me thoughtfully. "It doesn't shine quite so bright—but it's more cleaner."

I couldn't help smiling at this. "You know I sometimes wash *my* face, Bruno. The moon never does that."

"Oh, doosn't she though!" cried Bruno; and he leant forwards and added in a solemn whisper, "The moon's face gets dirtier and dirtier every night, till it's black all across. And then, when it's dirty all over—*so*—" (he passed his hand across his own rosy cheeks as he spoke) "then she washes it."

"Then it's all clean again, isn't it?"

"Not all in a moment," said Bruno. "What a deal of teaching oo wants! She washes it little by little—only she begins at the other edge, oo know.

By this time he was sitting quietly on the dead mouse with his arms folded, and the weeding wasn't getting on a bit: so I had to say "Work first, pleasure afterwards: no more talking till that bed's finished."

Chapter XV

Bruno's Revenge

AFTER that we had a few minutes of silence, while I sorted out the pebbles, and amused myself with watching Bruno's plan of gardening. It was quite a new plan to me: he always measured each bed before he weeded it, as if he was afraid the weeding would make it shrink; and once, when it came out longer than he wished, he set to work to thump the mouse with his little fist, crying out "There now! It's all gone wrong again! Why don't oo keep oor tail straight when I tell oo!"

"I'll tell oo what I'll do," Bruno said in a half-whisper, as we worked. "Oo like Fairies, don't oo?"

"Yes," I said: "of course I do, or I shouldn't have come here. I should have gone to some place where there are no Fairies."

Bruno laughed contemptuously. "Why, oo might as well say oo'd go to some place where there wasn't any air —supposing oo didn't like air!"

This was a rather difficult idea to grasp. I tried a change of subject. "You're nearly the first Fairy I ever saw. Have *you* ever seen any people besides me?"

"Plenty!" said Bruno. "We see 'em when we walk in the road."

"But they ca'n't see *you*. How is it they never tread on you?"

"Ca'n't *tread* on us," said Bruno, looking amused at my ignorance. "Why, suppose oo're walking, here—so—" (making little marks on the ground) "and suppose there's a Fairy—that's me—walking *here*. Very well then, oo put one foot here, and one foot here, and so oo doesn't tread on the Fairy."

This was all very well as an explanation, but it didn't convince me. "Why shouldn't I put one foot *on* the Fairy?" I asked.

"I don't know *why*," the little fellow said in a thoughtful tone. "But I know oo *wouldn't*. Nobody never walked on the top of a Fairy. Now I'll tell oo what I'll do, as oo're so fond of Fairies. I'll get oo an invitation to the Fairy-King's dinner-party. I know one of the head-waiters."

I couldn't help laughing at this idea. "Do the waiters invite the guests?" I asked.

"Oh, not *to sit down!*" Bruno said. "But to wait at table. Oo'd like that, wouldn't oo? To hand about plates, and so on."

"Well, but that's not so nice as sitting at the table, is it?"

"Of course it isn't," Bruno said, in a tone as if he rather pitied my ignorance; "but if oo're not even Sir Anything, oo ca'n't expect to be allowed to sit at the table, oo know."

I said, as meekly as I could, that I didn't expect it, but it was the only way of going to a dinner-party that I really enjoyed. And Bruno tossed his head, and said, in a rather offended tone, that I might do as I pleased—there were many he knew that would give their ears to go.

"Have you ever been yourself, Bruno?"

"They invited me once, last week," Bruno said, very gravely. "It was to wash up the soup-plates—no, the cheese-plates I mean—that was grand enough. And I waited at table. And I didn't hardly make only *one* mistake."

"What was it?" I said. "You needn't mind telling *me*."

"Only bringing scissors to cut the beef with," Bruno said carelessly. "But the grandest thing of all was, *I* fetched the King a glass of cider!"

"That *was* grand!" I said, biting my lip to keep myself from laughing.

"Wasn't it?" said Bruno, very earnestly. "Oo know it isn't every one that's had such an honour as *that!*"

This set me thinking of the various queer things we call "an honour" in this world, but which, after all, haven't a bit more honour in them than what Bruno enjoyed, when he took the King a glass of cider.

I don't know how long I might not have dreamed on in this way, if Bruno hadn't suddenly roused me. "Oh, come here quick!" he cried, in a state of the wildest excitement. "Catch hold of his other horn! I ca'n't hold him more than a minute!"

He was struggling desperately with a great snail, clinging to one of its horns, and nearly breaking his poor little back in his efforts to drag it over a blade of grass.

I saw we should have no more gardening if I let this sort of thing go on, so I quietly took the snail away, and put it on a bank where he couldn't reach it. "We'll hunt it afterwards, Bruno," I said, "if you really want to catch it. But what's the use of it when you've got it?"

"What's the use of a fox when oo've got it?" said Bruno. "I know oo big things hunt foxes."

I tried to think of some good reason why "big things" should hunt foxes, and he should not hunt snails, but none came into my head: so I said at last, "Well, I suppose one's as good as the other. I'll go snail-hunting myself some day."

"I should think oo wouldn't be so silly", said Bruno, "as to go snail-hunting by oorself. Why, oo'd never get the snail along, if oo hadn't somebody to hold on to his other horn!"

"Of course I sha'n't go *alone*," I said, quite gravely. "By the way, is that the best kind to hunt, or do you recommend the ones without shells?"

"Oh, no, we never hunt the ones without shells," Bruno said, with a little shudder at the thought of it. "They're always so cross about it; and then, if oo tumbles over them, they're ever so sticky!"

By this time we had nearly finished the garden. I had fetched some violets, and Bruno was just helping me to put in the last, when he suddenly stopped and said "I'm tired."

"Rest then," I said: "I can go on without you, quite well."

Bruno needed no second invitation: he at once began

arranging the dead mouse as a kind of sofa. "And I'll sing oo a little song," he said, as he rolled it about.

"Do," said I: "I like songs very much."

"Which song will oo choose?" Bruno said, as he dragged the mouse into a place where he could get a good view of me. " 'Ting, ting, ting' is the nicest."

There was no resisting such a strong hint as this: however, I pretended to think about it for a moment, and then said "Well, I like 'Ting, ting, ting' best of all."

"That shows oo're a good judge of music," Bruno said, with a pleased look. "How many hare-bells would oo like?" And he put his thumb into his mouth to help me to consider.

As there was only one cluster of hare-bells within easy reach, I said very gravely that I thought one would do *this* time, and I picked it and gave it to him. Bruno ran his hand once or twice up and down the flowers, like a musician trying an instrument, producing a most delicious delicate tinkling as he did so. I had never heard flower-music before—I don't think one can, unless one's in the "eerie" state—and I don't know quite how to give you an idea of what it was like, except by saying that it sounded like a peal of bells a thousand miles off. When he had satisfied himself that the flowers were in tune, he seated himself on the dead mouse (he never seemed really comfortable anywhere else), and, looking up at me with a merry twinkle in his eyes, he began. By the way, the tune was rather a curious one, and you might like to try it yourself, so here are the notes.

> *"Rise, oh, rise! The daylight dies:*
> *The owls are hooting, ting, ting, ting!*
> *Wake, oh, wake! Beside the lake*
> *The elves are fluting, ting, ting, ting!*
> *Welcoming our Fairy King,*
> *We sing, sing, sing."*

He sang the first four lines briskly and merrily, making the hare-bells chime in time with the music; but the last two he sang quite slowly and gently, and merely waved the flowers backwards and forwards. Then he left off to explain. "The Fairy-King is Oberon, and he lives across the lake—and sometimes he comes in a little boat—and we go and meet him—and then we sing this song, you know."

"And then you go and dine with him?" I said, mischievously.

"Oo shouldn't talk," Bruno hastily said: "it interrupts the song so."

I said I wouldn't do it again.

"I never talk myself when I'm singing," he went on very gravely: "so *oo* shouldn't either." Then he tuned the hare-bells once more, and sang:

> *"Hear, oh, hear! From far and near*
> *The music stealing, ting, ting, ting!*
> *Fairy bells adown the dells*
> *Are merrily pealing, ting, ting, ting!*
> *Welcoming our Fairy King,*
> *We ring, ring, ring.*
>
> *"See, oh, see! On every tree*
> *What lamps are shining, ting, ting, ting!*
> *They are eyes of fiery flies*
> *To light our dining, ting, ting, ting!*
> *Welcoming our Fairy King*
> *They swing, swing, swing.*
>
> *"Haste, oh, haste, to take and taste*
> *The dainties waiting, ting, ting, ting!*
> *Honey-dew is stored ——"*

"Hush, Bruno!" I interrupted in a warning whisper. "She's coming!"

Bruno checked his song, and, as she slowly made her way through the long grass, he suddenly rushed out headlong at her like a little bull, shouting "Look the other way! Look the other way!"

"Which way?" Sylvie asked, in rather a frightened tone, as she looked round in all directions to see where the danger could be.

"*That* way!" said Bruno, carefully turning her round with her face to the wood. "Now, walk backwards—walk gently—don't be frightened: oo sha'n't trip!"

But Sylvie *did* trip notwithstanding: in fact he led her, in his hurry, across so many little sticks and stones, that it was really a wonder the poor child could keep on her feet at all. But he was far too much excited to think of what he was doing.

I silently pointed out to Bruno the best place to lead her to, so as to get a view of the whole garden at once: it was a little rising ground, about the height of a potato; and, when they had mounted it, I drew back into the shade, that Sylvie mightn't see me.

I heard Bruno cry out triumphantly "*Now* oo may look!" and then followed a clapping of hands, but it was all done by Bruno himself. Sylvie was silent—she only stood and gazed with her hands clasped together, and I was half afraid she didn't like it after all.

Bruno too was watching her anxiously, and when she jumped down off the mound, and began wandering up and down the little walks, he cautiously followed her about, evidently anxious that she should form her own opinion of it all, without any hint from him. And when at last she drew a long breath, and gave her verdict—in a hurried whisper, and without the slightest regard to grammar—"It's the loveliest thing as I never saw in all my life before!" the little fellow looked as well pleased as if it had been given by all the judges and juries in England put together.

"And did you really do it all by yourself, Bruno?" said Sylvie. "And all for me?"

"I was helped a bit," Bruno began, with a merry little laugh at her surprise. "We've been at it all the afternoon —I thought oo'd like——" and here the poor little fellow's lip began to quiver, and all in a moment he burst out crying, and running up to Sylvie he flung his arms passionately round her neck, and hid his face on her shoulder.

There was a little quiver in Sylvie's voice too, as she whispered "Why, what's the matter, darling?" and tried to lift up his head and kiss him.

But Bruno only clung to her, sobbing, and wouldn't be comforted till he had confessed. "I tried—to spoil oor garden—first—but I'll never—never——" and then came another burst of tears, which drowned the rest of the sentence. At last he got out the words "I liked—putting in the flowers—for *oo*, Sylvie—and I never was so happy before." And the rosy little face came up at last to be kissed, all wet with tears as it was.

Sylvie was crying too by this time, and she said nothing but "Bruno, dear!" and "*I* never was so happy before," though why these two children who had never been so happy before should both be crying was a mystery to *me*.

I felt very happy too, but of course I didn't cry: "big things" never do, you know—we leave all that to the Fairies. Only I think it must have been raining a little just then, for I found a drop or two on my cheeks.

After that they went through the whole garden again, flower by flower, as if it were a long sentence they were spelling out, with kisses for commas, and a great hug by way of a full-stop when they got to the end.

"Doos oo know, that was my river-edge, Sylvie?" Bruno solemnly began.

Sylvie laughed merrily. "What *do* you mean?" she said. And she pushed back her heavy brown hair with both hands, and looked at him with dancing eyes in which the big tear-drops were still glittering.

Bruno drew in a long breath, and made up his mouth for

a great effort. "I mean re—venge," he said: "now oo under'tand." And he looked so happy and proud at having said the word right at last, that I quite envied him. I rather think Sylvie didn't "under'tand" at all; but she gave him a little kiss on each cheek, which seemed to do just as well.

So they wandered off lovingly together, in among the buttercups, each with an arm twined round the other, whispering and laughing as they went, and never so much as once looked back at poor me. Yes, once, just before I quite lost sight of them, Bruno half turned his head, and nodded me a saucy little good-bye over one shoulder. And that was all the thanks I got for *my* trouble. The very last thing I saw of them was this—Sylvie was stooping down with her arms round Bruno's neck, and saying coaxingly in his ear, "Do you know, Bruno, I've quite forgotten that hard word. Do say it once more. Come! Only this once, dear!"

But Bruno wouldn't try it again.

Chapter XVI

A Changed Crocodile

The Marvellous—the Mysterious—had quite passed out of my life for the moment: and the Common-place reigned supreme. I turned in the direction of the Earl's house, as it was now "the witching hour" of five, and I knew I should find them ready for a cup of tea and a quiet chat.

Lady Muriel and her father gave me a delightfully warm welcome. They were not of the folk we meet in fashionable drawing-rooms—who conceal all such feelings as they may chance to possess beneath the impenetrable mask of a conventional placidity. "The Man with the Iron Mask" was, no doubt, a rarity and a marvel in his own age: in modern London no one would turn his head to give him a second look! No, these were *real* people.

When they *looked* pleased, it meant that they *were* pleased: and when Lady Muriel said, with a bright smile, "I'm *very* glad to see you again!" I knew that it was *true*.

Still I did not venture to disobey the injunctions—crazy as I felt them to be—of the love-sick young Doctor, by so much as alluding to his existence: and it was only after they had given me full details of a projected Picnic, to which they invited me, that Lady Muriel exclaimed, almost as an after-thought, "and *do*, if you can, bring Doctor Forester with you! I'm sure a day in the country would do him good. I'm afraid he studies too much——"

It was "on the tip of my tongue" to quote the words "His only books are woman's looks!" but I checked myself just in time—with something of the feeling of one who has crossed a street, and has been all but run over by a passing "Hansom".

"—and I think he has too lonely a life," she went on, with a gentle earnestness that left no room whatever to suspect a double meaning. "*Do* get him to come! And don't forget the day, Tuesday week. We can drive you over. It would be a pity to go by rail—there is so much pretty scenery on the road. And our open carriage just holds four."

"Oh, *I'll* persuade him to come!" I said with confidence —thinking "it would take all *my* powers of persuasion to keep him away!"

The Picnic was to take place in ten days: and though Arthur readily accepted the invitation I brought him, nothing that I could say would induce him to call—either with me or without me—on the Earl and his daughter in the meanwhile. No: he feared to "wear out his welcome", he said: they had "seen enough of him for one while": and, when at last the day for the expedition arrived, he was so childishly nervous and uneasy that I thought it best so to arrange our plans that we should go separately to the house—my intention being to arrive some time after him, so as to give him time to get over a meeting.

With this object I purposely made a considerable circuit

on my way to the Hall (as we called the Earl's house): "and if I could only manage to lose my way a bit," I thought to myself, "that would suit me capitally!"

In this I succeeded better, and sooner, than I had ventured to hope for. The path through the wood had been made familiar to me, by many a solitary stroll, in my former visit to Elveston; and how I could have so suddenly and so entirely lost it—even though I *was* so engrossed in thinking of Arthur and his lady-love that I heeded little else—was a mystery to me. "And this open place", I said to myself, "seems to have some memory about it I cannot distinctly recall—surely it is the very spot where I saw those Fairy-Children! But I hope there are no snakes about!" I mused aloud, taking my seat on a fallen tree. "I certainly do *not* like snakes—and I don't suppose *Bruno* likes them, either!"

"No, he *doesn't* like them!" said a demure little voice at my side. "He's not *afraid* of them, you know. But he doesn't *like* them. He says they're too waggly!"

Words fail me to describe the beauty of the little group —couched on a patch of moss, on the trunk of the fallen tree, that met my eager gaze: Sylvie reclining with her elbow buried in the moss, and her rosy cheek resting in the palm of her hand, and Bruno stretched at her feet with his head in her lap.

"Too waggly?" was all I could say in so sudden an emergency.

"I'm not particular," Bruno said carelessly: "but I *do* like straight animals best——"

"But you like a dog when it wags its tail," Sylvie interrupted. "You *know* you do, Bruno!"

"But there's more of a dog, isn't there, Mister Sir?" Bruno appealed to me. "*You* wouldn't like to have a dog if it hadn't got nuffin but a head and a tail?"

I admitted that a dog of that kind would be uninteresting.

"There *isn't* such a dog as that," Sylvie thoughtfully remarked.

"But there *would* be," cried Bruno, "if the Professor shortened it up for us!"

"Shortened it up?" I said. "That's something new. How does he do it?"

"He's got a curious machine——" Sylvie was beginning to explain.

"A *welly* curious machine," Bruno broke in, not at all willing to have the story thus taken out of his mouth, "and if oo puts in—somefinoruvver—at *one* end, oo know —and he turns the handle—and it comes out at the uvver end, oh, ever so short!"

"As short as short!" Sylvie echoed.

"And one day—when we was in Outland, oo know— before we came to Fairyland—me and Sylvie took him a big Crocodile. And he shortened it up for us. And it *did* look so funny! And it kept looking round, and saying 'wherever *is* the rest of me got to?' And then its eyes looked unhappy——"

"Not *both* its eyes," Sylvie interrupted.

"Course not!" said the little fellow. "Only the eye that *couldn't* see wherever the rest of it had got to. But the eye that *could* see wherever——"

"How short *was* the Crocodile?" I asked, as the story was getting a little complicated.

"Half as short again as when we caught it—*so* long," said Bruno, spreading out his arms to their full stretch.

I tried to calculate what this would come to, but it was too hard for me. Please make it out for me, dear Child who reads this!

"But you didn't leave the poor thing so short as that, did you?"

"Well, no. Sylvie and me took it back again and we got it stretched to—to—how much was it, Sylvie?"

"Two times and a half, and a little bit more," said Sylvie.

"It wouldn't like that better than the other way, I'm afraid?"

"Oh, but it did though!" Bruno put in eagerly. "It *were*

proud of its new tail! Oo never saw a Crocodile so proud! Why it could go round and walk on the top of its tail, and along its back, all the way to its head!"

"Not *quite* all the way," said Sylvie. "It couldn't, you know."

"Ah, but it *did*, once!" Bruno cried triumphantly. "Oo weren't looking—but *I* watched it. And it walked on tipplety-toe, so as it wouldn't wake itself, 'cause it thought it were asleep. And it got both its paws on its tail. And it walked and it walked all the way along its back. And it walked and it walked on its forehead. And it walked a tiny little way down its nose! There now!"

This was a good deal worse than the last puzzle. Please, dear Child, help again!

"I don't believe no Crocodile never walked along its own forehead!" Sylvie cried, too much excited by the controversy to limit the number of her negatives.

"Oo don't know the *reason* why it did it!" Bruno scornfully retorted. "It had a welly good reason. I *heard* it say 'Why *shouldn't* I walk on my own forehead?' So a course it *did*, oo know!"

"If *that's* a good reason, Bruno," I said, "why shouldn't *you* get up that tree?"

"*Shall*, in a minute," said Bruno: "soon as we've done talking. Only two peoples *ca'n't* talk comfably togevver, when one's getting up a tree, and the other isn't!"

It appeared to me that a conversation would scarcely be "comfable" while trees were being climbed, even if *both* the "peoples" were doing it: but it was evidently dangerous to oppose any theory of Bruno's; so I thought it best to let the question drop, and to ask for an account of the machine that made things *longer*.

This time Bruno was at a loss, and left it to Sylvie. "It's like a mangle," she said: "if things are put in, they get squoze——"

"Squeezeled!" Bruno interrupted.

"Yes." Sylvie accepted the correction, but did not attempt to pronounce the word, which was evidently new to her. "They get—like that—and they come out, oh, ever so long!"

"Once," Bruno began again, "Sylvie and me writed——"

"Wrote!" Sylvie whispered.

"Well, we *wroted* a Nursery-Song, and the Professor mangled it longer for us. It were *'There was a little Man, And he had a little gun, And the bullets——'* "

"I know the rest," I interrupted. "But would you say it *long*—I mean the way that it came out of the mangle?"

"We'll get the Professor to *sing* it for you," said Sylvie. "It would spoil it to *say* it."

"I would like to meet the Professor," I said. "And I would like to take you all with me, to see some friends of mine, that live near here. Would you like to come?"

"I don't think the *Professor* would like to come," said Sylvie. "He's *very* shy. But *we'd* like it very much. Only we'd better not come *this* size, you know."

The difficulty had occurred to me already: and I had felt that perhaps there *would* be a slight awkwardness in introducing two such tiny friends into Society. "What size will you be?" I enquired.

"We'd better come as—common *children*," Sylvie thoughtfully replied. "That's the easiest size to manage."

"Could you come to-day?" I said, thinking "then we could have you at the Picnic!"

Sylvie considered a little. "Not *to-day*," she replied. "We haven't got the things ready. We'll come on—Tuesday next, if you like. And now, *really*, Bruno, you must come and do your lessons."

"I *wiss* oo wouldn't say *'really* Bruno!' " the little fellow pleaded, with pouting lips that made him look prettier than ever. "It *always* shows there's something horrid coming! And I wo'n't kiss you, if you're so unkind."

"Ah, but you *have* kissed me!" Sylvie exclaimed in merry triumph.

"Well then, I'll *un*kiss you!" And he threw his arms round her neck for this novel, but apparently not *very* painful, operation.

"It's *very* like *kissing*!" Sylvie remarked, as soon as her lips were again free for speech.

"Oo don't know *nuffin* about it! It were just the *conkery*!" Bruno replied with much severity, as he marched away.

Sylvie turned her laughing face to me. "Shall we come on Tuesday?" she said.

"Very well," I said: "let it be Tuesday next. But where *is* the Professor? Did he come with you to Fairyland?"

"No," said Sylvie. "But he promised he'd come and see us, *some* day. He's getting his Lecture ready. So he has to stay at home."

"At home?" I said dreamily, not feeling quite sure what she had said.

"Yes, Sir. His Lordship and Lady Muriel *are* at home. Please to walk this way."

Chapter XVII

The Three Badgers

STILL more dreamily I found myself following this imperious voice into a room where the Earl, his daughter, and Arthur, were seated. "So you're come *at last!*" said Lady Muriel, in a tone of playful reproach.

"I was delayed," I stammered. Though *what* it was that had delayed me I should have been puzzled to explain! Luckily no questions were asked.

The carriage was ordered round, the hamper, containing our contribution to the Picnic, was duly stowed away, and we set forth.

There was no need for *me* to maintain the conversation. Lady Muriel and Arthur were evidently on those most delightful of terms, where one has no need to check thought after thought, as it rises to the lips, with the fear "*this* will not be appreciated—*this* will give offence—*this* will sound too serious—this will sound flippant": like very old friends, in fullest sympathy, their talk rippled on.

"Why shouldn't we desert the Picnic and go in some other direction?" she suddenly suggested. "A party of four is surely self-sufficing? And as for *food*, our hamper——"

"Why *shouldn't* we? What a genuine *lady's* argument!" laughed Arthur. "A lady never knows on which side the *onus probandi*—the burden of proving—lies!"

"Do *men* always know?" she asked with a pretty assumption of meek docility.

"With *one* exception—the only one I can think of—Dr. Watts, who has asked the senseless question

> *'Why should I deprive my neighbour*
> *Of his goods against his will?'*

Fancy *that* as an argument for Honesty! His position seems to be 'I'm only honest because I see no reason to steal.' And the *thief's* answer is of course complete and crushing. 'I deprive my neighbour of his goods because I want them myself. And I do it against his will because there's no chance of getting him to consent to it!' "

"I can give you one other exception," I said: "an argument I heard only to-day—and *not* by a lady. 'Why shouldn't I walk on my own forehead?' "

"What a curious subject for speculation!" said Lady Muriel, turning to me, with eyes brimming over with laughter. "May we know who propounded the question? And *did* he walk on his own forehead?"

"I ca'n't remember *who* it was that said it!" I faltered. "Nor *where* I heard it!"

"Whoêver it was, I hope we shall meet him at the Picnic!" said Lady Muriel. "It's a *far* more interesting question than *'Isn't* this a picturesque ruin?' *'Aren't* those autumn-tints lovely?' I shall have to answer those two questions *ten* times, at least, this afternoon!"

"That's one of the miseries of Society!" said Arthur. "Why ca'n't people let one enjoy the beauties of Nature without having to *say* so every minute? Why should Life be one long Catechism?"

"It's just as bad at a picture-gallery," the Earl remarked. "I went to the R.A. last May, with a conceited young artist: and he *did* torment me! I wouldn't have minded his criticizing the pictures *himself*: but *I* had to agree with him—or else to argue the point, which would have been worse!"

"It was *depreciatory* criticism, of course?" said Arthur.

"I don't see the 'of course' at all."

"Why, did you ever know a conceited man dare to *praise* a picture? The one thing he dreads (next to not being noticed) is *to be proved fallible!* If you once *praise* a picture, your character for *infallibility* hangs by a thread. Suppose it's a figure-picture, and you venture to say 'draws well'. Somebody measures it, and finds one of the proportions an eighth of an inch wrong. *You* are disposed of as a critic! 'Did you say he draws *well*?' your friends enquire sarcastically, while you hang your head and blush. No. The only *safe* course, if any one says 'draws well', is to shrug your shoulders. '*Draws* well?' you repeat thoughtfully. 'Draws *well*? Humph!' That's the way to become a great critic!"

Thus airily chatting, after a pleasant drive through a few miles of beautiful scenery, we reached the *rendezvous* —a ruined castle—where the rest of the picnic-party were already assembled. We spent an hour or two in sauntering about the ruins: gathering at last, by common consent, into a few random groups, seated on the side of a mound, which commanded a good view of the old castle and its surroundings.

The momentary silence, that ensued, was promptly taken possession of—or, more correctly, taken into custody—by a Voice; a voice so smooth, so monotonous, so sonorous, that one felt, with a shudder, that any other conversation was precluded, and that, unless some desperate remedy were adopted, we were fated to listen to a Lecture, of which no man could foresee the end!

The Speaker was a broadly-built man, whose large, flat, pale face was bounded on the North by a fringe of hair, on the East and West by a fringe of whisker, and on the South by a fringe of beard—the whole constituting a uniform halo of stubbly whitey-brown bristles. His features were so entirely destitute of expression that I could not help saying to myself—helplessly, as if in the clutches of a night-mare—"they are only penciled in: no final touches as yet!" And he had a way of ending every sentence with a sudden smile, which spread like a ripple over that vast blank surface, and was gone in a moment, leaving behind it such absolute solemnity that I felt impelled to murmur "it was not *he*: it was somebody else that smiled!"

"Do you observe?" (such was the phrase with which the wretch began each sentence) "Do you observe the way in which that broken arch, at the very top of the ruin, stands out against the clear sky? It is placed *exactly* right: and there is *exactly* enough of it. A little more, or a little less, and all would be utterly spoiled!"

"Oh gifted architect!" murmured Arthur, inaudibly to all but Lady Muriel and myself. "Foreseeing the exact effect his work would have, when in ruins, centuries after his death!"

"And do you observe, where those trees slope down the hill," (indicating them with a sweep of the hand, and with all the patronising air of the man who has himself arranged the landscape), "how the mists rising from the river fill up *exactly* those intervals where we *need* indistinctness, for artistic effect? Here, in the foreground, a few clear touches are not amiss: but a *back*-ground without mist, you know! It is simply barbarous! Yes, we *need* indistinctness!"

The orator looked so pointedly at *me* as he uttered these words, that I felt bound to reply, by murmuring something to the effect that I hardly felt the need *myself*—and that I enjoyed looking at a thing, better, when I could *see* it.

"Quite so!" the great man sharply took me up. "From

your point of view, that is correctly put. But for any one who has a soul for *Art*, such a view is preposterous. *Nature* is one thing. *Art* is another. *Nature* shows us the world as it *is*. But *Art*—as a Latin author tells us—*Art*, you know—the words have escaped my memory——"

"*Ars est celare Naturam*," Arthur interposed with a delightful promptitude.

"Quite so!" the orator replied with an air of relief. "I thank you! *Ars est celare Naturam*—but that isn't it." And, for a few peaceful moments, the orator brooded, frowningly, over the quotation. The welcome opportunity was seized, and *another* voice struck into the silence.

"What a *lovely* old ruin it is!" cried a young lady in spectacles, the very embodiment of the March of Mind, looking at Lady Muriel, as the proper recipient of all really *original* remarks. "And *don't* you admire those autumn-tints on the trees? *I* do, *intensely*!"

Lady Muriel shot a meaning glance at me; but replied with admirable gravity. "Oh yes indeed, indeed! *So* true!"

"And isn't it strange", said the young lady, passing with startling suddenness from Sentiment to Science, "that the mere impact of certain coloured rays upon the Retina should give us such exquisite pleasure?"

"You have studied Physiology, then?" a certain young Doctor courteously enquired.

"Oh, *yes*! Isn't it a *sweet* Science?"

Arthur slightly smiled. "It seems a paradox, does it not," he went on, "that the image formed on the Retina should be inverted?"

"It *is* puzzling," she candidly admitted. "Why is it we do not *see* things upside-down?"

"You have never heard the Theory, then, that the *Brain* also is inverted?"

"No *indeed*! What a *beautiful* fact! But how is it *proved*?"

"*Thus*," replied Arthur, with all the gravity of ten Professors rolled into one. "What we call the *vertex* of the Brain is really its *base*: and what we call its *base* is really its *vertex*: it is simply a question of *nomenclature*."

This last polysyllable settled the matter. "How truly delightful!" the fair Scientist exclaimed with enthusiasm. "I shall ask our Physiological Lecturer why he never gave us that *exquisite* Theory!"

"I'd give something to be present when the question is asked!" Arthur whispered to me, as, at a signal from Lady Muriel, we moved on to where the hampers had been collected, and devoted ourselves to the more *substantial* business of the day.

We "waited" on ourselves, as the modern barbarism (combining two good things in such a way as to secure the discomforts of both and the advantages of neither) of having a picnic with servants to wait upon you, had not yet reached this out-of-the-way region—and of course the gentlemen did not even take their places until the ladies had been duly provided with all imaginable creature-comforts. Then I supplied myself with a plate of something solid and a glass of something fluid, and found a place next to Lady Muriel.

It had been left vacant—apparently, for Arthur, as a distinguished stranger: but he had turned shy, and had placed himself next to the young lady in spectacles, whose high rasping voice had already cast loose upon Society such ominous phrases as "Man is a bundle of Qualities!", "the Objective is only attainable through the Subjective!". Arthur was bearing it bravely: but several faces wore a look of alarm, and I thought it high time to start some less metaphysical topic.

"In my nursery days," I began, "when the weather didn't suit for an out-of-doors picnic, we were allowed to have a peculiar kind, that we enjoyed hugely. The table cloth was laid *under* the table, instead of upon it: we sat round it on the floor: and I believe we really enjoyed that extremely uncomfortable kind of dinner more than we ever did the orthodox arrangement!"

"I've no doubt of it," Lady Muriel replied. "There's nothing a well-regulated child hates so much as regularity. I believe a really healthy boy would thoroughly enjoy Greek Grammar—if only he might stand on his head to learn it! And your carpet-dinner certainly spared you *one* feature of a picnic, which is to me its chief drawback."

"The chance of a shower?" I suggested.

"No, the chance—or rather the certainty—of *live* things occurring in combination with one's food! *Spiders* are *my* bugbear. Now my father has *no* sympathy with that sentiment—*have* you, dear?" For the Earl had caught the word and turned to listen.

"To each his sufferings, all are men," he replied in the sweet sad tones that seemed natural to him: "each has his pet aversion."

"But you'll never guess *his*!" Lady Muriel said, with that delicate silvery laugh that was music to my ears.

I declined to attempt the impossible.

"He doesn't like *snakes*!" she said, in a stage whisper. "Now, isn't *that* an unreasonable aversion? Fancy not liking such a dear, coaxingly, *clingingly* affectionate creature as a snake!"

"Not like *snakes*!" I exclaimed. "Is such a thing possible?"

"No, he *doesn't* like them," she repeated with a pretty mock-gravity. "He's not *afraid* of them, you know. But he doesn't *like* them. He says they're too waggly!"

I was more startled than I liked to show. There was something so *uncanny* in this echo of the very words I had so lately heard from that little forest-sprite, that it was only by a great effort I succeeded in saying, carelessly, "Let us banish so unpleasant a topic. Wo'n't you sing us something, Lady Muriel? I know you *do* sing without music."

"The only songs I know—without music—are *desperately* sentimental, I'm afraid! Are your tears all ready?"

"Quite ready! Quite ready!" came from all sides, and Lady Muriel—not being one of those lady-singers who think it *de rigueur* to decline to sing till they have been petitioned three or four times, and have pleaded failure of memory, loss of voice, and other conclusive reasons for silence—began at once:

> "*There be three Badgers on a mossy stone,*
>   *Beside a dark and covered way:*
> *Each dreams himself a monarch on his throne,*
>   *And so they stay and stay—*
> *Though their old Father languishes alone,*
>   *They stay, and stay, and stay.*
>
> "*There be three Herrings loitering around,*
>   *Longing to share that mossy seat:*
> *Each Herring tries to sing what she has found*
>   *That makes Life seem so sweet.*
> *Thus, with a grating and uncertain sound,*
>   *They bleat, and bleat, and bleat.*
>
> "*The Mother-Herring, on the salt sea-wave,*
>   *Sought vainly for her absent ones:*
> *The Father-Badger, writhing in a cave,*
>   *Shrieked out 'Return, my sons!*
> *You shall have buns', he shrieked, 'if you'll behave!*
>   *Yea, buns, and buns, and buns!'*
>
> " '*I fear*', *said she*, '*your sons have gone astray?*
>   *My daughters left me while I slept.*'
> '*Yes'm,*' *the Badger said:* '*it's as you say.*'
>   '*They should be better kept.*'
> *Thus the poor parents talked the time away,*
>   *And wept, and wept, and wept.*"

Here Bruno broke off suddenly. "The Herrings' Song wants anuvver tune, Sylvie," he said. "And I ca'n't sing it —not wizout oo plays it for me!"

Instantly Sylvie seated herself upon a tiny mushroom, that happened to grow in front of a daisy, as if it were the most ordinary musical instrument in the world, and played on the petals as if they were the notes of an organ. And such delicious *tiny* music it was! Such teeny-tiny music!

Bruno held his head on one side, and listened very gravely for a few moments until he had caught the melody. Then the sweet childish voice rang out once more:

> "Oh, dear beyond our dearest dreams,
> Fairer than all that fairest seems!
> To feast the rosy hours away,
> To revel in a roundelay!
>   How blest would be
>   A life so free—
> Ipwergis-Pudding to consume,
> And drink the subtle Azzigoom!

> "And if, in other days and hours,
> Mid other fluffs and other flowers,
> The choice were given me how to dine—
> 'Name what thou wilt: it shall be thine!'
>   Oh, then I see
>   The life for me—
> Ipwergis-Pudding to consume,
> And drink the subtle Azzigoom!"

"Oo may leave off playing *now*, Sylvie. I can do the uvver tune much better wizout a compliment."

"He means 'without *accompaniment*,' " Sylvie whispered, smiling at my puzzled look: and she pretended to shut up the stops of the organ.

> "The Badgers did not care to talk to Fish:
>   They did not dote on Herrings' songs:
> They never had experienced the dish
>   To which that name belongs:
>   'And oh, to pinch their tails', (this was their wish),
>   'With tongs, yea, tongs, and tongs!' "

I ought to mention that he marked the parenthesis, in the air, with his finger. It seemed to me a very good plan. You know there's no *sound* to represent it—any more than there is for a question.

Suppose you have said to your friend "You are better to-day," and that you want him to understand that you are asking him a *question*, what can be simpler than just to make a "?" in the air with your finger? He would understand you in a moment!

> " '*And are not these the Fish,' the Eldest sighed.*
> '*Whose Mother dwells beneath the foam?'*
> '*They* are *the Fish!' the Second one replied.*
> '*And they have left their home!'*
> '*Oh wicked Fish,' the Youngest Badger cried,*
> '*To roam, yea, roam, and roam!'*

> "*Gently the Badgers trotted to the shore—*
> *The sandy shore that fringed the bay:*
> *Each in his mouth a living Herring bore—*
> *Those aged ones waxed gay:*
> *Clear rang their voices through the ocean's roar,*
> '*Hooray, hooray, hooray!'* "

"So they all got safe home again," Bruno said, after waiting a minute to see if *I* had anything to say: he evidently felt that *some* remark ought to be made. And I couldn't help wishing there were some such rule in Society, at the conclusion of a song—that the singer *herself* should say the right thing, and not leave it to the audience. Suppose a young lady has just been warbling ("with a grating and uncertain sound") Shelley's exquisite lyric "*I arise from dreams of thee*": how much nicer it would be, instead of *your* having to say "Oh, *thank* you, *thank* you!" for the young lady herself to remark, as she draws on her gloves, while the impassioned words "*Oh, press it to thine own, or it will break at last!*" are still ringing in your ears, "—but she wouldn't do it, you know. So it *did* break at last."

"And I *knew* it would!" she added quietly, as I started at the sudden crash of broken glass. "You've been holding it sideways for the last minute, and letting all the champagne run out! Were you asleep, I wonder? I'm *so* sorry my singing has such a narcotic effect!"

CHAPTER XVIII

Queer Street, Number Forty

LADY MURIEL was the speaker. And, for the moment, that was the only fact I could clearly realize. But how she came to be there—and how *I* came to be there—and how the glass of champagne came to be there—all these were questions which I felt it better to think out in silence, and not commit myself to any statement till I understood things a little more clearly.

"First accumulate a mass of Facts: and *then* construct a Theory." *That*, I believe, is the true Scientic Method. I sat up, rubbed my eyes, and began to accumulate Facts.

A smooth grassy slope, bounded, at the upper end, by venerable ruins half buried in ivy, at the lower, by a stream seen through arching trees—a dozen gaily-dressed people, seated in little groups here and there—some open hampers—the *débris* of a picnic—such were the *Facts* accumulated by the Scientific Researcher. And now, what deep, far-reaching *Theory* was he to construct from them? The Researcher found himself at fault. Yet stay! One Fact had escaped his notice. While all the rest were grouped in twos and in threes, *Arthur* was alone: while all tongues were talking, *his* was silent: while all faces were gay, *his* was gloomy and despondent. Here was a *Fact* indeed! The Researcher felt that a *Theory* must be constructed without delay.

Lady Muriel had just risen and left the party. Could *that* be the cause of his despondency? The Theory hardly rose to the dignity of a Working Hypothesis. Clearly more Facts were needed.

The Researcher looked round him once more: and now the Facts accumulated in such bewildering profusion, that the Theory was lost among them. For Lady Muriel had gone to meet a strange gentleman, just visible in the distance: and now she was returning with him, both of them talking eagerly and joyfully, like old friends who have been long parted: and now she was moving from group to group, introducing the new hero of the hour: and he, young, tall, and handsome, moved gracefully at her side, with the erect bearing and firm tread of a soldier. Verily, the Theory looked gloomy for Arthur! His eye caught mine, and he crossed to me.

"He is very handsome," I said.

"Abominably handsome!" muttered Arthur: then smiled at his own bitter words. "Lucky no one heard me but you!"

"Doctor Forester," said Lady Muriel, who had just joined us, "let me introduce to you my cousin Eric Lindon—*Captain* Lindon, I should say."

Arthur shook off his ill-temper instantly and completely, as he rose and gave the young soldier his hand. "I have heard of you," he said. "I'm very glad to make the acquaintance of Lady Muriel's cousin."

"Yes, that's all I'm distinguished for, *as yet!*" said Eric (so we soon got to call him) with a winning smile. "And I doubt", glancing at Lady Muriel, "if it even amounts to a good-conduct-badge! But it's something to begin with."

"You must come to my father, Eric," said Lady Muriel. "I think he's wandering among the ruins." And the pair moved on.

The gloomy look returned to Arthur's face: and I could see it was only to distract his thoughts that he took his place at the side of the metaphysical young lady, and resumed their interrupted discussion.

"Talking of Herbert Spencer," he began, "do you really find no *logical* difficulty in regarding Nature as a process of involution, passing from definite coherent homogeneity to indefinite incoherent heterogeneity?"

Amused as I was at the ingenious jumble he had made of Spencer's words, I kept as grave a face as I could.

"No *physical* difficulty," she confidently replied: "but I haven't studied *Logic* much. Would you *state* the difficulty?"

"Well," said Arthur, "do you accept it as self-evident?

Is it as obvious, for instance, as that 'things that are greater than the same are greater than one another'?"

"To *my* mind," she modestly replied, "it seems *quite* as obvious. I grasp *both* truths by intuition. But *other* minds may need some logical—I forget the technical terms."

"For a *complete* logical argument", Arthur began with admirable solemnity, "we need two prim Misses——"

"Of course!" she interrupted. "I remember that word now. And they produce——?"

"A Delusion," said Arthur.

"Ye—es?" she said dubiously. "I don't seem to remember that so well. But what is the *whole* argument called?"

"A Sillygism."

"Ah, yes! I remember now. But I don't need a Sillygism, you know, to prove that mathematical axiom you mentioned."

"Nor to prove that 'all angles are equal', I suppose?"

"Why, of course not! One takes such a simple truth as that for granted!"

Here I ventured to interpose, and to offer her a plate of strawberries and cream. I felt really uneasy at the thought that she *might* detect the trick: and I contrived, unperceived by her, to shake my head reprovingly at the pseudo-philosopher. Equally unperceived by her, Arthur slightly raised his shoulders, and spread his hands abroad, as who should say "What else can I say to her?" and moved away leaving her to discuss her strawberries by "involution", or any other way she preferred.

By this time the carriages, that were to convey the revelers to their respective homes, had begun to assemble outside the Castle-grounds: and it became evident—now that Lady Muriel's cousin had joined our party—that the problem, how to convey five people to Elveston, with a carriage that would only hold four, must somehow be solved.

The Honourable Eric Lindon, who was at this moment walking up and down with Lady Muriel, might have solved it at once, no doubt, by announcing his intention of returning on foot. Of *this* solution there did not seem to be the very smallest probability.

The next best solution, it seemed to me, was that *I* should walk home: and this I at once proposed.

"You're sure you don't mind?" said the Earl. "I'm afraid the carriage wo'n't take us all, and I don't like to suggest to Eric to desert his cousin so soon."

"So far from minding it," I said, "I should prefer it. It will give me time to sketch this beautiful old ruin."

"I'll keep you company," Arthur suddenly said. And, in answer to what I suppose was a look of surprise on my face, he said in a low voice, "I *really* would rather. I shall be quite *de trop* in the carriage!"

"I think I'll walk too," said the Earl. "You'll have to be content with *Eric* as your escort," he added, to Lady Muriel, who had joined us while he was speaking.

"You must be as entertaining as Cerberus—'three gentlemen rolled into one'—" Lady Muriel said to her companion. "It will be a grand military exploit!"

"A sort of Forlorn Hope?" the Captain modestly suggested.

"You *do* pay pretty compliments!" laughed his fair cousin. "Good day to you, gentlemen three—or rather deserters three!" And the two young folk entered the carriage and were driven away.

"How long will your sketch take?" said Arthur.

"Well," I said, "I should like an hour for it. Don't you think you had better go without me? I'll return by train. I know there's one in about an hour's time."

"Perhaps that *would* be best," said the Earl. "The Station is quite close."

So I was left to my own devices, and soon found a comfortable seat, at the foot of a tree, from which I had a good view of the ruins.

"It is a very drowsy day," I said to myself, idly turning over the leaves of the sketch-book to find a blank page. "Why, I thought you were a mile off by this time!" For, to my surprise, the two walkers were back again.

"I came back to remind you", Arthur said, "that the trains go every ten minutes——"

"Nonsense!" I said. "It isn't the Metropolitan Railway!"

"It *is* the Metropolitan Railway," the Earl insisted. "This is a part of Kensington."

"Why do you talk with your eyes shut?" said Arthur. "Wake up!"

"I think it's the heat that makes me so drowsy," I said, hoping, but not feeling quite sure, that I was talking sense. "Am I awake now?"

"I think *not*," the Earl judicially pronounced. "What do *you* think, Doctor? He's only got one eye open!"

"And he's snoring like anything!" cried Bruno. "Do wake up, you dear old thing!" And he and Sylvie set to work, rolling the heavy head from side to side, as if its connection with the shoulders was a matter of no sort of importance.

And at last the Professor opened his eyes, and sat up, blinking at us with eyes of utter bewilderment. "Would you have the kindness to mention", he said, addressing me with his usual old-fashioned courtesy, "whereabouts we are just now—and *who* we are, beginning with me?"

I thought it best to begin with the children. "This is Sylvie, Sir; and *this* is Bruno."

"Ah, yes! I know *them* well enough!" the old man murmured. "It's *myself* I'm most anxious about. And perhaps you'll be good enough to mention, at the same time, how I got here?"

"A harder problem occurs to *me*," I ventured to say: "and that is, how you're to get back again."

"True, true!" the Professor replied. "That's *the* Problem, no doubt. Viewed *as* a Problem, outside of oneself, it is a *most* interesting one. Viewed as a portion of one's own biography, it is, I must admit, very distressing!" He groaned, but instantly added, with a chuckle, "As to *myself*, I think you mentioned that I am——"

"Oo're the *Professor!*" Bruno shouted in his ear. "Didn't

oo know *that*? Oo've come from *Outland*! And it's *ever* so far away from here!"

The Professor leapt to his feet with the agility of a boy. "Then there's no time to lose!" he exclaimed anxiously. "I'll just ask this guileless peasant, with his brace of buckets that contain (apparently) water, if he'll be so kind as to direct us. Guileless peasant!" he proceeded in a louder voice. "Would you tell us the way to Outland?"

The guileless peasant turned with a sheepish grin. "Hey?" was all he said.

"The—way—to—Outland!" the Professor repeated.

The guileless peasant set down his buckets and considered. "Ah, dunnot——"

"I ought to mention," the Professor hastily put in, "that whatever you say will be used in evidence against you."

The guileless peasant instantly resumed his buckets. "Then ah says nowt!" he answered briskly, and walked away at a great pace.

The children gazed sadly at the rapidly vanishing figure. "He goes very quick!" the Professor said with a sigh. "But I *know* that was the right thing to say. I've studied your English Laws. However, let's ask this next man that's coming. He is *not* guileless, and he is *not* a peasant —but I don't know that either point is of vital importance."

It was, in fact, the Honourable Eric Lindon, who had apparently fulfilled his task of escorting Lady Muriel home, and was now strolling leisurely up and down the road outside the house, enjoying a solitary cigar.

"Might I trouble you, Sir, to tell us the nearest way to Outland!" Oddity as he was, in outward appearance, the Professor was, in that essential nature which no outward disguise could conceal, a thorough gentleman.

And, as such, Eric Lindon accepted him instantly. He took the cigar from his mouth, and delicately shook off the ash, while he considered. "The name sounds strange to me," he said. "I doubt if I can help you."

"It is not *very* far from *Fairyland*," the Professor suggested.

Eric Lindon's eye-brows were slightly raised at these words, and an amused smile, which he courteously tried to repress, flitted across his handsome face. "A trifle *cracked*!" he muttered to himself. "But what a jolly old patriarch it is!" Then he turned to the children. "And ca'n't *you* help him, little folk?" he said, with a gentleness of tone that seemed to win their hearts at once. "Surely *you* know all about it?

> '*How many miles to Babylon?*
> *Three-score miles and ten.*
> *Can I get there by candlelight?*
> *Yes, and back again!*' "

To my surprise, Bruno ran forwards to him, as if he were some old friend of theirs, seized the disengaged hand and hung on to it with both of his own: and there stood this tall dignified officer in the middle of the road, gravely swinging a little boy to and fro, while Sylvie stood ready to push him, exactly as if a real swing had suddenly been provided for their pastime.

"We don't want to get to *Babylon*, oo know!" Bruno explained as he swung.

"And it isn't *candlelight*: it's *daylight*!" Sylvie added, giving the swing a push of extra vigour, which nearly took the whole machine off its balance.

By this time it was clear to me that Eric Lindon was quite unconscious of my presence. Even the Professor and the children seemed to have lost sight of me: and I stood in the midst of the group, as unconcernedly as a ghost, seeing but unseen.

"How perfectly isochronous!" the Professor exclaimed with enthusiasm. He had his watch in his hand, and was carefully counting Bruno's oscillations. "He measures time quite as accurately as a pendulum!"

"Yet even pendulums," the good-natured young soldier observed, as he carefully released his hand from Bruno's grasp, "are not a joy *for ever!* Come, that's enough for one bout, little man! Next time we meet, you shall have another. Meanwhile you'd better take this old gentleman to Queer Street, Number——"

"*We'll* find it!" cried Bruno eagerly, as they dragged the Professor away.

"We are much indebted to you!" the Professor said, looking over his shoulder.

"Don't mention it!" replied the officer, raising his hat as a parting salute.

"*What* number did you say!" the Professor called from the distance.

The officer made a trumpet of his two hands. "Forty!" he shouted in stentorian tones. "And not *piano*, by any means!" he added to himself. "It's a mad world, my masters, a mad world!" He lit another cigar, and strolled on towards his hotel.

"What a lovely evening!" I said, joining him as he passed me.

"Lovely indeed," he said. "Where did *you* come from? Dropped from the clouds?"

"I'm strolling your way," I said: and no further explanation seemed necessary.

"Have a cigar?"

"Thanks: I'm not a smoker."

"Is there a Lunatic Asylum near here?"

"Not that I know of."

"Thought there might be. Met a lunatic just now. Queer old fish as ever I saw!"

And so, in friendly chat, we took our homeward ways, and wished each other "good-night" at the door of his hotel.

Left to myself, I felt the "eerie" feeling rush over me again. and saw, standing at the door of Number Forty, the three figures I knew so well.

"Then it's the wrong house?" Bruno was saying.

"No, no! It's the right *house*," the Professor cheerfully replied: "but it's the wrong *street*. *That's* where we've made our mistake! Our best plan, now will be to——"

It was over. The street was empty. Commonplace life was around me, and the "eerie" feeling had fled.

CHAPTER XIX

How to Make a Phlizz

THE week passed without any further communication with the "Hall", as Arthur was evidently fearful that we might "wear out our welcome"; but when, on Sunday morning, we were setting out for church, I gladly agreed to his proposal to go round and enquire after the Earl, who was said to be unwell.

Eric, who was strolling in the garden, gave us a good report of the invalid, who was still in bed, with Lady Muriel in attendance.

"Are you coming with us to church?" I enquired.

"Thanks, no," he courteously replied. "It's not—exactly—in my line, you know. It's an excellent institution—for the *poor*. When I'm with my own folk, I go, just to set them an example. But I'm not known *here:* so I think I'll excuse myself sitting out a sermon. Country-preachers are always so dull!"

Arthur was silent till we were out of hearing. Then he said to himself, almost inaudibly, *"Where two or three are gathered together in my name, there am I in the midst of them."*

"Yes," I assented: "no doubt that *is* the principle on which church-going rests."

"And when he *does* go," he continued (our thoughts ran so much together, that our conversation was often slightly elliptical), "I suppose he repeats the words '*I believe in the Communion of Saints*'?"

But by this time we had reached the little church, into which a goodly stream of worshippers, consisting mainly of fishermen and their families, was flowing.

The service would have been pronounced by any modern æsthetic religionist—or religious æsthete, which is it? —to be crude and cold: to me, coming fresh from the ever-advancing developments of a London church under a *soi-disant* "Catholic" Rector, it was unspeakably refreshing.

There was no theatrical procession of demure little choristers, trying their best not to simper under the admiring gaze of the congregation: the people's share in the service was taken by the people themselves, unaided, except that a few good voices, judiciously posted here and there among them, kept the singing from going too far astray.

There was no murdering of the noble music, contained in the Bible and the Liturgy, by its recital in a dead monotone, with no more expression than a mechanical talking-doll.

No, the prayers were *prayed*, the lessons were *read*, and—best of all—the sermon was *talked*; and I found myself repeating, as we left the church, the words of Jacob, when he *"awaked out of his sleep"*. " *'Surely the Lord is in this place! This is none other but the house of God, and this is the gate of heaven.'* "

"Yes," said Arthur, apparently in answer to my thoughts, "those 'high' services are fast becoming pure Formalism. More and more the people are beginning to regard them as 'performances', in which they only 'assist' in the French sense. And it is *specially* bad for the little boys. They'd be much less self-conscious as pantomime-fairies. With all that dressing-up, and stagy-entrances and exits, and being always *en evidence*, no wonder if they're eaten up with vanity, the blatant little coxcombs!"

When we passed the Hall on our return, we found the Earl and Lady Muriel sitting out in the garden. Eric had gone for a stroll.

We joined them, and the conversation soon turned on the sermon we had just heard, the subject of which was "selfishness".

"What a change has come over our pulpits", Arthur remarked, "since the time when Paley gave that utterly selfish definition of virtue, *'the doing good to mankind, in obedience to the will of God, and for the sake of ever-lasting happiness'!"*

Lady Muriel looked at him enquiringly, but she seemed to have learned by intuition, what years of experience had taught *me*, that the way to elicit Arthur's deepest thoughts was neither to assent nor dissent, but simply to *listen*.

"At that time," he went on, "a great tidal wave of selfishness was sweeping over human thought. Right and Wrong had somehow been transformed into Gain and Loss, and Religion had become a sort of commercial transaction. We may be thankful that our preachers are beginning to take a nobler view of life."

"But is it not taught again and again in the *Bible?*" I ventured to ask.

"Not in the Bible, as a *whole*," said Arthur. "In the Old Testament, no doubt, rewards and punishments are constantly appealed to as motives for action. That teaching is best for *children*, and the Israelites seem to have been, mentally, *utter* children. We guide our children thus, at first: but we appeal, as soon as possible, to their innate sense of Right and Wrong: and, when *that* stage is safely past, we appeal to the highest motive of all, the desire for likeness to, and union with, the Supreme Good. I think you will find that to be the teaching of the Bible, *as a whole*, beginning with *'that thy days may be long in the land'*, and ending with *'be ye perfect, even as your Father which is in heaven is perfect'*."

We were silent for awhile, and then Arthur went off on another tack. "Look at the literature of Hymns, now. How cankered it is, through and through, with selfishness! There are few human compositions more utterly degraded than some modern Hymns!"

I quoted the stanza.

> *"Whatever, Lord, we lend to Thee,*
> *Repaid a thousandfold shall be,*
> *Then gladly will we give to Thee,*
>   *Giver of all!"*

"Yes," he said grimly: "that is the typical stanza. And the very last charity-sermon I heard was infected with it. After giving many good reasons for charity, the preacher wound up with 'and, for all you give, you will be repaid a thousandfold!' Oh, the utter meanness of such a motive, to be put before men who *do* know what self-sacrifice is, who *can* appreciate generosity and heroism! Talk of Original *Sin!*" he went on with increasing bitterness. "Can you have a stronger proof of the Original Goodness there must be in this nation, than the fact that Religion has been preached to us, as a commercial speculation, for a century, and that we still believe in a God?"

"It couldn't have gone on so long", Lady Muriel musingly remarked, "if the Opposition hadn't been practically silenced—put under what the French call *la clôture*. Surely in any lecture-hall, or in private society, such teaching would soon have been hooted down?"

"I trust so," said Arthur: "and, though I don't want to see 'brawling in church' legalized, I must say that our preachers enjoy an *enormous* privilege—which they ill deserve, and which they misuse terribly. We put our man into a pulpit, and we virtually tell him 'Now, you may stand there and talk to us for half-an-hour. We wo'n't interrupt you by so much as a *word!* You shall have it all your own way!' And what does he give us in return? Shallow twaddle, that, if it were addressed to you over a dinner-table, you would think 'Does the man take me for a *fool?*' "

The return of Eric from his walk checked the tide of Arthur's eloquence, and, after a few minutes' talk on more conventional topics, we took our leave. Lady Muriel walked with us to the gate. "You have given me much to think about," she said earnestly, as she gave Arthur her hand. "I'm so glad you came in!" And her words brought a real glow of pleasure into that pale worn face of his.

On the Tuesday, as Arthur did not seem equal to more walking, I took a long stroll by myself, having stipulated that he was not to give the *whole* day to his books, but was to meet me at the Hall at about tea-time. On my way back, I passed the Station just as the afternoon-train came in sight, and sauntered down the stairs to see it come in. But there was little to gratify my idle curiosity: and, when the train was empty, and the platform clear, I found it was about time to be moving on, if I meant to reach the Hall by five.

As I approached the end of the platform, from which a steep irregular wooden staircase conducted to the upper world, I noticed two passengers, who had evidently arrived by the train, but who, oddly enough, had entirely escaped my notice, though the arrivals had been so few. They were a young woman and a little girl: the former, so far as one could judge by appearances, was a nurse-maid, or possibly a nursery-governess, in attendance on the child, whose refined face, even more than her dress, distinguished her as of a higher class than her companion.

The child's face was refined, but it was also a worn and sad one, and told a tale (or so I seemed to read it) of much illness and suffering, sweetly and patiently borne. She had a little crutch to help herself along with: and she was now standing, looking wistfully up the long staircase, and apparently waiting till she could muster courage to begin the toilsome ascent.

There are some things one *says* in life—as well as things one *does*—which come automatically, by *reflex action*, as the physiologists say (meaning, no doubt, action *without* reflection, just as *lucus* is said to be derived "*a non lucendo*"). Closing one's eyelids, when something seems to be flying into the eye, is one of those actions, and saying "May I carry the little girl up the stairs?" was another. It wasn't that any thought of offering help occurred to me, and that *then* I spoke: the first intimation I had, of being likely to make that offer, was the sound of my own voice, and the discovery that the offer had been made. The servant paused, doubtfully glancing from her charge to me, and then back again to the child. "Would you like it, dear?" she asked her. But no such doubt appeared to cross the child's mind: she lifted her arms eagerly to be taken up. "Please!" was all she said, while a faint smile flickered on the weary little face. I took her up with scrupulous care, and her little arm was at once clasped trustfully round my neck.

She was a *very* light weight—so light, in fact, that the ridiculous idea crossed my mind that it was rather easier going up, with her in my arms, than it would have been without her: and, when we reached the road above, with its cart-ruts and loose stones—all formidable obstacles for a lame child—I found that I had said "I'd better carry her over this rough place", before I had formed any *mental* connection between its roughness and my gentle little burden. "Indeed it's troubling you too much, Sir!" the maid exclaimed. "She can walk very well on the flat." But the arm, that was twined about my neck, clung just an atom more closely at the suggestion, and decided me to say "She's no weight, really. I'll carry her a little further. I'm going your way."

The nurse raised no further objection: and the next speaker was a ragged little boy, with bare feet, and a broom over his shoulder, who ran across the road, and pretended to sweep the perfectly dry road in front of us. "Give us a 'ap'ny!" the little urchin pleaded, with a broad grin on his dirty face.

"*Don't* give him a 'ap'ny!" said the little lady in my arms. The *words* sounded harsh: but the *tone* was gentleness itself. "He's an *idle* little boy!" And she laughed a laugh of such silvery sweetness as I had never yet heard from any lips but Sylvie's. To my astonishment, the boy actually *joined* in the laugh, as if there were some subtle sympathy between them, as he ran away down the road and vanished through a gap in the hedge.

But he was back in a few moments, having discarded his broom and provided himself, from some mysterious source, with an exquisite bouquet of flowers. "Buy a posy, buy a posy! Only a 'ap'ny!" he chanted, with the melancholy drawl of a professional beggar.

"*Don't* buy it!" was Her Majesty's edict as she looked down, with a lofty scorn that seemed curiously mixed with tender interest, on the ragged creature at her feet.

But this time I turned rebel, and ignored the royal commands. Such lovely flowers, and of forms so entirely new to me, were not to be abandoned at the bidding of any little maid, however imperious. I bought the bouquet: and the little boy, after popping the halfpenny into his mouth, turned head-over-heels, as if to ascertain whether the human mouth is really adapted to serve as a money-box.

With wonder, that increased every moment, I turned over the flowers, and examined them one by one: there was not a single one among them that I could remember having ever seen before. At last I turned to the nursemaid. "Do these flowers grow wild about here? I never saw——" but the speech died away on my lips. The nursemaid had vanished!

"You can put me down, *now*, if you like," Sylvie quietly remarked.

I obeyed in silence, and could only ask myself "Is this a *dream*?", on finding Sylvie and Bruno walking one on either side of me, and clinging to my hands with the ready confidence of childhood.

"You're larger than when I saw you last!" I began. "Really I think we ought to be introduced again! There's so much of you that I never met before, you know."

"Very well!" Sylvie merrily replied. "This is *Bruno*. It doesn't take long. He's only got one name!"

"There's *another* name to me!" Bruno protested, with a reproachful look at the Mistress of the Ceremonies. "And it's—'*Esquire*'!"

"Oh, of course. I forgot," said Sylvie. "Bruno—*Esquire*!"

"And did you come here to meet *me*, my children?" I enquired.

"You know I *said* we'd come on Tuesday," Sylvie explained. "Are we the proper size for common children?"

"Quite the right size for *children*," I replied, (adding mentally "though not *common* children, by any means!") "But what became of the nursemaid?"

"It are *gone*!" Bruno solemnly replied.

"Then it wasn't solid, like Sylvie and you?"

"No. Oo couldn't *touch* it, oo know. If oo walked *at* it, oo'd go right froo!"

"I quite expected you'd find it out, once," said Sylvie. "Bruno ran it against a telegraph post, by accident. And it went in two halves. But you were looking the other way."

I felt that I had indeed missed an opportunity: to witness such an event as a nursemaid going "in two halves" does not occur twice in a life-time!

"When did oo guess it were Sylvie?" Bruno enquired.

"I didn't guess it, till it *was* Sylvie," I said. "But how did you manage the nursemaid?"

"*Bruno* managed it," said Sylvie. "It's called a Phlizz."

"And how do you make a Phlizz, Bruno?"

"The Professor teached me how," said Bruno. "First oo takes a lot of air——"

"Oh, *Bruno*!" Sylvie interposed. "The Professor said you weren't to tell!"

"But who did her *voice*?" I asked.

"Indeed it's troubling you too much, Sir! She can walk very well on the flat."

Bruno laughed merrily as I turned hastily from side to side, looking in all directions for the speaker. "That were *me*!" he gleefully proclaimed, in his own voice.

"She can indeed walk very well on the flat," I said. "And I think *I* was the Flat."

By this time we were near the Hall. "This is where my friends live," I said. "Will you come in and have some tea with them?"

Bruno gave a little jump of joy: and Sylvie said "Yes, please. You'd like some tea, Bruno, wouldn't you? He hasn't tasted *tea*", she explained to me, "since we left Outland."

"And *that* weren't *good* tea!" said Bruno. "It were so *welly* weak!"

Chapter XX

Light Come, Light Go

LADY MURIEL's smile of welcome could not *quite* conceal the look of surprise with which she regarded my new companions.

I presented them in due form. "This is *Sylvie*, Lady Muriel. And this is *Bruno*."

"Any surname?" she enquired, her eyes twinkling with fun.

"No," I said gravely. "No surname."

She laughed, evidently thinking I said it in fun; and stooped to kiss the children—a salute to which *Bruno* submitted with reluctance: *Sylvie* returned it with interest.

While she and Arthur (who had arrived before me) supplied the children with tea and cake, I tried to engage the Earl in conversation: but he was restless and *distrait*, and we made little progress. At last, by a sudden question, he betrayed the cause of his disquiet.

"*Would* you let me look at those flowers you have in your hand?"

"Willingly!" I said, handing him the bouquet. Botany was, I knew, a favourite study of his: and these flowers were to me so entirely new and mysterious, that I was really curious to see what a botanist would say of them.

They did *not* diminish his disquiet. On the contrary, he became every moment more excited as he turned them over. "*These* are all from Central India!" he said, laying aside part of the bouquet. "They are rare, even there: and I have never seen them in any other part of the world. *These* two are Mexican—*This* one——" (He rose hastily and carried it to the window, to examine it in a better light, the flush of excitement mounting to his very forehead) "—is, I am nearly sure—but I have a book of Indian Botany here——" He took a volume from the book-shelves, and turned the leaves with trembling fingers. "Yes! Compare it with this picture! It is the exact duplicate! This is the flower of the Upas-tree, which usually grows only in the depths of forests; and the flower fades so quickly after being plucked, that it is scarcely possible to keep its form or colour even so far as the outskirts of the forest! Yet this is in full bloom! *Where* did you get these flowers?" he added with breathless eagerness.

I glanced at Sylvie, who, gravely and silently, laid her finger on her lips, then beckoned to Bruno to follow her, and ran out into the garden; and I found myself in the position of a defendant whose two most important witnesses have been suddenly taken away. "Let me give you the flowers!" I stammered out at last, quite "at my wit's end" as to how to get out of the difficulty. "You know much more about them than I do!"

"I accept them most gratefully! But you have not yet told me——" the Earl was beginning, when we were interrupted, to my great relief, by the arrival of Eric Lindon.

To *Arthur*, however, the newcomer was, I saw clearly, anything but welcome. His face clouded over: he drew a little back from the circle, and took no further part in the conversation, which was wholly maintained, for some minutes, by Lady Muriel and her lively cousin, who were discussing some new music that had just arrived from London.

"Do just try this one!" he pleaded. "The music looks easy to sing at sight, and the song's quite appropriate to the occasion."

"Then I suppose it's

> '*Five o'clock tea!*
> *Ever to thee*
> *Faithful I'll be,*
> *Five o'clock tea!*' "

laughed Lady Muriel, as she sat down to the piano, and lightly struck a few random chords.

"Not quite: and yet it *is* a kind of 'ever to thee faithfull I'll be!' It's a pair of hapless lovers: *he* crosses the briny deep: and *she* is left lamenting."

"That is *indeed* appropriate!" she replied mockingly, as he placed the song before her. "And am *I* to do the lamenting? And who for, if you please?"

She played the air once or twice through, first in quick, and finally in slow, time; and then gave us the whole song with as much graceful ease as if she had been familiar with it all her life:

> *"He steps so lightly to the land,*
> 　*All in his manly pride:*
> *He kissed her cheek, he pressed her hand,*
> 　*Yet still she glanced aside.*
> *'Too gay he seems,' she darkly dreams,*
> 　*'Too gallant and too gay*
> *To think of me—poor simple me—*
> 　*When he is far away!'*
>
> *'I bring my Love this goodly pearl*
> 　*Across the seas,' he said:*
> *'A gem to deck the dearest girl*
> 　*That ever sailor wed!'*
> *She clasps it tight: her eyes are bright:*
> 　*Her throbbing heart would say*
> *'He thought of me—he thought of me—*
> 　*When he was far away!'*
>
> *The ship has sailed into the West:*
> 　*Her ocean-bird is flown:*
> *A dull dead pain is in her breast,*
> 　*And she is weak and lone:*
> *Yet there's a smile upon her face,*
> 　*A smile that seems to say*
> *'He'll think of me—he'll think of me—*
> 　*When he is far away!*
>
> *'Though waters wide between us glide,*
> 　*Our lives are warm and near:*

> *No distance parts two faithful hearts—*
> *Two hearts that love so dear:*
> *And I will trust my sailor-lad,*
> *For ever and a day,*
> *To think of me—to think of me—*
> *When he is far away!'* "

The look of displeasure, which had begun to come over Arthur's face when the young Captain spoke of Love so lightly, faded away as the song proceeded, and he listened with evident delight. But his face darkened again when Eric demurely remarked "Don't you think 'my *soldier*-lad' would have fitted the tune just as well?"

"Why, so it would!" Lady Muriel gaily retorted. "Soldiers, sailors, tinkers, tailors, what a lot of words would fit in! I think 'my *tinker*-lad' sounds best. Don't *you?*"

To spare my friend further pain, I rose to go, just as the Earl was beginning to repeat his particularly embarrassing question about the flowers.

"You have not yet——"

"Yes, I've *had* some tea, thank you!" I hastily interrupted him. "And now we really *must* be going. Good evening, Lady Muriel!" And we made our adieux, and escaped, while the Earl was still absorbed in examining the mysterious bouquet.

Lady Muriel accompanied us to the door. "You *couldn't* have given my father a more acceptable present!" she said, warmly. "He is so passionately fond of Botany. I'm afraid *I* know nothing of the *theory* of it, but I keep his *Hortus Siccus* in order. I must get some sheets of blotting-paper, and dry these new treasures for him before they begin to fade."

"*That* wo'n't be no good at all!" said Bruno, who was waiting for us in the garden.

"Why wo'n't it?" said I. "You know I *had* to give the flowers, to stop questions."

"Yes, it ca'n't be helped," said Sylvie: "but they *will* be sorry when they find them gone!"

"But how will they go?"

"Well, I don't know *how*. But they *will* go. The nose-gay was only a *Phlizz*, you know. Bruno made it up.

These last words were in a whisper, as she evidently did not wish Arthur to hear. But of this there seemed to be little risk: he hardly seemed to notice the children, but paced on, silent and abstracted; and when, at the entrance to the wood, they bid us a hasty farewell and ran off, he seemed to wake out of a day-dream.

The bouquet vanished, as Sylvie had predicted; and when, a day or two afterwards, Arthur and I once more visited the Hall, we found the Earl and his daughter, with the old housekeeper, out in the garden, examining the fastenings of the drawing-room window.

"We are holding an Inquest," Lady Muriel said, advancing to meet us: "and we admit you, as Accessories before the Fact, to tell us all you know about those flowers."

"The Accessories before the Fact decline to answer *any* questions," I gravely replied. "And they reserve their defence."

"Well then, turn Queen's Evidence, please! The flowers have disappeared in the night," she went on, turning to Arthur, "and we are *quite* sure no one in the house has meddled with them. Somebody must have entered by the window——"

"But the fastenings have not been tampered with," said the Earl.

"It must have been while you were dining, my Lady," said the housekeeper.

"That was it," said the Earl. "The thief must have seen you bring the flowers", turning to me, "and have noticed that you did *not* take them away. And he must have known their great value—they are simply *priceless*!" he exclaimed, in sudden excitement.

"And you never told us how you got them!" said Lady Muriel.

"Some day," I stammered, "I may be free to tell you. Just now, would you excuse me?"

The Earl looked disappointed, but kindly said "Very well, we will ask no questions".

"But we consider you a *very* bad Queen's Evidence," Lady Muriel added playfully, as we entered the arbour. "We pronounce you to be an accomplice: and we sentence you to solitary confinement, and to be fed on bread and—butter. Do you take sugar?"

"It is disquieting, certainly," she resumed, when all "creature-comforts" had been duly supplied, "to find that the house has been entered by a thief—in this out-of-the-way place. If only the flowers had been *eatables*, one might have suspected a thief of quite another shape——"

"You mean that universal explanation for all mysterious disappearances, 'the *cat* did it'?" said Arthur.

"Yes," she replied. "What a convenient thing it would be if all thieves had the same shape! It's so confusing to have some of them quadrupeds and others bipeds!"

"It has occurred to me", said Arthur, "as a curious problem in Teleology—the Science of Final Causes," he added, in answer to an enquiring look from Lady Muriel.

"And a Final Cause is——?"

"Well, suppose we say—the last of a series of connected events—each of the series being the cause of the next—for whose sake the first event takes place."

"But the last event is practically an *effect* of the first, isn't it? And yet you call it a *cause* of it!"

Arthur pondered a moment. "The words are rather confusing, I grant you," he said. "Will this do? The last event is an effect of the first: but the *necessity* for that event is a cause of the *necessity* for the first."

"That seems clear enough," said Lady Muriel. "Now let us have the problem."

"It's merely this. What object can we imagine in the arrangement by which each different size (roughly speaking) of living creatures has its special shape? For instance, the human race has one kind of shape—bipeds. Another set, ranging from the lion to the mouse, are quadrupeds. Go down a step or two further, and you come to insects with six legs—hexapods—a beautiful name, is it not? But beauty, in our sense of the word, seems to diminish as we go down: the creature becomes more—I won't say 'ugly' of any of God's creatures—more uncouth. And, when we take the microscope, and go a few steps lower still, we come upon animalculæ, terribly uncouth, and with a terrible number of legs!"

"The other alternative," said the Earl, "would be a *diminuendo* series of repetitions of the same type. Never mind the monotony of it: let's see how it would work in other ways. Begin with the race of men, and the creatures they require: let us say horses, cattle, sheep, and dogs—we don't exactly require frogs and spiders, do we, Muriel?"

Lady Muriel shuddered perceptibly: it was evidently a painful subject. "We can dispense with *them*," she said gravely.

"Well, then we'll have a second race of men, half-a-yard high——"

"—who would have *one* source of exquisite enjoyment, not possessed by ordinary men!" Arthur interrupted.

"*What* source?" said the Earl.

"Why, the grandeur of scenery! Surely the grandeur of a mountain, to *me*, depends on its *size*, relative to me? Double the height of the mountain, and of course it's twice as grand. Halve *my* height, and you produce the same effect."

"Happy, happy, happy Small!" Lady Muriel murmured rapturously. "None but the Short, none but the Short, none but the Short enjoy the Tall!"

"But let me go on," said the Earl. "We'll have a third race of men, five inches high; a fourth race, an inch high——"

"They couldn't eat common beef and mutton, I'm sure!" Lady Muriel interrupted.

"True, my child, I was forgetting. Each set must have its own cattle and sheep."

"And its own vegetation," I added. "What could a cow, an inch high, do with grass that waved far above its head?"

"That is true. We must have a pasture within a pasture, so to speak. The common grass would serve our inch-high cows as a green forest of palms, while round the root of each tall stem would stretch a tiny carpet of microscopic grass. Yes, I think our scheme will work fairly well. And it would be very interesting, coming into contact with the races below us. What sweet little things the inch-high bull-dogs would be! I doubt if even *Muriel* would run away from one of them!"

"Don't you think we ought to have a *crescendo* series, as well?" said Lady Muriel. "Only fancy being a hundred yards high! One could use an elephant as a paper-weight, and a crocodile as a pair of scissors!"

"And would you have races of different sizes communicate with one another?" I enquired. "Would they make war on one another, for instance, or enter into treaties?"

"*War* we must exclude, I think. When you could crush a whole nation with one blow of your fist, you couldn't conduct war on equal terms. But anything, involving a collision of *minds* only, would be possible in our ideal world—for of course we must allow *mental* powers to all, irrespective of size. Perhaps the fairest rule would be that, the *smaller* the race, the *greater* should be its intellectual development!"

"Do you mean to say", said Lady Muriel, "that these manikins of an inch high are to *argue* with me?"

"Surely, surely!" said the Earl. "An argument doesn't depend for its logical force on the *size* of the creature that utters it!"

She tossed her head indignantly. "I would *not* argue with any man less than six inches high!" she cried. "I'd make him *work*!"

"What at?" said Arthur, listening to all this nonsense with an amused smile.

"*Embroidery*!" she readily replied. "What *lovely* embroidery they would do!"

"Yet, if they did it wrong," I said, "you couldn't *argue* the question. I don't know *why:* but I agree that it couldn't be done."

"The reason is," said Lady Muriel, "one couldn't sacrifice one's *dignity* so far."

"Of course one couldn't!" echoed Arthur. "Any more than one could argue with a potato. It would be altogether—excuse the ancient pun—*infra dig*.!"

"I doubt it," said I. "Even a pun doesn't *quite* convince me."

"Well, if that is *not* the reason," said Lady Muriel, "what reason would you give?"

I tried hard to understand the meaning of this question: but the persistent humming of the bees confused me, and there was a drowsiness in the air that made every thought stop and go to sleep before it had got well thought out: so all I could say was "That must depend on the *weight* of the potato".

I felt the remark was not so sensible as I should have liked it to be. But Lady Muriel seemed to take it quite as a matter of course. "In that case——" she began, but suddenly started, and turned away to listen. "Don't you hear him?" she said. "He's crying. We must go to him, somehow."

And I said to myself "That's very strange! I quite thought it was *Lady Muriel* talking to me. Why, it's *Sylvie* all the while!" And I made another great effort to say something that should have some meaning in it. "Is it about the potato?"

Chapter XXI

Through the Ivory Door

"I don't know," said Sylvie. "Hush! I must think. I could go to him, by myself, well enough. But I want *you* to come too."

"Let me go with you," I pleaded. "I can walk as fast as *you* can, I'm sure."

Sylvie laughed merrily. "What nonsense!" she cried. "Why, you ca'n't walk a bit! You're lying quite flat on your back! You don't understand these things."

"I can walk as well as *you* can," I repeated. And I tried my best to walk a few steps: but the ground slipped away backwards, quite as fast as I could walk, so that I made no progress at all. Sylvie laughed again.

"There, I told you so! You've no idea how funny you look, moving your feet about in the air, as if you were walking! Wait a bit. I'll ask the Professor what we'd better do." And she knocked at his study-door.

The door opened, and the Professor looked out. "What's that crying I heard just now?" he asked. "Is it a human animal?"

"It's a boy," Sylvie said.

"I'm afraid you've been teasing him?"

"No, *indeed* I haven't!" Sylvie said, very earnestly. "I *never* tease him!"

"Well, I must ask the Other Professor about it." He went back into the study, and we heard him whispering "small human animal—says she hasn't been teasing him—the kind that's called Boy——"

"Ask her *which* Boy," said a new voice. The Professor came out again.

"*Which* Boy is it that you haven't been teasing?"

Sylvie looked at me with twinkling eyes. "You dear old thing!" she exclaimed, standing on tip-toe to kiss him, while he gravely stooped to receive the salute. "How you *do* puzzle me! Why, there are *several* boys I haven't been teasing!"

The Professor returned to his friend: and this time the voice said "Tell her to bring them here—*all* of them!"

"I ca'n't, and I wo'n't!" Sylvie exclaimed, the moment he reappeared. "It's *Bruno* that's crying: and he's my brother: and, please, we *both* want to go: he ca'n't walk, you know: he's—he's *dreaming*, you know" (this in a whisper, for fear of hurting my feelings). "*Do* let's go through the Ivory Door!"

"I'll ask him," said the Professor, disappearing again. He returned directly. "He says you may. Follow me, and walk on tip-toe."

The difficulty with me would have been, just then, *not* to walk on tip-toe. It seemed very hard to reach down far enough to just touch the floor, as Sylvie led me through the study.

The Professor went before us to unlock the Ivory Door. I had just time to glance at the Other Professor, who was sitting reading, with his back to us, before the Professor showed us out through the door, and locked it behind us. Bruno was standing with his hands over his face, crying bitterly.

"What's the matter, darling?" said Sylvie, with her arms round his neck.

"Hurted mine self *welly* much!" sobbed the poor little fellow.

"I'm *so* sorry, darling! How ever *did* you manage to hurt yourself so?"

"Course I managed it!" said Bruno, laughing through his tears. "Does oo think nobody else but *oo* ca'n't manage things?"

Matters were looking distinctly brighter, now Bruno had begun to argue. "Come, let's hear all about it!" I said.

"My foot took it into its head to slip——" Bruno began.

"A foot hasn't got a head!" Sylvie put in, but all in vain.

"I slipted down the bank. And I tripted over a stone. And the stone hurted my foot! And I trod on a Bee. And the Bee stinged my finger!" Poor Bruno sobbed again. The complete list of woes was too much for his feelings. "And it knewed I didn't *mean* to trod on it!" he added, as the climax.

"That Bee should be ashamed of itself!" I said severely,

and Sylvie hugged and kissed the wounded hero till all
tears were dried.

"My finger's quite unstung now!" said Bruno. "Why
doos there be stones? Mister Sir, doos oo know?"

"They're good for *something*," I said: "even if we don't
know *what*. What's the good of *dandelions*, now?"

"Dindledums?" said Bruno. "Oh, they're ever so
pretty! And stones aren't pretty, one bit. Would oo like
some dindledums, Mister Sir?"

"Bruno!" Sylvie murmured reproachfully. "You
mustn't say 'Mister' and 'Sir' both at once! Remember
what I told you!"

"You told me I were to say 'Mister' when I spoked
about him, and I were to say 'Sir' when I spoked *to* him!"

"Well, you're not doing *both*, you know."

"Ah, but I *is* doing bofe, Miss Praticular!" Bruno exclaimed triumphantly. "I wishted to speak *about* the
Gemplun—and I wishted to speak *to* the Gemplun. So a
course I said 'Mister Sir'!"

"That's all right, Bruno," I said.

"*Course* it's all right!" said Bruno. "Sylvie just knows
nuffin at all!"

"There never *was* an impertinenter boy!" said Sylvie,
frowning till her bright eyes were nearly invisible.

"And there never was an ignoranter girl!" retorted
Bruno. "Come along and pick some dindledums. *That's
all she's fit for!*" he added in a very loud whisper to me.

"But why do you say 'Dindledums', Bruno? *Dandelions* is the right word."

"It's because he jumps about so," Sylvie said, laughing.

"Yes, that's it," Bruno assented. "Sylvie tells me the
words, and then, when I jump about, they get shooken
up in my head—till they're all froth!"

I expressed myself as perfectly satisfied with this explanation. "But aren't you going to pick me any dindledums, after all?"

"Course we will!" cried Bruno. "Come along, Sylvie!"

And the happy children raced away, bounding over the turf with the fleetness and grace of young antelopes.

"Then you didn't find your way back to Outland?" I said to the Professor.

"Oh yes, I did!" he replied, "We never got to Queer Street; but I found another way. I've been backwards and forwards several times since then. I had to be present at the Election, you know, as the author of the new Money-Act. The Emperor was so kind as to wish that *I* should have the credit of it. 'Let come what come may,' (I remember the very words of the Imperial Speech) 'if it *should* turn out that the Warden *is* alive, *you* will bear witness that the change in the coinage is the *Professor's* doing, not *mine!*' I never was so glorified in my life, before!" Tears trickled down his cheeks at the recollection, which apparently was not *wholly* a pleasant one.

"Is the Warden supposed to be *dead?*"

"Well, it's *supposed* so: but, mind you, *I* don't believe it! The evidence is *very* weak—mere hear-say. A wandering Jester, with a Dancing-Bear (they found their way into the Palace, one day) has been telling people he comes from Fairyland, and that the Warden died there. *I* wanted the Vice-Warden to question him, but, most unluckily, he and my Lady were always out walking when the Jester came round. Yes, the Warden's supposed to be dead!" And more tears trickled down the old man's cheeks.

"But what is the new Money-Act?"

The Professor brightened up again. "The Emperor started the thing," he said. "He wanted to make everybody in Outland twice as rich as he was before—just to make the new Government popular. Only there wasn't nearly enough money in the Treasury to do it. So *I* suggested that he might do it by doubling the value of every coin and bank-note in Outland. It's the simplest thing possible. I wonder nobody ever thought of it before! And you never saw such universal joy. The shops are full from morning to night. Everybody's buying everything!"

"And how was the glorifying done?"

A sudden gloom overcast the Professor's jolly face. "They did it as I went home after the Election," he mournfully replied. "It was kindly meant—but I didn't like it! They waved flags all round me till I was nearly blind: and they rang bells till I was nearly deaf: and they strewed the road so thick with flowers that I lost my way!" And the poor old man sighed deeply.

"How far is it to Outland?" I asked, to change the subject.

"About five days' march. But one *must* go back—occasionally. You see, as Court-Professor, I have to be *always* in attendance on Prince Uggug. The Empress would be *very* angry if I left him, even for an hour."

"But surely, every time you come here, you are absent ten days, at least?"

"Oh, more than that!" the Professor exclaimed. "A fortnight, sometimes. But of course I keep a memorandum of the exact time when I started, so that I can put the Court-time back to the very moment!"

"Excuse me," I said. "I don't understand."

Silently the Professor drew from his pocket a square gold watch, with six or eight hands, and held it out for my inspection. "This", he began, "is an Outlandish Watch——"

"So I should have thought."

"——which has the peculiar property that, instead of *its* going with the *time*, the *time* goes with *it*. I trust you understand me now?"

"Hardly," I said.

"Permit me to explain. So long as it is let alone, it takes its own course. Time has *no* effect upon it."

"I have known such watches," I remarked.

"It *goes*, of course, at the usual rate. Only the time has to go *with* it. Hence, if I move the hands, I change the time. To move them *forwards*, in *advance* of the true time, is impossible: but I can move them as much as a month *backwards*—that is the limit. And then you have the events all over again—with any alterations experience may suggest."

"*What* a blessing such a watch would be", I thought, "in real life! To be able to unsay some heedless word—to undo some reckless deed! Might I see the thing done?"

"With pleasure!" said the good natured Professor. "When I move *this* hand back to *here*", pointing out the place, "History goes back fifteen minutes!"

Trembling with excitement, I watched him push the hand round as he described.

"Hurted mine self *welly* much!"

Shrilly and suddenly the words rang in my ears, and, more startled than I cared to show, I turned to look for the speaker.

Yes! There was Bruno, standing with the tears running down his cheeks, just as I had seen him a quarter of an hour ago; and there was Sylvie with her arms round his neck!

I had not the heart to make the dear little fellow go through his troubles a second time, so hastily begged the Professor to push the hands round into their former position. In a moment Sylvie and Bruno were gone again, and I could just see them in the far distance, picking "dindledums".

"Wonderful, indeed!" I exclaimed.

"It has another property, yet more wonderful," said the Professor. "You see this little peg? That is called the 'Reversal Peg'. If you push it in, the events of the next hour happen in the reverse order. Do not try it now. I will lend you the Watch for a few days, and you can amuse yourself with experiments."

"Thank you very much!" I said as he gave me the Watch. "I'll take the greatest care of it—why, here are the children again!"

"We could only but find *six* dindledums," said Bruno, putting them into my hands, " 'cause Sylvie said it were time to go back. And here's a big blackberry for *ooself*! We couldn't only find but *two*!"

"Thank you: it's *very* nice," I said. "And I suppose *you* ate the other, Bruno?"

"No, I didn't," Bruno said, carelessly. "*Aren't* they pretty dindledums, Mister Sir?"

"Yes, very: but what makes you limp so, my child?"

"Mine foot's come *hurted* again!" Bruno mournfully replied. And he sat down on the ground, and began nursing it.

The Professor held his head between his hands—an attitude that I knew indicated distraction of mind. "Better rest a minute," he said. "It may be better then—or it may be worse. If only I had some of my medicines here! I'm Court-Physician, you know," he added, aside to me.

"Shall I go and get you some blackberries, darling?" Sylvie whispered, with her arms round his neck; and she kissed away a tear that was trickling down his cheek.

Bruno brightened up in a moment. "That *are* a good plan!" he exclaimed. "I thinks my foot would come *quite* unhurted, if I eated a blackberry—two or three blackberries—six or seven blackberries——"

Sylvie got up hastily. "I'd better go", she said, aside to me, "before he gets into the double figures!"

"Let me come and help you," I said. "I can reach higher up than you can."

"Yes, please," said Sylvie, putting her hand into mine: and we walked off together.

"Bruno *loves* blackberries," she said, as we paced slowly along by a tall hedge, that looked a promising place for them, "and it was so *sweet* of him to make me eat the only one!"

"Oh, it was *you* that ate it, then? Bruno didn't seem to like to tell me about it."

"No; I saw that," said Sylvie. "He's always afraid of being praised. But he *made* me eat it, really! I would much rather he—oh, what's that?" And she clung to my hand, half-frightened, as we came in sight of a hare, lying on its side with legs stretched out, just in the entrance to the wood.

"It's a *hare*, my child. Perhaps it's asleep."

"No, it isn't asleep," Sylvie said, timidly going nearer to look at it: "it's eyes are open. Is it—is it——" her voice dropped to an awe-struck whisper. "is it *dead*, do you think?"

"Yes, it's quite dead," I said, after stooping to examine it. "Poor thing! I think it's been hunted to death. I know the harriers were out yesterday. But they haven't touched it. Perhaps they caught sight of another, and left it to die of fright and exhaustion."

"Hunted to *death*?" Sylvie repeated to herself, very slowly and sadly. "I thought hunting was a thing they *played* at—like a game. Bruno and I hunt snails: but we never hurt them when we catch them!"

"Sweet angel!" I thought. "How am I to get the idea of *Sport* into your innocent mind?" And as we stood, hand-in-hand, looking down at the dead hare, I tried to put the thing into such words as she could understand. "You know what fierce wild-beasts lions and tigers are?" Sylvie nodded. "Well, in some countries men *have* to kill them, to save their own lives, you know."

"Yes," said Sylvie: "if one tried to kill *me*, Bruno would kill *it*—if he could."

"Well, and so the men—the hunters—get to enjoy it, you know: the running, and the fighting, and the shouting, and the danger."

"Yes," said Sylvie. "Bruno likes danger."

"Well, but, in *this* country, there aren't any lions and tigers, loose: so they hunt other creatures, you see." I hoped, but in vain, that this would satisfy her, and that she would ask no more questions.

"They hunt *foxes*," Sylvie said, thoughtfully. "And I think they *kill* them, too. Foxes are very fierce. I daresay men don't love them. Are hares fierce?"

"No," I said, "A hare is a sweet, gentle, timid animal— almost as gentle as a lamb."

"But, if men *love* hares, why—why———" her voice quivered, and her sweet eyes were brimming over with tears.

"I'm afraid they *don't* love them, dear child."

"All *children* love them," Sylvie said. "All *ladies* love them."

"I'm afraid even *ladies* go to hunt them sometimes."

Sylvie shuddered. "Oh, no, not *ladies!*" she earnestly pleaded. "Not Lady Muriel!"

"No, *she* never does, I'm sure—but this is too sad a sight for *you*, dear. Let's try and find some———"

But Sylvie was not satisfied yet. In a hushed, solemn tone, with bowed head and clasped hands, she put her final question. "Does GOD love hares?"

"Yes!" I said. "I'm *sure* He does! He loves every living thing. Even sinful *men*. How much more the animals, that cannot sin!"

"I don't know what 'sin' means," said Sylvie. And I didn't try to explain it.

"Come, my child," I said, trying to lead her away. "Wish good-bye to the poor hare, and come and look for blackberries."

"Good-bye, poor hare!" Sylvie obediently repeated, looking over her shoulder at it as we turned away. And then, all in a moment, her self-command gave way. Pulling her hand out of mine, she ran back to where the dead hare was lying, and flung herself down at its side in such an agony of grief as I could hardly have believed possible in so young a child.

"Oh, my darling, my darling!" she moaned over and over again. "And GOD meant your life to be so beautiful!"

Sometimes, but always keeping her face hidden on the ground, she would reach out one little hand, to stroke the poor dead thing, and then once more bury her face in her hands, and sob as if her heart would break.

I was afraid she would really make herself ill: still I thought it best to let her weep away the first sharp agony of grief: and, after a few minutes, the sobbing gradually ceased, and Sylvie rose to her feet, and looked calmly at me, though tears were still streaming down her cheeks.

I did not dare to speak again, just yet; but simply held out my hand to her, that we might quit the melancholy spot.

"Yes, I'll come now," she said. Very reverently she kneeled down, and kissed the dead hare; then rose and gave me her hand, and we moved on in silence.

A child's sorrow is violent, but short; and it was almost in her usual voice that she said, after a minute, "Oh, stop, stop! Here are some *lovely* blackberries!"

We filled our hands with fruit, and returned in all haste to where the Professor and Bruno were seated on a bank, awaiting our return.

Just before we came within hearing-distance, Sylvie checked me. "Please don't tell *Bruno* about the hare!" she said.

"Very well, my child! But why not?"

Tears again glittered in those sweet eyes, and she turned her head away, so that I could scarcely hear her reply. "He's—he's very *fond* of gentle creatures, you know. And he'd—he'd be so sorry! I don't want him to be made sorry."

"And *your* agony of sorrow is to count for nothing, then, sweet unselfish child!" I thought to myself. But no more was said till we had reached our friends; and Bruno was far too much engrossed, in the feast we had brought him, to take any notice of Sylvie's unusually grave manner.

"I'm afraid it's getting rather late, Professor?" I said.

"Yes, indeed," said the Professor. "I must take you all through the Ivory Door again. You've stayed your full time."

"Mightn't we stay a *little* longer!" pleaded Sylvie.

"Just *one* minute!" added Bruno.

But the Professor was unyielding. "It's a great privilege, coming through at all," he said. "We must go now." And we followed him obediently to the Ivory Door, which he threw open, and signed to me to go through first.

"You're coming too, aren't you?" I said to Sylvie.

"Yes," she said: "but you wo'n't see us after you've gone through."

"But suppose I wait for you outside?" I asked, as I stepped through the doorway.

"In that case," said Sylvie, "I think the potato would be *quite* justified in asking *your* weight. I can quite imagine a really *superior* kidney-potato declining to argue with any one under *fifteen stone!*"

With a great effort I recovered the thread of my thoughts. "We lapse very quickly into nonsense!" I said.

Chapter XXII

Crossing the Line

"Let us lapse back again," said Lady Muriel. "Take another cup of tea? I hope *that's* sound common sense?"

"And all that strange adventure", I thought, "has occupied the space of a single comma in Lady Muriel's speech! A single comma, for which grammarians tell us to 'count *one*'!" (I felt no doubt that the Professor had kindly put back the time for me, to the exact point at which I had gone to sleep.)

When a few minutes afterwards, we left the house, Arthur's first remark was certainly a strange one. "We've been there just *twenty minutes*," he said, "and I've done nothing but listen to you and Lady Muriel talking: and yet, somehow, I feel exactly as if *I* had been talking with her for an *hour* at least!"

And so he *had* been, I felt no doubt: only, as the time had been put back to the beginning of the *tête-à-tête* he referred to, the whole of it had passed into oblivion, if not into nothingness! But I valued my own reputation for sanity too highly to venture on explaining to *him* what had happened.

For some cause, which I could not at the moment divine, Arthur was unusually grave and silent during our walk home. It could not be connected with Eric Lindon, I thought, as he had for some days been away in London: so that, having Lady Muriel almost "all to himself"—for *I* was only too glad to hear those two conversing, to have any wish to intrude any remarks of my own—he *ought*, theoretically, to have been specially radiant and contented with life. "Can he have heard any bad news?" I said to myself. And, almost as if he had read my thoughts, he spoke.

"He will be here by the last train," he said, in the tone of one who is continuing a conversation rather than beginning one.

"Captain Lindon, do you mean?"

"Yes—Captain Lindon," said Arthur: "I said 'he', because I fancied we were talking about him. The Earl told me he comes to-night, though *to-morrow* is the day when he will know about the Commission that he's hoping for. I wonder he doesn't stay another day to hear the result, if he's really so anxious about it as the Earl believes he is."

"He can have a telegram sent after him," I said: "but it's not very soldier-like, running away from possible bad news!"

"He's a very good fellow," said Arthur: "but I confess it would be good news for *me*, if he got his Commission, and his Marching Orders all at once! I wish him all happiness—with *one* exception. Good night!" (We had reached home by this time.) "I'm not good company to-night—better be alone."

It was much the same, next day. Arthur declared he wasn't fit for Society, and I had to set forth alone for an afternoon-stroll. I took the road to the Station, and, at the point where the road from the "Hall" joined it, I paused, seeing my friends in the distance, seemingly bound for the same goal.

"Will you join us?" the Earl said, after I had exchanged greetings with him, and Lady Muriel, and Captain Lindon. "This restless young man is expecting a telegram, and we are going to the Station to meet it."

"There is also a restless young woman in the case," Lady Muriel added.

"That goes without saying, my child," said her father. "Women are *always* restless!"

"For generous appreciation of all one's *best* qualities," his daughter impressively remarked, "there's nothing to compare with a father, is there, Eric?"

"Cousins are not 'in it'," said Eric: and then somehow the conversation lapsed into two duologues, the younger folk taking the lead, and the two old men following with less eager steps.

"And when are we to see your little friends again?" said the Earl. "They are singularly attractive children."

"I shall be delighted to bring them, when I can," I said. "But I don't know, myself, when I am likely to see them again."

"I'm not going to question you," said the Earl: "but there's no harm in mentioning that Muriel is simply tormented with curiosity! We know most of the people about here, and she has been vainly trying to guess what house they can possibly be staying at."

"Some day I may be able to enlighten her: but just at present——"

"Thanks. She must bear it as best she can. *I* tell her it's a grand opportunity for practising *patience*. But she hardly sees it from that point of view. Why, there *are* the children!"

So indeed they were: waiting (for *us*, apparently) at a stile, which they could not have climbed over more than a few moments, as Lady Muriel and her cousin had passed it without seeing them. On catching sight of us, Bruno ran to meet us, and to exhibit to us, with much pride, the handle of a clasp-knife—the blade having been broken off—which he had picked up in the road.

"And what shall you use it for, Bruno?" I said.

"Don't know," Bruno carelessly replied: "must think."

"A child's first view of life", the Earl remarked, with that sweet sad smile of his, "is that it is a period to be spent in accumulating portable property. That view gets modified as the years glide away." And he held out his hand to Sylvie, who had placed herself by me, looking a little shy of him.

But the gentle old man was not one with whom any child, human of fairy, could be shy for long; and she had very soon deserted my hand for his—Bruno alone remaining faithful to his first friend. We overtook the other couple just as they reached the Station, and both Lady Muriel and Eric greeted the children as old friends—the latter with the words "So you got to Babylon by candle-light, after all?"

"Yes, and back again!" cried Bruno.

Lady Muriel looked from one to the other in blank astonishment. "What, *you* know them, Eric?" she exclaimed. "This mystery grows deeper every day!"

"Then we must be somewhere in the Third Act," said Eric. "You don't expect the mystery to be cleared up till the Fifth Act, do you?"

"But it's such a *long* drama!" was the plaintive reply. "We *must* have got to the Fifth Act by this time!"

"*Third* Act, I assure you," said the young soldier mercilessly. "Scene, a railway-platform. Lights down. Enter Prince (in disguise, of course) and faithful Attendant. *This* is the Prince—" (taking Bruno's hand) "and here stands his humble Servant! What is your Royal Highness's next command?" And he made a most courtier-like low bow to his puzzled little friend.

"Oo're *not* a Servant!" Bruno scornfully exclaimed. "Oo're a *Gemplun*!"

"*Servant*, I assure your Royal Highness!" Eric respectfully insisted. "Allow me to mention to your Royal Highness my various situations—past, present, and future."

"What did oo begin wiz?" Bruno asked, beginning to enter into the jest. "Was oo a shoe-black?"

"Lower than that, your Royal Highness! Years ago, I offered myself as a *Slave*—as a '*Confidential* Slave', I think it's called?" he asked, turning to Lady Muriel.

But Lady Muriel heard him not: something had gone wrong with her glove, which entirely engrossed her attention.

"Did oo get the place?" said Bruno.

"Sad to say, your Royal Highness, I did *not*! So I had to take a situation as—as *Waiter*, which I have now held for some years—haven't I?" He again glanced at Lady Muriel.

"Sylvie dear, *do* help me to button this glove!" Lady Muriel whispered, hastily stooping down, and failing to hear the question.

"And what will oo be *next*?" said Bruno.

"My next place will, I hope, be that of *Groom*. And after that——"

"Don't puzzle the child so!" Lady Muriel interrupted. "What nonsense you talk!"

"—after that," Eric persisted, "I hope to obtain the situation of *Housekeeper*, which—*Fourth Act!*" he proclaimed, with a sudden change of tone. "Lights turned up. Red lights. Green lights. Distant rumble heard. Enter a passenger-train!"

And in another minute the train drew up alongside of the platform, and a stream of passengers began to flow out from the booking office and waiting-rooms.

"Did you ever make *real* life into a drama?" said the Earl. "Now just try. I've often amused myself that way. Consider this platform as our stage. Good entrances and exits on *both* sides, you see. Capital background scene: real engine moving up and down. All this bustle, and people passing to and fro, must have been most carefully rehearsed! How naturally they do it! With never a glance at the audience! And every grouping is quite fresh, you see. No repetition!"

It really was admirable, as soon as I began to enter into it from this point of view. Even a porter passing, with a barrow piled with luggage, seemed so realistic that one was tempted to applaud. He was followed by an angry mother, with hot red face, dragging along two screaming children, and calling, to some one behind, "John! Come on!" Enter, John, very meek, very silent, and loaded with parcels. And he was followed, in his turn, by a frightened little nursemaid, carrying a fat baby, also screaming. All the children screamed.

"Capital byplay!" said the old man aside. "Did you notice the nursemaid's look of terror? It was simply *perfect!*"

"You have struck quite a new vein," I said. "To most of us Life and its pleasures seem like a mine that is nearly worked out."

"Worked out!" exclaimed the Earl. "For any one with true dramatic instincts, it is only the Overture that is ended! The real treat has yet to begin. You go to a theatre, and pay your ten shillings for a stall, and what do you get for your money? Perhaps it's a dialogue between a couple of farmers—unnatural in their overdone caricature of farmers' dress—more unnatural in their constrained attitudes and gestures—most unnatural in their attempts at ease and geniality in their talk. Go instead and take a seat in a third-class railway-carriage, and you'll get the same dialogue done *to the life*! Front-seats—no orchestra to block the view—and nothing to pay!"

"Which reminds me," said Eric. "There is nothing to pay on receiving a telegram! Shall we enquire for one?" And he and Lady Muriel strolled off in the direction of the Telegraph-Office.

"I wonder if Shakespeare had that thought in his mind", I said, "when he wrote 'All the world's a stage'?"

The old man sighed. "And so it is," he said, "look at it as you will. Life is indeed a drama; a drama with but few *encores*—and no *bouquets!*" he added dreamily. "We spend one half of it in regretting the things we did in the other half!"

"And the secret of *enjoying* it", he continued, resuming his cheerful tone, "is *intensity!*"

"But not in the modern æsthetic sense, I presume? Like the young lady, in Punch, who begins a conversation with 'Are you *intense?*' "

"By no means!" replied the Earl. "What I mean is intensity of *thought*—a concentrated *attention*. We lose half the pleasure we might have in Life, by not really *attending*. Take any instance you like: it doesn't matter *how* trivial the pleasure may be—the principle is the same. Suppose *A* and *B* are reading the same second-rate circulating-library novel. *A* never troubles himself to master the relationships of the characters, on which perhaps all the interest of the story depends: he 'skips' over all the descriptions of scenery, and every passage that looks rather dull: he doesn't half attend to the passages he does read: he goes on reading—merely from want of resolution to find another occupation—for hours after he ought to have put the book aside: and reaches the 'FINIS' in a state of utter weariness and depression! *B* puts his whole soul *into* the thing—on the principle that 'whatever is worth doing is worth doing *well*': he masters the genealogies: he calls up pictures before his 'mind's eye' as he reads about the scenery: best of all, he resolutely shuts the book at the end of some chapter, while his interest is yet at its keenest, and turns to other subjects; so that, when next he allows himself an hour at it, it is like a hungry man sitting down to dinner: and, when the book is finished, he returns to the work of his daily life like 'a giant refreshed'!"

"But suppose the book were really *rubbish*—nothing to repay attention?"

"Well, suppose it," said the Earl. "My theory meets *that* case, I assure you! *A* never finds out that it *is* rubbish, but maunders on to the end, trying to believe he's enjoying himself. *B* quietly shuts the book, when he's read a dozen pages, walks off to the Library, and changes it for a better! I have yet *another* theory for adding to the enjoyment of Life—that is, if I have not exhausted your patience? I'm afraid you find me a very garrulous old man."

"No indeed!" I exclaimed earnestly. And indeed I felt as if one *could* not easily tire of the sweet sadness of that gentle voice.

"It is, that we should learn to take our pleasures *quickly*, and our pains *slowly*."

"But why? I should have put it the other way, myself."

"By taking *artificial* pain—which can be as trivial as you please—*slowly*, the result is that, when *real* pain comes, however severe, all you need do is to let it go at its *ordinary* pace, and it's over in a moment!"

"Very true," I said, "but how about the *pleasure*?"

"Why, by taking it quick, you can get so much more into life. It takes *you* three hours and a half to hear and enjoy an opera. Suppose *I* can take it in, and enjoy it, in half-an-hour. Why, I can enjoy *seven* operas, while you are listening to *one*!"

"Always supposing you have an orchestra capable of *playing* them," I said. "And that orchestra has yet to be found!"

The old man smiled. "I have heard an air played," he said, "and by no means a short one—played right through, variations and all, in three seconds!"

"When? And how?" I asked eagerly, with a half-notion that I was dreaming again.

"It was done by a little musical-box," he quietly replied. "After it had been wound up, the regulator, or something, broke, and it ran down, as I said, in about three seconds. But it *must* have played all the notes, you know!"

"Did you *enjoy* it?" I asked, with all the severity of a cross-examining barrister.

"No, I didn't!" he candidly confessed. "But then, you know, I hadn't been trained to that kind of music!"

"I should much like to *try* your plan," I said, and, as Sylvie and Bruno happened to run up to us at the moment, I left them to keep the Earl company, and strolled along the platform, making each person and event play its part in an *extempore* drama for my especial benefit. "What, is the Earl tired of you already?" I said, as the children ran past me.

"No!" Sylvie replied with great emphasis. "He wants the evening-paper. So Bruno's going to be a little news-boy!"

"Mind you charge a good price for it!" I called after them.

Returning up the platform, I came upon Sylvie alone. "Well, child," I said, "where's your little news-boy? Couldn't he get you an evening-paper?"

"He went to get one at the book-stall at the other side," said Sylvie; "and he's coming across the line with it—oh, Bruno, you ought to cross by the bridge!" for the distant thud, thud, of the Express was already audible. Suddenly a look of horror came over her face. "Oh, he's fallen down on the rails!" she cried, and darted past me at a speed that quite defied the hasty effort I made to stop her.

But the wheezy old Station-Master happened to be close behind me: he wasn't good for much, poor old man, but he was good for this; and, before I could turn round, he had the child clasped in his arms, saved from the certain death she was rushing to. So intent was I in watching this scene, that I hardly saw a flying figure in a light grey suit, who shot across from the back of the platform, and was on the line in another second. So far as one could take note of time in such a moment of horror, he had about ten clear seconds, before the Express would be upon him, in which to cross the rails and to pick up Bruno. Whether he did so or not it was quite impossible to guess: the next thing one knew was that the Express had passed, and that, whether for life or death, all was over. When the cloud of dust had cleared away, and the line was once more visible, we saw with thankful hearts that the child and his deliverer were safe.

"All right!" Eric called to us cheerfully, as he recrossed the line. "He's more frightened than hurt!"

He lifted the little fellow up into Lady Muriel's arms, and mounted the platform as gaily as if nothing had happened: but he was as pale as death, and leaned heavily on the arm I hastily offered him, fearing he was about to faint. "I'll just—sit down a moment——" he said dreamily: "—where's Sylvie?"

Sylvie ran to him, and flung her arms round his neck, sobbing as if her heart would break. "Don't do that, my darling!" Eric murmured, with a strange look in his eyes. "Nothing to cry about now, you know. But you very nearly got yourself killed for nothing!"

"For Bruno!" the little maiden sobbed. "And he would have done it for me. Wouldn't you, Bruno?"

"Course I would!" Bruno said, looking round with a bewildered air.

Lady Muriel kissed him in silence as she put him down out of her arms. Then she beckoned Sylvie to come and take his hand, and signed to the children to go back to where the Earl was seated. "Tell him," she whispered with quivering lips, "tell him—all is well!" Then she turned to the hero of the day. "I thought it was *death*," she said. "Thank God, you are safe! Did you see how near it was?"

"I saw there was just time," Eric said lightly. "A soldier must learn to carry his life in his hand, you know. I'm all right now. Shall we go to the telegraph-office again? I daresay it's come by this time."

I went to join the Earl and the children, and we waited —almost in silence, for no one seemed inclined to talk, and Bruno was half-asleep on Sylvie's lap—till the others joined us. No telegram had come.

"I'll take a stroll with the children," I said, feeling that we were a little *de trop*, "and I'll look in, in the course of the evening."

"We must go back into the wood, now," Sylvie said, as soon as we were out of hearing. "We ca'n't stay this size any longer."

"Then you will be quite tiny Fairies, again, next time we meet?"

"Yes," said Sylvie: "but we'll be children again some day—if you'll let us. Bruno's very anxious to see Lady Muriel again."

"She are *welly* nice," said Bruno.

"I shall be very glad to take you to see her again," I said. "Hadn't I better give you back the Professor's Watch? It'll be too large for you to carry when you're Fairies, you know."

Bruno laughed merrily. I was glad to see he had quite recovered from the terrible scene he had gone through. "Oh, no, it wo'n't!" he said. "When *we* go small, *it'll* go small!"

"And then it'll go straight to the Professor," Sylvie added, "and you wo'n't be able to use it any more: so you'd better use it all you can, *now*. We *must* go small when the sun sets. Good-bye!"

"Good-bye!" cried Bruno. But their voices sounded very far away, and, when I looked round, both children had disappeared.

"And it wants only two hours to sunset!" I said as I strolled on. "I must make the best of my time!"

Chapter XXIII

An Outlandish Watch

As I entered the little town, I came upon two of the fishermen's wives interchanging that last word "which never was the last": and it occurred to me, as an experiment with the Magic Watch, to wait till the little scene was over, and then to "encore" it.

"Well, good night t'ye! And ye winna forget to send us word when your Martha writes?"

"Nay, ah winna forget. An' if she isn't suited, she can but coom back. Good night t'ye!"

A casual observer might have thought "and there ends

the dialogue!" That casual observer would have been mistaken.

"Ah, she'll like 'em, I war'n' ye! *They'll* not treat her bad, yer may depend. They're varry canny fowk. Good night!"

"Ay, they *are* that! Good night!"

"Good night! And ye'll send us word if she writes?"

"Aye, ah will, yer may depend! Good night t'ye!"

And at last they parted. I waited till they were some twenty yards apart, and then put the Watch a minute back. The instantaneous change was startling: the two figures seemed to flash back into their former places.

"—isn't suited, she can but coom back. Good night t'ye!" one of them was saying: and so the whole dialogue was repeated, and, when they had parted for the second time, I let them go their several ways, and strolled on through the town.

"But the real usefulness of this magic power", I thought, "would be to undo some harm, some painful event, some accident——" I had not long to wait for an opportunity of testing *this* property also of the Magic Watch, for, even as the thought passed through my mind, the accident I was imagining occurred. A light cart was standing at the door of the "Great Millinery Depôt" of Elveston, laden with card-board packing-cases, which the driver was carrying into the shop, one by one. One of the cases had fallen into the street. but it scarcely seemed worth while to step forward and pick it up, as the man would be back again in a moment. Yet, in that moment, a young man riding a bicycle came sharp round the corner of the street and, in trying to avoid running over the box, upset his machine, and was thrown headlong against the wheel of the spring-cart. The driver ran out to his assistance, and he and I together raised the unfortunate cyclist and carried him into the shop. His head was cut and bleeding; and one knee seemed to be badly injured; and it was speedily settled that he had better be conveyed at once to the only Surgery in the place. I helped them in emptying the cart, and placing in it some pillows for the wounded man to rest on; and it was only when the driver had mounted to his place, and was starting for the Surgery, that I bethought me of the strange power I possessed of undoing all this harm.

"Now is my time!" I said to myself, as I moved back the hand of the Watch, and saw, almost without surprise this time, all things restored to the places they had occupied at the critical moment when I had first noticed the fallen packing-case.

Instantly I stepped out into the street, picked up the box, and replaced it in the cart: in the next moment the bicycle had spun round the corner, passed the cart without let or hindrance, and soon vanished in the distance, in a cloud of dust.

"Delightful power of magic!" I thought. "How much of human suffering I have—not only relieved, but actually annihilated!" And, in a glow of conscious virtue, I stood watching the unloading of the cart, still holding the Magic Watch open in my hand, as I was curious to see what would happen when we again reached the exact time at which I had put back the hand.

The result was one that, if only I had considered the thing carefully, I might have foreseen: as the hand of the Watch touched the mark, the spring-cart—which had driven off, and was by this time half-way down the street, was back again at the door, and in the act of starting, while—oh woe for the golden dream of world-wide benevolence that had dazzled my dreaming fancy!—the wounded youth was once more reclining on the heap of pillows, his pale face set rigidly in the hard lines that told of pain resolutely endured.

"Oh mocking Magic Watch!" I said to myself, as I passed out of the little town, and took the seaward road that led to my lodgings. "The good I fancied I could do is vanished like a dream: the evil of this troublesome world is the only abiding reality!"

And now I must record an experience so strange, that I

think it only fair, before beginning to relate it, to release
my much-enduring reader from any obligation he may
feel to believe this part of my story, *I* would not have
believed it, I freely confess, if I had not seen it with my
own eyes: then why should I expect it of my reader, who,
quite possibly, has never seen anything of the sort?

I was passing a pretty little villa, which stood rather
back from the road, in its own grounds, with bright
flower-beds in front—creepers wandering over the walls
and hanging in festoons about the bow-windows—an easy-
chair forgotten on the lawn, with a newspaper lying near
it—a small pug-dog "couchant" before it, resolved to
guard the treasure even at the sacrifice of life—and a
front-door standing invitingly half-open. "Here is my
chance", I thought, "for testing the reverse action of the
Magic Watch!" I pressed the "reversal-peg" and walked
in. In *another* house, the entrance of a stranger might
cause surprise—perhaps anger, even going so far as to
expel the said stranger with violence: but *here*, I knew,
nothing of the sort could happen. The *ordinary* course of
events—first, to think nothing about me; then, hearing
my footsteps to look up and see me; and then to wonder
what business I had there—would be reversed by the
action of my Watch. They would *first* wonder who I was,
then see me, then look down, and think no more about me.
And as to being expelled with violence, *that* event would
necessarily come *first* in this case. "So, if I can once get
in," I said to myself, "all risk of *expulsion* will be over!"

The pug-dog sat up, as a precautionary measure, as I
passed; but, as I took no notice of the treasure he was
guarding, he let me go by without even one remonstrant
bark. "He that takes my life," he seemed to be saying,
wheezily, to himself, "takes trash: But he that takes the
Daily Telegraph——!" But this awful contingency I did
not face.

The party in the drawing-room—I had walked straight
in, you understand, without ringing the bell, or giving
any notice of my approach—consisted of four laughing

rosy children, of ages from about fourteen down to ten, who were, apparently, all coming towards the door (I found they were really walking *backwards*), while their mother, seated by the fire with some needle-work on her lap, was saying, just as I entered the room, "Now, girls, you may get your things on for a walk."

To my utter astonishment—for I was not yet accustomed to the action of the Watch—"all smiles ceased" (as Browning says) on the four pretty faces, and they all got out pieces of needle-work, and sat down. No one noticed *me* in the least, as I quietly took a chair and sat down to watch them.

When the needle-work had been unfolded, and they were all ready to begin, their mother said "Come, *that's* done, at last! You may fold up your work, girls." But the children took no notice whatever of the remark; on the contrary, they set to work at once sewing—if that is the proper word to describe an operation such as *I* had never before witnessed. Each of them threaded her needle with a short end of thread attached to the work, which was instantly pulled by an invisible force through the stuff, dragging the needle after it: the nimble fingers of the little sempstress caught it at th other side, but only to lose it again the next moment. And so the work went on, steadily undoing itself, and the neatly-stitched little dresses, or whatever they were, steadily falling to pieces. Now and then one of the children would pause, as the recovered thread became inconveniently long, wind it on a bobbin, and start again with another short end.

At last all the work was picked to pieces and put away, and the lady led the way into the next room, walking backwards, and making the insane remark "Not yet, dear: we *must* get the sewing done first." After which, I was not surprised to see the children skipping backwards after her, exclaiming "Oh, mother, it *is* such a lovely day for a walk!"

In the dining-room, the table had only dirty plates and empty dishes on it. However the party—with the addition of a gentleman, as good-natured, and as rosy, as the children—seated themselves at it very contentedly.

You have seen peopie eating cherry-tart, and every now and then cautiously conveying a cherry-stone from their lips to their plates? Well, something like that went on all through this ghastly—or shall we say "ghostly"?—banquet. An empty fork is raised to the lips: there it receives a neatly-cut piece of mutton, and swiftly conveys it to the plate, where it instantly attaches itself to the mutton already there. Soon one of the plates, furnished with a complete slice of mutton and two potatoes, was handed up to the presiding gentleman, who quietly replaced the slice on the joint, and the potatoes in the dish.

Their conversation was, if possible, more bewildering than their mode of dining. It began by the youngest girl suddenly, and without provocation, addressing her eldest sister. "Oh, you *wicked* story-teller!" she said.

I expected a sharp reply from the sister; but, instead of this, she turned laughingly to her father, and said, in a very loud stage-whisper, "To be a bride!"

The father, in order to do *his* part in a conversation that seemed only fit for lunatics, replied "Whisper it to me, dear."

But she *didn't* whisper (these children never did anything they were told): she said, quite loud, "Of course not! Everybody knows what *Dolly* wants!"

And little Dolly shrugged her shoulders, and said, with a pretty pettishness, "Now, Father, you're not to tease! You know I don't want to be bride's-maid to *anybody*!"

"And Dolly's to be the fourth," was her father's idiotic reply.

Here Number Three put in her oar. "Oh, it *is* settled, Mother dear, really and truly! Mary told us all about it. It's to be next Tuesday four weeks—and three of her cousins are coming to be bride's-maids—and——"

"*She* doesn't forget it Minnie!" the Mother laughingly replied. "I do wish they'd get it settled! I don't like long engagements."

And Minnie wound up the conversation—if so chaotic a series of remarks deserves the name—with "Only think! We passed the Cedars this morning, just exactly as Mary Davenant was standing at the gate, wishing good-bye to Mister—I forget his name. Of course we looked the other way."

By this time I was so hopelessly confused that I gave up listening, and followed the dinner down into the kitchen.

But to you, O hypercritical reader, resolute to believe no item of this weird adventure, what need to tell how the mutton was placed on the spit, and slowly unroasted—how the potatoes were wrapped in their skins, and handed over to the gardener to be buried—how, when the mutton had at length attained to rawness, the fire, which had gradually changed from red-heat to a mere blaze, died down so suddenly that the cook had only just time to catch its last flicker on the end of a match—or how the maid, having taken the mutton off the spit, carried it (backwards, of course) out of the house, to meet the butcher, who was coming (also backwards) down the road?

The longer I thought over this strange adventure, the more hopelessly tangled the mystery became: and it was a real relief to meet Arthur in the road, and get him to go with me up to the Hall, to learn what news the telegraph had brought. I told him, as we went, what had happened at the Station, but as to my further adventures I thought it best, for the present, to say nothing.

The Earl was sitting alone when we entered. "I am glad you are come in to keep me company," he said. "Muriel is gone to bed—the excitement of that terrible scene was too much for her—and Eric has gone to the hotel to pack his things, to start for London by the early train."

"Then the telegram has come!" I said.

"Did you not hear? Oh, I had forgotten: it came in after you left the Station. Yes, it's all right: Eric has got his commission; and, now that he has arranged matters with Muriel, he has business in town that must be seen to at once."

"What arrangement do you mean?" I asked with a sinking heart, as the thought of Arthur's crushed hopes came to my mind. "Do you mean that they are *engaged*?"

"They have been engaged—in a sense—for two years," the old man gently replied: "that is, he has had my promise to consent to it, so soon as he could secure a permanent and settled line in life. I could never be happy with my child married to a man without an object to live for— without even an object to die for!"

"I hope they will be happy," a strange voice said. The speaker was evidently in the room, but I had not heard the door open, and I looked around in some astonishment. The Earl seemed to share my surprise. "Who spoke?" he exclaimed.

"It was I," said Arthur, looking at us with a worn, haggard face, and eyes from which the light of life seemed suddenly to have faded. "And let me wish *you* joy also, dear friend," he added, looking sadly at the Earl, and speaking in the same hollow tones that had startled us so much.

"Thank you," the old man said, simply and heartily.

A silence followed: then I rose, feeling sure that Arthur would wish to be alone, and bade our gentle host "Good night": Arthur took his hand, but said nothing: nor did he speak again, as we went home, till we were in the house and had lit our bed-room candles. Then he said, more to himself than to me, *"The heart knoweth its own bitterness.* I never understood those words till now."

The next few days passed wearily enough. I felt no inclination to call again, by myself, at the Hall; still less to propose that Arthur should go with me: it seemed better to wait till Time—that gentle healer of our bitterest sorrows—should have helped him to recover from the first shock of the disappointment that had blighted his life.

Business, however, soon demanded my presence in town; and I had to announce to Arthur that I must leave him for a while. "But I hope to run down again in a month," I added. "I would stay now, if I could. I don't think it's good for you to be alone."

"No, I ca'n't face solitude, *here*, for long," said Arthur. "But don't think about *me*. I have made up my mind to accept a post in India, that has been offered me. Out there, I suppose I shall find something to live for; I ca'n't see *anything* at present. '*This life of mine I guard, as God's high gift, from scathe and wrong, Not greatly care to lose!*' "

"Yes," I said: "your name-sake bore as heavy a blow, and lived through it."

"A far heavier one than *mine*," said Arthur. "The woman *he* loved proved false. There is no such cloud as *that* on my memory of—of——" He left the name unuttered, and went on hurriedly. "But *you* will return, will you not?"

"Yes, I shall come back for a short time."

"Do," said Arthur: "and you shall write and tell me of our friends. I'll send you my address when I'm settled down."

Chapter XXIV

The Frogs' Birthday-Treat

AND so it came to pass that, just a week after the day when my Fairy-friends first appeared as Children, I found myself taking a farewell-stroll through the wood, in the hope of meeting them once more. I had but to stretch myself on the smooth turf, and the "eerie" feeling was on me in a moment.

"Put oor ear *welly* low down," said Bruno, "and I'll tell oo a secret! It's the Frogs' Birthday-Treat—and we've lost the Baby!"

"*What* Baby?" I said, quite bewildered by this complicated piece of news.

"The *Queen's* Baby, a course!" said Bruno. "Titania's Baby. And we's *welly* sorry. Sylvie, she's—oh so sorry!"

"*How* sorry is she?" I asked, mischievously.

"Three-quarters of a yard," Bruno replied with perfect solemnity. "And *I'm* a little sorry too," he added, shutting his eyes so as not to see that he was smiling.

"And what are you doing about the Baby?"

"Well, the *soldiers* are all looking for it—up and down —everywhere."

"The *soldiers*?" I exclaimed.

"Yes, a course!" said Bruno. "When there's no fighting to be done, the soldiers doos any little odd jobs, oo know."

I was amused at the idea of its being a "little odd job" to find the Royal Baby. "But how did you come to lose it?" I asked.

"We put it in a flower," Sylvie, who had just joined us, explained with her eyes full of tears. "Only we ca'n't remember *which*!"

"She says *us* put it in a flower," Bruno interrupted, " 'cause she doesn't want *I* to get punished. But it were really *me* what put it there. *Sylvie* were picking Dindledums."

"You shouldn't say '*us* put it in a flower'," Sylvie very gravely remarked.

"Well, *hus*, then," said Bruno. "I never *can* remember those horrid H's!"

"Let me help you to look for it," I said. So Sylvie and I made a "voyage of discovery" among all the flowers; but there was no Baby to be seen.

"What's become of Bruno?" I said, when we had completed our tour.

"He's down in the ditch there," said Sylvie, "amusing a young Frog."

I went down on my hands and knees to look for him, for I felt very curious to know how young Frogs *ought* to be amused. After a minute's search, I found him sitting at the edge of the ditch, by the side of the little Frog, and looking rather disconsolate.

"How are you getting on, Bruno?" I said, nodding to him as he looked up.

"Ca'n't amuse it no more," Bruno answered, very dolefully, " 'cause it wo'n't say what it would like to do next! I've showed it all the duck-weeds—and a live caddis-worm—but it wo'n't say nuffin! What—would oo—like?" he shouted into the ear of the Frog: but the little creature sat quite still, and took no notice of him. "It's deaf, I think!" Bruno said, turning away with a sigh. "And it's time to get the Theatre ready."

"Who are the audience to be?"

"Only but Frogs," said Bruno. "But they haven't comed yet. They wants to be drove up, like sheep."

"Would it save time", I suggested, "if I were to walk round with Sylvie, to drive up the Frogs, while you get the Theatre ready?"

"That are a good plan!" cried Bruno. "But where are Sylvie?"

"I'm here!" said Sylvie, peeping over the edge of the bank. "I was just watching two Frogs that were having a race."

"Which won it?" Bruno eagerly inquired.

Sylvie was puzzled. "He does ask such hard questions!" she confided to me.

"And what's to happen in the Theatre?" I asked.

"First they have their Birthday-Feast," Sylvie said: "then Bruno does some Bits of Shakespeare; then he tells them a Story."

"I should think the Frogs like the Feast best. Don't they?"

"Well, there's generally very few of them that get any. They will keep their mouths shut so tight! And it's just as well they do," she added, "because Bruno likes to cook it himself: and he cooks very queerly. Now they're all in. Would you just help me to put them with their heads the right way?"

We soon managed this part of the business, though the Frogs kept up a most discontented croaking all the time.

"What *are* they saying?" I asked Sylvie.

"They're saying 'Fork! Fork!' It's very silly of them! You're not going to *have* forks!" she announced with some severity. "Those that want any Feast have just got to open their mouths, and Bruno'll put some of it in!"

At this moment Bruno appeared, wearing a little white apron to show that he was a Cook, and carrying a tureen full of very queer-looking soup. I watched very carefully as he moved about among the Frogs; but I could not see that *any* of them opened their mouths to be fed—except one very young one, and I'm nearly sure it did it accidentally, in yawning. However, Bruno instantly put a large spoonful of soup into its mouth, and the poor little thing coughed violently for some time.

So Sylvie and I had to share the soup between us, and to *pretend* to enjoy it, for it certainly was *very* queerly cooked.

I only ventured to take *one* spoonful of it ("Sylvie's Summer-Soup," Bruno said it was), and must candidly confess that it was not *at all* nice; and I could not feel surprised that so many guests had kept their mouths shut up tight.

"What's the soup *made* of, Bruno?" said Sylvie, who had put a spoonful of it to her lips, and was making a wry face over it.

And Bruno's answer was anything but encouraging. "Bits of things!"

The entertainment was to conclude with "Bits of Shakespeare", as Sylvie expressed it, which were all to be done by Bruno, Sylvie being fully engaged in making the Frogs keep their heads towards the stage: after which Bruno was to appear in his real character, and tell them a Story of his own invention.

"Will the Story have a Moral to it?" I asked Sylvie, while Bruno was away behind the hedge, dressing for the first "Bit".

"I *think* so," Sylvie replied doubtfully. "There generally *is* a Moral, only he puts it in too soon."

"And will he *say* all the Bits of Shakespeare?"

"No, he'll only *act* them," said Sylvie. "He knows hardly any of the words. When I see what he's dressed like, I've to tell the Frogs what character it is. They're always in such a hurry to guess! Don't you hear them all saying 'What? What?'" And so indeed they were: it had only sounded like croaking, till Sylvie explained it, but I could now make out the "Wawt? Wawt?" quite distinctly.

"But why do they try to guess it before they see it?"

"I don't know," Sylvie said: "but they always *do*. Sometimes they begin guessing weeks and weeks before the day!"

(So now, when you hear the Frogs croaking in a particularly melancholy way, you may be sure they're trying to guess Bruno's next Shakespeare "Bit". Isn't *that* interesting?)

However, the chorus of guessing was cut short by Bruno, who suddenly rushed on from behind the scenes, and took a flying leap down among the Frogs, to re-arrange them.

For the oldest and fattest Frog—who had never been properly arranged so that he could see the stage, and so had no idea what was going on—was getting restless, and had upset several of the Frogs, and turned others round with their heads the wrong way. And it was no good at all, Bruno said, to do a "Bit" of Shakespeare when there was nobody to look at it (you see he didn't count *me* as anybody). So he set to work with a stick, stirring them up, very much as you would stir up tea in a cup, till most of them had at least *one* great stupid eye gazing at the stage.

"*Oo* must come and sit among them, Sylvie," he said in despair, "I've put these two side-by-side, with their noses the same way, ever so many times, but they *do* squarrel so!"

So Sylvie took her place as "Mistress of the Ceremonies", and Bruno vanished again behind the scenes, to dress for the first "Bit".

"Hamlet!" was suddenly proclaimed, in the clear sweet tones I knew so well. The croaking all ceased in a moment, and I turned to the stage, in some curiosity to see what Bruno's ideas were as to the behaviour of Shakespeare's greatest Character.

According to this eminent interpreter of the Drama, Hamlet wore a short black cloak (which he chiefly used for muffling up his face, as if he suffered a good deal from toothache), and turned out his toes very much as he walked. "To be or not to be!" Hamlet remarked in a cheerful tone, and then turned head-over-heels several times, his cloak dropping off in the performance.

I felt a little disappointed: Bruno's conception of the part seemed so wanting in dignity. "Wo'n't he say any more of the speech?" I whispered to Sylvie.

"I *think* not," Sylvie whispered in reply. "He generally turns head-over-heels when he doesn't know any more words."

Bruno had meanwhile settled the question by disappearing from the stage; and the Frogs instantly began inquiring the name of the next Character.

"You'll know directly!" cried Sylvie, as she adjusted two or three young Frogs that had struggled round with their backs to the stage. "Macbeth!" she added, as Bruno re-appeared.

Macbeth had something twisted round him, that went over one shoulder and under the other arm, and was meant, I believe, for a Scotch plaid. He had a thorn in his hand, which he held out at arm's length, as if he were a little afraid of it. "Is this a *dagger*?" Macbeth inquired, in a puzzled sort of tone: and instantly a chorus of "Thorn! Thorn!" arose from the Frogs (I had quite learned to understand their croaking by this time).

"It's a *dagger*!" Sylvie proclaimed in a peremptory tone. "Hold your tongues!" and the croaking ceased at once.

Shakespeare has not told us, so far as I know, that Macbeth had any such eccentric habit as turning head-over-heels in private life: but Bruno evidently considered it quite an essential part of the character, and left the stage in a series of somersaults. However, he was back again in a few moments, having tucked under his chin the end of a tuft of wool (probably left on the thorn by a wandering sheep), which made a magnificent beard, that reached nearly down to his feet.

"Shylock!" Sylvie proclaimed. "No, I beg your pardon!" she hastily corrected herself, "King Lear! I hadn't noticed the crown." (Bruno had very cleverly provided one, which fitted him exactly, by cutting out the centre of a dandelion to make room for his head.)

King Lear folded his arms (to the imminent peril of his beard) and said, in a mild explanatory tone, "Ay, every *inch* a king!" and then paused, as if to consider how this could best be proved. And here, with all possible deference to Bruno as a Shakespearean critic, I *must* express my opinion that the poet did *not* mean his three great tragic heroes to be so strangely alike in their personal habits; nor do I believe that he would have accepted the faculty of turning head-over-heels as any proof at all of royal descent. Yet it appeared that King Lear, after deep meditation, could think of no other argument by which to prove his kingship: and, as this was the last of the "Bits" of Shakespeare ("We never do more than *three*," Sylvie explained in a whisper), Bruno gave the audience quite a long series of somersaults before he finally retired, leaving the enraptured Frogs all crying out "More! More!" which I suppose was their way of encoring a performance. But Bruno wouldn't appear again, till the proper time came for telling the Story.

When he appeared at last in his *real* character, I noticed a remarkable change in his behaviour. He tried no more somersaults. It was clearly his opinion that, however suitable the habit of turning head-over-heels might be to such petty individuals as Hamlet and King Lear, it would never do for *Bruno* to sacrifice his dignity to such an extent. But it was equally clear that he did not feel entirely at his ease, standing all alone on the stage, with no costume to disguise him: and though he began, several times, "There were a Mouse——", he kept glancing up and down, and on all sides, as if in search of more comfortable quarters from which to tell the Story. Standing on one side of the stage, and partly overshadowing it, was a tall fox-glove, which seemed, as the evening breeze gently swayed it hither and thither, to offer exactly the sort of accommodation that the orator desired. Having once decided on his quarters, it needed only a second or two for him to run up the stem like a tiny squirrel, and to seat himself astride on the topmost bend, where the fairy-bells clustered most closely, and from whence he could look down on his audience from such a height that all shyness vanished, and he began his Story merrily.

"Once there were a Mouse and a Crocodile and a Man and a Goat and a Lion." I had never heard the "dramatis personæ" tumbled into a story with such profusion and in such reckless haste; and it fairly took my breath away. Even Sylvie gave a little gasp, and allowed three of the Frogs, who seemed to be getting tired of the entertainment, to hop away into the ditch, without attempting to stop them.

"And the Mouse found a Shoe, and it thought it were a Mouse-trap. So it got right in, and it stayed in ever so long."

"Why did it *stay* in?" said Sylvie. Her function seemed to be much the same as that of the Chorus in a Greek Play: she had to encourage the orator, and draw him out, by a series of intelligent questions.

" 'Cause it thought it couldn't get out again," Bruno explained. "It were a clever mouse. It knew it couldn't get out of traps!"

"But why did it go in at all?" said Sylvie.

"—and it jamp, and it jamp," Bruno proceeded, ignoring this question, "and at last it got right out again. And it looked at the mark in the Shoe. And the Man's name were in it. So it knew it wasn't its own Shoe."

"Had it thought it *was*?" said Sylvie.

"Why, didn't I tell oo it thought it were a *Mouse-trap*?' the indignant orator replied. "Please, Mister Sir, will oo make Sylvie attend?" Sylvie was silenced, and was all attention: in fact, she and I were most of the audience now, as the Frogs kept hopping away, and there were very few of them left.

"So the Mouse gave the Man his Shoe. And the Man were welly glad, 'cause he hadn't got but one Shoe, and he were hopping to get the other."

Here I ventured on a question. "Do you mean 'hopping', or 'hoping'?"

"Bofe," said Bruno. "And the Man took the Goat out of the Sack." ("We haven't heard of the *sack* before," I said. "Now you wo'n't hear of it again," said Bruno.) "And he said to the Goat, 'Oo will walk about here till I comes back.' And he went and he tumbled into a deep hole. And the Goat walked round and round. And it walked under the Tree. And it wug its tail. And it looked up in the Tree. And it sang a sad little Song. Oo never heard such a sad little Song!"

"Can you sing it, Bruno?" I asked.

"Iss, I can," Bruno readily replied. "And I sa'n't. It would make Sylvie cry——"

"It wouldn't!" Sylvie interrupted in great indignation. "And I don't believe the Goat sang it at all!"

"It did, though!" said Bruno. "It singed it right froo. I *sawed* it singing with its long beard——"

"It couldn't sing with its *beard*," I said, hoping to puzzle the little fellow: "a beard isn't a *voice*."

"Well then, *oo* couldn't walk with Sylvie!" Bruno cried triumphantly. "Sylvie isn't a *foot*!"

I thought I had better follow Sylvie's example, and be silent for a while. Bruno was too sharp for us.

"And when it had singed all the Song, it ran away— for to get along to look for the Man, oo know. And the Crocodile got along after it—for to bite it, oo know. And the Mouse got along after the Crocodile.

"Wasn't the Crocodile *running*?" Sylvie enquired. She appealed to me. "Crocodiles do run, don't they?"

I suggested "crawling" as the proper word.

"He wasn't running," said Bruno, "and he wasn't crawling. He went struggling along like a portmanteau. And he held his chin ever so high in the air——"

"What did he do *that* for?" said Sylvie.

"'Cause he hadn't got a toofache!" said Bruno. "Ca'n't oo make out *nuffin* wizout I 'splain it? Why, if he'd had a toofache, a course he'd have held his head down—like this—and he'd have put a lot of warm blankets round it!"

"If he'd *had* any blankets," Sylvie argued.

"Course he *had* blankets!" retorted her brother. "Doos oo think Crocodiles goes walks wizout blankets? And he frowned with his eyebrows. And the Goat was welly flightened at his eyebrows!"

"I'd never be afraid of *eyebrows*!" exclaimed Sylvie.

"I should think oo *would*, though, if they'd got a Crocodile fastened to them, like these had! And so the Man jamp, and he jamp, and at last he got right out of the hole."

Sylvia gave another little gasp: this rapid dodging about among the characters of the Story had taken away her breath.

"And he runned away—for to look for the Goat, oo know. And he heard the Lion grunting——"

"Lions don't grunt," said Sylvie.

"This one did," said Bruno. "And its mouth were like a large cupboard. And it had plenty of room in its mouth. And the Lion runned after the Man—for to eat him, oo know. And the Mouse runned after the Lion."

"But the Mouse was running after the *Crocodile*," I said: "he couldn't run after *both*!"

Bruno sighed over the density of his audience, but explained very patiently. "He *did* runned after *bofe*: 'cause they went the same way! And first he caught the Crocodile, and then he didn't catch the Lion. And when he'd caught the Crocodile, what doos oo think he did—'cause he'd got pincers in his pocket?"

"I ca'n't guess," said Sylvie.

"Nobody couldn't guess it!" Bruno cried in high glee. "Why, he wrenched out that Crocodile's toof!"

"*Which* tooth?" I ventured to ask.

But Bruno was not to be puzzled. "The toof he were going to bite the Goat with, a course!"

"He couldn't be sure about that", I argued, "unless he wrenched out *all* its teeth."

Bruno laughed merrily, and half sang, as he swung himself backwards and forwards, "He did—wrenched—out—*all* its teef!"

"Why did the Crocodile wait to have them wrenched out?" said Sylvie.

"It had to wait," said Bruno.

I ventured on another question. "But what became of the Man who said 'You may wait here till I come back'?"

"He didn't say 'Oo *may*'," Bruno explained. "He said, 'Oo *will*.' Just like Sylvie says to me 'Oo will do oor lessons till twelve o'clock.' Oh, I *wiss*," he added with a little sigh, "I *wiss* Sylvie would say 'Oo *may* do oor lessons'!"

This was a dangerous subject for discussion, Sylvie seemed to think. She returned to the Story. "But what became of the Man?"

"Well, the Lion springed at him. But it came so slow, it were three weeks in the air——"

"Did the Man wait for it all that time?" I said.

"Course he didn't!" Bruno replied, gliding head-first down the stem of the fox-glove, for the Story was evidently close to its end. "He sold his house, and he packed up his things, while the Lion were coming. And he went and he lived in another town. So the Lion ate the wrong man."

This was evidently the Moral: so Sylvie made her final proclamation to the Frogs. "The Story's finished! And whatever is to be *learned* from it," she added, aside to me, "I'm sure *I* don't know!"

I did not feel *quite* clear about it myself, so made no suggestion: but the Frogs seemed quite content, Moral or no Moral, and merely raised a husky chorus of "Off! Off!" as they hopped away.

Chapter XXV

Looking Eastward

"It's just a week", I said, three days later, to Arthur, "since we heard of Lady Muriel's engagement. I think *I* ought to call, at any rate, and offer my congratulations. Wo'n't you come with me?"

A pained expression passed over his face. "When must you leave us?" he asked.

"By the first train on Monday."

"Well—yes, I *will* come with you. It would seem strange and unfriendly if I didn't. But this is only Friday. Give me till Sunday afternoon. I shall be stronger then."

Shading his eyes with one hand, as if half-ashamed of the tears that were coursing down his cheeks, he held the other out to me. It trembled as I clasped it.

I tried to frame some words of sympathy; but they seemed poor and cold, and I left them unspoken. "Good night!" was all I said.

"Good night, dear friend!" he replied. There was a manly vigour in his tone that convinced me he was wrestling with, and triumphing over, the great sorrow that had so nearly wrecked his life—and that, on the stepping-stone of his dead self, he would surely rise to higher things!

There was no chance, I was glad to think, as we set out on Sunday afternoon, of meeting *Eric* at the Hall, as he had returned to town the day after his engagement was announced. *His* presence might have disturbed the calm —the almost unnatural calm—with which Arthur met the woman who had won his heart, and murmured the few graceful words of sympathy that the occasion demanded.

Lady Muriel was perfectly radiant with happiness: sadness could not live in the light of such a smile: and even Arthur brightened under it, and, when she remarked "You see I'm watering my flowers, though it *is* the Sabbath-Day," his voice had almost its old ring of cheerfulness as he replied "Even on the Sabbath-Day works of mercy are allowed. But this *isn't* the Sabbath-Day. The Sabbath-Day has ceased to exist."

"I know it's not *Saturday*," Lady Muriel replied: "but isn't Sunday often called 'the Christian Sabbath'?"

"It is so called, I think, in recognition of the *spirit* of the Jewish institution, that one day in seven should be a day of *rest*. But I hold that Christians are freed from the *literal* observance of the Fourth Commandment."

"Then where is our *authority* for Sunday observance?"

"We have, first, the fact that the seventh day was 'sanctified', when God rested from the work of Creation. That is binding on us as *Theists*. Secondly, we have the fact that 'the Lord's Day' is a *Christian* institution. That is binding on us as *Christians*."

"And your practical rules would be——?"

"First, as Theists, to keep it *holy* in some special way, and to make it, so far as is reasonably possible, a day of *rest*. Secondly, as *Christians*, to attend public worship."

"And what of *amusements*?"

"I would say of them, as of all kinds of *work*, whatever is innocent on a week-day, is innocent on Sunday, provided it does not interfere with the duties of the day."

"Then you would allow children to *play* on Sunday?"

"Certainly I should. Why make the day irksome to their restless natures?"

"I have a letter somewhere," said Lady Muriel, "from an old friend, describing the way in which Sunday was kept in her younger days. I will fetch it for you."

"I had a similar description, *vivâ voce*, years ago," Arthur said when she had left us, "from a little girl. It was really touching to hear the melancholy tone in which she said 'On Sunday I mustn't play with my doll! On Sunday I mustn't run on the sands! On Sunday I mustn't dig in the garden!' Poor child! She had indeed abundant cause for hating Sunday!"

"Here is the letter," said Lady Muriel, returning. "Let me read you a piece of it."

"When, as a child, I first opened my eyes on a Sunday-morning, a feeling of dismal anticipation, which began at least on the Friday, culminated. I knew what was before me, and my wish, if not my word, was 'Would God it were evening!' It was no day of rest, but a day of texts, of catechisms (Watts'), of tracts about converted swearers, godly char-women, and edifying deaths of sinners saved.

"Up with the lark, hymns and portions of Scripture had to be learned by heart till 8 o'clock, when there were family-prayers, then breakfast, which I was never able to enjoy, partly from the fast already undergone, and partly from the outlook I dreaded.

"At 9 came Sunday-School; and it made me indignant to be put into the class with the village-children, as well as alarmed lest, by some mistake of mine, I should be put below them.

"The Church-Service was a veritable Wilderness of Zin. I wandered in it, pitching the tabernacle of my thoughts on the lining of the square family-pew, the fidgets of my small brothers, and the horror of knowing that, on the Monday, I should have to write out, from memory, jottings of the rambling disconnected extempore sermon, which might have any text but its own, and to stand or fall by the result.

"This was followed by a cold dinner at 1 (servants to have no work), Sunday-School again from 2 to 4, and Evening-Service at 6. The intervals were perhaps the greatest trial of all, from the efforts I had to make, to be less than usually sinful, by reading books and sermons as barren as the Dead Sea. There was but one rosy spot, in the distance, all that day: and that was 'bed-time', which never could come too early!"

"Such teaching was well meant, no doubt," said Arthur; "but it must have driven many of its victims into deserting the Church-Services altogether."

"I'm afraid *I* was a deserter this morning," she gravely said. "I had to write to Eric. Would you—would you mind my telling you something he said about *prayer*? It had never struck me in that light before."

"In what light?" said Arthur.

"Why, that all Nature goes by fixed, regular laws— Science has proved *that*. So that asking God to *do* anything (except of course praying for *spiritual* blessings) is to expect a miracle: and we've no right to do *that*. I've not put it as well as *he* did: but that was the outcome of it, and it has confused me. Please tell me what you can say in answer to it."

"I don't propose to discuss *Captain Lindon's* difficulties," Arthur gravely replied; "specially as he is not present. But, if it is *your* difficulty," (his voice unconsciously took a tender tone) "then I will speak."

"It *is* my difficulty," she said anxiously.

"Then I will begin by asking 'Why did you except *spiritual* blessings?' Is not your mind a part of Nature?"

"Yes, but Free-Will comes in there—I can *choose* this or that; and God can influence my choice."

"Then you are not a Fatalist?"

"Oh, no!" she earnestly exclaimed.

"Thank God!" Arthur said to himself, but in so low a whisper that only *I* heard it. "You grant then that I can, by an act of free choice, move this cup", suiting the action to the word, "*this* way or *that* way?"

"Yes, I grant it."

"Well, let us see how far the result is produced by fixed laws. The *cup* moves because certain mechanical forces are impressed on it by my *hand*. My *hand* moves because certain forces—electric, magnetic, or whatever 'nerve-force' may prove to be—are impressed on it by my *brain*. This nerve-force, stored in the brain, would probably be traceable, if Science were complete, to chemical forces supplied to the brain by the blood, and ultimately derived from the food I eat and the air I breathe."

"But would not that be Fatalism? Where would Free-Will come in?"

"In *choice* of nerves," replied Arthur. "The nerve-force in the brain may flow just as naturally down one nerve as down another. We need something more than a fixed Law of Nature to settle *which* nerve shall carry it. That 'something' is Free-Will."

Her eyes sparkled. "I see what you mean!" she exclaimed. "Human Free-Will is an exception to the system of fixed Law. Eric said something like that. And then I think he pointed out that God can only influence Nature by influencing Human Wills. So that we *might* reasonably pray *'give us this day our daily bread'*, because many of the causes that produce bread are under Man's control. But to pray for rain, or fine weather, would be as unreasonable as——" she checked herself, as if fearful of saying something irreverent.

In a hushed, low tone, that trembled with emotion, and with the solemnity of one in the presence of death, Arthur slowly replied *"Shall he that contendeth with the Almighty instruct him?* Shall we, 'the swarm that in the noon-tide beam were born,' feeling in ourselves the power to direct, this way or that, the forces of Nature—of *Nature*, of which we form so trivial a part—shall we, in our boundless arrogance, in our pitiful conceit, *deny* that power to the Ancient of Days? Saying, to our Creator, 'Thus far and no further. Thou madest, but thou canst not rule!'?"

Lady Muriel had covered her face in her hands, and did not look up. She only murmured "Thanks, thanks!" again and again.

We rose to go. Arthur said, with evident effort, "One word more. If you would *know* the power of Prayer—in anything and everything that Man can need—*try* it. *Ask, and it shall be given you.* I—*have* tried it. I *know* that God answers prayer!"

Our walk home was a silent one, till we had nearly

reached the lodgings: then Arthur murmured—and it was almost an echo of my own thoughts—"*What knowest thou, O wife, whether thou shalt save thy husband?*"

The subject was not touched on again. We sat on, talking, while hour after hour, of this our last night together, glided away unnoticed. He had much to tell me about India, and the new life he was going to, and the *work* he hoped to do. And his great generous soul seemed so filled with noble ambition as to have no space left for any vain regret or selfish repining.

"Come, it is nearly morning!" Arthur said at last, rising and leading the way upstairs. "The sun will be rising in a few minutes: and, though I *have* basely defrauded you of your last chance of a night's rest here, I'm sure you'll forgive me: for I really *couldn't* bring myself to say 'Good night' sooner. And God knows whether you'll ever see me again, or hear of me!"

"*Hear* of you I am certain I shall!" I warmly responded, and quoted the concluding lines of that strange poem "Waring":

> "*Oh, never star*
> *Was lost here, but it rose afar!*
> *Look East, where whole new thousands are!*
> *In Vishnu-land what Avatar?*"

"Aye, look Eastward!" Arthur eagerly replied, pausing at the stair-case window, which commanded a fine view of the sea and the eastward horizon. "The West is the fitting tomb for all the sorrow and the sighing, all the errors and the follies of the Past: for all its withered Hopes and all its buried Loves! From the East comes new strength, new ambition, new Hope, new Life, new Love! Look Eastward! Aye, look Eastward!"

His last words were still ringing in my ears as I entered my room, and undrew the window-curtains, just in time to see the sun burst in glory from his ocean-prison, and clothe the world in the light of a new day.

"So may it be for him, and me, and all of us!" I mused.

"All that is evil, and dead, and hopeless, fading with the Night that is past! All that is good, and living, and hopeful, rising with the dawn of Day!

"Fading, with the Night, the chilly mists, and the noxious vapours, and the heavy shadows, and the wailing gusts, and the owl's melancholy hootings: rising, with the Day, the darting shafts of light, and the wholesome morning breeze, and the warmth of a dawning life, and the mad music of the lark! Look Eastward!

"Fading, with the Night, the clouds of ignorance, and the deadly blight of sin, and the silent tears of sorrow: and ever rising, higher, higher, with the Day, the radiant dawn of knowledge, and the sweet breath of purity, and the throb of a world's ecstasy! Look Eastward!

"Fading, with the Night, the memory of a dead love, and the withered leaves of a blighted hope, and the sickly repinings and moody regrets that numb the best energies of the soul: and rising, broadening, rolling upward like a living flood, the manly resolve, and the dauntless will, and the heavenward gaze of faith—*the substance of things hoped for, the evidence of things not seen!*

"Look Eastward! Aye, look Eastward!"

IV
Sylvie and Bruno
Concluded

Dreams, that elude the Maker's frenzied grasp—
Hands, stark and still, on a dead Mother's breast,
Which nevermore shall render clasp for clasp,
Or deftly soothe a weeping Child to rest—
In suchlike forms me listeth to portray
My Tale, here ended. Thou delicious Fay—
The guardian of a Sprite that lives to tease thee—
Loving in earnest, chiding but in play
The merry mocking Bruno! Who, that sees thee,
Can fail to love thee, Darling, even as I?—
My sweetest Sylvie we must say "Good-bye!"

PREFACE

LET me here express my sincere gratitude to the many Reviewers who have noticed, whether favourably or unfavourably, the previous Volume. Their unfavourable remarks were, most probably, well-deserved; the favourable ones less probably so. Both kinds have no doubt served to make the book known, and have helped the reading Public to form their opinions of it. Let me also here assure them that it is not from any want of respect for their criticisms, that I have carefully forborne from reading *any* of them. I am strongly of opinion that an author had far better *not* read any reviews of his books: the unfavourable ones are almost certain to make him cross, and the favourable ones conceited; and *neither* of these results is desirable.

Criticisms have, however, reached me from private sources, to some of which I propose to offer a reply.

One such critic complains that Arthur's strictures, on sermons and on choristers, are too severe. Let me say, in reply, that I do *not* hold myself responsible for *any* of the opinions expressed by the characters in my book. They are simply opinions which, it seemed to me, might probably be held by the persons into whose mouths I put them, and which were worth consideration.

Other critics have objected to certain innovations in spelling, such as "ca'n't", "wo'n't", "traveler". In reply, I can only plead my firm conviction that the popular usage is *wrong*. As to "ca'n't", it will not be disputed that, in all *other* words ending in "n't", these letters are an abbreviation of "not"; and it is surely absurd to suppose that, in this solitary instance, "not" is represented by " 't"! In fact "can't" is the *proper* abbreviation for "can it", just as "is't" is for "is it". Again, in "wo'n't", the first apostrophe is needed, because the word "would"

461

is here *abridged* into "wo": but I hold it proper to spell "don't" with only *one* apostrophe, because the word "do" is here *complete*. As to such words as "traveler", I hold the correct principle to be, to *double* the consonant when the accent falls on that syllable; otherwise to leave it *single*. This rule is observed in most cases (e.g. we double the "r" in "preferred", but leave it single in "offered"), so that I am only extending, to other cases, an existing rule. I admit, however, that I do not spell "parallel", as the rule would have it; but here we are constrained, by the etymology, to insert the double "l".

In the Preface to Vol. I. were two puzzles, on which my readers might exercise their ingenuity. One was, to detect the 3 lines of "padding", which I had found it necessary to supply in the passage extending from the top of p. 280 to the middle of p. 282. They are the 23rd, 24th and 25th lines of p. 281. The other puzzle was, to determine which (if any) of the 8 stanzas of the Gardener's Song (see pp. 294, 301, 303, 306, 314, 318, 342, 344) were adapted to the context, and which (if any) had the context adapted to them. The last of them is the only one that was adapted to the context, the "Garden-Door that opened with a key" having been substituted for some creature (a Cormorant, I think) "that nestled in a tree". At pp. 301, 314, and 342, the context was adapted to the stanza. At p. 306, neither stanza nor context was altered: the connection between them was simply a piece of good luck.

In the Preface to Vol. I., at pp. 255, 256, I gave an account of the making-up of the story of "Sylvie and Bruno". A few more details may perhaps be acceptable to my Readers.

It was in 1873, as I *now* believe, that the idea first occurred to me that a little fairy-tale (written, in 1867, for "Aunt Judy's Magazine", under the title "Bruno's Revenge") might serve as the nucleus of a longer story. This I surmise, from having found the original draft of the last paragraph of Vol. II., dated 1873. So that this paragraph has been waiting 20 years for its chance of emerging into print—more than twice the period so cautiously recommended by Horace for "repressing" one's literary efforts!

It was in February, 1885, that I entered into negotiations, with Mr. Harry Furniss, for illustrating the book. Most of the substance of *both* Volumes was then in existence in manuscript: and my original intention was to publish the *whole* story at once. In September, 1885, I received from Mr. Furniss the first set of drawings—the four which illustrate "Peter and Paul": in November, 1886, I received the second set—the three which illustrate the Professor's song about the "little man" who had "a little gun": and in January, 1887, I received the third set —the four which illustrate the "Pig-Tale".

So we went on, illustrating first one bit of the story, and then another, without any idea of sequence. And it was not till March, 1889, that, having calculated the number of pages the story would occupy, I decided on dividing it into *two* portions, and publishing it half at a time. This necessitated the writing of a *sort* of conclusion for the first Volume: and *most* of my Readers, I fancy, regarded this as the *actual* conclusion, when that Volume appeared in December, 1889. At any rate, among all the letters I received about it, there was only *one* which expressed *any* suspicion that it was not a *final* conclusion. This letter was from a child. She wrote "we were so glad, when we came to the end of the book, to find that there was no ending-up, for that shows us that you are going to write a sequel."

It may interest some of my Readers to know the *theory* on which this story is constructed. It is an attempt to show what might *possibly* happen, supposing that Fairies really existed; and that they were sometimes visible to us, and we to them; and that they were sometimes able to assume human form: and supposing, also, that human beings might sometimes become conscious of what goes on in the Fairy-world—by actual transference of their immaterial essence, such as we meet with in "Esoteric Buddhism".

I have supposed a Human being to be capable of various psychical states, with varying degrees of consciousness, as follows:

(*a*) the ordinary state, with no consciousness of the presence of Fairies;

(*b*) the "eerie" state, in which, while conscious of actual surroundings, he is *also* conscious of the presence of Fairies;

(*c*) a form of trance, in which, while *un*conscious of actual surroundings, and apparently asleep, he (i.e. his immaterial essence) migrates to other scenes, in the actual world, or in Fairyland, and is conscious of the presence of Fairies.

I have also supposed a Fairy to be capable of migrating from Fairyland into the actual world, and of assuming, at pleasure, a Human form; and also to be capable of various psychical states, viz.

(*a*) the ordinary state, with no consciousness of the presence of Human beings;

(*b*) a sort of "eerie" state, in which he is conscious, if in the actual world, of the presence of actual Human beings; if in Fairyland, of the presence of the immaterial essences of Human beings.

I will here tabulate the passages, in both Volumes, where abnormal states occur.

Vol. I.	Historian's Locality and	State.	Other Characters.
pp. 264–270	In train	*c*	Chancellor (*b*) p. 264.
277–289	do.	*c*	
294–301	do.	*c*	
303–310	At lodgings	*c*	
314–318	On beach	*c*	
319–350	At lodgings	*c*	S. and B. (*b*) pp. 338–341.
			Professor (*b*) p. 344.
355–370	In wood	*b*	Bruno (*b*) pp. 358–370.

Vol. I.	Historian's Locality and	State.	Other characters.
pp. 372–376	In wood, sleep-walking	c	S. and B. (b).
383–385	Among ruins	c	do. (b).
389, 390	do. dreaming	a	
391–393	do. sleep-walking	c	S. B. and Professor in Human form.
393	In street...........	b	
398–406	At station, &c.	b	S. and B. (b)
410–421	In garden..........	c	S. B. and Professor(b)
423–431	On road, &c.	a	S. and B. in Human form.
431–437	In street, &c........	a	
439–450	In wood	b	S. and B. (b).
Vol. II.			
pp. 474–482	In garden..........	b	S. and B. (b).
496–498	On road	b	do. (b).
498–511	do.	b	do. in Human form.
511–517	do.	b	do. (b).
547–578	In drawing-room ...	a	do. in Human form.
578–595	do. ...	c	do. (b).
603–607	In smoking-room ...	c	do. (b).
623–626	In wood	b	do. (a); Lady Muriel (b).
627–644	At lodgings	c	
646–669	do.	c	
673–end.	do.	b	

In the Preface to Vol. I., at pp. 255 and 256, I gave an account of the *origination* of some of the ideas embodied in the book. A few more such details may perhaps interest my Readers:

I. p. 361. The very peculiar use, here made of a dead mouse, comes from real life. I once found two very small boys, in a garden, playing a microscopic game of "Single-Wicket". The bat was, I think, about the size of a table-spoon; and the utmost distance attained by the ball, in its most daring flights, was some 4 or 5 yards. The *exact* length was of course a matter of *supreme* importance; and it was always carefully measured out (the batsman and the bowler amicably sharing the toil) with a dead mouse!

I. p. 388 The two quasi-mathematical Axioms, quoted

by Arthur at p. 388 of Vol. I. ("Things that are greater
than the same are greater than one another", and "All
angles are equal") were actually enunciated, in all seriousness, by undergraduates at a University situated not
100 miles from Ely.

II. p. 477. Bruno's remark ("I can, if I like, &c.") was
actually made by a little boy.

II. p. 478. So also was his remark ("I know what it
doesn't spell"). And his remark ("I just twiddled my
eyes, &c.") I heard from the lips of a little girl, who had
just solved a puzzle I had set her.

II. p. 501. Bruno's soliloquy ("For its father, &c.") was
actually spoken by a little girl, looking out of the window
of a railway-carriage.

II. p. 540. The remark, made by a guest at the dinner-
party, when asking for a dish of fruit ("I've been wishing
for them, &c.") I heard made by the great Poet-Laureate,
whose loss the whole reading-world has so lately had to
deplore.

II. p. 553. Bruno's speech, on the subject of the age of
"Mein Herr", embodies the reply of a little girl to the
question "Is your grandmother an *old* lady?" "I don't
know if she's an *old* lady," said this cautious young person; "she's *eighty-three*."

II. p. 573. The speech about "Obstruction" is no mere
creature of my imagination! It is copied *verbatim* from
the columns of the Standard, and was spoken by Sir
William Harcourt, who was, at the time, a member of
the "Opposition", at the "National Liberal Club", on
July the 16th, 1890.

II. p. 636. The Professor's remark, about a dog's tail,
that "it doesn't bite at *that* end", was actually made by a
child, when warned of the danger he was incurring by
pulling the dog's tail.

II. p. 657. The dialogue between Sylvie and Bruno,
which occupies lines 28 to 36, is a *verbatim* report (merely
substituting "cake" for "penny") of a dialogue overheard
between two children.

One story in this Volume—"Bruno's Picnic"—I can vouch for as suitable for telling to children, having tested it again and again; and, whether my audience has been a dozen little girls in a village-school, or some thirty or forty in a London drawing-room, or a hundred in a High School, I have always found them earnestly attentive, and keenly appreciative of such fun as the story supplied.

May I take this opportunity of calling attention to what I flatter myself was a successful piece of name-coining, at p. 283 of Vol. I. Does not the name "Sibimet" fairly embody the character of the Sub-Warden? The gentle Reader has no doubt observed what a singularly useless article in a house a brazen trumpet is, if you simply leave it lying about, and never blow it!

Readers of the first Volume, who have amused themselves by trying to solve the two puzzles propounded at page 257 of the Preface, may perhaps like to exercise their ingenuity in discovering which (if any) of the following parallelisms were intentional, and which (if any) accidental.

"Little Birds".   Events, and Persons.
Stanza 1. Banquet.
        2. Chancellor.
        3. Empress and Spinach (II. 635).
        4. Warden's Return.
        5. Professor's Lecture (II. 640).
        6. Other Professor's Song (I. 329).
        7. Petting of Uggug.
        8. Baron Doppelgeist.
        9. Jester and Bear (I. 321). Little Foxes.
       10. Bruno's Dinner-Bell; Little Foxes.

I will publish the answer to this puzzle in the Preface to a little book of "Original Games and Puzzles", now in course of preparation.

I have reserved, for the last, one or two rather more serious topics.

I had intended, in this Preface, to discuss more fully, than I had done in the previous Volume, the "Morality of Sport", with special reference to letters I have received from lovers of Sport, in which they point out the many great advantages which men get from it, and try to prove that the suffering, which it inflicts on animals, is too trivial to be regarded.

But, when I came to think the subject out, and to arrange the whole of the arguments "pro" and "con", I found it much too large for treatment here. Some day, I hope to publish an essay on this subject. At present, I will content myself with stating the net result I have arrived at.

It is, that God has given to Man an absolute right to take the *lives* of other animals, for *any* reasonable cause, such as the supply of food: but that He has *not* given to Man the right to inflict *pain*, unless when *necessary*: that mere pleasure, or advantage, does not constitute such a necessity: and, consequently, that pain, inflicted for the purposes of *Sport*, is cruel, and therefore wrong. But I find it a far more complex question than I had supposed; and that the "case", on the side of the Sportsman, is a much stronger one than I had supposed. So, for the present, I say no more about it.

Objections have been raised to the severe language I have put into the mouth of "Arthur", at p. 397, on the subject of "Sermons", and at pp. 395, 396, on the subjects of Choral Services and "Choristers".

I have already protested against the assumption that I am ready to endorse the opinions of characters in my story. But, in these two instances, I admit that I am much in sympathy with "Arthur". In my opinion, far too many sermons are expected from our preachers; and, as a consequence, a great many are preached, which are not worth listening to; and, as a consequence of *that*, we are very apt *not* to listen. The reader of this paragraph probably heard a sermon last Sunday morning? Well, let him, if he can, name the text, and state how the preacher treated it!

Then, as to "Choristers", and all the other accessories —of music, vestments, processions, &c.—which have come, along with them, into fashion—while freely admitting that the "Ritual" movement was sorely needed, and that it has effected a vast improvement in our Church-Services, which had become dead and dry to the last degree, I hold that, like many other desirable movements, it has gone too far in the opposite direction, and has introduced many new dangers.

For the Congregation this new movement involves the danger of learning to think that the Services are done *for* them; and that their bodily *presence* is all they need contribute. And, for Clergy and Congregation alike, it involves the danger of regarding these elaborate Services as *ends in themselves*, and of forgetting that they are simply *means*, and the very hollowest of mockeries, unless they bear fruit in our *lives*.

For the Choristers it seems to involve the danger of self-conceit, as described at p. 395 (N.B. "stagy-entrances" is a misprint for "stage-entrances"), the danger of regarding those parts of the Service, where their help is not required, as not worth attending to, the danger of coming to regard the Service as a mere outward form—a series of postures to be assumed, and of words to be said or sung, while the *thoughts* are elsewhere—and the danger of "familiarity" breeding "contempt" for sacred things.

Let me illustrate these last two forms of danger, from my own experience. Not long ago, I attended a Cathedral-Service, and was placed immediately behind a row of men, members of the Choir; and I could not help noticing that they treated the *Lessons* as a part of the Service to which they needed not to give *any* attention, and as affording them a convenient opportunity for arranging music-books, &c., &c. Also I have frequently seen a row of little choristers, after marching in procession to their places, kneel down, as if about to pray, and rise from their knees after a minute spent in looking about them, it being but too evident that the attitude was a mere mockery. Surely it is very dangerous, for these children, to thus accustom them to *pretend* to pray? As an instance of irreverent treatment of holy things, I will mention a custom, which no doubt many of my readers have noticed in Churches where the Clergy and Choir enter in procession, viz. that, at the end of the private devotions, which are carried on in the vestry, and which are of course inaudible to the Congregation, the final "Amen" is *shouted*, loud enough to be heard all through the Church. This serves as a signal, to the Congregation, to prepare to rise when the procession appears: and it admits of no dispute that it is for this purpose that it is thus shouted. When we remember to Whom that "Amen" is *really* addressed, and consider that it is here *used* for the same purpose as one of the Church-bells, we must surely admit that it is a piece of gross irreverence? To *me* it is much as if I were to see a Bible used as a footstool.

As an instance of the dangers, for the Clergy themselves, introduced by this new movement, let me mention the fact that, according to *my* experience, Clergymen of this school are *specially* apt to retail comic anecdotes, in which the most sacred names and words—sometimes actual texts from the Bible—are used as themes for jesting. Many such things are repeated as having been originally said by *children*, whose utter ignorance of evil must no doubt acquit *them*, in the sight of God, of all blame; but it must be otherwise for those who *consciously* use such innocent utterances as material for their unholy mirth.

Let me add, however, *most* earnestly, that I fully believe that this profanity is, in many cases, *un*conscious: the "environment" (as I have tried to explain at pp. 532, 533) makes all the difference between man and man; and I rejoice to think that many of these profane stories—which *I* find so painful to listen to, and should feel it a sin to repeat—give to *their* ears no pain, and to *their* consciences no shock; and that *they* can utter, not less sincerely than myself, the two prayers, "*Hallowed be Thy Name*," and "*from hardness of heart, and contempt of Thy Word and Commandment, Good Lord, deliver us!*" To which I would desire to add, for their sake and for my own, Keble's beautiful petition, "*help us, this and every day, To live more nearly as we pray!*" It is, in fact, for its *consequences*—for the grave dangers, both to speaker and to hearer, which it involves—rather than for what it is *in itself*, that I mourn over this clerical habit of profanity in social talk. To the *believing* hearer it brings the danger of loss of reverence for holy things, by the mere act of listening to, and enjoying, such jests; and also the temptation to retail them for the amusement of others. To the *unbelieving* hearer it brings a welcome confirmation of his theory that religion is a fable, in the spectacle of its accredited champions thus betraying their trust. And to the speaker himself it must surely bring the danger of *loss of faith*. For surely such jests, if uttered with no consciousness of harm, must necessarily be also uttered with no consciousness, at the moment, of the *reality* of God, as a *living being*, who hears all we say. And he, who allows himself the habit of thus uttering holy words, with no thought of their meaning, is but too likely to find that, for him, God has become a myth, and heaven a poetic fancy —that, for him, the light of life is gone, and that he is at heart an atheist, lost in "*a darkness that may be felt*".

There is, I fear, at the present time, an increasing tendency to irreverent treatment of the name of God and of subjects connected with religion. Some of our theatres are helping this downward movement by the gross caricatures of clergymen which they put upon the stage: some of our clergy are themselves helping it, by showing that they can lay aside the spirit of reverence, along with their surplices, and can treat as jests, when *outside* their churches, names and things to which they pay an almost superstitious veneration when *inside*: the "Salvation Army" has, I fear, with the best intentions, done much to help it, by the coarse familiarity with which they treat holy things: and surely every one, who desires to *live* in the spirit of the prayer *"Hallowed be Thy Name"*, ought to do what he can, however little that may be, to check it. So I have gladly taken this unique opportunity, however unfit the topic may seem for the Preface to a book of this kind, to express some thoughts which have weighed on my mind for a long time. I did not expect, when I wrote the Preface to Vol. I, that it would be read to any appreciable extent: but I rejoice to believe, from evidence that has reached me, that it *has* been read by many, and to hope that this Preface will also be so: and I think that, among them, some will be found ready to sympathize with the views I have put forwards, and ready to help, with their prayers and their example, the revival, in Society, of the waning spirit of reverence.

Christmas, 1893.

Chapter I

Bruno's Lessons

DURING the next month or two my solitary town-life seemed, by contrast, unusually dull and tedious. I missed the pleasant friends I had left behind at Elveston—the genial interchange of thought—the sympathy which gave to one's ideas a new and vivid reality: but, perhaps more than all, I missed the companionship of the two Fairies— or Dream-Children, for I had not yet solved the problem as to who or what they were—whose sweet playfulness had shed a magic radiance over my life.

In office-hours—which I suppose reduce most men to the mental condition of a coffee-mill or a mangle—time sped along much as usual: it was in the pauses of life, the desolate hours when books and newspapers palled on the sated appetite, and when, thrown back upon one's own dreary musings, one strove—all in vain—to people the vacant air with the dear faces of absent friends, that the real bitterness of solitude made itself felt.

One evening, feeling my life a little more wearisome than usual, I strolled down to my Club, not so much with the hope of meeting any friend there, for London was now "out of town", as with the feeling that here, at least, I should hear "sweet words of human speech", and come into contact with human thought.

However, almost the first face I saw there *was* that of a friend. Eric Lindon was lounging, with rather a "bored" expression of face, over a newspaper; and we fell into conversation with a mutual satisfaction which neither of us tried to conceal.

After a while I ventured to introduce what was just then the main subject of my thoughts. "And so the Doctor" (a name we had adopted by a tacit agreement, as a

473

convenient compromise between the formality of "Doctor Forester" and the intimacy—to which Eric Lindon hardly seemed entitled—of "Arthur") "has gone abroad by this time, I suppose? Can you give me his present address?"

"He is still at Elveston—I believe," was the reply. "But I have not been there since I last met you."

I did not know which part of this intelligence to wonder at most. "And might I ask—if it isn't taking too much of a liberty—when your wedding-bells are to—or perhaps they *have* rung, already?"

"No," said Eric, in a steady voice, which betrayed scarcely a trace of emotion: "*that* engagement is at an end. I am still 'Benedick the *un*married man'."

After this, the thick-coming fancies—all radiant with new possibilities of happiness for Arthur—were far too bewildering to admit of any further conversation, and I was only too glad to avail myself of the first decent excuse, that offered itself, for retiring into silence.

The next day I wrote to Arthur, with as much of a reprimand for his long silence as I could bring myself to put into words, begging him to tell me how the world went with him.

Needs must that three or four days—possibly more—should elapse before I could receive his reply; and never had I known days drag their slow length along with a more tedious indolence.

To while away the time, I strolled, one afternoon, into Kensington Gardens, and, wandering aimlessly along any path that presented itself, I soon became aware that I had somehow strayed into one that was wholly new to me. Still, my elfish experiences seemed to have so completely faded out of my life that nothing was further from my thoughts than the idea of again meeting my fairy-friends, when I chanced to notice a small creature, moving among the grass that fringed the path, that did not seem to be an insect, or a frog, or any other living thing that I could think of. Cautiously kneeling down, and making an *ex tempore* cage of my two hands, I imprisoned the little wanderer, and felt a sudden thrill of surprise and delight on discovering that my prisoner was no other than *Bruno* himself!

Bruno took the matter *very* coolly, and, when I had replaced him on the ground, where he would be within easy conversational distance, he began talking, just as if it were only a few minutes since last we had met.

"Doos oo know what the *Rule* is", he en quired, "when oo catches a Fairy, withouten its having tolded oo where it was?" (Bruno's notions of English Grammar had certainly *not* improved since our last meeting.)

"No," I said. "I didn't know there was any Rule about it."

"I *think* oo've got a right to *eat* me," said the little fellow, looking up into my face with a winning smile. "But I'm not pruffickly sure. Oo'd better not do it wizout asking."

It did indeed seem reasonable not to take so irrevocable a step as *that*, without due enquiry. "I'll certainly *ask* about it, first," I said. "Besides, I don't know yet whether you would be *worth* eating!"

"I guess I'm *deliciously* good to eat," Bruno remarked in a satisfied tone, as if it were something to be rather proud of.

"And what are you doing here, Bruno?"

"*That's* not my name!" said my cunning little friend. "Don't oo know my name's 'Oh Bruno!'? That's what Sylvie always calls me, when I says mine lessons."

"Well then, what are you doing here, oh Bruno?"

"Doing mine lessons, a-course!" With that roguish twinkle in his eye, that always came when he knew he was talking nonsense.

"Oh, *that's* the way you do your lessons, is it? And do you remember them well?"

"Always can 'member *mine* lessons," said Bruno. "It's *Sylvie's* lessons that's so *dreffully* hard to 'member!" He frowned, as if in agonies of thought, and tapped his fore-

head with his knuckles. "I *ca'n't* think enough to under
stand them!" he said despairingly. "It wants *double*
thinking, I believe!"

"But where's Sylvie gone?"

"That's just what *I* want to know!" said Bruno dis-
consolately. "What ever's the good of setting me lessons,
when she isn't here to 'splain the hard bits?"

"*I'll* find her for you!" I volunteered; and, getting up,
I wandered round the tree under whose shade I had been
reclining, looking on all sides for Sylvie. In another minute I *again* noticed some strange thing moving among the
grass, and, kneeling down, was immediately confronted
with Sylvie's innocent face, lighted up with a joyful surprise at seeing me, and was accosted, in the sweet voice I
knew so well, with what seemed to be the *end* of a sentence
whose beginning I had failed to catch.

"——and I think he ought to have *finished* them by
this time. So I'm going back to him. Will you come too?
It's only just round at the other side of this tree."

It was but a few steps for *me*; but it was a great
many for Sylvie; and I had to be very careful to walk
slowly, in order not to leave the little creature so far behind as to lose sight of her.

To find Bruno's *lessons* was easy enough: they appeared to be neatly written out on large smooth ivy-
leaves, which were scattered in some confusion over a
little patch of ground where the grass had been worn
away; but the pale student, who ought by rights to have
been bending over them, was nowhere to be seen: we
looked in all directions, for some time in vain; but
at last Sylvie's sharp eyes detected him, swinging on a
tendril of ivy, and Sylvie's stern voice commanded
his instant return to *terra firma* and to the business of
Life.

"Pleasure first and business afterwards" seemed to be
the motto of these tiny folk, so many hugs and kisses
had to be interchanged before anything else could be
done.

"Now, Bruno," Sylvie said reproachfully, "didn't I tell you you were to go on with your lessons, unless you heard to the contrary?"

"But I *did* heard to the contrary!" Bruno insisted, with a mischievous twinkle in his eye.

"*What* did you hear, you wicked boy?"

"It were a sort of noise in the air," said Bruno: "a sort of a scrambling noise. Didn't *oo* hear it, Mister Sir?"

"Well, anyhow, you needn't go to *sleep* over them, you lazy-lazy!" For Bruno had curled himself up, on the largest "lesson", and was arranging another as a pillow.

"I *wasn't* asleep!" said Bruno, in a deeply-injured tone. "When I shuts mine eyes, it's to show that I'm *awake*!"

"Well, how much have you learned, then?"

"I've learned a little tiny bit," said Bruno, modestly, being evidently afraid of overstating his achievement. "*Ca'n't* learn no more!"

"Oh Bruno! You know you *can*, if you like."

"Course I can, if I *like*," the pale student replied; "but I ca'n't if I *don't* like!"

Sylvie had a way—which I could not too highly admire —of evading Bruno's logical perplexities by suddenly striking into a new line of thought; and this masterly stratagem she now adopted.

"Well, I must say *one* thing——"

"Did oo know, Mister Sir," Bruno thoughtfully remarked, "that Sylvie ca'n't count? Whenever she says 'I must say *one* thing', I *know* quite well she'll say *two* things! And she always doos."

"Two heads are better than one, Bruno," I said, but with no very distinct idea as to what I meant by it.

"I shouldn't mind having two *heads*," Bruno said softly to himself: "one head to eat mine dinner, and one head to argue wiz Sylvie—doos oo think oo'd look prettier if oo'd got *two* heads, Mister Sir?"

The case did not, I assured him, admit of a doubt.

"The reason why Sylvie's so cross——" Bruno went on very seriously, almost sadly.

Sylvie's eyes grew large and round with surprise at this new line of enquiry—her rosy face being perfectly radiant with good humour. But she said nothing.

"Wouldn't it be better so tell me after the lessons are over?" I suggested.

"Very well," Bruno said with a resigned air: "only she wo'n't be cross then."

"There's only three lessons to do," said Sylvie. "Spelling, and Geography, and Singing."

"Not *Arithmetic*?" I said.

"No, he hasn't a head for Arithmetic——"

"Course I haven't!" said Bruno. "Mine head's for *hair*. I haven't got a *lot* of heads!"

"—and he ca'n't learn his Multiplication-table——"

"I like *History* ever so much better," Bruno remarked. "Oo has to *repeat* that Muddlecome table——"

"Well, and you have to repeat——"

"No, oo hasn't!" Bruno interrupted. "History repeats itself. The Professor said so!"

Sylvie was arranging some letters on a board—E—V—I—L. "Now, Bruno," she said, "what does *that* spell?"

Bruno looked at it, in solemn silence, for a minute. "I know what it *doesn't* spell!" he said at last.

"That's no good," said Sylvie. "What *does* it spell?"

Bruno took another look at the mysterious letters. "Why, it's 'LIVE', backwards!" he exclaimed. (I thought it was, indeed.)

"How *did* you manage to see that?" said Sylvie.

"I just twiddled my eyes," said Bruno, "and then I saw it directly. Now may I sing the King-fisher Song?"

"Geography next," said Sylvie. "Don't you know the Rules?"

"I think there oughtn't to be such a lot of Rules, Sylvie! I thinks——"

"Yes, there *ought* to be such a lot of Rules, you wicked,

wicked boy! And how dare you *think* at all about it? And shut up that mouth directly!"

So, as "that mouth" didn't seem inclined to shut up of itself, Sylvie shut it for him—with both hands—and sealed it with a kiss, just as you would fasten up a letter.

"Now that Bruno is fastened up from talking," she went on, turning to me, "I'll show you the Map he does his lessons on."

And there it was, a large Map of the World, spread out on the ground. It was so large that Bruno had to crawl about on it, to point out the places named in the "Kingfisher Lesson".

"When a King-fisher sees a Lady-bird flying away, he says '*Ceylon*, if you *Candia*!' And when he catches it, he says 'Come to *Media*! And if you're *Hungary* or thirsty, I'll give you some *Nubia*!' When he takes it in his claws, he says '*Europe*!' When he puts it into his beak, he says '*India*!' When he's swallowed it, he says '*Eton*!' That's all."

"That's *quite* perfect," said Sylvie. "Now, you may sing the King-fisher Song."

"Will *oo* sing the chorus?" Bruno said to me.

I was just beginning to say "I'm afraid I don't know the *words*", when Sylvie silently turned the map over, and I found the words were all written on the back. In one respect it was a *very* peculiar song: the chorus to each verse came in the *middle*, instead of at the *end* of it. However, the tune was so easy that I soon picked it up, and managed the chorus as well, perhaps, as it is possible for *one* person to manage such a thing. It was in vain that I signed to Sylvie to help me: she only smiled sweetly and shook her head.

> "*King Fisher courted Lady Bird—*
> **Sing Beans, sing Bones, sing Butterflies!**
> '*Find me my match,*' *he said,*
> '*With such a noble head—*
> *With such a beard, as white as curd—*
> *With such expressive eyes!*'

" '*Yet pins have heads,*' *said Lady Bird*—
Sing Prunes, sing Prawns, sing Primrose-Hill!
  '*And, where you stick them in,*
  They stay, and thus a pin
Is very much to be preferred
  To one that's never still!'

" '*Oysters have beards,*' *said Lady Bird*—
Sing Flies, sing Frogs, sing Fiddle-strings!
  '*I love them, for I know*
  They *never chatter so:*
They would not say one single word—
  Not if you crowned them Kings!'

" '*Needles have eyes,*' *said Lady Bird*—
Sing Cats, sing Corks, sing Cowslip-tea!
  '*And they are sharp—just what*
  Your Majesty is not:
So get you gone—'tis too absurd
  To come a-courting me!' "

"So he went away," Bruno added as a kind of post-script, when the last note of the song had died away, "Just like he always did."

"Oh, my *dear* Bruno!" Sylvie exclaimed, with her hands over her ears. "You shouldn't say 'like': you should say '*what*'."

To which Bruno replied, doggedly, "I only says 'what!' when oo doosn't speak loud, so as I can hear oo."

"Where did he go to?" I asked, hoping to prevent an argument.

"He went more far than he'd never been before," said Bruno.

"You should never say 'more far'," Sylvie corrected him: "you should say '*farther*'."

"Then *oo* shouldn't say 'more broth', when we're at dinner," Bruno retorted: "oo should say '*brother*'!"

This time Sylvie evaded an argument by turning away, and beginning to roll up the Map. "Lessons are over!" she proclaimed in her sweetest tones.

"And has there been no *crying* over them?" I enquired. "Little boys *always* cry over their lessons, don't they?"

"I never cries after twelve o'clock," said Bruno: " 'cause then it's getting so near to dinner-time."

"Sometimes, in the morning," Sylvie said in a low voice; "when it's Geography-day, and when he's been disobe——"

"*What* a fellow you are to talk, Sylvie!" Bruno hastily interposed. "Doos oo think the world was *made* for oo to talk in?"

"Why, where would you *have* me talk, then?" Sylvie said, evidently quite ready for an argument.

But Bruno answered resolutely. "I'm not going to argue about it, 'cause it's getting late, and there wo'n't be time—but oo's as 'ong as ever oo can be!" And he rubbed the back of his hand across his eyes, in which tears were beginning to glitter.

Sylvie's eyes filled with tears in a moment. "I didn't mean it, Bruno, *darling!*" she whispered; and the rest of the argument was lost "amid the tangles of Neæra's hair", while the two disputants hugged and kissed each other.

But this new form of argument was brought to a sudden end by a flash of lightning, which was closely followed by a peal of thunder, and by a torrent of raindrops, which came hissing and spitting, almost like live creatures, through the leaves of the tree that sheltered us. "Why, it's raining cats and dogs!" I said.

"And all the *dogs* has come down *first*," said Bruno: "there's nothing but *cats* coming down now!"

In another minute the pattering ceased, as suddenly as it had begun. I stepped out from under the tree, and found that the storm was over; but I looked in vain, on my return, for my tiny companions. They had vanished with the storm, and there was nothing for it but to make the best of my way home.

On the table lay, awaiting my return, an envelope of

that peculiar yellow tint which always announces a telegram, and which must be, in the memories of so many
of us, inseparably linked with some great and sudden
sorrow—something that has cast a shadow, never in this
world to be wholly lifted off, on the brightness of Life.
No doubt it has *also* heralded—for many of us—some
sudden news of joy; but this, I think, is less common:
human life seems, on the whole, to contain more of sorrow than of joy. And yet the world goes on. Who knows
why?

This time, however, there was no shock of sorrow to be
faced: in fact, the few words it contained ("Could not
bring myself to write. Come soon. Always welcome. A
letter follows this. Arthur.") seemed so like Arthur himself speaking, that it gave me quite a thrill of pleasure,
and I at once began the preparations needed for the
journey.

CHAPTER II

Love's Curfew

"FAYFIELD Junction! Change for Elveston!"
What subtle memory could there be, linked to these
commonplace words, that caused such a flood of happy
thoughts to fill my brain? I dismounted from the carriage in a state of joyful excitement for which I could not
at first account. True, I had taken this very journey, and
at the same hour of the day, six months ago; but many
things had happened since then, and an old man's memory has but a slender hold on recent events: I sought "the
missing link" in vain. Suddenly I caught sight of a bench
—the only one provided on the cheerless platform—with
a lady seated on it, and the whole forgotten scene flashed
upon me as vividly as if it were happening over again.

"Yes," I thought. "This bare platform is, for me, rich with the memory of a dear friend! She was sitting on that very bench, and invited me to share it, with some quotation from Shakespeare—I forget what. I'll try the Earl's plan for the Dramatization of Life, and fancy that figure to be Lady Muriel; and I wo'n't undeceive myself too soon!"

So I strolled along the platform, resolutely "making-believe" (as children say) that the casual passenger, seated on that bench, was the Lady Muriel I remembered so well. She was facing away from me, which aided the elaborate cheatery I was practising on myself: but, though I was careful, in passing the spot, to look the other way, in order to prolong the pleasant illusion, it was inevitable that, when I turned to walk back again, I should see who it was. It was Lady Muriel herself!

The whole scene now returned vividly to my memory; and, to make this repetition of it stranger still, there was the same old man, whom I remembered seeing so roughly ordered off, by the Station-Master, to make room for his titled passenger. The same, but "with a difference": no longer tottering feebly along the platform, but actually seated at Lady Muriel's side, and in conversation with her! "Yes, put it in your purse," she was saying, "and remember you're to spend it all for *Minnie*. And mind you bring her something nice, that'll do her real good! And give her my love!" So intent was she on saying these words, that, although the sound of my footstep had made her lift her head and look at me, she did not at first recognize me.

I raised my hat as I approached, and then there flashed across her face a genuine look of joy, which so exactly recalled the sweet face of Sylvie, when last we met in Kensington Gardens, that I felt quite bewildered.

Rather than disturb the poor old man at her side, she rose from her seat, and joined me in my walk up and down the platform, and for a minute or two our conversation was as utterly trivial and commonplace as if we were merely two casual guests in a London drawing-room. Each of us seemed to shrink, just at first, from touching on the deeper interests which linked our lives together.

The Elveston train had drawn up at the platform, while we talked; and, in obedience to the Station-Master's obsequious hint of "This way, my Lady! Time's up!", we were making the best of our way towards the end which contained the sole first-class carriage, and were just passing the now-empty bench, when Lady Muriel noticed, lying on it, the purse in which her gift had just been so carefully bestowed, the owner of which, all un-conscious of his loss, was being helped into a carriage at the other end of the train. She pounced on it instantly. "Poor old man!" she cried. "He mustn't go off, and think he's lost it!"

"Let *me* run with it! I can go quicker than you!" I said. But she was already half-way down the platform, flying ("running" is much too mundane a word for such fairy-like motion) at a pace that left all possible efforts of *mine* hopelessly in the rear.

She was back again before I had well completed my audacious boast of speed in running, and was saying, quite demurely, as we entered our carriage, "and you really think *you* could have done it quicker?"

"No, indeed!" I replied. "I plead 'Guilty' of gross ex-aggeration, and throw myself on the mercy of the Court!"

"The Court will overlook it—for this once!" Then her manner suddenly changed from playfulness to an anxious gravity.

"You are not looking your best!" she said with an anxious glance. "In fact, I think you look *more* of an invalid than when you left us. I very much doubt if London agrees with you?"

"It *may* be the London air," I said, "or it may be the hard work—or my rather lonely life: anyhow, I've *not* been feeling very well, lately. But Elveston will soon set me up again. Arthur's prescription—he's my doctor, you know, and I heard from him this morning—is 'plenty of ozone, and new milk, and *pleasant society*'!"

"Pleasant society?" said Lady Muriel, with a pretty make-believe of considering the question. "Well, really I don't know where we can find *that* for you! We have so few neighbours. But new milk we *can* manage. Do get it of my old friend Mrs. Hunter, up there, on the hill-side. You may rely upon the *quality*. And her little Bessie comes to school every day, and passes your lodgings. So it would be very easy to send it."

"I'll follow your advice with pleasure," I said; "and I'll go and arrange about it to-morrow. I know Arthur will want a walk."

"You'll find it quite an easy walk—under three miles, I think."

"Well, now that we've settled that point, let me retort your own remark upon yourself. I don't think *you're* looking quite your best!"

"I daresay not," she replied in a low voice; and a sudden shadow seemed to overspread her face. "I've had some troubles lately. It's a matter about which I've been long wishing to consult you, but I couldn't easily write about it. I'm *so* glad to have this opportunity!"

"Do you think", she began again, after a minute's silence, and with a visible embarrassment of manner most unusual in her, "that a promise, deliberately and solemnly given, is *always* binding—except, of course, where its fulfilment would involve some actual *sin*?"

"I ca'n't think of any other exception at this moment," I said. "That branch of casuistry is usually, I believe, treated as a question of truth and untruth——"

"Surely that *is* the principle?" she eagerly interrupted. "I always thought the Bible-teaching about it consisted of such texts '*lie not one to another*'?"

"I have thought about that point," I replied; "and it seems to me that the essence of *lying* is the intention of *deceiving*. If you give a promise, fully *intending* to fulfil it, you are certainly acting truthfully *then*; and, if you afterwards break it, that does not involve any *deception*. I cannot call it *untruthful*."

Another pause of silence ensued. Lady Muriel's face was hard to read: she looked pleased, I thought, but also puzzled; and I felt curious to know whether her question had, as I began to suspect, some bearing on the breaking off of her engagement with Captain (now Major) Lindon.

"You have relieved me from a great fear," she said; "but the thing is of course *wrong*, somehow. What texts would *you* quote, to prove it wrong?"

"Any that enforce the payment of *debts*. If *A* promises something to *B*, *B* has a claim upon *A*. And *A*'s sin, if he breaks his promise, seems to me more analogous to *stealing* than to *lying*."

"It's a new way of looking at it—to me," she said; "but it seems a *true* way, also. However, I wo'n't deal in generalities, with an old friend like you! For we *are* old friends, somehow. Do you know, I think we *began* as old friends?" she said with a playfulness of tone that ill accorded with the tears that glistened in her eyes.

"Thank you very much for saying so," I replied. "I like to think of you as an *old* friend," ("—though you don't look it!" would have been the almost necessary sequence, with any other lady; but she and I seemed to have long passed out of the time when compliments, or any such trivialities, were possible).

Here the train paused at a station, where two or three passengers entered the carriage; so no more was said till we had reached our journey's end.

On our arrival at Elveston, she readily adopted my suggestion that we should walk up together; so, as soon as our luggage had been duly taken charge of—hers by the servant who met her at the station, and mine by one of the porters—we set out together along the familiar lanes, now linked in my memory with so many delightful associations. Lady Muriel at once recommended the conversation at the point where it had been interrupted.

"You knew of my engagement to my cousin Eric. Did you also hear——"

"Yes," I interrupted, anxious to spare her the pain of giving any details. "I heard it had all come to an end."

"I would like to tell you how it happened," she said; "as that is the very point I want your advice about. I had long realized that we were not in sympathy in religious belief. His ideas of Christianity are very shadowy; and even as to the existence of a God he lives in a sort of dreamland. But it has not affected his life! I feel sure, now, that the most absolute Atheist *may* be leading, though walking blindfold, a pure and noble life. And if you knew half the good deeds——" she broke off suddenly, and turned away her head.

"I entirely agree with you," I said. "And have we not our Saviour's own promise that such a life shall surely lead to the light?"

"Yes, I know it," she said in a broken voice, still keeping her head turned away. "And so I told him. He said he would believe, for *my* sake, if he could. And he wished for *my* sake, he could see things as I did. But that is all wrong!" she went on passionately. "God *cannot* approve such low motives as that! Still it was not *I* that broke it off. I knew he loved me; and I had *promised*; and——"

"Then it was *he* that broke it off?"

"He released me unconditionally." She faced me again now, having quite recovered her usual calmness of manner.

"Then what difficulty remains?"

"It is *this*, that I don't believe he did it of his own free will. Now, supposing he hid it *against* his will, merely to satisfy my scruples, would not his claim on me remain just as strong as ever? And would not my promise be as binding as ever? My father says 'no'; but I ca'n't help fearing he is biased by his love for me. And I've asked no one else. I have many friends—friends for the bright sunny weather; not friends for the clouds and storms of life; not *old* friends like you!"

"Let me think a little," I said: and for some minutes we walked on in silence, while, pained to the heart at seeing the bitter trial that had come upon this pure and gentle soul, I strove in vain to see my way through the tangled skein of conflicting motives.

"If she loves him truly", (I seemed at last to grasp the clue to the problem) "is not *that*, for her the voice of God? May she not hope that she is sent to him, even as Ananias was sent to Saul in his blindness, that he may receive his sight?" Once more I seemed to hear Arthur whispering *"What knowest thou, O wife, whether thou shalt save thy husband?"* and I broke the silence with the words "If you still love him truly——"

"I do *not*!" she hastily interrupted. "At least—not in *that* way. I *believe* I loved him when I promised; but I was very young: it is hard to know. But, whatever the feeling was, it is dead *now*. The motive on *his* side is Love: on *mine* it is—Duty!"

Again there was a long silence. The whole skein of thought was tangled worse than ever. This time *she* broke the silence. "Don't misunderstand me!" she said. "When I said my heart was not *his*, I did not mean it was any one else's! At present I feel bound to *him*; and, till I know I am absolutely free, in the sight of God, to love any other than him, I'll never even *think* of any one else—in *that* way, I mean. I would die sooner!" I had never imagined my gentle friend capable of such passionate utterances.

I ventured on no further remark until we had nearly arrived at the Hall-gate; but, the longer I reflected, the clearer it became to me that no call of Duty demanded the sacrifice—possibly of the happiness of a life—which she seemed ready to make. I tried to make this clear to *her* also, adding some warnings on the dangers that surely awaited a union in which mutual love was wanting. "The only argument for it, worth considering," I said in conclusion, "seems to be his supposed *reluctance* in releasing you from your promise. I have tried to give to that argument its *full* weight, and my conclusion is that it does *not* affect the rights of the case, or invalidate the release he has given you. My belief is that you are *entirely* free to act as *now* seems right."

"I am *very* grateful to you," she said earnestly. "Believe it, please! I ca'n't put it into proper words!" and the subject was dropped by mutual consent: and I only learned, long afterwards, that our discussion had really served to dispel the doubts that had harassed her so long.

We parted at the Hall-gate, and I found Arthur eagerly awaiting my arrival; and, before we parted for the night, I had heard the whole story—how he had put off his journey from day to day, feeling that he *could* not go away from the place till his fate had been irrevocably settled by the wedding taking place: how the preparations for the wedding, and the excitement in the neighbourhood, had suddenly come to an end, and he had learned (from Major Lindon, who called to wish him good-bye) that the engagement had been broken off by mutual consent: how he had instantly abandoned all his plans for going abroad, and had decided to stay on at Elveston, for a year or two at any rate, till his newly-awakened hopes should prove true or false; and how, since that memorable day, he had avoided all meetings with Lady Muriel, fearing to betray his feelings before he had had any sufficient evidence as to how she regarded him. "But it is nearly six weeks since all that happened," he said in conclusion, "and we can meet in the ordinary way, now, with no need for any painful allusions. I would have written to tell you all this: only I kept hoping from day to day that—that there would be *more* to tell!"

"And how should there be *more*, you foolish fellow," I fondly urged, "if you never even go near her? Do you expect the offer to come from *her?*"

Arthur was betrayed into a smile. "No," he said, "I hardly expect *that*. But I'm a desperate coward. There's no doubt about it!"

"And what *reasons* have you heard of for breaking off the engagement?"

"A good many," Arthur replied, and proceeded to count them on his fingers. "First, it was found that she was dying of—something; so *he* broke it off. Then it was found that *he* was dying of—some other thing; so *she* broke it off. Then the Major turned out to be a confirmed gamester; so the *Earl* broke it off. Then the Earl insulted him; so the *Major* broke it off. It got a good deal broken off, all things considered!"

"You have all this on the very best authority, of course?"

"Oh, certainly! And communicated in the strictest confidence! Whatever defects Elveston society suffers from, *want of information* isn't one of them!"

"Nor *reticence*, either, it seems. But, seriously, do you know the real reason?"

"No, I'm quite in the dark."

I did not feel that I had any right to enlighten him; so I changed the subject, to the less engrossing one of "new milk", and we agreed that I should walk over, next day, to Hunter's farm, Arthur undertaking to set me part of the way, after which he had to return to keep a business engagement.

Chapter III

Streaks of Dawn

NEXT day proved warm and sunny, and we started early, to enjoy the luxury of a good long chat before he would be obliged to leave me.

"This neighbourhood has more than its due proportion of the *very* poor," I remarked, as we passed a group of hovels, too dilapidated to deserve the name of "cottages".

"But the few rich", Arthur replied, "give more than

their due proportion of help in charity. So the balance is kept."

"I suppose the *Earl* does a good deal?"

"He *gives* liberally; but he has not the health or strength to do more. Lady Muriel does more in the way of school-teaching and cottage-visiting than she would like me to reveal."

"Then *she*, at least, is not one of the 'idle mouths' one so often meets with among the upper classes. I have sometimes thought they would have a hard time of it, if suddenly called on to give their *raison d'être*, and to show cause why they should be allowed to live any longer!"

"The whole subject", said Arthur, "of what we may call 'idle mouths' (I mean persons who absorb some of the material *wealth* of a community—in the form of food, clothes, and so on—without contributing its equivalent in the form of productive *labour*) is a complicated one, no doubt. I've tried to think it out. And it seemed to me that the simplest form of the problem, to start with, is a community without *money*, who buy and sell by *barter* only; and it makes it yet simpler to suppose the food and other things to be capable of *keeping* for many years without spoiling."

"Yours is an excellent plan," I said. "What is your solution of the problem?"

"The commonest type of 'idle mouths' ", said Arthur, "is no doubt due to money being left by parents to their own children. So I imagined a man—either exceptionally clever, or exceptionally strong and industrious—who had contributed so much valuable labour to the needs of the community that its equivalent, in clothes, etc., was (say) five times as much as he needed for himself. We cannot deny his *absolute* right to give the superfluous wealth as he chooses. So, if he leaves *four* children behind him (say two sons and two daughters), with enough of all the necessaries of life to last them a life-time, I cannot see that the *community* is in any way wronged if they choose to do nothing in life but to 'eat, drink, and be merry'.

Most certainly, the community could not fairly say, in reference to *them*, '*if a man will not work, neither let him eat.*' Their reply would be crushing. 'The labour has already been *done*, which is a fair equivalent for the food we are eating; and you have had the benefit of it. On what principle of justice can you demand *two* quotas of work for *one* quota of food?' "

"Yet surely", I said, "there is something wrong *somewhere*, if these four people are well able to do useful work, and if that work is actually *needed* by the community, and they elect to sit idle?"

"I think there *is*," said Arthur: "but it seems to me to arise from a Law of God—that every one shall do as much as he can to help others—and not from any *rights*, on the part of the community, to exact labour as an equivalent for food that has already been fairly earned."

"I suppose the *second* form of the problem is where the 'idle mouths' possess *money* instead of *material* wealth?"

"Yes," replied Arthur: "and I think the simplest case is that of *paper*-money. *Gold* is itself a form of material wealth; but a bank-note is merely a *promise* to hand over so much *material* wealth when called upon to do so. The father of these four 'idle mouths', had done (let us say) five thousand pounds' worth of useful work for the community. In return for this, the community had given him what amounted to a written promise to hand over, whenever called upon to do so, five thousand pounds' worth of food, etc. Then, if he only uses *one* thousand pounds' worth himself, and leaves the rest of the notes to his children, surely they have a full right to *present* these written promises, and to say 'hand over the food, for which the equivalent labour has been already done'. Now I think *this* case well worth stating, publicly and clearly. I should like to drive it into the heads of those Socialists who are priming our ignorant paupers with such sentiments as 'Look at them bloated haristocrats! Doing not a stroke o' work for theirselves, and living on the sweat of *our* brows!' I should like to *force* them to see that the *money*, which those 'haristocrats' are spending, represents so much labour *already* done for the community, and whose equivalent, in *material* wealth, is *due from the community*."

"Might not the Socialists reply 'Much of this money does not represent *honest* labour *at all*. If you could trace it back, from owner to owner, though you might begin with several legitimate steps, such as gifts, or bequeathing by will, or 'value received', you would soon reach an owner who had no moral right to it but had got it by fraud or other crimes; and of course his successors in the line would have no better right to it than *he* had."

"No doubt, no doubt," Arthur replied. "But surely that involves the logical fallacy of *proving too much*? It is *quite* as applicable to *material* wealth, as it is to *money*. If we once begin to go back beyond the fact that the *present* owner of certain property came by it honestly, and to ask whether any previous owner, in past ages, got it by fraud, would *any* property be secure?"

After a minute's thought, I felt obliged to admit the truth of this.

"My general conclusion," Arthur continued, "from the mere standpoint of human *rights*, man against man, was this—that if some wealthy 'idle mouth', who has come by his money in a lawful way, even though not one atom of the labour it represents has been his own doing, chooses to spend it on his own needs, without contributing any labour to the community from whom he buys his food and clothes, that community has no *right* to interfere with him. But it's quite another thing, when we come to consider the *divine* law. Measured by *that* standard, such a man is undoubtedly doing wrong, if he fails to use, for the good of those in need, the strength or the skill, that God has given him. That strength and skill do *not* belong to the community, to be paid to *them* as a *debt*: they do *not* belong to the man *himself*, to be used for his *own* enjoyment: they *do* belong to God, to be used according to

His will; and we are not left in doubt as to what this will is. '*Do good, and lend, hoping for nothing again.*' "

"Anyhow," I said, "an 'idle mouth' very often gives away a great deal in charity."

"In *so-called* 'charity'," he corrected me. "Excuse me if I seem to speak *un*charitably. I would not dream of *applying* the term to any *individual*. But I would say, *generally*, that a man who gratifies every fancy that occurs to him—denying himself in *nothing*—and merely gives to the poor some part, or even *all*, of his *superfluous* wealth, is only deceiving himself if he calls it *charity*."

"But, even in giving away *superfluous* wealth, he *may* be denying himself the miser's pleasure in hoarding?"

"I grant you that, gladly," said Arthur. "Given that he *has* that morbid craving, he is doing a good deed in restraining it."

"But, even in spending on *himself*", I persisted, "our typical rich man often does good, by employing people who would otherwise be out of work: and that is often better than pauperizing them by *giving* the money."

"I'm glad you've said that!" said Arthur. "I would not like to quit the subject without exposing the *two* fallacies of that statement—which have gone so long uncontradicted that Society now accepts it as an axiom!"

"What are they?" I said. "I don't even see *one*, myself."

"One is merely the fallacy of *ambiguity*—the assumption that '*doing good*' (that is, benefiting somebody) is necessarily *a good thing to do* (that is, a *right* thing). The other is the assumption that, if one of two specified acts is *better* than another, it is necessarily a *good* act in itself. I should like to call this the fallacy of *comparison*—meaning that it assumes that what is *comparatively* good is therefore *positively* good."

"Then what is *your* test of a good act?"

"That it shall be *our best*," Arthur confidently replied. "And even *then* '*we are unprofitable servants*'. But let me illustrate the two fallacies. Nothing illustrates a fallacy so well as an extreme case, which fairly comes under it.

Suppose I find two children drowning in a pond. I rush in, and save one of the children, and then walk away, leaving the other to drown. Clearly I have '*done good*', in saving a child's life? But—— Again, supposing I meet an inoffensive stranger, and knock him down and walk on. Clearly that is '*better*' than if I had proceeded to jump upon him and break his ribs? But——"

"Those 'buts' are quite unanswerable," I said. "But I should like an instance from *real* life."

"Well, let us take one of those abominations of modern Society, a Charity-Bazaar. It's an interesting question to think out—how much of the money, that reaches the object in view, is *genuine* charity; and whether even *that* is spent in the *best* way. But the subject needs regular classification, and analysis, to understand it properly."

"I should be glad to *have* it analysed," I said: "it has often puzzled me."

"Well, if I am really not boring you. Let us suppose our Charity-Bazaar to have been organized to aid the funds of some Hospital: and that A, B, C *give* their services in making articles to sell, and in acting as salesmen, while X, Y, Z buy the articles, and the money so paid goes to the Hospital.

"There are two distinct species of such Bazaars: one, where the payment exacted is merely the *market-value* of the goods supplied, that is, exactly what you would have to pay at a shop: the other, where *fancy-prices* are asked. We must take these separately.

"First, the 'market-value' case. Here A, B, C are exactly in the same position as ordinary shopkeepers; the only difference being that they give the proceeds to the Hospital. Practically, they are *giving their skilled labour* for the benefit of the Hospital. This seems to me to be genuine charity. And I don't see how they could use it better. But X, Y, Z are exactly in the same position as any ordinary purchasers of goods. To talk of 'charity' in connection with *their* share of the business, is sheer nonsense. Yet they are very likely to do so.

"Secondly, the case of 'fancy-prices'. Here I think the simplest plan is to divide the payment into two parts, the 'market-value' and the excess over that. The 'market-value' part is on the same footing as in the first case: the *excess* is all we have to consider. Well, A, B, C do not *earn* it; so we may put *them* out of the question: it is a *gift*, from X, Y, Z, to the Hospital. And my opinion is that it is not given in the best way: far better buy what they choose to *buy*, and give what they choose to *give*, as two *separate* transactions: then there is *some* chance that their motive in giving may be real charity, instead of a mixed motive—half charity, half self-pleasing. 'The trail of the serpent is over it all.' And *therefore* it is that I hold all such spurious 'Charities' in *utter* abomination!" He ended with unusual energy, and savagely beheaded, with his stick, a tall thistle at the road-side, behind which I was startled to see Sylvie and Bruno standing. I caught at his arm, but too late to stop him. Whether the stick reached them, or not, I could not feel sure: at any rate they took not the smallest notice of it, but smiled gaily, and nodded to me: and I saw at once that they were only visible to *me*: the "eerie" influence had not reached to *Arthur*.

"Why did you try to save it?" he said. "*That's* not the wheedling Secretary of a Charity-Bazaar! I only wish it were!" he added grimly.

"Does oo know, that stick went right froo my head!" said Bruno. (They had run round to me by this time, and each had secured a hand.) "Just under my chin! I *are* glad I aren't a thistle!"

"Well, we've threshed *that* subject out, anyhow!" Arthur resumed. "I'm afraid I've been talking too much, for *your* patience and for my strength. I must be turning soon. This is about the end of my tether."

> "Take, O boatman, thrice thy fee;
> Take, I give it willingly;
> For, invisible to thee,
> Spirits twain have crossed with me!"

I quoted, involuntarily.

"For utterly inappropriate and irrelevant quotations," laughed Arthur, "you are 'ekalled by few, and excelled by none'!" And we strolled on.

As we passed the head of the lane that led down to the beach, I noticed a single figure moving slowly along it, seawards. She was a good way off, and had her back to us: but it was Lady Muriel, unmistakably. Knowing that Arthur had not seen her, as he had been looking, in the other direction, at a gathering rain-cloud, I made no remark, but tried to think of some plausible pretext for sending him back by the sea.

The opportunity instantly presented itself. "I'm getting tired," he said. "I don't think it would be prudent to go further. I had better turn here."

I turned with him, for a few steps, and as we again approached the head of the lane, I said, as carelessly as I could, "Don't go back by the road. It's too hot and dusty. Down this lane, and along the beach, is nearly as short; and you'll get a breeze off the sea."

"Yes, I think I will," Arthur began; but at that moment we came into sight of Lady Muriel, and he checked himself. "No, it's too far round. Yet it certainly *would* be cooler——" He stood, hesitating, looking first one way and then the other—a melancholy picture of utter infirmity of purpose!

How long this humiliating scene would have continued, if *I* had been the only external influence, it is impossible to say; for at this moment Sylvie, with a swift decision worthy of Napoleon himself, took the matter into her own hands. "You go and drive *her*, up this way," she said to Bruno. "I'll get *him* along!" And she took hold of the stick that Arthur was carrying, and gently pulled him down the lane.

He was totally unconscious that any will but his own was acting on the stick, and appeared to think it had taken a horizontal position simply because he was pointing with it. "Are not those *orchises* under the hedge there?" he said. "I think that decides me. I'll gather some as I go along."

Meanwhile Bruno had run on behind Lady Muriel, and, with much jumping about and shouting (shouts audible to no one but Sylvie and myself), much as if he were driving sheep, he managed to turn her round and make her walk, with eyes˜demurely cast upon the ground, in our direction.

The victory was ours! And, since it was evident that the lovers, thus urged together, *must* meet in another minute, I turned and walked on, hoping that Sylvie and Bruno would follow my example, as I felt sure that the fewer the spectators the better it would be for Arthur and his good angel.

"And what sort of meeting was it?" I wondered, as I paced dreamily on.

CHAPTER IV

The Dog-King

"THEY shooked hands," said Bruno, who was trotting at my side, in answer to the unspoken question.

"And they looked *ever* so pleased!" Sylvie added from the other side.

"Well, we must get on, now, as quick as we can," I said. "If only I knew the best way to Hunter's farm!"

"They'll be sure to know in this cottage," said Sylvie.

"Yes, I suppose they will. Bruno, would you run in and ask?"

Sylvie stopped him, laughingly, as he ran off. "Wait a minute," she said. "I must make you *visible* first, you know."

"And *audible* too, I suppose?" I said, as she took the

jewel, that hung round her neck, and waved it over his head, and touched his eyes and lips with it.

"Yes," said Sylvie: "and *once*, do you know, I made him *audible*, and forgot to make him *visible*! And he went to buy some sweeties in a shop. And the man *was* so frightened! A voice seemed to come out of the air, 'Please, I want two ounces of barley-sugar drops!' And a shilling came *bang* down upon the counter! And the man said 'I ca'n't *see* you!' And Bruno said 'It doosn't sinnify seeing *me*, so long as oo can see the *shilling*!' But the man said he never sold barley-sugar drops to people he couldn't *see*. So we had to—*Now*, Bruno, you're ready!" And away he trotted.

Sylvie spent the time, while we were waiting for him, in making *herself* visible also. "It's rather awkward, you know," she explained to me, "when we meet people, and they can see *one* of us, and ca'n't see the *other*!"

In a minute or two Bruno returned, looking rather disconsolate. "He'd got friends with him, and he were *cross*!" he said. "He asked me who I were. And I said 'I'm Bruno: who is *these* peoples?' And he said 'One's my half-brother, and t'other's my half-sister: and I don't want no more company! Go along with yer!' And I said 'I ca'n't go along *wizout* mine self!' And I said 'Oo shouldn't have *bits* of peoples lying about like that! It's welly untidy!' And he said 'Oh, don't talk to *me*!' And he pushted me outside! And he shutted the door!"

"And you never asked where Hunter's farm was?" queried Sylvie.

"Hadn't room for any questions," said Bruno. "The room were so crowded."

"Three people *couldn't* crowd a room," said Sylvie.

"They *did*, though," Bruno persisted. "*He* crowded it most. He's such a welly *thick* man—so as oo couldn't knock him down."

I failed to see the drift of Bruno's argument. "Surely *anybody* could be knocked down," I said: "thick or thin wouldn't matter."

"Oo couldn't knock *him* down," said Bruno. "He's more wide than he's high: so, when he's lying down he's more higher than when he's standing: so a-course oo couldn't knock him *down*!"

"Here's another cottage," I said: "*I'll* ask the way, *this* time."

There was no need to go in, this time, as the woman was standing in the doorway, with a baby in her arms, talking to a respectably dressed man—a farmer, as I guessed—who seemed to be on his way to the town.

"—and when there's *drink* to be had," he was saying, "he's just the worst o' the lot, is your Willie. So they tell me. He gets fairly mad wi' it!"

"I'd have given 'em the lie to their faces, a twelve-month back!" the woman said in a broken voice. "But a' canna noo! A' canna noo!" She checked herself on catching sight of us, and hastily retreated into the house, shutting the door after her.

"Perhaps you can tell me where Hunter's farm is?" I said to the man, as he turned away from the house.

"I can *that*, Sir!" he replied with a smile. "I'm John Hunter hissel, at your sarvice. It's nobbut half a mile further—the only house in sight, when you get round bend o' the road yonder. You'll find my good woman within, if so be you've business wi' *her*. Or mebbe I'll do as well?"

"Thanks," I said. "I want to order some milk. Perhaps I had better arrange it with your wife?"

"Aye," said the man. "*She* minds all *that*. Good day t'ye, Master—and to your bonnie childer, as well!" And he trudged on.

"He should have said '*child*', not '*childer*'," said Bruno. "Sylvie's not a *childer*!"

"He meant *both* of us," said Sylvie.

"No, he didn't!" Bruno persisted. "'cause he said 'bonnie', oo know!"

"Well, at any rate he *looked* at us both," Sylvie maintained.

"Well, then he *must* have seen we're not *both* bonnie!"

Bruno retorted. "A-*course* I'm much uglier than *oo*! Didn't he mean *Sylvie*, Mister Sir?" he shouted over his shoulder, as he ran off.

But there was no use in replying, as he had already vanished round the bend of the road. When we overtook him he was climbing a gate, and was gazing earnestly into the field, where a horse, a cow, and a kid were browsing amicably together. "For its father, a *Horse*," he murmured to himself. "For its mother, a *Cow*. For their dear little child, a *little* Goat, is the most curiousest thing I ever seen in my world!"

"Bruno's World!" I pondered. "Yes, I suppose every child has a world of his own—and every man, too, for the matter of that. I wonder if *that's* the cause for all the misunderstanding there is in Life?"

"That *must* be Hunter's farm!" said Sylvie, pointing to a house on the brow of the hill, led up to by a cart-road. "There's no other farm in sight, *this* way; and you *said* we must be nearly there by this time."

I had *thought* it, while Bruno was climbing the gate, but I couldn't remember having *said* it. However, Sylvie was evidently in the right. "Get down, Bruno," I said, "and open the gate for us."

"It's a good thing we's with oo, *isn't* it, Mister Sir?" said Bruno, as we entered the field. "That big dog might have bited oo, if oo'd been alone! Oo needn't be *flightened* of it!" he whispered, clinging tight to my hand to encourage me. "It aren't fierce!"

"Fierce!" Sylvie scornfully echoed, as the dog—a magnificent Newfoundland—that had come galloping down the field to meet us, began curveting round us, in gambols full of graceful beauty, and welcoming us with short joyful barks. "Fierce! Why, it's as gentle as a lamb! It's— why, Bruno, don't you know? It's——"

"So it *are*!" cried Bruno, rushing forwards and throwing his arms round its neck. "Oh, you *dear* dog!" And it seemed as if the two children would never have done hugging and stroking it.

"And how *ever* did he get *here?*" said Bruno. "Ask him, Sylvie. I doosn't know how."

And then began an eager talk in Doggee, which of course was lost upon *me*; and I could only *guess*, when the beautiful creature, with a sly glance at me, whispered something in Sylvie's ear, that *I* was now the subject of conversation. Sylvie looked round laughingly.

"He asked me who you are," she explained. "And I said '*He's our friend*'. And he said 'What's his name?' And I said 'It's *Mister Sir*'. And he said 'Bosh!' "

"What is 'Bosh!' in Doggee," I enquired.

"It's the same as in English," said Sylvie. "Only, when a *dog* says it, it's a sort of whisper, that's half a *cough* and half a *bark*. Nero, say '*Bosh!*' "

And Nero, who had now begun gamboling round us again, said "*Bosh!*" several times; and I found that Sylvie's description of the sound was perfectly accurate.

"I wonder what's behind this long wall?" I said, as we walked on.

"It's the *Orchard*," Sylvie replied, after a consultation with Nero. "See, there's a boy getting down off the wall, at that far corner. And now he's running away across the field. I do believe he's been stealing the apples!"

Bruno set off after him, but returned to us in a few moments, as he had evidently no chance of overtaking the young rascal.

"I couldn't catch him!" he said. "I wiss I'd started a little sooner. His pockets *was* full of apples!"

The Dog-King looked up at Sylvie, and said something in Doggee.

"Why, of *course* you can!" Sylvie exclaimed. "How stupid not to think of it! *Nero*'ll hold him for us, Bruno! But I'd better make him invisible, first." And she hastily got out the Magic Jewel, and began waving it over Nero's head, and down along his back.

"That'll do!" cried Bruno, impatiently. "After him, good Doggie!"

"Oh, Bruno!" Sylvie exclaimed reproachfully. "You

shouldn't have sent him off so quick! I hadn't done the tail!"

Meanwhile Nero was coursing like a greyhound down the field: so at least I concluded from all *I* could see of him—the long feathery tail, which floated like a meteor through the air—and in a very few seconds he had come up with the little thief.

"He's got him safe, by one foot!" cried Sylvie, who was eagerly watching the chase. "Now there's no hurry, Bruno!"

So we walked, quite leisurely, down the field, to where the frightened lad stood. A more curious sight I had seldom seen, in all my "eerie" experiences. Every bit of him was in violent action, except the left foot, which was apparently glued to the ground—there being nothing visibly holding it: while, at some little distance, the long feathery tail was waving gracefully from side to side, showing that Nero, at least, regarded the whole affair as nothing but a magnificent game of play.

"What's the matter with you?" I said, as gravely as I could.

"Got the crahmp in me ahnkle!" the thief groaned in reply. "An' me fut's gone to sleep!" And he began to blubber aloud.

"Now, look here!" Bruno said in a commanding tone, getting in front of him. "Oo've got to give up those apples!"

The lad glanced at me, but didn't seem to reckon *my* interference as worth anything. Then he glanced at Sylvie: *she* clearly didn't count for very much, either. Then he took courage. "It'll take a better man than any of *yer* to get 'em!" he retorted defiantly.

Sylvie stooped and patted the invisible Nero. "A *little* tighter!" she whispered. And a sharp yell from the ragged boy showed how promptly the Dog-King had taken the hint.

"What's the matter *now*?" I said. "Is your ankle worse?"

"And it'll get worse, and worse, and worse," Bruno solemnly assured him, "till oo gives up those apples!"

Apparently the thief was convinced of this at last, and he sulkily began emptying his pockets of the apples. The children watched from a little distance, Bruno dancing with delight at every fresh yell extracted from Nero's terrified prisoner.

"That's all," the boy said at last.

"It *isn't* all!" cried Bruno. "There's three more in that pocket!"

Another hint from Sylvie to the Dog-King—another sharp yell from the thief, now convicted of lying also—and the remaining three apples were surrendered.

"Let him go, please," Sylvie said in Doggee, and the lad limped away at a great pace, stooping now and then to rub the ailing ankle in fear, seemingly, that the "crahmp" might attack it again.

Bruno ran back, with his booty, to the orchard wall, and pitched the apples over it one by one. "I's welly afraid *some* of them's gone under the wrong trees!" he panted, on overtaking us again.

"The *wrong* trees!" laughed Sylvie. "Trees *ca'n't* do wrong! There's no such things as *wrong* trees!"

"Then there's no such things as *right* trees, neither!" cried Bruno. And Sylvie gave up the point.

"Wait a minute, please!" she said to me. "I must make Nero *visible*, you know!"

"No, *please* don't!" cried Bruno, who had by this time mounted on the Royal back, and was twisting the Royal hair into a bridle. "It'll be *such* fun to have him like this!"

"Well, it *does* look funny," Sylvie admitted, and led the way to the farm-house, where the farmer's wife stood, evidently much perplexed at the weird procession now approaching her. "It's summat gone wrong wi' my spectacles, I doubt!" she murmured, as she took them off, and began diligently rubbing them with a corner of her apron.

Meanwhile Sylvie had hastily pulled Bruno down from

his steed, and had just time to make His Majesty wholly visible before the spectacles were resumed.

All was natural, now; but the good woman still looked a little uneasy about it. "My eyesight's getting bad," she said, "but I see you *now*, my darlings! You'll give me a kiss, won't you?"

Bruno got behind me, in a moment: however Sylvie put up *her* face, to be kissed, as representative of *both*, and we all went in together.

CHAPTER V

Matilda Jane

"COME to me, my little gentleman," said our hostess, lifting Bruno into her lap, "and tell me everything."

"I ca'n't," said Bruno. "There wouldn't be time. Besides, I don't know everything."

The good woman looked a little puzzled, and turned to Sylvie for help. "Does he like *riding*?" she asked.

"Yes, I *think* so," Sylvie gently replied. "He's just had a ride on *Nero*."

"Ah, Nero's a grand dog, isn't he? Were you ever outside a *horse*, my little man?"

"*Always!*" Bruno said with great decision. "Never was *inside* one. Was *oo*?"

Here I thought it well to interpose, and to mention the business on which we had come, and so relieved her, for a few minutes, from Bruno's perplexing questions.

"And those dear children will like a bit of cake, *I'll* warrant!" said the farmer's hospitable wife, when the business was concluded, as she opened her cupboard, and brought out a cake. "And don't you waste the crust, little gentleman!" she added, as she handed a good slice of it to Bruno. "You know what the poetry-book says about wilful waste?"

"No, I don't," said Bruno. "What doos he say about it?"

"Tell him, Bessie!" And the mother looked down, proudly and lovingly, on a rosy little maiden, who had just crept shyly into the room, and was leaning against her knee. "What's that your poetry-book says about wilful waste?"

"*For wilful waste makes woeful want,*" Bessie recited, in an almost inaudible whisper: "*and you may live to say 'How much I wish I had the crust that then I threw away!'* "

"Now try if *you* can say it, my dear! *For wilful*——"

"*For wifful*—sumfinoruvver——" Bruno began, readily enough; and then there came a dead pause. "Ca'n't remember no more!"

"Well, what do you *learn* from it, then? You can tell us *that*, at any rate?"

Bruno ate a little more cake, and considered: but the moral did not seem to him to be a very obvious one.

"Always to——" Sylvie prompted him in a whisper.

"Always to——" Bruno softly repeated: and then, with sudden inspiration, "always to look where it goes to!"

"Where *what* goes to, darling?"

"Why the *crust*, a course!" said Bruno. "Then, if I lived to say '*How much I wiss I had the crust*——' (and all that), I'd know where I frew it to!"

This new interpretation quite puzzled the good woman. She returned to the subject of "Bessie". "Wouldn't you like to see Bessie's doll, my dears! Bessie, take the little lady and gentleman to see Matilda Jane!"

Bessie's shyness thawed away in a moment. "Matilda Jane has just woke up," she stated, confidentially, to Sylvie. "Won't you help me on with her frock? Them strings *is* such a bother to tie!"

"I can tie *strings*," we heard, in Sylvie's gentle voice, as the two little girls left the room together. Bruno ignored the whole proceeding, and strolled to the window, quite with the air of a fashionable gentleman. Little girls, and dolls, were not at all in his line.

And forthwith the fond mother proceeded to tell me (as what mother is not ready to do?) of all Bessie's virtues (and vices too, for the matter of that) and of the many fearful maladies which, notwithstanding those ruddy cheeks and that plump little figure, had nearly, time and again, swept her from the face of the earth.

When the full stream of loving memories had nearly run itself out, I began to question her about the working men of that neighbourhood, and specially the "Willie," whom we had heard of at his cottage. "He was a good fellow once," said my kind hostess: "but it's the drink has ruined him! Not that I'd rob them of the drink—it's good for the most of them—but there's some as is too weak to stand agin' temptations: it's a thousand pities, for *them*, as they ever built the Golden Lion at the corner there!"

"The Golden Lion?" I repeated.

"It's the new Public," my hostess explained. "And it stands right in the way, and handy for the workmen, as they come back from the brickfields, as it might be to-day, with their week's wages. A deal of money gets wasted that way. And some of 'em gets drunk."

"If only they could have it in their own houses——" I mused, hardly knowing I had said the words out loud.

"That's it!" she eagerly exclaimed. It was evidently a solution, of the problem, that she had already thought out. "If only you could manage, so's each man to have his own little barrel in his own house—there'd hardly be a drunken man in the length and breadth of the land!"

And then I told her the old story—about a certain cottager who bought himself a little barrel of beer, and installed his wife as bar-keeper: and how, every time he wanted his mug of beer, he regularly paid her over the counter for it: and how she never would let him go on "tick", and was a perfectly inflexible bar-keeper in never letting him have more than his proper allowance: and how, every time the barrel needed refilling, she had plenty to do it with, and something over for her money-box: and how, at the end of the year, he not only found

himself in first-rate health and spirits, with that unde-
finable but quite unmistakable air which always distin-
guishes the sober man from the one who takes "a drop
too much", but had quite a box full of money, all saved
out of his own pence!

"If only they'd all do like that!" said the good woman,
wiping her eyes, which were overflowing with kindly
sympathy. "Drink hadn't need to be the curse it is to
some——"

"Only a *curse*", I said, "when it is used wrongly. Any
of God's gifts may be turned into a curse, unless we use it
wisely. But we must be getting home. Would you call the
little girls? Matilda Jane has seen enough of company,
for *one* day, I'm sure!"

"I'll find 'em in a minute," said my hostess, as she rose
to leave the room. "Maybe that young gentleman saw
which way they went?"

"Where are they, Bruno?" I said.

"They ain't in the field," was Bruno's rather evasive
reply, " 'cause there's nothing but *pigs* there, and Sylvie
isn't a pig. Now don't interrupt me any more, 'cause I'm
telling a story to this fly; and it wo'n't attend!"

"They're among the apples, I'll warrant 'em!" said the
Farmer's wife. So we left Bruno to finish his story, and
went out into the orchard, where we soon came upon the
children, walking sedately side by side, Sylvie carrying
the doll, while little Bess carefully shaded its face, with a
large cabbage-leaf for a parasol.

As soon as they caught sight of us, little Bess dropped
her cabbage-leaf and came running to meet us, Sylvie
following more slowly, as her precious charge evidently
needed great care and attention.

"I'm its Mamma, and Sylvie's the Head-Nurse," Bessie
explained: "and Sylvie's taught me ever such a pretty
song, for me to sing to Matilda Jane!"

"Let's hear it once more, Sylvie," I said, delighted at
getting the chance I had long wished for, of hearing her
sing. But Sylvie turned shy and frightened in a moment.

"No, *please not!*" she said, in an earnest "aside" to me. "Bessie knows it quite perfect now. Bessie can sing it!"

"Aye, aye! Let Bessie sing it!" said the proud mother. "Bessie has a bonny voice of her own," (this again was an "aside" to me) "though I say it as shouldn't!"

Bessie was only too happy to accept the "encore". So the plump little Mamma sat down at our feet, with her hideous daughter reclining stiffly across her lap (it was one of a kind that wo'n't sit down, under *any* amount of persuasion), and, with a face simply beaming with delight, began the lullaby, in a shout that *ought* to have frightened the poor baby into fits. The Head-Nurse crouched down behind her, keeping herself respectfully in the background, with her hands on the shoulders of her little mistress, so as to be ready to act as Prompter, if required, and to supply "*each gap in faithless memory void*".

The shout, with which she began, proved to be only a momentary effort. After a very few notes, Bessie toned down, and sang on in a small but very sweet voice. At first her great black eyes were fixed on her mother, but soon her gaze wandered upwards, among the apples, and she seemed to have quite forgotten that she had any other audience than her Baby, and her Head-Nurse, who once or twice supplied, almost inaudibly, the right note, when the singer was getting a little "flat".

> "*Matilda Jane, you never look*
> *At any toy or picture-book:*
> *I show you pretty things in vain—*
> *You must be blind, Matilda Jane!*
>
> "*I ask you riddles, tell you tales,*
> *But all our conversation fails:*
> *You never answer me again—*
> *I fear you're dumb, Matilda Jane!*
>
> "*Matilda, darling, when I call,*
> *You never seem to hear at all:*
> *I shout with all my might and main—*
> *But you're so deaf, Matilda Jane!*

"Matilda Jane, you needn't mind:
For, though you're deaf, and dumb, and blind,
There's some one loves you, it is plain—
And that is me, Matilda Jane!"

She sang three of the verses in a rather perfunctory style, but the last stanza evidently excited the little maiden. Her voice rose, ever clearer and louder: she had a rapt look on her face, as if suddenly inspired, and, as she sang the last few words, she clasped to her heart the inattentive Matilda Jane.

"Kiss it now!" prompted the Head-Nurse. And in a moment the simpering meaningless face of the Baby was covered with a shower of passionate kisses.

"What a bonny song!" cried the Farmer's wife. "Who made the words, dearie?"

'I—I think I'll look for Bruno," Sylvie said demurely, and left us hastily. The curious child seemed always afraid of being praised, or even noticed.

"Sylvie planned the words," Bessie informed us, proud of her superior information: "and Bruno planned the music—and *I* sang it!" (this last circumstance, by the way, we did not need to be told).

So we followed Sylvie, and all entered the parlour together. Bruno was still standing at the window, with his elbows on the sill. He had, apparently, finished the story that he was telling to the fly, and had found a new occupation. "Don't imperrupt!" he said as we came in. "I'm counting the Pigs in the field!"

"How many are there?" I enquired.

"About a thousand and four," said Bruno.

"You mean 'about a thousand'," Sylvie corrected him. "There's no good saying '*and four*': you *ca'n't* be sure about the four!"

"And you're as wrong as ever!" Bruno exclaimed triumphantly. "It's just the *four* I *can* be sure about; 'cause they're here, grubbling under the window! It's the *thousand* I isn't pruffickly sure about!"

"But some of them have gone into the sty," Sylvie said, leaning over him to look out of the window.

"Yes," said Bruno; "but they went so slowly and so fewly, I didn't care to count *them*."

"We must be going, children," I said. "Wish Bessie good-bye." Sylvie flung her arms round the little maiden's neck, and kissed her: but Bruno stood aloof, looking unusually shy. ("I never kiss *nobody* but Sylvie!" he explained to me afterwards.) The Farmer's wife showed us out: and we were soon on our way back to Elveston.

"And that's the new public-house that we were talking about, I suppose?" I said, as we came in sight of a long low building, with the words "THE GOLDEN LION" over the door.

"Yes, that's it," said Sylvie. "I wonder if *her* Willie's inside? Run in, Bruno, and see if he's there."

I interposed, feeling that Bruno was, in a sort of way, in *my* care. "That's not a place to send a child into." For already the revellers were getting noisy: and a wild discord of singing, shouting, and meaningless laughter came to us through the open windows.

"They wo'n't *see* him, you know," Sylvie explained. "Wait a minute, Bruno!" She clasped the jewel, that always hung round her neck, between the palms of her hands, and muttered a few words to herself. What they were I could not at all make out, but some mysterious change seemed instantly to pass over us. My feet seemed to me no longer to press the ground, and the dream-like feeling came upon me, that I was suddenly endowed with the power of floating in the air. I could still just *see* the children: but their forms were shadowy and unsubstantial, and their voices sounded as if they came from some distant place and time, they were so unreal. However, I offered no further opposition to Bruno's going into the house. He was back again in a few moments. "No, he isn't come yet," he said. "They're talking about him inside, and saying how drunk he was last week."

While he was speaking, one of the men lounged out

through the door, a pipe in one hand and a mug of beer in the other, and crossed to where we were standing, so as to get a better view along the road. Two or three others leaned out through the open window, each holding his mug of beer, with red faces and sleepy eyes. "Canst see him, lad?" one of them asked.

"I dunnot know," the man said, taking a step forwards, which brought us nearly face to face. Sylvie hastily pulled me out of his way. "Thanks, child," I said. "I had forgotten he couldn't see us. What would have happened if I had stayed in his way?"

"I don't know," Sylvie said gravely. "It wouldn't matter to *us*; but *you* may be different." She said this in her usual voice, but the man took no sort of notice, though she was standing close in front of him, and looking up into his face as she spoke.

"He's coming now!" cried Bruno, pointing down the road.

"He be a-coomin noo!" echoed the man, stretching out his arm exactly over Bruno's head, and pointing with his pipe.

"Then *chorus* agin!" was shouted out by one of the red-faced men in the window: and forthwith a dozen voices yelled, to a harsh discordant melody, the refrain:

> "*There's him, an' yo', an' me,*
> *Roarin' laddies!*
> *We loves a bit o' spree,*
> *Roarin' laddies we,*
> *Roarin' laddies*
> *Roarin' laddies!*"

The man lounged back again to the house, joining lustily in the chorus as he went: so that only the children and I were in the road when "Willie" came up.

Chapter VI

Willie's Wife

HE made for the door of the public-house, but the children intercepted him. Sylvie clung to one arm; while Bruno, on the opposite side, was pushing him with all his strength, and many inarticulate cries of "Gee-up! Gee-back! Woah then!" which he had picked up from the waggoners.

"Willie" took not the least notice of them: he was simply conscious that *something* had checked him: and, for want of any other way of accounting for it, he seemed to regard it as his own act.

"I wunnut coom in," he said: "not to-day."

"A mug o' beer wunnut hurt 'ee!" his friends shouted in chorus. "*Two* mugs wunnut hurt 'ee! Nor a dozen mugs!"

"Nay," said Willie. "I'm agoan whoam."

"What, withouten thy drink, Willie man?" shouted the others. But "Willie man" would have no more discussion, and turned doggedly away, the children keeping one on each side of him, to guard him against any change in his sudden resolution.

For a while he walked on stoutly enough, keeping his hands in his pockets, and softly whistling a tune, in time to his heavy tread: his success, in appearing entirely at his ease, was *almost* complete; but a careful observer would have noted that he had forgotten the second part of the air, and that, when it broke down, he instantly began it again, being too nervous to think of another, and too restless to endure silence.

It was not the old fear that possessed him now—the old fear that had been his dreary companion every Saturday night he could remember as he had reeled along, steadying himself against gates and garden-palings, and when the shrill reproaches of his wife had seemed to his dazed brain only the echo of a yet more piercing voice within the intolerable wail of a hopeless remorse: it was a wholly new fear that had come to him now: life had taken on itself a new set of colours, and was lighted up with a new and dazzling radiance, and he did not see, as yet, how his home-life, and his wife and child, would fit into the new order of things: the very novelty of it all was, to his simple mind, a perplexity and an overwhelming terror.

And now the tune died into sudden silence on the trembling lips, as he turned a sharp corner, and came in sight of his own cottage, where his wife stood, leaning with folded arms on the wicket-gate, and looking up the road with a pale face, that had in it no glimmer of the light of hope—only the heavy shadow of a deep stony despair.

"Fine an' early, lad! Fine an' early!" the words might have been words of welcoming, but oh, the bitterness of the tone in which she said it! "What brings thee from thy merry mates, and all the fiddling and the jigging? Pockets empty, I doubt? Or thou'st come, mebbe, for to see thy little one die? The bairnie's clemmed, and I've nor bite nor sup to gie her. But what does *thou* care?" She flung the gate open, and met him with blazing eyes of fury.

The man said no word. Slowly, and with downcast eyes, he passed into the house, while she, half terrified at his strange silence, followed him in without another word; and it was not till he had sunk into a chair, with his arms crossed on the table and with drooping head, that she found her voice again.

It seemed entirely natural for us to go in with them: at another time one would have asked leave for this, but I felt, I knew not why, that we were in some mysterious way invisible, and as free to come and to go as disembodied spirits.

The child in the cradle woke up, and raised a piteous cry, which in a moment brought the children to its side: Bruno rocked the cradle, while Sylvie tenderly replaced the little head on the pillow from which it had slipped. But the mother took no heed of the cry, nor yet of the satisfied "coo" that it set up when Sylvie had made it happy again: she only stood gazing at her husband, and vainly trying, with white quivering lips (I believe she thought he was mad), to speak in the old tones of shrill upbraiding that he knew so well.

"And thou'st spent all thy wages—I'll swear thou hast —on the devil's own drink—and thou'st been and made thysen a beast again—as thou allus dost——"

"Hasna!" the man muttered, his voice hardly rising above a whisper, as he slowly emptied his pockets on the table. "There's th' wage, Missus, every penny on't."

The woman gasped and put one hand to her heart, as if under some great shock of surprise. "Then *how's* thee gotten th' drink?"

"*Hasna* gotten it," he answered her, in a tone more sad than sullen. "I hanna touched a drop this blessed day. No!" he cried aloud, bringing his clenched fist heavily down upon the table, and looking up at her with gleaming eyes, "nor I'll never touch another drop o' the cursed drink—till I die—so help me God my Maker!" His voice, which had suddenly risen to a hoarse shout, dropped again as suddenly: and once more he bowed his head, and buried his face in his folded arms.

The woman had dropped upon her knees by the cradle, while he was speaking. She neither looked at him nor seemed to hear him. With hands clasped above her head, she rocked herself wildly to and fro. "Oh my God! Oh my God!" was all she said, over and over again.

Sylvie and Bruno gently unclasped her hands and drew them down—till she had an arm round each of them, though she took no notice of them, but knelt on with eyes gazing upwards, and lips that moved as if in silent thanksgiving. The man kept his face hidden, and uttered no sound: but one could *see* the sobs that shook him from head to foot.

After a while he raised his head—his face all wet with tears. "Polly!" he said softly; and then, louder, "Old Poll!"

Then she rose from her knees and came to him, with a dazed look, as if she were walking in her sleep. "Who was it called me old Poll?" she asked: her voice took on it a tender playfulness: her eyes sparkled; and the rosy light of Youth flushed her pale cheeks, till she looked more like a happy girl of seventeen than a worn woman of forty. "Was that my own lad, my Willie, a-waiting for me at the stile?"

His face too was transformed, in the same magic light, to the likeness of a bashful boy: and boy and girl they seemed, as he wound an arm about her, and drew her to his side, while with the other hand he thrust from him the heap of money, as though it were something hateful to the touch. "Tak it, lass," he said, "tak it all! An' fetch us summat to eat: but get a sup o' milk, first, for t' bairn."

"My *little* bairn!" she murmured as she gathered up the coins. "My own little lassie!" Then she moved to the door, and was passing out, but a sudden thought seemed to arrest her: she hastily returned—first to kneel down and kiss the sleeping child, and then to throw herself into her husband's arms and be strained to his heart. The next moment she was on her way, taking with her a jug that hung on a peg near the door: we followed close behind.

We had not gone far before we came in sight of a swinging sign-board bearing the word "DAIRY" on it, and here she went in, welcomed by a little curly white dog, who, not being under the "eerie" influence, saw the children, and received them with the most effusive affection. When I got inside, the dairyman was in the act of taking the money. "Is't for thysen, Missus, or for t' bairn?" he asked, when he had filled the jug, pausing with it in his hand.

"For t' *bairn*!" she said, almost reproachfully. "Think'st tha I'd touch a drop *mysen*, while as *she* hadna got her fill?"

"All right, Missus," the man replied, turning away with the jug in his hand. "Let's just mak sure it's good measure." He went back among his shelves of milk-bowls, carefully keeping his back towards her while he emptied a little measure of cream into the jug, muttering to himself "mebbe it'll hearten her up a bit, the little lassie!"

The woman never noticed the kind deed, but took back the jug with a simple "Good evening, Master," and went her way: but the children had been more observant, and, as we followed her out, Bruno remarked "That were *welly* kind: and I loves that man: and if I was welly rich I'd give him a hundred pounds—and a bun. That little grummeling dog doosn't know its business!" He referred to the dairyman's little dog, who had apparently quite forgotten the affectionate welcome he had given us on our arrival, and was now following at a respectful distance, doing his best to *"speed the parting guest"* with a shower of little shrill barks, that seemed to tread on one another's heels.

"What *is* a dog's business?" laughed Sylvie. "Dogs ca'n't keep shops and give change!"

"Sisters' businesses *isn't* to laugh at their brothers," Bruno replied with perfect gravity. "And dogs' businesses is to *bark*—not like that: it should finish one bark before it begins another: and it should—Oh Sylvie, there's some dindledums!"

And in another moment the happy children were flying across the common, racing for the patch of dandelions.

While I stood watching them, a strange dreamy feeling came upon me: a railway-platform seemed to take the place of the green sward, and, instead of the light figure of Sylvie bounding along, I seemed to see the flying form of Lady Muriel; but whether Bruno had also undergone a transformation, and had become the old man whom she was running to overtake, I was unable to judge, so instantaneously did the feeling come and go.

When I re-entered the little sitting-room which I shared with Arthur, he was standing with his back to me, looking out of the open window, and evidently had not heard me enter. A cup of tea, apparently just tasted and pushed

aside, stood on the table, on the opposite side of which was
a letter, just begun, with the pen lying across it: an open
book lay on the sofa: the London paper occupied the easy
chair; and on the little table which stood by it, I noticed
an unlighted cigar and an open box of cigar-lights: all
things betokened that the Doctor, usually so methodical
and so self-contained, had been trying every form of
occupation, and could settle to none!

"This is very unlike *you*, Doctor!" I was beginning, but
checked myself, as he turned at the sound of my voice, in
sheer amazement at the wonderful change that had taken
place in his appearance. Never had I seen a face so radiant
with happiness, or eyes that sparkled with such unearthly
light! "Even thus", I thought, "must the herald-angel
have looked, who brought to the shepherds, watching
over their flocks by night, that sweet message of *'peace
on earth, good-will to men'*!"

"Yes, dear friend!" he said, as if in answer to the question that I suppose he read in my face. "It is true! It is
true!"

No need to ask *what* was true. "God bless you both!" I
said, as I felt the happy tears brimming to my eyes. "You
were made for each other!"

"Yes," he said, simply, "I believe we were. And *what*
a change it makes in one's Life! This isn't the same
world! That isn't the sky I saw yesterday! Those clouds—
I never saw such clouds in all my life before! They look
like troops of hovering angels!"

To *me* they looked very ordinary clouds indeed: but
then I had not fed *"on honeydew, And drunk the milk of
Paradise"*!

"She wants to see you—at once," he continued, de-
scending suddenly to the things of earth. "She says *that* is
the *one* drop yet wanting in her cup of happiness!"

"I'll go at once," I said, as I turned to leave the room.
"Wo'n't you come with me?"

"No, Sir!" said the Doctor, with a sudden effort—
which proved an utter failure—to resume his professional

manner. "Do I *look* like coming with you? Have you never heard that two is company, and——"

"Yes," I said, "I *have* heard it: and I'm painfully aware that *I* am *Number Three*! But, *when* shall we three meet again?"

"*When the hurly-burly's done!*" he answered with a happy laugh, such as I had not heard from him for many a year.

Chapter VII

Mein Herr

So I went on my lonely way, and, on reaching the Hall, I found Lady Muriel standing at the garden-gate waiting for me.

"No need to *give* you joy, or to *wish* you joy?" I began.

"None *whatever!*" she replied, with the joyous laugh of a child. "We *give* people what they haven't got: we *wish* for something that is yet to come. For me, it's all *here*! It's all *mine*! Dear friend," she suddenly broke off, "do you think Heaven ever begins on *Earth*, for any of us?"

"For *some*," I said. "For some, perhaps, who are simple and childlike. You know he said 'of such is the Kingdom of Heaven'."

Lady Muriel clasped her hands, and gazed up into the cloudless sky, with a look I had often seen in Sylvie's eyes. "I feel as if it had begun for *me*," she almost whispered. "I feel as if *I* were one of the happy children, whom He bid them bring near to Him, though the people would have kept them back. Yes, He has seen me in the throng. He has read the wistful longing in my eyes. He has beckoned me to Him. They have *had* to make way for me. He has taken me up in His arms. He has put His hands upon me and blessed me!" She paused, breathless in her perfect happiness.

"Yes," I said. "I think He has!"

"You must come and speak to my father," she went on, as we stood side by side at the gate, looking down the shady lane. But, even as she said the words, the "eerie" sensation came over me like a flood: I saw the dear old Professor approaching us, and also saw, what was stranger still, that he was visible to *Lady Muriel*!

What was to be done? Had the fairy-life been merged in the real life? Or was Lady Muriel "eerie" also, and thus able to enter into the fairy-world along with me? The words were on my lips ("I see an old friend of mine in the lane: if you don't know him, may I introduce him to you?") when the strangest thing of all happened: Lady Muriel spoke.

"I see an old friend of mine in the lane," she said: "if you don't know him, may I introduce him to you?"

I seemed to wake out of a dream: for the "eerie" feeling was still strong upon me, and the figure outside seemed to be changing at every moment, like one of the shapes in a kaleidoscope: now he was the *Professor*, and now he was somebody else! By the time he had reached the gate, he certainly was somebody else: and I felt that the proper course was for *Lady Muriel*, not for *me*, to introduce him. She greeted him kindly, and, opening the gate, admitted the venerable old man—a German, obviously—who looked about him with dazed eyes, as if *he*, too, had but just awaked from a dream!

No, it was certainly *not* the Professor! My old friend *could* not have grown that magnificent beard since last we met: moreover, he would have recognised *me*, for I was certain that *I* had not changed much in the time.

As it was, he simply looked at me vaguely, and took off his hat in response to Lady Muriel's words "Let me introduce Mein Herr to you"; while in the words, spoken in a strong German accent, "proud to make your acquaintance, Sir!" I could detect no trace of an idea that we had ever met before.

Lady Muriel led us to the well-known shady nook,

where preparations for afternoon-tea had already been made, and, while she went in to look for the Earl, we seated ourselves in two easy-chairs, and "Mein Herr" took up Lady Muriel's work, and examined it through his large spectacles (one of the adjuncts that made him so provokingly like the Professor). "Hemming pocket-handkerchiefs?" he said, musingly. "So *that* is what the English miladies occupy themselves with, is it?"

"It is the one accomplishment", I said, "in which Man has never yet rivalled Woman!"

Here Lady Muriel returned with her father; and, after he had exchanged some friendly words with "Mein Herr", and we had all been supplied with the needful "creature-comforts", the newcomer returned to the suggestive subject of Pocket-handkerchiefs.

"You have heard of Fortunatus's Purse, Miladi? Ah, so! Would you be surprised to hear that, with three of these leetle handkerchiefs, you shall make the Purse of Fortunatus, quite soon, quite easily?"

"Shall I indeed?" Lady Muriel eagerly replied, as she took a heap of them into her lap, and threaded her needle. "*Please* tell me how, Mein Herr! I'll make one before I touch another drop of tea!"

"You shall first," said Mein Herr, possessing himself of two of the handkerchiefs, spreading one upon the other, and holding them up by two corners, "you shall first join together these upper corners, the right to the right, the left to the left; and the opening between them shall be the *mouth* of the Purse."

A very few stitches sufficed to carry out *this* direction. "Now, if I sew the other three edges together", she suggested, "the bag is complete?"

"Not so, Miladi: the *lower* edges shall *first* be joined— ah, not so!" (as she was beginning to sew them together). "Turn one of them over, and join the *right* lower corner of the one to the *left* lower corner of the other, and sew the lower edges together in what you would call *the wrong way.*"

"*I* see!" said Lady Muriel, as she deftly executed the order. "And a very twisted, uncomfortable, uncanny-looking bag it makes! But the *moral* is a lovely one. Unlimited wealth can only be attained by doing things *in the wrong way!* And how are we to join up these mysterious—no, I mean *this* mysterious opening?" (twisting the thing round and round with a puzzled air). "Yes, it *is* one opening. I thought it was *two*, at first."

"You have seen the puzzle of the Paper Ring?" Mein Herr said, addressing the Earl. "Where you take a slip of paper, and join its ends together, first twisting one, so as to join the *upper* corner of *one* end to the *lower* corner of the *other*?"

"I saw one made, only yesterday," the Earl replied. "Muriel, my child, were you not making one, to amuse those children you had to tea?"

"Yes, I know that Puzzle," said Lady Muriel. "The Ring has only *one* surface, and only *one* edge, It's very mysterious!"

"The *bag* is just like that, isn't it?" I suggested. "Is not the *outer* surface of one side of it continuous with the *inner* surface of the other side?"

"So it is!" she exclaimed. "Only it *isn't* a bag, just yet. How shall we fill up this opening, Mein Herr?"

"Thus!" said the old man impressively, taking the bag from her, and rising to his feet in the excitement of the explanation. "The edge of the opening consists of *four* handkerchief edges, and you can trace it continuously, round and round the opening: down the right edge of *one* handkerchief, up the left edge of the *other*, and then down the left edge of the *one*, and up the right edge of the *other*!"

"So you can!" Lady Muriel murmured thoughtfully, leaning her head on her hand, and earnestly watching the old man. "And that *proves* it to be only *one* opening!"

She looked so strangely like a child, puzzling over a difficult lesson, and Mein Herr had become, for the moment, so strangely like the old Professor, that I felt utterly bewildered: the "eerie" feeling was on me in its full force, and I felt almost *impelled* to say "Do you understand it, Sylvie?" However I checked myself by a great effort, and let the dream (if indeed it *was* a dream) go on to its end.

"Now, this *third* handkerchief", Mein Herr proceeded, "has *also* four edges, which you can trace continuously round and round: all you need do is to join its four edges to the four edges of the opening. The Purse is then complete, and its outer surface——"

"*I* see!" Lady Muriel eagerly interrupted. "Its *outer* surface will be continuous with its *inner* surface! But it will take time. I'll sew it up after tea." She laid aside the bag, and resumed her cup of tea. "But why do you call it Fortunatus's Purse, Mein Herr?"

The dear old man beamed upon her, with a jolly smile, looking more exactly like the Professor than ever. "Don't you see, my child—I should say Miladi? Whatever is *inside* that Purse, is *outside* it; and whatever is *outside* it, is *inside* it. So you have all the wealth of the world in that leetle Purse!"

His pupil clapped her hands, in unrestrained delight. "I'll certainly sew the third handkerchief in—*some* time," she said: "but I wo'n't take up your time by trying it now. Tell us some more wonderful things, please!" And her face and her voice so *exactly* recalled Sylvie, that I could not help glancing round, half-expecting to see *Bruno* also!

Mein Herr began thoughtfully balancing his spoon on the edge of his teacup, while he pondered over this request. "Something wonderful—like Fortunatus's Purse? *That* will give you—when it is made—wealth beyond your wildest dreams: but it will not give you *Time!*"

A pause of silence ensued—utilized by Lady Muriel for the very practical purpose of refilling the teacups.

"In *your* country", Mein Herr began with a startling abruptness, "what becomes of all the wasted Time?"

Lady Muriel looked grave. "Who can tell?" she half-whispered to herself. "All one knows is that it is gone—past recall!"

"Well, in *my*—I mean in a country *I* have visited", said the old man, "they store it up: and it comes in *very* useful, years afterwards! For example, suppose you have a long tedious evening before you: nobody to talk to: nothing you care to do: and yet hours too soon to go to bed. How do *you* behave then?"

"I get *very* cross," she frankly admitted: "and I want to throw things about the room!"

"When that happens to—to the people I have visited, they never act *so*. By a short and simple process—which I cannot explain to you—they store up the useless hours: and, on some *other* occasion, when they happen to *need* extra time, they get them out again."

The Earl was listening with a slightly incredulous smile. "Why cannot you *explain* the process?" he enquired.

Mein Herr was ready with a quite unanswerable reason. "Because you have no *words*, in *your* language, to convey the ideas which are needed. I could explain it in—in—but you would not understand it!"

"No indeed!" said Lady Muriel, graciously dispensing with the *name* of the unknown language. "I never learnt it—at least, not to speak it *fluently*, you know. *Please* tell us some more wonderful things!"

"They run their railway-trains without any engines—nothing is needed but machinery to *stop* them with. Is *that* wonderful enough, Miladi?"

"But where does the *force* come from?" I ventured to ask.

Mein Herr turned quickly round, to look at the new speaker. Then he took off his spectacles, and polished them, and looked at me again, in evident bewilderment. I could see he was thinking—as indeed *I* was also—that we *must* have met before.

"They use the force of *gravity*," he said. "It is a force known also in *your* country, I believe?"

"But that would need a railway going *down-hill*," the Earl remarked. "You ca'n't have *all* your railways going down-hill?"

"They *all* do", said Mein Herr.

"Not from *both* ends?"

"From *both* ends."

"Then I give it up!" said the Earl.

"Can you explain the process?" said Lady Muriel. "Without using that language, that I ca'n't speak fluently?"

"Easily," said Mein Herr. "Each railway is in a long tunnel, perfectly straight: so of course the *middle* of it is nearer the centre of the globe than the two ends: so every train runs half-way *down*-hill, and that gives it force enough to run the *other* half *up*-hill."

"Thank you. I understand that perfectly," said Lady Muriel. "But the velocity, in the *middle* of the tunnel, must be something *fearful*!"

Mein Herr was evidently much gratified at the intelligent interest Lady Muriel took in his remarks. At every moment the old man seemed to grow more chatty and more fluent. "You would like to know our methods of *driving*?" he smilingly enquired. "To us, a run-away horse is of no import at all!"

Lady Muriel slightly shuddered. "To *us* it is a very real danger," she said.

"That is because your carriage is wholly *behind* your horse. Your horse runs. Your carriage follows. Perhaps your horse has the bit in his teeth. Who shall stop him? You fly, ever faster and faster! Finally comes the inevitable upset!"

"But suppose *your* horse manages to get the bit in his teeth?"

"No matter! We would not concern ourselves. Our horse is harnessed in the very centre of our carriage. Two wheels are in front of him, and two behind. To the roof is attached one end of a broad belt. This goes under the horse's body, and the other end is attached to a leetle—

what you call a 'windlass', I think. The horse takes the
bit in his teeth. He runs away. We are flying at ten miles
an hour! We turn our little windlass, five turns, six turns,
seven turns, and—poof! Our horse is off the ground! *Now*
let him gallop in the air as much as he pleases: our *carriage* stands still. We sit round him, and watch him till he
is tried. Then we let him down. Our horse is glad, very
much glad, when his feet once more touch the ground!"

"Capital!" said the Earl, who had been listening attentively. "Are there any other peculiarities in your carriages?"

"In the *wheels*, sometimes, my Lord. For your health,
you go to sea: to be pitched, to be rolled, occasionally to be
drowned. *We* do all that on land: we are pitched, as you;
we are rolled, as you; but *drowned*, no! There is no
water!"

"What are the wheels like, then?"

"They are *oval*, my Lord. Therefore the carriages rise
and fall."

"Yes, and pitch the carriage backwards and forwards:
but how do they make it *roll*?"

"They do not match, my Lord. The *end* of one wheel
answers to the side of the opposite wheel. So first one side
of the carriage rises, then the other. And it pitches all the
while. Ah, you must be a good sailor, to drive in our
boat-carriages!"

"I can easily believe it," said the Earl.

Mein Herr rose to his feet. "I must leave you now, Miladi," he said, consulting his watch. "I have another engagement."

"I only wish we had stored up some extra time!" Lady
Muriel said, as she shook hands with him. "Then we
could have kept you a little longer!"

"In *that* case I would gladly stay," replied Mein Herr.
"As it is—I fear I must say goodbye!"

"Where did you first meet him?" I asked Lady Muriel,
when Mein Herr had left us. "And where does he live?
And what is his real name?"

"We first—met—him——" she musingly replied, "really, I ca'n't remember *where*! And I've no idea where he lives! And I never heard any other name! It's very curious. It never occurred to me before to consider what a mystery he is!"

"I hope we shall meet again," I said: "he interests me very much."

"He will be at our farewell-party, this day fortnight," said the Earl. "Of course you will come? Muriel is anxious to gather all our friends around us once more, before we leave the place."

And then he explained to me—as Lady Muriel had left us together—that he was so anxious to get his daughter away from a place full of so many painful memories connected with the now-cancelled engagement with Major Lindon, that they had arranged to have the wedding in a month's time, after which Arthur and his wife were to go on a foreign tour.

"Don't forget Tuesday week!" he said as we shook hands at parting. "I only wish you could bring with you those charming children, that you introduced to us in the summer. Talk of the mystery of Mein Herr! That's *nothing* to the mystery that seems to attend *them*! I shall never forget those marvellous flowers!"

"I will bring them if I possibly can," I said. But how to *fulfil* such a promise, I mused to myself on my way back to our lodgings, was a problem entirely beyond my skill!

Chapter VIII

In a Shady Place

The ten days glided swiftly away: and, the day before the great party was to take place, Arthur proposed that we should stroll down to the Hall, in time for afternoon-tea.

"Hadn't you better go *alone?*" I suggested. "Surely *I* shall be very much *de trop?*"

"Well, it'll be a kind of *experiment*," he said. "*Fiat experimentum in corpore vili!*" he added, with a graceful bow of mock politeness towards the unfortunate victim. "You see I shall have to bear the sight, to-morrow night, of my lady-love making herself agreeable to everybody *except* the right person, and I shall bear the agony all the better if we have a dress-rehearsal beforehand!"

"*My* part in the play being, apparently, that of the sample *wrong* person?"

"Well, no," Arthur said musingly, as we set forth: "there's no such part in a regular company. 'Heavy Father'? *That* wo'n't do: that's filled already. 'Singing Chambermaid'? Well, the 'First Lady' doubles *that* part. 'Comic Old Man'? You're not comic enough. After all, I'm afraid there's no part for you but the 'Well-dressed Villain': only", with a critical side-glance, "I'm a *leetle* uncertain about the dress!"

We found Lady Muriel alone, the Earl having gone out to make a call, and at once resumed old terms of intimacy, in the shady arbour where the tea-things seemed to be always waiting. The only novelty in the arrangements (one which Lady Muriel seemed to regard as *entirely* a matter of course), was that two of the chairs were placed *quite* close together, side by side. Strange to say, *I* was not invited to occupy *either* of them!

"We have been arranging, as we came along, about letter-writing," Arthur began. "He will want to know how we're enjoying our Swiss tour: and of course we must pretend we *are?*"

"Of course," she meekly assented.

"And the skeleton-in-the-cupboard——" I suggested.

"—is always a difficulty", she quickly put in, "when you're travelling about, and when there are no cupboards in the hotels. However, *ours* is a *very* portable one; and will be neatly packed, in a nice leather case——"

"But please don't think about *writing*", I said, "when

you've anything more attractive on hand. I delight in *reading* letters, but I know well how tiring it is to *write* them."

"It *is*, sometimes," Arthur assented. "For instance, when you're very shy of the person you have to write to."

"Does that show itself in the *letter*?" Lady Muriel enquired. "Of course, when I hear any one *talking—you*, for instance—I can see how *desperately* shy he is! But can you see that in a *letter*?"

"Well, of course, when you hear any one talk *fluently* —*you*, for instance—you can see how desperately *un*-shy she is—not to say saucy! But the shyest and most intermittent talker must *seem* fluent in letter-writing. He may have taken half-an-hour to *compose* his second sentence; but there it is, close after the first!"

"Then letters don't express all that they *might* express?"

"That's merely because our system of letter-writing is incomplete. A shy writer *ought* to be able to show that he is so. Why shouldn't he make *pauses* in writing, just as he would do in speaking? He might leave blank spaces—say half a page at a time. And a *very* shy girl—if there *is* such a thing—might write a sentence on the *first* sheet of her letter—then put in a couple of blank sheets—then a sentence on the *fourth* sheet: and so on."

"I quite foresee that *we*—I mean this clever little boy and myself—" Lady Muriel said to me, evidently with the kind wish to bring me into the conversation, "—are going to become famous—of course all our inventions are common property now—for a new Code of Rules for Letter-writing! Please invent some more, little boy!"

"Well, another thing *greatly* needed, little girl, is some way of expressing that we *don't* mean anything."

"Explain yourself, little boy! Surely *you* can find no difficulty in expressing a *total* absence of meaning?"

"I mean that you should be able, when you *don't* mean a thing to be taken seriously, to express that wish. For human nature is so constituted that whatever you write seriously is taken as a joke, and whatever you mean as a joke is taken seriously! At any rate, it is so in writing to a *lady*!"

"Ah! you're not used to writing to ladies!" Lady Muriel remarked, leaning back in her chair, and gazing thoughtfully into the sky. "You should try."

"Very good," said Arthur. "How many ladies may I begin writing to? As many as I can count on the fingers of both hands?"

"As many as you can count on the *thumbs* of *one* hand!" his lady-love replied with much severity. "What a *very* naughty little boy he is! *Isn't* he?" (with an appealing glance at me).

"He's a little fractious," I said. "Perhaps he's cutting a tooth." While to myself I said "How *exactly* like Sylvie talking to Bruno!"

"He wants his tea." (The naughty little boy volunteered the information.) "He's getting very tired, at the mere *prospect* of the great party to-morrow!"

"Then he shall have a good rest before-hand!" she soothingly replied. "The tea isn't made yet. Come, little boy, lean well back in your chair, and think about nothing —or about *me*, whichever you prefer!"

"All the same, all the same!" Arthur sleepily murmured, watching her with loving eyes, as she moved her chair away to the tea table, and began to make the tea. "Then he'll wait for his tea, like a good, patient little boy!"

"Shall I bring you the London Papers?" said Lady Muriel. "I saw them lying on the table as I came out, but my father said there was nothing in them, except that horrid murder-trial." (Society was just then enjoying its daily thrill of excitement in studying the details of a specially sensational murder in a thieve's den in the East of London.)

"I have no appetite for horrors," Arthur replied. "But I hope we have learned the lesson they should teach us— though we are very apt to read it backwards!"

"You speak in riddles," said Lady Muriel. "Please explain yourself. See now," suiting the action to the word, "I am sitting at your feet, just as if you were a second Gamaliel! Thanks, no." (This was to me, who had risen to bring her chair back to its former place.) "Pray don't disturb yourself. This tree and the grass make a very nice easy-chair. *What* is the lesson that one always reads wrong?"

Arthur was silent for a minute. "I would like to be clear what it *is* I mean," he said, slowly and thoughtfully, "before I say anything to *you*—because you *think* about it."

Anything approaching to a compliment was so unusual an utterance for Arthur, that it brought a flush of pleasure to her cheek, as she replied "It is *you*, that give me the ideas to think about."

"One's first thought", Arthur proceeded, "in reading anything specially vile or barbarous, as done by a fellow-creature, is apt to be that we see a new depth of Sin revealed *beneath* us: and we seem to gaze down into that abyss from some higher ground, far apart from it."

"I think I understand you now. You mean that one ought to think—not 'God, I thank Thee that I am not as other men are'—but 'God, be merciful to me also, who might be, but for Thy grace, a sinner as vile as he!' "

"No," said Arthur. "I meant a great deal more than that."

She looked up quickly, but checked herself, and waited in silence.

"One must begin further back, I think. Think of some other man, the same age as this poor wretch. Look back to the time when they both began life—before they had sense enough to know Right from Wrong. *Then*, at any rate, they were equal in God's sight?"

She nodded assent.

"We have, then, two distinct epochs at which we may contemplate the two men whose lives we are comparing. At the first epoch they are, so far as moral responsibility is concerned, on precisely the same footing: they are alike incapable of doing right or wrong. At the second epoch the one man—I am taking an extreme case, for contrast —has won the esteem and love of all around him: his character is stainless, and his name will be held in honour hereafter: the other man's history is one unvaried record of crime, and his life is at last forfeited to the outraged laws of his country. Now what have been the causes, in each case, of each man's condition being what it is at the second epoch? They are of two kinds—one acting from within, the other from without. These two kinds need to be discussed separately—that is, if I have not already tired you with my prosing?"

"On the contrary," said Lady Muriel, "it is a special delight to me to have a question discussed in this way— analysed and arranged so that one can understand it. Some books, that profess to argue out a question, are to me intolerably wearisome, simply because the ideas are all arranged haphazard—a sort of 'first come, first served'."

"You are very encouraging," Arthur replied, with a pleased look. "The causes, acting from *within*, which make a man's character what it is at any given moment, are his successive acts of volition—that is, his acts of choosing whether he will do this or that."

"We are to assume the existence of Free-Will?" I said, in order to have that point made quite clear.

"If not," was the quiet reply, "*cadit quaestio:* and I have no more to say."

"We *will* assume it!" the rest of the audience—the majority, I may say, looking at it from Arthur's point of view—imperiously proclaimed. The orator proceeded.

"The causes, acting from *without*, are his surroundings —what Mr. Herbert Spencer calls his 'environment'. Now the point I want to make clear is this, that a man is responsible for his act of choosing, but *not* responsible for his environment. Hence, if these two men make, on some given occasion, when they are exposed to equal temptation, equal efforts to resist and to choose the right, their condition, in the sight of God, must be the same. If He is pleased in the one case, so will He be in the other; if displeased in the one case, so also in the other."

"That is so, no doubt: I see it quite clearly," Lady Muriel put in.

"And yet, owing to their different environments, the one may win a great victory over the temptation, while the other falls into some black abyss of crime."

"But surely you would not say those men were equally guilty in the sight of God?"

"Either that", said Arthur, "or else I must give up my belief in God's perfect justice. But let me put one more case, which will show my meaning even more forcibly. Let the one man be in a high social position—the other, say, a common thief. Let the one be tempted to some trivial act of unfair dealing—something which he can do with the absolute certainty that it will never be discovered—something which he can with perfect ease forbear from doing—and which he distinctly knows to be a sin. Let the other be tempted to some terrible crime—as men would consider it—but under an almost overwhelming pressure of motives—of course not *quite* overwhelming, as that would destroy all responsibility. Now, in this case, let the second man make a *greater* effort at resistance than the first. Also suppose *both* to fall under the temptation—I say that the second man is, in God's sight, *less* guilty than the other."

Lady Muriel drew a long breath. "It upsets all one's ideas of Right and Wrong—just at first! Why, in that dreadful murder-trial, you would say, I suppose, that it was possible that the least guilty man in the Court was the murderer, and that possibly the judge who tried him, by yielding to the temptation of making one unfair remark, had committed a crime outweighing the criminal's whole career!"

"Certainly I should," Arthur firmly replied. "It sounds like a paradox, I admit. But just think what a grievous sin it must be, in God's sight, to yield to some very slight temptation, which we could have resisted with perfect ease, and to do it deliberately, and in the full light of God's Law. What penance can atone for a sin like *that*?"

"I ca'n't reject your theory," I said. "But how it seems to widen the possible area of Sin in the world!"

"Is that so?" Lady Muriel anxiously enquired.

"Oh, not so, not so!" was the eager reply. "To me it seems to clear away much of the cloud that hangs over the world's history. When this view first made itself clear to me, I remember walking out into the fields, repeating to myself that line of Tennyson *'There seemed no room for sense of wrong!'* The thought, that perhaps the real guilt of the human race was infinitely less than I fancied it— that the millions, whom I had thought of as sunk in hopeless depths of sin, were perhaps, in God's sight, scarcely sinning at all—was more sweet than words can tell! Life seemed more bright and beautiful, when once that thought had come! *'A livelier emerald twinkles in the grass, A purer sapphire melts into the sea!'* " His voice trembled as he concluded, and the tears stood in his eyes.

Lady Muriel shaded her face with her hand, and was silent for a minute. "It is a beautiful thought," she said, looking up at last. "Thank you—Arthur, for putting it into my head!"

The Earl returned in time to join us at tea, and to give us the very unwelcome tidings that a fever had broken out in the little harbour-town that lay below us—a fever of so malignant a type that, though it had only appeared a day or two ago, there were already more than a dozen down in it, two or three of whom were reported to be in imminent danger.

In answer to the eager questions of Arthur—who of course took a deep scientific interest in the matter—he could give very few *technical* details, though he had met the local doctor. It appeared, however, that it was an almost *new* disease—at least in *this* century, though it *might* prove to be identical with the "Plague" recorded in History—*very* infectious, and frightfully rapid in its action. "It will not, however, prevent our party to-morrow," he said in conclusion. "None of the guests belong to the infected district, which is, as you know, exclusively peopled by fishermen: so you may come with out any fear."

Arthur was very silent, all the way back, and, on reach-ing our lodgings, immediately plunged into medical studies, connected with the alarming malady of whose arrival he had just heard.

CHAPTER IX

The Farewell-Party

ON the following day, Arthur and I reached the Hall in good time, as only a few of the guests—it was to be a party of eighteen—had as yet arrived; and these were talking with the Earl, leaving us the opportunity of a few words apart with our hostess.

"Who is that *very* learned-looking man with the large spectacles?" Arthur enquired. "I haven't met him here before, have I?"

"No, he's a new friend of ours," said Lady Muriel: "a German, I believe. He *is* such a dear old thing! And quite the most learned man I ever met—-with *one* exception, of course!" she added humbly, as Arthur drew himself up with an air of offended dignity.

"And the young lady in blue, just beyond him, talking to that foreign-looking man. Is *she* learned, too?"

"I don't know," said Lady Muriel. "But I'm told she's a wonderful piano-forte-player. I hope you'll hear her to-night. I asked that foreigner to take her in, because *he's* very musical, too. He's a French Count, I believe; and he sings *splendidly*!"

"Science—music—singing—you have indeed got a

complete party!" said Arthur. "I feel quite a privileged
person, meeting all these stars. I *do* love music!"

"But the party isn't *quite* complete!" said Lady Muriel.
"You haven't brought us those two beautiful children,"
she went on, turning to me. "He brought them here to tea,
you know, one day last summer," again addressing
Arthur: "and they *are* such darlings!"

"They are, *indeed*," I assented.

"But why haven't you brought them with you? You
promised my father you *would*."

"I'm very sorry," I said; "but really it was impossible
to bring them with me." Here I most certainly *meant* to
conclude the sentence: and it was with a feeling of utter
amazement, which I cannot adequately describe, that I
heard myself *going on speaking*. "—but they are to join
me here in the course of the evening" were the words,
uttered in *my* voice, and seeming to come from *my* lips.

"I'm *so* glad!" Lady Muriel joyfully replied. "I *shall* enjoy introducing them to some of my friends here! When
do you expect them?"

I took refuge in silence. The only *honest* reply would
have been "That was not *my* remark. *I* didn't say it, and
it isn't true!" But I had not the moral courage to make
such a confession. The character of a "lunatic" is not, I
believe, very difficult to *acquire*: but it is amazingly difficult to *get rid of:* and it seemed quite certain that any such
speech as *that* would *quite* justify the issue of a writ "*de
lunatico inquirendo*".

Lady Muriel evidently thought I had failed to hear her
question, and turned to Arthur with a remark on some
other subject; and I had time to recover from my shock of
surprise—or to awake out of my momentary "eerie" condition, whichever it was.

When things around me seemed once more to be real,
Arthur was saying "I'm afraid there's no help for it: they
must be finite in number."

"I should be sorry to have to believe it," said Lady
Muriel. "Yet, when one comes to think of it, there *are* no

new melodies, now-a-days. What people talk of as 'the last new song' always recalls to *me* some tune I've known as a child!"

"The day must come—if the world lasts long enough —" said Arthur, "when every possible tune will have been composed—every possible pun perpetrated—" (Lady Muriel wrung her hands, like a tragedy-queen) "and, worse than that, every possible *book* written! For the number of *words* is finite."

"It'll make very little difference to the *authors*," I suggested. "Instead of saying '*what* book shall I write?' an author will ask himself '*which* book shall I write?' A mere verbal distinction!"

Lady Muriel gave me an approving smile. "But *lunatics* would always write new books, surely?" she went on. "They *couldn't* write the sane books over again!"

"True," said Arthur. "But their books would come to an end, also. The number of lunatic *books* is as finite as the number of lunatics."

"And *that* number is becoming greater every year," said a pompous man, whom I recognized as the self-appointed showman on the day of the picnic.

"So they say," replied Arthur. "And, when ninety per cent. of us are lunatics," (he seemed to be in a wildly nonsensical mood) "the asylums will be put to their proper use."

"And that is——?" the pompous man gravely enquired

"*To shelter the sane!*" said Arthur. "*We* shall bar ourselves in. The lunatics will have it all their own way, *outside*. They'll do it a little queerly, no doubt. Railway-collisions will be always happening: steamers always blowing up: most of the towns will be burnt down: most of the ships sunk——"

"And most of the men *killed*!" murmured the pompous man, who was evidently hopelessly bewildered.

"Certainly," Arthur assented. "Till at last there will be *fewer* lunatics than sane men. Then *we* come out: *they* go in: and things return to their normal condition!"

The pompous man frowned darkly, and bit his lip, and folded his arms, vainly trying to think it out. "He is *jesting!*" he muttered to himself at last, in a tone of withering contempt, as he stalked away.

By this time the other guests had arrived; and dinner was announced. Arthur of course took down Lady Muriel: and *I* was pleased to find myself seated at her other side, with a severe-looking old lady (whom I had not met before, and whose name I had, as is usual in introductions, entirely failed to catch, merely gathering that it sounded like a compound-name) as my partner for the banquet.

She appeared, however, to be acquainted with Arthur, and confided to me in a low voice her opinion that he was "a very argumentative young man". Arthur, for his part, seemed well inclined to show himself worthy of the character she had given him, and, hearing her say "I never take wine with my soup!" (this was *not* a confidence to me, but was launched upon Society, as a matter of general interest), he at once challenged a combat by asking her "*when* would you say that property *commence* in a plate of soup?"

"This is *my* soup," she sternly replied: "and what is before you is *yours.*"

"No doubt," said Arthur: "but *when* did I begin to own it? Up to the moment of its being put into the plate, it was the property of our host: while being offered round the table, it was, let us say, held in trust by the waiter: did it become mine when I accepted it? Or when it was placed before me? Or when I took the first spoonful?"

"He is a *very* argumentative young man!" was all the old lady would say: but she said it audibly, this time, feeling that Society had a right to know it.

Arthur smiled mischievously. "I shouldn't mind betting you a shilling", he said, "that the Eminent Barrister next you" (It certainly *is* possible to say words so as to make them begin with capitals!) "ca'n't answer me!"

"I *never* bet," she sternly replied.

"Not even sixpenny points at *whist?*"

"*Never!*" she repeated. "*Whist* is innocent enough: but whist played for *money!*" She shuddered.

Arthur became serious again. "I'm afraid I ca'n't take that view," he said. "I consider that the introduction of small stakes for card-playing was one of the most *moral* acts Society ever did, *as* Society."

"How was it so?" said Lady Muriel.

"Because it took Cards, once for all, out of the category of games at which *cheating* is possible. Look at the way Croquet is demoralizing Society. Ladies are beginning to cheat at it, terribly: and, if they're found out, they only laugh, and call it fun. But when there's *money* at stake, that is out of the question. The swindler is *not* accepted as a wit. When a man sits down to cards, and cheats his friends out of their money, he doesn't get much *fun* out of it—unless he thinks it fun to be kicked down stairs!"

"If all gentlemen thought as badly of ladies as *you* do," my neighbour remarked with some bitterness, "there would be very few—very few——". She seemed doubtful how to end her sentence, but at last took "honeymoons" as a safe word.

"On the contrary," said Arthur, the mischievous smile returning to his face, "if only people would adopt *my* theory, the number of honeymoons—quite of a new kind —would be greatly increased!"

"May we hear about this new kind of honeymoon?" said Lady Muriel.

"Let X be the gentleman," Arthur began, in a slightly raised voice, as he now found himself with an audience of *six*, including "Mein Herr", who was seated at the other side of my polynomial partner. "Let X be the gentleman, and Y the lady to whom he thinks of proposing. He applies for an Experimental Honeymoon. It is granted. Forthwith the young couple—accompanied by the great-aunt of Y, to act as chaperone—start for a month's tour, during which they have many a moonlight-walk, and many a *tête-à-tête* conversation, and each can form a more correct estimate of the other's character, in four *weeks*, than would have been possible in as many *years*, when meeting under the ordinary restrictions of Society. And it is only after their *return* that X finally decides whether he will, or will not, put the momentous question to Y!"

"In nine cases out of ten", the pompous man proclaimed, "he would decide to break it off!"

"Then, in nine cases out of ten," Arthur rejoined, "an unsuitable match would be prevented, and *both* parties saved from misery!"

"The only really *unsuitable* matches", the old lady remarked, "are those made without sufficient *Money*. Love may come *afterwards*. Money is needed *to begin with*!"

This remark was cast loose upon Society, as a sort of general challenge; and, as such, it was at once accepted by several of those within hearing: *Money* became the key-note of the conversation for some time: and a fitful echo of it was again heard, when the dessert had been placed upon the table, the servants had left the room, and the Earl had started the wine in its welcome progress round the table.

"I'm very glad to see you keep up the old customs," I said to Lady Muriel as I filled her glass. "It's really delightful to experience, once more, the peaceful feeling that comes over one when the waiters have left the room—when one can converse without the feeling of being overheard, and without having dishes constantly thrust over one's shoulder. How much more sociable it is to be able to pour out the wine for the ladies, and to hand the dishes to those who wish for them!"

"In that case, kindly send those peaches down here," said a fat red-faced man, who was seated beyond our pompous friend. "I've been wishing for them—diagonally—for some time!"

"Yes, it *is* a ghastly innovation", Lady Muriel replied, "letting the waiters carry round the wine at dessert. For one thing, they *always* take it the wrong way round—which of course brings bad luck to *everybody* present!"

"Better go the *wrong* way than not go *at all!*" said our host. "Would you kindly help yourself?" (This was to the fat red-faced man.) "You are not a teetotaler, I think?"

"Indeed but I *am!*" he replied, as he pushed on the bottles. "Nearly twice as much money is spent in England on *Drink*, as on any other article of food. Read this card." (What faddist ever goes about without a pocketful of the appropriate literature?) "The stripes of different colours represent the amounts spent of various articles of food. Look at the highest three. Money spent on butter and on cheese, thirty-five millions: on bread, seventy millions: on *intoxicating liquors*, one hundred and thirty-six millions! If I had my way, I would close every public-house in the land! Look at that card, and read the motto. *That's where all the money goes to!*"

"Have you seen the *Anti-Teetotal Card?*" Arthur innocently enquired.

"No, Sir, I have not!" the orator savagely replied. "What is it like?"

"Almost exactly like this one. The coloured stripes are the same. Only, instead of the words 'Money spent on', it has 'Incomes derived from sale of'; and, instead of 'That's where all the money goes to', its motto is *'That's where all the money comes from!'* "

The red-faced man scowled, but evidently considered Arthur beneath his notice. So Lady Muriel took up the cudgels. "Do you hold the theory", she enquired, "that people can preach teetotalism more effectually by being teetotalers themselves?"

"Certainly I do!" replied the red-faced man. "Now, here is a case in point," unfolding a newspaper-cutting: "let me read you this letter from a teetotaler. *To the Editor. Sir, I was once a moderate drinker, and knew a man who drank to excess. I went to him. 'Give up this drink,' I said. 'It will ruin your health!' 'You drink,' he said: 'why shouldn't I?' 'Yes,' I said, 'but I know when to leave off.' He turned away from me. 'You drink in your way,' he said: 'let me drink in mine. Be off!' Then I saw that, to do any good with him, I must forswear drink. From that hour I haven't touched a drop!"*

"There! What do you say to *that*?" He looked round triumphantly, while the cutting was handed round for inspection.

"How very curious!" exclaimed Arthur when it had reached him. "Did you happen to see a letter, last week, about early rising? It was strangely like this one."

The red-faced man's curiosity was roused. "Where did it appear?" he asked.

"Let me read it to you," said Arthur. He took some papers from his pocket, opened one of them, and read as follows. *To the Editor. Sir, I was once a moderate sleeper, and knew a man who slept to excess. I pleaded with him. 'Give up this lying in bed,' I said. 'It will ruin your health!' 'You go to bed,' he said: 'why shouldn't I?' 'Yes,' I said, 'but I know when to get up in the morning.' He turned away from me. 'You sleep in your way,' he said: 'let me sleep in mine. Be off!' Then I saw that to do any good with him, I must forswear sleep. From that hour I haven't been to bed!"*

Arthur folded and pocketed his paper, and passed on the newspaper-cutting. None of us dared to laugh, the red-faced man was evidently so angry. "Your parallel doesn't run on all fours!" he snarled.

"*Moderate* drinkers never do so!" Arthur quietly replied. Even the stern old lady laughed at this.

"But it needs many other things to make a *perfect* dinner!" said Lady Muriel, evidently anxious to change the subject. "Mein Herr! What is *your* idea of a perfect dinner party?"

The old man looked around smilingly, and his gigantic spectacles seemed more gigantic than ever. "A *perfect* dinner-party?" he repeated. "First, it must be presided over by our present hostess!"

"That of *course*!" she gaily interposed. "But what *else*, Mein Herr?"

"I can but tell you what I have seen," said Mein Herr, "in mine own—in the country I have traveled in."

He paused for a full minute, and gazed steadily at the ceiling—with so dreamy an expression on his face, that I feared he was going off into a reverie, which seemed to be his normal state. However, after a minute, he suddenly began again.

"That which chiefly causes the failure of a dinner-party, is the running-short—not of meat, nor yet of drink, but of *conversation*."

"In an *English* dinner-party", I remarked, "I have never known *small-talk* run short!"

"Pardon me," Mein Herr respectfully replied, "I did not say 'small-talk'. I said 'conversation'. All such topics as the weather, or politics, or local gossip, are unknown among us. They are either vapid or controversial. What we need for *conversation* is a topic of *interest* and of *novelty*. To secure these things we have tried various plans— Moving-Pictures, Wild-Creatures, Moving-Guests, and a Revolving-Humorist. But this last is only adapted to *small* parties."

"Let us have it in four separate Chapters, please!" said Lady Muriel, who was evidently deeply interested—as, indeed, most of the party were, by this time: and, all down the table, talk had ceased, and heads were leaning forwards, eager to catch fragments of Mein Herr's oration.

"Chapter One! Moving-Pictures!" was proclaimed in the silvery voice of our hostess.

"The dining-table is shaped like a circular ring," Mein Herr began, in low dreamy tones, which, however, were perfectly audible in the silence. "The guests are seated at the inner side as well as the outer, having ascended to their places by a winding-staircase, from the room below. Along the middle of the table runs a little railway; and there is an endless train of trucks, worked round by machinery; and on each truck there are two pictures, leaning back to back. The train makes two circuits during dinner; and, when it has been *once* round, the waiters turn the pictures round in each truck, making them face the other way. Thus *every* guest sees *every* picture!"

He paused, and the silence seemed deader than ever. Lady Muriel looked aghast. "Really, if this goes on," she exclaimed, "I shall have to drop a pin! Oh, it's *my* fault, is it?" (In answer to an appealing look from Mein Herr.) "I was forgetting my duty. Chapter Two! Wild-Creatures!"

"We found the Moving-Pictures a *little* monotonous," said Mein Herr. "People didn't care to talk Art through a whole dinner; so we tried Wild-Creatures. Among the flowers, which we laid (just as *you* do) about the table, were to be seen, here a mouse, there a beetle; here a spider" (Lady Muriel shuddered), "there a wasp; here a toad, there a snake"; ("Father!" said Lady Muriel, plaintively. "Did you hear *that*?"); "so we had plenty to talk about!"

"And when you got stung——" the old lady began.

"They were all chained-up, dear Madam!"

And the old lady gave a satisfied nod.

There was no silence to follow, *this* time. "Third Chapter!" Lady Muriel proclaimed at once. "Moving-Guests!"

"Even the Wild-Creatures proved monotonous," the orator proceeded. "So we left the guests to choose their own subjects; and, to avoid monotony, we changed *them*. We made the table of *two* rings; and the inner ring moved slowly round, all the time, along with the floor in the middle and the inner row of guests. Thus *every* inner guest was brought face-to-face with *every* outer guest. It was a little confusing, sometimes, to have to *begin* a story to one friend and *finish* it to another; but *every* plan has its faults, you know."

"Fourth Chapter!" Lady Muriel hastened to announce. "The Revolving-Humorist!"

"For a *small* party we found it an excellent plan to have a round table, with a hole cut in the middle large enough to hold *one* guest. Here we placed our *best* talker. He revolved slowly, facing every other guest in turn: and he told lively anecdotes the whole time!"

"I shouldn't like it!" murmured the pompous man. "It would make me giddy, revolving like that! I should decline to——" here it appeared to dawn upon him that perhaps the assumption he was making was not warranted by the circumstances: he took a hasty gulp of wine, and choked himself.

But Mein Herr had relapsed into reverie, and made no further remark. Lady Muriel gave the signal, and the ladies left the room.

CHAPTER X

Jabbering and Jam

WHEN the last lady had disappeared, and the Earl, taking his place at the head of the table, had issued the military order "Gentlemen! Close up the ranks, if you please!" and when, in obedience to his command, we had gathered ourselves compactly round him, the pompous man gave a deep sigh of relief, filled his glass to the brim, pushed on the wine, and began one of his favourite orations. "They are charming, no doubt! Charming, but very frivolous. They drag us down, so to speak, to a lower level. They——"

"Do not all pronouns require antecedent *nouns*?" the Earl gently enquired.

"Pardon me," said the pompous man, with lofty condescension. "I had overlooked the noun. The ladies. We regret their absence. Yet we console ourselves. *Thought is free*. With them, we are limited to *trivial* topics—Art, Literature, Politics, and so forth. One can bear to discuss *such* paltry matters with a lady. But no man, in his senses —" (he looked sternly round the table, as if defying contradiction) "—ever yet discussed *WINE* with a lady!" He sipped his glass of port, leaned back in his chair, and slowly raised it up to his eye, so as to look through it at the lamp. "The vintage, my Lord?" he enquired, glancing at his host.

The Earl named the date.

"So I had supposed. But one likes to be certain. The *tint* is, perhaps, slightly pale. But the *body* is unquestionable. And as for the *bouquet*——"

Ah, that magic Bouquet! How vividly that magic word recalled the scene! The little beggar boy turning his somersault in the road—the sweet little crippled maiden in my arms—the mysterious evanescent nursemaid—all rushed tumultuously into my mind, like the creatures of a dream: and through this mental haze there still boomed on, like the tolling of a bell, the solemn voice of the great connoisseur of *WINE!*

Even *his* utterances had taken on themselves a strange and dream-like form. "No," he resumed—and *why* is it, I pause to ask, that, in taking up the broken thread of a dialogue, one *always* begins with this cheerless monosyllable? After much anxious thought, I have come to the conclusion that the object in view is the same as that of the schoolboy, when the sum he is working has got into a hopeless muddle, and when in despair he takes the sponge, washes it all out, and begins again. Just in the same way the bewildered orator, by the simple process of denying *everything* that has been hitherto asserted, makes a clean sweep of the whole discussion, and can "start fair" with a fresh theory. "No," he resumed: "there's nothing like cherry-jam, after all. That's what *I* say!"

"Not for *all* qualities!" an eager little man shrilly interposed. "For *richness* of general tone I don't say that it *has* a rival. But for *delicacy* of modulation—for what one may call the 'harmonics' of flavour—give *me* good old *raspberry*-jam!"

"Allow me one word!" The fat red-faced man, quite hoarse with excitement, broke into the dialogue. "It's too important a question to be settled by Amateurs! I can give you the views of a *Professional*—perhaps the most experienced jam-taster now living. Why, I've known him fix the age of strawberry-jam, to a *day*—and we all know what a difficult jam it is to give a date to—on a single tasting! Well, I put to him the *very* question you are discussing. His words were '*cherry*-jam is best, for mere *chiaroscuro* of flavour: *raspberry*-jam lends itself best to those resolved discords that linger so lovingly on the tongue: but, for rapturous *utterness* of saccharine perfection, it's *apricot-jam first and the rest nowhere*!' That was well put, *wasn't it?*"

"Consummately put!" shrieked the eager little man.

"I know your friend well," said the pompous man. "As a jam-taster, he has no rival! Yet I scarcely think——"

But here the discussion became general: and his words were lost in a confused medley of names, every guest sounding the praises of his own favourite jam. At length, through the din, our host's voice made itself heard. "Let us join the ladies!" These words seemed to recall me to waking life; and I felt sure that, for the last few minutes, I had relapsed into the "eerie" state.

"A strange dream!" I said to myself as we trooped upstairs. "Grown men discussing, as seriously as if they were matters of life and death, the hopelessly trivial details or mere *delicacies*, that appeal to no higher human function than the nerves of the tongue and palate! What a humiliating spectacle such a discussion would be in waking life!"

When, on our way to the drawing-room, I received from the housekeeper my little friends, clad in the daintiest of evening costumes, and looking, in the flush of expectant delight, more radiantly beautiful than I had ever seen them before. I felt no shock of surprise, but accepted the fact with the same unreasoning apathy with which one meets the events of a dream, and was merely conscious of a vague anxiety as to how they would acquit themselves in so novel a scene—forgetting that Court-life in Outland was as good training as they could need for Society in the more substantial world.

It would be best, I thought, to introduce them as soon

as possible to some good-natured lady-guest, and I
selected the young lady whose piano-forte-playing had
been so much talked of. "I am sure you like children," I
said. "May I introduce two little friends of mine? This is
Sylvie—and this is Bruno."

The young lady kissed Sylvie very graciously. She
would have done the same for *Bruno*, but he hastily drew
back out of reach. "Their faces are new to me," she said.
"Where do you come from, my dear?"

I had not anticipated so inconvenient a question; and,
fearing that it might embarrass Sylvie, I answered for
her. "They come from some distance. They are only here
just for this one evening."

"How far have you come, dear?" the young lady persisted.

Sylvie looked puzzled. "A mile or two, I *think*," she
said doubtfully.

"A mile or *three*," said Bruno.

"You shouldn't say 'a mile or *three*'," Sylvie corrected
him.

The young lady nodded approval. "Sylvie's quite right.
It isn't usual to say 'a mile or *three*'."

"It would be usual—if we said it often enough," said
Bruno.

It was the young lady's turn to look puzzled now. "He's
very quick, for his age!" she murmured. "You're not
more than seven, are you, dear?" she added aloud.

"I'm not so many as *that*," said Bruno. "I'm *one*.
Sylvie's *one*. Sylvie and me is *two*. *Sylvie* taught me to
count."

"Oh, I wasn't *counting* you, you know!" the young
lady laughingly replied.

"Hasn't oo *learnt* to count?" said Bruno.

The young lady bit her lip. "Dear! What embarrassing
questions he *does* ask!" she said in a half-audible "aside".

"Bruno, you shouldn't!" Sylvie said reprovingly.

"Shouldn't *what*?" said Bruno.

"You shouldn't ask—that sort of questions."

"*What* sort of questions?" Bruno mischievously persisted.

"What *she* told you not," Sylvie replied, with a shy glance at the young lady, and losing all sense of grammar in her confusion.

"Oo ca'n't pronounce it!" Bruno triumphantly cried. And he turned to the young lady, for sympathy in his victory. "I *knewed* she couldn't pronounce 'umbrella-sting'!"

The young lady thought it best to return to the arithmetical problem. "When I asked if you were *seven*, you know, I didn't mean 'how many *children*?' I meant 'how many *years*——' "

"Only got *two* ears," said Bruno. "Nobody's got *seven* ears."

"And you belong to this little girl?" the young lady continued, skilfully evading the anatomical problem.

"No I doosn't belong to *her*!" said Bruno. "Sylvie belongs to *me*!" And he clasped his arms round her as he added "She are my very mine!"

"And, do you know," said the young lady, "I've a little sister at home, exactly like *your* sister? I'm sure they'd love each other."

"They'd be very extremely useful to each other," Bruno said, thoughtfully. "And they wouldn't want no looking-glasses to brush their hair wiz."

"Why not, my child?"

"Why, each one would do for the other one's looking-glass a-course!" cried Bruno.

But here Lady Muriel, who had been standing by, listening to this bewildering dialogue, interrupted it to ask if the young lady would favour us with some music; and the children followed their new friend to the piano.

Arthur came and sat down by me. "If rumour speaks truly," he whispered, "we are to have a real treat!" And then, amid a breathless silence, the performance began.

She was one of those players whom Society talks of as "brilliant", and she dashed into the loveliest of Haydn's

Symphonies in a style that was clearly the outcome of years of patient study under the best masters. At first it seemed to be the perfection of piano-forte-playing; but in a few minutes I began to ask myself, wearily, "*What* is it that is wanting? *Why* does one get no pleasure from it?"

Then I set myself to listen intently to every note; and the mystery explained itself. There *was* an almost perfect mechanical *correctness*—and there was nothing else! False notes, of course, did not occur: she knew the piece too well for *that*; but there was just enough irregularity of *time* to betray that the player had no real "ear" for music—just enough inarticulateness in the more elaborate passages to show that she did not think her audience worth taking real pains for—just enough mechanical monotony of accent to take all *soul* out of the heavenly modulations she was profaning—in short, it was simply irritating; and, when she had rattled off the finale and had struck the final chord as if, the instrument being now done with, it didn't matter how many wires she broke, I could not even *affect* to join in the stereotyped "Oh, *thank* you!" which was chorused around me.

Lady Muriel joined us for a moment. "Isn't it *beautiful?*" she whispered to Arthur, with a mischievous smile.

"No, it isn't!" said Arthur. But the gentle sweetness of his face quite neutralized the apparent rudeness of the reply.

"Such execution, you know!" she persisted.

"That's what she *deserves*," Arthur doggedly replied: "but people are so prejudiced against capital——"

"Now you're beginning to talk nonsense!" Lady Muriel cried. "But you *do* like Music, don't you? You said so just now."

"Do I like *Music*?" the Doctor repeated softly to himself. "My dear Lady Muriel, there is Music and Music. Your question is painfully vague. You might as well ask 'Do you like *People*?'"

Lady Muriel bit her lip, frowned, and stamped with one tiny foot. As a dramatic, representation of ill-temper, it was distinctly *not* a success. However, it took in *one* of her audience, and Bruno hastened to interpose, as peace-maker in a rising quarrel, with the remark "*I* likes Peoples!"

Arthur laid a loving hand on the little curly head. "What? *All* Peoples?" he enquired.

"Not *all* Peoples," Bruno explained. "Only but Sylvie —and Lady Muriel—and him—" (pointing to the Earl) "and oo—and oo!"

"You shouldn't point at people," said Sylvie. "It's very rude."

"In Bruno's World," I said, "there are only *four* People—worth mentioning!"

"In Bruno's World!" Lady Muriel repeated thoughtfully. "A bright and flowery world. Where the grass is always green, where the breezes always blow softly, and the rain-clouds never gather; where there are no wild beasts, and no deserts——"

"There *must* be deserts," Arthur decisively remarked. "At least if it was *my* ideal world."

"But what possible use is there in a *desert*?" said Lady Muriel. "*Surely* you would have no wilderness in your ideal world?"

Arthur smiled. "But indeed I *would*!" he said. "A wilderness would be more necessary than a railway; and *far* more conducive to general happiness than church-bells!"

"But what would you use it for?"

"*To practise music in*," he replied. "All the young ladies, that have no ear for music, but insist on learning it, should be conveyed, every morning, two or three miles into the wilderness. There each would find a comfortable room provided for her, and also a cheap second-hand piano-forte, on which she might play for hours, without adding one needless pang to the sum of human misery!"

Lady Muriel glanced round in alarm, lest these barbarous sentiments should be overheard. But the fair musician was at a safe distance. "At any rate you must allow that she's a sweet girl?" she resumed.

"Oh, certainly. As sweet as *eau sucrée*, if you choose—and nearly as interesting!"

"You are incorrigible!" said Lady Muriel, and turned to me. "I hope you found Mrs. Mills an interesting companion?"

"Oh, *that's* her name, is it?" I said. "I fancied there was *more* of it."

"So there is: and it will be 'at your proper peril' (whatever that may mean) if you ever presume to address her as 'Mrs. Mills'. She is 'Mrs. Ernest—Atkinson—Mills'!"

"She is one of those would-be grandees," said Arthur, "who think that, by tacking on to their surname all their spare Christian-names, with hyphens between, they can give it an aristocratic flavour. As if it wasn't trouble enough to remember *one* surname!"

By this time the room was getting crowded, as the guests, invited for the evening-party, were beginning to arrive, and Lady Muriel had to devote herself to the task of welcoming them, which she did with the sweetest grace imaginable. Sylvie and Bruno stood by her, deeply interested in the process.

"I hope you like my friends?" she said to them. "Specially my dear old friend, Mein Herr (What's become of him, I wonder? Oh, there he is!), that old gentleman in spectacles, with a long beard!"

"He's a grand old gentleman!" Sylvie said, gazing admiringly at "Mein Herr", who had settled down in a corner, from which his mild eyes beamed on us through a gigantic pair of spectacles. "And what a lovely beard!"

"What does he call his-self?" Bruno whispered.

"He calls himself 'Mein Herr'," Sylvie whispered in reply.

Bruno shook his head impatiently. "That's what he calls his *hair*, not his *self*, oo silly!" He appealed to me. "What doos he call his *self*, Mister Sir?"

"That's the only name *I* know of," I said. "But he looks very lonely. Don't you pity his grey hairs?"

"I pities his *self*," said Bruno, still harping on the misnomer; "but I doosn't pity his *hair*, one bit. His *hair* ca'n't feel!"

"We met him this afternoon," said Sylvie. "We'd been to see Nero, and we'd had *such* fun with him, making him invisible again! And we saw that nice old gentleman as we came back."

"Well, let's go and talk to him, and cheer him up a little," I said: "and perhaps we shall find out what he calls himself."

Chapter XI

The Man in the Moon

THE children came willingly. With one of them on each side of me, I approached the corner occupied by "Mein Herr". "You don't object to *children*, I hope?" I began.

"*Crabbed age and youth cannot live together!*" the old man cheerfully replied, with a most genial smile. "Now take a good look at me, my children! You would guess me to be an *old* man, wouldn't you?"

At first sight, though his face had reminded me so mysteriously of "the Professor", he had seemed to be decidedly a *younger* man: but, when I came to look into the wonderful depth of those large dreamy eyes, I felt, with a strange sense of awe, that he was incalculably *older*: he seemed to gaze at us out of some by-gone age, centuries away.

"I don't know if oo're an *old* man," Bruno answered, as the children, won over by the gentle voice, crept a little closer to him. "I thinks oo're *eighty-three*."

"He is very exact!" said Mein Herr.

"Is he anything like right?" I said.

"There are reasons," Mein Herr gently replied, "reasons which I am not at liberty to explain, for not mentioning *definitely* any Persons, Places, or Dates. One remark only

I will permit myself to make—that the period of life, between the ages of a hundred-and-sixty-five and a hundred-and-seventy-five, is a specially *safe* one."

"How do you make that out?" I said.

"Thus. You would consider swimming to be a very safe amusement, if you scarcely ever heard of any one dying of it. Am I not right in thinking that you never heard of any one dying between those two ages?"

"I see what you mean," I said: "but I'm afraid you ca'n't prove *swimming* to be safe, on the same principle. It is no uncommon thing to hear of some one being *drowned*."

"In *my* country," said Mein Herr. "no one is *ever* drowned."

"Is there no water deep enough?"

"Plenty! But we ca'n't *sink*. We are all *lighter than water*. Let me explain," he added, seeing my look of surprise. "Suppose you desire a race of *pigeons* of a particular shape or colour, do you not select, from year to year, those that are nearest to the shape or colour you want, and keep those, and part with the others?"

"We do," I replied. "We call it 'Artificial Selection'."

"Exactly so," said Mein Herr. "Well, *we* have practised that for some centuries—constantly selecting the *lightest* people: so that, now, *everybody* is lighter than water."

"Then you never can be drowned at *sea*?"

"Never! It is only on the *land*—for instance, when attending a play in a theatre—that we are in such a danger."

"How can that happen at a *theatre*?"

"Our theatres are all *underground*. Large tanks of water are placed above. If a fire breaks out, the taps are turned, and in one minute the theatre is flooded, up to the very roof! Thus the fire is extinguished."

"*And* the audience, I presume?"

"That is a minor matter," Mein Herr carelessly replied. "But they have the comfort of knowing that, whether drowned or not, they are all *lighter than water*. We have not yet reached the standard of making people lighter than *air*: but we are *aiming* at it; and, in another thousand years or so——"

"What doos oo do wiz the peoples that's too heavy?" Bruno solemnly enquired.

"We have applied the same process," Mein Herr continued, not noticing Bruno's question, "to many other purposes. We have gone on selecting *walking-sticks*—always keeping those that walked *best*—till we have obtained some, that can walk by themselves! We have gone on selecting *cotton-wool*, till we have got some lighter than air! You've no idea what a useful material it is! We call it 'Imponderal'."

"What do you use it for?"

"Well, chiefly for *packing* articles, to go by Parcel-Post. It makes them weigh *less than nothing*, you know."

"And how do the Post Office people know what you have to pay?"

"That's the beauty of the new system!" Mein Herr cried exultingly. "They pay *us*: we don't pay *them*! I've often got as much as five shillings for sending a parcel."

"But doesn't your Government object?"

"Well, they *do* object a little. They say it comes so expensive, in the long run. But the thing's as clear as daylight, by their own rules. If I send a parcel, that weighs a pound *more* than nothing, I *pay* three-pence: so, of course, if it weighs a pound *less* than nothing, I ought to *receive* three-pence."

"It is *indeed* a useful article!" I said.

"Yet even 'Imponderal' has its disadvantages," he resumed. "I bought some, a few days ago, and put it into my *hat*, to carry it home, and the hat simply floated away!"

"Had oo some of that funny stuff in oor hat *to-day*?" Bruno enquired. "Sylvie and me saw oo in the road, and oor hat were ever so high up! Weren't it, Sylvie?"

"No, that was quite another thing," said Mein Herr. "There was a drop or two of rain falling: so I put my hat on the top of my stick—as an umbrella, you know. As I came along the road", he continued, turning to me, "I was overtaken by——"

"—a shower of rain?" said Bruno.

"Well, it *looked* more like the tail of a dog," Mein Herr replied. "It was the most curious thing! Something rubbed affectionately against my knee. And I looked down. And I could see *nothing*! Only, about a yard off, there was a dog's tail, wagging, all by itself!"

"Oh, *Sylvie*!" Bruno murmured reproachfully. "Oo didn't finish making him visible!"

"I'm *so* sorry!" Sylvie said, looking very penitent. "I meant to rub it along his back, but we were in such a hurry. We'll go and finish him to-morrow. Poor thing! Perhaps he'll get no supper to-night!"

"*Course* he won't!" said Bruno. "Nobody never gives bones to a dog's tail!"

Mein Herr looked from one to the other in blank astonishment. "I do not understand you," he said. "I had lost my way, and I was consulting a pocket-map, and somehow I had dropped one of my gloves, and this invisible *Something*, that had rubbed against my knee, actually brought it back to me!"

"Course he did!" said Bruno. "He's *welly* fond of fetching things."

Mein Herr looked so thoroughly bewildered that I thought it best to change the subject. "What a useful thing a pocket-map is!" I remarked.

"That's another thing we've learned from *your* Nation," said Mein Herr, "map-making. But we've carried it much further than *you*. What do you consider the *largest* map that would be really useful?"

"About six inches to the mile."

"Only *six inches*!" exclaimed Mein Herr. "We very soon got to six *yards* to the mile. Then we tried a *hundred* yards to the mile. And then came the grandest idea of all! We actually made a map of the country, on the scale of *a mile to the mile*!"

"Have you used it much?" I enquired.

"It has never been spread out, yet," said Mein Herr: "the farmers objected: they said it would cover the whole country, and shut out the sunlight! So we now use the country itself, as its own map, and I assure you it does nearly as well. Now let me ask you *another* question. What is the smallest *world* you would care to inhabit?"

"*I* know!" cried Bruno, who was listening intently. "I'd like a little teeny-tiny world, just big enough for Sylvie and me!"

"Then you would have to stand on opposite side of it," said Mein Herr. "And so you would never see your sister *at all*!"

"And I'd have no *lessons*," said Bruno.

"You don't mean to say you've been trying experiments in *that* direction!" I said.

"Well, not *experiments* exactly. We do not profess to *construct* planets. But a scientific friend of mine, who has made several balloon-voyages, assures me he has visited a planet so small that he could walk right round it in twenty minutes! There had been a great battle, just before his visit, which had ended rather oddly: the vanquished army ran away at full speed, and in a very few minutes found themselves face-to-face with the victorious army, who were marching home again, and who were so frightened at finding themselves between *two* armies, that they surrendered at once! Of course that lost them the battle, though, as a matter of fact, they had killed *all* the soldiers on the other side."

"Killed soldiers *ca'n't* run away," Bruno thoughtfully remarked.

" 'Killed' is a technical word," replied Mein Herr. "In the little planet I speak of, the bullets were made of soft black stuff, which marked everything it touched. So, after a battle, all you had to do was to count how many soldiers on each side were 'killed'—that means 'marked on the *back*', for marks in *front* didn't count."

"Then you couldn't 'kill' any, unless they ran away?" I said.

"My scientific friend found out a better plan than *that*. He pointed out that, if only the bullets were sent *the other way round the world*, they would hit the enemy in the *back*. After that, the *worst* marksmen were considered the *best* soldiers; and *the very worst of all* always got First Prize."

"And how did you decide which was *the very worst of all*?"

"Easily. The *best* possible shooting is, you know, to hit what is exactly in *front* of you: so of course the *worst* possible is to hit what is exactly *behind* you."

"They were strange people in that little planet!" I said.

"They were indeed! Perhaps their method of *government* was the strangest of all. In *this* planet, I am told, a Nation consists of a number of Subjects, and one King: but, in the little planet I speak of, it consisted of a number of *Kings*, and one *Subject*!"

"You say you are 'told' what happens in *this* planet," I said. "May I venture to guess that you yourself are a visitor from some *other* planet?"

Bruno clapped his hands in his excitement. "Is oo the Man-in-the-Moon?" he cried.

Mein Herr looked uneasy. "I am *not* in the Moon, my child," he said evasively. "To return to what I was saying. I think *that* method of government ought to answer *well*. You see, the Kings would be sure to make Laws contradicting each other: so the Subject could never be punished, because, *whatever* he did he'd be obeying *some* Law."

"And, whatever he did, he'd be *dis*obeying *some* Law!" cried Bruno. "So he'd *always* be punished!"

Lady Muriel was passing at the moment, and caught the last word. "Nobody's going to be punished *here*!" she said, taking Bruno in her arms. "This is Liberty-Hall! Would you lend me the children for a minute?"

"The children desert us, you see," I said to Mein Herr,

as she carried them off: "so we old folk must keep each other company!"

The old man sighed. "Ah, well! We're old folk *now*; and yet I was a child myself, once—at least I fancy so."

It *did* seem a rather unlikely fancy, I could not help owning to myself—looking at the shaggy white hair, and the long beard—that he could *ever* have been a child. "You are fond of young people?" I said.

"Young *men*," he replied. "Not of *children* exactly. I used to teach young men—many a year ago—in my dear old University!"

"I didn't quite catch its *name*?" I hinted.

"I did not name it," the old man replied mildly. "Nor would you know the name if I did. Strange tales I could tell you of all the changes I have witnessed there! But it would weary you, I fear."

"No, *indeed*!" I said. "Pray go on. What kind of changes?"

But the old man seemed to be more in a humour for questions than for answers. "Tell me," he said, laying his hand impressively on my arm, "tell me something. For I am a stranger in your land. and I know little of *your* modes of education: yet something tells me *we* are further on than *you* in the eternal cycle of change—and that many a theory *we* have tried and found to fail, *you* also will try, with a wilder enthusiasm: you also will find to fail, with a bitterer despair!"

It was strange to see how, as he talked, and his words flowed more and more freely, with a certain rhythmic eloquence, his features seemed to glow with an inner light, and the whole man seemed to be transformed, as if he had grown fifty years younger in a moment of time.

CHAPTER XII

Fairy-Music

THE silence that ensued was broken by the voice of the musical young lady, who had seated herself near us, and was conversing with one of the newly-arrived guests. "Well!" she said in a tone of scornful surprise. "We *are* to have something new in the way of music, it appears!"

I looked round for an explanation, and was nearly as much astonished as the speaker herself: it was *Sylvie* whom Lady Muriel was leading to the piano!

"Do try it, my darling!" she was saying. "I'm sure you can play very nicely!"

Sylvie looked round at me, with tears in her eyes. I tried to give her an encouraging smile, but it was evidently a great strain on the nerves of a child so wholly unused to be made an exhibition of, and she was frightened and unhappy. Yet here came out the perfect sweetness of her disposition: I could see that she was resolved to forget herself, and do her best to give pleasure to Lady Muriel and her friends. She seated herself at the instrument, and began instantly. Time and expression, so far as one could judge, were perfect: but her touch was one of such extraordinary lightness that it was at first scarcely possible, through the hum of conversation which still continued, to catch a note of what she was playing.

But in a minute the hum had died away into absolute silence, and we all sat, entranced and breathless, to listen to such heavenly music as none then present could ever forget.

Hardly touching the notes at first, she played a sort of introduction in a minor key—like an embodied twilight; one felt as though the lights were growing dim, and a mist were creeping through the room. Then there flashed through the gathering gloom the first few notes of a melody so lovely, so delicate, that one held one's breath, fearful to lose a single note of it. Ever and again the music dropped into the pathetic minor key with which it had begun, and, each time that the melody forced its way, so to speak, through the enshrouding gloom into the light of day, it was more entrancing, more magically sweet. Under the airy touch of the child, the instrument actually seemed to *warble*, like a bird. *"Rise up, my love, my fair one,"* it seemed to sing, *"and come away! For lo, the winter is past, the rain is over and gone; the flowers appear on the earth; the time of the singing of birds is come!"* One could fancy one heard the tinkle of the last few drops, shaken from the trees by a passing gust—that one saw the first glittering rays of the sun, breaking through the clouds.

The Count hurried across the room in great excitement. "I *cannot* remember myself", he exclaimed, "of the name of this so charming an air! It is of an opera, most surely. Yet not even will the *opera* remind his name to me! What you call him, dear child?"

Sylvie looked round at him with a rapt expression of face. She had ceased playing, but her fingers still wandered fitfully over the keys. All fear and shyness had quite passed away now, and nothing remained but the pure joy of the music that had thrilled our hearts.

"The title of it!" the Count repeated impatiently. "How call you the opera?"

"I don't know what an opera *is*," Sylvie half-whispered.

"How, then, call you the *air*?"

"I don't know any name for it," Sylvie replied, as she rose from the instrument.

"But this is marvellous!" exclaimed the Count, following the child, and addressing himself to me, as if I were the proprietor of this musical prodigy, and so *must* know the origin of her music. "You have heard her play this, sooner—I would say 'before this occasion'? How call you the air?"

I shook my head; but was saved from more questions

by Lady Muriel, who came up to petition the Count for
a song.

The Count spread out his hands apologetically, and
ducked his head. "But, Milady, I have already respected
—I would say prospected—all your songs; and there shall
be none fitted to my voice! They are not for basso voices!"

"Wo'n't you look at them again?" Lady Muriel im-
plored.

"Let's help him!" Bruno whispered to Sylvie. "Let's
get him—*you* know!"

Sylvie nodded. "Shall *we* look for a song for you?"
she said sweetly to the Count.

"Mais *oui*!" the little man exclaimed.

"Of course we may!" said Bruno, while, each taking
a hand of the delighted Count, they led him to the music-
stand.

"There is still hope!" said Lady Muriel over her shoulder, as she followed them.

I turned to "Mein Herr", hoping to resume our interrupted conversation. "You were remarking——" I
began: but at this moment Sylvie came to call Bruno,
who had returned to my side, looking unusually serious.
"*Do* come, Bruno!" she entreated. "You know we've
nearly found it!" Then, in a whisper, "The locket's in
my *hand*, now. I couldn't get it out while they were
looking!"

But Bruno drew back. "The man called me names,"
he said with dignity.

"What names?" I enquired with some curiosity.

"I asked him", said Bruno, "which sort of song he liked.
And he said '*A* song of *a* man, not of *a* lady'. And I said
'Shall Sylvie and me find you the song of Mister Tottles?'
And he said 'Wait, eel!' And I'm *not* an eel, oo know!"

"I'm *sure* he didn't mean it!" Sylvie said earnestly.
"It's something French—you know he ca'n't talk English
so well as——"

Bruno relented visibly. "Course he knows no better, if
he's Flench! Flenchmen *never* can speak English so

goodly as *us!*" And Sylvie led him away, a willing captive.

"Nice children!" said the old man, taking off his spectacles and rubbing them carefully. Then he put them on again, and watched with an approving smile, while the children tossed over the heap of music, and we just caught Sylvie's reproving words, "We're *not* making hay, Bruno!"

"This has been a long interruption to our conversation," I said. "Pray let us go on!"

"Willingly!" replied the gentle old man. "I was much interested in what you——" He paused a moment, and passed his hand uneasily across his brow. "One forgets," he murmured. "What was I saying? Oh! Something you were to tell me. Yes. Which of your teachers do you value the most highly, those whose words are easily understood, or those who puzzle you at every turn?"

I feel obliged to admit that we generally admired most the teachers we couldn't quite understand.

"Just so," said Mein Herr. "That's the way it begins. Well, *we* were at that stage some eighty years ago—or was it ninety? Our favourite teacher got more obscure every year; and every year we admired him more—just as *your* Art-fanciers call *mist* the fairest feature in a landscape, and admire a view with frantic delight when they can see nothing! Now I'll tell you how it ended. It was Moral Philosophy that our idol lectured on. Well, his pupils couldn't make head or tail of it, but they got it all by heart; and, when Examination-time came, they wrote it down; and the Examiners said 'Beautiful! (What depth!'"

"But what good was it to the young men *afterwards?*"

"Why, don't you see?" replied Mein Herr. "*They* became teachers in their turn, and *they* said all these things over again; and *their* pupils wrote it all down; and the Examiners accepted it; and nobody had the ghost of an idea what it all meant!"

"And how did it end?"

"It ended this way. We woke up one fine day, and found there was no one in the place that knew *anything* about Moral Philosophy. So we abolished it, teachers, classes, examiners, and all. And if any one wanted to learn anything about it, he had to make it out for himself; and after another twenty years or so there were several men that really knew something about it! Now tell me another thing. How long do you teach a youth before you examine him, in your Universities?"

I told him, three or four years.

"Just so, just what *we* did!" he exclaimed. "We taught 'em a bit, and, just as they were beginning to take it in, we took it all out again! We pumped our wells dry before they were a quarter full—we stripped our orchards while the apples were still in blossom—we applied the severe logic of arithmetic to our chickens, while peacefully slumbering in their shells! Doubtless it's the early bird that picks up the worm—but if the bird gets up so outrageously early that the worm is still deep underground, what *then* is its chance of a breakfast?"

Not much, I admitted.

"Now see how that works!" he went on eagerly. "If you want to pump your wells so soon—and I suppose you tell me that is what you *must* do?"

"We must," I said. "In an over-crowded country like this, nothing but Competitive Examinations——"

Mein Herr threw up his hands wildly. "What, *again?*" he cried. "I thought it was dead, fifty years ago! Oh this Upas tree of Competitive Examinations! Beneath whose deadly shade all the original genius, all the exhaustive research, all the untiring life-long diligence by which our fore-fathers have so advanced human knowledge, must slowly but surely wither away, and give place to a system of Cookery, in which the human mind is a sausage, and all we ask is, how much indigestible stuff can be crammed into it!"

Always, after these bursts of eloquence, he seemed to forget himself for a moment, and only to hold on to the thread of thought by some single word. "Yes, *crammed*," he repeated. "We went through all that stage of the disease—had it bad, I warrant you! Of course, as the Examination was all in all, we tried to put in just what was wanted—and the *great* thing to aim at was, that the Candidate should know absolutely *nothing* beyond the needs of the Examination! I don't say it was ever *quite* achieved: but one of my own pupils (pardon an old man's egotism) came very near it. After the Examination, he mentioned to me the few facts which he knew but had *not* been able to bring in, and I can assure you they were trivial, Sir, absolutely trivial!"

I feebly expressed my surprise and delight.

The old man bowed, with a gratified smile, and proceeded. "At that time, no one had hit on the much more rational plan of watching for the individual scintillations of genius, and rewarding them as they occurred. As it was, we made our unfortunate pupil into a Leyden-jar, charged him up to the eyelids—then applied the knob of a Competitive Examination, and drew off one magnificent spark, which very often cracked the jar! What mattered *that*? Ee labeled it 'First Class Spark', and put it away on the shelf."

"But the more rational system——?" I suggested.

"Ah, yes! *that* came next. Instead of giving the whole reward of learning in one lump, we used to pay for every good answer as it occurred. How well I remember lecturing in those days, with a heap of small coins at my elbow! It was 'A *very* good answer, Mr. Jones!' (that meant a shilling, mostly). 'Bravo, Mr. Robinson!' (that meant half-a-crown). Now I'll tell you how *that* worked. Not one single fact would any of them take in, without a fee! And when a clever boy came up from school, he got paid more for learning than we got paid for teaching him! Then came the wildest craze of all."

"What, *another* craze?" I said.

"It's the last one," said the old man. "I must have tired you out with my long story. Each College wanted to get the clever boys: so we adopted a system which we had heard was very popular in England: the Colleges competed against each other, and the boys let themselves out to the highest bidder! What geese we were! Why, they were bound to come to the University *somehow*. We needn't have paid 'em! And all our money went in getting clever boys to come to one College rather than another! The competition was so keen, that at last mere money-payments were not enough. Any College, that wished to secure some specially clever young man, had to waylay him at the station, and hunt him through the streets. The first who touched him was allowed to have him."

"That hunting-down of the scholars, as they arrived, must have been a curious business," I said. "Could you give me some idea of what it was like?"

"Willingly!" said the old man. "I will describe to you the very last Hunt that took place, before that form of Sport (for it was actually reckoned among the *Sports* of the day: we called it 'Cub-Hunting') was finally abandoned. I witnessed it myself, as I happened to be passing by at the moment, and was what we called 'in at the death'. I can see it now!" he went on in an excited tone, gazing into vacancy with those large dreamy eyes of his. "It seems like yesterday; and yet it happened——" He checked himself hastily, and the remaining words died away into a whisper.

"*How* many years ago did you say?" I asked, much interested in the prospect of at last learning *some* definite fact in his history.

"*Many* years ago," he replied. "The scene at the Railway-Station had been (so they told me) one of wild excitement. Eight or nine Heads of Colleges had assembled at the gates (no one was allowed inside), and the Station-Master had drawn a line on the pavement, and insisted on their all standing behind it. The gates were flung open! The young man darted through them, and fled like lightning down the street, while the Heads of Colleges actually *yelled* with excitement on catching sight of him! The Proctor gave the word, in the old statutory form, *'Semel! Bis! Ter! Currite!'*, and the Hunt began! Oh, it was a fine sight, believe me! At the first corner he dropped his Greek Lexicon: further on, his railway-rug: then various small articles: then his umbrella: lastly, what I suppose he prized most, his hand-bag; but the game was up: the spherical Principal of—of——"

"Of *which* College?" I said.

"—of *one* of the Colleges", he resumed, "had put into operation the Theory—his own discovery—of Accelerated Velocity, and captured him just opposite to where I stood. I shall never forget that wild breathless struggle! But it was soon over. Once in those great bony hands, escape was impossible!"

"May I ask why you speak of him as the *'spherical'* Principal?" I said.

"The epithet referred to his *shape*, which was a perfect *sphere*. You are aware that a bullet, another instance of a perfect sphere, when falling in a perfectly straight line, moves with Accelerated Velocity?"

I bowed assent.

"Well, my spherical friend (as I am proud to call him) set himself to investigate the *causes* of this. He found them to be *three*. One; that it is a perfect *sphere*. Two; that it moves in a *straight line*. Three; that its direction is *not upwards*. When these three conditions are fulfilled, you get Accelerated Velocity."

"Hardly," I said: "if you will excuse my differing from you. Suppose we apply the theory to *horizontal* motion. If a bullet is fired *horizontally*, it——"

"—it does *not* move in a *straight line*," he quietly finished my sentence for me.

"I yield the point," I said. "What did your friend do next?"

"The next thing was to apply the theory, as you rightly suggest, to *horizontal* motion. But the moving body, ever tending to *fall*, needs *constant support*, if it is to move in a true horizontal line. 'What, then,' he asked himself, 'will give *constant support to a moving body?*' And his answer was *'Human legs!' That* was the discovery that immortalized his name!"

"His name being——?" I suggested.

"I had not mentioned it," was the gentle reply of my most unsatisfactory informant. "His next step was an obvious one. He took to a diet of suet-dumplings, until his body had become a perfect sphere. *Then* he went out for his first experimental run—which nearly cost him his life!"

"How was *that*?"

"Well, you see, he had no idea of the *tremendous* new Force in Nature that he was calling into play. He began too fast. In a very few minutes he found himself moving at a hundred miles an hour! And, if he had not had the presence of mind to charge into the middle of a hay-stack (which he scattered to the four winds) there can be no doubt that he would have left the Planet he belonged to, and gone right away into Space!"

"And how came that to be the *last* of the Cub-Hunts?" I enquired.

"Well, you see, it led to a rather scandalous dispute between two of the Colleges. *Another* Principal had laid his hand on the young one, so nearly at the same moment as the *spherical* one, that there was no knowing which had touched him first. The dispute got into print, and did us no credit, and, in short, Cub-Hunts came to an end. Now I'll tell you what cured us of that wild craze of ours, the bidding against each other, for the clever scholars, just as if they were articles to be sold by auction! Just when the craze had reached its highest point, and when one of the Colleges had actually advertised a Scholarship of one thousand pounds *per annum*, one of our tourists brought us the manuscript of an old African legend—I happen to have a copy of it in my pocket. Shall I translate it for you?"

"Pray go on," I said, though I felt I was getting *very* sleepy.

Chapter XIII

What Tottles Meant

MEIN HERR unrolled the manuscript, but, to my great surprise, instead of *reading* it, he began to *sing* it, in a rich mellow voice that seemed to ring through the room.

"One thousand pounds per annuum
Is not so bad a figure, come!"
Cried Tottles. "And I tell you, flat,
A man may marry well on that!
To say 'the Husband needs the Wife'
Is not the way to represent it.
The crowning joy of Woman's life
Is Man!" said Tottles (and he meant it).

The blissful Honey-moon is past:
The Pair have settled down at last:
Mamma-in-law their home will share,
And make their happiness her care.
"Your income is an ample one:
Go it, my children!" (And they went it).
"I rayther think this kind of fun
Wo'n't last!" said Tottles (and he meant it).

They took a little country-box—
A box at Covent Garden also:
They lived a life of double-knocks,
Acquaintances began to call so:
Their London house was much the same
(It took three hundred, clear, to rent it):
"Life is a very jolly game!"
Cried happy Tottles (and he meant it).

"Contented with a frugal lot"
(He always used that phrase at Gunter's),
He bought a handy little yacht—
A dozen serviceable hunters—

The fishing of a Highland Loch—
A sailing-boat to circumvent it—
"The sounding of that Gaelic 'och'
Beats me*!" said Tottles (and he meant it).*

Here, with one of those convulsive starts that wake
one up in the very act of dropping off to sleep, I became
conscious that the deep musical tones that thrilled me
did *not* belong to Mein Herr, but to the French Count.
The old man was still conning the manuscript.

"I *beg* your pardon for keeping you waiting!" he said.
"I was just making sure that I knew the English for all
the words. I am quite ready now." And he read me the
following Legend:

"In a city that stands in the very centre of Africa, and
is rarely visited by the casual tourist, the people had always bought eggs—a daily necessary in a climate where
egg-flip was the usual diet—from a Merchant who came
to their gates once a week. And the people always bid
wildly against each other: so there was quite a lively
auction every time the Merchant came, and the last egg
in his basket used to fetch the value of two or three
camels, or thereabouts. And eggs got dearer every week.
And still they drank their egg-flip, and wondered where
all their money went to.

"And there came a day when they put their heads together. And they understood what donkeys they had
been.

"And next day, when the Merchant came, only *one*
Man went forth. And he said 'Oh, thou of the hook-nose
and the goggle-eyes, thou of the measureless beard, how
much for that lot of eggs?'

"And the Merchant answered him 'I *could* let thee have
that lot at ten thousand piastres the dozen'.

"And the Man chuckled inwardly, and said '*Ten*
piastres the dozen I offer thee, and no more, oh descen-
dant of a distinguished grandfather!'

"And the Merchant stroked his beard, and said 'Hum!

I will await the coming of thy friends.' So he waited. And the Man waited with him. And they waited both together."

"The manuscript breaks off here," said Mein Herr, as he rolled it up again; "but it was enough to open our eyes. We saw what simpletons we had been—buying our Scholars much as those ignorant savages bought their eggs—and the ruinous system was abandoned. If only we could have abandoned, along with it, all the *other* fashions we had borrowed from you, instead of carrying them to their logical results! But it was not to be. What ruined my country, and drove me from my home, was the introduction—into the *Army*, of all places—of your theory of Political Dichotomy!"

"Shall I trouble you too much," I said, "if I ask you to explain what you mean by 'the Theory of Political Dichotomy'?"

"No trouble at all!" was Mein Herr's most courteous reply. "I quite enjoy talking, when I get so good a listener. What started the thing, with us, was the report brought to us, by one of our most eminent statesmen, who had stayed some time in England, of the way affairs were managed there. It was a political necessity (so he assured us, and we believed him, though we had never discovered it till that moment) that there should be *two* Parties, in every affair and on every subject. In *Politics*, the two Parties, which you had found it necessary to institute, were called, he told us, 'Whigs' and 'Tories'."

"That must have been some time ago?" I remarked.

"It *was* some time ago," he admitted. "And this was the way the affairs of the British Nation were managed. (You will correct me if I misrepresent it. I do but repeat what our traveler told us.) These two Parties—which were in chronic hostility to each other—took turns in conducting the Government; and the Party, that happened *not* to be in power, was called the 'Opposition', I believe?"

"That is the right name," I said. "There have always

been, so long as we have had a Parliament at all, *two*
Parties, one 'in', and one 'out'."

"Well, the function of the 'Ins' (if I may so call them)
was to do the best they could for the national welfare—
in such things as making war or peace, commercial
treaties, and so forth?"

"Undoubtedly," I said.

"And the function of the 'Outs' was (so our traveler
assured us, though we were very incredulous at first) to
prevent the 'Ins' from succeeding in any of these things?"

"To *criticize* and to *amend* their proceedings," I corrected him. "It would be *unpatriotic* to *hinder* the Government in doing what was for the good of the Nation!
We have always held a *Patriot* to be the greatest of heroes,
and an *unpatriotic* spirit to be one of the worst of human
ills!"

"Excuse me for a moment," the old gentleman courteously replied, taking out his pocket-book. "I have a few
memoranda here, of a correspondence I had with our
tourist, and, if you will allow me, I'll just refresh my
memory—although I quite agree with you—it is, as you
say, one of the worst of human ills——" And, here Mein
Herr began singing again.

> But oh, the worst of human ills
> (Poor Tottles found) are "little bills"!
> And, with no balance in the Bank
> What wonder that his spirits sank?
> Still, as the money flowed away,
> He wondered how on earth she spent it.
> "You cost me twenty pounds a day,
> At least!" cried Tottles (and he meant it).
>
> She sighed. "Those Drawing Rooms, you know!
> I really never thought about it:
> Mamma declared we ought to go—
> We should be Nobodies without it.
> That diamond-circlet for my brow—
> I quite believed that she had sent it,

Until the Bill came in just now——'
"Viper!" *cried Tottles (and he meant it).*

Poor Mrs. T. could bear no more, ·
But fainted flat upon the floor.
Mamma-in-law, with anguish wild,
Seeks, all in vain, to rouse her child.
"Quick! Take this box of smelling-salts!
Don't scold her, James, or you'll repent it,
She's a dear girl, with all her faults——"
"She is!" *groaned Tottles (and he meant it).*

"I was a donkey", Tottles cried,
"To choose your daughter for my bride!
'Twas you that bid us cut a dash!
'Tis you have brought us to this smash!
You don't suggest one single thing
That can in any way prevent it——
"Then what's the use of arguing?"
"Shut up!" *cried Tottles (and he meant it).*

Once more I started into wakefulness, and realized that Mein Herr was not the singer. He was still consulting his memoranda.

"It is exactly what my friend told me," he resumed, after conning over various papers. " '*Unpatriotic*' is the very word I had used, in writing to him, and '*hinder*' is the very word he used in his reply! Allow me to read you a portion of his letter:

" '*I can assure you,' he writes, 'that, unpatriotic as you may think it, the recognized function of the 'Opposition' is to hinder in every manner not forbidden by the Law, the action of the Government. This process is called 'Legitimate Obstruction': and the greatest triumph the 'Opposition' can ever enjoy, is when they are able to point out that, owing to their 'Obstruction', the Government have failed in everything they have tried to do for the good of the Nation!'* "

"Your friend has not put it *quite* correctly," I said. "The Opposition would no doubt be glad to point out that the Government had failed *through their own fault* but *not* that they had failed on account of *Obstruction!*"

"You think so?" he gently replied. "Allow me now to read to you this newspaper-cutting, which my friend enclosed in his letter. It is part of the report of a public speech, made by a Statesman who was at the time a member of the 'Opposition':

" '*At the close of the Session, he thought they had no reason to be discontented with the fortunes of the campaign. They had routed the enemy at every point. But the pursuit must be continued. They had only to follow up a disordered and dispirited foe.*' "

"Now to what portion of your national history would you guess that the speaker was referring?"

"Really, the number of *successful* wars we have waged during the last century", I replied, with a glow of British pride, "is *far* too great for me to guess, with any chance of success, *which* it was we were then engaged in. However. I will name '*India*' as the most probable. The Mutiny was no doubt, all but crushed, at the time that speech was made. What a fine, manly, *patriotic* speech it must have been!" I exclaimed in an outburst of enthusiasm.

"You think so?" he replied, in a tone of gentle pity. "Yet my friend tells me that the '*disordered and dispirited foe*' simply meant the Statesmen who happened to be in power at the moment; that the '*pursuit*' simply meant 'Obstruction'; and that the words '*they had routed the enemy*' simply meant that the 'Opposition' had succeeded in hindering the Government from doing any of the work which the Nation had empowered them to do!"

I thought it best to say nothing.

"It seemed queer to *us*, just at first," he resumed, after courteously waiting a minute for me to speak: "but, when once we had mastered the idea, our respect for your Nation was so great that we carried it into every department of life! It was '*the beginning of the end*' with us. My country never held up its head again!" And the poor old gentleman sighed deeply.

"Let us change the subject," I said. "Do not distress yourself, I beg!"

"No, no!" he said, with an effort to recover himself. "I had rather finish my story! The next step (after reducing our Government to impotence, and putting a stop to all useful legislation, which did not take us long to do) was to introduce what we called 'the glorious British Principle of Dichotomy' into *Agriculture*. We persuaded many of the well-to-do farmers to divide their staff of labourers into two Parties, and to set them one against the other. They were called, like our political Parties, the 'Ins' and the 'Outs': the business of the 'Ins' was to do as much of ploughing, sowing, or whatever might be needed, as they could manage in a day, and at night they were paid according to the amount they had *done*: the business of the 'Outs' was to hinder them, and *they* were paid for the amount they had *hindered*. The farmers found they had to pay only *half* as much wages as they did before, and they didn't observe that the amount of work done was only a *quarter* as much as was done before: so they took it up quite enthusiastically, *at first*."

"And *afterwards*——?" I enquired.

"Well, *afterwards* they didn't like it quite so well. In a very short time, things settled down into a regular routine. No work *at all* was done. So the 'Ins' got no wages, and the 'Outs' got full pay. And the farmers never discovered, till most of them were ruined, that the rascals had agreed to manage it so, and had shared the pay between them! While the thing lasted, there were funny sights to be seen! Why, I've often watched a ploughman, with two horses harnessed to the plough, doing his best to get it *forwards*; while the opposition-ploughman, with three donkeys harnessed at the *other* end, was doing *his* best to get it *backwards*! And the plough never moving an inch, *either* way!"

"But *we* never did anything like *that*!" I exclaimed.

"Simply because you were less *logical* than we were," replied Mein Herr. "There is *sometimes* an advantage in being a donk—Excuse me! No *personal* allusion intended. All this happened *long ago*, you know!"

"Did the Dichotomy-Principle succeed in *any* direction?" I enquired.

"In *none*," Mein Herr candidly confessed. "It had a *very* short trial in *Commerce*. The shop-keepers *wouldn't* take it up, after once trying the plan of having half the attendants busy in folding up and carrying away the goods which the other half were trying to spread out upon the counters. They said the Public didn't like it!"

"I don't wonder at it," I remarked.

"Well, we tried 'the British Principle' for some years. And the end of it all was——" His voice suddenly dropped, almost to a whisper; and large tears began to roll down his cheeks. "—the end was that we got involved in a war; and there was a great battle, in which we far out-numbered the enemy. But what could one expect, when only *half* of our soldiers were fighting, and the other half pulling them back? It ended in a crushing defeat—an utter rout. This caused a Revolution; and most of the Government were banished. I myself was accused of Treason, for having so strongly advocated 'the British Principle'. My property was all forfeited, and—and—I was driven into exile! 'Now the mischief's done,' they said, 'perhaps you'll kindly leave the country?' It nearly broke my heart, but I had to go!"

The melancholy tone became a wail: the wail became a chant: the chant became a song—though whether it was *Mein Herr* that was singing, this time, or somebody else, I could not feel certain.

> "*And, now the mischief's done, perhaps*
> *You'll kindly go and pack your traps?*
> *Since* two (*your daughter and your son*)
> *Are Company, but* three *are none.*
> *A course of saving we'll begin:*
> *When change is needed,* I'll *invent it.*

Don't think to put your *finger in*
This *pie!" cried Tottles* (*and he meant it*).

The music seemed to die away. Mein Herr was again speaking in his ordinary voice. "Now tell me one thing more," he said. "Am I right in thinking that in *your* Universities, though a man may reside some thirty or forty years, you examine him, once for all, at the end of the first three or four?"

"That is so, undoubtedly," I admitted.

"Practically, then, you examine a man at the *beginning* of his career!" the old man said to himself rather than to me. "And what guarantee have you that he *retains* the knowledge for which you have rewarded him—beforehand, as *we* should say?"

"None," I admitted, feeling a little puzzled at the drift of his remarks. "How do *you* secure that object?"

"By examining him at the *end* of his thirty or forty years—not at the beginning," he gently replied. "On an average, the knowledge then found is about one-fifth of what it was at first—the process of forgetting going on at a very steady uniform rate—and he, who forgets *least*, gets *most* honour, and most rewards."

"Then you give him the money when he needs it no longer? And you make him live most of his life on *nothing*!"

"Hardly that. He gives his orders to the tradesmen: they supply him, for forty, sometimes fifty years, at their own risk: then he gets his Fellowship—which pays him in *one* year as much as *your* Fellowships pay in fifty— and then he can easily pay all his bills, with interest."

"But suppose he fails to get his Fellowship? That must occasionally happen."

"That occasionally happens." It was Mein Herr's turn, now, to make admissions.

"And what becomes of the tradesmen?"

"They calculate accordingly. When a man appears to be getting alarmingly ignorant, or stupid, they will sometimes refuse to supply him any longer. You have no idea with what enthusiasm a man will begin to rub up his forgotten sciences or languages, when his butcher has cut off the supply of beef and mutton!"

"And who are the Examiners?"

"The young men who have just come, brimming over with knowledge. You would think it a curious sight," he went on, "to see mere boys examining such old men. I have known a man set to examine his own grandfather. It was a little painful for both of them, no doubt. The old gentleman was as bald as a coot——"

"How bald would that be?" I've no idea why I asked this question. I felt I was getting foolish.

Chapter XIV

Bruno's Picnic

"As *bald* as bald," was the bewildering reply. "Now, Bruno, I'll tell you a story."

"And I'll tell *oo* a story," said Bruno, beginning in a great hurry for fear of Sylvie getting the start of him: "once there were a Mouse—a little tiny Mouse—such a tiny little Mouse! Oo never saw such a tiny Mouse——"

"Did nothing ever happen to it, Bruno?" I asked. "Haven't you anything more to tell us, besides its being so tiny?"

"Nothing never happened to it," Bruno solemnly replied.

"Why did nothing never happen to it?" said Sylvie, who was sitting, with her head on Bruno's shoulder, patiently waiting for a chance of beginning *her* story.

"It were too tiny," Bruno explained.

"*That's* no reason!" I said. "However tiny it was, things might happen to it."

Bruno looked pityingly at me, as if he thought me very

stupid. "It were too tiny," he repeated. "If anything happened to it, it would die—it were so *very* tiny!"

"Really that's enough about its being tiny!" Sylvie put in. Haven't you invented any more about it?"

"Haven't invented no more yet."

"Well, then, you shouldn't begin a story till you've invented more! Now be quiet, there's a good boy, and listen to *my* story."

And Bruno, having quite exhausted all his inventive faculty, by beginning in too great a hurry, quietly resigned himself to listening. "Tell about the other Bruno, please," he said coaxingly.

Sylvie put her arms round his neck, and began:—

"The wind was whispering among the trees," ("That wasn't good manners!" Bruno interrupted. "Never mind about manners," said Sylvie) "and it was evening—a nice moony evening, and the Owls were hooting——"

"Pretend they weren't Owls!" Bruno pleaded, stroking her cheek with his fat little hand. "I don't like Owls. Owls have such great big eyes. Pretend they were Chickens!"

"Are you afraid of their great big eyes, Bruno?" I said.

"Aren't *'fraid* of nothing," Bruno answered in as careless a tone as he could manage: "they're ugly with their great big eyes. I think if they cried, the tears would be as big—oh, as big as the moon!" And he laughed merrily. "Doos Owls cry ever, Mister Sir?"

"Owls cry never," I said gravely, trying to copy Bruno's way of speaking: "they've got nothing to be sorry for, you know."

"Oh, but they have!" Bruno exclaimed. "They're ever so sorry, 'cause they killed the poor little Mouses!"

"But they're not sorry when they're *hungry*, I suppose?"

"Oo don't know nothing about Owls!" Bruno scornfully remarked. "When they're hungry, they're very, *very* sorry they killed the little Mouses, 'cause if they *hadn't* killed them there'd be sumfin for supper, oo know!"

Bruno was evidently getting into a dangerously inventive state of mind, so Sylvie broke in with "Now I'm going on with the story. So the Owls—the Chickens, I mean —were looking to see if they could find a nice fat Mouse for their supper——"

"Pretend it was a nice 'abbit!" said Bruno.

"But it *wasn't* a nice habit, to kill Mouses," Sylvie argued. "I ca'n't pretend *that*!"

"I didn't say '*habit*', oo silly fellow!" Bruno replied with a merry twinkle in his eye. " '*abbits*—that runs about in the fields!"

"Rabbit? Well it can be a Rabbit, if you like. But you mustn't alter my story so much, Bruno. A Chicken *couldn't* eat a Rabbit!"

"But it might have wished to see if it could try to eat it."

"Well, it wished to see if it could try—oh, really, Bruno, that's nonsense! I shall go back to the Owls."

"Well, then, pretend they hadn't great eyes!"

"And they saw a little Boy," Sylvie went on, disdaining to make any further corrections. "And he asked them to tell him a story. And the Owls hooted and flew away——" ("Oo shouldn't say '*flewed*'; oo should say '*flied*'," Bruno whispered. But Sylvie wouldn't hear.) "And he met a Lion. And he asked the Lion to tell him a story. And the Lion said 'yes', it would. And, while the Lion was telling him the story, it nibbled some of his head off——"

"Don't say 'nibbled'!" Bruno entreated. "Only little things nibble—little thin sharp things, with edges——"

"Well, then, it '*nubbled*'," said Sylvie. "And when it had nubbled *all* his head off, he went away, and he never said 'thank you'!"

"That were very rude," said Bruno. "If he couldn't speak, he might have nodded—no, he couldn't nod. Well, he might have shaked *hands* with the Lion!"

"Oh, I'd forgotten that part!" said Sylvie. "He *did*

shake hands with it. He came back again, you know, and he thanked the Lion very much, for telling him the story."

"Then his head had growed up again?" said Bruno.

"Oh yes, it grew up in a minute. And the Lion begged pardon, and said it wouldn't nubble off little boys' heads —not never no more!"

Bruno looked much pleased at this change of events. "Now that are a *really* nice story!" he said. "*Aren't* it a nice story, Mister Sir?"

"Very," I said. "I would like to hear another story about that Boy."

"So would *I*,' said Bruno, stroking Sylvie's cheek again. "*Please* tell about Bruno's Picnic; and don't talk about *nubbly* Lions!"

"I wo'n't, if it frightens you," said Sylvie.

"*Flightens* me!" Bruno exclaimed indignantly. "It isn't *that*! It's 'cause 'nubbly' 's such a grumbly word to say— when one person's got her head on another person's shoulder. When she talks like that," he exclaimed to me, "the talking goes down bofe sides of my face—all the way to my chin—and it *doos* tickle so! It's enough to make a beard grow, that it is!"

He said this with great severity, but it was evidently meant for a joke: so Sylvie laughed—a delicious musical little laugh, and laid her soft cheek on the top of her brother's curly head, as if it were a pillow, while she went on with the story. "So this Boy——"

"But it wasn't *me*, oo know!" Bruno interrupted. "And oo needn't try to look as if it was, Mister Sir!"

I represented, respectfully, that I was trying to look as if it wasn't.

"—he was a middling good Boy——"

"He were a *welly* good Boy!" Bruno corrected her. "And he never did nothing he wasn't told to do——"

"*That* doesn't make a good Boy!" Sylvie said contemptuously.

"*That do* make a good Boy!" Bruno insisted.

Sylvie gave up the point. "Well, he was a *very* good Boy, and he always kept his promises, and he had a big cupboard——"

"—for to keep all his promises in!" cried Bruno.

"If he kept *all* his promises," Sylvie said, with a mischievous look in her eyes, "he wasn't like *some* Boys I know of!"

"He had to put *salt* with them, a-course," Bruno said gravely: "oo ca'n't keep promises when there isn't any salt. And he kept his birthday on the second shelf."

"How long did he keep his birthday?" I asked. "I never can keep *mine* more than twenty-four hours."

"Why, a birthday *stays* that long by itself!" cried Bruno. "Oo doosn't know how to keep birthdays! This Boy kept *his* a whole year!"

"And then the next birthday would begin," said Sylvie. "So it would be his birthday *always*."

"So it were," said Bruno. "Doos *oo* have treats on *oor* birthday, Mister Sir?"

"Sometimes," I said.

"When oo're *good*, I suppose?"

"Why, it *is* a sort of treat, being good, isn't it?" I said.

"A sort of *treat*!" Bruno repeated. "It's a sort of *punishment*, I think!"

"Oh, Bruno!" Sylvie interrupted, almost sadly. "How *can* you?"

"Well, but it *is*," Bruno persisted. "Why, look here, Mister Sir! *This* is being good!" And he sat bolt upright, and put on an absurdly solemn face. "First oo must sit up as straight as pokers——"

"—as *a* poker," Sylvie corrected him.

"—as straight as *pokers*," Bruno firmly repeated. "Then oo must clasp oor hands—*so*. Then—'Why hasn't 'oo brushed oor hair? Go and brush it *toreckly*!' Then—'Oh, Bruno, oo mustn't dog's-ear the daisies!' Did oo learn *oor* spelling wiz daisies, Mister Sir?"

"I want to hear about that Boy's *Birthday*," I said.

Bruno returned to the story instantly. "Well, so this Boy said 'Now it's my Birthday!' And so—I'm tired!" he suddenly broke off, laying his head in Sylvie's lap. "Sylvie knows it best. Sylvie's grown-upper than me. Go on, Sylvie!"

Sylvie patiently took up the thread of the story again. "So he said 'Now it's my Birthday. Whatever shall I do to keep my Birthday?' All *good* little Boys—" (Sylvie turned away from Bruno, and made a great pretence of whispering to *me*) "—all *good* little Boys—Boys that learn their lessons quite perfect—they always keep their birthdays, you know. So of course *this* little Boy kept *his* Birthday."

"Oo may call him Bruno, if oo like," the little fellow carelessly remarked. "It weren't *me*, but it makes it more interesting."

"So Bruno said to himself 'The properest thing to do is to have a Picnic, all by myself, on the top of the hill. And I'll take some Milk and some Bread, and some Apples: and first and foremost, I want some *Milk*!' So, first and foremost, Bruno took a milk-pail——"

"And he went and milkted the Cow!" Bruno put in.

"Yes," said Sylvie, meekly accepting the new verb. "And the Cow said 'Moo! What are you going to do with all that Milk?' And Bruno said 'Please'm, I want it for my Picnic.' And the Cow said 'Moo! But I hope you wo'n't *boil* any of it?' And Bruno said 'No, *indeed* I wo'n't! New Milk's so nice and so warm, it wants no boiling!'"

"It doesn't want no boiling," Bruno offered as an amended version.

"So Bruno put the Milk in a bottle. And then Bruno said 'Now I want some Bread!' So he went to the Oven, and he took out a delicious new Loaf. And the Oven——".

"—ever so light and so puffy!" Bruno impatiently corrected her. "Oo shouldn't leave out so many words!"

Sylvie humbly apologized. "—a delicious new Loaf,

ever so light and so puffy. And the Oven said——" Here Sylvie made a long pause. "Really I don't know *what* an Oven begins with, when it wants to speak!"

Both children looked appealingly at me; but I could only say, helplessly, "I haven't the least idea! *I* never heard an Oven speak!"

For a minute or two we all sat silent; and then Bruno said, very softly, "Oven begins wiz 'O'."

"*Good* little boy!" Sylvie exclaimed. "He does his spelling *very* nicely. *He's cleverer than he knows!*" she added, aside, to *me*. "So the Oven said 'O! What are you going to do with all that Bread?' And Bruno said 'Please—' Is an Oven 'Sir' or ' 'm', would you say?" She looked to me for a reply.

"*Both*, I think," seemed to me the safest thing to say.

Sylvie adopted the suggestion instantly. "So Bruno said 'Please, Sirm, I want it for my Picnic.' And the Oven said 'O! But I hope you wo'n't *toast* any of it?' And Bruno said, 'No, *indeed* I wo'n't! New Bread's so light and so puffy, it wants no toasting!' "

"It never doesn't want no toasting," said Bruno. "I *wiss* oo wouldn't say it so short!"

"So Bruno put the Bread in the hamper. Then Bruno said 'Now I want some Apples!' So he took the hamper, and he went to the Apple-Tree, and he picked some lovely ripe Apples. And the Apple-Tree said——" Here followed another long pause.

Bruno adopted his favourite expedient of tapping his forehead; while Sylvie gazed earnestly upwards, as if she hoped for some suggestion from the birds, who were singing merrily among the branches overhead. But no result followed.

"What *does* an Apple-Tree begin with, when it wants to speak?" Sylvie murmured despairingly, to the irresponsive birds.

At last, taking a leaf out of Bruno's book, I ventured on a remark. "Doesn't 'Apple-Tree' always begin with Eh!'?"

"Why, of *course* it does! How *clever* of you!" Sylvie cried delightedly.

Bruno jumped up, and patted me on the head. I tried not to feel conceited.

"So the Apple-Tree said 'Eh! What are you going to do with all those Apples?' And Bruno said 'Please, Sir, I want them for my Picnic.' And the Apple-Tree said 'Eh! But I hope you wo'n't *bake* any of them?' And Bruno said 'No, *indeed* I wo'n't! Ripe Apples are so nice and so sweet, they want no baking!' "

"They never doesn't——" Bruno was beginning, but Sylvie corrected herself before he could get the words out.

" 'They never doesn't nohow want no baking.' So Bruno put the Apples in the hamper, along with the Bread, and the bottle of Milk. And he set off to have a Picnic, on the top of the hill, all by himself——"

"He wasn't greedy, oo know, to have it all by himself," Bruno said, patting me on the cheek to call my attention; " 'cause he hadn't got no brothers and sisters."

"It was very sad to have no *sisters*, wasn't it?" I said.

"Well, I don't know," Bruno said thoughtfully; " 'cause he hadn't no lessons to do. So he didn't mind."

Sylvie went on. "So, as he was walking along the road, he heard behind him such a curious sort of noise—a sort of a Thump! Thump! Thump! 'Whatever *is* that?' said Bruno. 'Oh, I know!' said Bruno. 'Why, it's only my Watch a-ticking!' "

"*Were* it his Watch a-ticking?" Bruno asked me, with eyes that fairly sparkled with mischievous delight.

"No doubt of it!" I replied. And Bruno laughed exultingly.

"Then Bruno thought a little harder. And he said 'No! it *ca'n't* be my Watch a-ticking; because I haven't *got* a Watch!' "

Bruno peered up anxiously into my face, to see how I took it. I hung my head, and put a thumb into my mouth, to the evident delight of the little fellow.

"So Bruno went a little further along the road. And

then he heard it again, that queer noise—Thump!
Thump! Thump! 'Whatever *is* that?' said Bruno. 'Oh, I
know!' said Bruno. 'Why, it's only the Carpenter a-
mending my Wheelbarrow!' "

"*Were* it the Carpenter a-mending his Wheelbarrow?"
Bruno asked me.

I brightened up, and said "It *must* have been!" in a
tone of absolute conviction.

Bruno threw his arms round Sylvie's neck. "Sylvie!"
he said, in a perfectly audible whisper. "He says it *must*
have been!"

"Then Bruno thought a little harder. And he said 'No!
It *ca'n't* be the Carpenter a-mending my Wheelbarrow,
because I haven't *got* a Wheelbarrow!' "

This time I hid my face in my hands, quite unable to
meet Bruno's look of triumph.

"So Bruno went a little further along the road. And
then he heard that queer noise again—Thump! Thump!
Thump! So he thought he'd look round, *this* time, just
to *see* what it was. And what should it be but a great
Lion!"

"A great big Lion," Bruno corrected her.

"A great big Lion. And Bruno was ever so frightened,
and he ran——"

"No, he wasn't *flightened* a bit!" Bruno interrupted.
(He was evidently anxious for the reputation of his name-
sake.) "He runned away to get a good look at the Lion;
'cause he wanted to see if it were the same Lion what
used to nubble little Boys' heads off; and he wanted to
know how big it was!"

"Well, he ran away, to get a good look at the Lion.
And the Lion trotted slowly after him. And the Lion
called after him, in a very gentle voice, 'Little Boy, little
Boy! You needn't be afraid of *me*! I'm a very *gentle* old
Lion now. I *never* nubble little Boys' heads off, as I used
to do.' And so Bruno said 'Don't you *really*, Sir? (Then
what do you live on?' And the Lion——"

"Oo *see* he weren't a bit flightened!" Bruno said to me

patting my cheek again. " 'cause he remembered to call it 'Sir', oo know."

I said that no doubt that was the *real* test whether a person was frightened or not.

"And the Lion said 'Oh, I live on bread-and-butter, and cherries, and marmalade, and plum-cake—' "

"—and *apples*!" Bruno put in.

"Yes, 'and apples'. And Bruno said 'Wo'n't you come with me to my Picnic?' And the Lion said 'Oh, I should like it *very much indeed*!' And Bruno and the Lion went away together." Sylvie stopped suddenly.

"Is that *all*?" I asked, despondingly.

"Not *quite* all," Sylvie slily replied "There's a sentence or two more. Isn't there, Bruno?"

"Yes," with a carelessness that was evidently put on: "just a sentence or two more."

"And, as they were walking along, they looked over a hedge, and who should they see but a little black Lamb! And the Lamb was ever so frightened. And it ran——"

"It were *really* flightened!" Bruno put in.

"It ran away. And Bruno ran after it. And he called 'Little Lamb! You needn't be afraid of *this* Lion! It *never* kills things! It lives on cherries, and marmalade—' "

"—and *apples*!" said Bruno. 'Oo *always* forgets the apples!"

"And Bruno said 'Wo'n't you come with us to my Picnic?' And the Lamb said 'Oh, I should like it *very much indeed*, if my Ma will let me!' And Bruno said 'Let's go and ask your Ma!' And they went to the old Sheep. And Bruno said 'Please, may your little Lamb come to my Picnic?' And the Sheep said 'Yes, if it's learnt all its lessons.' And the Lamb said 'Oh yes, Ma! I've learnt *all* my lessons!' "

"Pretend it hadn't any lessons!" Bruno earnestly pleaded.

"Oh, that would never do!" said Sylvie. "I ca'n't leave out all about the lessons! And the old Sheep said 'Do you know your A B C yet? Have you learnt A?' And the

Lamb said 'Oh yes, Ma! I went to the A-field, and I helped them to make A!' 'Very good, my child! And have you learnt B?' 'Oh yes, Ma! I went to the B-hive, and the B gave me some honey!' 'Very good, my child! And have you learnt C?' 'Oh yes, Ma! I went to the C-side, and I saw the ships sailing on the C!' 'Very good, my child! You may go to Bruno's Picnic.' "

"So they set off. And Bruno walked in the middle, so that the Lamb mightn't see the Lion——"

"It were *flightened*," Bruno explained.

"Yes, and it trembled so; and it got paler and paler; and, before they'd got to the top of the hill, it was a *white* little Lamb—as white as snow!"

"But *Bruno* weren't flightened!" said the owner of that name. "So *he* staid black!"

"No, he *didn't* stay black! He staid *pink*!" laughed Sylvie. "I shouldn't kiss you like this, you know, if you were *black*!"

"Oo'd *have* to!" Bruno said with great decision. "Besides, Bruno wasn't *Bruno*, oo know—I mean, Bruno wasn't *me*—I mean—don't talk nonsense, Sylvie!"

"I wo'n't do it again!" Sylvie said very humbly. "And so, as they went along, the Lion said 'Oh, I'll tell you what I used to do when I was a young Lion. I used to hide behind trees, to watch for little Boys.' " (Bruno cuddled a little closer to her.) " 'And, if a little thin scraggy Boy came by, why, I used to let him go. But, if a little fat juicy——' "

Bruno could bear no more. "Pretend he wasn't juicy!" he pleaded, half-sobbing.

"Nonsense, Bruno!" Sylvie briskly replied. "It'll be done in a moment! '—if a little fat juicy Boy came by, why, I used to spring out and gobble him up! Oh, you've no *idea* what a delicious thing it is—a little juicy Boy!' And Bruno said 'Oh, if you please, Sir, *don't* talk about eating little boys! It makes me so *shivery*!' "

The real Bruno shivered, in sympathy with the hero.

"And the Lion said 'Oh, well, we wo'n't talk about it,

then! I'll tell you what happened on my wedding-day——' "

"I like *this* part better," said Bruno, patting my cheek to keep me awake.

" 'There was, oh, such a lovely wedding-breakfast! At *one* end of the table there was a large plum-pudding. And at the other end there was a nice roasted *Lamb*! Oh, you've no *idea* what a delicious thing it is—a nice roasted Lamb!' And the Lamb said 'Oh, if you please, Sir, *don't* talk about eating Lambs! It makes me so *shivery*!' And the Lion said 'Oh, well, we wo'n't talk about it, then!' "

CHAPTER XV

The Little Foxes

"So, when they got to the top of the hill, Bruno opened the hamper: and he took out the Bread, and the Apples, and the Milk: and they ate, and they drank. And when they'd finished the Milk, and eaten half the Bread and half the Apples, the Lamb said 'Oh, my paws is so sticky! I want to wash my paws!' And the Lion said 'Well, go down the hill, and wash them in the brook, yonder. We'll wait for you!' "

"It never comed back!" Bruno solemnly whispered to me.

But Sylvie overheard him. "You're not to whisper, Bruno! It spoils the story! And when the Lamb had been gone a long time, the Lion said to Bruno 'Do go and see after that silly little Lamb! It must have lost its way.' And Bruno went down the hill. And when he got to the brook, he saw the Lamb sitting on the bank: and who should be sitting by it but an old Fox!'

'Don't know who *should* be sitting by it," Bruno

said thoughtfully to himself. "A old Fox *were* sitting by it."

"And the old Fox were saying," Sylvie went on, for once conceding the grammatical point. " 'Yes, my dear, you'll be ever so happy with us, if you'll only come and see us! I've got three little Foxes there, and we do love little Lambs so dearly!' And the Lamb said 'But you never *eat* them, do you, Sir?' And the Fox said 'Oh, no! What, *eat* a Lamb? We never *dream* of doing such a thing!' So the Lamb said 'Then I'll come with you.' And off they went, hand in hand."

"That Fox were welly extremely wicked, *weren't* it?" said Bruno.

"No, no!" said Sylvie, rather shocked at such violent language. "It wasn't quite so bad as that!"

"Well, I mean, it wasn't nice," the little fellow corrected himself.

"And so Bruno went back to the Lion. 'Oh, come quick!' he said. 'The Fox has taken the Lamb to his house with him! I'm *sure* he means to eat it!' And the Lion said 'I'll come as quick as ever I can!' And they trotted down the hill."

"Do oo think he caught the Fox, Mister Sir?" said Bruno. I shook my head, not liking to speak: and Sylvie went on.

"And when they got to the house, Bruno looked in at the window. And there he saw the three little Foxes sitting round the table, with their clean pinafores on, and spoons in their hands——"

"Spoons in their hands!" Bruno repeated in an ecstasy of delight.

"And the Fox had got a great big knife—all ready to kill the poor little Lamb——" ("Oo needn't be flightened, Mister Sir!" Bruno put in, in a hasty whisper.)

"And just as he was going to do it, Bruno heard a great ROAR——" (The real Bruno put his hand into mine, and held tight), "and the Lion came *bang* through the door, and the next moment it had bitten off the old

Fox's head! And Bruno jumped in at the window, and went leaping round the room, and crying out 'Hooray! Hooray! The old Fox is dead! The old Fox is dead!' "

Bruno got up in some excitement. "May I do it now?" he enquired.

Sylvie was quite decided on this point. "Wait till afterwards," she said. "The speeches come next, don't you know? You always love the speeches, *don't* you?"

"Yes, I doos," said Bruno: and sat down again.

"The Lion's speech. 'Now, you silly little Lamb, go home to your mother, and never listen to old Foxes again. And be very good and obedient.' "

"The Lamb's speech. 'Oh, indeed, Sir, I will, Sir!' and the Lamb went away." ("But *oo* needn't go away!" Bruno explained. "It's quite the nicest part—what's coming now!" Sylvie smiled. She liked having an appreciative audience.)

"The Lion's speech to Bruno. 'Now, Bruno, take those little Foxes home with you, and teach them to be good obedient little Foxes! Not like that wicked old thing there, that's got no head!' " ("That hasn't got no head," Bruno repeated.)

"Bruno's speech to the Lion. 'Oh, indeed, Sir, I will, Sir!' And the Lion went away." ("It gets betterer and betterer, now," Bruno whispered to me, "right away to the end!")

"Bruno's speech to the little Foxes. 'Now, little Foxes, you're going to have your first lesson in being good. I'm going to put you into the hamper, along with the Apples and the Bread: and you're not to eat the Apples: and you're not to eat the Bread: and you're not to eat *anything*—till we get to my house: and then you'll have your supper.' "

"The little Foxes' speech to Bruno. The little Foxes said nothing.

"So Bruno put the Apples into the hamper—and the little Foxes—and the Bread—" ("They had picnicked all the Milk," Bruno explained in a whisper) "—and he set off to go to his house." ("We're getting near the end now," said Bruno.)

"And, when he had got a little way, he thought he would look into the hamper, and see how the little Foxes were getting on."

"So he opened the door——" said Bruno.

"Oh, Bruno!" Sylvie exclaimed, "*you're* not telling the story! So he opened the door, and behold, there were no Apples! So Bruno said 'Eldest little Fox, have *you* been eating the Apples?' And the eldest little Fox said 'No no no!' " (It is impossible to give the tone in which Sylvie repeated this rapid little 'No no no!' The nearest I can come to it is to say that it was much as if a young and excited duck had tried to quack the words. It was too quick for a quack, and yet too harsh to be anything else.) "Then he said 'Second little Fox, have *you* been eating the Apples?' And the second little Fox said 'No no no!' Then he said 'Youngest little Fox, have *you* been eating the Apples?' And the youngest little Fox *tried* to say 'No no no!' but its mouth was so full, it couldn't, and it only said 'Wauch! Wauch! Wauch!' And Bruno looked into its mouth. And its mouth was full of Apples! And Bruno shook his head, and he said 'Oh dear, oh dear! What bad creatures these Foxes are!' "

Bruno was listening intently: and, when Sylvie paused to take breath, he could only just gasp out the words "About the Bread?"

"Yes," said Sylvie, "the Bread comes next. So he shut the door again; and he went a little further; and then he thought he'd just peep in once more. And behold, there was no Bread!" ("What do 'behold' *mean*?" said Bruno. "Hush!" said Sylvie.) "And he said 'Eldest little Fox, have *you* been eating the Bread?' And the eldest little Fox said 'No no no!' 'Second little Fox, have *you* been eating the Bread?' And the second little Fox only said 'Wauch! Wauch! Wauch!' And Bruno looked into its mouth, and its mouth was full of Bread!" ("It might have chokeded it," said Bruno.) "So he said 'Oh dear, oh dear! What *shall* I do with these Foxes?' And he went a little further." ("Now comes the most interesting part," Bruno whispered.)

"And when Bruno opened the hamper again, what do you think he saw?" ("Only *two* Foxes!" Bruno cried in a great hurry.) "You shouldn't tell it so quick. However, he *did* see only *two* Foxes. And he said 'Eldest little Fox, have you been eating the youngest little Fox?' And the eldest little Fox said 'No no no!' 'Second little Fox, have *you* been eating the youngest little Fox?' And the second little Fox did its very best to say 'No no no!' but it could only say 'Weuchk! Weuchk! Weuchk!' And when Bruno looked into its mouth, it was half full of Bread, and half full of Fox!" (Bruno said nothing in the pause this time. He was beginning to pant a little, as he knew the crisis was coming.)

"And when he'd got nearly home, he looked once more into the hamper, and he saw——"

"Only——" Bruno began, but a generous thought struck him, and he looked at me. "*Oo* may say it, *this* time, Mister Sir!" he whispered. It was a noble offer, but I wouldn't rob him of the treat. "Go on, Bruno," I said, "you say it much the best." "Only—but—*one*—Fox!" Bruno said with great solemnity.

" 'Eldest little Fox,' " Sylvie said, dropping the narrative-form in her eagerness, " 'you've been *so* good that I can hardly believe *you've* been disobedient: but I'm *afraid* you've been eating your little sister?' And the eldest little Fox said 'Whihuauch! Whihuauch!' and then it choked. And Bruno looked into its mouth, and it *was* full!" (Sylvie paused to take breath, and Bruno lay back among the daisies, and looked at me triumphantly. "Isn't it *grand*, Mister Sir?" said he. I tried hard to assume a critical tone. "It's grand," I said: "but it frightens one so!" "Oo may sit a little closer to *me*, if oo like," said Bruno.)

"And so Bruno went home: and took the hamper into the kitchen, and opened it. And he saw——" Sylvie looked at *me*, this time, as if she thought I had been rather neglected and ought to be allowed *one* guess, at any rate.

"He ca'n't guess!" Bruno cried eagerly. "I 'fraid I *must* tell him! There weren't—*nuffin* in the hamper!" I shivered in terror, and Bruno clapped his hands with delight. "He *is* flightened, Sylvie! Tell the rest!"

"So Bruno said 'Eldest little Fox, have you been eating *yourself*, you wicked little Fox?' And the eldest little Fox said 'Whihuauch!' And then Bruno saw there was only its *mouth* in the hamper! So he took the mouth, and he opened it, and shook, and shook! And at last he shook the little Fox out of its own mouth! And then he said 'Open your mouth again, you wicked little thing!' And he shook, and shook! And he shook out the second little Fox! And he said 'Now open *your* mouth!' And he shook, and shook! And he shook out the youngest little Fox, and all the Apples, and all the Bread!

"And then Bruno stood the little Foxes up against the wall: and he made them a little speech. 'Now, little Foxes, you've begun very wickedly—and you'll have to be punished. First you'll go up to the nursery, and wash your faces, and put on clean pinafores. Then you'll hear the bell ring for supper. Then you'll come down: and *you wo'n't have any supper*: but you'll have a good *whipping*! Then you'll go to bed. Then in the morning you'll hear the bell ring for breakfast. *But you wo'n't have any breakfast!* You'll have a good *whipping*! Then you'll have your lessons. And, perhaps, if you're *very* good, when dinner-time comes, you'll have a little dinner, and no more whipping!' " ("How *very* kind he was!" I whispered to Bruno. "*Middling* kind," Bruno corrected me gravely.)

"So the little Foxes ran up to the nursery. And soon Bruno went into the hall, and rang the big bell. 'Tingle, tingle, tingle! Supper, supper, supper!' Down came the little Foxes, in such a hurry for their supper! Clean pinafores! Spoons in their hands! And, when they got into the dining-room, there was ever such a white table-cloth on the table! But there was nothing on it but a big whip. And they had *such* a whipping!" (I put my handkerchief to my eyes, and Bruno hastily climbed upon my knee and stroked my face. "Only *one* more whipping, Mister Sir!" he whispered. "Don't cry more than oo ca'n't help!")

"And the next morning early, Bruno rang the big bell again. 'Tingle, tingle, tingle! Breakfast, breakfast, breakfast!' Down came the little Foxes! Clean pinafores! Spoons in their hands! No breakfast! Only the big whip! Then came lessons," Sylvie hurried on, for I still had my handkerchief to my eyes. "And the little Foxes were ever so good! And they learned their lessons backwards, and forwards, and upside-down. And at last Bruno rang the big bell again. 'Tingle, tingle, tingle! Dinner, dinner, dinner!' And when the little Foxes came down——" ("Had they clean pinafores on?" Bruno enquired. "Of course!" said Sylvie. "And spoons?" "Why, you *know* they had!" "Couldn't be *certain*," said Bruno.) "— they came as slow as slow! And they said 'Oh! There'll be no dinner! There'll only be the big whip!' But, when they got into the room, they saw the most *lovely* dinner!" ("Buns?" cried Bruno, clapping his hands.) "Buns, and cake, and——" ("—and jam?" said Bruno.) "Yes, jam— and soup—and——" ("—and *sugar plums*!" Bruno put in once more; and Sylvie seemed satisfied.)

"And ever after that, they *were* such good little Foxes! They did their lessons as good as gold—and they never did what Bruno told them not to—and they never ate each other any more—and *they never ate themselves*!"

The story came to an end so suddenly, it almost took my breath away; however I did my best to make a pretty speech of thanks. "I'm sure it's very—very—very much so, I'm sure!" I seemed to hear myself say.

Chapter XVI

Beyond These Voices

"I DIDN'T quite catch what you said!" were the next words that reached my ear, but certainly *not* in the voice either of Sylvie or of Bruno, whom I could just see, through the crowd of guests, standing by the piano, and listening to the Count's song. Mein Herr was the speaker. "I didn't quite catch what you said!" he repeated. "But I've no doubt you take *my* view of it. Thank you *very* much for your kind attention. There is only but *one* verse left to be sung!" These last words were not in the gentle voice of Mein Herr, but in the deep bass of the French Count. And, in the silence that followed, the final stanza of "Tottles" rang through the room.

> *See now this couple settled down*
> *In quiet lodgings, out of town:*
> *Submissively the tearful wife*
> *Accepts a plain and humble life:*
> *Yet begs one boon on bended knee:*
> *"My ducky-darling, don't resent it!*
> *Mamma might come for two or three——"*
> *"NEVER!" yelled Tottles. And he meant it.*

The conclusion of the song was followed by quite a chorus of thanks and compliments from all parts of the room, which the gratified singer responded to by bowing low in all directions. "It is to me a great privilege", he said to Lady Muriel, "to have met with this so marvellous a song. The accompaniment to him is so strange, so mysterious: it is as if a new music were to be invented! I will play him once again so as that to show you what I mean." He returned to the piano, but the song had vanished.

The bewildered singer searched through the heap of music lying on an adjoining table, but it was not there, either. Lady Muriel helped in the search: others soon joined: the excitement grew. "What *can* have become of it?" exclaimed Lady Muriel. Nobody knew: one thing only was certain, that no one had been near the piano since the Count had sung the last verse of the song.

"Nevare mind him!" he said, most good-naturedly. "I shall give it you with memory alone!" He sat down, and began vaguely fingering the notes; but nothing resembling the tune came out. Then he, too, grew excited. "But what oddness! How much of singularity! That I might lose, not the words alone, but the tune also—that is quite curious, I suppose?"

We all supposed it, heartily.

"It was that sweet little boy, who found it for me," the Count suggested. "Quite perhaps *he* is the thief?"

"Of course he is!" cried Lady Muriel. "Bruno! Where are you, my darling?"

But no Bruno replied: it seemed that the two children had vanished as suddenly, and as mysteriously, as the song.

"They are playing us a trick?" Lady Muriel gaily exclaimed. "This is only an *ex tempore* game of Hide-and-Seek! That little Bruno is an embodied Mischief!"

The suggestion was a welcome one to most of us, for some of the guests were beginning to look decidedly uneasy. A general search was set on foot with much enthusiasm: curtains were thrown back and shaken, cupboards opened, and ottomans turned over; but the number of possible hiding-places proved to be strictly limited; and the search came to an end almost as soon as it had begun.

"They must have run out, while we were wrapped up in the song," Lady Muriel said, addressing herself to the Count, who seemed more agitated than the others; "and no doubt they've found their way back to the housekeeper's room."

"Not by *this* door!" was the earnest protest of a knot of two or three gentlemen, who had been grouped round the door (one of them actually leaning against it) for the last half-hour, as they declared. "*This* door has not been opened since the song began!"

An uncomfortable silence followed this announcement. Lady Muriel ventured no further conjectures, but quietly examined the fastenings of the windows, which opened as doors. They all proved to be well fastened, *inside*.

Not yet at the end of her resources, Lady Muriel rang the bell. "Ask the housekeeper to step here," she said, "and to bring the children's walking-things with her."

"I've brought them, my Lady," said the obsequious housekeeper, entering after another minute of silence. "I thought the young lady would have come to my room to put on her boots. Here's your boots, my love!" she added cheerfully, looking in all directions for the children. There was no answer, and she turned to Lady Muriel with a puzzled smile. "Have the little darlings hid themselves?"

"I don't see them, just now," Lady Muriel replied, rather evasively. "You can leave their things here, Wilson. *I'll* dress them, when they're ready to go."

The two little hats, and Sylvie's walking-jacket, were handed round among the ladies, with many exclamations of delight. There certainly was a sort of witchery of beauty about them. Even the little boots did not miss their share of favourable criticism. "Such natty little things!" the musical young lady exclaimed, almost fondling them as she spoke. "And what tiny tiny feet they must have!"

Finally, the things were piled together on the centre-ottoman, and the guests, despairing of seeing the children again, began to wish good-night and leave the house.

There were only some eight or nine left—to whom the Count was explaining, for the twentieth time, how he had had his eye on the children during the last verse of the song; how he had then glanced round the room, to see what effect "de great chest-note" had had upon his audience; and how, when he looked back again, they had both disappeared—when exclamations of dismay began to be heard on all sides, the Count hastily bringing his story to an end to join in the outcry.

The walking-things had all disappeared!

After the utter failure of the search for the *children*, there was a very half-hearted search made for their *apparel*. The remaining guests seemed only too glad to get away, leaving only the Count and our four selves.

The Count sank into an easy-chair, and panted a little.

"Who then *are* these dear children, I pray you?" he said. "Why come they, why go they, in this so little ordinary a fashion? That the music should make itself vanish—that the hats, the boots, should make themselves to vanish—how is it, I pray you?"

"I've no idea where they are!" was all I could say, on finding myself appealed to, by general consent, for an explanation.

The Count seemed about to ask further questions, but checked himself.

"The hour makes himself to become late," he said. "I wish to you a very good night, my Lady. I betake myself to my bed—to dream—if that indeed I be not dreaming now!" And he hastily left the room.

"Stay awhile, stay awhile!" said the Earl, as I was about to follow the Count. "*You* are not a guest, you know! Arthur's friend is at *home* here!"

"Thanks!" I said, as with true English instincts, we drew our chairs together round the fire-place, though no fire was burning—Lady Muriel having taken the heap of music on her knee, to have one more search for the strangely-vanished song.

"Don't you sometimes feel a wild longing", she said, addressing herself to me, "to have something more to do with your hands, while you talk, than just holding a cigar, and now and then knocking off the ash? Oh, I know all that you're going to say!" (This was to Arthur, who appeared about to interrupt her.) "The Majesty of Thought supersedes the work of the fingers. A Man's severe thinking, *plus* the shaking-off a cigar-ash, comes to the same total as a Woman's trivial fancies, *plus* the most elaborate embroidery. *That's* your sentiment, isn't it, only better expressed?"

Arthur looked into the radiant, mischievous face, with a grave and very tender smile. "Yes," he said resignedly: "that is my sentiment, exactly."

"Rest of body, and activity of mind," I put in. "Some writer tells us *that* is the acme of human happiness."

"Plenty of *bodily* rest, at any rate!" Lady Muriel replied, glancing at the three recumbent figures around her. "But what you call activity of *mind*——"

"—is the privilege of young Physicians *only*," said the Earl. "We old men have no claim to be active. *What can an old man do but die?*"

"A good many other things, I should *hope*," Arthur said earnestly.

"Well, maybe. Still you have the advantage of me in many ways, dear boy! Not only that *your* day is dawning while *mine* is setting, but your *interest* in Life—somehow I ca'n't help envying you *that*. It will be many a year before you lose your hold of *that*."

"Yet surely many human interests *survive* human Life?" I said.

"Many do, no doubt. And *some* forms of Science; but only *some*, I think. Mathematics, for instance: *that* seems to possess an endless interest: one ca'n't imagine *any* form of Life, or *any* race of intelligent beings, where Mathematical truth would lose its meaning. But I fear *Medicine* stands on a different footing. Suppose you discover a remedy for some disease hitherto supposed to be incurable. Well, it is delightful for the moment, no doubt —full of interest—perhaps it brings you fame and fortune. But what then? Look on, a few years, into a life where disease has no existence. What is your discovery worth, *then*? Milton makes Jove promise too much. '*Of so much fame in heaven expect thy meed.*' Poor comfort when one's 'fame' concerns matters that will have ceased to have a meaning!"

"At any rate one wouldn't care to make any *fresh*

medical discoveries," said Arthur. "I see no help for *that* —though I shall be sorry to give up my favourite studies. Still, medicine, disease, pain, sorrow, sin—I fear they're all linked together. Banish sin, and you banish them all!"

"*Military* science is a yet stronger instance," said the Earl. "Without sin, *war* would surely be impossible. Still any mind, that has had in this life any keen interest, not in *itself* sinful, will surely find itself *some* congenial line of work hereafter. Wellington may have no more *battles* to fight—and yet—

> '*We doubt not that, for one so true,*
> *There must be other, nobler work to do,*
> *Than when he fought at Waterloo,*
> *And Victor he must ever be!*' "

He lingered over the beautiful words, as if he loved them: and his voice, like distant music, died away into silence.

After a minute or two he began again. "If I'm not wearying you, I would like to tell you an idea of the future Life which has haunted me for years, like a sort of waking nightmare—I ca'n't reason myself out of it."

"Pray do," Arthur and I replied, almost in a breath. Lady Muriel put aside the heap of music, and folded her hands together.

"The one idea", the Earl resumed, "that has seemed to me to overshadow all the rest, is that of *Eternity*—involving, as it seems to do, the necessary *exhaustion* of all subjects of human interest. Take Pure Mathematics, for instance—a Science independent of our present surroundings. I have studied it, myself, a little. Take the subject of circles and ellipses—what we call 'curves of the second degree'. In a future Life, it would only be a question of so many years (or *hundreds* of years, if you like), for a man to work out *all* their properties. Then he *might* go to curves of the third degree. Say *that* took ten times as long (you see we have *unlimited* time to deal with). I can hardly imagine his *interest* in the subject holding out even for those; and, though there is no limit to the *degree* of the curves he might study, yet surely the time, needed to exhaust *all* the novelty and interest of the subject, would be absolutely *finite*? And so of all other branches of Science. And, when I transport myself, in thought, through some thousands or millions of years, and fancy myself possessed of as much Science as one created reason can carry, I ask myself 'What then? With nothing more to learn, can one rest content on *knowledge*, for the eternity yet to be lived through?' It has been a very wearying thought to me. I have sometimes fancied one *might*, in that event, say 'It is better *not* to be', and pray for personal *annihilation*—the Nirvana of the Buddhists.''

"But that is only half the picture," I said. "Besides working for *oneself*, may there not be the helping of *others*?"

"Surely, surely!" Lady Muriel exclaimed in a tone of relief, looking at her father with sparkling eyes.

"Yes," said the Earl, "so long as there *were* any others needing help. But, given ages and ages more, surely all created reasons would at length reach the same dead level of *satiety*. And *then* what is there to look forward to?"

"I know that weary feeling," said the young Doctor. "I have gone through it all, more than once. Now let me tell you how I have put it to myself. I have imagined a little child, playing with toys on his nursery-floor, and yet able to *reason*, and to look on, thirty years ahead. Might he not say to himself 'By that time I shall have had enough of bricks and ninepins. How weary Life will be!' Yet, if we look forward through those thirty years, we find him a great statesman, full of interests and joys far more intense than his baby-life could give—joys wholly inconceivable to his baby-mind—joys such as no baby-language could in the faintest degree describe. Now, may not our life, a million years hence, have the same relation, to our life now, that the man's life has to the child's? And, just as one might try, all in vain, to express to that child, in the language of bricks and ninepins, the meaning of 'politics', so perhaps all those descriptions of Heaven, with its music, and its feasts, and its streets of gold, may be only attempts to describe, in *our* words, things for which we *really* have no words at all. Don't you think that, in *your* picture of another life, you are in fact transplanting that child into political life, without making any allowance for his growing up?"

'I think I understand you," said the Earl. "The music of Heaven *may* be something beyond our powers of thought. Yet the music of Earth is sweet! Muriel, my child, sing us something before we go to bed!"

"Do," said Arthur, as he rose and lit the candles on the cottage-piano, lately banished from the drawing-room to make room for a "semi-grand". "There is a song here, that I have never heard you sing.

> *'Hail to thee, blithe spirit!*
> *Bird thou never wert,*
> *That from Heaven, or near it,*
> *Pourest thy full heart!'* "

he read from the page he had spread open before her.

"And our little life here", the Earl went on, "is, to that grand time, like a child's summer-day! One gets tired as night draws on," he added, with a touch of sadness in his voice, "and one gets to long for bed! For those welcome words 'Come, child, 'tis bed-time!' "

Chapter XVII

To the Rescue!

"It *isn't* bed-time!" said a sleepy little voice. "The owls hasn't gone to bed, and I s'a'n't go to seep wizout oo sings to me!"

"Oh, Bruno!" cried Sylvie. "Don't you know the owls

have only just got up? But the *frogs* have gone to bed, ages ago.'

"Well, *I* aren't a frog," said Bruno.

"What shall I sing?" said Sylvie, skilfully avoiding the argument.

"Ask Mister Sir," Bruno lazily replied, clasping his hands behind his curly head, and lying back on his fern-leaf, till it almost bent over with his weight. "This aren't a comfable leaf, Sylvie. Find me a comfabler—please!" he added, as an after-thought, in obedience to a warning finger held up by Sylvie. "I doosn't like being feet-up-wards!"

It was a pretty sight to see—the motherly way in which the fairy-child gathered up her little brother in her arms, and laid him on a stronger leaf. She gave it just a touch to set it rocking, and it went on vigorously by it-self, as if it contained some hidden machinery. It cer-tainly wasn't the wind, for the evening-breeze had quite died away again, and not a leaf was stirring over our heads.

"Why does that one leaf rock so, without the others?" I asked Sylvie. She only smiled sweetly and shook her head. "I don't know *why*," she said. "It always does, if it's got a fairy-child on it. It *has* to, you know."

"And can people see the leaf rock, who ca'n't see the Fairy on it?"

"Why, of course!" cried Sylvie. "A leaf's a leaf, and everybody can see it; but Bruno's Bruno, and they ca'n't see *him*, unless they're eerie, like you."

Then I understood how it was that one sometimes sees —going through the woods in a still evening—one fern-leaf rocking steadily on, all by itself. Haven't you ever seen that? Try if you can see the fairy-sleeper on it, next time; but don't *pick* the leaf, whatever you do; let the little one sleep on!

But all this time Bruno was getting sleepier and sleep-ier. "Sing, sing!" he murmured fretfully, Sylvie looked to me for instructions. "What shall it be?" she said.

"Could you sing him the nursery-song you once told me of?" I suggested. "The one that had been put through the mind-mangle, you know. *'The little man that had a little gun,'* I think it was."

"Why, that are one of the *Professor's* songs!" cried Bruno. "I likes the little man; and I likes the way they spinned him—like a teetle-totle-tum." And he turned a loving look on the gentle old man who was sitting at the other side of his leaf-bed, and who instantly began to sing, accompanying himself on his Outlandish guitar, while the snail, on which he sat, waved its horns in time to the music.

> *In stature the Manlet was dwarfish—*
> *No burly big Blunderbore he:*
> *And he wearily gazed on the crawfish*
> *His Wifelet had dressed for his tea.*
> *"Now reach me, sweet Atom, my gunlet,*
> *And hurl the old shoelet for luck:*
> *Let me hie to the bank of the runlet,*
> *And shoot thee a Duck!"*
>
> *She has reached him his minikin gunlet:*
> *She has hurled the old shoelet for luck:*
> *She is busily baking a bunlet,*
> *To welcome him home with his Duck.*
> *On he speeds, never wasting a wordlet,*
> *Though thoughtlets cling, closely as wax,*
> *To the spot where the beautiful birdlet*
> *So quietly quacks.*
>
> *Where the Lobsterlet lurks, and the Crablet*
> *So slowly and sleepily crawls:*
> *Where the Dolphin's at home, and the Dablet*
> *Pays long ceremonious calls:*
> *Where the Grublet is sought by the Froglet:*
> *Where the Frog is pursued by the Duck:*
> *Where the Ducklet is chased by the Doglet—*
> *So runs the world's luck!*

He has loaded with bullet and powder:
   His footfall is noiseless as air:
But the Voices grow louder and louder,
   And bellow, and bluster, and blare.
They bristle before him and after,
   They flutter above and below,
Shrill shriekings of lubberly laughter,
          Weird wailings of woe!

They echo without him, within him:
   They thrill through his whiskers and beard:
Like a teetotum seeming to spin him,
   With sneers never hitherto sneered.
"Avengement," they cry, "on our Foelet!
   Let the Manikin weep for our wrongs!
Let us drench him, from toplet to toelet,
          With Nursery-Songs!

"He shall muse upon 'Hey! Diddle! Diddle!'
   On the Cow that surmounted the Moon:
He shall rave of the Cat and the Fiddle,
   And the Dish that eloped with the Spoon:
And his soul shall be sad for the Spider,
   When Miss Muffet was sipping her whey,
That so tenderly sat down beside her,
          And scared her away!

"The music of Midsummer-madness
   Shall sting him with many a bite,
Till, in rapture of rollicking sadness,
   He shall groan with a gloomy delight:
He shall swathe him, like mists of the morning,
   In platitudes luscious and limp,
Such as deck, with a deathless adorning,
          The Song of the Shrimp!

"When the Ducklet's dark doom is decided,
   We will trundle him home in a trice:
And the banquet, so plainly provided,
   Shall round into rose-buds and rice:

In a blaze of pragmatic invention
 He shall wrestle with Fate, and shall reign:
But he has not a friend fit to mention,
  So hit him again!"

He has shot it, the delicate darling!
 And the Voices have ceased from their strife:
Not a whisper of sneering or snarling,
 As he carries it home to his wife:
Then, cheerily champing the bunlet
 His spouse was so skilful to bake,
He hies him once more to the runlet,
  To fetch her the Drake!

"He's sound asleep now," said Sylvie, carefully tucking in the edge of a violet-leaf, which she had been spreading over him as a sort of blanket: "good night!"

"Good night!" I echoed.

"You may well say 'good night'!" laughed Lady Muriel, rising and shutting up the piano as she spoke. "When you've been nid—nid—nodding all the time I've been singing for your benefit! What was it all about, now?" she demanded imperiously.

"Something about a duck?" I hazarded. "Well, a bird of some kind?" I corrected myself, perceiving at once that *that* guess was wrong, at any rate.

"*Something about a bird of some kind!*" Lady Muriel repeated, with as much withering scorn as her sweet face was capable of conveying. "And that's the way he speaks of Shelley's Sky-Lark, is it? When the Poet particularly says '*Hail to thee, blithe spirit!* Bird *thou never wert!*' "

She led the way to the smoking-room, where, ignoring all the usages of Society and all the instincts of Chivalry, the three Lords of the Creation reposed at their ease in low rocking-chairs, and permitted the one lady who was present to glide gracefully about among us, supplying our wants in the form of cooling drinks, cigarettes, and lights. Nay, it was only *one* of the three who had the chivalry to go beyond the common-place "thank you", and to quote the Poet's exquisite description of how Geraint, when waited on by Enid, was moved

> *"To stoop and kiss the tender little thumb*
> *That crossed the platter as she laid it down,"*

and to suit the action to the word—an audacious liberty for which, I feel bound to report, he was *not* dūly reprimanded.

As no topic of conversation seemed to occur to any one, and as we were, all four, on those delightful terms with one another (the only terms, I think, on which any friendship, that deserves the name of *intimacy*, can be maintained) which involve no sort of necessity for *speaking* for mere speaking's sake, we sat in silence for some minutes.

At length I broke the silence by asking "Is there any fresh news from the harbour about the Fever?"

"None since this morning," the Earl said, looking very grave. "But that was alarming enough. The Fever is spreading fast: the London doctor has taken fright and left the place, and the only one now available isn't a regular doctor at all: he is apothecary, and doctor, and dentist, and I don't know what other trades, all in one. It's a bad outlook for those poor fishermen—and a worse one for all the women and children."

"How many are there of them altogether?" Arthur asked.

"There were nearly one hundred, a week ago," said the Earl: "but there have been twenty or thirty deaths since then."

"And what religious ministrations are there to be had?"

"There are three brave men down there," the Earl replied, his voice trembling with emotion, "gallant heroes as ever won the Victoria Cross! I am certain that no one of the three will ever leave the place merely to save his own life. There's the Curate: his wife is with him: they have no children. Then there's the Roman Catholic Priest. And there's the Wesleyan Minister. They go amongst their own flocks mostly; but I'm told that those who are dying like to have *any* of the three with them. How slight the barriers seem to be that part Christian from Christian, when one has to deal with the great facts of Life and the reality of Death!"

"So it must be, and so it should be——" Arthur was beginning, when the front-door bell rang, suddenly and violently.

We heard the front-door hastily opened, and voices outside: then a knock at the door of the smoking-room, and the old house-keeper appeared, looking a little scared.

"Two persons, my Lord, to speak with Dr. Forester."

Arthur stepped outside at once, and we heard his cheery "Well, my men?" but the answer was less audible, the only words I could distinctly catch being "ten since morning, and two more just——"

"But there *is* a doctor there?" we heard Arthur say: and a deep voice, that we had not heard before, replied "Dead, Sir. Died three hours ago."

Lady Muriel shuddered, and hid her face in her hands: but at this moment the front-door was quietly closed, and we heard no more.

For a few minutes we sat quite silent: then the Earl left the room, and soon returned to tell us that Arthur had gone away with the two fishermen, leaving word that he would be back in about an hour. And, true enough, at the end of that interval—during which very little was said, none of us seeming to have the heart to talk—the front-door once more creaked on its rusty hinges, and a step was heard in the passage, hardly to be recognized as Arthur's, so slow and uncertain was it, like a blind man feeling his way.

He came in, and stood before Lady Muriel, resting one hand heavily on the table, and with a strange look in his eyes, as if he were walking in his sleep.

"Muriel—my love——" he paused, and his lips quivered: but after a minute he went on more steadily.

"Muriel—my darling—they—*want* me—down in the harbour."

"*Must* you go?" she pleaded, rising and laying her hands on his shoulders, and looking up into his face with her great eyes brimming over with tears. "Must *you* go, Arthur? It may mean—death!"

He met her gaze without flinching. "It *does* mean death," he said, in a husky whisper: "but—darling—I am *called*. And even my life itself——" His voice failed him, and he said no more.

For a minute she stood quite silent, looking upwards with a helpless gaze, as if even prayer were now useless, while her features worked and quivered with the great agony she was enduring. Then a sudden inspiration seemed to come upon her and light up her face with a strange sweet smile. "*Your* life?" she repeated. "It is not *yours* to give!"

Arthur had recovered himself by this time, and could reply quite firmly, "That is true," he said. "It is not *mine* to give. It is *yours*, now, my—wife that is to be! And you —do *you* forbid me to go? Will you not spare me, my own beloved one?"

Still clinging to him, she laid her head softly on his breast. She had never done such a thing in my presence before, and I knew how deeply she must be moved. "I *will* spare you", she said, calmly and quietly, "to God."

"And to God's poor," he whispered.

"And to God's poor," she added. "When must it be, sweet love?"

"To-morrow morning," he replied. "And I have much to do before then."

And then he told us how he had spent his hour of absence. He had been to the Vicarage, and had arranged for the wedding to take place at eight the next morning (there was no legal obstacle, as he had, some time before this, obtained a Special Licence) in the little church we knew so well. "My old friend here", indicating me, "will act as 'Best Man', I know: your father will be there to give you away: and—and—you will dispense with bride's-maids, my darling?"

She nodded: no words came.

"And then I can go with a willing heart—to do God's work—knowing that we are *one*—and that we are together in *spirit*, though not in bodily presence—and are most of all together when we pray! Our *prayers* will go up together——"

"Yes, yes!" sobbed Lady Muriel. "But you must not stay longer now, my darling! Go home and take some rest. You will need all your strength to-morrow——"

"Well, I will go," said Arthur. "We will be here in good time to-morrow. Good night, my own own darling!"

I followed his example, and we two left the house together. As we walked back to our lodgings, Arthur sighed deeply once or twice, and seemed about to speak—but no words came, till we had entered the house, and had lit our candles, and were at our bedroom-doors. Then Arthur said "Good night, old fellow! God bless you!"

"God bless you!" I echoed from the very depths of my heart.

We were back again at the Hall by eight in the morning, and found Lady Muriel and the Earl, and the old Vicar, waiting for us. It was a strangely sad and silent party that walked up to the little church and back; and I could not help feeling that it was much more like a funeral than a wedding: to Lady Muriel it *was* in fact, a funeral rather than a wedding, so heavily did the presentiment weigh upon her (as she told us afterwards) that her newly-won husband was going forth to his death.

Then we had breakfast; and, all too soon, the vehicle was at the door, which was to convey Arthur, first to his lodgings, to pick up the things he was taking with him, and then as far towards the death-stricken hamlet as it was considered safe to go. One or two of the fishermen were to meet him on the road, to carry his things the rest of the way.

"And are you quite sure you are taking all that you will need?" Lady Muriel asked.

"All that I shall need as a *doctor*, certainly. And my own personal needs are few: I shall not even take any of my own wardrobe—there is a fisherman's suit, ready-made, that is waiting for me at my lodgings. I shall only take my watch, and a few books, and—stay—there *is* one book I should like to add, a pocket-Testament—to use at the bedsides of the sick and dying——"

"Take mine!" said Lady Muriel: and she ran upstairs to fetch it. "It has nothing written in it but 'Muriel'," she said as she returned with it: "shall I inscribe——"

"No, my own one," said Arthur, taking it from her. "What *could* you inscribe better than that? Could any human name mark it more clearly as my own individual property? Are *you* not mine? Are you not," (with all the old playfulness of manner) "as Bruno would say, 'my *very mine*'?"

He bade a long and loving adieu to the Earl and to me, and left the room, accompanied only by his wife, who was bearing up bravely, and was—*outwardly*, at least—less overcome than her old father. We waited in the room a minute or two, till the sounds of wheels had told us that Arthur had driven away; and even then we waited still, for the step of Lady Muriel, going upstairs to her room, to die away in the distance. Her step, usually so light and joyous, now sounded slow and weary, like one who plods on under a load of hopeless misery; and I felt almost as hopeless, and almost as wretched as she. "Are we four destined *ever* to meet again, on this side the grave?" I asked myself, as I walked to my home. And the tolling of a distant bell seemed to answer me, "No! No! No!"

CHAPTER XVIII

A Newspaper-Cutting

EXTRACT FROM THE "FAYFIELD CHRONICLE".

Our readers will have followed with painful interest, the accounts we have from time to time published of the terrible epidemic which has, during the last two months, carried off most of the inhabitants of the little fishing-harbour adjoining the village of Elveston. The last survivors, numbering twenty-three only, out of a population which, three short months ago, exceeded one hundred and twenty, were removed on Wednesday last, under the authority of the Local Board, and safely lodged in the County Hospital: and the place is now veritably "a city of the dead", without a single human voice to break its silence.

The rescuing party consisted of six sturdy fellows—fishermen from the neighbourhood—directed by the resident Physician of the Hospital, who came over for that purpose, heading a train of hospital-ambulances. The six men had been selected—from a much larger number who had volunteered for this peaceful "forlorn hope"—for their strength and robust health, as the expedition was considered to be, even now, when the malady has expended its chief force, not unattended with danger.

Every precaution that science could suggest, against the risk of infection, was adopted: and the sufferers were tenderly carried on litters, one by one, up the steep hill, and placed in the ambulances which, each provided with a hospital nurse, were waiting on the level road. The fifteen miles, to the Hospital, were done at a walking-pace, as some of the patients were in too prostrate a condition to bear jolting, and the journey occupied the whole afternoon.

The twenty-three patients consist of nine men, six women, and eight children. It has not been found possible to identify them all, as some of the children—left with no surviving relatives—are infants: and two men and one woman are not yet able to make rational replies, the brain-powers being entirely in abeyance. Among a more well-to-do race, there would no doubt have been names marked on the clothes; but here no such evidence is forthcoming.

Besides the poor fishermen and their families, there were but five persons to be accounted for: and it was ascertained, beyond

*a doubt, that all five are numbered with the dead. It is a melan-
choly pleasure to place on record the names of these genuine
martyrs—than whom none, surely, are more worthy to be entered
on the glory-roll of England's heroes! They are as follows:*

*The Rev. James Burgess, M.A., and Emma his wife. He was
the Curate at the Harbour, not thirty years old, and had been
married only two years. A written record was found in their
house, of the dates of their deaths.*

*Next to theirs we will place the honoured named of Dr.
Arthur Forester, who, on the death of the local physician, nobly
faced the imminent peril of death, rather than leave these poor
folk uncared for in their last extremity. No record of his name,
or of the date of his death, was found: but the corpse was easily
identified, although dressed in the ordinary fisherman's suit
(which he was known to have adopted when he went down there),
by a copy of the New Testament, the gift of his wife, which was
found, placed next his heart, with his hands crossed over it. It
was not thought prudent to remove the body, for burial elsewhere:
and accordingly it was at once committed to the ground, along
with four others found in different houses, with all due reverence.
His wife, whose maiden name was Lady Muriel Orme, had been
married to him on the very morning on which he undertook his
self-sacrificing mission.*

*Next we record the Rev. Walter Saunders, Wesleyan Min-
ister. His death is believed to have taken place two or three
weeks ago, as the words "Died October 5" were found written
on the wall of the room which he is known to have occupied—the
house being shut up, and apparently not having been entered for
some time.*

*Last—though not a whit behind the other four in glorious self-
denial and devotion to duty—let us record the name of Father
Francis, a young Jesuit Priest who had been only a few months
in the place. He had not been dead many hours when the explor-
ing party came upon the body, which was identified, beyond the
possibility of doubt, by the dress, and by the crucifix which was,
like the young Doctor's Testament, clasped closely to his heart.*

*Since reaching the hospital, two of the men and one of the
children have died. Hope is entertained for all the others: though
there are two or three cases where the vital powers seem to be so
entirely exhausted that it is but "hoping against hope" to regard
ultimate recovery as even possible.*

Chapter XIX

A Fairy-Duet

THE year—what an eventful year it had been for me!—
was drawing to a close, and the brief wintry day hardly
gave light enough to recognize the old familiar objects,
bound up with so many happy memories, as the train
glided round the last bend into the station, and the hoarse
cry of "Elveston! Elveston!" resounded along the platform.

It was sad to return to the place, and to feel that I
should never again see the glad smile of welcome, that
had awaited me here so few months ago. "And yet, if I
were to find him here," I muttered, as in solitary state I
followed the porter, who was wheeling my luggage on a
barrow, "and if he *were* to '*strike a sudden hand in mine,
And ask a thousand things of home,*' I should not—no, '*I
should not feel it to be strange*'!"

Having given directions to have my luggage taken to
my old lodgings, I strolled off alone, to pay a visit, before
settling down in my own quarters, to my dear old friends
—for such I indeed felt them to be, though it was barely
half a year since first we met—the Earl and his widowed
daughter.

The shortest way, as I well remembered, was to cross
through the churchyard. I pushed open the little wicket-
gate and slowly took my way among the solemn mem-
orials of the quiet dead, thinking of the many who had,
during the past year, disappeared from the place, and had
gone to "join the majority". A very few steps brought me
in sight of the object of my search. Lady Muriel, dressed
in the deepest mourning, her face hidden by a long crape
veil, was kneeling before a little marble cross, round
which she was fastening a wreath of flowers.

The cross stood on a piece of level turf, unbroken by
any mound, and I knew that it was simply a memorial-

cross, for one whose dust reposed elsewhere, even before reading the simple inscription:

In loving Memory of
ARTHUR FORESTER, M.D.
whose mortal remains lie buried by the sea:
whose spirit has returned to God who gave it.

"GREATER LOVE HATH NO MAN THAN THIS, THAT A MAN LAY DOWN HIS LIFE FOR HIS FRIENDS."

She threw back her veil on seeing me approach, and came forwards to meet me, with a quiet smile, and far more self-possessed than I could have expected.

"It is quite like old times, seeing *you* here again!" she said, in tones of genuine pleasure. "Have you been to see my father?"

"No," I said: "I was on my way there, and came through here as the shortest way. I hope he is well, and you also?"

"Thanks, we are both quite well. And you? Are you any better yet?"

"Not much better, I fear: but no worse, I am thankful to say."

"Let us sit here awhile, and have a quiet chat," she said. The calmness—almost indifference—of her manner quite took me by surprise. I little guessed what a fierce restraint she was putting upon herself.

"One can be so quiet here," she resumed. "I come here every—every day."

"It is very peaceful," I said.

"You got my letter?"

"Yes, but I delayed writing. It is so hard to say—on *paper*——"

"I know. It was kind of you. You were with us when we saw the last of——" She paused a moment, and went on more hurriedly. "I went down to the harbour several times, but no one knows which of those vast graves it is. However, they showed me the house he died in: that was

some comfort. I stood in the very room where—where——"
She struggled in vain to go on. The flood-gates had given
way at last, and the outburst of grief was the most terrible I had ever witnessed. Totally regardless of my presence, she flung herself down on the turf, burying her face
in the grass, and with her hands clasped round the little
marble cross. "Oh, my darling, my darling!" she sobbed.
"And God meant your life to be so beautiful!"

I was startled to hear, thus repeated by Lady Muriel,
the very words of the darling child whom I had seen
weeping so bitterly over the dead hare. Had some mysterious influence passed, from that sweet fairy-spirit, ere she
went back to Fairyland, into the human spirit that loved
her so dearly? The idea seemed too wild for belief. And
yet, are there not *more things in heaven and earth than are
dreamt of in our philosophy*?

"God *meant* it to be beautiful," I whispered, "and surely it *was* beautiful? God's purpose never fails!" I dared
say no more, but rose and left her. At the entrance-gate
to the Earl's house I waited, leaning on the gate and
watching the sun set, revolving many memories—some
happy, some sorrowful—until Lady Muriel joined me.

She was quite calm again now. "Do come in," she said.
"My father will be so pleased to see you!"

The old man rose from his chair, with a smile, to welcome me; but his self-command was far less than his
daughter's, and the tears coursed down his face as he
grasped both my hands in his, and pressed them warmly.

My heart was too full to speak; and we all sat silent for
a minute or two. Then Lady Muriel rang the bell for tea.
"You *do* take five o'clock tea, I know!" she said to me,
with the sweet playfulness of manner I remembered so
well, "even though you *ca'n't* work your wicked will on
the Law of Gravity, and make the teacups descend into
Infinite Space, a little faster than the tea!"

This remark gave the tone to our conversation. By a
tacit mutual consent, we avoided, during this our first
meeting after her great sorrow, the painful topics that

filled our thoughts, and talked like light-hearted children who had never known a care.

"Did you ever ask yourself the question," Lady Muriel began, *à propos* of nothing, "what is the *chief* advantage of being a Man instead of a Dog?"

"No, indeed," I said: "but I think there are advantages on the *Dog's* side of the question as well."

"No doubt," she replied, with that pretty mock-gravity that became her so well: "but, on *Man's* side, the chief advantage seems to me to consist in *having pockets*! It was borne in upon me—upon *us*, I should say; for my father and I were returning from a walk—only yesterday. We met a dog carrying home a bone. What it wanted it for, I've no idea: certainly there was no *meat* on it——"

A strange sensation came over me, that I had heard all this, or something exactly like it, before: and I almost expected her next words to be "perhaps he meant to make a cloak for the winter?" However what she really said was "and my father tried to account for it by some wretched joke about *pro bono publico*. Well, the dog laid down the bone—*not* in disgust with the pun, which would have shown it to be a dog of taste—but simply to rest its jaws, poor thing! I *did* pity it so! Won't you join my *Charitable Association for supplying dogs with pockets?* How would *you* like to have to carry your walking-stick in your mouth?"

Ignoring the difficult question as to the *raison d'être* of a walking-stick, supposing one had no *hands*, I mentioned a curious instance, I had once witnessed, of reasoning by a dog. A gentleman, with a lady, and child, and a large dog, were down at the end of a pier on which I was walking. To amuse his child, I suppose, the gentleman put down on the ground his umbrella and the lady's parasol, and then led the way to the other end of the pier, from which he sent the dog back for the deserted articles. I was watching with some curiosity. The dog came racing back to where I stood, but found an unexpected difficulty in picking up the things it had come for. With the umbrella in its mouth, its jaws were so far apart that it could get no firm grip on the parasol. After two or three failures, it paused and considered the matter.

Then it put down the umbrella and began with the parasol. Of course that didn't open its jaws nearly so wide, and it was able to get a good hold of the umbrella, and galloped off in triumph. One couldn't doubt that it had gone through a real train of logical thought.

"I entirely agree with you," said Lady Muriel: "but don't orthodox writers condemn that view, as putting Man on the level of the lower animals? Don't they draw a sharp boundary-line between Reason and Instinct?"

"That certainly *was* the orthodox view, a generation ago," said the Earl. "The truth of Religion seemed ready to stand or fall with the assertion that Man was the only reasoning animal. But that is at an end now. Man can still claim *certain* monopolies—for instance, such a use of *language* as enables us to utilize the work of many, by 'division of labour'. But the belief, that we have a monopoly of *Reason*, has long been swept away. Yet no catastrophe has followed. As some old poet says, '*God is where he was*'."

"Most religious believers would *now* agree with Bishop Butler," said I, "and not reject a line of argument, even if it led straight to the conclusion that animals have some kind of *soul*, which survives their bodily death."

"I *would* like to know *that* to be true!" Lady Muriel exclaimed. "If only for the sake of the poor horses. Sometimes I've thought that, if anything *could* make me cease to believe in a God of perfect justice, it would be the sufferings of horses—without guilt to deserve it, and without any compensation!"

"It is only part of the great Riddle," said the Earl, "why innocent beings *ever* suffer. It *is* a great strain on Faith—but not a *breaking* strain, I think."

"The sufferings of *horses*", I said, "are chiefly caused by *Man's* cruelty. So *that* is merely one of the many instances of Sin causing suffering to others than the Sinner

himself. But don't you find a greater difficulty in sufferings inflicted by animals upon each other? For instance, a
cat playing with a mouse. Assuming it to have no *moral*
responsibility, isn't that a greater mystery than a man
over-driving a horse?"

"I think it *is*," said Lady Muriel, looking a mute appeal
to her father.

"What right have we to make that assumption?" said
the Earl. "*Many* of our religious difficulties are merely
deductions from unwarranted assumptions. The wisest
answer to most of them, is, I think, '*behold, we know not
anything*'."

"You mentioned 'division of labour', just now," I said.
"Surely it is carried to a wonderful perfection in a hive of
bees?"

"So wonderful—so entirely super-human—" said the
Earl, "and so entirely inconsistent with the intelligence
they show in other ways—that I feel no doubt at all that
it is *pure* Instinct, and *not*, as some hold, a very high
order of Reason. Look at the utter stupidity of a bee,
trying to find its way out of an open window! It *doesn't*
try, in any reasonable sense of the word: it simply bangs
itself about! We should call a puppy *imbecile*, that behaved
so. And yet we are asked to believe that its intellectual
level is above Sir Isaac Newton!"

"Then you hold that *pure* Instinct contains no *Reason*
at all?"

"On the contrary," said the Earl, "I hold that the work
of a bee-hive involves Reason of the *highest* order. But
none of it is done by the *Bee*. *God* has reasoned it all out,
and has put into the mind of the Bee the *conclusions*, only,
of the reasoning process."

"But how do their minds come to work *together*?" I
asked.

"What right have we to assume that they *have* minds?"

"Special pleading, special pleading!" Lady Muriel cried,
in a most unfilial tone of triumph. "Why, you yourself
said, just now, 'the mind of the Bee'!"

"But I did *not* say '*minds*', my child," the Earl gently replied. "It has occurred to me, as the most probable solution of the 'Bee'-mystery, that a swarm of Bees *have only one mind among them*. We often see one mind animating a most complex collection of limbs and organs, *when joined together*. How do we know that any material connection is necessary? May not mere neighbourhood be enough? If so, a swarm of bees is simply a single animal whose many limbs are not quite close together!"

"It is a bewildering thought," I said, "and needs a night's rest to grasp it properly. Reason and Instinct *both* tell me I ought to go home. So, good-night!"

"I'll 'set' you part of the way," said Lady Muriel. "I've had no walk to-day. It will do me good, and I have more to say to you. Shall we go through the wood? It will be pleasanter than over the common, even though it *is* getting a little dark."

We turned aside into the shade of interlacing boughs, which formed an architecture of almost perfect symmetry, grouped into lovely groined arches, or running out, far as the eye could follow, into endless aisles, and chancels, and naves, like some ghostly cathedral, fashioned out of the dream of a moon-struck poet.

"Always, in this wood," she began after a pause (silence seemed natural in this dim solitude), "I begin thinking of Fairies! May I ask you a question?" she added hesitatingly. "Do you believe in Fairies?"

The momentary impulse was so strong to tell her of my experiences in this very wood, that I had to make a real effort to keep back the words that rushed to my lips. "If you mean, by 'believe', 'believe in their *possible* existence', I say 'Yes'. For their *actual existence*, of course, one would need *evidence*."

"You were saying, the other day", she went on, "that you would accept *anything*, on good evidence, that was not *à priori* impossible. And I think you named *Ghosts* as an instance of a *provable* phenomenon. Would *Fairies* be another instance?"

"Yes, I think so." And again it was hard to check the wish to say more: but I was not yet sure of a sympathetic listener.

"And have you any theory as to what sort of place they would occupy in Creation? Do tell me what you think about them! Would they, for instance (supposing such beings to exist), would they have any moral responsibility? I mean" (and the light bantering tone suddenly changed to one of deep seriousness) "would they be capable of *sin*?"

"They can reason—on a lower level, perhaps, than men and women—never rising, I think, above the faculties of a child; and they have a moral sense, most surely. Such a being, without *free will*, would be an absurdity. So I am driven to the conclusion that they *are* capable of sin."

"You believe in them?" she cried delightedly, with a sudden motion as if about to clap her hands. "Now tell me, have you any reason for it?"

And still I strove to keep back the revelation I felt sure was coming. "I believe that there is *life* everywhere —not *material* only, not merely what is palpable to our senses—but immaterial and invisible as well. We believe in our own immaterial essence—call it 'soul', or 'spirit', or what you will. Why should not other similar essences exist around us, *not* linked on to a visible and *material* body? Did not God make this swarm of happy insects, to dance in this sunbeam for one hour of bliss, for no other object, that we can imagine, than to swell the sum of conscious happiness? And where shall we dare to draw the line, and say 'He has made all these and no more'?"

"Yes, yes"! she assented, watching me with sparkling eyes. "But these are only reasons for not *denying*. You have more reasons than this, have you not?"

"Well, yes," I said, feeling I might safely tell all now. "And I could not find a fitter time or place to say it. I have *seen* them—and in this very wood!"

Lady Muriel asked no more questions. Silently she paced at my side, with head bowed down and hands clasped tightly together. Only, as my tale went on, she drew a little short quick breath now and then, like a child panting with delight. And I told her what I had never yet breathed to any other listener, of my double life, and, more than that (for *mine* might have been but a noonday-dream), of the double life of those two dear children.

And when I told her of Bruno's wild gambols, she laughed merrily; and when I spoke of Sylvie's sweetness and her utter unselfishness and trustful love, she drew a deep breath, like one who hears at last some precious tidings for which the heart has ached for a long while; and the happy tears chased one another down her cheeks.

"I have often longed to meet an angel," she whispered, so low that I could hardly catch the words. "I'm *so* glad I've seen Sylvie! My heart went out to the child the first moment that I saw her—Listen!" she broke off suddenly. "That's Sylvie singing! I'm sure of it! Don't you know her voice?"

"I have heard *Bruno* sing, more than once," I said: "but I never heard Sylvie."

"I have only heard her *once*," said Lady Muriel. "It was that day when you brought us those mysterious flowers. The children had run out into the garden; and I saw Eric coming in that way, and went to the window to meet him: and Sylvie was singing, under the trees, a song I had never heard before. The words were something like 'I think it is Love, I feel it is Love'. Her voice sounded far away, like a dream, but it was beautiful beyond all words—as sweet as an infant's first smile, or the first gleam of the white cliffs when one is coming *home* after weary years—a voice that seemed to fill one's whole being with peace and heavenly thoughts—Listen!" she cried, breaking off again in her excitement. "That *is* her voice, and that's the very song!"

I could distinguish no words, but there was a dreamy sense of music in the air that seemed to grow ever louder and louder, as if coming nearer to us. We stood quite silent, and in another minute the two children appeared, coming straight towards us through an arched opening among the trees. Each had an arm round the other, and the setting sun shed a golden halo round their heads, like what one sees in pictures of saints. They were looking in our direction, but evidently did not see us, and I soon made out that Lady Muriel had for once passed into a condition familiar to *me*, that we were both of us "eerie", and that, though we could see the children so plainly, we were quite invisible to *them*.

The song ceased just as they came into sight: but, to my delight, Bruno instantly said "Let's sing it all again, Sylvie! It *did* sound so pretty!" And Sylvie replied "Very well. It's *you* to begin, you know."

So Bruno began, in the sweet childish treble I knew so well:

> "*Say, what is the spell, when her fledgelings are cheeping,*
> *That lures the bird home to her nest?*
> *Or wakes the tired mother, whose infant is weeping,*
> *To cuddle and croon it to rest?*
> *What's the magic that charms the glad babe in her arms,*
> *Till it cooes with the voice of the dove?*"

And now ensued quite the strangest of all the strange experiences that marked the wonderful year whose history I am writing—the experience of *first* hearing Sylvie's voice in song. Her part was a very short one—only a few words—and she sang it timidly, and very low indeed, scarcely audibly, but the *sweetness* of her voice was simply indescribable; I have never heard any earthly music like it.

> "*'Tis a secret, and so let us whisper it low—*
> *And the name of the secret is Love!*"

On me the first effect of her voice was a sudden sharp pang that seemed to pierce through one's very heart. (I had felt such a pang only once before in my life, and it had been from *seeing* what, at the moment, realized one's idea of perfect beauty—it was in a London exhibition, where, in making my way through a crowd, I suddenly met, face to face, a child of quite unearthly beauty.) Then came a rush of burning tears to the eyes, as though one could weep one's soul away for pure delight. And lastly there fell on me a sense of awe that was almost terror— some such feeling as Moses must have had when he heard the words *"Put off thy shoes from off thy feet, for the place whereon thou standest is holy ground"*. The figures of the children became vague and shadowy, like glimmering meteors: while their voices rang together in exquisite harmony as they sang:

> *"For I think it is Love,*
> *For I feel it is Love,*
> *For I'm sure it is nothing but Love!"*

By this time I could see them clearly once more. Bruno again sang by himself:

> *"Say, whence is the voice that, when anger is burning,*
> *Bids the whirl of the tempest to cease?*
> *That stirs the vexed soul with an aching—a yearning*
> *For the brotherly hand-grip of peace?*
> *Whence the music that fills all our being—that thrills*
> *Around us, beneath, and above?"*

Sylvie sang more courageously, this time: the words seemed to carry her away, out of herself:

> *" 'Tis a secret: none knows how it comes, how it goes:*
> *But the name of the secret is Love!"*

And clear and strong the chorus rang out:

> *"For I think it is Love,*
> *For I feel it is Love,*
> *For I'm sure it is nothing but Love!"*

Once more we heard Bruno's delicate little voice alone:

"Say whose is the skill that paints valley and hill,
Like a picture so fair to the sight?
That flecks the green meadow with sunshine and shadow,
Till the little lambs leap with delight?"

And again uprose that silvery voice, whose angelic sweetness I could hardly bear:

" 'Tis a secret untold to hearts cruel and cold,
Though 'tis sung, by the angels above,
In notes that ring clear for the ears that can hear—
And the name of the secret is Love!"

And then Bruno joined in again with

"For I think it is Love,
For I feel it is Love,
For I'm sure it is nothing but Love!"

"That *are* pretty!" the little fellow exclaimed, as the children passed us—so closely that we drew back a little to make room for them, and it seemed we had only to reach out a hand to touch them: but this we did not attempt.

"No use to try and stop them!" I said, as they passed away into the shadows. "Why, they could not even *see* us!"

"No use at all," Lady Muriel echoed with a sigh. "One would *like* to meet them again, in living form! But I feel, somehow, *that* can never be. They have passed out of *our* lives!" She sighed again; and no more was said, till we came out into the main road, at a point near my lodgings.

"Well, I will leave you here," she said. "I want to get back before dark: and I have a cottage-friend to visit, first. Good night, dear friend! Let us see you soon—and often!" she added, with an affectionate warmth that went to my very heart. *"For those are few we hold as dear!"*

"Good night!" I answered. "Tennyson said that of a worthier friend than me."

"Tennyson didn't know what he was talking about!" she saucily rejoined, with a touch of her old childish gaiety, and we parted.

CHAPTER XX

Gammon and Spinach

M Y landlady's welcome had an extra heartiness about it: and though, with a rare delicacy of feeling, she made no direct allusion to the friend whose companionship had done so much to brighten life for me, I felt sure that it was a kindly sympathy with my solitary state that made her so specially anxious to do all she could think of to ensure my comfort, and make me feel at home.

The lonely evening seemed long and tedious: yet I lingered on, watching the dying fire, and letting Fancy mould the red embers into the forms and faces belonging to bygone scenes. Now it seemed to be Bruno's roguish smile that sparkled for a moment, and died away: now it was Sylvie's rosy cheek: and now the Professor's jolly round face, beaming with delight. "You're welcome, my little ones!" he seemed to say. And then the red coal, which for the moment embodied the dear old Professor, began to wax dim, and with its dying lustre the words seemed to die away into silence. I seized the poker, and with an artful touch or two revived the waning glow, while Fancy—no coy minstrel she—sang me once again the magic strain I loved to hear.

"You're welcome, little ones!" the cheery voice repeated. "I told them you were coming. Your rooms are all ready for you. And the Emperor and the Empress— well, I think they're rather pleased than otherwise! In fact, Her Highness said 'I hope they'll be in time for the Banquet!' Those were her very words, I assure you!"

"Will Uggug be at the Banquet?" Bruno asked. And both children looked uneasy at the dismal suggestion.

"Why, of course he will!" chuckled the Professor. "Why, it's his *birthday*, don't you know? And his health will be drunk, and all that sort of thing. What would the Banquet be without *him*?"

"Ever so much nicer," said Bruno. But he said it in a *very* low voice, and nobody but Sylvie heard him.

The Professor chuckled again. "It'll be a jolly Banquet, now *you've* come, my little man! I *am* so glad to see you again!"

"I 'fraid we've been very long in coming," Bruno politely remarked.

"Well, yes," the Professor assented. "However, you're very short, now you're come: that's *some* comfort." And he went on to enumerate the plans for the day. "The Lecture comes first," he said. "*That* the Empress *insists* on. She says people will eat so much at the Banquet, they'll be too sleepy to attend to the Lecture afterwards— and perhaps she's right. There'll just be a little *refreshment*, when the people first arrive—as a kind of surprise for the Empress, you know. Ever since she's been—well, not *quite so* clever as she once was—we've found it desirable to concoct little surprises for her. *Then* comes the Lecture——"

"What? The Lecture you were getting ready—ever so long ago?" Sylvie enquired.

"Yes—that's the one," the Professor rather reluctantly admitted. "It *has* taken a goodish time to prepare. I've got so many other things to attend to. For instance, I'm Court-Physician. I have to keep all the Royal Servants in good health—and that reminds me!" he cried, ringing the bell in a great hurry. "This is Medicine-Day! We only give Medicine once a week. If we were to begin giving it every day, the bottles would *soon* be empty!"

"But if they were ill on the *other* days?" Sylvie suggested.

"What, ill on the wrong *day*!" exclaimed the Professor.

"Oh, that would never do! A Servant would be dismissed *at once*, who was ill on the wrong day! This is the Medicine for *to-day*," he went on, taking down a large jug from a shelf. "I mixed it, myself, first thing this morning. Taste it!" he said, holding out the jug to Bruno. "Dip in your finger, and taste it!"

Bruno did so, and made such an excruciatingly wry face that Sylvie exclaimed in alarm, "Oh, Bruno, you mustn't!"

"It's welly extremely nasty!" Bruno said, as his face resumed its natural shape.

"Nasty?" said the Professor. "Why, of *course* it is! What would Medicine be, if it wasn't *nasty*?"

"Nice," said Bruno.

"I was going to say—" the Professor faltered, rather taken aback by the promptness of Bruno's reply, "—that *that* would never do! Medicine *has* to be nasty, you know. Be good enough to take this jug, down into the Servants' Hall," he said to the footman who answered the bell: "and tell them it's their Medicine for *to-day*."

"Which of them is to drink it?" the footman asked, as he carried off the jug.

"Oh, I've not settled *that* yet!" the Professor briskly replied. "I'll come and settle that, soon. Tell them not to begin, on any account, till I come! It's really *wonderful*", he said, turning to the children, "the success I've had in curing Diseases! Here are some of my memoranda." He took down from the shelf a heap of little bits of paper, pinned together in twos and threes. "Just look at *this* set, now. '*Under-Cook Number Thirteen recovered from Common Fever—Febris Communis*.' And now see what's pinned to it. '*Gave Under-Cook Number Thirteen a Double Dose of Medicine.' That's* something to be proud of, *isn't* it?"

"But which happened *first*?" said Sylvie, looking very much puzzled.

The Professor examined the papers carefully. "They are not *dated*, I find," he said with a slightly dejected air: "so I fear I ca'n't tell you. But they *both* happened: there's no doubt of *that*. The *Medicine's* the great thing, you know. The *Diseases* are much less important. You can keep a *Medicine*, for years and years: but nobody ever wants to keep a *Disease*! By the way, come and look at the platform. The Gardener asked me to come and see if it would do. We may as well go before it gets dark."

"We'd like to, very much!" Sylvie replied. "Come, Bruno, put on your hat. Don't keep the dear Professor waiting!"

"Ca'n't find my hat!" the little fellow sadly replied. "I were rolling it about. And it's rolled itself away!"

"Maybe it's rolled in *there*," Sylvie suggested, pointing to a dark recess, the door of which stood half open: and Bruno ran in to look. After a minute he came slowly out again, looking very grave, and carefully shut the cupboard door after him.

"It aren't in there," he said, with such unusual solemnity, that Sylvie's curiosity was aroused.

"What *is* in there, Bruno?"

"There's cobwebs—and two spiders—" Bruno thoughtfully replied, checking off the catalogue on his fingers, "—and the cover of a picture-book—and a tortoise—and a dish of nuts—and an old man."

"An old man!" cried the Professor, trotting across the room in great excitement. "Why, it must be the Other Professor, that's been lost for ever so long!"

He opened the door of the cupboard wide: and there he was, the Other Professor, sitting in a chair, with a book on his knee, and in the act of helping himself to a nut from a dish, which he had taken down off a shelf just within his reach. He looked round at us, but said nothing till he had cracked and eaten the nut. Then he asked the old question. "Is the Lecture all ready?"

"It'll begin in an hour," the Professor said, evading the question. "First, we must have something to surprise the Empress. And then comes the Banquet——"

"The Banquet!" cried the Other Professor, springing up, and filling the room with a cloud of dust. Then I'd better go and—and brush myself a little. What a state I'm in!"

"He *does* want brushing!" the Professor said, with a critical air. "Here's your hat, little man! I had put it on by mistake. I'd quite forgotten I had *one* on, already. Let's go and look at the platform."

"And there's that nice old Gardener singing still!" Bruno exclaimed in delight, as we went out into the garden. "I do believe he's been singing that very song ever since we went away!"

"Why, of course he has!" replied the Professor. "It wouldn't be the thing to leave off, you know."

"Wouldn't be *what* thing?" said Bruno: but the Professor thought it best not to hear the question. "What are you doing with that hedgehog?" he shouted at the Gardener, whom they found standing upon one foot, singing softly to himself, and rolling a hedgehog up and down with the other foot.

"Well, I wanted fur to know what hedgehogs lives on: so I be a-keeping this here hedgehog—fur to see if it eats potatoes——"

"Much better keep a potato," said the Professor; "and see if hedgehogs eat it!"

"That be the roight way, sure-ly!" the delighted Gardener exclaimed. "Be you come to see the platform?"

"Aye, aye!" the Professor cheerily replied. "And the children have come back, you see!"

The Gardener looked round at them with a grin. Then he led the way to the Pavilion; and as he went he sang:

> "*He looked again, and found it was*
> *A Double Rule of Three:*
> '*And all its Mystery*', *he said,*
> '*Is clear as day to me!*' "

"You've been *months* over that song," said the Professor. "Isn't it finished yet?"

"There be only one verse more," the Gardener sadly replied. And, with tears streaming down his cheeks, he sang the last verse:

> *"He thought he saw an Argument*
> *That proved he was the Pope:*
> *He looked again, and found it was*
> *A Bar of Mottled Soap.*
> *'A fact so dread', he faintly said,*
> *'Extinguishes all hope!'"*

Choking with sobs, the Gardener hastily stepped on a few yards ahead of the party, to conceal his emotion.

"Did *he* see the Bar of Mottled Soap?" Sylvie enquired, as we followed.

"Oh, certainly!" said the Professor. "That song is his own history, you know."

Tears of an ever-ready sympathy glittered in Bruno's eyes. "I's *welly* sorry he isn't the Pope!" he said. "Aren't *you* sorry, Sylvie?"

"Well—I hardly know," Sylvie replied in the vaguest manner. "Would it make him any happier?" she asked the Professor.

"It wouldn't make the *Pope* any happier," said the Professor. "Isn't the platform *lovely*?" he asked, as we entered the Pavilion.

"I've put an extra beam under it!" said the Gardener, patting it affectionately as he spoke. "And now it's that strong, as—as a mad elephant might dance upon it!"

"Thank you *very* much!" the Professor heartily rejoined. "I don't know that we shall exactly require—but it's convenient to know." And he led the children upon the platform, to explain the arrangements to them. "Here are three seats, you see, for the Emperor and the Empress and Prince Uggug. But there must be two more chairs here!" he said, looking down at the Gardener. "One for Lady Sylvie, and one for the smaller animal!"

"And may I help in the Lecture?" said Bruno. "I can do some conjuring tricks."

"Well, it's not exactly a *conjuring* lecture," the Professor said, as he arranged some curious-looking machines on the table. "However, what can you do? Did you ever go through a table, for instance?"

"Often!" said Bruno. "*Haven't* I, Sylvie?"

The Professor was evidently surprised, though he tried not to show it. "This must be looked into," he muttered to himself, taking out a note-book. "And first—what kind of table?"

"Tell him!" Bruno whispered to Sylvie, putting his arms round her neck.

"Tell him yourself," said Sylvie.

"Ca'n't," said Bruno. "It's a *bony* word."

"Nonsense!" laughed Sylvie. "You can say it well enough, if you only try. Come!"

"Muddle——" said Bruno. "That's a bit of it."

"*What* does he say?" cried the bewildered Professor.

"He means the multiplication-table," Sylvie explained.

The Professor looked annoyed, and shut up his note-book again. "Oh, that's *quite* another thing," he said.

"It are ever so many other things," said Bruno. "*Aren't* it, Sylvie?"

A loud blast of trumpets interrupted this conversation. "Why, the entertainment has *begun*!" the Professor exclaimed, as he hurried the children into the Reception-Saloon. "I had no idea it was so late!"

A small table, containing cake and wine, stood in a corner of the Saloon; and here we found the Emperor and Empress waiting for us. The rest of the Saloon had been cleared of furniture, to make room for the guests. I was much struck by the great change a few months had made in the faces of the Imperial Pair. A vacant stare was now the *Emperor's* usual expression; while over the face of the *Empress* there flitted, ever and anon, a meaningless smile.

"So you're come at last!" the Emperor sulkily remarked, as the Professor and the children took their places. It was evident that he was *very* much out of temper: and we were not long in learning the cause of this. He did not consider the preparations, made for the Imperial party, to be such as suited their rank. "A common mahogany table!" he growled, pointing to it contemptuously with his thumb. "Why wasn't it made of gold, I should like to know?"

"It would have taken a very long——" the Professor began, but the Emperor cut the sentence short.

"Then the cake! Ordinary plum! Why wasn't it made of—of——" He broke off again. "Then the wine! Merely old Madeira! Why wasn't it——? Then this chair! That's worst of all. Why wasn't it a throne? One *might* excuse the other omissions, but I *ca'n't* get over the chair!"

"What *I* ca'n't get over", said the Empress, in eager sympathy with her angry husband, "is the *table!*"

"Pooh!" said the Emperor.

"It is much to be regretted!" the Professor mildly replied, as soon as he had a chance of speaking. After a moment's thought he strengthened the remark. *"Everything"*, he said, addressing Society in general, "is *very much* to be regretted!"

A murmur of "Hear, hear!" rose from the crowded Saloon.

There was a rather awkward pause: the Professor evidently didn't know how to begin. The Empress leant forwards, and whispered to him. "A few jokes, you know, Professor—just to put people at their ease!"

"True, true, Madam!" the Professor meekly replied. "This little boy——"

"Please don't make any jokes about me!" Bruno exclaimed, his eyes filling with tears.

"I wo'n't if you'd rather I didn't," said the kind-hearted Professor. "It was only something about a Ship's Buoy: a harmless pun—but it doesn't matter." Here he turned to the crowd and addressed them in a loud voice. "Learn your A's!" he shouted. "Your B's! Your C's! and your D's! *Then* you'll be at your ease!"

There was a roar of laughter from all the assembly,

and then a great deal of confused whispering. "*What* was it he said? Something about bees, I fancy——"

The Empress smiled in her meaningless way, and fanned herself. The poor Professor looked at her timidly: he was clearly at his wits' end again, and hoping for another hint. The Empress whispered again.

"Some spinach, you know, Professor, as a surprise."

The Professor beckoned to the Head-Cook, and said something to him in a low voice. Then the Head-Cook left the room, followed by all the other cooks.

"It's difficult to get things started," the Professor remarked to Bruno. "When once we get started, it'll go on all right, you'll see."

"If oo want to startle people", said Bruno, "oo should put live frogs on their backs."

Here the cooks all came in again, in a procession, the Head-Cook coming last and carrying something, which the others tried to hide by waving flags all round it. "Nothing but flags, Your Imperial Highness! Nothing but flags!" he kept repeating, as he set it before her. Then all the flags were dropped in a moment, as the Head-Cook raised the cover from an enormous dish.

"What is it?" the Empress said faintly, as she put her spy-glass to her eye. "Why, it's *Spinach*, I declare!"

"Her Imperial Highness is surprised," the Professor explained to the attendants: and some of them clapped their hands. The Head-Cook made a low bow, and in doing so dropped a spoon on the table, as if by accident, just within reach of the Empress, who looked the other way and pretended not to see it.

"I *am* surprised!" the Empress said to Bruno. "Aren't you?"

"Not a bit," said Bruno. "I heard——" but Sylvie put her hand over his mouth, and spoke for him. "He's rather tired, I think. He wants the Lecture to begin."

"I want the *supper* to begin," Bruno corrected her.

The Empress took up the spoon in an absent manner, and tried to balance it across the back of her hand, and in doing this she dropped it into the dish: and, when she took it out again, it was full of spinach. "How curious!" she said, and put it into her mouth. "It tastes just like *real* spinach! I thought it was an imitation—but I do believe it's real!" And she took another spoonful.

"It wo'n't be real much longer," said Bruno.

But the Empress had had enough spinach by this time, and somehow—I failed to notice the exact process—we all found ourselves in the Pavilion, and the Professor in the act of beginning the long-expected Lecture.

CHAPTER XXI

The Professor's Lecture

"IN Science—in fact, in most things—it is usually best *to begin at the beginning*. In *some* things, of course, it's better to begin at the *other* end. For instance, if you wanted to paint a dog green, it *might* be best to begin with the *tail*, as it doesn't bite at *that* end. And so——"

"May *I* help oo?" Bruno interrupted.

"Help me to do *what*?" said the puzzled Professor, looking up for a moment, but keeping his finger on the book he was reading from, so as not to lose his place.

"To paint a dog green!" cried Bruno. "Oo can begin wiz its *mouf*, and I'll——"

"No, no!" said the Professor. "We haven't got to the *Experiments* yet. And so", returning to his note-book, "I'll give you the Axioms of Science. After that I shall exhibit some Specimens. Then I shall explain a Process or two. And I shall conclude with a few Experiments. An *Axiom*, you know, is a thing that you accept without contradiction. For instance, if I were to say 'Here we are!', that would be accepted without any contradiction, and it's a nice sort of remark to *begin* a conversation with. So it would be an *Axiom*. Or again, supposing I were to say, 'Here we are not!', *that* would be——"

"—a fib!" cried Bruno.

"Oh, *Bruno!*" said Sylvie in a warning whisper. "Of course it would be an *Axiom*, if the Professor said it!"

"—that would be accepted, if people were civil," continued the Professor; "so it would be *another* Axiom."

"It *might* be an Axledum," Bruno said: "but it wouldn't be *true!*"

"Ignorance of Axioms", the Lecturer continued, "is a great drawback in life. It wastes so much time to have to say them over and over again. For instance, take the Axiom, '*Nothing is greater than itself*'; that is, '*Nothing can contain itself.*' How often you hear people say 'He was so excited, he was quite unable to contain himself.' Why, *of course* he was unable! The *excitement* had nothing to do with it!"

"I say, look here, you know!" said the Emperor, who was getting a little restless. "How many Axioms are you going to give us? At *this* rate, we sha'n't get to the *Experiments* till to-morrow-week!"

"Oh, sooner than *that*, I assure you!" the Professor replied, looking up in alarm. "There are only," (he referred to his notes again) "only *two* more, that are really *necessary.*"

"Read 'em out, and get on to the *Specimens*," grumbled the Emperor.

"The *First* Axiom", the Professor read out in a great hurry, "consists of these words, '*Whatever is, is.*' And the Second consists of *these* words, '*Whatever isn't, isn't.*' We will now go on to the *Specimens*. The first tray contains Crystals and other Things." He drew it towards him, and again referred to his notebook. "Some of the labels —owing to insufficient adhesion——" Here he stopped again, and carefully examined the page with his eye-glass. "I ca'n't read the rest of the sentence," he said at last, "but it *means* that the labels have come loose, and the Things have got mixed——"

"Let *me* stick 'em on again!" cried Bruno eagerly, and began licking them, like postage-stamps, and dabbing them down upon the *Crystals* and the other Things. But the Professor hastily moved the tray out of his reach. "They *might* get fixed to the *wrong* Specimens, you know!" he said.

"Oo shouldn't have any *wrong* peppermints in the tray!" Bruno boldly replied. "*Should* he, Sylvie?"

But Sylvie only shook her head.

The Professor heard him not. He had taken up one of the bottles, and was carefully reading the label through his eye-glass. "Our first Specimen———" he announced, as he placed the bottle in front of the other Things, "is— that is, it is called———" here he took it up, and examined the label again, as if he thought it might have changed since he last saw it, "is called Aqua Pura—common water—the fluid that cheers—"

"Hip! Hip! Hip!" the Head-Cook began enthusiastically.

"—but *not* inebriates!" the Professor went on quickly, but only just in time to check the "Hooroar!" which was beginning.

"Our second Specimen", he went on, carefully opening a small jar, "is—" here he removed the lid, and a large beetle instantly darted out, and with an angry buzz went straight out of the Pavilion, "—is—or rather, I should say," looking sadly into the empty jar, "it *was*— a curious kind of Blue Beetle. Did anyone happen to re-mark—as it went past—three blue spots under each wing?"

Nobody had remarked them.

"Ah, well!" the Professor said with a sigh. "It's a pity. Unless you remark that kind of thing *at the moment*, it's very apt to get overlooked! The *next* Specimen, at any rate, will not fly away! It is—in short, or perhaps, more correctly, at *length*—an *Elephant*. You will observe———" Here he beckoned to the Gardener to come up on the platform, and with his help began putting together what looked like an enormous dog-kennel, with short tubes projecting out of it on both sides.

"But we've seen *Elephants* before," the Emperor grumbled.

"Yes, but not through a *Megaloscope*!" the Professor eagerly replied. "You know you ca'n't see a *Flea*, properly, without a *magnifying*-glass—what we call a *Microscope*. Well, just in the same way, you ca'n't see an *Elephant*, properly without a *minimifying*-glass. There's one in each of these little tubes. And *this* is a *Megaloscope*! The Gardener will now bring in the next Specimen. Please open *both* curtains, down at the end there, and make way for the Elephant!"

There was a general rush to the sides of the Pavilion, and all eyes were turned to the open end, watching for the return of the Gardener, who had gone away singing *"He thought he saw an Elephant That practised on a Fife!"* There was silence for a minute: and then his harsh voice was heard again in the distance. *"He looked again*—come up then! *He looked again, and found it was*—woa back! *and found it was A letter from his*—make way there! He's a-coming!"

And in marched or waddled—it is hard to say which is the right word—an Elephant, on its hind-legs, and playing on an enormous fife which it held with its fore-feet.

The Professor hastily threw open a large door at the end of the Megaloscope, and the huge animal, at a signal from the Gardener, dropped the fife, and obediently trotted into the machine, the door of which was at once shut by the Professor. "The Specimen is now ready for observation!" he proclaimed. "It is exactly the size of the common Mouse—*Mus Communis!*"

There was a general rush to the tubes, and the spectators watched with delight the minikin creature, as it playfully coiled its trunk round the Professor's extended finger, finally taking its stand upon the palm of his hand, while he carefully lifted it out, and carried it off to exhibit to the Imperial party.

"Isn't it a *darling*?" cried Bruno. "May I stroke it, please? I'll touch it *welly* gently!"

The Empress inspected it solemnly with her eye-glass. "It is very small," she said in a deep voice. "Smaller than elephants usually are, I believe?"

The Professor gave a start of delighted surprise. "Why, that's *true!*" he murmured to himself. Then louder, turning to the audience, "Her Imperial Highness has made a remark which is perfectly sensible!" And a wild cheer arose from that vast multitude.

"The next Specimen", the Professor proclaimed, after carefully placing the little elephant in the tray, among the Crystals and other things, "is a *Flea*, which we will enlarge for the purposes of observation." Taking a small pill-box from the tray, he advanced to the Megaloscope, and reversed all the tubes. "The Specimen is ready!" he cried, with his eye at one of the tubes, while he carefully emptied the pill-box through a little hole at the side. "It is now the size of the Common Horse—*Equus Communis!*"

There was another general rush, to look through the tubes, and the Pavilion rang with shouts of delight, through which the Professor's anxious tones could scarcely be heard. "Keep the door of the Microscope *shut!*" he cried. "If the creature were to escape, *this size*, it would——" But the mischief was done. The door had swung open, and in another moment the Monster had got out, and was trampling down the terrified, shrieking spectators.

But the Professor's presence of mind did not desert him. "Undraw those curtains!" he shouted. It was done. The Monster gathered its legs together, and in one tremendous bound vanished into the sky.

"Where *is* it?" said the Emperor, rubbing his eyes.

"In the next Province, I fancy," the Professor replied. "That jump would take it at *least* five miles! The next thing is to explain a Process or two. But I find there is hardly room enough to operate—the smaller animal is rather in my way——"

"Who does he mean?" Bruno whispered to Sylvie.

"He means *you!*" Sylvie whispered back. "Hush!"

"Be kind enough to move—angularly—to *this* corner," the Professor said, addressing himself to Bruno.

Bruno hastily moved his chair in the direction indicated. "Did I move angrily enough?" he inquired. But the Professor was once more absorbed in his Lecture, which he was reading from his note-book.

"I will now explain the process of—the name is blotted, I'm sorry to say. It will be illustrated by a number of—of——" here he examined the pages for some time, and at last said "It seems to be either 'Experiments' or 'Specimens'——"

"Let it be *Experiments*," said the Emperor. "We've seen plenty of *Specimens*."

"Certainly, certainly!" the Professor assented. "We will have some Experiments."

"May *I* do them?" Bruno eagerly asked.

"Oh dear no!" The Professor looked dismayed. "I really don't know what would happen if *you* did them!"

"Nor nobody doosn't know what'll happen if *oo* doos them!" Bruno retorted.

"Our First Experiment requires a Machine. It has two knobs—only *two*—you can count them, if you like."

The Head-Cook stepped forwards, counted them, and retired satisfied.

"Now you *might* press those two knobs together—but that's not the way to do it. Or you *might* turn the Machine upside-down—but *that's* not the way to do it!"

"What *are* the way to do it?" said Bruno, who was listening very attentively.

The Professor smiled benignantly. "Ah, yes!" he said, in a voice like the heading of a chapter. "The Way To Do It! Permit me!" and in a moment he had whisked Bruno upon the table. "I divide my subject", he began, "into three parts——"

"I think I'll get down!" Bruno whispered to Sylvie. "It aren't nice to be divided!"

"He hasn't got a knife, silly boy!" Sylvie whispered in reply. "Stand still! You'll break all the bottles!"

"The first part is to take hold of the knobs," putting them into Bruno's hands. "The second part is——" Here he turned the handle, and, with a loud "Oh!", Bruno dropped both the knobs, and began rubbing his elbows.

The Professor chuckled in delight. "It had a sensible effect. *Hadn't* it?" he enquired.

"No, it hadn't a *sensible* effect!" Bruno said indignantly. "It were very silly indeed. It jingled my elbows, and it banged my back, and it crinkled my hair, and it buzzed among my bones!"

"I'm sure it *didn't*!" said Sylvie. "You're only inventing!"

"Oo doesn't know nuffin about it!" Bruno replied. "Oo wasn't there to see. Nobody ca'n't go among my bones. There isn't room!"

"Our Second Experiment", the Professor announced, as Bruno returned to his place, still thoughtfully rubbing his elbows, "is the production of that seldom-seen-but-greatly-to-be-admired phenomenon, Black Light! You have seen White Light, Red Light, Green Light, and so on: but never, till this wonderful day, have any eyes but mine seen *Black Light*! This box", carefully lifting it upon the table, and covering it with a heap of blankets, "is quite full of it. The way I made it was this—I took a lighted candle into a dark cupboard and shut the door. Of course the cupboard was then full of *Yellow* Light. Then I took a bottle of Black ink, and poured it over the candle: and, to my delight, every atom of the Yellow Light turned *Black*! That was indeed the proudest moment of my life! Then I filled a box with it. And now —would anyone like to get under the blankets and see it?"

Dead silence followed this appeal: but at last Bruno said *"I'll* get under, if it won't jingle my elbows."

Satisfied on this point, Bruno crawled under the blankets, and, after a minute or two, crawled out again, very hot and dusty, and with his hair in the wildest confusion.

"What did you see in the box?" Sylvie eagerly enquired.

"I saw *nuffin*!" Bruno sadly replied. "It were too dark!"

"He has described the appearance of the thing exactly!" the Professor exclaimed with enthusiasm. "Black Light, and Nothing, look so extremely alike, at first sight, that I don't wonder he failed to distinguish them! We will now proceed to the Third Experiment."

The Professor came down, and led the way to where a post had been driven firmly into the ground. To one side of the post was fastened a chain, with an iron weight hooked on to the end of it, and from the other side projected a piece of whalebone, with a ring at the end of it. "This is a *most* interesting Experiment!" the Professor announced. "It will need *time*, I'm afraid: but that is a trifling disadvantage. Now observe. If I were to unhook this weight, and let go, it would fall to the ground. You do not deny *that*?"

Nobody denied it.

"And in the same way, if I were to bend this piece of whalebone round the post—thus—and put the ring over this hook—thus—it stays bent: but, if I unhook it, it straightens itself again. You do not deny *that*?"

Again, nobody denied it.

"Well, now, suppose we left things just as they are, for a long time. The force of the *whalebone* would get exhausted, you know, and it would stay bent, even when you unhooked it. Now, *why* shouldn't the same thing happen with the *weight*? The *whalebone* gets so used to being bent, that it ca'n't *straighten* itself any more. Why shouldn't the *weight* get so used to being held up, that it ca'n't *fall* any more? That's what *I* want to know!"

"That's what *we* want to know!" echoed the crowd.

"How long must we wait?" grumbled the Emperor.

The Professor looked at his watch. "Well, I *think* a thousand years will do to *begin* with," he said. "Then we will cautiously unhook the weight: and, if it *still* shows (as perhaps it will) a *slight* tendency to fall, we will hook it on to the chain again, and leave it for *another* thousand years."

Here the Empress experienced one of those flashes of Common Sense which were the surprise of all around her. "Meanwhile there'll be time for another Experiment," she said.

"There will *indeed*!" cried the delighted Professor. "Let us return to the platform, and proceed to the *Fourth* Experiment!"

"For this concluding Experiment, I will take a certain Alkali, or Acid—I forget which. Now you'll see what will happen when I mix it with Some—" here he took up a bottle, and looked at it doubtfully, "—when I mix it with—with Something——"

Here the Emperor interrupted. "What's the *name* of the stuff?" he asked.

"I don't remember the *name*," said the Professor: "and the label has come off." He emptied it quickly into the other bottle, and, with a tremendous bang, both bottles flew to pieces, upsetting all the machines, and filling the Pavilion with thick black smoke. I sprang to my feet in terror, and—and found myself standing before my solitary hearth, where the poker, dropping at last from the hand of the sleeper, had knocked over the tongs and the shovel, and had upset the kettle, filling the air with clouds of steam. With a weary sigh, I betook myself to bed.

Chapter XXII

The Banquet

"*Heaviness may endure for a night: but joy cometh in the morning.*" The next day found me quite another being. Even the memories of my lost friend and companion were sunny as the genial weather that smiled around me. I did not venture to trouble Lady Muriel, or her father, with another call so soon: but took a walk into the country, and only turned homewards when the low sunbeams warned me that day would soon be over.

On my way home, I passed the cottage where the old man lived, whose face always recalled to me the day when I first met Lady Muriel; and I glanced in as I passed, half-curious to see if he were still living there.

Yes: the old man was still alive. He was sitting out in the porch, looking just as he did when I first saw him at Fayfield Junction—it seemed only a few days ago!

"Good evening!" I said, pausing.

"Good evening, Maister!" he cheerfully responded. "Wo'n't ee step in?"

I stepped in, and took a seat on the bench in the porch. "I'm glad to see you looking so hearty," I began. "Last time, I remember, I chanced to pass just as Lady Muriel was coming away from the house. Does she still come to see you?"

"Ees," he answered slowly. "She has na forgotten me. I don't lose her bonny face for many days together. Well I mind the very first time she come, after we'd met at Railway Station. She told me as she come to mak' amends. Dear child! Only think o' that! To mak' amends!"

"To make amends for what?" I enquired. "What could *she* have done to need it?"

"Well, it were loike this, you see? We were both on us a-waiting fur t' train at t' Junction. And I had setten mysen down upat t' bench. And Station-Maister, *he* comes and he orders me off—fur t' mak' room for her Ladyship, you understand?"

"I remember it all," I said. "I was there myself, that day."

"*Was* you, now? Well, an' she axes my pardon fur 't. Think o' that, now! *My* pardon! An owd ne'er-do-weel like me! Ah! She's been here many a time, sin' then.

Why, she were in here only yestere'en, as it were, a-sittin',
as it might be, where you're a-sitting now, an' lookin'
sweeter and kinder nor an angel! An' she says 'You've
not got your Minnie, now,' she says, 'to fettle for ye.'
Minnie was my grand-daughter, Sir, as lived wi' me.
She died, a matter of two months ago—or it may be three.
She was a bonny lass—and a good lass, too. Eh, but life
has been rare an' lonely without her!''

He covered his face in his hands: and I waited a minute
or two, in silence, for him to recover himself.

"So she says, 'Just tak' *me* fur your Minnie!' she says.
'Didna Minnie mak' your tea fur you?' says she. 'Ay,'
says I. An' she mak's the tea. 'An' didna Minnie light
your pipe?' says she. 'Ay,' says I. An' she lights the pipe
for me. 'An' didna Minnie set out your tea in t' porch?'
An' I says 'My dear,' I says, 'I'm thinking you're Minnie
hersen!' An' she cries a bit. We both on us cries a bit——''

Again I kept silence for a while.

"An' while I smokes my pipe, she sits an' talks to me—
as loving an' as pleasant! I'll be bound I thowt it were
Minnie come again! An' when she gets up to go, I says
'Winnot ye shak' hands wi' me?' says I. An' she says
'Na,' she says: 'a cannot *shak' hands* wi' thee!'' she says.''

"I'm sorry she said *that*," I put in, thinking it was the
only instance I had ever known of pride of rank showing
itself in Lady Muriel.

"Bless you, it werena *pride!*'' said the old man, reading
my thoughts. "She says '*Your* Minnie never *shook hands*
wi' you!' she says. 'An' *I'm* your Minnie now,' she says.
An' she just puts her dear arms about my neck—and she
kisses me on t' cheek—an' may God in Heaven bless
her!'' And here the poor old man broke down entirely,
and could say no more.

"God bless her!'' I echoed. "And good night to you!''
I pressed his hand, and left him. "Lady Muriel,'' I said
softly to myself as I went homewards, "truly you know
how to 'mak' amends'!''

Seated once more by my lonely fireside, I tried to recall

the strange vision of the night before, and to conjure up the face of the dear old Professor among the blazing coals. "That black one—with just a touch of red—would suit him well," I thought. "After such a catastrophe, it would be sure to be covered with black stains—and he would say:

"The result of *that* combination—you may have noticed?—was an *Explosion*! Shall I repeat the Experiment?"

"No, no! Don't trouble yourself!" was the general cry. And we all trooped off, in hot haste, to the Banqueting-Hall, where the feast had already begun.

No time was lost in helping the dishes, and very speedily every guest found his plate filled with good things.

"I have always maintained the principle," the Professor began, "that it is a good rule to take some food—occasionally. The great advantage of dinner-parties——" he broke off suddenly. "Why, actually here's the Other Professor!" he cried. "And there's no place left for him!"

The Other Professor came in reading a large book, which he held close to his eyes. One result of his not looking where he was going was that he tripped up, as he crossed the Saloon, flew up into the air, and fell heavily on his face in the middle of the table.

"*What* a pity!" cried the kind-hearted Professor, as he helped him up.

"It wouldn't be *me*, if I didn't trip," said the Other Professor.

The Professor looked much shocked. "Almost *anything* would be better than *that*!" he exclaimed. "It never does", he added, aside to Bruno, "to be anybody else, does it?"

To which Bruno gravely replied "I's got nuffin on my plate."

The Professor hastily put on his spectacles, to make sure that the *facts* were all right, to begin with: then he turned his jolly round face upon the unfortunate owner of the empty plate. "And what would you like next, my little man?"

"Well," Bruno said, a little doubtfully, "I think I'll take some plum-pudding, please—while I think of it."

"Oh, Bruno!" (This was a whisper from Sylvie.) "It isn't good manners to ask for a dish before it comes!"

And Bruno whispered back "But I might forget to ask for some, when it comes, oo know—I *do* forget things, sometimes," he added, seeing Sylvie about to whisper more.

And *this* assertion Sylvie did not venture to contradict.

Meanwhile a chair had been placed for the Other Professor, between the Empress and Sylvie. Sylvie found him a rather uninteresting neighbour: in fact, she couldn't afterwards remember that he had made more than *one* remark to her during the whole banquet, and that was "What a comfort a Dictionary is!" (She told Bruno, afterwards, that she had been too much afraid of him to say more than "Yes, Sir" in reply: and that had been the end of their conversation. On which Bruno expressed a very decided opinion that *that* wasn't worth calling a "conversation" at all. "Oo should have asked him a riddle!" he added triumphantly. "Why, *I* asked the Professor *three* riddles! One was that one you asked me in the morning, 'How many pennies is there in two shillings?' And another was——" "Oh, Bruno!" Sylvie interrupted. "*That* wasn't a riddle!" "It *were*!" Bruno fiercely replied.)

By this time a waiter had supplied Bruno with a plateful of *something*, which drove the plum-pudding out of his head.

"Another advantage of dinner-parties", the Professor cheerfully explained, for the benefit of anyone that would listen, "is that it helps you to *see* your friends. If you want to *see* a man, offer him something to eat. It's the same rule with a mouse."

"This Cat's very kind to the Mouses," Bruno said, stooping to stroke a remarkably fat specimen of the race, that had just waddled into the room, and was rubbing itself affectionately against the leg of his chair. "Please, Sylvie, pour some milk in your saucer. Pussie's ever so thirsty!"

"Why do you want *my* saucer?" said Sylvie. "You've got one yourself!"

"Yes, I know," said Bruno: "but I wanted *mine* for to give it some *more* milk in."

Sylvie looked unconvinced: however it seemed quite impossible for her *ever* to refuse what her brother asked: so she quietly filled her saucer with milk, and handed it to Bruno, who got down off his chair to administer it to the cat.

"The room's very hot, with all this crowd," the Professor said to Sylvie. "I wonder why they don't put some lumps of ice in the grate? You fill it with lumps of coal in the winter, you know, and you sit around it and enjoy the warmth. How jolly it would be to fill it now with lumps of ice, and sit round it and enjoy the coolth!"

Hot as it was, Sylvie shivered a little at the idea. "It's very cold *outside*," she said. "My feet got almost frozen to-day."

"That's the *shoemaker's* fault!" the Professor cheerfully replied. "How often I've explained to him that he *ought* to make boots with little iron frames under the soles, to hold lamps! But he never *thinks*. No one would suffer from cold, if only they would *think* of those little things. I always use hot ink, myself, in the winter. Very few people ever think of *that*! Yet how simple it is!"

"Yes, it's very simple," Sylvie said politely. "Has the cat had enough?" This was to Bruno, who had brought back the saucer only half-emptied.

But Bruno did not hear the question. "There's somebody scratching at the door and wanting to come in," he said. And he scrambled down off his chair, and went and cautiously peeped out through the door-way.

"Who was it wanted to come in?" Sylvie asked, as he returned to his place.

"It were a Mouse," said Bruno. "And it peepted in. And it saw the Cat. And it said 'I'll come in another day.' And I said 'Oo needn't be flightened. The Cat's *welly* kind to Mouses.' And it said 'But I's got some imporkant business, what I *must* attend to.' And it said 'I'll call again to-morrow.' And it said 'Give my love to the Cat.'"

"What a fat cat it is!" said the Lord Chancellor, leaning across the Professor to address his small neighbour. "It's quite a wonder!"

"It was awfully fat when it camed in," said Bruno: "so it would be more wonderfuller if it got thin all in a minute."

"And that was the reason, I suppose," the Lord Chancellor suggested, "why you didn't give it the rest of the milk?"

"No," said Bruno. "It was a betterer reason. I tooked the saucer up 'cause it were so discontented!"

"It doesn't look so to *me*," said the Lord Chancellor. "What made you think it was discontented?"

"'Cause it grumbled in its throat."

"Oh, Bruno!" cried Sylvie. "Why, that's the way cats show they're *pleased*!"

Bruno looked doubtful. "It's not a good way," he objected. "Oo wouldn't say *I* were pleased, if I made that noise in my throat!"

"What a singular boy!" the Lord Chancellor whispered to himself: but Bruno had caught the words.

"What do it mean to say 'a *singular* boy'?" he whispered to Sylvie.

"It means *one* boy," Sylvie whispered in return. "And *plural* means two or three."

"Then I's welly glad I *is* a singular boy!" Bruno said with great emphasis. "It would be *horrid* to be two or three boys! P'raps they wouldn't play with me!"

"Why *should* they?" said the Other Professor, suddenly waking up out of a deep reverie. "They might be asleep, you know."

"Couldn't, if *I* was awake," Bruno said cunningly.

"Oh, but they might indeed!" the Other Professor protested. "Boys don't all go to sleep at once, you know. So these boys—but who are you talking about?"

"He *never* remembers to ask that first!" the Professor whispered to the children.

"Why, the rest of *me*, a-course!" Bruno exclaimed triumphantly. "Supposing I was two or three boys!"

The Other Professor sighed, and seemed to be sinking back into his reverie; but suddenly brightened up again, and addressed the Professor. "There's nothing more to be done *now*, is there?"

"Well, there's the dinner to finish," the Professor said with a bewildered smile: "and the heat to bear. I hope you'll enjoy the dinner—such as it is; and that you wo'n't mind the heat—such as it isn't."

The sentence *sounded* well, but somehow I couldn't quite understand it; and the Other Professor seemed to be no better off. "Such as it isn't *what*?" he peevishly enquired.

"It isn't as hot as it might be," the Professor replied, catching at the first idea that came to hand.

"Ah, I see what you mean *now*!" the Other Professor graciously remarked. "It's very badly expressed, but I quite see it *now*! Thirteen minutes and a half ago," he went on, looking first at Bruno and then at his watch as he spoke, "you said 'this Cat's very kind to the Mouses.' It must be a singular animal!"

"So it *are*," said Bruno, after carefully examining the Cat, to make sure how many there were of it.

"But how do you know it's kind to the Mouses—or, more correctly speaking, the *Mice*?"

" 'Cause it *plays* with the Mouses," said Bruno; "for to amuse them, oo know."

"But that is just what I *don't* know," the Other Professor rejoined. "My belief is, it plays with them to *kill* them!"

"Oh, that's quite a *accident*!" Bruno began, so eagerly, that it was evident he had already propounded this very difficulty to the Cat. "It 'splained all that to me, while it were drinking the milk. It said 'I teaches the Mouses new games: the Mouses likes it ever so much.' It said 'Sometimes little accidents happens: sometimes the Mouses kills theirselves.' It said 'I's always *welly* sorry, when the Mouses kills theirselves.' It said——"

"If it was so *very* sorry," Sylvie said, rather disdainfully, "it wouldn't *eat* the Mouses after they'd killed themselves!"

But this difficulty, also, had evidently not been lost sight of in the exhaustive ethical discussion just concluded. "It said——" (the orator constantly omitted, as superfluous, his own share in the dialogue, and merely gave us the replies of the Cat) "It said 'Dead Mouses *never* objecks to be eaten.' It said 'There's no use wasting good Mouses.' It said 'Wifful——' sumfinoruvver. It said 'And oo may live to say "How much I wiss I had the Mouse that then I frew away!"' It said——"

"It hadn't *time* to say such a lot of things!" Sylvie interrupted indignantly.

"Oo doesn't know how Cats speaks!" Bruno rejoined contemptuously. "Cats speaks *welly* quick!"

Chapter XXIII

The Pig-Tale

By this time the appetites of the guests seemed to be nearly satisfied, and even *Bruno* had the resolution to say, when the Professor offered him a fourth slice of plum-pudding, "I thinks three helpings is enough!"

Suddenly the Professor started as if he had been electrified. "Why, I had nearly forgotten the most important part of the entertainment! The Other Professor is to recite a Tale of a Pig—I mean a Pig-Tale," he corrected himself. "It has Introductory Verses at the beginning, and at the end."

"It ca'n't have Introductory Verses at the *end*, can it?" said Sylvie.

"Wait till you hear it," said the Professor: "then you'll see. I'm not sure it hasn't some in the *middle*, as well." Here he rose to his feet, and there was an instant silence through the Banqueting-Hall: they evidently expected a speech.

"Ladies, and gentlemen," the Professor began, "the Other Professor is so kind as to recite a Poem. The title of it is 'The Pig-Tale'. He never recited it before!" (General cheering among the guests.) "He will never recite it again!" (Frantic excitement, and wild cheering all down the hall, the Professor himself mounting the table in hot haste, to lead the cheering, and waving his spectacles in one hand and a spoon in the other.)

Then the Other Professor got up, and began:

> *Little Birds are dining*
> *Warily and well,*
> *Hid in mossy cell:*
> *Hid, I say, by waiters*
> *Gorgeous in their gaiters—*
> *I've a Tale to tell.*

> *Little Birds are feeding*
> *Justices with jam,*
> *Rich in frizzled ham:*
> *Rich, I say, in oysters*
> *Haunting shady cloisters—*
> *That is what I am.*

> *Little Birds are teaching*
> *Tigresses to smile,*
> *Innocent of guile:*
> *Smile, I say, not smirkle—*
> *Mouth a semicircle,*
> *That's the proper style.*

Little Birds are sleeping
All among the pins,
Where the loser wins:
Where, I say, he sneezes
When and how he pleases—
So the Tale begins.

There was a Pig that sat alone
Beside a ruined Pump:
By day and night he made his moan—
It would have stirred a heart of stone
To see him wring his hoofs and groan,
Because he could not jump.

A certain Camel heard him shout—
A Camel with a hump.
"Oh, is it Grief, or is it Gout?
What is this bellowing about?"
That Pig replied, with quivering snout,
"Because I cannot jump!"

That Camel scanned him, dreamy-eyed.
"Methinks you are too plump.
I never knew a Pig so wide—
That wobbled so from side to side—
Who could, however much he tried,
Do such a thing as jump!

"Yet mark those trees, two miles away,
All clustered in a clump:
If you could trot there twice a day,
Nor ever pause for rest or play,
In the far future—Who can say?—
You may be fit to jump."

That Camel passed, and left him there,
Beside the ruined Pump.
Oh, horrid was that Pig's despair!
His shrieks of anguish filled the air.
He wrung his hoofs, he rent his hair,
Because he could not jump.

There was a Frog that wandered by—
A sleek and shining lump:
Inspected him with fishy eye,
And said "O Pig, what makes you cry?"
And bitter was that Pig's reply,
   "Because I cannot jump!"

That Frog he grinned a grin of glee,
And hit his chest a thump.
"O Pig," he said, "be ruled by me,
And you shall see what you shall see.
This minute, for a trifling fee,
   I'll teach you how to jump!

"You may be faint from many a fall,
And bruised by many a bump:
But, if you persevere through all,
And practise first on something small,
Concluding with a ten-foot wall,
   You'll find that you can jump!"

That Pig looked up with joyful start:
   "Oh Frog, you are a trump!
Your words have healed my inward smart—
Come, name your fee and do your part:
Bring comfort to a broken heart,
   By teaching me to jump!"

"My fee shall be a mutton-chop,
   My goal this ruined Pump.
Observe with what an airy flop
I plant myself upon the top!
Now bend your knees and take a hop,
   For that's the way to jump!"

Uprose that Pig, and rushed, full whack,
   Against the ruined Pump:
Rolled over like an empty sack,
And settled down upon his back,
While all his bones at once went "Crack!"
   It was a fatal jump.

When the Other Professor had recited this Verse, he went across to the fire-place, and put his head up the chimney. In doing this, he lost his balance, and fell head-first into the empty grate, and got so firmly fixed there that it was some time before he could be dragged out again.

Bruno had had time to say "I thought he wanted to see how many peoples was up the chimbley."

And Sylvie had said "*Chimney*—not chimbley."

And Bruno had said "Don't talk 'ubbish!"

All this, while the Other Professor was being extracted.

"You must have blacked your face!" the Empress said anxiously. "Let me send for some soap?"

"Thanks, no," said the Other Professor, keeping his face turned away. "Black's quite a respectable colour. Besides, soap would be no use without water——"

Keeping his back well turned away from the audience, he went on with the Introductory Verses:

> *Little Birds are writing*
> *Interesting books,*
> *To be read by cooks:*
> *Read, I say, not roasted—*
> *Letterpress, when toasted,*
> *Loses its good looks.*

> *Little Birds are playing*
> *Bagpipes on the shore,*
> *Where the tourists snore:*
> *"Thanks!" they cry. "'Tis thrilling!*
> *Take, oh take this shilling!*
> *Let us have no more!"*

> *Little Birds are bathing*
> *Crocodiles in cream,*
> *Like a happy dream:*
> *Like, but not so lasting—*
> *Crocodiles, when fasting,*
> *Are not all they seem!*

That Camel passed, as Day grew dim
  Around the ruined Pump.
"O broken heart! O broken limb!
It needs", that Camel said to him,
"Something more fairy-like and slim,
  To execute a jump!"

That Pig lay still as any stone,
  And could not stir a stump:
Nor ever, if the truth were known,
Was he again observed to moan,
Nor ever wring his hoofs and groan,
  Because he could not jump.

That Frog made no remark, for he
  Was dismal as a dump:
He knew the consequence must be
That he would never get his fee—
And still he sits, in miserie,
  Upon that ruined Pump!

"It's a miserable story!" said Bruno. "It begins miserably, and it ends miserablier. I think I shall cry. Sylvie, please lend me your handkerchief."

"I haven't got it with me," Sylvie whispered.

"Then I wo'n't cry," said Bruno manfully.

"There are more Introductory Verses to come," said the Other Professor, "but I'm hungry." He sat down, cut a large slice of cake, put it on Bruno's plate, and gazed at his own empty plate in astonishment.

"Where did you get that cake?" Sylvie whispered to Bruno.

"He gived it me," said Bruno.

"But you shouldn't ask for things! You *know* you shouldn't!"

"I *didn't* ask," said Bruno, taking a fresh mouthful: "he *gived* it me."

Sylvie considered this for a moment: then she saw her way out of it. "Well, then, ask him to give *me* some!"

"You seem to enjoy that cake?" the Professor remarked.

"Doos that mean 'munch'?" Bruno whispered to Sylvie.

Sylvie nodded. "It means 'to munch' and 'to *like* to munch'."

Bruno smiled at the Professor. "I *doos* enjoy it," he said.

The Other Professor caught the word. "And I hope you're enjoying *yourself*, little Man?" he enquired.

Bruno's look of horror quite startled him. "No, *indeed* I aren't!" he said.

The Other Professor looked thoroughly puzzled. "Well, well!" he said. "Try some cowslip wine!" And he filled a glass and handed it to Bruno. "Drink this, my dear, and you'll be quite another man!"

"Who shall I be?" said Bruno, pausing in the act of putting it to his lips.

"Don't ask so many questions!" Sylvie interposed, anxious to save the poor old man from further bewilderment. "Suppose we get the Professor to tell us a story."

Bruno adopted the idea with enthusiasm. "*Please* do!" he cried eagerly. "Sumfin about tigers—and bumble-bees—and robin-redbreasts, oo knows!"

"Why should you always have *live* things in stories?" said the Professor. "Why don't you have events, or circumstances?"

"Oh, *please* invent a story like that!" cried Bruno.

The Professor began fluently enough. "Once a coincidence was taking a walk with a little accident, and they met an explanation—a *very* old explanation—so old that it was quite doubled up, and looked more like a conundrum——" he broke off suddenly.

"*Please* go on!" both children exclaimed.

The Professor made a candid confession. "It's a very difficult sort to invent, I find. Suppose Bruno tells one, first."

Bruno was only too happy to adopt the suggestion.

"Once there were a Pig, and a Accordion, and two jars of Orange-marmalade——"

"The *dramatis personæ*," murmured the Professor. "Well, what then?"

"So, when the Pig played on the Accordion," Bruno went on, "one of the Jars of Orange-marmalade didn't like the tune, and the other Jar of Orange-marmalade did like the tune—I *know* I shall get confused among those Jars of Orange-marmalade, Sylvie!" he whispered anxiously.

"I will now recite the other Introductory Verses," said the Other Professor.

> *Little Birds are choking*
> *Baronets with bun,*
> *Taught to fire a gun:*
> *Taught, I say, to splinter*
> *Salmon in the winter—*
> *Merely for the fun.*
>
> *Little Birds are hiding*
> *Crimes in carpet-bags,*
> *Blessed by happy stags:*
> *Blessed, I say, though beaten—*
> *Since our friends are eaten*
> *When the memory flags.*
>
> *Little Birds are tasting*
> *Gratitude and gold,*
> *Pale with sudden cold:*
> *Pale, I say, and wrinkled—*
> *When the bells have tinkled,*
> *And the Tale is told.*

"The next thing to be done", the Professor cheerfully remarked to the Lord Chancellor, as soon as the applause, caused by the recital of the Pig-Tale, had come to an end, "is to drink the Emperor's health, is it not?"

"Undoubtedly!" the Lord Chancellor replied with much solemnity, as he rose to his feet to give the necessary directions for the ceremony. "Fill your glasses!" he thundered. All did so, instantly. "Drink the Emperor's health!" A general gurgling resounded all through the Hall. "Three cheers for the Emperor!" The faintest possible sound followed *this* announcement: and the Chancellor, with admirable presence of mind, instantly proclaimed "A speech from the Emperor!"

The Emperor had begun his speech almost before the words were uttered. "However unwilling to be Emperor —since you all wish me to be Emperor—you know how badly the late Warden managed things—with such enthusiasm as you have shown—he persecuted you—he taxed you too heavily—you know who is fittest man to be Emperor—my brother had no sense——"

How long this curious speech might have lasted it is impossible to say, for just at this moment a hurricane shook the palace to its foundations, bursting open the windows, extinguishing some of the lamps, and filling the air with clouds of dust, which took strange shapes in the air, and seemed to form words.

But the storm subsided as suddenly as it had risen— the casements swung into their places again: the dust vanished: all was as it had been a minute ago—with the exception of the Emperor and Empress, over whom had come a wondrous change. The vacant stare, the meaningless smile, had passed away: all could see that these two strange beings had returned to their senses.

The Emperor continued his speech as if there had been no interruption. "And we have behaved—my wife and I —like two arrant Knaves. We deserve no better name. When my brother went away, you lost the best Warden you ever had. And I've been doing my best, wretched hypocrite that I am, to cheat you into making me an Emperor. Me! One that has hardly got the wits to be a shoe-black!"

The Lord Chancellor wrung his hands in despair. "He is mad, good people!" he was beginning. But both speeches stopped suddenly—and, in the dead silence that followed, a knocking was heard at the outer door.

"What is it?" was the general cry. People began running in and out. The excitement increased every moment. The Lord Chancellor, forgetting all the rules of Court-ceremony, ran full speed down the hall, and in a minute returned, pale and gasping for breath.

Chapter XXIV

The Beggar's Return

"Your Imperial Highnesses!" he began. "It's the old Beggar again! Shall we set the dogs at him?"

"Bring him here!" said the Emperor.

The Chancellor could scarcely believe his ears. "*Here*, your Imperial Highness? Did I rightly understand——"

"Bring him here!" the Emperor thundered once more. The Chancellor tottered down the hall—and in another minute the crowd divided, and the poor old Beggar was seen entering the Banqueting-Hall.

He was indeed a pitiable object: the rags, that hung about him, were all splashed with mud: his white hair and his long beard were tossed about in wild disorder. Yet he walked upright, with a stately tread, as if used to command: and—strangest sight of all—Sylvie and Bruno came with him, clinging to his hands, and gazing at him with looks of silent love.

Men looked eagerly to see how the Emperor would receive the bold intruder. Would he hurl him from the steps of the daïs? But no. To their utter astonishment, the Emperor knelt as the beggar approached, and with bowed head murmured "Forgive us!"

"Forgive us!" the Empress, kneeling at her husband's side, meekly repeated.

The Outcast smiled. "Rise up!" he said. "I forgive you!" And men saw with wonder that a change had passed over the old beggar, even as he spoke. What had seemed, but now, to be vile rags and splashes of mud, were seen to be in truth kingly trappings, broidered with gold, and sparkling with gems. All knew him now, and bent low before the Elder Brother, the true Warden.

"Brother mine, and Sister mine!" the Warden began, in a clear voice that was heard all through that vast hall. "I come not to disturb you. Rule on, as Emperor, and rule wisely. For I am chosen King of Elfland. To-morrow I return there, taking nought from thence, save only— save only——" his voice trembled, and with a look of ineffable tenderness, he laid his hands in silence on the heads of the two little ones who clung around him.

But he recovered himself in a moment, and beckoned to the Emperor to resume his place at the table. The company seated themselves again—room being found for the Elfin-King between his two children—and the Lord Chancellor rose once more, to propose the next toast.

"The next toast—the hero of the day—why, he isn't here!" he broke off in wild confusion.

Good gracious! Everybody had forgotten Prince Uggug!

"He was told of the Banquet, of course?" said the Emperor.

"Undoubtedly!" replied the Chancellor. "*That* would be the duty of the Gold Stick in Waiting."

"Let the Gold Stick come forwards!" the Emperor gravely said.

The Gold Stick came forwards. "I attended on His Imperial Fatness," was the statement made by the trembling official. "I told him of the Lecture and the Banquet——."

"What followed!" said the Emperor: for the unhappy man seemed almost too frightened to go on.

"His Imperial Fatness was graciously pleased to be sulky. His Imperial Fatness was graciously pleased to box my ears. His Imperial Fatness was graciously pleased to say 'I don't care!'"

"'Don't-care' came to a bad end," Sylvie whispered to Bruno. "I'm not sure, but I *believe* he was hanged."

The Professor overheard her. "*That* result", he blandly remarked, "was merely a case of mistaken identity."

Both children looked puzzled.

"Permit me to explain. 'Don't-care' and 'Care' were twin-brothers. 'Care', you know, killed the Cat. And they caught 'Don't-care' by mistake, and hanged him instead. And so 'Care' is alive still. But he's very unhappy without his brother. That's why they say 'Begone, dull Care!' "

"Thank you!" Sylvie said, heartily. "It's very extremely interesting. Why, it seems to explain *everything*!"

"Well, not quite *everything*," the Professor modestly rejoined. "There are two or three scientific difficulties——"

"What was your general impression as to His Imperial Fatness?" the Emperor asked the Gold Stick.

"My impression was that His Imperial Fatness was getting more——"

"More *what*?"

All listened breathlessly for the next word.

"More PRICKLY!"

"He must be sent for *at once*!" the Emperor exclaimed. And the Gold Stick went off like a shot. The Elfin-King sadly shook his head. "No use, no use!" he murmured to himself. "Loveless, loveless!"

Pale, trembling, speechless, the Gold Stick came slowly back again.

"Well?" said the Emperor. "Why does not the Prince appear?"

"One can easily guess," said the Professor. "His Imperial Fatness is, without doubt, a little preoccupied."

Bruno turned a look of solemn enquiry on his old friend. "What do that word mean?"·

But the Professor took no notice of the question. He was eagerly listening to the Gold Stick's reply.

"Please your Highness! His Imperial Fatness is——" Not a word more could he utter.

The Empress rose in an agony of alarm. "Let us go to him!" she cried. And there was a general rush for the door.

Bruno slipped off his chair in a moment. "May we go too?" he eagerly asked. But the King did not hear the question, as the Professor was speaking to him. "*Preoccupied*, your Majesty!" he was saying. "That is what he is, no doubt!"

"May we go and see him?" Bruno repeated. The King nodded assent, and the children ran off. In a minute or two they returned, slowly and gravely. "Well?" said the King. "What's the matter with the Prince?"

"He's—what *you* said," Bruno replied looking at the Professor. "That hard word." And he looked to Sylvie for assistance.

"Porcupine," said Sylvie.

"No, no!" the Professor corrected her. " '*Pre-occupied*,' you mean."

"No, it's *porcupine*," persisted Sylvie. "Not that other word at all. And please will you come? The house is all in an uproar." ("And oo'd better bring an uproar-glass wiz oo!" added Bruno.)

We got up in great haste, and followed the children upstairs. No one took the least notice of *me*, but I wasn't at all surprised at this, as I had long realized that I was quite invisible to them all—even to Sylvie and Bruno.

All along the gallery, that led to the Prince's apartment, an excited crowd was surging to and fro, and the Babel of voices was deafening: against the door of the room three strong men were leaning, vainly trying to shut it—for some great animal inside was constantly bursting it half open, and we had a glimpse, before the men could push it back again, of the head of a furious wild beast, with great fiery eyes and gnashing teeth. Its voice was a sort of mixture—there was the roaring of a lion, and the bellowing of a bull, and now and then a scream like a gigantic parrot. "There is no judging by the voice!" the Professor cried in great excitement. "What is it?" he shouted to the men at the door. And a general chorus of voices answered him "Porcupine! Prince Uggug has turned into a Porcupine!"

"A new Specimen!" exclaimed the delighted Professor. "Pray let me go in. It should be labeled at once!"

But the strong men only pushed him back. "Label it, indeed! Do you want to be eaten up?" they cried.

"Never mind about Specimens, Professor!" said the Emperor, pushing his way through the crowd. "Tell us how to keep him safe!"

"A large cage!" the Professor promptly replied. "Bring a large cage," he said to the people generally, "with strong bars of steel, and a portcullis made to go up and down like a mouse-trap! Does anyone happen to have such a thing about him?"

It didn't sound a likely sort of thing for anyone to have about him; however, they brought him one directly: curiously enough, there happened to be one standing in the gallery.

"Put it facing the opening of the door, and draw up the portcullis!" This was done in a moment.

"Blankets now!" cried the Professor. "This is a most interesting Experiment!"

There happened to be a pile of blankets close by: and the Professor had hardly said the word, when they were all unfolded and held up like curtains all around. The Professor rapidly arranged them in two rows, so as to make a dark passage, leading straight from the door to the mouth of the cage.

"Now fling the door open!" This did not need to be done: the three men had only to leap out of the way, and the fearful monster flung the door open for itself, and, with a yell like the whistle of a steam-engine, rushed into the cage.

"Down with the portcullis!" No sooner said than done: and all breathed freely once more, on seeing the Porcupine safely caged.

The Professor rubbed his hands in childish delight. "The Experiment has succeeded!" he proclaimed. "All that is needed now is to feed it three times a day, on chopped carrots and——"

"Never mind about its food, just now!" the Emperor interrupted. "Let us return to the Banquet. Brother, will you lead the way?" And the old man, attended by his children, headed the procession down stairs. "See the fate of a loveless life!" he said to Bruno, as they returned to their places. To which Bruno made reply, "I always loved Sylvie, so I'll never get prickly like that!"

"He *is* prickly, certainly," said the Professor, who had caught the last words, "but we must remember that, however porcupiny, he is royal still! After this feast is over, I'm going to take a little present to Prince Uggug—just to soothe him, you know: it isn't pleasant living in a cage."

"What'll you give him for a birthday-present?" Bruno enquired.

"A small saucer of chopped carrots," replied the Professor. "In giving birthday-presents, *my* motto is—cheapness! I should think I save forty pounds a year by giving —oh, *what* a twinge of pain!"

"What is it?" said Sylvie anxiously.

"My old enemy!" groaned the Professor. "Lumbago— rheumatism—that sort of thing. I think I'll go and lie down a bit." And he hobbled out of the Saloon, watched by the pitying eyes of the two children.

"He'll be better soon!" the Elfin-King said cheerily. "Brother!" turning to the Emperor, "I have some business to arrange with you to-night. The Empress will take care of the children." And the two Brothers went away together, arm-in-arm.

The Empress found the children rather sad company. They could talk of nothing but "the dear Professor", and "what a pity he's so ill", till at last she made the welcome proposal "Let's go and see him!"

The children eagerly grasped the hands she offered them: and we went off to the Professor's study, and found him lying on the sofa, covered up with blankets, and reading a little manuscript-book. "Notes on Vol. Three!" he murmured, looking up at us. And there, on a table near him, lay the book he was seeking when first I saw him.

"And how are you now, Professor?" the Empress asked, bending over the invalid.

The Professor looked up, and smiled feebly. "As devoted to your Imperial Highness as ever!" he said in a weak voice. "All of me, that is not Lumbago, is Loyalty!"

"A sweet sentiment!" the Empress exclaimed with tears in her eyes. "You seldom hear anything so beautiful as that—even in a Valentine!"

"We must take you to stay at the seaside," Sylvie said, tenderly. "It'll do you ever so much good! And the Sea's so grand!"

"But a Mountain's grander!" said Bruno.

"What is there grand about the Sea?" said the Professor. "Why, you could put it all into a teacup!"

"*Some* of it," Sylvie corrected him.

"Well, you'd only want a certain number of teacups to hold it *all*. And *then* where's the grandeur? Then as to a Mountain—why, you could carry it all away in a wheelbarrow, in a certain number of years!"

"It wouldn't look grand—the bits of it in the wheelbarrow," Sylvie candidly admitted.

"But when oo put it together again——" Bruno began.

"When you're older," said the Professor, "you'll know that you *ca'n't* put Mountains together again so easily! One lives and one learns, you know!"

"But it needn't be the *same* one, need it?" said Bruno. "Wo'n't it do, if *I* live, and if *Sylvie* learns?"

"I *ca'n't* learn without living!" said Sylvie.

"But I *can* live without learning!" Bruno retorted. "Oo just try me!"

"What I meant, was—" the Professor began, looking much puzzled, "—was—that you don't know *everything*, you know."

"But I *do* know everything I know!" persisted the little fellow. "I know ever so many things! Everything, 'cept the things I *don't* know. And Sylvie knows all the rest."

The Professor sighed, and gave it up. "Do you know what a Boojum is?"

"*I* know!" cried Bruno. "It's the thing what wrenches people out of their boots!"

"He means 'bootjack'," Sylvie explained in a whisper.

"You ca'n't wrench people out of *boots*," the Professor mildly observed.

Bruno laughed saucily. "Oo *can*, though! Unless they're *welly* tight in."

"Once upon a time there was a Boojum——" the Professor began, but stopped suddenly. "I forget the rest of the Fable," he said. "And there was a lesson to be learned from it. I'm afraid I forget *that* too."

"*I'll* tell oo a Fable!" Bruno began in a great hurry. "Once there were a Locust, and a Magpie, and a Engine-driver. And the Lesson is, to learn to get up early——"

"It isn't a bit interesting!" Sylvie said contemptuously. "You shouldn't put the Lesson so soon."

"When did you invent that Fable?" said the Professor. "Last week?"

"No!" said Bruno. "A deal shorter ago than that, Guess again!"

"I ca'n't guess," said the Professor. "How long ago?"

"Why, it isn't invented yet!" Bruno exclaimed triumphantly. "But I *have* invented a lovely one! Shall I say it?"

"If you've *finished* inventing it," said Sylvie. "And let the Lesson be 'to try again'!"

"No," said Bruno with great decision. "The Lesson are '*not* to try again'!" "Once there were a lovely china man, what stood on the chimbley-piece. And he stood, and he stood. And one day he tumbleded off, and he didn't hurt his self one bit. Only he *would* try again. And the next time he tumbleded off, he hurted his self welly much, and breaked off ever so much varnish."

"But how did he come back on the chimney-piece after his first tumble?" said the Empress. (It was the first sensible question she had asked in all her life.)

"*I* put him there!" cried Bruno.

"Then I'm afraid you know something about his tumbling," said the Professor. "Perhaps you pushed him?"

To which Bruno replied, very seriously, "Didn't pushed him *much*—he were a *lovely* china man," he added hastily, evidently very anxious to change the subject.

"Come, my children!" said the Elfin-King, who had just entered the room. "We must have a little chat together, before you go to bed." And he was leading them away, but at the door they let go his hands, and ran back again to wish the Professor good night.

"Good night, Profesor, good night!" And Bruno solemnly shook hands with the old man, who gazed at him with a loving smile, while Sylvie bent down to press her sweet lips upon his forehead.

"Good night, little ones!" said the Professor. "You may leave me now—to ruminate. I'm as jolly as the day is long, except when it's necessary to ruminate on some very difficult subject. All of me," he murmured sleepily as we left the room, "all of me, that isn't *Bonhommie*, is Rumination!"

"*What* did he say, Bruno?" Sylvie enquired, as soon as we were safely out of hearing.

"I *think* he said 'All of me that isn't Bone-disease is Rheumatism.' Whatever *are* that knocking, Sylvie?"

Sylvie stopped, and listened anxiously. It sounded like some one kicking at a door, "I *hope* it isn't that Porcupine breaking loose!" she exclaimed.

"Let's go on!" Bruno said hastily. "There's nuffin to wait for, oo know!"

Chapter XXV

Life Out of Death

THE sound of kicking, or knocking, grew louder every moment: and at last a door opened somewhere near us. "Did you say 'come in!' Sir?" my landlady asked timidly.

"Oh yes, come in!" I replied. "What's the matter?"

"A note has just been left for you, Sir, by the baker's boy. He said he was passing the Hall, and they asked him to come round and leave it here."

The note contained five words only. "Please come at once. Muriel."

A sudden terror seemed to chill my very heart. "The Earl is ill!" I said to myself. "Dying, perhaps!" And I hastily prepared to leave the house.

"No bad news, Sir, I hope?" my landlady said, as she saw me out. "The boy said as some one had arrived unexpectedly——"

"I hope that is it!" I said. But my feelings were those of fear rather than of hope: though, on entering the house, I was somehat reassured by finding luggage lying in the entrance, bearing the initials "E. L."

"It's only Eric Lindon after all!" I thought, half relieved and half annoyed. "Surely she need not have sent for me for *that*!"

Lady Muriel met me in the passage. Her eyes were gleaming—but it was the excitement of joy, rather than of grief. "I have a surprise for you!" she whispered.

"You mean that Eric Lindon is here?" I said, vainly trying to disguise the involuntary bitterness of my tone. " '*The funeral baked meats did coldly furnish forth the marriage-tables*,'" I could not help repeating to myself. How cruelly I was misjudging her!

"No, no!" she eagerly replied. "At least—Eric *is* here. But——" her voice quivered, "but there is *another*!"

No need for further question. I eagerly followed her in. There on the bed, he lay—pale and worn—the mere shadow of his old self—my old friend come back again from the dead!

"Arthur!" I exclaimed. I could not say another word.

"Yes, back again, old boy!" he murmured, smiling as I grasped his hand. "*He*", indicating Eric, who stood near, "saved my life—*He* brought me back. Next to God, we must thank *him*, Muriel, my wife!"

Silently I shook hands with Eric, and with the Earl: and with one consent we moved into the shaded side of the room, where we could talk without disturbing the invalid, who lay, silent and happy, holding his wife's hand in his, and watching her with eyes that shone with the deep steady light of Love.

"He has been delirious till to-day," Eric explained in a low voice: "and even to-day he has been wandering more than once. But the sight of *her* has been new life to him." And then he went on to tell us, in would-be careless tones —I knew how he hated any display of feeling—how he had insisted on going back to the plague-stricken town, to bring away a man whom the doctor had abandoned as dying, but who *might*, he fancied, recover if brought to the hospital: how he had seen nothing in the wasted features to remind him of Arthur, and only recognized him when he visited the hospital a month after: how the doctor had forbidden him to announce the discovery, saying that any shock to the over-taxed brain might kill him at once: how he had stayed on at the hospital, and nursed the sick man by night and day—all this with the studied indifference of one who is relating the commonplace acts of some chance acquaintance!

"And this was his *rival*!" I thought. "The man who had won from him the heart of the woman he loved!"

"The sun is setting," said Lady Muriel, rising and leading the way to the open window. "Just look at the western sky! What lovely crimson tints! We shall have a glorious day to-morrow——" We had followed her across the room, and were standing in a little group, talking in low tones in the gathering gloom, when we were startled by the voice of the sick man, murmuring words too indistinct for the ear to catch.

"He is wandering again," Lady Muriel whispered, and returned to the bedside. We drew a little nearer also: but no, this had none of the incoherence of delirium. "*What reward shall I give unto the Lord*", the tremulous lips were saying, "*for all the benefits that He hath done unto me? I will receive the cup of salvation, and call—and call——*" but here the poor weakened memory failed, and the feeble voice died into silence.

His wife knelt down at the bedside, raised one of his arms, and drew it across her own, fondly kissing the thin white hand that lay so listlessly in her loving grasp. It seemed to me a good opportunity for stealing away without making her go through any form of parting: so, nodding to the Earl and Eric, I silently left the room. Eric followed me down the stairs, and out into the night.

"Is it Life or Death?" I asked him, as soon as we were far enough from the house for me to speak in ordinary tones.

"It is *Life*!" he replied with eager emphasis. "The doctors are quite agreed as to *that*. All he needs now, they say, is rest, and perfect quiet, and good nursing. He's quite sure to get rest and quiet, here: and, as for the nursing, why, I think it's just *possible*——" (he tried hard to make his trembling voice assume a playful tone) "he may even get fairly well nursed, in his present quarters!"

"I'm sure of it!" I said. "Thank you so much for coming out to tell me!" And, thinking he had now said all he had come to say, I held out my hand to bid him good night. He grasped it warmly, and added, turning his face away as he spoke, "By the way, there is one other thing I wanted to say, I thought you'd like to know that—that I'm not—not in the mind I was in when last we met. It isn't—that I can accept Christian belief—at least, not yet. But all this came about so strangely. And she had prayed, you know. And I had prayed. And—and" his voice broke, and I could only just catch the concluding words, "*there is a God that answers prayer! I know it for* certain now." He wrung my hand once more, and left me suddenly. Never before had I seen him so deeply moved.

So, in the gathering twilight, I paced slowly homewards, in a tumultuous whirl of happy thoughts: my heart seemed full, and running over, with joy and thankfulness: all that I had so fervently longed for, and prayed for, seemed now to have come to pass. And, though I reproached myself, bitterly, for the unworthy suspicion I had for one moment harboured against the true-hearted Lady Muriel, I took comfort in knowing it had been but a passing thought.

Not Bruno himself could have mounted the stairs with so buoyant a step, as I felt my way up in the dark, not pausing to strike a light in the entry, as I knew I had left the lamp burning in my sitting-room.

But it was no common *lamplight* into which I now stepped, with a strange, new, dreamy sensation of some subtle witchery that had come over the place. Light, richer and more golden than any lamp could give, flooded the room, streaming in from a window I had somehow never noticed before, and lighting up a group of three shadowy figures, that grew momently more distinct—a grave old man in royal robes, leaning back in an easy chair, and two children, a girl and a boy, standing at his side.

"Have you the Jewel still, my child?" the old man was saying.

"Oh, *yes!*" Sylvie exclaimed with unusual eagerness.

"Do you think I'd *ever* lose it or forget it?" She undid the ribbon round her neck, as she spoke, and laid the Jewel in her father's hand.

Bruno looked at it admiringly. "What a lovely brightness!" he said. "It's just like a little red star! May I take it in my hand?"

Sylvie nodded: and Bruno carried it off to the window, and held it aloft against the sky, whose deepening blue was already spangled with stars. Soon he came running back in some excitement. "Sylvie! Look here!" he cried. "I can see right through it when I hold it up to the sky.

And it isn't red a bit: it's, oh such a lovely blue! And the words are all different! Do look at it!"

Sylvie was quite excited, too, by this time; and the two children eagerly held up the Jewel to the light, and spelled out the legend between them, "ALL WILL LOVE SYLVIE."

"Why, this is the *other* Jewel!" cried Bruno. "Don't you remember, Sylvie? The one you *didn't* choose!"

Sylvie took it from him, with a puzzled look, and held it, now up to the light, now down. "It's blue, *one* way," she said softly to herself, "and it's red the *other* way! Why, I thought there were *two* of them—Father!" she suddenly exclaimed, laying the Jewel once more in his hand, "I do believe it was the *same* Jewel all the time!"

"Then you choosed it from *itself*," Bruno thoughtfully remarked. "Father, *could* Sylvie choose a thing from itself?"

"Yes, my own one," the old man replied to Sylvie, not noticing Bruno's embarrassing question, "it *was* the same Jewel—but you chose quite right." And he fastened the ribbon round her neck again.

"SYLVIE WILL LOVE ALL—ALL WILL LOVE SYLVIE." Bruno murmured, raising himself on tiptoe to kiss the "little red star". "And, when you look *at* it, it's red and fierce like the sun—and, when you look *through* it, it's gentle and blue like the sky!"

"God's own sky," Sylvie said, dreamily.

"God's own sky," the little fellow repeated, as they stood, lovingly clinging together, and looking out into the night. "But oh, Sylvie, what makes the sky such a *darling* blue?"

Sylvie's sweet lips shaped themselves to reply, but her voice sounded faint and very far away. The vision was fast slipping from my eager gaze: but it seemed to me, in that last bewildering moment, that not Sylvie but an angel was looking out through those trustful brown eyes, and that not Sylvie's but an angel's voice was whispering

"IT IS LOVE."

V
Verse

PREFACE TO
THE HUNTING OF THE SNARK

IF—and the thing is wildly possible—the charge of
writing nonsense were ever brought against the author of
this brief but instructive poem, it would be based, I feel
convinced, on the line (in p. 684)

"Then the bowsprit got mixed with the rudder sometimes:"

In view of this painful possibility, I will not (as I might)
appeal indignantly to my other writings as a proof that I
am incapable of such a deed: I will not (as I might) point
to the strong moral purpose of this poem itself, to the
arithmetical principles so cautiously inculcated in it, or to
its noble teachings in Natural History—I will take the
more prosaic course of simply explaining how it happened.

The Bellman, who was almost morbidly sensitive about
appearances, used to have the bowsprit unshipped once
or twice a week to be revarnished; and it more than once
happened, when the time came for replacing it, that no
one on board could remember which end of the ship it
belonged to. They knew it was not of the slightest use to
appeal to the Bellman about it—he would only refer to
his Naval Code, and read out in pathetic tones Admiralty
Instructions which none of them had ever been able to
understand—so it generally ended in its being fastened
on, anyhow, across the rudder. The helmsman[1] used to
stand by with tears in his eyes: *he* knew it was all wrong,
but alas! Rule 42 of the Code, "*No one shall speak to the*

---

[1] This office was usually undertaken by the Boots, who found in
it a refuge from the Baker's constant complaints about the insufficient blacking of his three pairs of boots.

Man at the Helm," had been completed by the Bellman himself with the words *"and the Man at the Helm shall speak to no one."* So remonstrance was impossible, and no steering could be done till the next varnishing day. During these bewildering intervals the ship usually sailed backwards.

As this poem is to some extent connected with the lay of the Jabberwock, let me take this opportunity of answering a question that has often been asked me, how to pronounce "slithy toves". The "i" in "slithy" is long, as in "writhe"; and "toves" is pronounced so as to rhyme with "groves". Again, the first "o" in "borogoves" is pronounced like the "o" in "borrow". I have heard people try to give it the sound of the "o" in "worry". Such is Human Perversity.

This also seems a fitting occasion to notice the other hard words in that poem. Humpty-Dumpty's theory, of two meanings packed into one word like a portmanteau, seems to me the right explanation for all.

For instance, take the two words "fuming" and "furious". Make up your mind that you will say both words, but leave it unsettled which you will say first. Now open your mouth and speak. If your thoughts incline ever so little towards "fuming", you will say "fuming-furious"; if they turn, by even a hair's breadth, towards "furious", you will say "furious-fuming"; but if you have that rarest of gifts, a perfectly balanced mind, you will say "frumious".

Supposing that, when Pistol uttered the well-known words—

"Under which king, Bezonian? Speak or die!"

Justice Shallow had felt certain that it was either William or Richard, but had not been able to settle which; so that he could not possibly say either name before the other, can it be doubted that, rather than die, he would have gasped out "Rilchiam!"

Girl with a boyish garb for boyish task,
    Eager she wields her spade: yet loves as well
Rest on a friendly knee, intent to ask
    The tale he loves to tell.

Rude spirits of the seething outer strife,
    Unmeet to read her pure and simple spright,
Deem, if you list, such hours a waste of life,
    Empty of all delight!

Chat on, sweet Maid, and rescue from annoy
    Hearts that by wiser talk are unbeguiled.
Ah, happy he who owns that tenderest joy,
    The heart-love of a child!

Away, fond thoughts, and vex my soul no more!
    Work claims my wakeful nights, my busy days—
Albeit bright memories of that sunlit shore
    Yet haunt my dreaming gaze!

THE HUNTING OF THE SNARK

The Landing

"JUST the place for a Snark!" the Bellman cried,
  As he landed his crew with care;
Supporting each man on the top of the tide
  By a finger entwined in his hair.

"Just the place for a Snark! I have said it twice:
  That alone should encourage the crew.
Just the place for a Snark! I have said it thrice:
  What I tell you three times is true."

The crew was complete: it included a Boots—
  A maker of Bonnets and Hoods—
A Barrister, brought to arrange their disputes—
  And a Broker, to value their goods.

A Billiard-marker, whose skill was immense,
  Might perhaps have won more than his share—
But a Banker, engaged at enormous expense,
  Had the whole of their cash in his care.

There was also a Beaver, that paced on the deck,
  Or would sit making lace in the bow:
And had often (the Bellman said) saved them from wreck
  Though none of the sailors knew how.

There was one who was famed for the number of things
  He forgot when he entered the ship:
His umbrella, his watch, all his jewels and rings,
  And the clothes he had bought for the trip.

He had forty-two boxes, all carefully packed,
   With his name painted clearly on each:
But, since he omitted to mention the fact,
   They were all left behind on the beach.

The loss of his clothes hardly mattered, because
   He had seven coats on when he came,
With three pair of boots—but the worst of it was,
   He had wholly forgotten his name.

He would answer to "Hi!" or to any loud cry,
   Such as "Fry me!" or "Fritter my wig!"
To "What-you-may-call-um!" or "What-was-his-name!"
   But especially "Thing-um-a-jig!"

While, for those who preferred a more forcible word,
   He had different names from these:
His intimate friends called him "Candle-ends",
   And his enemies "Toasted-cheese".

"His form is ungainly—his intellect small—"
   (So the Bellman would often remark)—
"But his courage is perfect! And that, after all,
   Is the thing that one needs with a Snark."

He would joke with hyænas, returning their stare
   With an impudent wag of the head:
And he once went a walk, paw-in-paw, with a bear,
   "Just to keep up its spirits," he said.

He came as a Baker: but owned, when too late—
   And it drove the poor Bellman half-mad—
He could only bake Bridecake—for which, I may state,
   No materials were to be had.

The last of the crew needs especial remark,
   Though he looked an incredible dunce:
He had just one idea—but, that one being "Snark",
   The good Bellman engaged him at once.

He came as a Butcher: but gravely declared,
　　When the ship had been sailing a week,
He could only kill Beavers. The Bellman looked scared,
　　And was almost too frightened to speak:

But at length he explained, in a tremulous tone,
　　There was only one Beaver on board;
And that was a tame one he had of his own,
　　Whose death would be deeply deplored.

The Beaver, who happened to hear the remark,
　　Protested, with tears in its eyes,
That not even the rapture of hunting the Snark
　　Could atone for that dismal surprise!

It strongly advised that the Butcher should be
　　Conveyed in a separate ship:
But the Bellman declared that would never agree
　　With the plans he had made for the trip:

Navigation was always a difficult art,
　　Though with only one ship and one bell:
And he feared he must really decline, for his part,
　　Undertaking another as well.

The Beaver's best course was, no doubt, to procure
　　A second-hand dagger-proof coat—
So the Baker advised it—and next, to insure
　　Its life in some Office of note:

This the Baker suggested, and offered for hire
　　(On moderate terms), or for sale,
Two excellent Policies, one Against Fire
　　And one Against Damage From Hail.

Yet still, ever after that sorrowful day,
　　Whenever the Butcher was by,
The Beaver kept looking the opposite way,
　　And appeared unaccountably shy.

FIT THE SECOND

The Bellman's Speech

THE Bellman himself they all praised to the skies—
    Such a carriage, such ease and such grace!
Such solemnity, too! One could see he was wise,
    The moment one looked in his face!

He had bought a large map representing the sea,
    Without the least vestige of land:
And the crew were much pleased when they found it to be
    A map they could all understand.

"What's the good of Mercator's North Poles and Equa-
        tors,
    Tropics, Zones, and Meridian Lines?"
So the Bellman would cry: and the crew would reply
    "They are merely conventional signs!

"Other maps are such shapes, with their islands and
        capes!
    But we've got our brave Captain to thank"
(So the crew would protest) "that he's bought *us* the
        best—
    A perfect and absolute blank!"

This was charming, no doubt: but they shortly found out
    That the Captain they trusted so well
Had only one notion for crossing the ocean,
    And that was to tingle his bell.

He was thoughtful and grave—but the orders he gave
    Were enough to bewilder a crew.
When he cried "Steer to starboard, but keep her head
        larboard!"
    What on earth was the helmsman to do?

Then the bowsprit got mixed with the rudder sometimes:
  A thing, as the Bellman remarked,
That frequently happens in tropical climes,
  When a vessel is, so to speak, "snarked".

But the principal failing occurred in the sailing,
  And the Bellman, perplexed and distressed,
Said he *had* hoped, at least, when the wind blew due East,
  That the ship would *not* travel due West!

But the danger was past—they had landed at last,
  With their boxes, portmanteaus, and bags:
Yet at first sight the crew were not pleased with the view
  Which consisted of chasms and crags.

The Bellman perceived that their spirits were low,
  And repeated in musical tone
Some jokes he had kept for a season of woe—
  But the crew would do nothing but groan.

He served out some grog with a liberal hand,
  And bade them sit down on the beach:
And they could not but own that their Captain looked
    grand,
  As he stood and delivered his speech.

"Friends, Romans, and countrymen, lend me your ears!"
  (They were all of them fond of quotations:
So they drank to his health, and they gave him three
    cheers,
  While he served out additional rations).

"We' have sailed many months, we have sailed many
    weeks,
  (Four weeks to the month you may mark),
But never as yet ('tis your Captain who speaks)
  Have we caught the least glimpse of a Snark!

"We have sailed many weeks, we have sailed many days,
　(Seven days to the week I allow),
But a Snark, on the which we might lovingly gaze,
　We have never beheld till now!

"Come, listen, my men, while I tell you again
　The five unmistakable marks
By which you may know, wheresoever you go,
　The warranted genuine Snarks.

"Let us take them in order. The first is the taste,
　Which is meagre and hollow, but crisp:
Like a coat that is rather too tight in the waist,
　With a flavour of Will-o'-the-Wisp.

"Its habit of getting up late you'll agree
　That it carries too far, when I say
That it frequently breakfasts at five-o'clock tea,
　And dines on the following day.

"The third is its slowness in taking a jest.
　Should you happen to venture on one,
It will sigh like a thing that is deeply distressed:
　And it always looks grave at a pun.

"The fourth is its fondness for bathing-machines,
　Which it constantly carries about,
And believes that they add to the beauty of scenes—
　A sentiment open to doubt.

"The fifth is ambition. It next will be right
　To describe each particular batch:
Distinguishing those that have feathers, and bite,
　From those that have whiskers, and scratch.

"For, although common Snarks do no manner of harm,
　Yet I feel it my duty to say
Some are Boojums——" The Bellman broke off in alarm,
　For the Baker had fainted away.

Fit the Third

The Baker's Tale

They roused him with muffins—they roused him with
    ice—
    They roused him with mustard and cress—
They roused him with jam and judicious advice—
    They set him conundrums to guess.

When at length he sat up and was able to speak,
    His sad story he offered to tell;
And the Bellman cried "Silence! Not even a shriek!"
    And excitedly tingled his bell.

There was silence supreme! Not a shriek, not a scream,
    Scarcely even a howl or a groan,
As the man they called "Ho!" told his story of woe
    In an antediluvian tone.

"My father and mother were honest, though poor——"
    "Skip all that!" cried the Bellman in haste.
"If it once becomes dark, there's no chance of a Snark—
    We have hardly a minute to waste!"

"I skip forty years," said the Baker in tears,
    "And proceed without further remark
To the day when you took me aboard of your ship
    To help you in hunting the Snark.

"A dear uncle of mine (after whom I was named)
    Remarked, when I bade him farewell——"
"Oh, skip your dear uncle!" the Bellman exclaimed,
    As he angrily tingled his bell.

"He remarked to me then," said that mildest of men,
    " 'If your Snark be a Snark, that is right:

Fetch it home by all means—you may serve it with greens
   And it's handy for striking a light.

" 'You may seek it with thimbles—and seek it with care—
   You may hunt it with forks and hope;
You may threaten its life with a railway-share;
   You may charm it with smiles and soap——' "

("That's exactly the method," the Bellman bold
   In a hasty parenthesis cried,
"That's exactly the way I have always been told
   That the capture of Snarks should be tried!")

" 'But oh, beamish nephew, beware of the day,
   If your Snark be a Boojum! For then
You will softly and suddenly vanish away,
   And never be met with again!'

"It is this, it is this that oppresses my soul,
   When I think of my uncle's last words:
And my heart is like nothing so much as a bowl
   Brimming over with quivering curds!

"It is this, it is this——" "We have had that before!"
   The Bellman indignantly said.
And the Baker replied "Let me say it once more.
   It is this, it is this that I dread!

"I engage with the Snark—every night after dark—
   In a dreamy delirious fight:
I serve it with greens in those shadowy scenes,
   And I use it for striking a light:

"But if ever I meet with a Boojum. that day,
   In a moment (of this I am sure),
I shall softly and suddenly vanish away—
   And the notion I cannot endure!"

FIT THE FOURTH

The Hunting

THE Bellman looked uffish, and wrinkled his brow.
　"If only you'd spoken before!
It's excessively awkward to mention it now,
　With the Snark, so to speak, at the door!

"We should all of us grieve, as you well may believe,
　If you never were met with again—
But surely, my man, when the voyage began,
　You might have suggested it then?

"It's excessively awkward to mention it now—
　As I think I've already remarked."
And the man they called "Hi!" replied, with a sigh,
　"I informed you the day we embarked.

"You may charge me with murder—or want of sense—
　(We are all of us weak at times):
But the slightest approach to a false pretence
　Was never among my crimes!

"I said it in Hebrew—I said it in Dutch—
　I said it in German and Greek:
But I wholly forgot (and it vexes me much)
　That English is what you speak!"

" 'Tis a pitiful tale," said the Bellman, whose face
　Had grown longer at every word:
"But, now that you've stated the whole of your case,
　More debate would be simply absurd.

"The rest of my speech" (he exclaimed to his men)
　"You shall hear when I've leisure to speak it.
But the Snark is at hand, let me tell you again!
　'Tis your glorious duty to seek it!

"To seek it with thimbles, to seek it with care;
　To pursue it with forks and hope;
To threaten its life with a railway-share;
　To charm it with smiles and soap!

"For the Snark's a peculiar creature, that wo'n't
　Be caught in a commonplace way.
Do all that you know, and try all that you don't:
　Not a chance must be wasted to-day!

"For England expects—I forbear to proceed:
　'Tis a maxim tremendous, but trite:
And you'd best be unpacking the things that you need
　To rig yourselves out for the fight."

Then the Banker endorsed a blank cheque (which he
　　　crossed),
　And changed his loose silver for notes:
The Baker with care combed his whiskers and hair,
　And shook the dust out of his coats:

The Boots and the Broker were sharpening a spade—
　Each working the grindstone in turn:
But the Beaver went on making lace, and displayed
　No interest in the concern:

Though the Barrister tried to appeal to its pride,
　And vainly proceeded to cite
A number of cases, in which making laces
　Had been proved an infringement of right.

The maker of Bonnets ferociously planned
　A novel arrangement of bows:
While the Billiard-marker with quivering hand
　Was chalking the tip of his nose.

But the Butcher turned nervous, and dressed himself fine,
　With yellow kid gloves and a ruff—

Said he felt it exactly like going to dine,
　　Which the Bellman declared was all "stuff".

"Introduce me, now there's a good fellow," he said,
　　"If we happen to meet it together!"
And the Bellman, sagaciously nodding his head,
　　Said "That must depend on the weather."

The Beaver went simply galumphing about,
　　At seeing the Butcher so shy:
And even the Baker, though stupid and stout,
　　Made an effort to wink with one eye.

"Be a man!" said the Bellman in wrath, as he heard
　　The Butcher beginning to sob.
"Should we meet with a Jubjub, that desperate bird,
　　We shall need all our strength for the job!"

Fit the Fifth

The Beaver's Lesson

They sought it with thimbles, they sought it with care;
　　They pursued it with forks and hope;
They threatened its life with a railway-share;
　　They charmed it with smiles and soap.

Then the Butcher contrived an ingenious plan
　　For making a separate sally;
And had fixed on a spot unfrequented by man,
　　A dismal and desolate valley.

But the very same plan to the Beaver occurred:
　　It had chosen the very same place:
Yet neither betrayed, by a sign or a word,
　　The disgust that appeared in his face.

Each thought he was thinking of nothing but "Snark"
    And the glorious work of the day;
And each tried to pretend that he did not remark
    That the other was going that way.

But the valley grew narrower and narrower still,
    And the evening got darker and colder,
Till (merely from nervousness, not from good will)
    They marched along shoulder to shoulder.

Then a scream, shrill and high, rent the shuddering sky
    And they knew that some danger was near:
The Beaver turned pale to the tip of its tail,
    And even the Butcher felt queer.

He thought of his childhood, left far behind—
    That blissful and innocent state—
The sound so exactly recalled to his mind
    A pencil that squeaks on a slate!

" 'Tis the voice of the Jubjub!" he suddenly cried.
    (This man, that they used to call "Dunce".)
"As the Bellman would tell you." he added with pride,
    "I have uttered that sentiment once.

" 'Tis the note of the Jubjub! Keep count, I entreat.
    You will find I have told it you twice.
'Tis the song of the Jubjub! The proof is complete.
    If only I've stated it thrice."

The Beaver had counted with scrupulous care,
    Attending to every word:
But it fairly lost heart, and outgrabe in despair,
    When the third repetition occurred.

It felt that, in spite of all possible pains,
    It had somehow contrived to lose count,
And the only thing now was to rack its poor brains
    By reckoning up the amount.

"Two added to one—if that could but be done",
  It said, "with one's fingers and thumbs!"
Recollecting with tears how, in earlier years,
  It had taken no pains with its sums.

"The thing can be done," said the Butcher, "I think.
  The thing must be done, I am sure.
The thing shall be done! Bring me paper and ink,
  The best there is time to procure."

The Beaver brought paper, portfolio, pens,
  And ink in unfailing supplies:
While strange creepy creatures came out of their dens,
  And watched them with wondering eyes.

So engrossed was the Butcher, he heeded them not,
  As he wrote with a pen in each hand,
And explained all the while in a popular style
  Which the Beaver could well understand.

"Taking Three as the subject to reason about—
  A convenient number to state—
We add Seven, and Ten, and then multiply out
  By One Thousand diminished by Eight.

"The result we proceed to divide, as you see,
  By Nine Hundred and Ninety and Two:
Then subtract Seventeen, and the answer must be
  Exactly and perfectly true.

"The method employed I would gladly explain,
  While I have it so clear in my head,
If I had but the time and you had but the brain—
  But much yet remains to be said.

"In one moment I've seen what has hitherto been
  Enveloped in absolute mystery,
And without extra charge I will give you at large
  A Lesson in Natural History."

In his genial way he proceeded to say
  (Forgetting all laws of propriety,
And that giving instruction, without introduction,
  Would have caused quite a thrill in Society),

"As to temper the Jubjub's a desperate bird.
  Since it lives in perpetual passion:
Its taste in costume is entirely absurd—
  It is ages ahead of the fashion:

"But it knows any friend it has met once before:
  It never will look at a bribe:
And in charity-meetings it stands at the door,
  And collects—though it does not subscribe.

"Its flavour when cooked is more exquisite far
  Than mutton, or oysters, or eggs:
(Some think it keeps best in an ivory jar,
  And some, in mahogany kegs:)

"You boil it in sawdust: you salt it in glue:
  You condense it with locusts and tape:
Still keeping one principal object in view—
  To preserve its symmetrical shape."

The Butcher would gladly have talked till next day,
  But he felt that the Lesson must end,
And he wept with delight in attempting to say
  He considered the Beaver his friend:

While the Beaver confessed, with affectionate looks
  More eloquent even than tears,
It had learned in ten minutes far more than all books
  Would have taught it in seventy years.

They returned hand-in-hand, and the Bellman, unmanned
  (For a moment) with noble emotion,
Said "This amply repays all the wearisome days
  We have spent on the billowy ocean!"

Such friends, as the Beaver and Butcher became,
  Have seldom if ever been known;
In winter or summer, 'twas always the same—
  You could never meet either alone.

And when quarrels arose—as one frequently finds
  Quarrels will, spite of every endeavour—
The song of the Jubjub recurred to their minds,
  And cemented their friendship for ever!

FIT THE SIXTH

The Barrister's Dream

THEY sought it with thimbles, they sought it with care;
  They pursued it with forks and hope;
They threatened its life with a railway-share;
  They charmed it with smiles and soap.

But the Barrister, weary of proving in vain
  That the Beaver's lace-making was wrong,
Fell asleep, and in dreams saw the creature quite plain
  That his fancy had dwelt on so long.

He dreamed that he stood in a shadowy Court,
  Where the Snark, with a glass in its eye,
Dressed in gown, bands, and wig, was defending a pig
  On the charge of deserting its sty.

The Witnesses proved, without error or flaw,
  That the sty was deserted when found:
And the Judge kept explaining the state of the law
  In a soft under-current of sound.

The indictment had never been clearly expressed,
  And it seemed that the Snark had begun,
And had spoken three hours, before any one guessed
  What the pig was supposed to have done.

The Jury had each formed a different view
   (Long before the indictment was read),
And they all spoke at once, so that none of them knew
   One word that the others had said.

"You must know——" said the Judge: but the Snark ex-
   claimed "Fudge!
   That statute is obsolete quite!
Let me tell you, my friends, the whole question depends
   On an ancient manorial right.

"In the matter of Treason the pig would appear
   To have aided, but scarcely abetted:
While the charge of Insolvency fails, it is clear,
   If you grant the plea 'never indebted'.

"The fact of Desertion I will not dispute:
   But its guilt, as I trust, is removed
(So far as relates to the costs of this suit)
   By the Alibi which has been proved.

"My poor client's fate now depends on your votes."
   Here the speaker sat down in his place,
And directed the Judge to refer to his notes
   And briefly to sum up the case.

But the Judge said he never had summed up before;
   So the Snark undertook it instead,
And summed it so well that it came to far more
   Than the Witnesses ever had said!

When the verdict was called for, the Jury declined,
   As the word was so puzzling to spell;
But they ventured to hope that the Snark wouldn't mind
   Undertaking that duty as well.

So the Snark found the verdict, although, as it owned,
   It was spent with the toils of the day:

When it said the word "GUILTY!" the Jury all groaned
    And some of them fainted away.

Then the Snark pronounced sentence, the Judge being
        quite
    Too nervous to utter a word:
When it rose to its feet, there was silence like night,
    And the fall of a pin might be heard.

"Transportation for life" was the sentence it gave,
    "And *then* to be fined forty pound."
The Jury all cheered, though the Judge said he feared
    That the phrase was not legally sound.

But their wild exultation was suddenly checked
    When the jailer informed them, with tears,
Such a sentence would have not the slightest effect,
    As the pig had been dead for some years.

The Judge left the Court, looking deeply disgusted
    But the Snark, though a little aghast,
As the lawyer to whom the defence was intrusted,
    Went bellowing on to the last.

Thus the Barrister dreamed, while the bellowing seemed
    To grow every moment more clear:
Till he woke to the knell of a furious bell,
    Which the Bellman rang close at his ear.

FIT THE SEVENTH

The Banker's Fate

THEY sought it with thimbles, they sought it with care;
    They pursued it with forks and hope;
They threatened its life with a railway-share;
    They charmed it with smiles and soap.

And the Banker, inspired with a courage so new
    It was matter for general remark,
Rushed madly ahead and was lost to their view
    In his zeal to discover the Snark.

But while he was seeking with thimbles and care,
    A Bandersnatch swiftly drew nigh
And grabbed at the Banker, who shrieked in despair,
    For he knew it was useless to fly.

He offered large discount—he offered a cheque
    (Drawn "to bearer") for seven-pounds-ten:
But the Bandersnatch merely extended its neck
    And grabbed at the Banker again.

Without rest or pause—while those frumious jaws
    Went savagely snapping around—
He skipped and he hopped, and he floundered and flopped,
    Till fainting he fell to the ground.

The Bandersnatch fled as the others appeared
    Led on by that fear-stricken yell:
And the Bellman remarked "It is just as I feared!"
    And solemnly tolled on his bell.

He was black in the face, and they scarcely could trace
    The least likeness to what he had been:
While so great was his fright that his waistcoat turned
        white—
    A wonderful thing to be seen!

To the horror of all who were present that day,
    He uprose in full evening dress,
And with senseless grimaces endeavoured to say
    What his tongue could no longer express.

Down he sank in a chair—ran his hands through his
        hair—
    And chanted in mimsiest tones

Words whose utter inanity proved his insanity,
　　While he rattled a couple of bones.

"Leave him here to his fate—it is getting so late!"
　　The Bellman exclaimed in a fright.
"We have lost half the day. Any further delay,
　　And we sha'n't catch a Snark before night!"

FIT THE EIGHTH

The Vanishing

THEY sought it with thimbles, they sought it with care;
　　They pursued it with forks and hope;
They threatened its life with a railway-share;
　　They charmed it with smiles and soap.

They shuddered to think that the chase might fail,
　　And the Beaver, excited at last,
Went bounding along on the tip of its tail,
　　For the daylight was nearly past.

"There is Thingumbob shouting!" the Bellman said.
　　"He is shouting like mad, only hark!
He is waving his hands, he is wagging his head,
　　He has certainly found a Snark!"

They gazed in delight, while the Butcher exclaimed
　　"He was always a desperate wag!"
They beheld him—their Baker—their hero unnamed—
　　On the top of a neighbouring crag,

Erect and sublime, for one moment of time,
　　In the next, that wild figure they saw
(As if stung by a spasm) plunge into a chasm,
　　While they waited and listened in awe.

"It's a Snark!" was the sound that first came to their ears,
   And seemed almost too good to be true.
Then followed a torrent of laughter and cheers:
   Then the ominous words "It's a Boo——"

Then, silence. Some fancied they heard in the air
   A weary and wandering sigh
That sounded like "—jum!" but the others declare
   It was only a breeze that went by.

They hunted till darkness came on, but they found
   Not a button, or feather, or mark,
By which they could tell that they stood on the ground
   Where the Baker had met with the Snark.

In the midst of the word he was trying to say,
   In the midst of his laughter and glee,
He had softly and suddenly vanished away—
   For the Snark *was* a Boojum, you see.

EARLY VERSE

MY FAIRY
(1845)

I HAVE a fairy by my side
   Which says I must not sleep,
When once in pain I loudly cried
   It said "You must not weep".

If, full of mirth, I smile and grin,
   It says "You must not laugh";
When once I wished to drink some gin
   It said "You must not quaff".

When once a meal I wished to taste
   It said "You must not bite";
When to the wars I went in haste
   It said "You must not fight".

"What may I do?" at length I cried,
   Tired of the painful task.
The fairy quietly replied,
   And said "You must not ask".

Moral: "You mustn't."